NEW DIR

Spring 2000

NINA BERBEROVA

THE LADIES FROM ST. PETERSBURG. Tr. by Schwartz. Three Russian novellas. "One of the Best Books of 1998." —*The New York Times*. $12.95 pbk.

JULIO CORTÁZAR

62: A MODEL KIT. Tr. by Rabassa. The classic 1968 novel about a European "city" is back in print. "Beautifully written." —*The New York Times.* $14.00 pbk.

H.D.

PILATE'S WIFE. Ed. w/intro. by Burke. Never before published 1929 novel. A feminist, spiritual version of the crucifixion of Jesus. $12.95 pbk. original.

SHUSAKU ENDO

FIVE BY ENDO. Tr. by Gessel. Japanese stories. "A master of the interior monologue."—Robert Coles, *The N.Y. Times Bk. Rev. An ND Bibelot.* $7.00 pbk.

THALIA FIELD

POINT AND LINE. New poetry. "Beautiful in ways we can scarcely imagine." —Carole Maso. "A real pleasure." —*Publishers Weekly*. $14.95 pbk. orig.

LARS GUSTAFSSON

ELEGIES AND OTHER POEMS. Ed. by Middleton. Poetry. A companion volume to *The Stillness of the World before Bach* (ND, 1988). $13.95 pbk. orig.

JAVIER MARÍAS

WHEN I WAS MORTAL. Tr. by Jull Costa. A dozen stories by Marías, "justly considered the most talented Spanish author alive" (*Il Messaggero*). $21.95 cl.

TOBY OLSON

HUMAN NATURE. New poetry. "A master's work without question, his own defining; time out of mind." —Robert Creeley. $14.95 pbk. orig.

MICHAEL PALMER

THE PROMISES OF GLASS. First new poetry since *At Passages* (ND, 1995). "One of America's most important poets."—*The Harvard Review.* $21.95 cl.

VICTOR PELEVIN

THE BLUE LANTERN. Tr. by Bromfield. Pelevin's stories now in pbk. "A finger-clickingly contemporary voice."—*The N.Y. Times Mag.* $12.95 pbk.

W. G. SEBALD

VERTIGO. Tr. by Hulse. Sebald's *(The Emigrants)* first novel. "One of the most exciting...of contemporary European writers."—*New Republic.* $23.95 cl.

MURIEL SPARK

MEMENTO MORI. Novel. A group of elderly friends in 1950s London. "Chillingly brilliant." —Tennessee Williams. *An ND Classic.* $11.95 pbk.

PAUL WEST

THE DRY DANUBE: A HITLER FORGERY. Hitler's "memoir" of his years as a failed art student. "West is a master."—*Wash. Post Bk. World.* $21.95 cl.

TENNESSEE WILLIAMS

STAIRS TO THE ROOF. Ed. w/intro. by Hale. First pub. of a Depression play, "a prayer for the wild of heart who are kept in cages" (TW). $11.95 pbk. orig.

COMING UP IN THE FALL

Conjunctions:35

AMERICAN POETRY

States of the Art

For fall 2000, *Conjunctions* completes the second of its two-volume project that began with this *American Fiction* issue. *Conjunctions:35, American Poetry: States of the Art,* will publish over sixty American poets whose work explores and redefines the boundaries of contemporary American poetry.

The issue will gather newly commissioned and unpublished work from a diverse group of poets—young voices to recognized masters. Together with this *American Fiction* issue, *Conjunctions:35, American Poetry: States of the Art* will be a necessary tool for anyone interested in the American poem as it enters the new century.

Among those whose work will appear in the issue are Barbara Guest, John Ashbery, Robert Creeley, Ann Lauterbach, C. D. Wright, Jackson Mac Low, Elaine Equi, Martine Bellen, John Yau, Robert Kelly, Mei-mei Berssenbrugge, Cole Swensen, Susan Howe, Keith Waldrop, Gustaf Sobin, Leslie Scalapino, Jorie Graham, John Taggart, Forrest Gander, Anne Waldman, Paul Hoover, Myung Mi Kim, Mark McMorris, Arthur Sze, Camille Guthrie, Melanie Neilson, Marjorie Welish, Charles North, Andrew Schelling, Charles Bernstein, Sam Hamill, Nathaniel Mackey, Peter Gizzi, Reginald Shepherd, Rosmarie Waldrop, and many others.

Bradford Morrow edits both volumes. For updates on contributors and previews of work, visit our website at www.conjunctions.com.

Yearly subscriptions to *Conjunctions* are only $18 for two issues—some 800 pages of contemporary and historical literature and art. Please send your check to *Conjunctions,* Bard College, Annandale-on-Hudson, NY 12504. Subscriptions can also be made over the Internet at www.conjunctions.com or by telephoning us at (914) 758-1539.

CONJUNCTIONS

Bi-Annual Volumes of New Writing

Edited by
Bradford Morrow

Contributing Editors
Walter Abish
Chinua Achebe
John Ashbery
Mei-mei Berssenbrugge
Guy Davenport
Elizabeth Frank
William H. Gass
Jorie Graham
Robert Kelly
Ann Lauterbach
Norman Manea
Patrick McGrath
Joanna Scott
Mona Simpson
Nathaniel Tarn
Quincy Troupe
William Weaver
John Edgar Wideman

published by Bard College

EDITOR: Bradford Morrow
MANAGING EDITOR: Michael Bergstein
SENIOR EDITORS: Robert Antoni, Martine Bellen, Peter Constantine, Elaine Equi, Brian Evenson
ASSOCIATE EDITORS: Jedediah Berry, Jonathan Safran Foer, Catherine Kasper
ART EDITORS: Anthony McCall, Norton Batkin
PUBLICITY: Mark R. Primoff
WEBMASTERS: Brian Evenson, Michael Neff
EDITORIAL ASSISTANTS: Devin Irby, Rabia Sandage, Courtney Scott, Alan Tinkler

CONJUNCTIONS is published in the Spring and Fall of each year by Bard College, Annandale-on-Hudson, NY 12504. This issue is made possible in part with the generous funding of the National Endowment for the Arts, and with public funds from the New York State Council on the Arts, a State Agency. We are also very grateful for a gift from an anonymous donor.

SUBSCRIPTIONS: Send subscription orders to CONJUNCTIONS, Bard College, Annandale-on-Hudson, NY 12504. Single year (two volumes): $18.00 for individuals; $25.00 for institutions and overseas. Two years (four volumes): $32.00 for individuals; $45.00 for institutions and overseas. Patron subscription (lifetime): $500.00. Overseas subscribers please make payment by International Money Order. For information about subscriptions, back issues and advertising, call Michael Bergstein at 914-758-1539 or fax 914-758-2660.

All editorial communications should be sent to Bradford Morrow, *Conjunctions,* 21 East 10th Street, New York, NY 10003. Unsolicited manuscripts cannot be returned unless accompanied by a stamped, self-addressed envelope.

Conjunctions is listed and indexed in the American Humanities Index.

Visit the *Conjunctions* website at www.conjunctions.com.

Copyright © 2000 CONJUNCTIONS.

Cover design by Anthony McCall Associates, New York. Photo collage: Michael Eastman.

All rights reserved. No part of this book may be reproduced or transmitted in any form or by any means, electronic or mechanical, including photocopying, recording or by any information storage and retrieval system, without permission in writing from the Publisher.

Printers: Edwards Brothers.

Typesetter: Bill White, Typeworks.

ISSN 0278-2324

ISBN 0-941964-50-7

Manufactured in the United States of America.

TABLE OF CONTENTS

AMERICAN FICTION
States of the Art

EDITOR'S NOTE . . . 7

John Edgar Wideman, *Two Stories* . . . 9

Mary Caponegro, *Ashes Ashes We All Fall Down* . . . 12

Sandra Cisneros, *Mexico Next Right* . . . 25

Paul West, *The Dark* . . . 29

Padgett Powell, *Mrs. Hollingsworth's List* . . . 40

Maureen Howard, *Inishmurray* . . . 55

Paul Auster, *Accident Report* . . . 61

Kathryn Davis, From *Versailles* . . . 66

Steve Erickson, *Swan Lake* . . . 69

William T. Vollmann, *The Sleepwalker* . . . 93

Alexander Theroux, *Laura Warholic* . . . 107

Mayra Montero, *El Hombre Pollack* (with a translation from Spanish by Edith Grossman) . . . 120

Edwidge Danticat, *Dies Irae* . . . 128

Rikki Ducornet, *The Battlefields of Shiraz* . . . 137

Dale Peck, *Fever Dreams: A Geography of Mind* . . . 144

Rick Moody, *Pan's Fair Throng* . . . 157

Joyce Carol Oates, *Four Dark Tales* . . . 167

Richard Powers and Bradford Morrow, *A Dialogue* . . . 171

Leslie Marmon Silko, *Introduction to a Book Titled* Blue Sevens, or Protect Yourself From Witchcraft While You Get Rich . . . 189

Ann Beattie, *The Big-Breasted Pilgrim* . . . 196

A. M. Homes, *Please Remain Calm* . . . 232

Paul LaFarge, *Lost and Legendary Aviators* 239
Robert Coover, *Alice in the Time of the Jabberwock* 245
Julia Alvarez, *Our Father* 271
Lois-Ann Yamanaka, *Wake* 282
Lydia Davis, *Happy Memories* 290
William H. Gass, *In Camera* 293
Joanna Scott, *An Interview by Bradford Morrow* 342
Jessica Hagedorn, *Requiem for a Prodigal Son* 353
Ben Marcus, *The Technology of Silence* 357
Christopher Sorrentino, *Stalingrad* 368
Brian Evenson, *Calling the Hour* 390
Diane Williams, *In the Lightly Moderate Vivid Deep* 392
Matthew Derby, *Joy of Eating* 395
Robert Antoni, *My Grandmother's Tale of How the Iguana Got Her Wrinkles, or The True Tale of El Dorado* 399
Pamela Ryder, *Overland* 418
Han Ong, *Obituary* 432
Russell Banks, *The Moor* 441
Rosario Ferré, *Flight of the Swan* 448
Ana Castillo, *Uitzilintzin, Uitzilintzin: Love Medicine for Sale* 456
David Shields, *The Ecstasy of Looking: Six Proofs* 459
Jonathan Safran Foer, *Finitude: From the Permanent Collection* 464
Carole Maso, *The Names* 474
NOTES ON CONTRIBUTORS 478

EDITOR'S NOTE

EVERY MEANINGFUL WORK OF FICTION changes the nature of fiction itself. It modifies what the imaginative reader—each writer's kindred collaborator—understands the state of the art to be. Narrative is a voluble, mercurial, vigorous entity, and all the more so in the hands of a spirited reader. This gathering of American fiction is offered to just that reader, one who treasures the language that chronicles its story as much as the story itself. One who sees in the style of storytelling a coequal parable, be it a subtle murmur, an emphatic music that belies or underscores, a swift shiver of difference in the voicing of something known but not appreciated before in quite that way. All the writers here in their very different ways are gymnasts of the word, namers naming their world with the vitality of an Adam designating the first birds. From John Edgar Wideman's story about stories—what questions they pose, what answers—to Carole Maso's on the enchanted process of a mother's titling her child, these are works about the world as a worded place.

And yet none of these writers of American fiction renounce their deeply felt personal ethics, their well-considered politics, in favor of Onan, of sheer aesthetics for aesthetics' sake. Steve Erickson's post-apocalyptic urban waterworld, Leslie Marmon Silko's shrewd travesty of a particularly egregious American dream, Russell Banks's portrait of unlikely lovers caught in the irrevocable throes of merely living their lives, Paul West's lucid vision of souls wrested from earth by the banality of violence—these works invite moral contemplation about history and its possible future.

How interesting, too, that so many of these American writers—three generations, ranging from twenty-three to seventy-five—cast their gazes beyond America proper, as if to engage the homeland by silhouette, by some process of witnessing what it isn't. Or what it might be in the companioning face of the rest of the world. Jessica Hagedorn's Manila, Julia Alvarez's Quebec, Rosario Ferré's Moscow, William T. Vollmann's Nazi Germany, Paul Auster's Paris, Edwidge Danticat's Haiti, Christopher Sorrentino's Stalingrad, Mayra Montero's Havana, Sandra Cisneros's Mexican border, Robert Antoni's Trinidad, Maureen Howard's Ireland, Kathryn Davis's Versailles, Rikki Ducornet's Shiraz . . . not to mention Robert Coover's reimagined Wonderland, Ben Marcus's otherwhere, the surreal Africa of Pamela Ryder. All this outward visioning nicely counterpoints the American scapes so deftly drawn by Ann Beattie, Han

Ong, Joyce Carol Oates, Padgett Powell, Alexander Theroux and the other superb fiction writers collected here, making one realize once more how intimate the world has become, how international the American eye.

An anthology of this compass is, of course, always the result of work by many people. I would particularly like to thank Joanna Scott, Robert Coover, Susan Bergholz, William Gass, Robert Antoni, Martine Bellen and Mei-mei Berssenbrugge for their ideas and help. And, as ever, thanks to all those people at Bard College whose commitment helps make this project thrive.

—Bradford Morrow
8 April 2000
New York City

In Memoriam

John Hawkes
1926–1998

"The author is his own best angleworm and the sharper the barb with which he fishes himself out of the darkness the better."

Two Stories
John Edgar Wideman

STORIES

—for TH

A MAN WALKING in the rain eating a banana. Where is he coming from. Where is he going. Why is he eating a banana. How hard is the rain falling. Where did he get the banana. What is the banana's name. How fast is the man walking. Does he mind the rain. What does he have on his mind. Who is asking all these questions. Who is supposed to answer them. Why. Does it matter. How many questions about a man walking in the rain eating a banana are there. Is the previous question one of them or is it another kind of question, not about the man or the walking or the rain. If not, what's it a question about. Does each question raise another question. If so, what's the point. If not, what will the final question be. Does the man know any of the answers. Does he enjoy bananas. Walking in the rain. Can the man feel the weight of eyes on him, the weight of questions. Why does the banana's bright yellow seem the only color, the last possible color remaining in a gray world with a gray scrim of rain turning everything grayer. I know question after question after question. The only answer I know is this: all the stories I could make from this man walking in the rain eating a banana would be sad, unless I'm behind a window with you looking out at him.

John Edgar Wideman

A HUNDRED YARDS AWAY. ROWING.

SUMMER AFTER SUMMER in an adirondack chair on this room-sized dock I've sat watching the lake's moods.

I watched a man, old and slight, in a white T-shirt and white billed cap, row across my field of vision, a distance of miles or inches depending on where you draw the line. For ten minutes or so he'd be out there on the water, about a hundred yards away, disappearing after he's worked his way across the mouth of the cove whose deep curve shelters this dock. In about a quarter hour he'd be visible again, still a hundred yards distant, rowing steadily with the same unhurried strokes back the way he'd come until he vanishes once more beyond the border of trees to the east.

Afternoons around five-thirty every fair day and probably the foul ones I didn't risk outdoors, he would rachet past in his clunky, aluminum boat, oars hinged to skinny arms, propelling himself backward through the water.

One summer a small black and white dog appeared in the rowboat. For a number of seasons the pair of them every day, man rowing in the stern, dog an ornament on the prow, across and back, master and pet, a fixture of waning afternoons.

Once on the breeze I thought I heard the man singing to the dog or the dog singing to the man. Sitting stiffly upright on its haunches, a spotted dog, two heads shorter than its companion, no hat, a beautiful voice if indeed it was the dog I heard singing.

Then one summer the man must have lost his dog or dog lost his man because a woman perched day after day at the end of the boat where the spotted dog had always perched, back to the man, gazing straight ahead. She never sang, but her lean silhouette as dependable, as cut from paper as the little dog's. A turban of twisted white hair raised her as tall from waist up as the white-hatted man at the oars. Man and woman matched bookends with invisible volumes between them, like brackets of a parenthesis, like the outstretched arms shaping this cove, holding some things in, keeping others out.

I remember wondering if the woman would reappear the following summer. Or a different lady or different dog. But the man and his boat didn't return for many seasons.

Years went by. Stories, but I couldn't write them.

The next and last time I saw the rowboat it was empty, except for the man drawing himself stroke by stroke through bright, morning water. A different time of day but somehow I knew he was still dedicated to vigorous exercise, a punctual daily outing.

Same man no doubt and I had to admit, watching him row past, how much I'd missed his comings and goings. Why couldn't I recollect how long since I'd seen him last. Years and years, too many to count, gone the instant his boat popped from behind the green curtain of trees and glided into the cove's mouth. A thousand years, no years, no time passing between a distant memory and the sudden sight of him rowing, unchanged, a hundred yards away, as if he'd never been absent, paralleling the razor-straight seam of the lake's far shore, below which on some windless mornings the woods are doubled, upside-down, flawless in a dark mirror.

He hailed me, acknowledged my presence that morning for the first time in all my years of watching.

Ahoy, ahoy, he might have shouted, one oar's dripping blade levered high out of the water and waved, a gesture I would have imagined him far too old and frail to perform.

Ahoy, ahoy, bouncing off the sounding board of water too late to reach me. My rotted chair scaffolding for intricate miles of webbing.

Ashes Ashes We All Fall Down

Mary Caponegro

EVERY NIGHT, CARTER SLEEPS beside a woman not his wife and feels both virtuous and guilty; virtuous, because the woman not his wife is not a mistress, either, but his mother, to whose side he cleaves in part to spare his wife, and guilty, because despite the cumulative nights of sacrifice, he cannot save his mother, for whose sake he nevertheless continues to deprive his wife—his wife who has her own legitimate needs, but who, because of these merciless circumstances, receives only the dregs of his attention and energy. How can he, how can the cosmos, justify it? How has all this come to pass? How has Carter come to find himself at age thirty-six in the house in which he grew up, on the far side of a hospital bed with broken crank, with his wife asleep, at least at rest (he hopes) upstairs in the twin bed which once was his, and will in years to come be their child's, and which will soon be insufficient to accommodate her? Furthermore, how can Carter possibly be sufficiently husband and sufficiently son to a wife who is with child, to a mother who is near death, the cruel irony of which timing he has become inured, given in his more philosophical moments to considering ineluctable? And if by some perverse coincidence the day of birth and death should coincide? He would have to choose whom to attend, to be cursed by the living or the dead: by his wife, who asks so little, almost too little of him, but who will no doubt consider it her obligation at some point to disclose to their child the anguished story of a father who made a reservation for his offspring's birth but stood him or her up—or by his mother, who after all blessed him with life, and disclosed to him reluctantly, gradually, in response to his importunate inquiries, the story of the complications of that event: his birth, which she in some sense nearly missed herself!

Or perhaps this curse, thinks Carter, is not a property of the future but of the past, more disconcerting still, a property transcending time, intrinsic to his nature. Perhaps curse and Carter go together, like failing and falling, like loving and losing, like causing, by means of some subtle, mysterious yet insidious mechanism situated elusively between a sin of commission and a sin of omission, an accident to befall the very ones one wants least in the world to be afflicted, one's daughter or mother or wife. But perhaps Carter is letting his imagination get carried away with him. It is not the first time he has entertained such a notion, and far from the last. How is a man to occupy his mind in such a state—when time is measured by a pendulum that doubles as a magic wand—correction: as a metal wand that travels over Carter's mother's sagging breast, and then his wife's distended belly, in search of likely (in the former) or less likely (in the latter) complications, supplemented by the purpose of not second-guessing sex.

It is easy enough to be carried away in these circumstances: surrounded, rather sandwiched, by beloved but bloated female bodies—in fact, the sense of a woman as robust, independent and sexual is already like some ancient myth (I'm sleeping with two women, jokes Carter to himself, and I'm not getting any!)—riddled with anxiety, anticipation, inadequacy, fatigue, awakened every hour, seemingly on the hour, to fetch or soothe or fuss and increasingly to engage in absurd exchanges that perpetuate this, he feels lately, largely losing battle between goodwill and futility.

Which takes today the form of lozenges. The triviality of it astounds him, and yet does not mitigate the violence of his feeling. Innocent cardboard box of innocent lemon drops. She wants one. He refuses. She begs him. He will not relent. Why can't Carter be as stubborn as the cosmos?—as frugal, as intractable, as niggardly with what is his to give? Meting out bizarre exchanges, substitutions, symmetries? Eye for an eye, tooth for a tooth. His child will, he presumes, he hopes, have two eyes, two hands, ten toes, and in accordance with the laws of nature now grows, right on schedule, in its mother's womb, with heart and liver protruding since the second month, as his wife's midsection swells, and as his mother's tumor burgeons in distorted mimicry.

As cruel as that would now appear to any uninitiated observer: one without a history, one who *hadn't* observed her nearly choke already several times. How can he responsibly let her suck them lying down? Nor can she easily sit up, so obviously he must forbid those ostensibly innocent lemon discs, not even candies, technically—and yet for her, refreshment, stimulation, her only sensual opportunity; he must deny her, he has denied his dying mother not just a stupid candy but Capital S Sensation! She may partake neither of sweet nor sour. How she must resent his parroting, "It's for your own good."

(As he resents—despite his best intentions—her every-minute-on-the-minute request for what she knows he must continue to refuse her.) "Don't you get it? Don't you get it, Mom? It isn't safe." A cough drop as luxury, how pathetic. And how strange on the eve, as it were, of being a father, he endures, in fact creates, this role reversal, knows he should instead be playful, resort to their shared idioms, euphemisms, coded intimacies of old ("Cat got your tongue?" she used to say to him affectionately, whenever he was shy in front of others; later, he to her, when one of her episodes commenced, or passed, to signal, "Mommy shouldn't be ashamed of this" (though Carter was afraid))—their banter much more tender than what passes, later, between Carter and his daughter, when she's older, when she's fresh. "Now don't be sassy, missy." "Name's not missy, CAR-TER." It's a stage, they'll assure each other, he and Andrea, as Emily drags them through the terrible twos, fours, sixes, eights, and even tens and twelves, for heaven's sake. "A daughter shouldn't call her father Carter, missy." "Name's not missy, sissy!" "That's enough. Upstairs, go to your room."

They strike a bargain. Suck to a timer. He borrows the kitchen gadget whose tick and ding he so resents, yet has deigned to use when concocting meals of her choosing in homage to some Platonic idea of appetite. (He'd always get it wrong, it seemed, the timing or the recipes, and on those rare occasions he'd succeed, it seemed both Andrea and his mother couldn't surmount their respective nauseas. Then if next time he brought home meager takeout, assuming meager hunger, one might say, "Today's a good day, I have quite an appetite," or "No, I haven't been nauseous since the first trimester, honey.") But today is not, by anybody's reckoning, a good day. Today requires strategy. And Carter has devised one. If she will be willing to surrender it, the lemon drop, at thirty seconds (approximately the time she can sustain sitting?) then she can wet her whistle in increments. "OK, Mom?" Carter pleads. "Is that all right with you, Mom? How about a deal?"

Easier said than done, and the saying was chore enough, worn down as Carter is by now, and how much more his mother must be, he thinks, on last legs, with precious little ambulation, dependent on her son who is not by nature the sort to make the grand gesture—would not, for example, be likely to carry wife over threshold on honeymoon, can barely manage lugging the TV back and forth—from her (once his) room upstairs to his mother's bedroom ("Wee Willy Winky," Carter sometimes has the irresistible urge to sing in stupid voice, "runs through the town, upstairs, downstairs . . .") and means to buy the second TV just as soon as he gets a moment. Where is a man to find that ever-elusive moment between ferrying her to the bathroom, to dining room, to automobile, to hospital, barely time to catnap, until the set reduced to the fewest props: the porta-potty, basin, tray and bell, wife's intercom and shared TV. By then the chemo-lite, as he refers to it, is her sole outing (complete with festive milk shake after), or if she is in a whimsical (read reckless) mood, corned beef on rye. "Oh Carter, you didn't!" when he tells his wife, who even if she wanted has no option to indulge in pickles and ice cream or the like brought home by faithful unencumbered hubby. Nobody eats corned beef on rye after chemo! Not even *your* mother. Chemo my ass, Chemo-on-rye. For which if he would build a ramp the carrying would be obviated; a wheelchair could do all the work transporting, but that, feels Carter, would be cheating. For does not she who carried him nine months deserve the cradle of his arms? Does not his name imply a beast of burden? Cart her. What he was born to do but didn't know till now. He'd carry her up a mountain if he had to—and he wants to—huffing, puffing, granted, but he'd gladly climb—though no doubt once atop the summit only to run into God of Abraham, who'd say, "Now Carter, by the way, today I bid you sacrifice your only mother for your at-the-moment only child. OK with you, pal?"

Carried him for nine but now has only six to live—the cliché of it: six months to live—like some made-for-TV movie—he flew in just in time, yes, right on cue to hear the news from a compassionate oncologist who nonetheless the moment she perceived his tears seemed put off. Carter has a theory that regardless of how much women claim they want more sensitive, more vulnerable men, more demonstrative men, if male tears shed themselves in public, it's as if an angel farted. Indeed, he felt as if he smelled when she proceeded to outline the kinds of chemotherapy or radiation they might try, the risks, the gains . . . at this point. Surely he could offer six months to his dying mother—who gave him several exclusively while she turned inward from the world, attending only to his nurture, even if they were the most important six months of his marriage, the development of his first and likely only child, even if it necessitated sacrificing his wife's ease and joy—his wife who did not have an easy road to—or through—pregnancy. She had to "lie in" as they called it. One of the obstetricians in her group apparently said, "We mustn't rock the boat, must not upset the apple cart"—that vessel, in each case, the uterus, he presumes. "Don't have to snag the bag," the same (wouldn't you know he'd be the one on call?) will later say when she comes in with amniotic sac already ruptured, just in time. Later still, she will attempt to explain to Carter the sensation of the episiotomy—"they think it's all one pain, you're in agony anyway, why not slice? But there are nerves in there, they should only know—a separate, distinct sear." (Thank God they're spared the circumcision decision with the daughter. From the sonogram forward he feels relieved.)

Ding. But not the timer this time—the doorbell. "Give me the lozenge, Mom. Come on." Who could it be? A rare event the doorbell ringing here. Oh God, he hopes it's not the priest. (She couldn't have called by herself, could she?) No. "I've got to get the door, Mom, and I can't have you in here alone with that lozenge. Please, Mom." He is reluctant but not squeamish when he inserts his (after washing) hand, reminded of dear old Sloopy who when ill could only be persuaded (read coerced) to take a pill the way the vet suggested, clamping closed her jaws until she had no option but to swallow, and of how no pill would save her when she raided the Easter basket—or was it Christmas stocking—of its foil-wrapped chocolate candy, foil intact. His basket he had left unguarded downstairs. He had killed her. (Easter—always honored by his mother because Jesus from the dead was like a woman from a coma. "Should have named me Lazarus, for Chrissake," he once said in irritation, then regretted.)

It rings again. Goddamn that bell. They'll wake poor Andrea. "Mom, be reasonable, I've got to answer that." How easy it is to slide his hand—a man should not be so familiar with his mother's mouth, is it unseemly? But hadn't he stood sentry half his life, grasping a wadded handkerchief, ready to place between her teeth at each incipient seizure? Hadn't he won over teacher after teacher by appearing first and every day of school, not especially well-groomed and yet seeming so due to the neatly folded hanky perpetually in his pocket, the talisman as pragmatic as symbolic whose true significance he did not to any one of them reveal? It could happen to anyone. He dreaded it when she had them, and yet he prayed to the very God his mother urged him to believe in that he be present when they did occur—to be her little helper, to protect her. (The least he could do, considering their origin—mingled, after all, with his.) From his youngest years he'd memorized the drill. Check for no constriction, no obstruction. That instruction conspicuously absent, noticed Carter, from both primary and secondary school curricula. For years he was afraid to kiss a girl the sexy way for fear of choking her, no other boy he knew had any such concerns; some worried later to be swallowed up or gnawed when girls went down on them, but no vagina dentata fear in Carter, nor stereotypical one-track male mind; his one track was the trachea, and the desperate wish to keep that passageway open for breath. Only to his wife could he confide his fear—his wife who instead of laughing, seemed so tender, understanding and relieved. "I knew you weren't a lousy kisser." Forgave his tongue's tentativity. How could such a man begin to be equipped to tell a son the facts of life? Hence Carter's joy, call it relief, when through the marvels of technology, he learns he is to be a daughter's father, not a son's.

"Now spit it out, Mom. 'Cause you promised me." And finally she does. He grabs a tissue as he races to the door but not in time to prevent a third chime. "OK, OK, I'm here," and there before his eyes is Andy—no, Jerry—is it Becker?) Who could forget that jaw? But nearly bald already? After a moment of confusion he recognizes the "fraternity brother" with whom he used to get a ride up to school after vacations from how many years ago, and just the kind of guy to ring a doorbell relentlessly. "Carter, man. How's it going?"

"Well, that's a long story, I'm afraid. What can I do for you, Jerry? Still live here in town?" And Jerry stands explaining that he never really left and that's just fine, and he commutes to work, stays in the city overnight two days a week sometimes three, and doesn't mind at all, but his mom told him Carter's mom was sick and he thought he'd stop by to see if Carter needed anything and does he?

Does he ever, Carter thinks but doesn't say, and finally, against his better judgment, takes Jerry down to the cluttered finished basement where they occasionally had a beer together in the old days and takes a break, thinking it might be good for everyone concerned, and hell, why not go get a beer for both of them? Just sit and shoot the shit with someone neither wife nor mother, someone neutral, talk about some stupid subject hopefully irrelevant to sickness, health or birth or death. But Jerry asks again how Carter is, and doesn't even smile when Carter, desperate, says, "It's like this, Jerry . . . since we're old fraternity brothers, I can trust you, right? . . . I'm sleeping with two women and I'm not getting any!" Jerry definitely does not take his cue and join him in uproarious preinebriated laughter. He looks, instead, uncomfortable, then looks Carter in the eye and asks, "So what kind of cancer is it, buddy?"

Which, when he later tells (confesses really) his reaction, to his wife, makes him feel chastened. "It's a reasonable question, Carter, really—different cancers behave differently, after all." And she should know, far better than he, being officially "pre"-cancerous before her surgery. Dysplasia. A pity, such a lovely word. Dysplasia Annabella Carcinoma—there's a name to give one's daughter. Would the beauty justify the stigma? Certainly apposite, in this case. He vividly recalls Andrea's anecdote about the ob/gyn intern, sweating and fumbling as he tried to guide his speculum to perform the pelvic exam on/in an interior no longer as intact. She found it funny, in a way. Almost. He does admire her equilibrium. Besides, she told him, all she cared about was his conclusion: what they'd cut away would not preclude her having children. But Carter, far less reasonable than his better half, is agitated—from the doorbell, from the cough drops, from the day after day in the landscape of someone else's disease, sandwiched as he is between his post-precancerous pre-postpartum wife and his postcancerous pre-posthumous mother—buffering and ferrying and shepherding from hospital bed at home to hospital proper from pre-op to post-op to "Hear the heartbeat honey, can you feel the kick?" while life kicks him again and again and again in the balls, as God the referee counts theatrically from one to ten. Seven, eight, nine, oh shit, he's up again, there's Carter for another round. Dizzy, staggering, but on his feet, Wee Willy Winky, headless chicken, well-intentioned idiot!

"What kind of cancer *isn't* it, you mean, by now?" he wants to shout to Jerry, perhaps does raise his voice, perhaps screams only in his head—"in all its metastatic splendor, taking dominion over every fucking organ, every tissue, every cell." What difference does it make in the end what kind it is or was? Do people offering condolences after car crashes inquire, "And was she killed then by an S.U.V.? A Pontiac? A Ford?" Only the brilliant steel-trap-minded Scandinavian technicians racing to the scene would ask such questions, do their calculations, draw conclusions, make suggestions. But for the *next* guy, not for *that* poor slob. He's dead already. Better luck next time, you six-feet-under fool, with *next* year's model, *next* year's air-bagged, all-wheeled coffin, *next* year's chemo, on the cusp of *next* year's surrogate incurable horror to replace whatever medical research just resolved. For the greater good, for the greater good at least of those who could afford the most solid crashworthy car, the most seamless surgical procedure, the most durable immuno-friendly genes. Maybe just a bunch of curious, bloodthirsty Swedes in need of titillation? Not an engineer in the lot! Who gives a fuck what kind of cancer? Carter doesn't. He hates the shared letters of his name—

also caretaker, though, he realizes, hates his own propensity to perseverate on such decorative esoterics as aural associations and slippery semantics. In times when sex is lacking in his life, supposes he indulges all the more in mental masturbation. To distract himself from counting down and balancing the equation of his daughter's forming organs, limbs against his mother's wasting same.

Meanwhile the God of Abraham looks down from cloud-surrounded mountain, holding up fingers, keeping tabs, correcting Carter's math: "eye = eye, tooth = tooth. Shave off intestine, send to fetus," crosses off another number on his godly character. But in the short space between prodrome and seizure, and longer space between seizure and prodrome, how is a boy to occupy his mind if not with mystical hooey, desperate nonsense, superstition (certainly not with the equivalent of the calculatons of Swedish engineers who certainly were not there to prevent the accident that put his mother in a coma that made the better part of *his* (that is hers with him) pregnancy more than literally lying-in, and set the stage for later seizures (never right at the times of stress but after, he recalls) that were the formative landmarks of his life! (His life now measured by the six months of his mother's time on earth, the same interval until his child's debut into the very world from which his mother, day by day, recedes.) His life engendered by a miracle (so called) of *his* evolving consciousness inside the body of a woman who had temporarily surrendered such.

All of which inspired—for good or ill—his wife to think that *all* is possible, no obstacle too great in pregnancy, that romanticized miraculous-mother-nature vision with which Carter feels *all* too familiar, and so even after the trauma of one lying-in affair whose punctuation equalled nearly not arriving, she will, approximately two years later say, "Let's try again, let's do it one more time, no matter what the risk, I'll be too old soon." And he will guardedly assent, and she will readily conceive, and will enjoy, this time, a smooth and virtually unimpeded nine months. Not a single complication. Carter will be thrilled to bring then three-year-old Emily to meet her brand-new baby sister, find his perfect parking space on level three, what luck, the same floor as maternity, and goes to take the flowers from the trunk and suddenly she isn't there. Emily isn't there. "Emmy. EMMY. Where are you, darling? This isn't hide and seek, sweetheart. Please answer daddy." Stern now: "*Emily.*" Looks in the car and under, repeats procedure, then looks in and under all the cars parked beside them. "EMILY." He's panicking. How can he visit Andrea now? How could some sicko child snatcher be so swift and crafty as to lie in wait outside the hospital's maternity ward? Has malevolence become so customized as that? In this marvelous burgeoning-with-progress, this tumescent-with-terrificness twenty-first century? And then her distant voice: "Daddy, I'm bad." What, is he hearing things now? Hearing voices? Coming from below, it seems? Alice down the rabbit hole? And he peers down the gap that is the absent portion of the floor's right angle to the wall and sees her standing there. Emily, how in the world? A cat landing on its feet? Thank God. "Wait I'm coming down, darling. Stay right there." He races down the stairs. "Daddy, I'm bad." Daughter, I'm worse. I'm cursed, and by extension so are you. Accidents await me to happen. All my life. He can't tell Andrea. Doesn't. "Not a word to mommy, OK?" (What, should he try to sue the hospital, the contractor who built the booby-trapped garage? Until at home that evening poor dear little thing starts vomiting violently. And he thinks, did I ruin her in those crucial several hours of assuming all's well that seems? Back to the hospital: CAT scans and e-grams and all *is* eventually well, but Andrea spends the night hobbling back and forth between emergency and maternity in the interstices of their newborn's feedings. And assuring Carter all is well, who had intended to be reassuring *her.* (He fashions analogies for his own private standardized test: Labor is to pregnancy as plane . . . When the trip there is smooth you know the return is bound to be hell. No such thing as a free . . .) No repercussions, admits Carter, though he never rests assured, never takes his eyes off her from that point on. For years his vigilance will envelop her, as if his eyes could cushion her every action, every gesture, until he realizes he's been duped again. She was a decoy.

"I guess I better be going," says Andy/Jerry Becker. "You've got so much to take care of," after Carter's outburst. "Sorry if I upset you, buddy." And Carter will feel rotten about losing it like that, and make it up to him much later, after Jerry has his own kid, a kid who won't enjoy the vigilance that Carter offers Emily and who will be blessedly oblivious to danger, with the advantage of a father who possesses utter equanimity, and seems genuinely unperturbed by any incident, while Carter knows no haven but anxiety. He envies Jerry's joking manner when his son, then later daughter, bumps his or her head and he, instead of panicking, says, "There goes Harvard." Hugs the kid, dries tears, says soothing words and carries on. There goes Harvard—no big deal, imagine that. The guy's a card, that Jerry.

"Yea, hey, sorry, Jerry. Got to check on my mom. Listen . . . thanks for coming." Sees him up and out and hurries to the bedroom where he sees his mother clutching something in each hand—is that a mirror in her left, where did she get that, didn't get it from the dresser, did she? Didn't get up out of bed while he—yes, she's about to put the lozenge in her mouth again, he's just in time, "I told you, Mom, *no cough drops.*" And suddenly overcome with irritation takes the box and throws it at the wall—it makes a pathetic sound between a thud and splat—and a rain of lemon hail pours down in lieu of afternoon sunlight. Seeing that she still clutches a single lozenge, he starts wrestling it away from her, she pleading for its custody. He feels both foolish and driven—chagrined and indignant. Touched that she must have thought that to watch herself sucking would be a way to duplicate his vigilance—he stayed too long in the basement. "Don't exert yourself please, Momma, give it to me, would you please?" "I need to ask you something, honey." "I told you, Mom. Don't ask again. It's for your own . . ." "No, I need . . ." She's breathing weakly. What is he, crazy? Wrestling with his dying mother exerting HER. ". . . To ask you something else." Suddenly he comes to sense, relents, releases her hand, so she in turn can unfist the translucent disc, bring her palm up to her face, let down the mirror, look him in the eye and say, "Tell me the truth, please, Carter." What is she about to ask? (The man on the phone, with the accent—asking about the accident, expressing concern, he never told—so many years ago. A touch of the proscriptive in his manner even then?) "Am I this yellow?" And he realizes all at once what the mirror was for—that her mission was not one of oral gratification this time, but a layman's—woman's—a lying-in-laywoman's-homespun diagnostic tool to see how jaundiced she'd become, the damn cancer having spread now to the liver, good as over, six months having shrunk to five four three two—no one even pretending they could save her, just assuage her pain, sustain some strength at best, and yes, how better than with chemo-lite? Embellished placebo lets you go through all the motions without many side effects and without ANY lasting good result: drive in, hook up your IV, get your hopes up, get up, go home, all for what? To pass the time in counting down from six to five to four to three to two to . . .

Won that round, OK. And how? By bullying his poor, defenseless, dearest, dying mother. What is his problem? A control freak? Is that what he's become? Straightjacketing experience? His own, his unborn children's, mother's, wife's? Has he no trust in life? No faith? "No priest! Please God, no priest," he yells when she, intuiting the end is near, requests communion. "I hate to tell you, Mom, that host is no more salubrious than a lemon drop." This Christian nonsense all began because of *his* birth, because she regained consciousness for *that* event—not a death but a birth-bed conversion in this case. Because she, like Sleeping Beauty, awoke to bear a healthy, two-eyed, ten-toed baby boy who became, eventually, a man of some intelligence, of perhaps greater than average sensitivity, not particularly good-looking, admittedly, but a certain kind of ladies' man, no womanizer but a certain sensibility that appealed to certain women, always faithful to his wife with the exception of this call it metaphysical transgression, this inadvertent infidelity, divided loyalty, sleeping nightly by his dying mother so he won't disturb his wife's sleep. But consequently cannot pay attention as he should to all the needs of either woman. Sometimes pays attention to the wrong things, sometimes stubborn, even obstinate—doesn't build a ramp so almost drops his mother carrying her to the car, doesn't hire a nurse or contact hospice since he feels he should provide all care, gets worn out, run down, and compromises pregnant wife and dying mother's immunity through exposure to his own germs. "Oh ye of little faith, of little sense, of little luck," bellows the mountain-topping, cloud-surrounded voice, "you'll see the pattern in the lives of those who fail to pay attention. And by the way, say three Hail Marys, two Our Fathers, take two lemon lozenges and call me in the morning—that is, if you're still alive."

Carter, in his middle age, will feel schooled, brutally, in the nuances of paying attention. He will, in retrospect, conclude he paid attention to the wrong things: to the wrong child, to the first and not the second, with whom he foolishly assumed he could be more relaxed, knowing, by then, the ropes. Because the first looked with disgust as he hovered over soccer practice, and as he subsequently expressed dismay that field hockey should demand a girl to wield a stick as well as run, two activities which should be mutually exclusive, for heaven's sake—the sight of that entangled nest of ball and sticks and feet enough to make him vomit. She laughed at him and said, "That's the game, sillydaddy" (his nickname based upon a squishy product in an egg because he once complained that he was putty in her hands) and in later years, "The point of playing, it's exciting, Dad, I like that." (No more daddy-I'm-bad, now it's daddy-you're-dumb.) Fortunately, the second, less fearless, less adventurous (less fresh as well—at least thus far), content to find adventure in the simple things: wading pool and sandbox and ring around the rosy, swing behind which he could stand and push, meting out velocity, in pocketful of posies, innocuous pink bicycle with training wheels, which when removed at the appropriate time should present no obstacle—first a little tentative, of course, he'll stand beside her balancing, providing her support until she balances intuitively, "No, Daddy, let me do it now, alone," then giddy with it up and down the street as he applauds each triumphant return.

"Last time, OK, sweetheart?" "OK, Daddy. This is my masterpiece!" (Where did she learn the word? Not from her sister, who he knows already salts vocabulary with vulgar words.) She's off in a blur of pink handlebars and purple jacket. Her favorite colors this month. Swaying ponytail. And suddenly the pink and purple blur flops sideways. "Corey? Sweetheart?" Déjà vu is disconcerting, Carter finds. Any minute tears, no doubt, but he will dry them. It's not Formula One racing after all, it isn't snowboarding, jet skiing, sky jumping, only an innocent pink bicycle sans training wheels on an insipid suburban sidewalk, the same upon which Carter learned to ride—"Corey, Daddy's coming," Daddy's running, Daddy can't run fast enough to offer consolation for the skinned knee or loose tooth, maybe bumped head to boot, at worst, dislocated elbow. "Corey, darling"—why is she not getting up? I'm coming, sweetpea. Why is she not opening her eyes? (Show me those lovely blue-grey eyes.) Innocuous concuss innocuous concuss innocuous pink bicycle should harbor no relation to insidious concussion, nor to headaches whose severity increases exponentially in later years, all encoded in a black spot on a bright screen, four minutes unconsciousness, four minutes of lost, irreplaceable cells, cat got your scan, eye for an eye and a brain for a brain. Yes, there goes Harvard, there goes Barnard, there goes Stanford and Haverford, U.B. and U.C. and SUNY and CUNY and Payless Community College as well, there goes health and happiness, here comes hell. And sure enough, here comes Carter to inhabit it, right on cue, feels right at home in tragedy. For causality read enemy. His life a perpetual prodrome to emotional seizure. How can life be whole again, he wonders. Often wonders. Ashes, ashes—for hospice read hubris—we all fall . . .

Her back hurts. Will he rub it for her? Of course I will. A Tylenol to ease the pain? What, is she kidding? One placebo good as any other, he supposes. Her shaking hand can hardly hold the cup. "Of course you're not that yellow, Mama, meant to tell you yesterday, last week, last month, last . . . tell me, though, now you tell *me* the truth, am I this callow? Please forgive me." Feels tears welling up.

Blinks them back. Hands on her sallow skin, all tenderness to soothe her wasting flesh, then both doze for who knows how long. Carter, groggy after what seems this time more than fitful catnapped sleep, observes her parted lips, coated with that whitish film, her skin cool. Holds her hand in his to warm it. Squeezes. "Cat got your nap?" Whispers it again. Then Andrea has come, as in a dream, to help him ascertain if this cold body's chill reads temperature of death. How did she get here? Knows she shouldn't use the stairs alone, in her condition. All in white and huge she stands before him, nudges him to wakefulness. At what point, Andrea, he wants to ask, does sleep concede to death? And at what point does death yield grief? When, exactly when, does grief commence in earnest? And what is its configuration: mountain, ocean, column, vector, black hole? A revolutionary universe with its own laws, its own specific gravity? A world without end, Amen? Here they are now, both his charges, both his life's loves in the same room. He is momentarily whole. Ever-shrinking Willy Winky need no longer run: upstairs, downstairs . . . "Carter, Carter, please get up, we have to go, we have to go right now, my water broke." And then a dam inside him bursts to marry hers, and he can't hold it back.

Mexico Next Right
Sandra Cisneros

NOT LIKE ON THE TRIPLE A ATLAS from orange to pink, but at a stoplight in a rippled heat and a dizzy gasoline stink, the United States ends all at once, a tangled shove of red lights from cars and trucks waiting their turn to get past the bridge. Miles and miles. —Oh my Got, Father says in his gothic English. —Holy cripes! says Mother fanning herself with a Texaco roadmap.

I forgot the light, white and stinging like an onion. I remembered the bugs, a windshield spotted with yellow. I remembered the heat, a sun that melts into the bones like Ben-Gay. I remembered how big Texas is. —Are we in Mexico yet? —No, not yet. [Sleep, wake up.] —Are we in Mexico yet? —Still Texas. [Sleep, wake up.] —Are we . . . —Christ almighty!!!

But the light. That I don't remember forgetting until I remember it.

We've crossed Illinois, Missouri, Oklahoma and Texas, singing all the songs we know. "The Moon Man Mambo" from our favorite Rocky and Bullwinkle album. *Ah, ah, aaaah! Scrooch, doobie-doobie, doobie-do. Swing your partner from planet to planet when you dooooo the moon man mamboooo!* The songs from *The Wizard of Oz* but with the words changed. *We're off to see the* abuela, *the* abuela *from Mexico City, because, because, because, because, becaaaause! Because of the wonderful things she does. . . .* Even though she's never done anything special. We sing TV commercials. *Get the blanket with the A, you can trust the big red A. Get the blanket made with acrylon today. . . . Knock on any Norge, knock on any Norge, hear the secret sound of quality, knock on any Norge! Years from now you'll be glad you chose Norge.* The *Yogi Bear Show* theme song. *He will sleep till noon but before it's dark, he'll have every picnic basket that's in Jellystone Park. . . . Coco Wheats, Coco Wheats can't be beat. It's the creamy hot cereal with the cocoa treat. . . .* And "Maria" from *West Side Story.*

Diarrhea, I just met a girl with diarrhea. . . . Until Mother yells, —Will you shut your *hocicos* or do I have to shut them for you?!!!

But crossing the border, nobody feels like singing. Everyone hot and sticky and in a bad mood, hair stiff from riding with the windows open, the backs of the knees sweaty, a little circle of spit next to where my head fell asleep; good lucky Father thought to sew beach towel slipcovers for our new car.

No more billboards announcing the next Stuckey's candy store, no more truck-stop donuts or roadside picnics with bologna-and-cheese sandwiches and cold bottles of 7-Up—*You like it. It like you.* Now we'll drink fruit-flavored sodas, tamarind, apple, pineapple; Pato Pascual with Donald Duck on the bottle, or Lulú, Betty Boop soda, or the one we hear on the radio with the happy song. *Todo mundo a refrescarse. Jarritos que buenos son. Por su sabor que buenos son.*

As soon as we cross the bridge everything switches to another language. *Toc* says the light switch in this country; at home it says *click. Honk,* say the cars at home; here they say *tán-tán-tán.* The *scrip-scrape-scrip* of highheels across saltillo floor tiles. The angry lion growl of the corrugated curtains when the shopkeepers roll them open each morning, and the lazy lion roar at night when they pull them shut. The *pick, pick, pick* of somebody's faraway hammer. Church bells over and over, all day, even when it's not o'clock. Roosters. The hollow echo of a dog barking. Bells from skinny horses pulling tourists in a carriage, clip-clop on cobblestones and big chunks of horse *caquita* tumbling out of them like shredded wheat.

Sweets sweeter, colors brighter, the bitter more bitter. A cage of parrots all the rainbow colors of Lulú sodas. Pushing a window out to open it instead of pulling it up. A cold slash of door latch in your hand instead of the dull round doorknob. Tin sugar spoon and how surprised the hand feels because it's so light. Children walking to school in the morning with their hair still wet from the morning bath. Mopping with a purple rag on a stick called *la jerga* instead of a mop. The fat lip of a soda pop bottle when you tilt your head back and drink. Birthday cakes walking out of a bakery without a box, just like that, on a wooden plate. And the metal tongs and tray when you buy Mexican sweet bread, help yourself. Corn flakes served with *hot* milk! A balloon painted with wavy pink stripes wearing a paper hat. A milk gelatin with a fly like a little black raisin rubbing its hands. Light and heavy, loud and soft, thud and ting and ping.

Churches the color of *flan.* Vendors selling slices of *jícama* with chile, lime juice and salt. Balloon vendors. The vendor of flags. The corn on the cob vendor. The pork rind vendor. The fried banana vendor. The pancake vendor. The vendor of strawberries in cream. The vendor of rainbow *pirulis,* of apple bars, of *tejocotes* bathed in caramel. The merengue man. The ice cream vendor—*A very good ice cream at five pesos.* The coffee man with the coffeemaker on his back and a paper cup dispenser, the cream-and-sugar boy scuttling alongside him.

Little girls in Sunday dresses like lace bells, like umbrellas, like parachutes, the more lace and fru-fru the better. Houses painted purple, electric blue, tiger orange, aquamarine, a yellow like a taxicab, hibiscus red with a yellow and green fence. Above doorways, faded wreaths from an anniversary or a death till the wind and rain erase them. A woman in an apron scrubbing the sidewalk in front of her house with a pink plastic broom and a bright green bucket filled with suds. A workman carrying a long metal pipe on his shoulder whistling *ffsttt-fffft* to warn people watch out, the pipe longer than he is tall, almost putting out someone's eye, *ya mero*—but he doesn't does he? *Ya mero, pero no.* Almost, but not quite. *Sí, pero no.* Yes, but no.

Fireworks displays, piñata makers, palm weavers. Pens—*Five different styles, they cost us a lot!* A restaurant called His Majesty, the Taco. The napkins little triangles of hard paper with the name printed on one side. Breakfast: a basket of *pan dulce,* Mexican sweetbread; hotcakes with honey; or steak; *frijoles* with fresh cilantro; *mollete;* or scrambled eggs with chorizo; eggs *a la mexicana* with tomato, onion and chile; or *huevos rancheros.* Lunch: lentil soup; fresh baked crusty *bolillos;* carrots with lime juice; *carne asada;* abalone; tortillas. Because we are sitting outdoors, Mexican dogs under the Mexican tables. —I can't stand dogs under the table when I'm eating. Mother complains, but as soon as we shoo two away, four others trot over.

Sandra Cisneros

The smell of diesel exhaust, the smell of somebody roasting coffee, the smell of hot corn tortillas along with the *pat-pat* of the women's hands making them, the sting of roasting chiles in your throat and in your eyes. Sometimes a smell in the morning, very cool and clean that makes you sad. And a night smell when the stars open white and soft like fresh *bolillo* bread. Every year I cross the border, it's the same—my mind forgets. But my body always remembers.

The Dark
Paul West

—for Bradford Morrow

Diagnosis of a Troop Train

Think of kings. If they cannot impose themselves upon commoners, or just a few folk with almost comparable titles, they sink into an ooze of moldy celery and black bones, where, my dears, they do not belong. Even as Prince of Wales, before he became the monarch Edward VII, Edward fancied the regal pile known as Sandringham, bought it for a quarter of a million pounds in 1862, and lived the happiest years of his life there, soothing himself and enlivening his guests, so much so that, when they left, he had them weighed, always testing that weight against the one they had on arriving, and thus proving to them, and himself, how well they had eaten and swilled. Ah, he sighed at the weight of those going away, little pondering the weight that might have been lost by someone addicted to abnormal sexual activity or another one whose taste lay in foods other than Windsor soup, roast beef, rice pudding (the staples) and (the coup de grâce) turbot *poché dans le pipi du petit Jésus ou pipi d'ange*. You went from common or garden fare to heaven in just a few mouthfuls, though of course habitual visitors soon knew whose *pipi* it was. Edward would have lost face if departure had revealed a new lightness, a loss. We can only surmise that certain leave-takers were not weighed or perhaps remained behind, walled up out of spite with enough sherry to last them the final week. It was safer to trough, and then be whisked back to London by special train.

Balancing his guests, however, with ponderous weights and a week's virtually force-fed mutton, say, was not the only imposition the king inflicted upon his creatures: through carefully selected minions he ran the whole piece as an estate, requiring gamekeepers, gardeners, masons, carpenters, cooks and maids, valets and stablehands and farriers, more than a hundred, all of whom, it is said, took pride in a kind of ancestral squalor, honored by sheer service to an institution almost too vast, and too bemired in pomp, for them to comprehend. Each stuck to his job, thrilling if he could do the work assigned, knowing he was among the chosen, called to the highest service until the end of his days. Men tugged forelock after removing humble cap, women curtseyed and simpered. It was what used to be called an imperial going-on, something between a jamboree and a durbah, with the king at a convenient distance except to his gilded cronies. He owned the place, of course, and its serfs, who were buried nowhere else.

By 1915, in the early years of the Great War, the hundred or so had tripled, not only a mob of the useful but, to some, a mythic contingent of the noble, the kept, the destined: their children's children would remain here, by royal appointment, until the next assassination. Nothing could be stauncher or stabler. It reminded the more thoughtful among the king's guests of the incessantly busy hive recommended by an old scholar named Mandeville: the epitome of the successful, stratified society that nothing could disrupt. King Edward became King George, who would become King George the Sixth, whose line would persist until all the names had been used up, which was never, not even after George the Nth. True, a certain loyal despondency afflicted those who worked on the estate, but they had been, as the phrase had it, "spoken for," and that was that. Besides, family skill passed on, and entire generations of the better schooled would run then abandon the beloved ground. It would rapidly approach perfection under some distant king whose bowels emptied into the same mahogany-mounted trough used by his ancestors.

All might have gone well if Edward the Seventh, who took the same name as Edward the Confessor of yore, had not decided that his honor-bound estate needed not only a staff but an army too, and these would be *territorials,* yeomen and guardians of the land, as anyone of the king's guests could prove, recalling rusty Latin. To Captain Frank Beck, he of the bushy mustache and Airedale eyes, fell the task of recruiting and drilling the more-than-willing troops, who got extra pay for their military services, most of all when they strode abroad (the Kings said "soared") to fight Johnny Turk and the Kaiser's spike-helmeted demons.

"No, not you, Beck, you shall not go." A king's protest.

Respectfully unheeded. "If *they* go, so must I, sire."

One war fast turns into another; only the armies remain the same, hordes of cannon-fodder. And the glorious image of Captain Beck, smoking pipe and brandishing his shooting stick (folding cane with a collapsible seat), urged his men on against the Turks and the Huns, crying "Come on, Sandringhams!" as if exhorting his old school's rugby team. By the time he had emptied his revolver he was dead, along with the one-hundred-strong cross section of genteel and genteel-addicted soldiery massed devoutly behind him. They did not all have Tennyson's Light Brigade in mind, but Captain Beck did, and he had already schooled his men, through tent-flap chat at midnight and exhortation at dawn, that if they died in action their debt would have been paid. Only honor and incessant rest awaited them. Restrained, mustached, neat, humbled men going to war, and then gone, certainly not to rise again.

Except for the New Zealanders, a crew little given to hyperbole and therefore taken seriously, who claimed to have seen the Sandringhams, of the Fifth Battalion Norfolk Regiment march forward into a rosy cloud, a bizarre huge puff of grotesque fleshliness, and gradually lift upward, borne there by some force that wafted them off the ground. Then they were gone. It was still August 12, 1915, but they were nowhere to be seen, enclosed in the ascending fluff. They had advanced toward a dense wood and not come out the other side, even Frank Beck, too old to serve, too honorable to let them face hell alone.

There had, of course, been several other such incidents, mystically contrived, as when the Angel of Mons had flown over during a British retreat, or when a ghastly German major cantered through the British trenches on the eve of an attack. Desperation hopes, the saving grace of wives and sweethearts left behind to imagine horrors while trapping mice and cooking porridge. A hundred men from a compact society, ascending like khaki gossamer, perhaps softened the image of war, inducing a renewed nostalgic longing for time off spent in the apple orchard or quaffing ale at the local pub. But who believed it, swallowed the image of Sergeant Cuthbert climbing or Lieutenant Aylesbury gliding, a flash-forward to the sky divers of the distant far end of the century? It might be fair to say they all believed it, for solace, and debunked it for common sense. Word of their demise would follow, and that would be the end of talk. They prepared for the worst in lenient stoicism, and boiled their kettles.

Thus their story was born, or at least the start of its onset, with the estate's huge retinue cast in the role of plaintive angels gone to glory: helpless, disciplined, and loyal to a T. It was not a bad reputation to have, going out in such style, never having heard of the Chief Constable who said style used to be ninety percent police work. True in their case, anyway as, called to the colors, they went in much the same mood as you would quell a riot or a backstairs melodrama. Heroes all, from private to captain, each endowed with a fleck of pride from royal affiliation. Dead together, they stayed together in that slowly rising cloud.

At least they did so until another story invaded the holy precinct of the first. A priest had discovered a mass grave in the wood they marched into, with not a rank omitted: the captain who had been the estate agent, gamekeepers and foremen become sergeants, farm-hands who had volunteered to be the rank and file of a miniature army so close-knit and orderly it seemed to belong only to peace-time. All from the same place, they ended up ensemble, and news of their deaths brought about a tide of sentimental loathing predicated on one of those Last Remarks that so haunt the minds of military historians and album makers.

Private John Dye apocalyptically to Captain Beck: "I don't think we are going to be made very welcome here, sir."

Smiling, Beck agreed. "I don't think we will, Dye."

Having thus settled their minds, they got on with it, minds fixed on the King, whom they were deputizing for. Given imperfect maps, bogus information and muddled orders from above (not Beck's), they marched into an ambush; a position that had been found empty by a patrol had filled up overnight, and it was into this trap that two cigarette-smoking colonels led them, brandishing canes above their heads. Now that the slowly ascending cloud had been disposed of (rising toward an angel overflying, perhaps), the wood caught fire. Those who were not cut down by machine-gun fire were burned to death. Telegrams eventually went out, describing them, at first, as merely missing, not even "believed killed." The king himself cabled General Sir Ian Hamilton, the British Commander, demanding to know the fate of his people, otherwise known as the Sandringham Company. Back came the shuddering, top-secret answer: "I am mortified to tell you that there is no news, none that is reliable, sire, beyond the disappearance of 14 officers and some 250 men. Captain F. R. Beck also missing. The battalion performed with ardor and dash."

At this point, the flummoxed king began a new habit. Confounded by, at first, a levitation, then by a cremation, he kept pursing his lips as if masticating a final morsel, which was only sometimes there. Always readjusting the set of his mouth, he resembled someone trying to speak through closed lips, but never finding the words, so that he seemed to have acquired a fresh tic of acute oral diffidence. The war went on, but his attention had fixed on the one event and could not see beyond it.

Newspapers and parliamentary questions kept the horror alive for years, even after the site had been excavated and all bodies removed (some forever missing). Later massacres ousted it, especially those of World War Two, a bravura mess famous for its superior carnage. The dead Sandringhams were replaced, their families compensated, a shoal of medals bestowed, and toil in the fields, with horses and cattle, roasts and B and S (brandy and soda) resumed. The horror of it, the local disaster so far away, had become merely nominal, recounted in chimney corners on especially stormy nights or in church on the occasion of marriage services, but lost and wasted as beyond remedy.

Even the ghastly truth that each soldier had been shot in the head had never been made public. An Essex vicar, Charles Pierrepoint Edwards, winner of the Military Cross for rescuing wounded men from no man's land, had returned to the Continent after the war and, mustering his own labor force, discovered 180 bodies, 122 of them men of the 5th Norfolks. On his return, he submitted a formal report to the War Office, but suppressing the plain signs of massacre. They had been shot on the field of honor, not by an execution squad. Had this news leaked out, it would surely have sounded odd, inadequate, spurious. Had there been enough enemy soldiers in the wood to carry out an act so fiendish? As it was, Parson Edwards, M.C., became revered as the hero who went back. What was Hamilton to answer to his king? "Sire, I have just sent them all to their deaths in pursuance of yet another bungled onslaught. Forgive me." A more modern opinion would have diagnosed the event as clusterfuck swathed in awe and mystery. A troop of amateur soldiers had been wiped out, and the king had to make his own peace, in the end managing to fire Hamilton for both tact and deceit.

Even this wretched finale would perhaps have sunk into the cloudy ignominy of modern history (a bad day in a worse galaxy) if another story had not begun to seep through from France: not a levitation, not a massacre, but a grandiose consummation the French themselves called *"un avènement"* (a coming or advent), after a phrase in a carol. Parson Edwards, M.C. had told only half the truth, or perhaps only one quarter of it, discovering corpses certainly, but also something else predicated on what many had come to regard as a fallible French fable, thunderously wonderful, satisfactory in outline, but not to be taken to heart. Lingering in the gloaming, he had spotted a set of steps leading, he presumed, to a bunker or shrapnel shelter, just as likely to contain bodies as the soil he stood on. Down he went, tentatively, flashlight quivering, only to hear the sound of music, at which he started up again, startled, and thinking he was too old for song, if only he could come back in a hundred years, when this and all else was impossible. He halted at the top of the much-worn steps and breathed in the cool demeanor of the splintered beeches, glad to be alive in the cradle of the peace, or at least in the manger of postwar delirium.

Then he went down again, toward a dim-lit door, which he kicked open in the rough manner of one alive affronting the dead, faintly aware that the door should not have been there at all, but blown to smithereens. There was a rumor. No, he dismissed it: a slander on deserters, no more than that. Something French, like that French johnny's tribute to dead friends, the war dead, in something about the tomb of Couperin. Not an insensitive man by any means; his very feat had won him reclame and dignity; he knew something about Butterworth and the poets Owen, Thomas, Kilmer and Rosenberg. So who was rejoicing down there, behind the door? To a lonely bugle sound? Not the dead composer, the dead poets. He did what we can always do, gradually tightening the focus of our eyes from blur to accuracy, at last taking in what was there all the time, but scrambled motley. How pale those faces, how awkward the ruined legs and arms, how matted-disheveled the blood-caked hair. The unwashed dead for some inexplicable reason were revelling, a militia of underground Eurydices who had not looked back at the Orpheus of war. But were they really the dead or those who had escaped?

Then something came to him, the patina of a rumor that said a battalion-sized group of deserters from all nations had taken to living underground in an archipelago of caves, emerging at night to steal food and fuel. All this beneath the battlegrounds of Franco-Germany. Edwards had poo-poohed this story when he first heard it, but was it more preposterous than levitation or atrocity? Why, the Germans here still wore their spiked coal-scuttle helmets, the British officers their collars and ties, their Sam Browne belts worn diagonally across the chest and swung over the shoulder beneath the epaulet. Now he too was an Orpheus in this underworld, observing one Austrian with a cat, whose coat he caressed while murmuring encouragement, almost as if hypnotizing the creature. Where had the cat come from? That was an easy question compared with a hundred others that occurred to him, concerning numbers, surgery, what was inimical, what was worth living for in such a state of eminent ruin. Were there, he wondered, enough of these runaways to start another war? Had they no idea that hostilities had ended? Was it not simpler for them to march upward and out and, at long last, seek medical aid? Parson Edwards felt he was missing something vital, something that, say, an atheist would have picked up on by now, or even a professional soldier. Survivors entombed by their own will, he murmured, and attempted to join in the revelry, but found himself oddly fended off, looked past and through by ex-soldiers of all kinds, all bound together by some secretive esprit de corps. Perhaps what he heard as voices was an aural illusion created—he gasped—by some interminable gramophone: a bakelite chorus of more or less soldierly songs or lewd military stories unfit for mixed company. It was almost the same feeling he had had when the war was going full tilt, when he purloined a line from Shakespeare ("Now thrive the armorers"), and pondered the sequence implied in the concept of replacement, especially among Royal Flying Corps pilots: After only a week, a pilot was dead, and his replacement, a beardless youth with a dozen flying hours, was due, only to be replaced a week later. To go unreplaced for a month, a pilot had to be mighty lucky, keeping his replacement at bay but only in the end to give way, shot down at last. Surely, he often wondered before he won his Military Cross, the commanding officer who sent these youths aloft could see into the future, at least two or three replacements ahead, so much so that he developed a special approach to death and substitution: not merely the vaunted indifference of a man chewing on the loneliness of command, but a view of humanity that was generic. "Allee samee," as the French stooge would cry in a postwar movie called *Lafayette Escadrille,* about American pilots who, also, lived only a week before yielding. "American bums," he called them as he rousted them from comfy beds at dawn for the next patrol. Parson Edwards, like all infantrymen yearning skyward, saw this movie during the peace, appalled by the casual callousness, just the same emotion he picked up underground from the lost legion.

Yet he still missed something vital to the puzzle.

As did his son, visiting the same place years later, observing the same mannikins or figurines, still presumably raiding local farms at night, unhindered by peacetime police. *How* he wondered, now at last believing his father's weird tales.

And *his* own son, in succession, or replacement, appalled by the phenomenon that had astonished his father and his father's father. He could only presume that the same goings-on had gone on right through the Second World War and the ensuing peace, when Europe began to unite. It was, however, only *his* son who, having made the same vain pilgrimage to the same area, began to see the light: the soldiers underground were fulfilling some kind of bargain, otherwise they would have broken free, leapt out into the sunlight or the dank cold, and taken their place among the living, gauchos released from long penance, or, their red-rimmed eyes refracting tears, just watching ducks fly over in V formation.

These, young Pierrepoint Pierrepoint told himself, were truly the dead, and no more shilly-shally about that. The living dead, he added. But why? It so happened he was an actuary with a developed interest in astronomy, an addict of such wonders as the Pistol Star, the brightest in the Milky Way, on the brink of blowing up in a supernova, or the so-called Arches cluster, 150 stars cramped together to form the outline of the Firth of Forth bridge in Scotland.

Now he saw something he should have guessed, rolling round and around in his mind the notion that the tug exerted by all the stars in our Galaxy is not enough to hold it together. Some huge halo of dark matter has to keep the rotor stars and the boiling gas at the fringe of the Galaxy from just whizzing away, out of control. Surely, some almost unimaginable halo of stuff, reaching millions of miles beyond the known outline of the Milky Way, sheaths it, curtails it. So he developed his theory, reckoning a departing soul weighs a gram, say, as has been demonstrated, and that one gram multiplied by all the souls that have known death makes enough weight to keep the Galaxy in rein. He has no idea how many, but in the finicky blasé fashion of actuaries, he knows it is bound to be enough.

So, then, the underground anteroom of the dead was always a waiting room in perpetual motion, multiplied by all the battlefields on earth, a keen corporate symbol for those who find a grave below and a civilian soul wafting on high too abstract for humane thought. Since this discovery, his friends have considered applying for a rubber room on his behalf, unable to believe or discredit him, but certain the entire equation is a more complex exchange than Pierrepoint Pierrepoint thinks it is. After all, are there no dead souls in other galaxies—the hopping fecopod in Sculptor's Cartwheel Galaxy, the crumb lizard in the Cygnus Loop supernova remnant, the Egg Nebula's dune-fondler, or the nitric eel, the hot-brain potamus—just aching to keep things together?

Bad case of undistributed middle, they say of him, reminding him the family name evokes Albert Pierrepoint, old-time hangman-barkeep of the king. What manner of death goes on today?

GROPING

There are fragrant summer nights when, out at the telescope with his thermos of cocoa and (naturally) a brown-caked mouth, he peers and thinks he sees, no he knows he sees, well past the imagining of any other dreamer, the faintest wisp that moves just a fraction like a dead caterpillar poised in blueberry jello, a phantom entity that keeps the Milky Way intact, fed a constant diet of transmuted souls, a gram per head, a reinforcement of billions over time, delicate as someone sipping lye with lemon, not quite matching the thousand angels that dance on the head of a pin, no, not reverse angels but similar, inhaling the invisible stream of souls that, recruited from dissonant midnight or a noon full of pealing bells, endlessly swarm upward unweighed but fractionally redeemed. These souls, he knows now, have been *bought,* like those in some medieval tracts, not bought *off* with its suggestion of bribery, but caught up by the velvet touch of need, a tit offered for the full, dejected tat of the body. It stands to sense, says Pierrepoint Pierrepoint, each one of us in the tiniest way a superintendent-to-be. Sometimes he felt just like the backyard squirrels who, as fall wore on, instead of running around the full right angle of his flowerbeds, cut off the corner along the wooden crossbars installed for strength. The cold was coming, right from space.

Having latched onto something mesmerically profound, Pierrepoint Pierrepoint may still be said to be not "making it," as we say nowadays. Out there at the lens, thinking he is watching the automatic recycling of human and inhuman souls, almost like the watcher in the poem who writes Shelley's *The Triumph of Life,* he contents himself by sweetening bronze tea with sticky, spermy condensed milk spilled from a churchkeyed can, giving the tea an aroma of dry mustard mixed with wet bubblegum. The more he delves into the eternity of futurity, the universe's need for death to hold it together like that famous expanding currant cake of the astronomers, the more he peers his way into the lattices of life, into the minutest pinholes where ships in bottles contain bottles with ships in them, and so forth, and spiders in aircraft hangars of olden times rig webs across the evenly spaced wing ribs of planes whose fabric has torn just enough to permit the installation of baby turnstiles. "This way to heaven, folks." In these in-and-out times he is the boy whose father has gone away, leaving the son in charge of simple multiplication cards only to return and find him spouting calculus at what seems the same age, able to figure out the tall grasses along the driveway and which of them has a salient winter configuration called E Pluribus Grass Plaza.

Something has come loose in his mind, freeing him, or his mind has come loose amid the swarm of particulars, setting all of them free as well. Now he asks his wife Gloria to notice the bizarre chime in the voices of the actress Joan Severance and the actor Peter Coyote. They belong to him now. At the jeweler's, when Lauren Lyuba shows him something, she adjusts her speech, almost saying the coo of "cool," but recovering just in time to pronounce it "sophisticated"; she changes her tune according to a customer's degree of suavity, at least as she sees it. He gets all this in a flash, as he does the opaque glare of homicidal bluestockings and the almost watery sounds that squirrels make along their tree trunks, sunlight tweaking the manias of both. He even knows, having been attuned to the way puns abolish time, that in the kingdom of the marsupials an aspirant is called a wallabe. From things and creatures about to die, he does not turn away but reinforces his gaze upon them, knowing they all hold the universe together: God's country estate as he now sees it. He cuts himself some slack, no longer bound by paternal will or royal fiat, but a loose cannon in the cheaper seats up front where he can see the mesh on which the projected picture floats, and behind it the twisted faces of the prematurely doomed.

Gloria Pierrepoint thinks he's gone daffy, what with his wobbly walk and teary eyes, and she cannot fathom why he now thinks all women are Libras. "You'd never trust a Virgo," he murmurs, "or a twin, or even an archer, would you now?" If she had a rolling pin handy, she'd wallop him with it, she an Aries, but she keeps still lest the most minor movement on her part stir him to violence. One of the pills he has to take will pass through him, yielding up all its goodness (so the leaflet says), reappearing skeletally firm like the cross section of a parrot's backbone. He understands this fact and likes it, clearer than anyone about a clutch of birthday balloons whose helium floats them perpendicular but never enough to free them from a circular disc of what seems fireclay that anchors them just enough, this beautifully judged as neither too heavy nor too light, with the whole balloonery hovering on the point of buffoonery, but never quite making it. Just, he says, like the dear old universe, outbound but tethered just the right amount, a quality we call cliff-hanger poise, Gloria, it's when we hold two magnets together and you feel the pull between them and muscle it as a living force, almost a protoplasm, a fluid, weakening as you pull them apart, coming on strong as your limp wrists weaken and you creep them together, as in Goethe, the *ewig Weibliche,* he says to his absent wife, who has left him for Omaha.

By day, he fixes on the crows that never seem to migrate, seduced by the promise of eternal roadkill; but they do come fluttering down, like pieces of black umbrella dislodged from higher up, and this pleases him, proves he's on the right track, shrugging his way from Cyrano de Bergerac's *Give me giants* to Sancho Panza's *What giants?* His world is held together by what's small.

He has even, in his serious classic cups, suggested that the amalgamated souls of the dead-and-gone fuse to form massive compact halo objects familiarly known as elderly white dwarfs that shift only slightly and exhibit a faint blue tinge out there in Deep Field North. Ho-hum, they tell him, chiding his trance, but he answers only with a sedate mumble. The brown on his lips and teeth dries and cakes, his mouth open wide. He knows no chill. His eye is on the target, his mind on the guide-rail to the Galaxy.

Mrs. Hollingsworth's List
Padgett Powell

GROCERIES

MRS. HOLLINGSWORTH LIKES to traipse. Her primary worry is thinning hair, though this has not happened yet. She enjoys a solidarity with fruit. She is wistful for the era in which hatboxes proliferated, though a hatbox is not something even her grandmother may have owned. More probably what she wants is hatboxes themselves, without the era or the hats. But the proud firm utility of the hatbox requires a hat and an era for its dignity; otherwise it is a relic. She does not want relics. Her husband is indistinct. She regards friendly dogs with suspicion. Her daughters have lost touch with her, or she with them, or both; it is the same thing, she thinks, or it is not the same thing, which means it may as well be the same thing: so much is pointless this way, indifferent, moot, or *mute* as a friend of hers says. Not a friend, but a friendly man whom she cannot bring herself to correct when he says "mute" for "moot," for then she might have to go on and indict his entire presumption to teach at the community college, inspiring roomfuls of college hopefuls to say "mute" for "moot" and filling them with other malaprops, and if she indicts him on that presumption she'd need go on and indict him for the presumption of his smug liberalness and for affecting to like film as Art and not movies as entertainment and for getting his political grooming from the smug liberalness and film-as-Art throat clearing of National Public Radio, and all of this, since it would be but the first strike in taking on the entire army of modest Americans who believe themselves superior to other Americans (but not to any foreigners, except dictators) mostly by virtue of their doing nothing but electing to think themselves superior—all of this would be unwise, or moot, and indeed she may as well be mute, maybe the oaf was on to something.

She wanted to summon a plumber and pour something caustic down the crack of his ass when he exposed it to her, as he invariably would, assuming the plumbing position. Drano, she thought, *trés apropos*. She had learned recently that the British term for the propensity for the working man to expose himself in this way was "showing builder's bottom." That was a lovely touch of noblesse oblige, of gently receding Empire. She was less gentle in her apprehension that the entire world and everyone in it was showing its ass. She was not unaware, and not happy, that this apprehension linked her closely to the film-as-Art side of the herd, and she would go to a movie with a plumber wearing no pants at all before she'd go to some *noire* with a man in slacks, but still she found herself actually calculating the drift of things if one were to try to burn a builder's bottom. She figured on this seriously all one morning until finally she faced it: it had come to this, had it? Her mind had gone. The practical consequences of her symbolically telling the world to pull its goddamn pants up filled up her otherwise empty head at age fifty. It had all come to this. Muriatic acid for the driveway contractor, liquid chlorine for the pool man, shot of Raid for the bug man, upgrade the plumber to a bead of molten solder. When this nonsense left her mind alone, she thought about the Civil War. How a woman could be prevented from doing anything but thinking of builder's bottom, and of all which that represented, and of all her impotence at reversing the disposition of the human world to show its ass, was owing somehow to the Civil War. The American Civil War, arguably as silly a war as they come, she was virtually ignorant of. She was not better informed of any war, actually, save for perhaps the Second World War and Vietnam, on a very topical basis. And she knew of one man who had been in Korea. But the Civil War . . . was beginning to haunt her.

She could not reckon this sudden absorption with it given how vastly uninformed she was of it. Manassas was molasses, Sharpsburg was Dullsville; the March to the Sea was no more than Hard To Lee. Her images of the dead, which she did know to nearly exceed all our other wars combined, were not those of the bodies themselves that the wet-plate photography so in its infancy had allegedly recorded in such stunning graphic. She kept seeing not bodies but crows on them. To her, true torment was not death but a crow.

The thousands of baleful tears shed then now went, she thought, into laundry softener—the women threw these handkerchiefs of the laundromat into their machines as they had thrown kerchiefs at military parades. The result was every bit as good: things smelled sweet and the women felt good about themselves. Their men marched on in the perfume of goodfeeling and put their cell phones to their heads and zeroed in on the enemy and fired nonsense at him all day. They had learned from Vietnam how to drop smoke on the enemy to better his targeting. There was much information. It was not clear when everyone had stopped believing in himself.

A prison term today was not the worst thing that could obtain, she thought. Nothing was. Nothing was the end of the world. All could be surmised and survived. Death and rape were just particularly bad. We were mature. But crows could land, after all; they need not fly all day long. And you had to regard them.

She knew that the Confederate mint in Columbia had printed its worthless millions and stood today in vacant ruin, but virtually intact, for sale at too high a price to sell to whoever would turn it into a museum or a mall. She knew that Appomattox is a National Park, fully restored, visited by thousands of tourists a year. She knew that only 4 percent of the final site of the Lost Cause is original, based on the number of original bricks to the total number of unoriginal bricks used in the restoration. She knew that this restoration had had to commence from the very archaeological digs that discovered the outlines of the original foundation of the house where it all ended. None of the original bricks was even in its original location. Only some stones of the hearth are in the same place. Beyond that, only the air *space* is the original thing, where it was. Maybe a piece of furniture or two that Grant and Lee might have *looked* at. And she knew about Lee's ingenious battle orders the Yankees found wrapped around lost cigars. That business amazed and frightened her. And the name Nathan Bedford Forrest was in her head like the hook of a pop-radio tune. In her grasp of it all he was a man who had somehow never been beaten in a war that was lost from the start. She knew more than she knew she knew.

On her kitchen table she noticed an odd, tall can of Ronson's Lighter Fluid. There had not been a cigarette lighter of the sort that required this fuel in this house in she would guess twenty years. It would squirt down a builder's bottom as pretty as you please. She chuckled. She was not herself, she thought, or she was, perhaps, and she chuckled again.

Were men who could not keep their pants up a function of the Civil War? Were women who put up with them a function of the Civil War? Was having yourself an indistinct husband a function of the Civil War? Was finding a strange bottle of flammable petroleum distillate beside your grocery list a function of the Civil War? Was chuckling and not knowing what was yourself and what was not yourself a function of the Civil War? Was not really caring at this point "who you were," and finding the phrase itself a hint risible, a function of the Civil War? She sat down at the table and wrote on her grocery list, "A mule runs across Durham, on fire," and then, dissatisfied with one item, sat down to augment the list.

Cornpone

Mrs. Hollingsworth wrote on:

A mule runs through Durham, on fire. No—there is something on his back, on fire. Memaw gives chase, with a broom, with which she attempts to whap out the fire on the mule. The mule keeps running. The fire appears to be fueled by paper of some sort, in a saddlebag or satchel tied on the mule. There is of course a measure of presumption in crediting Memaw with trying to put out the fire; it is difficult for the innocent witness to know that she is not just beating the mule, or hoping to, and that the mule happens to be on fire, and that that does not affect Memaw one way or another. But we have it on private authority, our own, that Memaw is attempting to save the paper, not gratuitously beat the mule, or even punitively beat the mule. Memaw is not a mule beater.

The paper is Memaw's money, perhaps (our private authority accedes this is likely), which money Pawpaw has strapped onto his getaway mount, perhaps (our private authority credits him with strapping the satchel on, but hesitates to characterize his sitting the mule as he is as a deliberate, intelligent attempt to actually "get away"); that is to say, we are a little out on a limb when we call the mule, as we brazenly do, the mount on which he hoped to get away, and might have, had he not, as he sat the plodding mule, carelessly dumped the lit contents of the bowl of his corncob pipe over his shoulder onto the satchel on the mule's back, thereby setting the fire and setting the mule into a motion more vigorous than a plod. A mule in a motion more vigorous than a plod with a fire on its back attracts more attention than, etc.

Memaw, we have it on private authority, solid, was initially, with her broom, after Pawpaw himself, before he set fire to the satchel behind him, so the argument that Pawpaw might have effected a clean getaway without the attention-getting extras of a trotting mule on fire is somewhat compromised. Memaw, with her broom, has merely changed course; she wants, now, to prevent her money's burning more than Pawpaw's leaving, though should Pawpaw get away, with the money unburnt, she presumably loses it all the same. That loss, of unburnt money, might prove temporary: unburnt money is recoverable, sometimes, if the thieves are not vigilant of their spoils, if the police are vigilant of their responsibilities, if good citizens who find money are honest and return it, etc. But burnt money is not recoverable, except in certain technical cases involving banks and demonstrable currency destruction and mint regulations allowing issue of new currency to replace the old, which cases Memaw would be surprised to hear about. And it is arguable that, were she indeed whapping Pawpaw and not the fire behind him, her object might not be to prevent his leaving but to accelerate it.

So Memaw is now whapping not the immediate person of Pawpaw but the fire behind him. It is not to be determined if Pawpaw fully appreciates the situation. He may think Memaw's consistent failure to strike *him* with the broom is a function of her indextrous skill with the broom used in this uncustomary manner. We are unable, even with the considerable intelligence available from our private authority, to hazard whether he knows the area to his immediate rear is in flames. Why Memaw would prefer to extinguish the fire rather than annul his escape or punish him for it is almost certainly beyond the zone of his ken. We have this on solid private authority, our own, our own *army* of private authority, in which we hold considerable rank. Pawpaw is holding his seat, careful to keep his clean corncob pipe from the reach of Memaw's broom, errant or not. Were the pipe to be knocked from his hand, either by a clean swipe that lofts it into the woods or by a glancing blow that puts it in the dirt at the mule's hustling feet, he would dismount to retrieve the pipe and thereby quit his escape. It is likely that Memaw and the burning mule would continue their fiery voyage, leaving him there inspecting his pipe for damage.

The mule is an intellectual among mules, and probably among the people around him, but we, the people around him, intellectuals among people or not, as per our test scores, our universities and degrees therefrom, and our disposition to observe public broadcasting, and with the entire army of private authority we command, cannot know what he knows. It is improbable that he knows of

Pawpaw's betrayal, of Memaw's hurt rage, of the accidental nature of the fire, of the denominations of the currency, of the improbable chance that among the money are dear letters to Memaw before she was Memaw that she does not want Pawpaw to discover, even after he has left her and might be presumed to be no longer jealous of her romantic affairs. It is not certain that he, the mule, knows his back, or something altogether too close to his back, is on fire. It is certain, beyond articulated speculation, that he senses his back is hot and that the kind of noise and the kinds of colors which make him hot and nervous when he is too near them are on his back. He has elected to flee, or is compelled to flee. Nervousness puts him in a predisposition to flee. A woman with a broom, a two-legger with any sort of prominent waving appendage, coming at him puts him in full disposition to flee, which he does, which increases the unnerving noises and colors and heat on his back, confirming him in the rectitude of this course of action, notwithstanding certain arguments which he has almost certainly never heard and might or might not comprehend were he to hear them that he'd be better off standing still.

That is Memaw's position: If the bastard would just stand still, she could save him *and* the money. She could get Lonnie Sipple's letters out of the money, get the money out of the bag, then get Pawpaw, as he stupidly yet sits the mule guarding his pipe, which she could verily whap into the woods with one shot, and then get Pawpaw and the mule on down the road, where they are fool enough to think they want to go. She knows the mule is not fool enough to want to go down the road—the mule would appear to be a faultless fellow until caught up in human malfeasance and crossfire and dithered by it; plus, he is on fire—but she is going to uncharitably link him to Pawpaw during the inexact thinking that prevails during domestic opera of this sort. This is precisely the kind of inexact thinking in which it does not occur to one that burnt money can be replaced at a bank under certain technical circumstances which make one nervous to speculate upon in the event that the money concerned is one's own. But now that the army of our private authority has revealed the further intelligence of the existence of personal letters—which we suspect it could have revealed sooner were relations between us, the rank, and it, the file, better—also in the satchel, we know that the money was never Memaw's first concern in her zealous whapping of the fire on the mule. And we know that Memaw, no matter how inexact her thinking during domestic opera of this sort, is not inclined to think that letters, like money, can be replaced, under certain technical circumstances, after they are burnt. Letters of the sort she is protecting now, in fact, are themselves but the thinnest substitute for, papery vestiges of, the irreplaceable tender emotions they recall, tender emotions she held and that held her in a state of rapt euphoria some thirty years ago, emotions she can but vaguely recollect when she holds the letters in her rare few moments of calm, tired tranquility. She and Lonnie Sipple are only nineteen years old, they kiss without the nuisances of whiskey and whiskers and malodorous thrusting, without the complications of bearing children, and Lonnie Sipple has not yet been found with the pitchfork tine through his heart.

Pawpaw is, in contrast to Lonnie Sipple in this recollected tender tranquility, and in the loud, mean, prevailing domestic opera which surrounds her small tranquilities like a flood tide, a piece of shit that thinks it won World War II and thereby earned the right to be every kind of shitass it is possible to be on Earth, and then some, if there is any then some. This, his single-handed winning of WWII, is inextricably and inexplicably a function of his people's collective losing of the Civil War eighty years before.

Memaw did not become Memaw until she allowed herself to be linked to Pawpaw via a civil ceremony during the post-War frenzy of imprudent coupling that wrought more harm to the country, she now thinks, than Hirohito. She had a normal name and was normal herself. She was Sally, and a fond uncle would call her Salamander, which now, against Memaw, sounds charming. And Pawpaw had been Henry Stiles until two minutes after the ceremony when people seemed to come out of the woods and the woodwork, all calling him Pawpaw and her nothing, ignoring her for a full two years, it seems, until slowly addressing her, tentatively at first but then unerringly, as Memaw. She was powerless to stop this phenomenon; it was not unlike a slow, rising tide, unnoticed until it is too late to escape. There she had been, first on a wide isolated silent mudflat of wedding-gift Tupperware and their VFW mortgage, and then in a sudden full sea of *Memaw* and only a thin horizon of sky and water around her. It stunned her to hear "Memaw makes the best cornpone," stunned her into hearing it again and again, and then Sally was never heard of or from again, and she was not a Salamander but a Hellbender.

We have it from the army of private authority that dogs love Memaw. Two dogs are, in fact, at her heels as she herself dogs the heels of the mule, of which dogging she is tiring, and Pawpaw, who dropped his pipe and voluntarily quit the mule to retrieve it, having grown complacent with his surmise that his pipe is unhurt, is in an awkward amalgam of embarrassment and fatigue and uncertainty as to what to do now. Memaw is between him and his burning getaway mule, and he is more winded than Memaw and the mule, so that the matter of his skirting around Memaw and overtaking the mule himself is out of the question. He is somewhat concerned—even the innocent witness can deduce this, by the nervous motions of his feet when she turns occasionally to glare at him and point one long finger at him—that Memaw will desist pursuit of the burning mule and come after him, which will put him in the face-losing position of having to retreat.

Keeping his distance, as he is, he has had occasion to pick up pieces of charred currency and an envelope with a cancelled stamp on it dated 1943, which he knows was the War because he knows (first to bloom in his troubled brain at this moment, this is to say) of the 1943 steel penny, a copper-conservation thing owing to the War, which he knows (second to bloom) he was in, which he knows (third) because he won it. The letter is addressed to Sally Palmer in a handwriting not his own.

This was the best grocery list Mrs. Hollingsworth had ever conceived. There were things on it that obviously suggested you need not go to the store only to be disappointed in not getting them. She sat at her table marvelling at the fun of such a grocery list. She was going to make a few of these. Yessireebob, she said to herself, slapping at a fly. This was a bit more like it. She studied for a moment her linoleum floor, which had a nice, old agate speckle to it, and made a sound like something breaking when you walked on it.

Bluegill

Mrs. Hollingsworth had read or heard some things about Nathan Bedford Forrest. She had to have. It was the name of the high school. Had she read of him as well? The idea formed in her mind that he had been indomitable; he had been the War's Achilles. Achilles with pinworms and slaves besmirching his heroic profile. Had she heard, even, that the South could have won had he been given broader command? He seemed listable.

She put him on:

A man who has seen Forrest catches two bluegill at one time on his single hook, on his cane pole, noticing as he does, inexplicably, an exotic fish—parrot fish? yellowtail?—in the water. The fish is as odd as his vision of the Civil War figure: a strange waking dream of a man on a horse larger and louder than Hollywood, whom he somehow knew to be representing Nathan Bedford Forrest. In the same spirit of unblinking improbability he saw what looked like a pompano in the dark lake, now the two bluegill. He enters the dockhouse to show the improbable catch to his wife. In the dim shack he sees a leg in tight polyester shorts hanging awkwardly off a cot, and as the party wakes up he realizes the leg is not his wife's. "Excuse me, Sir—Ma'am," he says to a fogged woman who looks like his father's sister a bit, but more bleached. He intends to explain everything, including how and why a man up to something, as it appears a man this close to a strange woman sleeping must be, would not come up on her like this with two fish on a pole. Only an honest bumbler would do that. Why this woman is where his wife should be, and in a drunken stupor, he cannot begin to decide. He says to her as she begins to focus on him for an explanation of his intrusion, holding forth the two fish, "The escapees of the hattism of dived-in-ness." By "hattism of dived-in-ness" he seems to mean regularity of conformity.

The man was named Lonnie Sipple before he forgot who he was because of his broken heart.

Forrest

—Do you see our leader with his hair on fire riding like—

—No.

—the wind?

—I didn't even see that he was on a horse.

—You'd better get with it, then. If your leader rides by with his hair on fire slapping at you with the flat of his sabre so as to inspire you, or goad you, or outright scare you to heroics beyond yourself, and taking up falterers by the collar and throwing them to constitute roadblocks before other falterers, and otherwise threatening them with sufficient otherworldy gesture that they become convinced simple mortality is less dreadful than what he promises them if they run, and so they decide to turn and fight, and thank him later, whether they are dead or alive—if you do not see this going on about you, you are in trouble.

—I did not see "my leader." I am not aware that I am being led. Or that I follow.

—Then you are in deep, deep trouble, my friend. I should take this can of Ronson here—who bought this? for what? very pretty can—and set *your* hair on fire.

—Maybe you should.

—This can reminds me of a bad high-school football uniform, the loud blue and yellow combo. Hard to win in that rig.

—Red and black beat that every time.

—There's Forrest again!

—Where?

—*Right there!*

—I can't see him.

—It is true, then. Some people see him, and some do not.

—I'd just as soon not.

—Frankly, I do not know that you are wrong. Because I do not know what to do with myself when I have seen him ride through a town square, horse and hair aflame, salt and leather and sweat and steel penetrating the trailing air, and a malaise of sadness and loss consuming all witness to him, leaving us diffident and afraid and idle in his wake.

—Maybe you should shoot him.

—The bullet would tink off him like a piece of errant solder. It would lie molten and deformed, splashed in the dirt. One side of it would shine and the other would be dulled by annealed dirt. It would be a symbol. Of something.

—Indeed. But what?

—I would not know. I failed Symbol.

—I failed Meta-everything

—High-five to that! But still, I can see Forrest, and you cannot.

—You have not failed Forrest.

—No, I have not. I will not fail Forrest. Forrest was made so that a man, even a confused one, a little afraid, or a lot, might not fail him, and thereby might not fail himself.

—He sounds like Jesus, sort of. But I failed Jesus, too.

—Let's not get into that. This is enough: a man whose head and horse is on fire storms through town squares under my minute inspection. He is either there, invisible to the townsfolk his passing would otherwise knock down or blow down, or he is only there in my perhaps specially tuned vision. To me it does not matter how he exists, or why. I see him, he leads, I follow. Sometimes that means I go into the closest cafe on the square and have coffee. But I do what I can do. Even the terms of society are clear in a cafe after Forrest passes. The waitress in white or light green is tired but polite. The drunk is at the counter. The regulars are at their table, sclerotic and suspendered, gouty and flushed and content. And I am I, on my Mars, dithered even by the choices on a country breakfast menu, so all I have is coffee. But I have seen Forrest. I am not doing badly.

Room

The man who has seen Forrest takes a room over the cafe. How long he will want the room he does not know. It is white. The floor is oak, a gymnasium certainty to it, clean and hard. He wants nothing on it. He has one chair, by the window. There is a radio. It is black and on, but silent. A red stereo-indicator light shows, and a comforting green luminescent tuning band. The man is unsure whether he has found this appliance (improbable) or brought it (improbable). The tuning band shows the same comforting green light that originally issued from radium in such an application. He considers, not seriously, throwing the radio out the window.

Out the window, on the courthouse lawn, wearing blazing white shirts and loose herringbone trousers held up by handsome suspenders, are three or four or five or six or seven black men who appear to be ancient. Realistically—a word or notion that rolls saltily and oddly in the man's head like an olive—they are probably seventy years old, but the impression they give is that they were alive when the great Minie'-ball debate over their fate took place. Like the radio, they too are on and silent and improbably placed. What they are discussing the man has no idea, in their immaculate clothes, consummately sober and peaceful and wise-looking, immutable agreeable whiskate.

The man turns and looks at his four plain walls and regards them as an invitation to rest.

Down on the courthouse lawn, he makes four plain mistakes.

—Gentlemen (#1), what town is this? I mean (#2), I've been driving and enjoying the scenery (#3) and my map is torn right where I think this is, I can't read where I am, I think.

—Where your map?

—In my car.
—Where your car?
The man waves vaguely behind himself (#4). He looks up at the window of his new room. He sees himself smiling and smirking at his intelligence-gathering mission among the seated sages.
—Holly Spring.
—Holly Spring what?
—Holly Spring *what* what?
—Which Holly Spring?
—*This* Holly Spring.
—Which *state* Holly Spring?
—*State?*
—He say his map bad.
—His map *real* bad.
—Missippi.
—Mississippi?
—Missippi.
The man waves to himself in his window, not concealing his waving to no one from the dark sages, which is not mistake #5. It says to them, Lost? Maybe loster than you think, Gentlemen.
He claims his room for his rest.
The bed is as loose in its springs as a hammock. The sheet is a coarse, clean muslin which is very agreeable to the touch, as is his near engulfment into the slung posture of the mattress. He hears a noise, probably under the floor, probably a rat.
What he would like it to be is a woman. He thinks: tunneling her way to me. Let her emerge from this clean, hard floor, splintering it with her desire for me, and let me bathe her and place her on a pallet on the floor and behold her. Let us eat. Let us have each other in a fresh way in a fresh start and keep it fresh, keep it starting. To have a woman in perpetual start!

Woman

Emerging from the floor, she is gauzy, dark, as if seen through frosted glass, full red lips prominent. At this moment, before the ruination can begin, the man is happy. He has been a Gila monster and is now a puppy. The woman has strong hands and does not fidget with them. This, the man says, let us keep it to this. His lips are numb.
—Wait until you get a load of Forrest.

The woman posts herself on the chair by the window, and the man watches her watch for Forrest. Her red lips are blued with the pressure of her determination.

—Were you Lonnie?

—Were you Sally?

—Shh.

MOTHER OF FATHER, FLAT OF KNIFE

Fist, skull, stomp, gouge, *ride!* Forrest says, when you are the fustest with the mostest until you are the leastest with the lastest. (Mrs. Hollingsworth thought Forrest actually said some of this.) He is through the Gentlemen of ebony tribal regalness and elegant white shirts in an unseen unfelt blast of oilcloth and horse lather and unsmelt tang of silver spur, the flat of his saber in abeyance.

The man who can see him recalls that the mother of his father would slap his father with the flat of her carving knife. She was a great proud carver, which women seldom are, of ham and tongue, and she did not like pickers picking at her work. Her knife was red-handled and pitted, a blackened steel that showed a shiny edge. She slapped the hands of children regularly with it. She could tell a child a lie.

Forrest is a ghostly trail of dust and sweat and malice, a struck chord of straining tack and sheathed weapon and purpose. His lips are set in a line not unlike the new woman's, but they do not show the blue of the pressure of determination, as hers do. Forrest's lips are easy, deliberate without deliberation, exactly like a horse's lips. He is an animal, all right, the man says. Did you see him?

—I saw him. I thought him wizened—I read that he declined.

—Declined what?

—No, *declined.* Fell off some. Withered. At the end.

—If he declined, Lord let him not incline.

—No.

FIRST BREAST NOT OF ONE'S MOTHER

When his grandmother, who could tell a child a lie, with pleasure, pursing her lips after it in a satisfied way, as if savoring a chocolate, died, Lonnie Sipple cried. The look on his grandmother's face when she told him a lie was the same look on her face when she played poker.

When he met Sally Palmer, and with his lips lifted her breast by a gentle pursing of the flesh just below her nipple, and felt the orange-like weight of her breast, it was the last clear moment of sanity and purpose on Earth he would know. It was possibly the first such moment, but he cannot remember anything before the moment, and cannot precisely recall the moment itself, and all since has been a sloppiness in his head and his heart.

He did not die of a pitchfork tine to the heart. That was Romantic palaver of the burning-mule stripe, and far too easy. He did in fact once *find* a tine, isolated and alone, in a field, but it did not touch his heart. It had about it a roughened, pitted quality, not unlike his grandmother's carving knife. All steel, he thinks, was more or less alike in those days.

Ride, Slide

"Most times Forrest rides," Mrs. Hollingsworth began her list one day, thinking of the way the teenagers in the neighborhood talk and slink around, or slump around. Most time Mist Forrest ride but sometime he slide.

Sometime he take off his butternut duster look like Peterman catalogue, and his Victoria Secret garter belt and all, and grease hisself up naked as a jaybird and say, Okay, I fight all you, black white blue gray I don't care. Ya'll come on. And people being dumb as shit, they come on, and they get they ass *whup.*

He so good he go to a wrassling tournament in Turkey once, during a time when he spose be recovering from a ball to the hip, which is how you say he got shot in them days. Never heard that about no Vietnam: my buddy he took dis ball to the hip, but he rode on! Shit. Em all saying, Found my buddy wid his balls in his mouf! Everybody drunk and all, going to the VA get pills. But back in Forrest time, it was ball to the hip, like soccer, and you went on, and went back later and kilt mo yankee. One time I say to this honky on his bicycle, Clean up America, Kill a redneck today! and it kind of surprise him. I guess since I *look* white and all. I'own know why he surprise, actually. Near everything surprise the white boy, that why he so *white.* He sur*prise!* all the time.

But Forrest he go to Turkey one time on hip-ball furlough and get in a wrassling tournament to hep speed his recovery and he line up and grap holt em boys all grease up and naked and he a *natural.* He just as good as them what done this all they life, and then they see it gerng be more to it than that. He git worked up and start slobbering on they ass. He slobber so much he win; they think he sick or got rabies or something. They start call him Deve, mean camel, he slobber so much like a camel slobber when it wrestle a camel. Deve win entire damn show. The Camel is very good, they say, Deve cok iyi. Then Forrest take his trophy and have a beer with them and come home and don't win the rest of the war cause Prez Davis homo for Genel Bragg, who don't like Forrest and won't give him no guns and shit. Which it is maybe good for us on skateboards and in these humongoid pants and all today, because Forrest they say hard on the nigga, so he ain't gone cut no wigga no slack either, and we be in it, too, if he'd a won, but I don't know if he so hard on the black man as all that, cause one time a man say to Forrest, Hey Genel, how come you so hard on the Negro?

I ain't hard on the Negro, Genel Forrest say. *Jesus* hard on the Negro, buddyro.

Mrs. Hollingsworth was pretty pleased with that, and she knew that no raphead dufus rebel on a skateboard could come up with it (and she wondered how she knew of Braxton Bragg's vendetta for Forrest), or sound like that if he did. It was *her* grocery list. She was no longer shopping for the mundane.

She sat her days at her kitchen table with a pot of something cooking slowly on the stove, a small blue flame and a small gurgle in the room with her. Anyone who saw her making this prodigious, preposterous list saw nothing awry. Her indistinct husband remained indistinct. She was beginning to enjoy a new kind of freedom, one that she hadn't suspected existed. She was shopping in heaven, and hell.

Inishmurray
Maureen Howard

HUGH BYRNES WAS EVER THE BOY. His people were fishermen. As children we rowed out for the fun of it, our little tub of a boat built by his father, a plaything in a world without toys. And there was the gift of our wits—dividing school prizes between us, vying to be head of the class. A kid's competition and far from true. We loved each other. Granted a dispensation from our village life that was narrow and hard for other children, indulged by the Byrnes and the Boyles as though changelings, once swans perhaps, or naked infants sprouting seraphs' wings. We caught sea trout in our net and gathered wild cherries walking the distance to Drontheim. On in this way Hugh and I, till the Christian Brothers came prospecting and took him away. I was left behind, at that time nursing my mother. When he returned at term's end, all was the same, our back talk masking affection, our roughhouse the unwitting touches of children. As the years passed our bodies broke the charm—diddies poking the thick wool of my jumpers, downy hair on his chin. Strange to each other. At Christmas, arm wrestling on the table rock, I was no match for him.

"You've gone boggie."

"That I have." For I was soft on Hugh Byrnes and filled my head with dreams while I turned my mother's bruised body this way and that in the bed, her flesh rubbed raw from the coarse linen sheet. I dreamed of the train ride to Cork where he was with the Fathers who gave him Latin, Greek and philosophical studies. There I'd work in a shop, selling ribbons or farmer cheese or female remedies—what matter the goods. Cook his fry ups, go about the city with my hair bobbed. Never once did I think I would marry Hugh, the flat clank of our chapel bell ringing. I was well aware the fathers had taken him to be a priest. He spoke now of theology added to his studies, but never a word to me of his calling. We were eighteen when he came back at Easter and appeared once at our door, cap in hand, to say it was a blessing my mother gone to her reward, shuffling the worn words from his mouth. On the Saturday he did not come to the dances, the half sets and waltzing. I heard he went out for the catch with his brothers where they set him up like a passenger. Though he lifted a glass at Hurley's, he'd never again be one of us.

But I would not have my dreams done and over. When the Byrnes walked down our lane, I called from the half-door, "Have you no use for me, Hugh?"

"How could that be, Nuala?"

"You might come by."

"I might do that," he said. I cared not at all what they thought of a girl who put herself forward. So it started—our crossing the out-fields that led down to the cove, the old haunts. He told me of gods, of their wars he read in the Greek and of the rowdy scholars, not the seminarians, who were his friends. He had spent holy week fasting, wearing out his knees in contemplation. Easter being over, he was released to the world. I believed that world was me. April, warmer than April, the broom early golden, birds busy in the hedgerows.

"Let's go out in the little boat?"

"Nuala, we would sink it. The great size of us."

He held out his hand to prove its span, a smooth hand that turned the pages of a book. Then I kissed the cup of it and let my lips stray to the Mount of Venus. He pulled back only to take the pins out of my hair, spill it loose, wild as I wore it when we were children gathering shells. Now isn't that the darling story? Lovers in a mist by the sea like the postcards with words the tourists can't read in the Gaelic. Inishmurray, the island I had never crossed to, lay before us.

"What a pity," I said, "to have the island so near and never see it." We paused in our kisses, trailed down to the shore. "A pity to always look on."

"It's nothing but rocks. Rocks and poteen."

I stroked his soft hand. "Will you take me?"

"It's more than a man can row."

"You must take me."

"Nuala, don't go on in this way."

But I would have my voyage. "Alf Ternan sails out for a fee."

And next day we found Alf, an ancient party who lived with his yellow dog in a hut of bark and sticks. No one knew how he came to live by the boulders. Some said he was a shell-shocked Aussie who never found his way home and some that he had been a barrister in Westport and some that he was in the Royal Navy, and that Alf once taught at the big houses, children of the gentry, a Protestant who did not choose to come among us. The few words I traded with Ternan, his accent was not Sligo. He carried himself tall, looking sharp at the horizon as if, weighing his pollack and herring in at the dock, he was still out to sea, content with that distance. His beard was a grey thicket rough as the coat of his dog. The strangest thing about Alf was his boat, fast and slim built with two masts. The fishermen spoke of it with reverence, an aristocrat among their castle yawls with the single spirit sails. It was said by some women that in summer Alf sailed the open waters to Galway Bay where his wife lay long buried.

I paid him more than he'd fish out that morning, money taken from a little chamois purse, hoarded shillings and sixpence, given to me by my mother on her last day. I rode out to Grange on Hugh's handlebars, the sky a fine blue above us. When we cast off, Alf did not like the undertow or the excitable froth on the water. Later we would be reminded—sun in the morning, a storm at day's end—but it was more than I wished for sailing away, as though we were leaving the small white cottages, the cattle grazing and the church steeples poking the sky, leaving it all behind. The yellow dog sniffed the air and yowled, then cowered at Alf's feet. Later they would say the wind picked up from the Southwest, that fishermen let down their sheets and rowed in early. By the end of that day Alf Ternan, waiting for us off Inishmurray, was swept under the terrible sea. We did not hear his masts crack in the gale, nor the dog who swam ashore yapping for his master.

Like all lovers, we thought the island was our own and took no account of the few people and their cattle who still lived on its rocky soil. An old woman with a witch's wen on her nose swatted flies off the cod drying in the sun by her door. She wondered at our arrival and remarked that Gallagher did not travel out on this day. Oh, I'd known supplies came by motor boat from the Killybeg store but wanted to spend the legacy of my mother's purse on my romantic adventure. We walked at a fair pace through the grassland with nothing in sight till a rotted wood post pointed to the antiquities. Hugh knew the sacred books of this place had been destroyed by heathens, knew as much of the early Christians who built these dwellings as he did of the pagan gods he read of in Cork. There was now this breach of his learning between us.

"Sea pinks," I cried. "The field entire with bluebells!" I stooped to show him the soft feathers of an eider duck nesting. I had Hugh and didn't give a damn for the ruins of a monastery, Sixth Century

A.D. It seemed we might be free of all histories, let the present consume us.

Nothing but rocks, he had said, but as we entered the stone cashel that enclosed the ruins he knew the burial places, separate for men and women, the holy wells and the upright slabs inscribed with crosses. We stood by a mound of stones. You could not live in our village and not hear of these stones. "The Clocha Breacha," Hugh named it with a touch of awe. Some foolishness they told of—walking counter clockwise against the sun then flipping them, you laid a curse. I turned a stone.

"Nuala," he scolded.

Laughing, I turned another. He pulled me from them, solemn as a saint, then came to himself and we climbed the highest rampart, ate oatcakes and the brown eggs I had boiled at dawn. Sharing warm orange squash, we looked back to the dark bay and out to the moody Atlantic. We were that high on our crumbling wall. At the inquest we would say the shadow of grey clouds upon the sea was at a great distance, that in our explorations we did not track the time of day.

All at once the fierce rain was on us. We ran for a stone hut and there we lay.

"How long would that be?" they asked us.

Time enough for our drenched clothes to come off in a fury. Time for his mouth on my swollen nipples and trembling thighs. I was wet with desire. The exact blue of Byrnes's eyes? I can no longer say. I believe he had the dent of the Devil's kiss in his chin. Yet I am a scholar in my own right and for many years I pictured with accuracy his rusty pubic hair, that particular gleaming shaft, the dark cutaneous pouch of the scrotum as though a perfect illustration of penis erectile projected on a slide in my classroom. I bled freely on our bed of rocks. His seed sweet to me as honey. Isn't that how I might tell it if, as a nurse, I had not followed the practical course of my profession?

"How long, Miss Boyle?"

"Till the storm was over."

And then the sky was strangely bright, the sun still as a brass cymbal not rung. Retracing our path to the shore, we spoke all that nonsense, stuff and nonsense of sweethearts, as the barnacle geese quacked above the moor. The houses were shuttered, but the woman with the wen on her nose was hanging her cod out after the storm. She knew the hour we had come to the island by the light as it fell on her floor and would tell to the minute when we passed again, so disheveled.

The dog yelped when we found him, then fell at our feet whining. His heart beat, beat hard against my hand, yellow dog of mixed breed, Alf Ternan's companion. The mutt led us to the splintered masts and all that was left of the canvas flapping.

"Look what we've done," Hugh's face ashen with shame. "Look what we have brought about, Nuala."

"An act of God!"

Wasn't that the stupid cry, for it was God who Hugh Byrnes chose in that moment, pushing my body from him, though when questioned he did not betray me, not a word of my inheritance spent, not a clue to our carnal knowledge. He spoke of our touring the oratories. "We took shelter in a beehive as the stone huts of the island are called." Quite the scholar of Inishmurray, master of more than Christian tales. In the barracks at Mullaghmore, Byrnes told these dark legends with authority, from the pulpit as it were. He spoke of our viewing the cursing stones, made it clear we'd not turned them at all.

An oddly pleasant gathering with the constables more curious in the matter of the illegal whiskey of the island than the death of a stranger among us, poor Alf sealed in his coffin boards. Had we spotted jugs of poteen? A still or keg hidden in the boulders? We had not which was the truth of it and the Sergeant himself broke into the mockery of an Inishmurray song—

> *We keep our own distillery; no taxes do we pay.*
> *May the Lord protect my island home that lies in*
> *Sligo Bay.*

Death was then declared accidental over a cup of tea, Alf Ternan's remains assigned to the Protestant graveyard. I've heard the sirens' whine far, then near the swift whoosh of gurneys rushed to emergency with bodies mangled, bleeding, the flesh ruptured, seared. Frayed wire and flame, ice storm, foot on the peddle as the mind wanders. Not all the stories of happenstance nor frail logic of the calculated risk will solve the mystery—why an experienced sailor lost his long wager with the sea waiting among the rocks for two foolish lovers. Our sailor washed up with my mother's purse in his pocket. I did not claim it. No fault was found in his death beyond the great swell of the sea, but my man walked from me. Escorted by his brothers in a donkey cart, Byrnes boarded the train to Cork, back to his blessed studies.

I went mad with the loss of him and mourned the waste of my body. My ripe breasts, full hips and what lay between were a ruin to me like the ancient stones of that island. In a week I gained my own story, it's a favorite don't you know, the girl who failed to seduce a priest from his calling. To prove the brittle shell of my beauty, I offered myself. Any man could have a go at me. Our schoolroom teacher who lived with his Ma, dug her garden—limp till I worked him over. The bottle boy at the pub who took me against the wall, the husband of Minnie O'Toole who butchered our cow, the father of twelve who thought never to take a plunge again, and the chief constable who gave me the eye at the inquest, thumping me in the back of his Morris van. Feverish with lust, I walked the one lane of our village at dusk, hair down as it once pleased my lover. On in this way, till the women came up to the door of our cottage in their Sunday shawls, women from the village and beyond. I well knew them, but could not name one biddie for you now. They pronounced me wanton, a harlot, strumpet—such old-fashioned words. One, a prosperous farmer's wife in hat and crocheted gloves, was willing to pay my way to Limerick or Dublin, a city that could handle a slut. Another suggested the mad house in Knocknarea.

I had been washing up. With the wet rag in my hand, I shooed them away like chicks at the door, then heard my father behind me, quite sober that morning. He still wore the black band of my mother's death on his sleeve. Matt Boyle turned them out at our gate, though he knew it was true what was said of his daughter in Hurley's. A woman with a tattered shawl detached herself from the party, ran back up our path. I see the malice in her eyes, the tobacco stain on her lips, the skin crazed like the bark of a creel. I hear her whispered secret, "You are the very Magdalene."

A memorable day, sealed slick, tight as a scar.

Accident Report
Paul Auster

1.

WHEN A. WAS A YOUNG WOMAN in San Francisco and just starting out in life, she went through a desperate period in which she almost lost her mind. In the space of just a few weeks, she was fired from her job, one of her best friends was murdered when thieves broke into her apartment at night, and A.'s beloved cat became seriously ill. I don't know the exact nature of the illness, but it was apparently life-threatening, and when A. took the cat to the vet, he told her that the cat would die within a month unless a certain operation was performed. She asked him how much the operation would cost. He toted up the various charges for her, and the amount came to three hundred twenty-seven dollars. A. didn't have that kind of money. Her bank account was down to almost zero, and for the next several days she walked around in a state of extreme distress, alternately thinking about her dead friend and the impossible sum needed to prevent her cat from dying: three hundred twenty-seven dollars.

One day she was driving through the Mission and came to a stop at a red light. Her body was there, but her thoughts were somewhere else, and in the gap between them, in that small space that no one has fully explored but where we all sometimes live, she heard the voice of her murdered friend. *Don't worry,* the voice said. *Don't worry. Things will get better soon.* The light turned green, but A. was still under the spell of this auditory hallucination, and she did not move. A moment later, a car rammed into her from behind, breaking one of the taillights and crumpling the fender. The man who was driving that car shut off his engine, climbed out of the car, and walked over to A. He apologized for doing such a stupid thing. No, A. said, it was my fault. The light turned green and I didn't go. But the man insisted that he was the one to blame. When he learned that A. didn't have collision insurance (she was too poor for luxuries like that), he offered to pay for any damages that had been done to her car. Get an estimate on what it will cost, he said, and send me the bill. My insurance company will take care of it. A. continued to protest, telling the man that he wasn't responsible for the accident, but he wouldn't take no for an answer, and finally she gave in. She took the car to a garage and asked the mechanic to assess the costs of repairing the fender and the tail-light. When she returned several hours later, he handed her a written estimate. Give or take a penny or two, the amount came to exactly three hundred twenty-seven dollars.

2.

W., the friend from San Francisco who told me that story, has been directing films for twenty years. His latest project is based on a novel that recounts the adventures of a mother and her teenage daughter. It is a work of fiction, but most of the events in the book are taken directly from the author's life. The author, now a grown woman, was once the teenage daughter, and the mother in the story—who is still alive—was her real mother.

W.'s film was shot in Los Angeles. A famous actress was hired to play the role of the mother, and according to what W. told me on a recent visit to New York, the filming went smoothly and the production was completed on schedule. Once he began to edit the movie, however, he decided that he wanted to add a few more scenes, which he felt would greatly enhance the story. One of them included a shot of the mother parking her car on a street in a residential neighborhood. The location manager went out scouting for an appropriate street, and eventually one was chosen—arbitrarily, it would seem, since one Los Angeles street looks more or less like any other. On the appointed morning, W., the actress, and the film crew gathered on the street to shoot the scene. That car that the actress was supposed to drive was parked in front of a house—no particular house, just one of the houses on that street—and as my friend and his leading lady stood on the sidewalk discussing the scene and the possible ways to approach it, the door of that house burst open and a woman came running out. She appeared to be laughing and screaming at the same time. Distracted by the commotion, W. and the actress stopped talking. A screaming and laughing woman was running across the front lawn, and she was headed straight for them. I don't know how big the lawn was. W. neglected to mention that detail when he told the story, but in my mind I see it as large, which would have given the woman a considerable distance to cover before she reached the sidewalk and announced who she was. A moment like that deserves to be prolonged, it seems to me—if only by a few seconds—for the thing that was about to happen was so improbable, so outlandish in its defiance of the odds, that one wants to savor it for a few extra seconds before letting go of it. The woman running across the lawn was the novelist's mother. A fictional character in her daughter's book, she was also her real mother, and now, by pure accident, she was about to meet the woman who was playing that fictional character in a film based on the book in which her character had in fact been herself. She was real, but she was also imaginary. And the actress who was playing her was both real and imaginery as well. There were two of them standing on the sidewalk that morning, but there was also just one. Or perhaps it was the same one twice. According to what my friend told me, when the women finally understood what had happened, they threw their arms around each other and embraced.

3.

Last September, I had to go to Paris for a few days, and my publisher booked a room for me in a small hotel on the Left Bank. It's the same hotel they use for all their authors, and I had already stayed there several times in the past. Other than its convenient location—midway down a narrow street just off the Boulevard Saint-Germain—there is nothing even remotely interesting about this hotel. Its rates are modest, its rooms are cramped, and it is not mentioned in any guide book. The people who run it are pleasant enough, but it is no more than a drab and inconspicuous hole-in-the-wall, and except for a couple of American writers who have the same French publisher I do, I have never met anyone who has stayed there. I mention this fact because the obscurity of the hotel plays a part in the story. Unless one stops for a moment to consider how many hotels there are in Paris (which attracts more visitors than any other city in the world) and then further considers how many rooms there are in those hotels (thousands, no doubt tens of thousands), the full import of what happened to me last year will not be understood.

I arrived at the hotel late—more than an hour behind schedule—and checked in at the front desk. I went upstairs immediately after that. Just as I was putting my key into the door of my room, the telephone started to ring. I went in, tossed my bag on the floor, and picked up the phone, which was set into a nook in the wall just beside the bed, more or less at pillow level. Because the phone was turned in toward the bed, and because the cord was short, and because the one chair in the room was out of reach, it was necessary to sit down on the bed in order to use the phone. That's what I did, and as I talked to the person on the other end of the line, I noticed a piece of paper lying under the desk on the other side of the room. If I had been anywhere else, I wouldn't have been in a position to see it. The dimensions of the room were so tight that the space between the desk and the foot of the bed was no more than four or five feet. From my vantage point at the head of the bed, I was in the only place that provided a low enough angle of the floor to see what was under the desk. After the conversation was over, I got off the bed, crouched down under the desk, and picked up the piece of paper. Curious, of course, always curious, but not at all expecting to find anything out of the ordinary. The paper turned out to be one of those little message forms they slip under your door in European hotels. To ______ and From ______, the date and the time, and then a blank square below for the message. The form had been folded in three, and printed out in block letters on the outer fold was the name of one of my closest friends. We don't see each other often (O. lives in Canada), but we have been through a number of memorable experiences together, and there has never been anything but the greatest affection between us. Seeing his name on the message form made me very happy. We hadn't spoken in a while, and I had had no inkling that he would be in Paris when I was there. In those first moments of discovery and incomprehension, I assumed that O. had somehow gotten wind of the fact that I was coming and had called the hotel to leave a message for me. The message had been delivered to my room, but whoever had brought it up had placed it carelessly on the edge of the desk, and it had blown onto the floor. Or else that person had accidentally dropped it (the chambermaid?) while preparing the room for my arrival. One way or the other, neither explanation was very plausible. The angle was wrong, and unless someone had kicked the message after it had fallen to the floor, the paper couldn't have been lying so far under the desk. I was already beginning to reconsider my hypothesis when something more important occurred to me. O.'s name was on the outside of the message form. If the message had been meant for me, my name would have been there. The recipient was the one whose name belonged on the outside, not the sender, and if my name wasn't there, it surely wasn't going to be anywhere else. I opened the message and read it. The sender was someone I had never heard of—but the recipient was indeed O. I rushed downstairs and asked the clerk at the front desk if O. was still there. It was a stupid question, of course, but I asked it anyway. How could O. be there if he was no longer in his room? I was there now, and O.'s room was no longer his room but mine. I asked the clerk when he had checked out. An hour ago, the clerk said. An hour ago I had been sitting in a taxi at the edge of Paris, stuck in a traffic jam. If I had made it to the hotel at the expected time, I would have run into O. just as he was walking out the door.

From Versailles

Kathryn Davis

MY SOUL IS GOING ON A TRIP. I want to talk about her. I want to talk about her. Why would anyone ever want to talk about anything else?

My soul is a girl: she is just like me. She is fifteen years old and has been promised in marriage to the French Dauphin, who also has a soul, though more visible and worldly, its body already formed (so I've been told) from layers of flesh and fat. In France they piss into chamber pots made of lapis, and dine on common garden slugs. In France their hands smell like vanilla and they shoot their *flechès d'amour* indiscriminately in all directions, owing to their taste for books pernicious to religion and morals.

My soul is also powerful, but like a young girl it has wishes and ideas—yes!—a soul can have ideas like a mind does. "Toinette, Toinette, you must pay attention," or so I can still hear Abbé Vermond implore, waving a book in my face when all I wanted to do was dance dance dance, as if he actually believed that to be light of heart is the same as being light of head.

We traveled in a carriage coated with glass and lined with pale blue satin, beautifully swift, magnificently sprung. The end of April and the clouds compact and quick moving, the fields turning from pale to deeper green, and the fruit trees' veiled heads humming with bees. From Vienna to Molck, from the valley of the Danube to the castle of Nymphenburg, whose inhabitants behaved like swine. Bells pealed all along our route and uniformed men shot off guns; little girls tossed flower petals in our path. The white horses of the Danube were here one minute, gone the next; one minute we slipped into the Black Forest's long cool shadows, the next out onto a hot sunny plain.

"The world where you must pass your life is but transitory," or so advised my papa from beyond the grave. "There is naught save eternity that is without end." In my lap I had my dear little pug, the smell of whose ears will always be sweeter to me than all the perfumes of Araby and the scent of heliotrope combined.

Twenty thousand horses stabled along the road from Vienna to

Strasbourg—no sooner did one of our steeds begin to lather up and stumble than it was ground into cat meat and a new one found to take its place. Serving women, hairdressers, dressmakers, surgeons, furriers, chaplains, apothecaries, cooks. One supper alone consisted of 150 chickens, 270 pounds of beef, 220 pounds of veal, 55 pounds of bacon, 50 pigeons, 300 eggs.

I was eager to please, though that meant something other than acquiesce to another's desire. Pleasing meant my own desire: the place where my body and soul met, like the musician's bow bearing down on the string, teasing a sound out: *ah ah ah ah ah!*

My soul thought she'd be happy, and then, one day, she'd die.

But, "die."

What does this mean?

One day Antoinette will not exist, though her soul will continue to flourish.

And WHO IS THAT? WHAT IS THAT?

By the time we stopped for supper at the Abbey of Schuttern I had no appetite at all, even though the nuns tried tempting me with pilchards and apricots and kugelhopf; I admit I wept a little. It was the sixth of May; we'd been on the road for over two weeks. From my bedroom window I could see the Rhine, which looked wide and flat and the color of lead, and the light on it looked like the pilchards had, silver and skinny and unappetizing. I heard a door creak, the sound of footsteps. Angry voices arguing below, fighting over the wording in the *consegna,* by which I was to be deeded away like a cottage or a plot of land to the people of France. A fork of lightning over the Rhine, and the Lorelei's long ghostly arm lifting to meet it . . .

But Mama would never let me get away with such silly thoughts—I missed her so much I thought I'd die. "You must eat everything on your plate, Antonia. No picking and choosing. Why have you not eaten all your fish? How many times must I tell you that the child who gives in to foolish fears will never amount to much as an adult. Come here, let me take a good look at you"—peering at me through a magnifying glass—"you seem so small for your age. How is your health?" Her white white hair and her white white teeth, one of which she'd had extracted while giving birth to me. Antoinette and a decayed molar, both of us born around eight o'clock in the evening, All Souls Day, 1755.

It was getting dark; the moon was coming up over the river. At home Carlotta would be saying her prayers and Maxie sneaking cheese to his pet mouse, poor Anna lying there with her hands folded across her chest like an effigy of herself, unable to stop coughing. Joseph and Christina, Elizabeth and Karl. Amalia, Leopold, Johanna, Josepha. Mama sitting in her private apartments, sipping her warm milk and signing state papers. Her head shorn and the walls draped in black ever since Papa's death, which she recorded in her prayer book—"Emperor Francis I, my husband, died on the 18th of August at half past nine o'clock. Our happy marriage lasted 29 years, 6 months and 6 days, 1,540 weeks, 10,781 days, 258,774 hours"—despite his numerous and humiliating infidelities.

At least I had my little pug with me, *Gott sei dank!* Tomorrow I would stop speaking German forever, but not tonight. I could see where we were headed and it was black as pitch.

Swan Lake

Steve Erickson

1.

SOMETIMES I'M PARALYZED BY MY LOVE for him. When he calls me from his little bed I know I'm not supposed to answer because that's the way he learns to go back to sleep on his own. Every night when I'm putting him to bed I say now listen Kirk you're getting to be a big boy, you have to learn to go to sleep on your own, do you understand? and he says Yes please. And then in the middle of the night he calls and, you know, I can't resist. It's the way he calls, not sleepy, not frightened, not crying, but very determined and aware and awake—"Mama?" I can hear the question mark so insistent it's not a question . . . it would break my heart not to answer.

In my heart he opens the door to this vast impassable terrain of fear. It's a fear stretching out beyond these young years of mine when mortality's supposed to be so inconceivable . . . and my own mortality *is* inconceivable, until I consider his—then it's existence itself that's inconceivable. How have moms down through the ages survived their love for their kids? The thought of his mortality is abysmal to me.

We were at a fair yesterday down by the lakeside and a vendor had in captivity one of the owls that have invaded the city ever since the lake first appeared a couple of years ago. She was explaining to some other mom's kid how, far up in the sky, the owl can hear a human heartbeat—and even at that very moment, I thought to myself, this owl could hear Kirk's little heart as I stood there holding him in my arms. Could it have heard his heart in my belly three years ago? Was this my first betrayal of my boy, his very birth, exposing him to the peril of owls that hear heartbeats? Every night I wait for the sun to set before writing this, and there it goes now, slipping down behind the San Vicente Bridge that crosses the lake to the northwest, I see it from my window . . . the sun goes down, the sky goes dark, the lake goes black, and owls swoop across the rising moon like leaves blown loose from a phantasmagoric tree twisting up out of the ground—and my voice rises from the crypt of my consciousness shaking words off like topsoil. Kirk and I are bonded by a cord of blood that runs from his heart to my thighs. Menstrual waves crash against the inner beach of my belly.

2.

I started this journal in Tokyo and then stopped a few weeks after I got pregnant, when I thought I had miscarried, and then started again after I got back to L.A. That was around the time the lake first appeared, right before Kirk was born. Of course the lake was already there before that, before anyone realized it was ever going to turn into an actual lake. The center is near where Hollywood Boulevard used to meet Laurel Canyon Boulevard, a bare puddle the morning it first bubbled up, no one thinking anything about it until however long it was before it cut Laurel Canyon off from the city altogether.

Since the city was in the middle of one of its usual droughts, a lake that appeared from nowhere and kept getting bigger ought to have been a little suspicious but I guess that's easy to say in retrospect. "What's that old machinery out there in the water all this time?" the writer down the hall asked me not that long ago, staring in the distance out his window, and I said, "Pumps from when they tried to drain it." As usual Kirk was busy demolishing the guy's apartment, sitting over in the corner pulling all the tape out of a video. "Hey!" I yelled. He stopped long enough to gauge whether this admonition was to be taken any more seriously than my others, before returning to the task at hand. "Hey!" I said again, "stop!"

"No please." He continued to unspool the tape. The writer over by the window glanced at Kirk unfazed. "Sorry," I mumbled, "my kid's wrecking your video—"

"When did they try to drain it?"

"When it didn't, you know, disappear of its own accord . . . evaporate or whatever—" Lunging for the video on the floor he'd just disemboweled, Kirk squalled "Mine! Mine!" as I snatched him up in my arms. "At that point no one understood yet it was filling up from a hole in the bottom. . . . Knock it off!"

"They ever figure out whether the water was coming from the sea?"

I shook my head, "There's no salt." The edge of the lake had just reached south of Sunset. Some weeks later it was almost all the way to Fountain Avenue, which meant it was only a couple of blocks from our hotel here at the top of what's now called the St. James Peninsula, named after the fancy hotel up on the Strip I can still see from my window. I used to sit watching it during feeding right after Kirk was born, lavender and magenta kliegs on the walls and the Sky Bar where young glam Hollywood drank martinis. But as the lake moved down Sunset and overtook it, you could see the kliegs go out and darkness move up the St. James Hotel floor by floor until it was all dead: "It would have gone anyway of its own volition," Doc said, "rotted by decadence from the bottom up"—as close as I've ever heard her to sounding judgmental about anything, and the only time I've ever heard her sound almost glad to see a building die. In the old rundown hotel here where Kirk and I live, some on the first floor have already started moving out.

3.

You'll spend your whole life, Doc said when I told her this dream I had, *making peace with your true nature*—whatever *that* means. Kirk was a few months old then. In the dream I was lying on the banks of what was once Laurel Avenue, near the old Thirties apartment where F. Scott Fitzgerald used to live when he was writing for the movies, I was lying there hypnotically fixed on the center of the lake.

Lying there in my dream suddenly I was acutely aware of my own womb predating me. I was suddenly aware of my womb being older than me—down inside me I could hear historical rumors, spasms of collective memory rippling outward, up to my lungs and down to my thighs . . . it infuriated me. It seemed so typical of everything—after all, do men's dicks predate *them?* I asked indignantly, maybe out loud or only in my head . . . in a dream it's hard to know—and in my heart I rejected it, this part of me that was my son's first home; and then in a surge of guilt and self-loathing, I rejected him. And then realized, in the dream, he wasn't there. Looking around frantically, from the water in front of me to the trees on the banks behind me, I sprang up from where I sat—and opened my eyes to find myself sitting up in my bed still in the grip of a tedious maternal instinct I can't ignore. . . .

No doubt about it, my little Kierkegaard's my little wild man. He runs around the apartment naked and his little flapdoodle sticking straight out and his treasured balloons flying along behind him, one string in each hand. Before I had him I had this idea babies were amorphous lumps of human clay that take distinct shape only over time . . . but he was half wildman half zenbaby right out of the chute—before, actually. In those last couple of months in the womb he was somersaulting in my belly hourly all ready to get out and wreck some videos. The couple of weeks between the time I got back from Tokyo, where I lived and worked for a year as a memory girl in Kabucki-cho, and when he was born we'd go down to the lake which at that time was still small enough you could walk around the whole thing in ten minutes except the part cut off by the Hollywood Hills, and we'd sit watching the water, and it was the only time he settled down inside me, mesmerized by the lake beyond my belly. In the first days after he was born, when the lake started spreading west down what was then the Strip, we'd watch it together from the window of our room as he lay in my arms, and I'd think he was asleep and then look to see his eyes open and calm, gazing at the lake and—I swear, I swear—smiling. "Big Agua," he started calling it when he turned two, having picked up the Spanish I don't know where, same place he learned to call the moon luna.

The lake was starting to get a lot of attention then, sightseers coming and going, city officials and geological experts standing around scratching their heads. Over the months of that first year everyone was kind of enchanted by the lake, however much consternation it caused schedules and traffic and bus lines—that's when the gondolas and rowboats came out, drifting across the surface of the water as it turned from the indigo of morning to the blaze of late afternoon . . . sailing in and out of the red light that poured over the hills like a lake of fire bursting the levee of the sun. Charred palms sutured the horizon. A makeshift harbor was built over by the now-flooded Château Marmont. Parasols came back into fashion that autumn, women walking the lakeshore with them and twirling them from their boats, so on Saturdays especially there was this panorama of spinning colored spheres floating above the surface of the lake and in its reflection. . . .

"Balloons!" Kirk would point when he saw the parasols, because that was when to him anything round and airborne was a balloon . . . and before everything was a balloon it was a bubble, back when he liked to blow the bubbles in his bath. By the lake he would blow bubbles from a bubble wand I bought him, as I lay in the grass reading. . . . "Put down book please," he commanded, grabbing the Proust from my hands. So we blew bubbles together, watching them float to the grass where those that didn't burst would settle like dew.

He'd smash them with his foot. "Smash the bubbles!" I'd cry, and he'd smash them, "Pap," and then I felt funny, it somehow seemed wrong to encourage him to smash something as delicate as a bubble. "Pap, pap, pap," he'd go. One afternoon he blew a particularly large balloon and said, out of nowhere, "This one's for my daddy," and it caught my breath—he had never mentioned his father before, and never has since . . . I didn't know he even knew what a daddy was. "This one's for my daddy," and the bubble slowly tumbled down through the air before us like a little spinning world, and when it landed it didn't pop and he didn't smash it, he just watched it there on the grass for a long time until it finally burst on its own.

My kid's beautiful. What else is a mom going to say, right? Except that my kid is actually beautiful . . . the moment he was born they held him up for me to look at slackjawed, stupefied—me, not him . . . "This child is beautiful," the Egyptian nurse assured me the next day in some wonder, and I had finally come enough out of my fog to crack "Yeah but you tell all mothers that," and thinking about it a moment she looked over both shoulders before she whispered back, "Well, yes, I do. But this child is *beautiful*" . . . and so he is. Which he sure didn't get from his mother or father, so go figure—he's a throwback to someone I can't even begin to know, never having known either my own mother or father. . . . Don't know where he ot the hair that shines brilliant gold in the sun or the sea-green eyes flecked with amber or the sanguine knowing mouth of a rapt mad monk. People's attraction to him is remarkable, when he was younger I'd push him in the stroller around the lake and people would gawk as though there was something slightly supernatural about the perfection of him, and not just little old grandmothers either—"Hey, cute baby, man!" some tattooed skinhead psychopath would interrupt his mayhem long enough to stop and exclaim. If anything, it worries me he's this beautiful. I worry life will let him get away with too much, given how he's a wily charmer on top of it, sweet and good-natured but already determined to run the show, musical in his self-assured defiance: "Noooooooo, please," demurring an urgently needed diaper in a lilting singsong voice. Giving orders at the age of two, Do this please! do that please!—a very *polite* dictator. "La-la!" he orders at night when I'm putting him to sleep, Il Duce's way of telling me he wants me to sing to him. "More la-la please!" means, Keep singing. "Bigger la-la please!" means, Sing louder.

But you know, I decided Kirk would be OK the afternoon he was playing with Parker from downstairs, the other baby in the hotel.

About eight months younger than Kirk, black, deaf and mute, and as with Kirk his father vanished into the ether of time before Parker could even commit him to memory, and his mother goes off to work at a tedious job she's ecstatic to have, answering telephones for the city, dropping Parker off at some daycare where they barely have a clue how to deal with normal babies let alone one who can't hear or speak. After a while the daycare tells her they can't handle him and so she has to find another daycare and in the meantime, if I'm free, sometimes I'll take him for a few hours until whatever babysitter Angela's been able to arrange shows up. Sometimes in return Angela takes Kirk. Sometimes on weekends she and I and the two kids go down to the lake where they play together . . . and this one afternoon was when I saw it—Angela saw it too.

It wasn't a big deal. Kirk and Parker each sat in their little folding chairs with balloons we'd bought them, tied to their wrists, Kirk a yellow one and Parker a blue one, and Parker pulled the string on his only to watch it float up and out over the water . . . it was a moment before he realized it wasn't going to come back. Then he tried to cry, which was much more terrible than any actual little-kid cry, because it was a cry caught in his heart no one could hear, and he was wracked by the eternal futility of cries he can't voice and balloons that never return. No matter how much Angela tried to comfort him he was inconsolable—until Kirk got up from his folding chair, walked over to Parker, pulled the string of his own balloon from his wrist with one hand and, with the other, handed it to Parker. Parker took the balloon and stopped crying.

Angela looked at me with this odd expression that almost made *me* cry except I never cry, the only times I've cried since I was three years old was when Kirk was born and the time in Tokyo I was sure I miscarried him. Maybe other two-year-olds do what Kirk did, maybe they do it all the time, what do I know? but I was under the distinct impression empathy was something we don't learn until five or six—so it cast a kind of spell on us, Kirk's gesture of silently giving his balloon to Parker . . . there almost seemed something a little otherworldly about it, and for a long time neither Angela nor I said anything. Kirk walked back to his chair and sat down and watched the lake. . . .

I used to be a notorious smart-ass—well, notorious to myself anyway. Always with the smart answer . . . but I'm not that smart anymore. I think having a kid rounds off the edges where there are edges and put new edges where everything's rounded off. There's no great revelation in having a child—you think you're going to be transformed, you'll somehow become a deeper, more substantial human being—but there's no change in me that I can tell other than all the new ways I've become afraid. Having never known either my mother or father, fuck knows I'm no advocate for parenthood. I can't tell it's made me a whit wiser or less trivial, really, or older except in the ways I'm not ready to be older. All I do know is the meaning of myself begins and ends with my boy, where I didn't know there even was a meaning before. All I know is he's the shore of the lake of my life where before maybe I knew there was a lake out there *somewhere* but had no clue where. It doesn't mean there's nothing of *me.* There's always been a *me* there, I know that. But it means he's the single lit lantern on the road to Me, dangling from the branch of experience that overhangs my night of doubt.

My name is Kristin. In July I'll be twenty-one.

4.

As the lake gets bigger, the power starts going out in parts of the city. You can tell from their pinpoint flickering in the wind off the lake that the lights in the faraway windows on the other side of the water are lanterns and candles, like fireflies hovering against the black hills on the distant shore.

Soon the city started rewriting all the addresses. Without me over-explaining it here, each new address has two parts, one fixing its place on the lake's perimeter and the other its distance from the lake's center. The Hotel Hamblin here where I rent a room for Kirk and me on a more or less permanent basis is PSW47/V180, for instance, which means it's 470 yards west of the southernmost point on the lake's edge, and 1,800 yards from the center—and of course as these addresses get bigger, they render the earlier addresses obsolete. PSW47/V170, for instance, doesn't exist anymore, it's now underwater. L.A. is a city of drowning addresses. At first people wondered: if the P was for "perimeter" and the SW for "southwest," then what was "V" for? If the V part of the address was the distance from the center of the lake, why wasn't it a "C" address, or M for "middle" or B for "bull's-eye"? It turned out V was for "vortex," and when that got out everyone kind of freaked. A rather poor choice of words, "vortex"—leave it to a bureaucrat to get poetic at exactly the wrong moment. Vortex sounds like a drain. It gives the impression not only something's coming up from the hole at the bottom of the lake, but something's going down too.

Not that long ago I got a letter addressed to Kristin Blu, and since my last name is Blumenthal I assumed it was for me, till I opened it. *My beautiful K* it began, and right then and there I knew he had the wrong girl, *labial jewel, riverine rapture* and so on and so forth in that vein, for the first few letters anyway, until they became more and more bitter, ecstasy replaced by bile as one after another went unanswered. They were signed by "W." Soon the letters started coming every day, each more furious and desperate than the last and each enclosing a small piece of an old photo which I stuck to our hotel wall with the other pieces, waiting for the complete portrait to fall into place.

Of course as each letter became more tormented, it occurred to me to write W and put him out of his misery. I felt guiltier and guiltier reading them—I mean, I had no excuses after the first one, did I? I mean, after the first one it was pretty obvious the letters weren't for me. But there was no return address on any of the envelopes and I guess it never occurred to him they might be going to the wrong address. It became pretty obvious to me pretty quickly that W is what I've always called a point-misser. Everyone misses the point now and then but some people are just born missing the point. It never occurred to W there might be any other possible reason his labial jewel wasn't answering. His desire was, you know, so grand and uncompromising and rigid he'd rather assume she was rejecting him than that something as banal as the incompetency of the postal service could be at fault. Some part of him wanted to judge her monstrously, some part of him wanted to be a martyr for cunnilingus rather than a prisoner of chance.

There was something else about the letters. Something clandestine, subterranean: *The lake,* he finally wrote in one, *is coming for me,* and the moment I read it I saw him somewhere out there in the city barricaded away, building an ark. *In China they would have found me by now.* I don't know how long it was, at least fifteen or twenty letters, before I finally noticed the letters weren't actually addressed to PSW47/V180 but V170.

When I saw this I grabbed Kirk—at the moment busy trying to demolish my carefully constructed jigsaw of the little pieces of W's photo attached to the wall—and went up the stairs the three floors to the Hamblin rooftop where a panoramic view of the lake stretched all the way from Hollywood in the northeast to the San Vicente Bridge in the west. There out in the water, about a thousand yards away on a more or less straight line from us to the center of the lake, rose an old abandoned apartment building like my own . . . and I knew right away it was PSW47/V170 where she lived. It was dusk, light failing at our backs, and only after Kirk and I stood there awhile watching the black of the water meet the black of the hills beyond, darkness slowly swallowing up V170 in the distance, did a light flicker in one of its faraway windows, clear as could be since every other window was dark, and just like I knew that was her address, when that light appeared I knew it was her, and she was still out there, alone, waiting for word from him.

5.

When I can scrape up money for childcare or Angela here in the hotel can watch Kirk a few hours, like most people in the city since the lake came I cobble together what jobs I can, including the one with Doc and the one for the writer down the hall. A desperate over-the-hill novelist who checked in for a few days in order to finish this screenplay he saw as his last best chance to salvage a career, he wound up staying a week and then two and then a month and now he's been here almost a year. The screenplay never gets finished and meanwhile his wife and son who live on the other side of the city come see him like relatives visiting an inmate. At the end of each reunion there's this tearful clutching between the three of them like the scene in a prison movie where they talk on a telephone divided by a window as their fingertips touch each other on opposite sides of the glass. Since he can check out of the hotel and go home anytime he wants, it's hard to figure. After a while he had been here so long that once, when he tried to leave, he couldn't find his way out and wound up knocking on my door asking if I'd go do some shopping for him and that's how I got to know him.

Day after day and night after night he sits in his room gazing morosely at his blank computer screen and drinking tequila and watching old movies stacked up in the corner, staring at the growing lake out his window, never answering except to a secret knock while bellmen slip him notes under the door wondering when he's going to check out. I read some of his script and maybe I'm wrong but toward the end I thought the main character—a chick punk singer—sounded a little like me. It wasn't the best movie but I'm sure there have been worse. I think his big problem is he hasn't the slightest idea how to write women characters, but he looks completely baffled when you try and tell him this . . . "What do you mean?" he says.

"What do I mean? I mean every female character is a stripper or porn star or sex slave."

He's thunderstruck by this epiphany. "Are you sure?" he says.

"Yes I'm sure."

He ponders this awhile more. "What about Tara Spectaculara?"

"Tara Spectaculara? The amazonian motorcycle queen with the huge tits? The one in the black leather jacket that's . . . how did you put it?"—flipping through the script—". . . 'unzipped so far it threatens the space-time continuum'?"

"Uh," he's thinking furiously, "well, these characters," he finally clears his throat, "are, you know . . . they're just, uh . . . the *forbidden iconography of the male psyche. . . .*"

"Oh, well, in that case. 'Forbidden iconography of the male psyche,' that's OK then. Stupid me, I thought this Tara was just your basic male wangie."

"Male what?"

"Wangie."

"I don't know what that is."

"Sure you do." Talk about a point-misser! This guy is, like, a *serial* point-misser. Anyway this is when he got the idea of passing me off as the writer of the script, that's the way his twisted mind works. He's convinced Hollywood isn't going to have any interest in failed literary-type novelists, better if a script filled with male wangies about rockerbabes and motorcycle queens, submitted to guy-studio-execs with heads full of their own male-wangies, is written by a twenty-year-old punk chick who would be expected to have special credibility on the subject of rockerbabes and motorcycle queens since undoubtedly I live with a harem of them, which of course is the biggest male wangie of all. So for a while one of my jobs has been to run around town sitting sullenly in Century City offices listening to why I'm being turned down—which is to say why he's being turned down—and I guess I have to admit on some level I must find this guy just pathetic enough to feel bad for him, since I keep doing it even though it's obviously never going to pay me anything, my five percent of the script contingent on someone actually buying it.

At the beginning the lake was banked on the north side of the Strip but when the dam there broke and the ensuing deluge cut most of the city in two, and before the San Vicente Bridge when all the east-west bus routes had to detour down to Venice Boulevard before turning back up the Peninsula formed by the La Cienega and Crescent Heights rivers, it fucked up my other part-time job as Doc's nurse/assistant. The couple of times I was late I could tell she was annoyed, which was mortifying given Doc is a fount of patience . . . she's just one of those people you never want to let down. Truth is I've never quite figured out what I contribute to her work except to take the patient's various atmospheric readings and hand her whatever instruments she needs—last time I think her irritation with me was aggravated by the fact that the diagnosis hadn't gone well and she was breaking the bad news to the habitants just as I got there, breathless from having run the half mile from the bus.

"It's dying," she had just told them . . . they were still standing on the front lawn arm in arm, looking at the terminal house stunned. I think because there's something so strong and deep about Doc, people find this sort of bluntness easier to accept—there's a manner about even her most ominous prognosis that says both: This is the way it is; and it breaks my heart. The habitants can tell she feels as bad as they do and I can tell it too, watching her move through the sick house from room to room in a bubble of stillness, running her fingers along the walls and the doorframes and the windowsills, pressing the side of her face against the plaster, listening for the heart. When she does this, her lined face glows with the flash of both twilight and dawn at the same time . . . all right, you can tell I'm in love with her. Her eyes older than her face and her smile younger, her hair lost between the gold of yesterday and the silver of tomorrow, serenity woven in the air around her like a glistening web . . . truth is, this job isn't much more lucrative than trying to peddle Jainlight's script, but I do it because I covet my moments with her. Sometimes I dream at night she's my mother I never knew, which isn't totally impossible, since Doc never says much about her past, like there's some unapproachable pain there, a lost lover or, worse, a lost child. . . .

She presses her face against the wall and closes her eyes, listening to the fading life of the house . . . once I saw a tear run down her cheek. "But, what makes it die?" I ask, and she shrugs, "Well," in that voice you can sometimes barely hear, it's so calm, "as with people it's not always easy to say. I just know it's slipping away. I can just hear it in the walls, I can just feel death spreading through the baseboards or see it in the ceilings, the ebbing of life. Sometimes it's just old age. Sometimes it's something unbearably sad that's taken place, that the house never recovers from—an untimely death, the end of a marriage, an act of violence or despair, something only the house knows . . . something only the house has seen, a betrayal the house absorbs into itself while shielding the habitants from its secret. Sometimes when a house dies, it's an act of sacrifice."

But what happens when the house can't stand its secrets anymore, that's what I want to know. What happens when the house starts telling the secrets back because it can't bear to bear them. Maybe the writer down the hall can't finish his script because the Hamblin constantly whispers in his head and his own thoughts drown in the muttering. Back in the Twenties when producers and studio chefs kept their girlfriends and mistresses here, what secrets did the walls hear then that now they can't keep anymore?

A few nights after Doc said this, Angela was working a night shift and Parker was staying over, sleeping in Kirk's room when I heard "Mama?"—that insistent question mark I can't resist, as emphatic as a period. . . . There was something different about it this time, though, he was *whispering* it, and when it was obvious he wasn't going to go back to sleep on his own, I went in to see him. He was standing in his crib in the dark, hair white in the moon through his window. "Mama," he whispered again and pointed at Parker, lying in his own crib Angela had brought up. . . . Flailing in the air, Parker's tiny hands formed strange, half-formed patterns as there twitched in his sleeping face a whimper he couldn't say. Momentarily alarmed in his two-year-old way, Kirk reached up his arms to me and I picked him up and held him awhile, but then, after watching Parker a few more minutes, he strained to get down, so I set him on the floor and together we continued to silently watch Parker's tiny hands fluttering in the air before him.

I finally realized Parker was dreaming. With his hands he was talking in his sleep. I looked around at the dark room, shadows throbbing with secrets of abandonment. Kirk stood there with his hand in mine "listening" to Parker's dream of lost daddies, before he let go and went to Parker's bedside and placed his small palm on the younger boy's brow. Immediately calmed by Kirk's touch, Parker dropped his arms to his sides and slept peacefully.

6.

Sitting by the lake before Kirk was born I would sing a song to him inside me. It's an old song and I don't know where I first heard it, I think it's an ancient folk ballad, or maybe a hymn. After he was born I would sing it to him at night as a lullaby.

We were born before the wind
Also younger than the sun

Like when I was a kid, Kirk used to never cry. He only started crying lately . . . I think he somehow got it in his head I was going to disappear. If I go in the next room I think he somehow gets it in his head I'll never come back. I'll be in the next room and suddenly he's wailing for me—and it was just lately I realized that, as much as anything else, his call of "Mama?" in the middle of the night, with its question mark so insistent it's a period, was nothing more or less than to make sure I was still there, that I hadn't vanished from his life. I don't know where he got this idea he would be left all alone in the world. Consumed by guilt I wrack my brain trying to figure out what I might have done that gave him this idea, but honest I can't think of anything, and I wonder if it's like his premature empathy—a premature sense that everything is fleeting.

When Kirk was a year old, the lake had gotten big enough there was a fog off the water in the mornings and evenings that climbed the Hollywood moors and wound through the city. A big chunk of the hills broke off and tumbled down into the lake and onto the shore, including a huge rock as tall as a house that landed near where Kirk and I would blow bubbles . . . of course I couldn't get it out of my head, what might have happened if we had been there when this monster rock came crashing down—I'm haunted by such possibilities on an hourly basis. Kirk always likes to throw rocks in the lake so I told him to go throw this one. He looked at it awhile with suspicion, then, surmounting his doubt, went over and put his little hands on the towering rock and pushed with all his might while I laughed. "Too big," he somberly announced, his spirit far bigger than the rest of him, far bigger than me, almost as big as the rock.

I'm not a religious person but after Kirk was born I started praying. Every night, "Dear God do whatever you want to me but don't let anything bad happen to my boy." And then it occurred to me if God wanted to punish me, I had just given him a pretty good hint how to go about it, and now God's just one more thing I have to protect him from.

Around the time he was eighteen months old, the city finally sent some divers down into the lake to try and figure out exactly what was in the hole at the bottom. This got a lot of attention, half the town out there watching the divers in their black wetsuits slip over the side of the boat and disappear and then come back up. Every time they came back up there seemed to be much conferring back and forth with various officials on the boat. Everyone figured there'd be some sort of press conference or announcement at the end but there was no announcement, instead everyone on the boat immediately hurried to their cars and drove off—pretty quickly it seemed to me. After that, no city officials came to the lake anymore, but for a week or so afterward everyone else who had been at the lake watching the divers would stand staring at the water as though an answer would come floating up any moment.

I don't know anything about higher math but in the more complicated equations I always assume there must be a chaos factor somewhere . . . or maybe that's what math tries to avoid. I guess maybe math is about factoring *out* the chaos, determining a definite value for everything . . . in science, chaos isn't about true randomness, of course. Science doesn't allow for the possibility of true chaos—only for an unknown order that calls itself chaos. I mean, if that butterfly flapping his wings in South America twenty years ago really did in some way cause my English muffin to burn this morning, that's not randomness, that's cause-and-effect of a truly huge sort, the exact opposite of chaos. My kid is the chaos factor in the equation of my existence, the thing that makes true the math of my days. For a while it made me nuts, the way I guess all kids make their parents nuts, his havoc . . . and then it finally occurred to me his chaos was an unknown order, his havoc was a rearrangement of the world in a way that marked his entrances into it and his exits from it. And so on the occasions I didn't immediately try to curb his chaos, when I sat back and watched just how far he would take it, I could almost see the unknown order—the morning he was ten months old, still learning to crawl, and he removed all my books from the bottom shelf (he had already learned just how much I loved my books) and then, when the shelf was cleared, put the books back one by one. Not in *my* order, which was really no particular order, but in some order of his own, that in the large scheme of things made as much sense as any other. So maybe there are revelations in having a kid after all.

He's now in that phase all two-year-olds go through where everything is Why? You have to go to bed, wildman. "Why?" Because it's night time. "Why?" Because the sun's gone to sleep. "Why?" Because the earth turns. "Why?" Don't kid yourself thinking this is the charming curiosity of childhood—this is a premeditated, cold-blooded campaign to exhaust all answers, including the answer of infinity.

Like I've done since I was a kid myself, on the wall of our apartment I tack articles about things that fascinate me and pictures of things that inspire me, and I had tacked up the little pieces of the photo that W was sending his lover, trying to assemble them into the whole, not knowing how many more fragments might be to come—and the morning I got what turned out to be the last letter, Kirk had taken all the pieces off the wall and stuck them back in different places, completely upsetting my very meticulous efforts. For ten minutes I screamed at him about it. Then, feeling shitty, I promised him we could go to the lake, and I dressed him and we grabbed the bus to the San Vicente Bridge and crossed to the other side and walked over to the lake hand in hand and sat on a small beach below the hills where I fell asleep in the sun, I don't know how long. I woke with a start. I woke in full panic—that I'd dozed off with Kirk sitting there in the sand not six fatal feet from the water. In this split second I woke I was consumed with all the remorse and grief and guilt that constantly hibernates in me, just waiting for the unspeakable tragedy I spend so much of my love for him dreading, the tragedy whose name my remorse and grief and guilt already bear. But there he was, hunkered down in the sand by the water in that way he sits sometimes, not on his butt but in a crouch, studying the view in front of him, and only when my brain assured itself he was OK did I realize he was peeling one page after another from my Proust and throwing them in the lake, and I almost started screaming at him again. But instead I walked over and just sat down with him, our feet in the water, the two of us together watching the pages of the book float out toward the center of the lake, little paper boats with sails made of reverie.

K, beautiful betrayer, begins W's last letter, *Mao of my desire, killer of my trust. Were I to have foreseen this silence from you all those years ago in that murderous moment that made me so anonymously famous I could have stood up to nothing, rather I would have accepted the chains of the passionless, the defeated, the tyrannized, the hopeless. . . . What do you suppose I saw in the barrel of that gun rolling toward me if not your face? What do you suppose made me brave? What do you suppose was the mouth of freedom I longed to kiss if not yours? Do you really think I did it just to thrill the world? In that last moment before I slipped into the confessional of history, forever pulling its curtain closed behind my innocence, before I dropped through the earth so as to make my way eastward to you over the years, I heard your sixteen-year-old dreams in my ears drowning out every scream of danger: I peered in the hole of the gun before me and saw your sixteen-year-old legs open to me—and so leaned forward to taste your promise there. Stepped to the right so there could be no eluding my fate, stepped to the left so there oculd be no eluding your whisper of love, clutching in my fist your yellow dress that the world took for a banner of freedom. Begged for destiny to flatten me against the Square beneath my feet. Begged for the explosion of the gun in whose smoke was written the way you belonged to me. Bitch. Whore. History's fucking tourist. Why don't you write me? How can you not write me? How can you not answer! With the passage of time have I become so merely* quaint, *as my photo recedes into the world's nostalgia? Bitch. . . . Kristin . . . please. Love me and I will redeem the ways I've become passé. Answer me. . . . Cunt! no. . . . Please. Love me and I will service you night and day on the Tiananmen of our appetites. Love me and in a moment I will ruthlessly trade the word freedom on the tip of my tongue for the opiate drop of your release. Love me and I will take on the lake for you, I will take on the world for you, again. . . .*

Enclosed with the letter were the two final pieces of the photo, one small round orb of black, one small orb of white—the eyes of his portrait, each a different color. But when I put all the other pieces on the wall back in some semblance of the way I had before Kirk scrambled them that morning, and then added the two eyes, his face still didn't come together except as a crazy abstraction. I kept rearranging the pieces, this way and that . . . sometimes they formed a cracked vase, sometimes a cloud passing before the moon, sometimes a flower floating above the sea, each of the images somehow *off,* straining for a cohesiveness the pieces didn't believe, until I fell asleep again and woke to find once again Kirk had taken all the pieces down and, the way he used to do with my books, put them back. He was just adding the two eyes about the time I opened my own.

Except they weren't eyes. One was the livid hole of the barrel of a gun on a military tank sitting on a flat paved open space . . . behind it was a second tank, with a third behind that and a fourth behind that. The other was the back of the dark head of the tiny man standing ramrod straight in front of the tank, arms straight at his sides, holding in one hand a pale cloth. A pretty famous picture, I guess, from not that long ago in the last century, but I was very little at the time so it wasn't something I knew all that much about, and I couldn't help feeling disappointed I'd put so much time and energy into coming up with just a man blocking a line of tanks, in the same way that, over the years, W had become bitter about having dared and risked so much only so now love could forsake him. That night, singing Kirk to sleep, I strained for a view of her window out there in the lake but it was impossible from my own window, so once I put Kirk down in his crib, locking the door of our room behind me I went back up to the hotel roof hoping to catch sight of her light—but I never did. In the blackness of the night and fog I couldn't make out her building at all, though I knew it was out there; I would have waited all night just to catch sight of her candle, but I didn't like leaving Kirk alone downstairs too long.

7.

Two days ago the lake reached the Hamblin. It happened some time in the middle of the night, and we woke the next morning to find the water up the steps of the eastern entrance, which is now the back way but was once the hotel's front foyer where eighty years ago fancy cars rolled up the circular drive to drop off studio bosses and their starlets. Bobbing in the lake outside the hotel was a silver gondola that shone in the sunlight like a bullet. It belongs to the hotel manager . . . he was prepared, I guess. Next morning water filled most of the first floor corridor, the gondola drifting up and down the hall.

I wouldn't have involved Doc at all if just once more I'd seen the other Kristin's light in her window—but now that the lake's reached the hotel, something's happened to me, I feel the situation's urgent in a way I don't understand. There have been no more letters from W. Once Kirk put the pieces of the photo together he didn't mix them up anymore, but sits on the floor silently looking at it. I don't know whether it's that Doc is so wise nothing surprises her, or incredulity just isn't in her repertoire of responses, but when I showed her the photo she didn't say anything either, she just looked at it a long time, at one point lifting her fingers as though she might touch it and glean something, before pulling back as though it was sacred. When she finally spoke, out on the lake halfway to the deserted building, it was only, "Are you sure which window is hers?" and of course I wasn't sure at all, I just thought we'd figure it out when we got there. I kept looking over my shoulder to see if maybe the hotel manager had sent the lake cops after us to retrieve his gondola, or if Kirk was watching our journey across the Big Agua from the roof with Angela and Parker . . . I hoped he had stopped crying. Soon the lake was too deep for the gondola pole and I had to take over at the oars.

There aren't many people out on the lake anymore. As it's gotten bigger and bigger, it's lost its charm. There have been accidents lately, people who have sailed out and not been seen again. It took us a little more than an hour to get to the abandoned apartment building that was once just a ten-minute walk away—and then we had to sail around it to dock the gondola somewhere it wouldn't drift off. We finally went in through the building's garage, now flooded with only a few feet between the water and the ceiling . . . there were stairs where once had been a furnace room. Where the water met the stairs we were able to get out and drag the gondola up the steps.

Out on the water I had started to tell Doc everything about W's letters but she raised her hand to stop me, as though too much information would only prejudice her diagnosis. Truthfully, I'm not sure we ever would have known for sure which was K's room if not for . . . well, if it hadn't become obvious. I'd only seen the light in her window in the dark from a distance, when it isn't that easy to count windows or floors, and from outside a building far away you think you can kind of guess where something is, and then you get inside and it's not so clear. We kept going through one deserted room after another, trying to find it before late afternoon turned to twilight, and then we found it, and for once even Doc was impressed.

It was my room, or a version of it—articles tacked to the walls, if not the same articles, books on the shelves with a lot of the same titles as mine, same Proust and Kierkegaard and Cendrars and Flannery O'Connor and the Brontës except now mildewed, there was the same photo, except not in pieces, of W as a young Chinese student standing before the tanks. There was a child's bedroom except it was that of an older child, about ten maybe with a small bed instead of a crib, Japanese animé posters instead of cartoon animals, and no sooner do we step into the room than Doc reels as though she's been hit, she even staggers a little, catching herself against the door with one hand and holding her forehead with the other.

From up over the hills in the far west come the first wave of owls, still so far away their shadows on my back skitter up my spine like small black spiders. Reflexively I turn to face the sun through the window, squinting for sight of the owls and looking toward my own building on the other side of the lake, hoping Angela has scurried Kirk to safety. For a while Doc seems frozen where she stands. With a kind of hesitation I've never seen in her before, she lays her hands on the walls and slowly moves through the room from the far doorway, already darkening with night, into the part of it that's blood-red with sunset, as though she's melting into the decomposed smear of the dead day, hands spreading out away from her until it's like she's scorched to the wall, face burned in the plaster. She doesn't make any sound at all for a moment. Then I hear this cry—a sound so convulsive at first I think it's coming from someone else in the room, or from the room itself—and she drops to the floor. The grief on her face is so huge her face is trying to catch up to it. Her eyes and mouth are so stricken they're incapable of tears or sound . . . and, well, I just wish I hadn't seen it. I just wish I hadn't seen it, because some last shred of trust in me shatters when I see her fall apart like this, some small capacity for faith I didn't even know I still had, until this moment when I know I don't have it anymore. Doc the quietly indomitable, who tends to sick and dying houses with the sort of resolve where strength trumps sympathy every time, lies at my feet waiting for whatever she's sensed in this room to recede just far enough away she can finally lower all her defenses against it and break down.

Just standing there I don't know whether I feel more terrified or betrayed, because this isn't my role with Doc, to comfort her. It's her role to comfort me, and I can't even bring myself to go near her, all I can do is crouch on the floor studying her from somewhere near the new sea-level: best I can offer is eye contact, if she wants it.

She never tells me what the walls said. She never tells me what she saw in the yawn of the floor beneath her. "What's the matter with you!" is all I can finally scream at her out on the lake, after waiting almost an hour in that room for Doc to get herself together or for the other Kristin to show up, which we both know isn't going to happen, until finally it starts to get so dark I know we have to get back to the gondola if we're going to find our way back through the building and across the water. "Why are you acting like this?" I scream, hysterical with disillusion, "it's just another dead building . . . !" The whole trip back across the water she doesn't look at me at all, just sitting in the gondola staring straight ahead of her in this blank way, until all I can say is, "I depended on you to be better and stronger and braver and wiser than I can ever be," and then, before the final fall of darkness, she finally looks straight at me, the mouth once younger than the rest of her now old, the eyes once older now ancient, and the hair once lost in time now having found its way home to tomorrow.

8.

I'm lying naked on the Laurel banks. In reality there are no such banks anymore, they're long since underwater, but in my dream there's no lake, just the banks where I lie at war with my womb. It grows dark. We are well into the hour of the owls. From out of the trees behind me I hear him come, and I close my eyes and wait, feel his hands on my feet and feel him lower himself to my thighs. He puts his tongue inside me. Mao of my desire, killer of my trust: I feel his words make their way up inside me. At the moment of my life's most unwilling orgasm I grab him by his black Chinese hair, and my water breaks—am I pregnant? I wonder in the dream—and the torrent that pours from me down Hollywood Boulevard sweeps in its path the Chevron at the corner of Sunset and Laurel Canyon (in reality now long gone, like the banks), rushes down the street and ebbs for a moment before streaming down the Strip . . . the force of it tears W from me. Last I see of him he's caught in the racing flood somewhere down Crescent Heights, trying to keep his head above the water as his arms wave frantically to grab on to something—I laugh out loud at the sight of it. Then in the last gush here comes little Kierkegaard, and I reach to catch him as he leaves me, but slick with afterbirth he slips from my hands, caught in an undertow that burps him up once at the center of the lake before pulling him back down.

I wake. I bolt upright from my dream. Because my thighs are damp, for a moment I'm confused, still in the dream, believing I've really given birth to the lake . . . I can still smell the dream. My heart pounds with fear. I lunge at the white waves of the bed before me to catch my child I've ejected so cruelly, all before my consciousness understands it was a dream—but I can still smell the dream. Finally understanding it's a dream I catch my breath in the dark to wonder what's wrong . . . and look out the window above my bed and in the light of the moon see the ripples of the lake below me. Then I realize I haven't heard his "Mama?" like he always calls, and I stumble from the bed through the apartment to his room.

An amniotic fog fills the room . . . I can barely see him through it. The smell of birth and the lake is overpowering. I move through the vapor to his crib where he sleeps too soundly, and pick him up . . . he barely stirs. He mumbles of monkeys and dinosaurs—he has a monkey book, *I Am a Little Monkey,* and a dinosaur book, *I Am a Big Dinosaur,* he likes me to read him at night—and his face glistens from the fog off the lake. I take him from his room and shut his door behind me. I take him to my bed and put him on the pillow next to mine, where he goes on sleeping.

I don't sleep. The rest of the night I sit up in the bed, placing my body as a barrier between him and the window with the lake beyond it. The rest of the night I sit up watching the center of the lake. Watching and waiting, my heart still pounds from my dream, but now it isn't a dream.

The lake is coming for him.

9.

Like last night, when I wake this morning it takes a moment to realize that what unsettles me is the silence. The hotel's quiet, there are no sounds in the hall or in the room above or below me. Kirk still sleeps on the pillow, which is unusual—almost always he wakes before I do. I lean over him inches from his face and listen to his breathing, watch his little chest rise and fall. I get up from the bed only sort of remembering at the last moment to pull on a robe . . . the world's never been as casual about its nakedness as I am. I walk out in the hall and down to the writer's room, my ear at the door listening for the sound of old movies or maybe even the tapping on the computer of him working, but I don't hear anything.

It's still early enough the hall lights are on except, I notice, in the eastern end of the hotel, and I realize this part of the hotel has lost power. I go back to my room and Kirk still sleeps on the pillow—and leaning back out the window that I looked from only hours ago last night, the black waters of the lake have already pushed past our room. The lake extends north to the hills, only a sliver of the top of the Peninsula still dry land, and soon that will be gone too.

The lake is coming for him. Sometimes I'm paralyzed by my love for him. . . . Some time in the last few hours, between dream and dawn, like a thought cast adrift waiting for me to rescue it, I know in no way I can explain that it doesn't matter where we go, if doesn't matter how far we try to get away, the lake will keep coming for him, and that I can't be paralyzed anymore. Down in the hole of the lake, down in the opening of the birth canal where the earth broke its water, lurks my son's doom and I must stop it. I have to shake myself loose of the love that holds me down and find inside me the love that will save him. I have to go to war with the womb of the earth that would reclaim him. With Kirk in hand I walk back down the hall to the writer's room, and when he doesn't answer my knock, when the door turns unlocked in my hand, movie videos are still on the floor inside, pages of script are still on the desk, there are clothes in the closet though the guy is nowhere to be seen. We go downstairs to Angela and Parker's room, to see if maybe I can leave Kirk with them, and they're gone too, door standing open and crib hastily ransacked . . . the water is only a few feet below their window. A couple of hours from now it will rise high enough to slosh into the apartment. Around noon the power goes out in the rest of the hotel, and I know there's just Kirk and me now, I know we're the last light burning in the window for some other mother to see from some other window in the future, west gazing at the east like the future gazes at the past. When the hotel manager's deserted silver gondola washes up on the stairs just below our floor, I know it's a sign.

In my heart my boy opens the floodgate to a vast unnavigable sea of fear; but I must close that gate. I reproach myself when I look at him at the other end of the gondola with no life jacket, boat precarious in the lake beneath us. His hair shines in the sun above. Looking east I'm not sure anymore how far the lake goes, though in the distance I still see Wilshire office complexes and maybe hear cars. Nobody else is on the lake. The afternoon passes, we sail quietly through the labyrinth of old Hollywood buildings that rise from the black water like the heads of granite fetuses the earth has miscarried. Out in deeper water the black of the lake frames Kirk's golden head. Scraps of wood from the disintegrating Château Marmont harbor drift by. Of course my little wildman seems to have no fear at all. From his two-year-old perspective this all seems inconceivably cool. As we follow the hills around to the northeast, the lake is still just shallow enough I can push us most of the way with the pole . . . Kirk wants to push the pole. "I want to push the pole please!" he demands. He starts to stand in the gondola to come take the pole and I explode with terror: "Sit down!" I scream at him, and he starts to cry. He cries and cries and for a while I just sit there at my end of the boat trying to get it together, then gingerly move to the middle of the boat to pull him to me for a moment and hold him. The way he clutches me I know he's more afraid than I thought. "Sorry, wildman," I whisper in his ear over and over, "sorry," and I almost turn the boat back to the Peninsula . . . but I know what I know, and I must do what I must do. "La-la please, Mama," he says, his whisper matching mine, conspiratorial.

And when the foghorn blows
You know I will be coming home

and by four-thirty we circle round the bend at Laurel Canyon and push our way up the watery ravine where we once watched the city divers swim down to the bottom of the lake.

And when the foghorn blows
I want to hear it,
I don't have to fear it . . .
And I want to rock your gypsy soul

and the sound of loons echoes around us in the growing fog. In the wind on the banks of the lake we can see flapping the tents from the abandoned fair where one afternoon we saw close up the owl that hears human heartbeats. By now the lake has taken most of the old fairground . . . in a long dark row the empty tents billow and collapse, black mouths blowing their secrets out over the lake.

We reach the lake's center. The hole at the bottom is somewhere below us. "Listen to me, wildman," I say as calmly as possible, lowering myself over the side of the gondola into the water.

He's puzzled. "Mama in Big Agua?"

"Yes, Mama's going in the Big Agua for a minute. Just for a minute, do you understand?"

He blinks at me in the twilight.

"Just for a minute. . . ." Please don't cry, it will break my heart. I'm already starting to shiver, and I don't want him to see that.

"Why?"

"So it can't hurt you anymore. Do you understand?"

He nods his head.

Don't ask me why. There isn't time for your whys. "But you have to sit here in the boat very still. Very, very still. You have to sit here and wait for me to come back, you can't move at all or else you could fall in—"

"No Big Agua for me," he reasons.

"No Big Agua for you. So you sit very still, OK?"

"Yes please."

"Mama will be right back for you. All right?"

"Yes please."

"I'll be gone just a minute."

He watches me silently. He doesn't cry.

"I love you, Kirk."

"Mama come back?"

"Right back."

He blinks at me a moment. "Yes, please."

I look around me, and for a moment the chill of the water passes. My eyes drink in everything, they're thirsty like they know something I don't . . . the twilight is the kind of blue you see maybe once in a lifetime, only once. In the wind I hear the murmur of the fluttering tents on the lakeshore, and I know I have only minutes before the sky fills with owls that can hear his heart—and suddenly I can hear his heart myself, its tiny steady thump in the whisper of the tents on the water. I reach over and take Kirk's hand in mine and press it, and before he can cry or try and grab me I take as deep a breath as I can, and slip down into the water.

Sinking, I can still hear his heart. Looking up one last time, I can see him leaning over the edge of the boat peering down at me, his small head a shimmery gold sphere floating above the lake like the parasols of autumn.

The Sleepwalker

William T. Vollmann

It is generally understood, however, that there is an inner ring of superior persons to whom the whole work has a most urgent and searching philosophical and social significance. I profess to be such a superior person . . .

—George Bernard Shaw, *The Perfect Wagnerite: A Commentary on the Niblung's Ring* (1898)

1.

THEIR SLAVE-SISTER GUTHRÚN, marriaged-chained to Huns on the other side of the dark wood, sent Gunnar and Hogni a ring wound around with wolf's hair to warn them not to come; but such devices cannot be guaranteed even in dreams. As the two brothers gazed across the hall-fire at the emissary who sat expectantly or ironically silent in the high-seat, Hogni murmured: Our way'd be fairly fanged, if we rode to claim the gifts he promises us! . . . — And then, raising golden mead-horns in the toasts which kingship requires, they accepted the Hunnish invitation. They could do nothing else, being trapped, as I said, in a fatal dream. While their vassals wept, they sleepwalked down the wooden hall, helmed themselves, mounted horses, and galloped through Myrkvith Forest to their foemen's castle where Guthrún likewise wept to see them, crying: Betrayed! — Gunnar replied: Too late, sister . . .—for when dreams become nightmares it is ever too late.

When on Z-Day 1936 the Chancellor of Germany, a certain Adolf Hitler, orders twenty-five thousand soldiers across six bridges into the Rhineland Zone, he too fears the future. Unlike Gunnar, he appears pale. Frowning, he grips his left wrist in his right. He's forsworn mead. He eats only fruits, vegetables and little Viennese cakes. Clenching his teeth, he strides anxiously to and fro. But slowly his voice deepens, becomes a snarling shout. He swallows. His voice sinks. In a monotone he announces: *At this moment, German troops are on the march.*

What will the English answer? Nothing, for it's Saturday, when every lord sits on his country estate, counting money, drinking champagne with Jews. The French are more inclined than they to prove his banesmen . . .

Here comes an ultimatum! His head twitches like a gun recoiling on its carriage. He grips the limp forelock which perpetually falls across his face. But then the English tell the French: *The Germans, after all, are only going into their own back garden.* — By then it's too late, too late.

I know what *I* should have done, if I'd been the French, laughs Hitler. I should have *struck!* And I should not have allowed a single German soldier to cross the Rhine!

To his vassals and henchmen in Munich he chants: *I go the way that Providence dictates, with the assurance of a sleepwalker.* — They applaud him. The white-armed Hunnish maidens scream with joy.

2.

In an Austrian crowd gathered to celebrate his march into Vienna (triple-angled shadows of bodies on parade, boxy tanks, goose steps, up-pointed rifles), a woman bays before the rest: *Heil Hitler!* — Children pelt his motorcade with flowers. His tanks fly both German and Austrian flags. He drafts a law to join Austria to Germany within twenty-four hours. He's bringing them home to the Reich, he says, his smile as friendly as when he leans across the desk to sign another nonaggression treaty with the credulous dwarfs of Nifleheim.

Dwarfs indeed! With his hands raised up (he's so pale against his own ink-blot moustache), he imparts the following unalterable truth: In this world, there are only dwarfs and giants. And *I* know who is whom!

While the sleepwalker looks on, wolf-hearted Göring, his creation, explains that Czechoslovakia is *a trifling piece of Europe.* (Brownshirts have already appeared on the premises, welcoming the sleepwalker with their chin-straps, banners, wreaths. Soon they will write JEW on Jewish windows, and shake their fists. In the next act, as the curtains get drawn up from the stage columns, we'll see his police coming metal-headed and rigid in the tumbrils to take Jews and hostages away.) Göring continues: The Czechs, a vile race of dwarfs without any culture—nobody even knows where they came from—are oppressing a civilized race; and behind them, together with Moscow, there can be seen the everlasting face of the Jewish fiend!

And Czechoslovakia vanishes like a handful of books flying into flames by night. Children in England and France begin trying on gas masks in anticipation of the sleepwalker's marching columns.

Now beneath the vast gilded eagle in the Reichstag, he sets herds of tanks browsing on the Polish meadows. Bombs fall like clashes of cymbals; arms swing in unison for his government of national recovery.

3.

He hesitates again. He fears what lies before him in Myrkvith Forest. Not that hesitation's practical—hasn't he already accepted the aliens' invitation to the contest? He dreads their spider-holes and deceits, but war's begun; he must roll honorably forth.

He craves to clear his mind. Yes, the curtain's risen, but he needs to lose himself one last time within the curved black *Schalldeckel* which conceals the tunnel to the orchestra pit beneath the stage. From nothingness he came. Would he'd come from a solid wooden hall like Gunnar and Hogni! Well, he'll *dream* Germany solid. Homeless, amorphous, he relaxes into nothingness whenever no one can see. He needs to be his velvet-puddled self, but fears disclosure, and, worse yet, fears his nothingness itself. He imagines how Gunnar felt when the Huns buried him alive in the snake pit. In his dreams he sometimes becomes a black bag filled with serpents. He wakes up vomiting, but the serpents will not crawl out his throat.

Gunnar had a harp; he played the snakes to sleep—all of them but one. And the sleepwalker, he masks himself in music.

4.

The sleepwalker's minions have built him a dream called Eagle's Nest—an eyrie rightly named, for doesn't he possess the droning eagles of steel which are now preying upon Poland? (Each Stuka's but an emanation of his right arm cutting through the air.) Eagle's Nest is reached first by way of a winding mountain road, which conveys the acolyte to the bronze portal, then by a dripping marble corridor through the rock, and finally by a brass elevator up into the heights, a hundred and sixty-five feet—why, that's even taller than the chimney will reach at Auschwitz! Here he can gaze down upon his world of henchmen, kinsmen and foemen. All the way to Poland he can see pale, flashing hands clapping, and frozen, pale faces beneath steel helmets uplifted to seek out his hoarse, loud, bullying voice. Just as at Bayreuth one finds singers and listeners sharing the same darkness, so Hitler and his vassals now dream their way through the great night he's spider-spun out of his own fear and hate, weaving strands of blackness thicker and thicker across the sky until the lights have dimmed—indeed, indeed, just as at Bayreuth (Wagner's innovation this; before him, the frivolous music-munchers sauntered in whenever they felt like it, the opera house illuminated to accommodate them, so that musicians and trappings could be seen, rendering the singers no more than human.). And at his command, liegemen launch eastward his bride-tokens of phosphorous, lead and steel.

5.

Shooting down come the Stukas, straight down, Polish streets spreading out before them like bloodstains, then bombs fall; flames take wing; people scream and run right into the machine guns. The Stukas soar, disdaining now those crooked, blackened ruins which foemen deserve, their bridges brokenly dangling in rivers.

6.

His pale, alert, immobile face watches the victory parade, his eyes like a bird's. Wagner had steam machines and colored lights at Bayreuth; *he* has the many-plumed smoke of ruined Warsaw. And all is as it was before—the same long columns of listeners at Party rallies, long squares of people, mobile barracks drawn up to hear him shouting, warning and exhorting his children of all ages. In comes the Gestapo, drawing up new lists of names, confiscating old ones. In Austria they'd accompanied their sleepwalker's voice less obviously, in much the same way that the Wagnerian orchestra lurks in the darkness past the *Schalldeckel.* They arrested three-quarters of a million people in Vienna on the first day of reunification, but softly. In Poland they need not be soft. They're backed by all good Germans, down to the last heil-smiling ladies and girls, each of whom agrees with him that his foreign adventures had better be, in his own terrifying phrase, *sealed in blood.* They seek themselves in the sleepwalker's pale mute face, his wrist clasping wrist as he endures the honors on his fiftieth birthday, sipping at the rasping static of an infinite cheer.

. 7.

On 23 July 1940 he meets Kubizek at Bayreuth. Kubizek's his old friend from his student days (if we grant that he ever had a friend). Rejected twice for artistic studies, the sleepwalker had stolen away from the unfated other youth to become a tramp. Years he'd spent then imprisoned within the *Schalldekel!* His life had supplied him with no indications of scale whatsoever; he could have been a giant or a dwarf depending on the size of the trees in the painted backdrop where the aliens, solid people, applauded far above his head. But then came a magic drumbeat; and suddenly our sleepwalker became one of the soldiers waving from the troop trains of 1914, and very soon desperately running through sharp-angled trenches, fleeing the gas bombs against which the handkerchiefs tied over their mouths could do less than Gunnar's harp. Kubizek might have admired him then, for he distinguished himself, but . . . But now that he's Führer he need be ashamed of nothing anymore. Troops are waving from the trains again. A huge swastika has overhung him ever since he became legal dictator.

He's already promised to support the artistic studies of Kubizek's children at the expense of the state. He's taken a very kind interest, yes he has. He's even sent Kubizek tickets to the *Ring*.

Of those four operas, "Das Rheingold" is his favorite. (The dwarfs are starving Jewish children with weary old faces, and men with pipe-stem arms.) Could it be his fondness for the music which enthralls him too deeply to remember Kubizek here? Actually he's very interested in the directing. Next comes "Die Walküre," where at the Magic Fire Music, the self-willed, virginal heroine's safely walled to sleep by searchlights like unto the flames inside the skeletons of French and Belgian houses, where weeping, gesturing neighbors bury the dead in deep craters. The sleepwalker has already noted Kubizek's frantic applause during the Ride of the Valkyries (a stunning, chilling, remorseless hymn to war, which thanks to the subterranean architecture gets necessarily softened and diffused a little at Bayreuth). He thinks to invite him up to his private box, but just then Frau Goebbels and her husband make a scene about some infidelity. . . . Now it's already time for "Siegfried," which he wishes to enjoy almost alone with Speer, so that they can whisper in each other's ears about new buildings.

At last, during the first intermission of "Götterdammerung" he finds time for the meeting. He dreads it; he wishes he'd never been persuaded into it by his own sentimentality. He has no time for such nonentities as August Kubizek.

Shyly, Kubizek congratulates him on conquering France. He replies: And here I have to stand by and watch the war robbing me of my best years. . . . We are getting old, Kubizek. — Kubizek bows and nods, not knowing what to say.

And yet, the sleepwalker says, and yet, *this* . . . You remember how we used to stand for hours on end for Wagner, because we could not afford to sit? You remember how "Götterdammerung" made us weep?

Yes, my Führer . . .

It's like a bath in steel, I tell you. After Wagner, I feel hardened and refreshed . . .

He returns to his box to sit rapturous until the end of the final act, when the devoted woman sets everything she loves on fire, and buildings collapse like sand castles, windowed facades slowly falling to the street, becoming dust and broken glass.

Kubizek in his humbler box remembers how when they were youths together the sleepwalker once wrote a *Hymn to the Beloved* to a tall and slender fair-haired girl named Stephanie Jansten, but never ever spoke to her. O yes, fair-haired! Why, she was as blonde as the smoke which now rises up from all the synagogues! Sometimes the sleepwalker was resolved on suicide for hours on end, but he said that Stephanie must be ready to die with him.

To the stage comes torchlight, wavering columns of light. When the sleepwalker shouts, they shout and thunder, their arms flashing up and down while his stiff boys bang drums. The sleepwalker speaks, or Siegfried sings; it matters not to the rigidly attentive faces. Light gleams on the side of his face.

8.

In 1941 he attacks his ally Russia. War on all fronts! Now Germany's safely surrounded by a wall of fire! How long will it take to reduce that empire to a smear beneath his boots? Three weeks, probably, but in this world exactitude sometimes fails. At Bayreuth, for example, the "Rheingold" has been performed in two-and-a-quarter hours, but sometimes it can take as long as three.

For this Russian campaign he selects a snippet of Liszt's *Preludes* to be played on the radio as a victory fanfare.

9.

The sleepwalker charmingly smiles as with both his hands he clasps the wrist of Wagner's granddaughter Verena.

Yes, my Führer, she murmurs. I will give orders that no one is to disturb you.

He enters his private box at the rear wall. He gazes down across the empty seats, which resemble the keyboard of an immense typewriter upon which he might compose any musical score he pleases.

I will not allow this war to hinder my objectives, he whispers to himself.

Russia will not die. Russia is coming at him like the dragon-worm which will rise up at the end of the world, bearing corpses in its claws. The aliens have tricked him, as he always knew they would. But he's raised the goblet of promise. He must continue on.

10.

Another weakling, another little shirker requests permission to report. The sleepwalker gazes at him with angry eyes.

The shirker complains about certain extreme measures. What a gallows-raven he is! He croaks and croaks. (In the *Ring*, don't even gods have to trick the dwarfish Jewish capitalist and even rob him in order to save the world?) The sleepwalker stares him down, but the shirker will not dwindle. On the conference room table there at Wolf's Lair, he lays out photographs of hungry street crowds in the Warsaw Ghetto, of children's faces like weeping skulls, pale, immobile bodies on the pavement, skinny, pale people lying in crowds on hay mattresses.

A secretary gasps.

The sleepwalker whirls to kiss her hand. — Never mind, child, he comforts her. She smiles, rushes from the room.

The shirker whines on and on. He's sure that this matter was never brought to the Führer's attention before. Of course the Jews are our misfortune , but this . . .

And the sleepwalker? He flicks at one of the photographs with his thumbnail. The mouth tightens.

11.

Another general insists on disturbing him with bad news of the Russian advance. He says that conditions are degenerating along the entire front.

Well, let them degenerate! he rages. All the better for me!

Yes, my Führer. But our own troops are freezing to death. Just yesterday I saw—

The sleepwalker covers his ears. — Perhaps I'm too sensitive, he replies.

12.

The workers have gathered before him into rectangular armies. Swastika standards begin marching in file down a long well of futurity. They shout; he waits, expressionless and dour. Long before the first Blood Purge of 1934 they'd seen him striding up to the dais of destiny, standing atop an immense dais with a swastika on the wall nearest his feet. Now they must all be conscripted, their factories to become still another front. He needs gold rings and henchmen.

He speaks of spiritual matters. Only they can save his grey cathedrals and greatcoats from the Russian Jews, who return to life no matter how many of them he burns. The workers must build new breastworks. Aren't they all answerable to the war dead? Even women will have to labor now, in spite of all his principles. Emergencies require extreme measures. Didn't Siegmund mate with his own sister to save the blood of their race?

And the workers listen. They honor his sacrifice. They will not bereave him of his war. Like the crowd at the Opera House, they offer him "stormy applause." At his drumbeat comes the gorgeous flash of ten thousand spades raised upon the Labor Front. In his honor, the German women have strung buntings upon their gingerbread houses. Soon enemy bombs will tumble upon them, and he'll turn away, his face milkily shining by torchlight.

13.

He always attends the first cycle at Bayreuth every year. This time again he comes early. At Bayreuth the stage is roofless like bombarded Stalingrad. The sleepwalker paces unyieldingly in his private box, brooding down the fan-shaped tiers of empty seats. He strokes the Corinthian columns. He unbuttons the collar of his shirt. He can almost hear the breathing of Verena Wagner outside. The *Schalldeckel* gapes before him: music's open grave. Like the bridegroom who longs to meet his bride beneath the linen sheets, he craves this hollow of secret repose. Only there can he hoard himself safe from the others whom he must ever watch with turning head. His magic renews itself there; he sleeps without dreaming.

And so he descends into the *Schalldeckel.* The old floorboards creak beneath his jackbooted tread. Coldheartedly nervous, he grips his sweaty forelock, gibbering softly to himself, wondering where to rest. But this time, beyond the darkness he spies the flickering fires of fire courts! Call him not afraid. He's the blond against the dark. But it's *so* dark, just as it once was during the previous World War when he was young and blinded by poison gas. . . . He strides blindly forward. Don't his own soldiers hunker down to run through tunnels in the ruins even though flashes of Russian rocket-light and snakes of flame pursue them?

The flames lunge up. A tall woman stands ahead. He scarcely comes up to her knees. The pupils of her eyes resemble sparks from the spearpoints of Valkyries. Jealous that blackness is not his alone, he halts, mistrusting, his own eyes glaring like twin red rings.

She clenches her fist. Then he knows he's on trial. Momentarily he awakes, staring candidly at her with his wide, piercing eyes. He thrusts his head back, speaks from the chin. He's somber, godlike, expressionless. Dreaming an answer to what she hasn't yet said, he tells her that in the operas, Wotan's noblest striving is for his own supplanting. He doesn't care if he loses the war, if he can only keep the Jews from getting back the magic ring.

Why, then, it's well for you, she replies.

What do they name you?

Laugh-at-Wailing.

Who gave you birth?

Fire's my father. *Doom* is my mother called.

And why do you await me here?

To tell you what you've always known—that you were born guilty and overmastered, that the nothingness you burn for refuses to receive you, that olden treasures grow corrupted at your touch.

The sleepwalker screams: It's all treason! Now I know why my Russian offensive's failed! That's my justification. If I was fated, then how was I to blame? You Jewish bitches have opposed me at every step, but do you think I care? I'll annihilate you; I'll exterminate you all! You think you're immortal, but I'll test you with every poisoned acid there is! I've always been too lenient. Well, that's about to change. I'll have you broken without mercy; I know what it takes; I'll wear you down . . .

But *Laugh-at-Wailing* answers with a chuckle like a rattle of futurity, like bones jiggling inside a procession of pale coffins across the scorched earth of liberated Auschwitz.

I won't give up! cries the sleepwalker. I don't care if it's useless!

The Valkyrie stands silent.

So then, in a pleading tone, he whispers: *Why did you make me?* I never wanted to be made . . .

For propaganda, of course. It's all in your own book. How can we persuade others to be good, without evil we can point to?

Mercurially calming himself, he smiles and remarks: You might as well have spared yourself the trouble. What did you think I'd do—walk sheepishly to the gallows? Do you think I've never been judged before?

I don't need opinions, little man.

And you truly believe I'll deviate one hair's breadth from the course I've laid out for myself? You think you can goad me into doing anything more extreme than I would do in any case? Are you so hopeful? Why, then, *it's well for you.*

He withdraws, escorted almost into the light by goblins like Russian tanks scuttering across ruins. He's in a panic. He rushes home to Berlin, where he can closet himself with Speer and gaze down at the Grand Avenue of postwar Berlin, modeled at one to one thousand scale. Speer's cabinetmakers built the new Opera House at one to fifty scale, and over here there'll be a cinema for the masses. Every edifice will be the same height.

With deferential formality, Speer asks his opinion on some aspect of the Central Railroad Station. Carefully, the sleepwalker tries out the Valkyrie's phrase: *I don't need opinions.* I already see everything.

Speer stares woodenly. The sleepwalker feels inspired.

14.

And now what? The inclined arm replicated a millionfold, the knife-edge hand, the shouting voices of his echoers, his chin-strapped orators, all sing out to stand firm. Germany lies obediently below him, like an aerial view of fields, a corduroy of bodies who soon will fight in Russia, shivering, warmed only by the pain of their own wounds. His swastika banners are grass-blades in an infinite meadow of war. Up standards! *Sieg Heil!* He's guarded by grimy soldiers with deep-sunk eyes. Comes the great battle between Siegmund and Hunding; then long lines of gravediggers are carting corpses two by two to the open pit; down the chute they go; then we paper them over, and add a sprinkle of dirt, hastily so that we will not get into even more trouble with the Germans who have dressed us in the striped uniforms and pale wrinkles of concentration-camp inmates and who are even now building our doom out of squat towers and barbed wire.

15.

Italy falls, but the sleepwalker knows how to save her from the Jews. Parachutes as beautiful as white flowers bloom upon the skies which he's now capturing. Black columns of smoke have translated the beaches of Normandy into the stage darkness after an intermission. In the next act he must sing of retreating German troops, of dead horses and throttled light. The inky moustache in his grey face, the black, gaping mouth, and above all the raised hands of him suck new blood down the marching orchard-lanes of swastika standards. Before him, beyond his warriors hunched under their caps, he seems to see a plain of faces and lights. Increasingly golden, this country draws him on beyond himself. Now he comprehends in his soul why Gunnar and Hogni could not resist the Hunnish invitation: Although it meant doom and sister-woe, at least they'd win that brilliant-if-sinister moment of light when they drew near their foe-men's forecourts. Futurity shone like a flame-flicker reflected on gold foil. They knew they'd be greeted by raised arms and faces, faces more pale and numerous than raindrops. The sleepwalker mutters, as he did on the eve of the Russian campaign: *The world will hold its breath . . .*

16.

Soothed by the solid row of columns marching alongside the seats at Bayreuth, he fingers the acanthus scrolls. He helps Verena Wagner with gifts of munificent gold. Soon his *Ring* will begin again. He'll watch it from start to finish, without fail. He always keeps his promises.

17.

A horizontal salute from Hitler in the clouds! The sleepwalker dreams his face away from the long line of German prisoners of war so ragged and dirty, who march off to Soviet Arctic prisons, their jaws bound up in blankets and rags. Meanwhile, his own lines of slave workers march feebly past ruined apartments and railroad sidings. His dreams are shriveling and scorching. His henchmen have given over running across each other's corpses in Africa. Shells and flames, tanks in snow, ice-maned horses, siege guns echoing in the wind, all these assault his dreams as the Russian Frost-Giants come west.

18.

Now he dwells within walls of smoke. Flames rush up his staircases; chandeliers transform themselves into scorched spiders. The light excites him. In the distance he can see electric glows of barbed wire. To fight the Jews, his henchmen have built many a city of factories in the snow whose long alleys of barbed wire are signposted by frozen, snowy corpses with outstretched arms. Heaps of jawbones, mountains of pliers mark the spots where his vassals extract gold teeth from the living and the dead. Lives blow away like waves of sand. If he can only dream this dream a little longer, they'll all be safely up the chimney. But where are his muscled heroes with their swords? Are they all dead? Snowy Russian tanks breast bluish flames and bluish snow to conquer Auschwitz, where more than seven tons of human hair await transshipment. A parade of skinny, dessicated corpses comes forth to tell lies and inspire new Jewish conspiracies.

19.

When the captive Gunnar told the Huns that he'd only reveal to them the hoard of the Niflungs (whose gold shone even brighter than the vertical gleams of sunlight upon marching SS boots) on condition that they cut out Hogni's heart, they tried to trick his rich-wrought mind by carrying to him a mere thrall's heart upon a board; but he knew his brother's heart would never quiver in terror as that one did even in death. Helpless before his cleverness, they killed Hogni then, who laughed as he died. Then Gunnar said that since only he remained to tell the secret, he had no more fear, for tell he never would.

When they lowered Gunnar into the slimy dungeon of adders, he played upon his harp so beautifully that all the serpents slept. Yet finally he wearied, and from that ball of reptiles he perforce lay upon rose up one to bite his liver, and so he perished there in the darkness of snakes.

Knowing her duty, valiant Guthrún served up her own sons' hearts to the husband who'd slain her brothers. After that she razed the castle by fire.

The sleepwalker in his pale gray coat (our memories of him have become so gray and grainy) craves to be another Gunnar. Isn't he a harpist, too? Hasn't he always been able to lull all snakes to sleep until now? And his Germany, she shall be Guthrún. Germany must die ferocious, burning down everything . . .

20.

On 12 April 1945, the Berlin Philharmonic presents Brünnhilde's last aria and the finale from "Götterdammerung." He's seen "Götterdammerung" more than a hundred times. Each time, his brain burns anew in flames of salmon-colored gold. Silhouettes of hanged corpses comprise the perimeter of his now-miniscule empire. A civilian hostage raises both arms. Where now his cruelly smiling pale young faces under steel helmets? Where now his myriad marchers on a hill, following the swastika flag? — In Siberia, or dead under mud or pale cobblestones! The radio which once spread his words like epidemics now pulses meaninglessly: *Complete obliteration . . . shameful . . . solemn promise . . .* The Russians have already reached Myrkvith Forest; waves of American Jews hem them in on all other fronts. Verena Wagner decides to plan a *Ring* without swastikas for 1946. Shadowy night crowds burn their uniforms, which were sewn and ornamented in his image. Other crowds in striped uniforms begin emerging from the lane of barbed wire. Mountains of shoes which from a distance resemble herrings in a tin memorialize those who will nevermore come forth. And the sleepwalker dreams. He gives orders to execute all the new traitors. Germany will be safe. Smiling at last in his address to the schoolboys who've hopelessly fought for him against the parades of Russian tanks now entering Berlin, he speaks of their common lineage, then hands out tokens like unto the ancient rings of red gold. The boys shout: *Heil Hitler!* Closing his eyes, he remembers how five years ago his long lines of victorious warriors passed through the Arc de Triomphe while he paid homage to Napoleon. But the world of the old gods was corrupt; it had to be smashed. He does not tell the boys this. It is too late for any explanations. A few days later, weird-ringed by Russian flames, the sleepwalker and his secret bride kill themselves.

21.

In his very first speech as Chancellor he'd cried: I have steadfastly refused to come to the people with cheap promises! — Then he'd pointed to his heart. But now what promises has Gunnar to harp on for all these ungrateful snakes? He tires now; his music stops. Shyly he confesses: On the day following the end of the Bayreuth Festival, I'm gripped by a great sadness—as when one strips the Christmas tree of its ornaments . . .

His music stops, his Berliners running behind mounds of rubble, flames winging out of windows, for he's lost this game of draughts which the gods once played with golden figures, but even yet he guards hope, for Roosevelt is dead; Stalin and Churchill are falling out; and that most ancient of all Norse prophecies sighs upon the lips of the moldy, grassy Mother who periodically arises from this grave-infested earth: Someday, perhaps even in the meadows of Poland where his herds of tanks recently gamboled, *the golden figures, the far-famed ones, will be found again, which they possessed in olden days.* And then, beneath an even, searing light, he'll win back his city all of gold, whose monuments and plazas remain unmarred by humanity.

Laura Warholic

Alexander Theroux

LAURA'S OLD FLAT ON RAVEN ST. was an ill-lit reptillary of soiled clothes, strewn papers and broken shades. It was situated in the narrow warren of drab back lots and the maze of ugly one-way streets between the river and Central Sq. with its pointless traffic islands on the top floor or a gray three-decker. Trucks juddered by, cars sped past. There were several stick-thin little kids jumping around on the high front cement stoop, small girls with fallen ankle-socks and torn frocks, desperate hair, and empty eyes. Eida, the oldest, about eight years old, disliked Laura and often called her brash names. A rickety stairway led up through the darkness. It was always depressing inside. Some of her drawings, legs like arms, heads like buttocks, hung on the walls in her room and on the back of the door. She had attended Parsons School of Design in New York but had wasted her parents' money on a degree she had never put to use, simply because she not only could not draw but even on a merely conceptual level hadn't the slightest gift for, a word she loved to use, "rendering." The decor was terse. There was the Iggy Pop poster on the wall. The Joel Witkin reproduction of the dead fat man sitting in a chair, headless, wearing only a pair of socks, as if her very picture partner, a grotesque double in madness, sorely saddened Eyestones, and he turned away. There were two other rooms on that floor, those of her two, mostly absent roommates, the only rooms that showed even a semblance of neatness.

A bare bulb hung from the ceiling on a wire in Laura's room. It smelled of Lysol or Dettol or some industrial cleaner. A brownish water came from the faucets of the sink, rusted with orange scour. A ragged blind hung slantways in the one cracked window, as well as the plastic curtain stained by years of hard water that hung celluloid-stiff in the shower stall reminded Eugene Eyestones of hot-sheet joints rented by the day in Saigon. The bedcover, with its rumpled blankets, was a trash heap of cracker boxes, empty coffee cups, candy wrappers, half-eaten tins of tuna fish, spilled milk, assorted other dropping and piles of old yellowing tabloids, *National Enquirer*s and

Stars and *Globes*, which her grandmother sent her from Syracuse on a weekly basis. "How can you sleep with the sound of traffic outside?" asked Eugene. She was making abrupt, squirrel-like movements to straighten the place out. "I masturbate," she said, shrugging. She looked at him and said sarcastically, "Slick mittens, you know? Petting snoopy. Rolling the mink. Buttering the bead." She kick-slid a box sideways. "I have a Prelude 3 vibrator, my pink pearl," she said. "You think I'm a bad girl, don't you? Shallow. Vulgar. Fill in the blank."

Her room smelt of applesnails. The potato-colored wallpaper, mottled with stains, was unpeeling in flaps all around. The room was particularly hideous. There was an empty dampness to the place. The kitchen was a cubbyhole, the floor uncarpeted, the chairs worn, and on a lazy-top formica table in one main room a coarse sheet of kapok served for a tablecloth. A plain bookcase in the room was filled with odd paperbacks on punk music, a few psychology and self-help books, and piles of 'zines, her primary reading. "Dan, a friend of mine in San Francisco, has most of my books, the bastard, and better return them. Boxes of them." All the contents of the room, crowded with boxes and trash, seemed to push the air out of the room. There was a sense of brownness, a coalescent odor of damp books and unwashed blankets, of cats and illness, of must and sadness and the sebum of her body. It was Upsidedownland! The Wherehouse! Eyestones referred to the place as "Bluegate Fields," from *The Picture of Dorian Gray.* A batch of snapshots Laura had taken of herself in her San Francisco digs, several showing her fully naked, wearing scarves, smeared with lipstick, were stuck in a mirror, along with snipped-out pictures from various magazines of people like Sandra Bernhard, Juliette Lewis, Laura Dern and the cadaverous singer Patti Smith, the kind of rude, homely women with whom, always in a ghostly validation of herself and with enough disillusioned wittiness to maintain irony, Laura insistently identified and madly sought to defend. Another wrinkled snapshot with a dog-eared corner, once ripped in two, now cellophaned, of a flaccid-faced man slipped out. Eugene held it up to look at it.

Her roommates. Maudie, a big blonde, and Wing, the Chinese woman, were not in sight. They were rarely there the few times he'd visited. They disliked Laura for her indifference and standoffishness and so avoided her themselves. Wing was softly graceful and darkly pretty and from the very first time he was introduced to her Eyestones wishes he had been able to be with her. There was on a mantle an athletic cup, Robin Zander's, with three dimes and four pennies in it. "You like that, huh? Look at this, puppy knees," she demoted, holding up some pieces of limp leather, demonstrating proudly that she was a complete hedonist. "A pair of drumgloves of Cheap Trick's." Laura slammed the one open window to stifle the shouts of the children outside and went to the bathroom. Everywhere in the room were stacked piles of cassettes, records, CDs and LPs. A broken box of sanitary napkins had been left open. Jars of Vaseline. Boxes of Kim-Wipes. A yellowing wardrobe, next to a heap of laundry, overflowed with cheap clothes of the thrift-shop and jumble-sale variety. "Who's the older man in the photo?"

"My father."

He was white and looked as though he had been processed in cold water, like a kosher chicken, with all his blood removed by way of his being salted. Selfish-looking and pinched, he held up a hand.

"There's a can of instant coffee in the pantry," shouted Laura through the open door of the bathroom where she squatted, peeing. "At least there was. I've got nothing else to offer you." "I thought you drank only Starbuck's." She piped up, shiny as chrome, "Only when you're buying." Her habits bore the random antietiquette of Generation Xers, ruleless, indifferent and slack. And flooding in on him as he stood there, in a place he had avoided so long, was the recollection, as if united, of all her lax behavior, a regime she always defended whenever he tried to discuss it with her, not with words but with an attitude of wooden-faced stupidity, sideways and self-absorbed, that one notices in the squint of golfers following a shot or on the face of a cheesy drummer sitting above his traps and smugly working his brushes. She never thanked anybody for favors. She never finished reading a book. She lost or misplaced any gifts you gave her, bracelets, rings, books. She read other people's mail. She was always late and rarely kept appointments. She had accumulated huge library fines. She was sloth-slow, getting out of a car, answering a question, forming a thought. She never ate all the food on her plate. She didn't know how to cook a meal, set a table, use a napkin, serve a plate. Polish? She *swept* rugs to clean them. If order were a test of sanity in a room, this room, this dark place—this woman—was bedlam itself. Her only loyalty seemed to be what she compiled in her witchy journal, her daybook listing the crimes of others against her, forgetting her own poisonous gossip that she always gave to the new man in her life of all the previous ones. "You'd be humiliated if you knew what she said about you," said Disknickers, with whom Laura once had an affair during a month when Eyestones had gone to San Diego, told him in a moment of confidence.

She wrote with difficulty, letters and such. Her handwriting was so spidery—upside marginalia and loops and erasures and superadded balloons and scratchings out—that reading any page or two that she wrote became a truly cognitive task, particularly because the paper she always employed and sent, fraying down one side, were always in bunches of disparate pages carelessly ripped out of various notebooks and added to sheets or other shapes and sizes. What were the differences in writing between men and women, Eyestones wondered? Whatever. It seemed to him a perfect if oblique idea for one of his columns. Were the sexes revealed in their syntax? Did the plush adjective, the reticent question mark, the soft reliance on the weak comma, undermining solid vehemence, reveal in the composing mind girlish diffidence? Was a terse, laconic style a man's? Caesurae proof women weakly had to tell us when to take a breath? For that matter, weren't female broadcasters and reporters on television always trying to sound like men, with that ersatz gruffiness and chin-firm delivery, all underlining voices and stridency? Laura, who always awkwardly held a pen, and wrote, with her right thumb literally wrapped around it and over the index finger—it was not so much held as gripped—habitually penned over words and letters, almost perversely, making double lines with every stroke, multiple exposure lines, as if she intentionally used a double-nib to give a drunken or ringing look to whatever she wrote or redid or traced over, all of it causing in Eyestones, whenever he tried to read one, a kind of retinal headache. In any case, this became the formal cause of his setting out one day with resolve to buy her this particular present and why, after work, he had come by this night.

Eyestones had bought her a typewriter. It was a lovely leaf-green Hermes 9, Swiss made and rock solid. He lifted it onto the table and lifted off the shell cover. Laura looked down on it as antedeluvian. "No one fucking even knows how these work anymore," she declared, typically negative, lethargically and disconsolately slapping the carriage side to side. She looked at him and smiled angrily, as if she wanted it well known that something was being fobbed off on her, and when she did, her long nose reached her mouth so wide that it seemed she was swallowing her nose.

"It's an appliance of science."

"For fuddy-duddies."

"I've used one all my life."

"That long?" He looked at her. "Wasn't that way back when electric light bulbs came to a point, *hon?*" she asked, dotting the sarcasm with a bit of savoring delight.

The Man With The Faraway Eyes regarded the ghost of folly and felt as he usually did after giving her something, anything, that it was pointless.

"Try?" he pleaded. He tossed onto the bed several boxes of typewriter ribbons and, opening another, slitting the cellophane, handed her the two small interlocking wheels. "Look closely. 320 thread-counts per square inch. Only Egyptian Pima, or Sea Island cotton, goes higher," he said. "It's the tightest fabric on earth. Look. Try pulling it. If you wanted, you could hang Virginia hams from it."

Laura stepped over the gift.

Ling from nowhere suddenly emerged from her room. She wore a robe of orchid satin, had no makeup on, and her short hair was brushed behind her ears. She kept custody of the eyes. She set a mug down in the pantry and simply passed through to the other room. She had long legs, and the uncomplicated photogenic features of her chalk-white skin, gracefully pretty, appeared to be a sort of lamp.

"Don't hold it against me that this place is such a lame-ass mess," Laura grizzled, suddenly growing meaner, having witnessed Ling walk by. She kicked a dusty box under the bed and hurled a blanket over a pile of trash. "You do, you know. Hold things against me. You're critical. You don't accept me for what or who I am." He said nothing but thought: *don't you see that if one were not critical, by allowing your slovenliness, I could end up that way myself?* Still, he pitied her in that room. There was no warmth, nothing to come home to. He dreaded going there. She was caverned off from everything, and whereas at one time she never came out, now that once she did, she rarely went back. From outside came cries in unison from the small girls jump-rope style, "*Scarecrow! Scarecrow! Scarecrow!*" Eugene went to look down, hefting up the sill, but Laura slammed down the window. "Cunts," she muttered.

On the wall, along with a recently added poster, taken in Boston, or a rock group he had never heard of called The Craven Slucks—four pie-faced dunces in aviator sunglasses and black leather jackets—were taped more of her own bad drawings, crutched anatomies and softball heads and thick clubs standing for human arms and legs in a series of sketches done in a weekly "figure composition" class she had begun attending, deformed, slanting females, for the most part, differentiated from the other sex only by the usual display of vulvas that every cranky feminist with a crayon or charcoal always unapologetically insists we see in detail and the ungainly prominence of buttocks the size of beach umbrellas by which as sort of academic space filler she seemed to be somehow trying to compensate for her own narrow imagination. "I hate living in this fucking place. Ling with all her lists and *thingies!* Mary let a friend of hers sleep in my own bed a few weekends ago. Can you believe it? "Eyestones only wondered where she had spent that same weekend, but he never asked that question which once he would have, but not anymore. "So what happens? I have to dish out money I don't have to buy a lock for the door. And you wouldn't be wicked fucking bummed?" she paused. "Watch out! That chair is dodgy. I got it thrifting at Morgan Memorial." She flung a broken cup into a trash box. "But remember when I asked if I could move in with you? You didn't want me." "It's not that I didn't want you." "You didn't!" she cried. "Don't deny it. I offered to clean your bathroom, to housekeep, to do washing. I care for you. I'm faithful to you. I don't look at anyone else. I'm interested only in you."

Memories create expectations, and he knew she came to him with a vision of defiance that sought compensation for everything prevented her in life. It was the nature of her "enthusiasm." She had no faith, as such, didn't believe in God or in anything, for that matter, but oddly, perhaps because of that, with an almost icy stare at the improvident and unobliging universe maintained the secular hope that *because* of that lack of faith, a total indifference to the supernatural, people like her, above all, deserved the help that believers—she inevitably saw such people as wealthy because they were wealthier than she—could provide. Nothing less would suffice for her. It was a mess. A big C.F., thought Eugene. A Charlie Foxtrot. A cluster fuck. An operation ending up in confusion.

"Faithful, did you say?" asked Eugene.

"I don't lie," she lied, and as a displacement activity space-cadeted out into the hallway. "I'll be right back. I have to call my grandmother in Syracuse," she called over her shoulder. Whispering, she ducked her head into Mary's room and asked, "Will you let me borrow a sexy dress for a special occasion?" "Which one?" Laura smiled her big red smile. "That plum 'barbed wire' dress you have? It protects the property but doesn't hide the view."

Eugene adjusted the ribbon in the typewriter. He thought of that word: *faithful—to what?* He knew she was lying, of course. She had an intimacy issue, to start with, and her low, fishy, underhanded imitations of caring were too obvious to hide, and whatever she promised, his mind in the matter was like a dead car battery that would not turn over. What she failed to see in herself was her eternal but unabated desperation. She was her mother again: merely the thin concave of the fat convex. She was also one of those driven, demented, Dionysian obsessives and ultra energetic sex-hysterics who, for all her protests of love for you, was the kind of person who as soon as you turned your back could fall in love with a UPS delivery man or a thin waiter serving a cutlet or any garage mechanic doing a lube who smiled at her, defending such a thing with almost astro-cartographical surety, and then disappear with him without one look back or a single regret. It happened all the time. He knew she had slept with—was still sleeping with, for all he knew—Disknickers. Saturday night and Sunday morning was not a social dichotomy with her; she slept with men on Saturday night and merely overslept with them the next morning. It was her only vocation. Everything else was an alias. A shadow artist, a shadow friend. A shadow lover. A shadow woman.

Once when her name came up at the office by way of a Mutrux comment regarding Eugene's complaint about the insistent subterranean hum of Laura's neurotic jealousies, coupled with her own deceit, Wrongarski breezily and with a fussy limp wrist quoted Cecil Parker's comment on Ingrid Bergman in *Indiscreet,* "There is no sincerity like a woman telling a lie."

Laura didn't love Eyestones. She didn't hate him. Other people for her did not really even register in matters of consequence. She did not feel the asperity of such notions. She was outside—beyond—such choices. She was interested only in herself, in getting by, in eating well, in finding men, and in not having to work in the attempt to achieve any of it. Whenever he tried to question her about where she was going in life, for her *own* benefit, her heart sealed up, as soundless and as airless and as remote as the moon.

"Who are these people?" asked Eugene, pointing to the poster of the wall of The Craven Slucks in their pretentious leathers. She explained that they were a local band. She grinned with that wide red mouth and flapped her ornithomimic arms and said, "I can't help myself, Cookie Puss."

"Who are you," asked Eugene, "The Four Tops?"

Laura grew cool. Eugene often felt that coldness coming from her. But her rooms also had a toxic effect on him whenever he visited her there, which over the course of the years he knew her had only happened twice. Suicide Alley. Nightmare Abbey. Bluegate Fields. Whenever he suggested that she move somewhere else, she would curse her high rent with alarm, invariably failing to mention how Curbstepper had several times lowered it for her, a subject that Eugene, closing his eyes with a growing sense of exasperation, did not want to pursue, such were its unsavory implications and meanings, but as she had bad short-term memory and often asked for money from Eyestones she invariably blundered when referencing her rental fee by never using the same figure twice, a sum that over the course of time was reported in diminishing returns.

She opened her refrigerator. "Want something—? "To eat?" he asked. "There's nothing here." On one shelf was a jar of bulk mustard, a bitten Chipwich, and an unwrapped, half-eaten, encrusted quesadilla that smelled. She took out a small package of stale Hostess Sno-Balls, shrugged, and ate them herself. He had never seen red nails which did not make the most fragile of fingers seem blunt and soiled. Her upside-down notions defeated all his attempts to change her ways, but her unsinkable urge to unvanish always left him with a feeling that she needed his help. She remained contentious, never content. "Won't your father help you out a bit?" She coldly looked back at him. What was it he so disliked in her empty stare as she sat there, an empty Mettlach stein with a wagging metal lid of a head? The indistinctness of her anger or peevishness or disgust was as inexplicable as the closeted nature of her affairs, which were even stranger because sharing was foreign to her utterly. What we do not say! How we cannot say it! Living her life, excusing it by *pretending* to live it, for she did nothing, a way of throwing shade. Over the years, month after month, day in and day out, as he had tried not to see her, she harrassed and annoyed the bejesus out of him, telephoning him, appearing on his doorstep, always insistently repeating, "I miss your company," and "It's so lonely listening to the wind and rain beating against the windows and the omnipresent traffic noises here," and "I need you" and 'Please don't desert me, please?" He heard: I need someone to take care of me and need to be with other men.

"I hate this place."

"Get out," said Eyestones. "*Face* getting out. Rely on yourself. You're always looking for shortcuts."

"I'm not brave."

"Fair enough," he said, remembering Quangtri. "But courage is not the absence of fear, only the disregard of it. Work at it. For your own control."

Laura sat down. "I fucking *hate* my life," she snapped and angrily kicked aside a pile of old LPs, which shot across the floor, revealing the gum-colored album covers of all her former favorite groups and singers, a revelation to Eyestones as blackly depressing as her mood: Bread, Yanni, Zamfir and His Pan Flute, John Tesh, Barry Manilow, Up With People, Neil Diamond, Wayne Newton, Hall & Oates, Kenny G.—singers she now loathed. Why was change in her always an about-face? Didn't hysterics often have erotic fits, sensory hallucinations, vivid sexual dreams? Was the disordered mind often—always?—sexual? Always mixed messages. Changed opinions. Altered states.

It was classic indirection. To him it was exactly like the confusion all policemen enjoy making by way of the traffic jams they often purposely create, letting chaos prevail, in order to look important in the midst of the chaos, or, similarly, the perplexity that venal, smug professors cause in classrooms by pretentiously overcomplicating simple problems in order to bewilder hapless students and so appear more brilliant. The odd truth was that Eugene, who felt a parallel vice in himself, saw enough in his own shortcomings to keep himself from judging her: *I disbelieve in myself because I no longer believe that there is a secret something inside me which, when I pray, seems worthy enough to merit they be answered.*

Was he using her himself, by indirection, to study the threnody-befucked oddities of love and sex? Was he himself a threat by example, an interlocuter, a videophile who cared for nothing but only to learn? Worse, as he listened to her, time after time, was he not uncaring, distracted as he was by looking with love into the winter sky toward that hopeful constellation and his scintillant nebula?

They sat there in silence. Eugene, who would have once fought to straighten her out, had given up. At one time, it would have seemed obscene. He had been true blue to her from the first time they met. Long before he had seen Rapunzel, he had given up on Laura because she was unfaithful—had no faith. To the true heart, but to any fool, as well, it is always understood that there are always better-looking people, for anybody, far prettier girls, much handsomer men, to be seen with, to talk to, to walk with along the beach, to share dreams with and live and die for. While fidelity understands this, love blesses it. Was that not what love was? The acceptance of someone *for* their faults? Laura had neither belief nor conviction in it. Cheating for her was an ongoing policy, the matrix, the mechanics, of merely waiting for the opportunity to do so. She once threatened to jump off the Citizens Bank Building, next to where she worked, if he did not love her, while later that very same week he had heard she had been making secret liaisons, not only with black Jamm the Wesort, but with a bald man named Harry whose name Eyestones's typist had given her in passing when, driven by jealousy, she had telephoned Kate the typist to ascertain whether Eugene Eyestones had once had an affair with *her!*

She suspected everybody. She was insanely jealous of girls of thirteen, of older women, of waitresses, particularly of waitresses—Creedmore at Totaljew's with her black-cherry hair she despised—but the sexual manifestations of jealousy masked other feelings. How odd, thought Eyestones, that its presence and its absence may denote abnormality *or* normality! Jealousy with Laura as with many women, he realized, often meant, not that she was passionately in love with her lover, but rather that she was infuriated with herself, often thinking that if he really knew her, he would never be satisfied with *her.* It was an emotion that only aped passion. Desire manqué. Farce. The mad Dionysian, he knew, was always projecting her own excessive and morbid sexual hysteria onto others, but now that jealousy, those erototropic drives, those deep, primal cravings, riddling morbid urgencies, involuntary lusts, he realized, represented a line of self-distrust, self-loathing, even if it did seem that she was in the hell of love. It had to do with belittling the object of her love, so that *she* could find height. My God, thought Eyestones, Ratnaster should interview her!

Ironically, Eyestones had inadvertently found several receipts on Laura's windowsill going back a year from the Velour Motel, a low box of broken shadows and unshapely brick, where in a spate of nightly chicane Laura of a night ended up with some local creep or cum-traveler trying to find love. It did not obtain anymore, as he thought lovingly of Rapunzel, but Laura had a great talent for taking the heart out of any situation that gave him joy even in the best of days, which was bad enough, until he realized that with her, no matter the man, she was only temporizing. There was no foundation to build on any level with her. Love was an orphan in their midst, he saw from the first, unavoidably finding in her lack of principles that this poor thing not only hadn't the slightest conception herself of what commitment meant, but what it was to be a woman. As was always the case with Eyestones, came a balancing truth, and with it, again, from Laura another idea for a column for *Bowls* by default. Had not Hosea the prophet still loved his adulteress wife, Gomer, in spite of her sins? Raised three children not his? It was the first time, he realized, we were given a conception of Yahweh as a god of love, not merely power and justice and lack of mercy. It immediately brought him back to an immediate concern.

"Laura, I didn't come over only to drop off the typewriter. There is something else I wanted to—well, mention. I'm worried about you," he said, wistfully regarding the room that looked like a geosynclinal trough, with its warped walls and sunken floors and poor light. An upended Elmo chair. Empty Big Gulp cups under the bed. Crumpled popcorn bags. Unreturned videocassettes. It was redolent with years of mustiness. Was it the closet that gave off the acrid odor of bad water, mushrooms, and bracket fungus or that pile of bent shoes or simply the drab, communicating foreignness of that whole listing wooden crate of a building on River St.? The way he got it, she was used to living in squats like this with various bumbandits, half-educated no-hopers, and dump-help to share paying the rent. He remembered that Laura was of Polish extraction, born like collapse in the Cayuga swamps near the slough of Syracuse. Sister of three "double-yokers." Unmarried name Shqumb, which sounded like an anagram. Awful parents who hated her. One niggardly, the other a nitwit. All monologues, no dialogue. All stuck in hopeless gridlock. "Did you hear me?"

Ignoring him, she asked, "Have you seen my banana clip?"

Stumbling over her LPs and fumbling through a grotty pile of unboxed cassettes, she picked one up and shoved it into her recorder. "Do you know 'Live at Budokan'? 'Surrender'? 'Need Your Love'? 'Clock Strikes Ten'? Oh, I'm sick of Cheap Trick. Wait." She quickly changed her mind, flashing through another pile and picked another one. "Boss Hog! I saw them at the Middle East. Boss Hog is Jon Spencer's other band. He's a slight, skinny, white-hipster kid from New York City. I saw the Jon Spencer Blues Explosion in San Francisco. I was like *whoa!* Listen closely! When he does that amped-up blues thing, audiences always go wild. It is *sooo* trippy! Live, local, and late-breaking! Listen to that idiosyncratic singing style full of growls, hiccups, shouts, and wailing." It was her new vocabulary. She was only reconfirming that she had met somebody new, some rocker or hair metal top or ephedrine cocinero from some concert or record shop or "scene" or other. She flipped her hair. "But it rocks out in a serious way, it's not jokey, it's what guys at the Middle East, the club over in Central Sq., call 'killer'—you know, as in 'killer riffs,' 'killer hooks,' a 'killer set!'? No holds barred blues-rock. Bang your head! Bang your head! Feed the noise! *Jesus, don't hit those pipes, will you?* Watch it! Sit over there. John Spencer also has a weird handmade antenna-like thing that produces a goofy outer-space sound and strange feedback effects—he'll fool around with that during a solo and sing through a little gizmo that distorts his voice, and he also plays harmonica well." She folded her arms. "Have you like even heard of the Jon Spencer Blues Explosion? Do you like hair metal? Are you into psychotropical funk?" Was her sex drive, he wondered, cyclical or periodic? She was thirty-six years old! Like Prufrock. Halfway through life! Sterility. No mermaids singing. It wasn't possible, but it was! When you can't live life, thought Eugene, unreality is less a great skill than a sanctuary.

"So," asked Laura, "have you ever heard of The Craven Slucks? This group in Cambridge? They're geniuses."

"Did you hear what I said?"

She snatched out the tape and stomped into the bathroom and came out after minutes.

"Yes, yes, yes," she said flatly. "I want to improve." She sighed, whuffing and walking around picking her teeth with her ATM card, as if she had chosen not to read his thoughts but come to her own conclusions. She had heard enough of his no-guts/no-glory speeches. She sat down, but said nothing more. Her generic defense came with a stock vocabulary.

Eyestones unhooked his thick eyeglasses and wiped his tired eyes.

"You don't even listen."

She shook her inner ear with a probing little finger, withdrew it to find a speck of wax, and rubbed it on her jeans. She sat back, folded her arms, exhaled, and stared at him—her pupils unequal—with a kind of stupid, open-eyed lack of cooperation.

Where *was* she?

Didn't she *care?*

The search is proof of what we *are!*

"You jilted Mutrux." He paused. "Didn't you?"

She shrugged. As soon as a person finds that she cannot go to Paris, she finds a reason she cannot go to Paris.

"Please," he said, holding up his hand. "He hates you. But it's worse." She folded her arms, a flaunting listener.

"I think Curbstepper is dangerous," said Eugene, regarding her air of nonchalance and tepid curiosity. How he had once pitied her! At one time he had wanted to take her dear sweet self and bundle her in the warmest blankets and hold her in his arms and kiss her face until she melted. No longer. There were even times when he told her that she was pretty, but she never developed enough confidence to accept a compliment and usually responded to praise with some goofy action, as though trying to divert one's gaze from her looks. Eugene had cared once, he did. Now when he regarded her he was only looking through red rain, painfully thinking of her and isolation and how her parents, hating each other, troubled by her chaotic life and irresponsibilities and already having had two children with Downs syndrome, had wanted desperately to be rid of her. We should always be careful what we get used to. Laura folded, then refolded, her arms, looking sexless as sans culottes. Eugene used a lot of his favorite words: *dialectic, try, solidarity, unique, conscience, begin, begin again, results, hope,* and avoided others, *bakery, bakery, bakery,* words which like a warm wind blew tropically into his sleepiness, and he leaned his head on the sofa, abstractedly watching the dark, dark, dark windows.

He slept an hour there, dreaming of Rapunzel, whose angelic face became part of the ceiling, appearing like a Fra Lippo Lippi angel, as if over the nave of his private church. He whispered a thought to God. The benefit of real prayer, he realized, is that, when aware you're pious, that's your comfort. You could read by the light of her smile, her blond porcelain beauty. O swirl of stars! Orion's nebula! With a buoyant white force Eyestones knew he was in love with her. He was suddenly restless and by eight-thirty decided to leave, said good-bye to Laura, tangled on her side of the bed, mutt-snoring away in a big dead blanket and a pile of gray sheets. "Keep your hands above the blanket," Eugene whispered, pronked upward with joy, and dressing in a matter of seconds, took the old wooden stairs three at a time and scooted back home.

Waking, Laura checked her watch, stood up, ran to the telephone, and quickly dialed a number at the music club in Central Square, called the Middle East.

"Jeff?"

El Hombre Pollack

Mayra Montero

HOY HE VISTO LA CASA de mi padre. La vi tal como era, con la terraza circular y la fachada en piedra. Fue en un libro sobre arquitectura, un regalo de cumpleaños que me trajo Sara, la mejor amiga de mi mujer. Me dijo: "Mira, Esteban, las casas de La Habana", y tuve una corazonada. No sé por qué me imaginé que iba a encontrarla allí. O sí, creo que lo sé: la casa fue bastante célebre en sus tiempos, tenía lo que la gente dio en llamar "baño romano", que no era más que una piscina íntima, y en ese irónico aposento, en ese espacio concebido quién sabe para qué locuras, yo me gané la indiferencia y el rencor. A los diez años, acabé con mi vida.

Puse la mano sobre una de las fotografías. Allí estaban la torre-mirador y la techumbre en tejas, y a su lado otra imagen: el patio central y el pórtico con sus columnas, cada columna de un mármol diferente, como quiso papá. Ocupando toda una página del libro estaba el "baño romano", los muebles y las buganvillas alrededor del estanque, y el hemiciclo con la estatua de Afrodita. Lo de la estatua no fue idea del arquitecto americano—Pollack no era un hombre de excesos—sino de su colaborador cubano, un muchacho graduado de la Universidad de Columbia; se llamaba Mendoza y mis padres le dieron mano libre.

He oído decir que mucha gente muere el día de su cumpleaños; hoy pensé que ése sería mi caso. Al ver las fotos, sentí que se me apretaba el pecho, me tembló una mano, sólo la mano izquierda, y estuve a punto de llamar a mi mujer, pero la escuché conversando con Sara y tuve ese gesto postrero de resignación: más valía que no me viera morir, que se enterara luego, cuando viniera a ofrecerme una copa, o cuando se acercara para ver ella también las casas de La Habana. En el primer momento creería que estaba dormido, pero enseguida notaría mi mano agarrotada; me tocaría la frente para sentir mi piel, la piel en solitario es la última certeza. Más tarde, al ver el libro abierto, al mirar la página que quedó marcada y leer el pie de foto: "Baño romano de la casa de los Vilardell", caería en la cuenta de los motivos de mi muerte súbita. Sólo a ella pude contarle parte

That Man, Pollack
Mayra Montero

—Translated from Spanish by Edith Grossman

TODAY I SAW MY FATHER'S HOUSE. I saw it just the way it used to be, with its circular terrace and stone facade. It was in a book on architecture, a birthday present given to me by Sara, my wife's best friend. She said to me: "Look, Esteban, the houses of Havana," and I had a premonition. I don't know why I imagined I would find it there. Or rather, I think I do know why: the house was fairly well known in its day; it had what people insisted on calling a "Roman bath," which was nothing more than an indoor pool, and in that ironic chamber, that space conceived for who knows what acts of madness, I attained indifference and rancor. At the age of ten, I put an end to my life.

I placed my hand on one of the photographs. There were the lookout tower and tiled roof, and next to them another image: the central courtyard and arcade, each column made of a different marble, just as Papá wanted. Occupying an entire page of the book was the "Roman bath," the furniture and bougainvillea around the pool, and the semicircle with the statue of Aphrodite. The statue wasn't the American architect's idea—Pollack was not a man given to excess—but his Cuban collaborator's, a boy with a degree from Columbia University; his name was Mendoza and my parents gave him a free hand.

I've heard that many people die on their birthdays; today I thought it would happen to me. When I saw the photographs, I felt a tightening in my chest; one of my hands, the left, began to tremble, and I was about to call my wife, but I heard her talking to Sara and I made a final gesture of resignation: it would be better if she didn't see me die, if she found out later when she came in to offer me a drink or to have a look at the houses of Havana. At first she would think I was asleep, but then she would notice my clenched hand and touch my forehead to feel my skin, just the skin is definitive proof. And when she saw the book and the page it was opened to, and read at the bottom of the photo, "Roman bath in the Vilardell house," she would understand the reasons for my sudden death. She was the only one to whom I could tell part of what had happened, a long time after we

de lo que había pasado, mucho después de que nos casáramos, cuando nuestro propio hijo era un niño de diez años. Ella lloró un poquito, me abrazó por la espalda y susurró: "Cuánto lo siento, Esteban".

Poco a poco me fui apaciguando, la mano me dejó de temblar y volví a mirar el libro. "Papá", me oí decir. ¿Cuántos años llevaba sin recordar la cara de mi padre? ¿Y la de mi madre? ¿Cuántos años estuve tratando de recuperar su voz, una voz que se cerró una noche, y que me fue negada desde ese instante y para siempre?

Volví a la foto del "baño romano". Miré las celosías que cerraban los intercolumnios, recordé el olor de la madera fina y volví a pensar en la luz, la que entraba desde el techo, como en un impluvium pompeyano, y la que se filtraba por las ventanitas, tan finamente rebanada, tan de color de mantequilla. Mamá pasaba parte de su vida allí, rodeada de belleza, cubierta por aquella luz. Sólo una vez la vi con aquel hombre, el arquitecto Pollack. Llegué temprano del colegio y, al pasar, oí algunos susurros, me detuve a mirar: mi madre, sentada junto a la piscina, hablaba con dulzura, y el hombre Pollack, parado en el extremo opuesto, sólo miraba al suelo. Desde ese día me grabé su rostro: los ojos pequeños, la nariz ganchuda, una boquita intensa de maledicencia y furia. O acaso no, acaso aquella boca era perfecta y complaciente, la furia y la maledicencia tenían que estar en mí. Recuerdo que esa tarde entré al "baño romano" y me interpuse: abracé a mi madre, que me preguntó si no iba a merendar. Yo la miré y sentí que había algo en ella que me traicionaba. No era la forma en que trataba a Pollack, sino todo lo contrario: en su manera de ignorarlo, en la distancia que ponía entre ambos, presentí una cercanía abominable, una complicidad con garras, como una fiera que aullaba de dolor.

Hay un escrito en este libro en que mencionan a los arquitectos y hablan del dueño de la casa, ponen el nombre de mi padre, que se dedicaba al tabaco, pero en el fondo era un artista: pintó los paneles del techo, pintó retratos de mamá y retratos míos. A mí dejó de retratarme a los 10 años, hay una ruptura en ese tiempo, una frontera que crucé a empujones. En el libro confirman lo que ya me habían dicho los amigos: la casa está deshabitada, en ruinas; el órgano que había en la sala desapareció hace años, y la estatua de Afrodita fue robada; el hemiciclo se cayó en pedazos. Me pregunto qué aguas podridas llenarán ahora el estanque de mi madre.

Pacífico se llamaba nuestro chófer. Murió una noche del mes de agosto. Había entrado a la casa en busca de mi padre y se desplomó en la galería que daba al patio. Era un hombre grueso y al caer su

married, when our own son was a boy of ten. She cried a little, put her arms around me, and whispered, "I'm so sorry, Esteban."

Gradually I began to calm down, my hand stopped trembling, and I looked at the book again. "Papá," I heard myself say. How many years was it since I had recalled my father's face? And my mother's? For how many years had I been trying to retrieve her voice, a voice that shut off one night and was denied to me from that moment on and forever after?

I returned to the photograph of the "Roman bath." I looked at the lattices that filled the spaces between the columns, remembered the scent of fine wood, and thought again about the light, the light that came in through the ceiling, as it did in a Pompeian impluvium, and the delicately patterned, buttery light filtering in through the windows. Mamá spent part of her life there, surrounded by beauty, bathed in that light. I saw her only once with that man, the architect Pollack. I came home early from school, and as I passed by I heard murmurs and stopped to look: my mother, sitting next to the pool, was speaking gently, and that man, Pollack, standing at the far end of the room, simply looked at the floor. Ever since that day his face has been etched in my mind: narrow eyes, hooked nose, mouth tight with filthy talk and rage. Or perhaps not, perhaps that mouth was perfect and amiable, and the rage and filthy talk had to be in me. I remember I went into the "Roman bath" that afternoon and positioned myself between them: I hugged my mother and she asked me if I wasn't going to have a snack. I looked at her and felt that something in her was betraying me. It was not her treatment of Pollack but just the opposite: in the way she ignored him, in the distance she placed between the two of them, I could sense an abhorrent closeness, a complicity with claws, like an animal howling in pain.

There's a text in the book that mentions the architects and discusses the owner of the house; my father's name is there; he worked in the tobacco business but basically he was an artist: he painted the ceiling panels, he painted portraits of Mamá and of me. He stopped painting me when I was ten, there was a break then, a frontier I was pushed across. The book confirms what friends already had told me: the house stands empty, in shambles; the organ in the living room disappeared years ago, and the statue of Aphrodite was stolen; the semicircle fell into ruins. I wonder what kind of stagnant water now fills my mother's pool.

Our chauffeur's name was Pacífico. He died one night in the month of August. He had come into the house looking for my father

cabeza se abrió como una fruta. Le sangraba casi todo: la nariz, la boca, las orejas. Mamá vino corriendo desde su habitación; papá, que estaba en el estudio, se acercó con un frasco de amoniaco, pero todo fue en balde. Las dos sirvientas se agacharon y le sostuvieron la cabeza, y papá puso dos dedos sobre el cuello de Pacifico. "Está muerto", dijo, y las sirvientas rompieron a llorar. Mi madre me hizo un gesto: "Ve a tu habitación, Esteban".

No tuvo que decirlo dos veces, a mí también me apetecía alejarme. Salí disparado, pero, en lugar de ir a mi habitación, me fui a la de ella. Abrí la puerta y me tiré en su cama, que era más blanda que la mía; pateé las sábanas con mis zapatos, me revolqué con furia, con un súbito dolor tan silencioso como la muerte que había dejado fuera. Luego me levanté y me acerqué al escritorio, que con la prisa había quedado abierto, tuve un ataque pasajero de locura, no puedo explicarlo de otro modo. Saqué papeles, cartas y tarjetas; tiré las fotos de sus amigas, y de los hijos de sus amigas. Lo estrujé casi todo en mis manos, y lo que no pude estrujar, lo pisoteé sobre la alfombra. Entonces me fijé en los papeles que estaban sobre el escritorio. Uno era un borrador, con algunas frases tachadas; el otro era la carta que mi madre estaba pasando a limpio cuando la llamaron por lo de Pacífico. La leí entera, pero con los años sólo se me quedó esta frase: "Es el aspecto íntimo de nuestra relación lo que me causa este gran sentimiento de culpa". El aspecto íntimo eran los pechos de mamá, su vientre que yo vi una vez, el espejismo brutal que eran sus nalgas, y ésas también las había visto. No lo pensé dos veces: mi corazón amargo y vengador se llenó de una desesperada euforia. Salí de la habitación con aquellos papeles en la mano, caminé lentamente por la galería, pasé junto al "baño romano" y vi que por la claraboya entraba una luz trémula, que es la luz del fondo de la noche. Al atravesar el patio escuché las hojas de los plátanos batiéndose y me paré aturdido porque el mármol de una de las columnas me recordó la sangre de Pacífico. Seguí adelante y me detuve al lado de mi padre. Ya nadie estaba inclinado sobre el chófer, lo habían cubierto con una sábana y una de las sirvientas limpiaba la sangre que había corrido por el suelo. Yo levanté la mano y le mostré los papeles a mi padre. Él me miró sin comprender, supongo que pensaría que eran dibujos. Pero entonces oyó el grito de mamá, ella los reconoció y me dijo: "¿Qué haces con eso?". Corrió hacia nosotros, intentó recuperar sus cartas, pero ya era tarde. Mi padre hizo un gesto para esquivarla y luego continuó leyendo. Cuando terminó, o cuando hubo leído suficiente, vino hacia mí, puso sus manos sobre mis hombros y me

and collapsed in the gallery that led to the courtyard. He was a heavy man, and when he fell his head split open like a fruit. Almost everything was bleeding: his nose, his mouth, his ears. Mamá came running from her room; Papá, who was in his studio, brought in a bottle of sal ammoniac, but there was nothing to be done. The two maids crouched down and held his head, and Papá placed two fingers on Pacífico's neck. "He's dead," he said, and the maids burst into tears. My mother signalled to me and said: "Go to your room, Esteban."

She didn't have to say it twice: I wanted to get away from there, too. I ran out, but instead of going to my room, I went to hers. I opened the door and threw myself on her bed, which was softer than mine; I kicked the sheets with my shoes, I tossed back and forth in a frenzy, feeling a sudden pain as silent as the death I had left outside. Then I got up and went to her desk; in her hurry she had left it open, and I suffered an attack of temporary insanity; I can't explain it any other way. I pulled out papers, letters, cards; I threw down the photographs of her friends and her friends' children. I crumpled almost everything in my hands, and what I couldn't crumple I ground into the rug with my feet. Then I looked at the papers on her desk. One was a rough draft, with some lines crossed out; the other was the clean copy of the letter my mother had been writing when they called her because of what had happened to Pacífico. I read all of it, but after so many years this is the only sentence I still remember: "It is the intimate aspect of our relationship that causes this immense feeling of guilt in me." The intimate aspect meant Mamá's breasts, her belly, I saw that once, the merciless illusion of her buttocks, I had seen them, too. I didn't need to think it over: my bitter, vengeful heart filled with a desperate euphoria. I left the room holding those papers in my hand, walked slowly through the gallery, passed the "Roman bath," and saw a faint glow coming in through the skylight, the light of deep night. When I crossed the courtyard I heard the leaves of the plantain trees brushing against one another, and I stopped in bewilderment because the marble of one of the columns reminded me of Pacífico's blood. I continued walking until I reached my father. Nobody was bending over the chauffeur now; he had been covered with a sheet, and one of the maids was washing away the blood that had run along the floor. I raised my hand and showed the papers to my father. He looked at me, uncomprehending; I suppose he thought they were drawings. But then he heard Mamá's cry, she recognized the papers and shouted at me: "What are you doing with them?" She ran toward us and tried to recover her letters, but it was

sacudió; luego me dio una bofetada que me lanzó sobre el cadáver de Pacífico. Me manché de sangre y empecé a gritar. Mi madre desapareció y una de las sirvientas me ayudó a ponerme de pie.

Al día siguiente toda la casa era un silencio. Sólo recuerdo eso: la quietud y la tristeza. El lugar donde cayó el chófer estaba limpio y mamá no se dejó ver en todo el día.. Mi padre sólo dijo "buen provecho" cuando nos sentamos a la mesa, mamá comió sola en su cuarto, debo decir que jamás volvió a comer conmigo. Ocho años después me fui a la Universidad de Columbia, me hice arquitecto como el hombre Pollack, y en muy contadas ocasiones regresé a la Habana.

La casa la cerró mi madre. Mi padre ya había muerto cuando ella decidió dejarlo todo. Se estableció en Bermudas, nunca supe por qué en ese lugar, ni tampoco con quién. Al morir ella, alguien me remitió una nota que me había dejado: "Si vuelves algún día a La Habana, hazme el favor de demoler la casa". Pensaba hacerlo, tuve esperanzas hasta que los amigos empezaron a contarme que todo estaba en ruinas. Hoy lo confirmo en este libro. Aquí está la casa de mi padre, el pórtico con sus columnas y el "baño romano" con su maldito signo: la estatua de Afrodita que nunca nos gustó, ni al hombre Pollack ni tampoco a mí.

too late. My father sidestepped her and went on reading. When he finished, or when he had read enough, he came over to me, put his hands on my shoulders, and shook me; then he slapped me so hard I fell across Pacífico's corpse. I was smeared with blood and began to scream. My mother disappeared and one of the maids helped me to my feet.

The next day the entire house was filled with silence. That's all I remember: the quiet and the sadness. The place where the chauffeur had fallen was clean, and Mamá did not show herself all day. The only thing my father said when we sat down at the table was "enjoy the meal"; Mamá ate alone in her room; I should add that she never ate with me again. Eight years later I enrolled at Columbia University; I became an architect like that man, Pollack, and rarely returned to Havana.

My mother closed the house. My father had already died when she decided to leave it all behind. She moved to Bermuda; I never knew why she went there, or with whom. When she died, someone forwarded a note she had left for me; "If you ever go back to Havana, please tear down the house." I planned to, I intended to, until my friends began to tell me it was all in ruins. I've confirmed it today in this book. Here is my father's house, the arcade with its columns and the "Roman bath" with its evil portent: the statue of Aphrodite that we never liked, not that man, Pollack, and not me.

Dies Irae

Edwidge Danticat

HE CAME TO KILL THE PREACHER. So he arrived early. Extra early. A whole two hours before the evening service would begin. The sun had not yet set when he plowed his red Beetle within a few inches of a row of market women who had lined themselves along where he had imagined the curb might be, to sell all kinds of things, from grilled peanuts to packs of cigarettes. He wanted a perfect view of the church entrance in case the opportunity came to do the job from inside the car without his having to get out and soil his shoes. He didn't care about witnesses; he could see the market women venturing a glimpse of his elephantine frame shifting now and again to better fit between the car seat and the steering wheel, his wide belly spilling over his belt to touch the lower end of the dashboard.

Later, one of the market women, who did not want her name used, would tell the Human Rights people, "He looked like a pig in a calabash sitting there. Yes, I watched him. For a long time. I was wishing to frighten him with my old eyes. I belong to that church; I didn't want to see my pastor die."

Rumors had been spreading for a while that the preacher had enemies in high places. His Baptist church was the largest in Bel-Air, one of the poorest, yet most politicized communities in Haiti's capital, a neighborhood which one American journalist described in an Associate Press article as "a hilly slum with an enviable view of the cobalt sea of Port-au-Prince harbor," before adding parenthetically, "Wasn't it Langston Hughes who said that misery is living in a place that everyone calls a slum but you call home?"

The church itself was called L'Eglise Baptiste des Anges, The Baptist Church of the Angels, which was printed on a wooden sign over the front doors. Above the sign was the first angel himself, Jesus, scrawny with a hollowed ivory face. The preacher had a radio show which aired at seven A.M. every Sunday morning on Radio Lumière so that those who could not visit his tabernacle could listen to his sermons before they went about their holy day. The rumors of the preacher's imminent encounter with the forces in power started as soon as he had begun broadcasting his sermons on the radio the year before. Those at the national palace who monitored such things were at first annoyed and then enraged that he wasn't sticking to "The more you suffer on earth, the more glorious your heavenly reward" script. In his radio sermons, later elaborated during midmorning services, the preacher called on the ghosts of brave men and women in the Bible who had fought tyrants and had nearly died, for their beliefs. (He began adding women since his wife had passed away six months before.) He exalted Queen Esther who had intervened to halt a planned massacre of her people, Daniel who had tamed lions intended to devour him, David who had pebbled Goliath's defeat, Jonah who had risen out of the belly of a beast.

"And what will we do with our beast?" The preacher encouraged his followers to chant from beside their radios at home, as well as from the long timber benches of his sanctuary. He liked to imagine the whole country screaming, "What will we do with our beast?" from the top of their voices until Heaven would be tormented by their cries and direct them to an answer.

The church members who were the most loyal of the radio listeners, when they were visited at home in the middle of the night and dragged away for questioning in the torture cells at Fort Dimanche, would all bravely answer the same way when asked what they thought the preacher meant when he demanded "What will we do with our beast?"

"We are Christians," they would say, "when we talk about the beast, we mean Satan, the devil."

The Human Rights people, when they gathered in hotel bars at the end of long days of secretly counting corpses and typing single-spaced reports, would speak of the flock's devotion to the preacher, adding, "These people didn't have far to go to find their devils. Their devils weren't imagined; they were real."

Not all the church members agreed with the preacher's political line. Some would even tell you "If the pastor continues like this, I leave the church. He should think about his life. He should think about his young daughter and granddaughter."

The preacher was thinking about his family. Or what was left of it.

So much so that soon after he had buried his fifty-two-year-old wife six months before, he had immediately made a request to the Canadian embassy for a visa for his daughter. The embassy, however, was not granting visas to poor pregnant women, so he had waited for his granddaughter to be born before making another request. Now they were hopeful for word from the embassy, so his daughter and granddaughter could leave for Montreal to which his sister and five cousins had fled.

All of this was in the preacher's file, on which Jacques Badagris had briefed himself before he came.

The light of day vanished as Badagris waited, the market women exchanging places around him, the day brokers going home to be replaced by night vendors who sold fried meats, plaintains, more peanuts, cigarettes and cigars, late into the night. Among the dusk travelers were the colleagues in uniform. He didn't know them intimately, but recognized a few. Those he did know loved to wear their uniforms, even though he didn't think they should on jobs like this. Not that there was anything low profile about this job. He was sure that even before the uniforms had arrived some of the neighborhood people, upon observing him, had already gone off to warn the preacher. He was equally certain that neither he nor his uniformed acquaintances would deter the preacher. The preacher would come and the evening service would go on. For if the preacher didn't come it would mean that the devil had won, the devil of his own fear.

The preacher did not live far away. There were men, agents, even now in front of his modest four-room concrete house waiting to get him in case he tried to run. Somehow Badagris found it hard to imagine the preacher even being afraid. Perhaps he too was falling for the religious propaganda. The preacher was not like the others, who in the last hours before their arrests would attempt to plot impossible escapes, running to relatives, to parcel out their goods and their children.

In his work, there were many approaches. Some of his colleagues tried to go as far from the neighborhoods where they grew up as possible when doing a job like this. Others relished going back to the people in their home areas, people who had refused cough syrup for a mother or sister as she sat up the whole night coughing up blood. Some would rather disappear the schoolteachers who told them they had heads like mules and were made of peasant stock so they'd never learn to read and write. Others wanted to take revenge on the girls who were too self-important, who never smiled when their names were called or when they were whistled at. Others still wanted to beat the girls' parents for asking their last names and judging their lineage not illustrious enough. But he himself liked to work on people he didn't know, people he could imagine and create all sort of evil tales around. For example, he could tell himself before killing the preacher that being Catholic, he wasn't supposed to like the Protestants, anyway. They didn't dance. They made their women dress in white and cover their heads. They were always talking or singing about the devil, using biblical symbolism that could easily be misinterpreted.

The preacher had had plenty of warning, he told himself: the night before the president had appeared on television and announced the execution of nineteen high-level officers who had betrayed him. Now every order coming from the national palace could be a test of an enlisted man's loyalty. They had already given the preacher a few direct warnings. The wife of a rival preacher had been convinced to poison the preacher's wife's coffee during a women's auxiliary meeting. Still the preacher had simply prayed over his wife's body and had taken her to her family village in the mountains to be buried in the grave behind the family's ancestral house.

Badagris tapped his index finger on the forty-five tucked away against his spine. It was a nervous habit, something he did whenever he was caught up in too much thinking. He was thinking of getting out for a while, moving to Florida, maybe New York, make himself part of the Haitian community there to keep an eye on the little movements that were fueling the expatriate invasions at the borders. He could infiltrate the art galleries where the exiled intellectuals met to drink coffee and talk revolutions. But none of this could happen until he killed the preacher.

Badagris peeked out of the window and asked one of the boys who were studying in a group under the streetlamp to get him a pack of cigarettes—Comme Il Faut, red. He was not even thirty years old, yet three different doctors had warned him about cancer. His voice was growing hoarse, his throat itching inside, from a place he couldn't scratch. But he couldn't do without the smoke, the tar and the temporary cloudiness the cigarettes allowed him, no more than he could do without his five-star Babancourt, a glass over a game of checkers with the smartest of the prisoners at the barracks. Sometimes he would convince them that if they won they could live, something which gave them a glint of hope unlike anything he's ever seen in human eyes, except maybe during a fight when someone whose throat you'd wrapped your hands around is suddenly on top of you squeezing tightly for his life. The night before, perhaps as his mind was preparing him for the preacher, he dreamed that he was leaving Haiti dressed as a nun after the government had fallen. Perhaps it was a sign from the gods he told himself, warning him to get out. He didn't want to wait until he was too old to get out. But when they had dropped the preacher on his lap, there was no way he could say no. That might hint that he was disloyal and he could not afford disloyal.

The boy came back with the cigarettes and a withered copy of a history book tucked under his arm. He let the boy have three gourdes of his change in honor of a past he could not deny. His parents were peasants with a ton of land that they lost when the regime came to power in 1957. Some big chef had decided he wanted to build a summer home on most of it. That's when he had joined the Miliciens, the Volunteers for National Security. It began when the Volunteers came to his town busing people to go to the capital to a presidential rally. They wanted bodies to listen to one of the president's Flag Day speeches. People had wanted to go home for their hats, but there was no time for that. Hats had been prepared for them with the president's name printed on them. There were many solemn faces on the camion that day but his was not one of them. He was going to the city where by craning his neck he could see the president of his country. On the bus that day he smoked his first pipe at twenty-two, drank his first cup of homemade moonshine. One of the silent objectors who had been trying to numb himself before the rally had passed the pipe and moonshine to him. With that first drink and smoke, he had finally become a man.

When he got to the city, he followed the throng of people through to the palace lawns. He was mesmerized by the procession of humanity, standing before the whitest and biggest building he had ever seen. Decorating the terraces were men with rifles dressed in uniforms with golden ropes like those he had studied in pictures of the fathers of the independence in his own boyhood history book. And finally the president slipping out onto the balcony dressed like the guardian of the cemetery in a black suit and black hat with the forty-five at his side. When he saw the president's face, he decided he would never go back, would never work the land like Azaka again, never carry a knapsack on his back and a machete in his hand. He listened for hours as the president read what seemed like a whole hundred-page book, in perfect nasal French. The tall *grimèl* woman in a teal dress at the president's side, fresh and buoyant as an azalea floating in a stream through the whole thing. He had wondered if she had a gun under her dress and would not have been surprised if she had. He didn't move his head the whole time the president was speaking. After the third, fourth and fifth hour of the speech, though, he found himself dreaming. He thought he saw a flock of thousands of winged women circling the palace from above, angry sibyls hissing proverbs through the speech.

Later he would tell his daughter, "I thought they were angels, marionettes, maybe a soul for each of us standing there in the sun."

And later still, the daughter would tell the truth commission, "I didn't realize he was a spiritual man."

Still this had to happen before, before . . . He couldn't kill the preacher and let it fade into silence the way the preacher's wife's demise had. He also could not make a martyr out of the preacher man, fuel his followers' boldness and rage. The preacher's death had to make noise but only so it could frighten the flock; it had to be used as a warning. The trouble was that the preacher himself was also learned at the game. The preacher too wanted whatever happened to him to be used in his favor.

The young boy was standing there not moving, even after he had given him the money. Badagris pulled an additional five gourdes bill from his pocket and handed it to the boy. He suddenly wanted to have some company, so he decided to engage the boy in conversation. There was a part of him that wished he could buy that child a future, buy all children like that boy a future. Perhaps not the future he's had himself, not the path his life had taken, but another kind of life.

"What do you study?" he asked the boy.

The boy replied, "History."

And he asked the boy to recite him the lesson of the day. The boy stammered and was nervous as if recalling school punishments, rulers on the knuckles, harsh words from the teachers for not getting his lesson right. He asked to see the boy's palms, for you could always tell how bright a student was, or how good he was at memorizing the lessons of the day, by examining his palms and knuckles for ruler calluses and splinter marks. He saw that the boy's hands were callused indeed, but maybe it wasn't because he was dumb, but because he didn't have the proper light in his house, or because he had a book with missing pages, or because he didn't get a chance to eat a hearty breakfast of herrings and eggs, cornmeal or spaghetti every morning. He gave the boy yet another five gourdes and shushed him away. Too much was gathering in his head now around the boy's fate. He watched as the boy bought himself some gum and a cigarette, inhaling deeply, trying to form a film of tar in the air. The boy bought a handful of goat meat and fried plantains, too, and shared them with his friends.

The boy, Lutin, would later tell a Reuters journalist, "We saw him sit there all afternoon. I bought him cigarettes. With the money he gave me extra, I bought supper and gum and shared with my friends." But the boy would not mention the cigarettes he had gotten for himself.

With the smoke clouding his lungs, Badagris suddenly longed for some rum. He yearned for dominoes, sweet words, a bare thigh to run his hand up and down on, some close dancing, a girl to shine his expensive belt buckle with the tip of her belly button. But all this would have to wait until the preacher was dead. And so he watched the boys suck the marrow out of the fried goat bones until the bones squeaked like flutes and he thought of how hungry he had been after the president's speech when the crowd was left to find its own way home and when one of the men in denim had approached him and asked him whether he wanted to join the Volunteers. He got fifty gourdes, an identification card, a bright more-indigo-than-blue denim uniform, a forty-five and the privilege of marching in all the national holiday parades. He was king. Okay maybe not king, but a highly valued court jester, since he didn't like the uniform. He thought it made him look like a dancer in a folklore show waiting for the drums to begin. And so he asked to wear regular clothes, eagerly provided for him when he appeared at the rich merchants' shops, and showed his volunteers membership card. His favorite line for them was, "I volunteered to protect national security. Unfortunately, or fortunately as you like, this includes your own."

The merchants usually fell for that line and with these words restaurants fed him, a landlord in a middle class neighborhood housed him, married women slept with him, virgins gave in to him, and the people who had looked down on him and his family in the past, well now they came all the way from Léogane to ask him for favors. Dressed in their best outfits, they came to the little office he closed off for himself in one of the back cells at Fort Dimanche and called him "Sergeant." Some even blasphemously ennobled him "Little President."

"It's been ten days," they would say, "since my son was taken." "My daughter is gone," they would cry, "and I know it was not of her will."

Whenever he wanted to, he could solve the problem simply by writing a note to the Léogane chefs who, because he was in the capital, deemed his position above their own. The only time he had made a trip back to Léogane was when both his mother and father had died of what was reported to him as sudden illnesses within days of one another. After burying his parents, he went and talked to the chef who had taken over their land. He told him, "We're all the same now, but I will never forget what you did to my parents. Now I am the one whom everyone comes to in the capital when you do something bad to them. A closed mouth doesn't catch flies, so I won't say anymore, but watch yourself now." It was a simple monologue that, even though it didn't get him back his father's land, stopped the requests for favors from the hometown for a while.

The way he acted at the inquisitions in his private cell in Fort Dimanche earned him a reputation. He was the one who came up with the most memorable psychical and psychological tortures. He was suffering, he knew it now, from what one of his father's contemporaries, the novelist Jacques Stephen Alexis, had called the hazards of the job. (*Tu deviens un véritable gendarme, un bourreau.*) It was becoming like any other job. He liked questioning the prisoners, teaching them to play bezik, have them staple clothespins to their ears as if it would help to save their lives. He liked to paddle them with braided cowhide. Sometimes he would stand on their backs and jump up and down like a drunk on a tripoline.

When one of the women who had been his prisoner in Ford Dimanche was interviewed for an uncompleted documentary in her tiny Haitian restaurant in New Rochelle, New York, the gaunt, stoop-shouldered octogenarian would say, "He told me he loved women and said, 'I truly hate to unwoman you.' "

On the videotape, the woman, who did not want her name used, was nervously biting the inside of her lower lip when she recalled his words. By the time she was finished talking about him, her mouth was filled with blood.

"He would wound you and then try to soothe you with words," she said. "He was God."

The Battlefields of Shiraz
Rikki Ducornet

IT WAS MY TWELFTH SUMMER. Father and I entered into a symbolic relationship with Mother of such intensity that even now I find it almost impossible to undo the mental knots we tied in our attempt to restrain her. That summer the city of Cairo took on the mystical and metaphysical features of one of those cryptic Roman paintings so prized by scholars in which each element has an allegorical significance: we saw signs of her everywhere. And I who had never much thought about her, I thought about her all the time. Her naked body rocking with laughter was the glyph beneath which the city pulsed; it haunted our nights—Father's and mine. When I visited the museum with Father—and, like the war games he played with Ramses Ragab, these visits took place in the early morning—I expected to see her materialize in every room. This was foolish; as much as she loved the Sporting Club, Mother hated museums. But I wanted to see her; I wanted her to return. I chose to petition an admirable lion's head in Room 46. I wanted Mother back not because I loved her (I think, in fact, that I had come to violently dislike her), but because it was unbearable to know she was *out there,* invisible and unfathomable, like a force of nature.

I wanted to keep my eye on her, to watch her eat in that absent way she had, to hear her voice rising and falling in the night, to stumble upon her barefoot, her mind elsewhere, pacing the hallway before dawn. I also left instructions with a lion-headed waterspout. Understand that I had chosen lions only because of a fabulous head in Room 46—its beauty and size. Once that decision had been made, I found myself appealing to lions whenever I saw one. (Like Venice, Cairo was riddled with lions.)

After our visit to the museum, Father and I would find a garden and a quiet place to sit. We sat, often in silence, and sometimes for hours. Or we would take a long walk, to the Suq el-Nahassin, perhaps, to wander in the stunning cacophony, the sound of hammers making it impossible to think, the brass and copper trays and barber's basins, dazzling in the light of late morning, making it impossible to see.

"Egyptians," Ramses Ragab once said to me over breakfast (it was a habit of ours to share a late breakfast when he and Father had finished their game of war), "have always believed in magic." This all-pervasive way of seeing and being in the world had taken hold of Father and me. "When I was a boy," Ramses Ragab said also, "my grandfather once sent me to Khedr el-Attar to buy a powder made of salamanders—a cure, or so he thought, for impotency."

Father and I would explore Khedr el-Attar, too, reeling under the influence of things we could not name but which filled the air with the scent of vanished times. Further the streets smelled of new soap and then, suddenly, of lamb kidney toasting over open fires, reminding us that we had been wandering all day. Stumbling out of the maze of streets, Father would hail a cab and off we'd go to the Komais Restaurant, or the Paris Café. There, while waiting for dinner, we would gorge on pickles, Father mopping his face with his handkerchief and more than once muttering: "She's been here." Then, I too could smell Mother's perfume. When, after dinner, he overturned his empty cup and asked our waiter to read his fortune, the waiter said: "Your heart is empty," proving himself a worthy reader, "and it won't be filled for a long time."

I do not think Father was himself aware of how irrational he had become. He would look to the street and the sky for signs, signs which were the indication of Mother's movements, revelations as to the tenor of her moods and the nature of her thoughts. For the most part, Father, if clearly eccentric, appeared to be as rational as ever, but then something would occur, evidence of the—I can only find one word—the *superstitious* nature of his thinking. For example, one morning as we loitered in a park, we saw a battle between two turtledoves. The female, coy as a cat, stood by. Father said: "Your mother is like her. She will not wander far." And it is true, she was in the vicinity. She had taken rooms in a somewhat worn but elegant building on Kasr el-Nil above the shop of a wealthy rug dealer, not far from the costly Hôtel Métropolitain, and therefore, not far from the museum.

I did not see it then as clearly as I do now; after all, I too was infected. But the empirical capacity of Father's mind—which had so often in the past impressed the world—had been violently disrupted. This new version of Father was more and more often incompatible with the old. But it was summer and he was able to blame his odd behavior on the heat. Because, to a certain extent, he was aware of it. Just after the incident with the doves—we were crossing Soliman

Pacha Place—he clicked his tongue as if to scold himself and said: "What nonsense I am speaking!" Caressing my cheek and grinning in that winning way he had he added: "How exhausting summer is!" Yet, despite such moments of lucidity, Father persisted in what I can only call this new peculiarity of thought—peculiarity that at the time was part and parcel of the mysterious world around us: Cairo, its fabulous museums, the fantastical sprawl of Egypt, the desert so near at hand, Mother's maddening absence and soon: Ramses Ragab's *Kosmètèrion!* That summer there was no such thing as *ordinary thinking.* The universe had gone topsy-turvy, and the profusion of games—for they took place several times a week—was just a small part of it. We did not know it yet, but Mother was taking on the attributes of myth. It should come as no surprise that I once awakened from shattering dreams, my heart pounding, to find Father in the kitchen nibbling toast. We had both dreamed the same dream: that we had been bandaged up like corpses! (And surely this explains—why has it not occurred to me before?—my life's delight in liberating mummies from their gum-infested cloth to see the caramelized flesh clinging to the redundant, yet invariably startling, bone!)

Father, in his fez and holding a diminutive aerostatic globe, was stretched out on the Shiraz. As I entered the room, Ramses Ragab, dressed in a dazzling white linen suit and smelling of labdanum, stood up and held out his hand. An astonishing hand: the nails were polished and shone like mirrors, and he was missing a thumb.

"We are," he explained with a self-mocking smile, "about to begin the battle of Fleuris."

They played at dawn because of the heat of summer. Father said he could think at dawn and at dusk only; the rest of the day he was "stunned." But I knew he played at war at dawn because his nights were cruel and long. The games gave him a reason to face the day; thanks to Ramses Ragab and the battle of Fleuris, he could look forward to the early hours rather than lie awake dreading another day without Mother.

As Father was engaged in the deployment of his troops, I asked Ramses Ragab—always a more precipitous player—what the aerostatic globe, now hanging from the ceiling by a hook, was for.

"It is for Captain Coutelle," he explained, nervously smoothing his hair with those marvelous fingers; "armed with a telescope and suspended far above the capacity of the Austrian musketry, he shall watch the battle unscathed." Peering into the montgolfier's basket, I saw a little lead soldier. "Captain Coutelle is furnished with a large ball of twine," Ramses Ragab continued. "This he will use to send messages—wrapped around rocks—to the French army."

"If he sends too many messages," Father mumbled from the floor with apparent seriousness, "he'll lose his ballast and sail into the sun."

I learned that Captain Coutelle could not maneuver his balloon himself, but was pulled about by means of a heavy cord. This operation was manned by no less than one-hundred and fifty foot soldiers. Rising to his knees, Father said wistfully: "This is how it all looked to Coutelle," and he pointed out the one-hundred and fifty foot soldiers. Ruled by a set of handsome bakelite dice, there was a chance they would all be wiped out by cannon fire and Coutelle lost to the wind. "He may land up in Iceland," Father laughed, bitterly, I thought.

You have understood that in Father's house, chess was just the tip of the iceberg. The games he played with Ramses Ragab (and on occasion with Boris Popov, a Russian colleague at the University) were a direct expression of the profound shift that had taken place in his mind. "The player," Father liked to say, "as does any man, struggles against the imposition of rules. The rules are essential, but it is equally important to know how best to bend them."

The playing field—in this case the sumptuous Shiraz, a carpet that looked like it had been woven of butterflies, and the very same Shiraz upon which Mother had entertained strangers, afforded a place where old patterns could be disrupted, new patterns found. For example, when Father and his new friend played at Waterloo, Napoleon always had a chance, as did the dervishes at Dongola. (Later that summer Kitchener's head would be set out on a toothpick pike.) Ruled by what he himself called *gamblesomeness,* Father, when he was not playing chess, played at war—and he played (the words belong to Ramses Ragab) *a deep game.* He never played poker—"a low game and a game of cheats"—nor Go (because he invariably lost). I should add that Father sometimes used the word 'game' in a novel way. He had a 'game' of Austrians, a 'game' of Abysinnians, and even a 'game' of camels. If Father was ruled by gamblesomeness, I think of this now, Mother *was* game. Her playing field was love, if not the love of Father. Nor, it is clear now, did she love me.

To continue: as beautiful as these games were, as beautiful as

Father's lead soldiers looked that morning set out on the blazing hearth of the Shiraz, their beauty was not the point. Father was not after an aesthetic charge so much as fulfilling a magical aim. Time and time again, all summer long, Father and Ramses Ragab would alter the course of History. This is not to say that aesthetics were absent. My father painted his armies with the delight of a pastry cook icing cakes. He relished sticking feathers to helmets with a spot of glue, and he had set out a naked brunette—to scale—standing up to her knees in a little painted pool; "The victor," he grinned, "may claim her."

"Beauty is double sixes," Ramses Ragab had laughed. "She is ascendant."

"I do not blame her," Father said then, and it was—I am certain—the first time he had referred in public to what had transpired. He said nothing else. Ramses Ragab dropped to his knees and looked on—we both did—as Father continued to set out his men, row after row of them.

Beauty is ascendant. I thought the remark obscure, but then I found it compelling. I had, just the week before, spent another dimly mysterious and tender morning along with Father at the Cairo museum, looking at the figures and forms of the dead. The alabaster face of Queen Ahmòse-nefertiri and Princess Sit-hathor-iunet, and even General Sepi—although his coffin is the oldest in the museum—were so beautiful they took the breath away. (General Sepi's corneas were carved of rock crystal!)

"Let the battle begin!" Father then exclaimed, easing himself back on the heels of his fancy leather pumps. The room took on the scent of mastic; in the kitchen our servant Beybars was busy fumigating the coffee cups. In a moment he would bring the coffee to the two men on a tiny tinned copper tray—a charming ritual that was taking place all over the city.

"On commence!" Ramses Ragab agreed as with a certain violence he rattled the dice in his fist. The men tossed to see who would go first. *"En avant!"* cried Father.

I left then, and wandered into Mother's abandoned room. Her dressing table, now distressingly free of clutter, had been a place of passion. At that table, before her mirror—a thing of such splendor and so heavy it would take two strong men to carry it off when, a week or so later, she sent for it—she had made her mortal face into something (Ramses Ragab's word comes to me) *ascendant.*

His word was also hers. Mother owned a book—one of the few

books I had ever seen her read—which offered a studio photograph of Irene Dunne wearing pearls and standing beside a horrible *faux* Chinese lamp, in what Mother called an *ascendant* pose. But if you could tear your eyes from her ideal qualities, you would see that the carpet above which Ms. Dunne, in very high heels, appeared to levitate—was both threadbare and missing an entire corner. Clearly the photo was meant to be cropped. *Odd* (Mother's word for me even then), it was the missing corner that captured my attention. It was a reminder of mortality, like a fly poised on the hand of a queen.

"She's just like one of those twenty-first dynasty corpses!" I exclaimed when, in an attempt to educate me, Mother released the precious volume from her vanity drawer.

"What the *fuck*," growled Mother.

"Like Ramses II's *corpse*," I insisted. "With pepper up the nose. I mean . . ." I blurted, stubborn despite the withering influence of my mother's outrage, "she only, uh . . . *looks* ascendant." And I began to tell her the extraordinary things I had learned during those precious moments when Ramses Ragab and Father would leave the battleground for breakfast and, while Mother was at the hairdresser or who knows where, discuss what Father called "Ragab's Mysteries." I told Mother that the Pharaoh's brain had been pulled from the skull through the nostrils with an iron hook, and the anus plugged with an onion.

"Not an *ordinary* onion—"

"You're a jerk." Mother inhaled on her cigarette deeply.

"Tut's nails were tied on with strings," I continued, somewhat pompously (a trait inherited from Father), "so that they wouldn't fall out." I felt like sobbing.

"*Christ.*" said Mother.

Ramses Ragab had been a student of archeology, but the study of mummies revealed a greater interest—he called it *an infatuation* with plants: their "First Qualities."

"Cassia, myrrh, lavender, oris, santal, rose, bergamot, anise, almond . . . I loved these things" he told me, "for their fragrances which caused me no end of delight, and for the mysteries of their medicinal properties which evoked the deepest reveries I had ever known and the greatest bliss. And I wondered: if a corpse could be secured from the immodest ravages of time by the precious oils of plants, then a savant use of them must protect the beauty of the living—not an original thought, but compelling to me. I decided to devote myself to chemistry—analytical, biological and pathological, and pharmacology—chemical and galenical; I studied toxicology and crystallography; I even studied alchemy! Then one marvelous afternoon I came upon Publius Ovidus Naso's *Cosmetica . . .*"

And so we came to that extraordinary place of his invention, Ramses Ragab's marvelous *Maison des Parures,* his *Kosmètèrion.* (Yet, lest you think that I was a lugubrious child, before moving on I think it best to add that if I was smitten by corpses, corpses—it must be said—which had been washed thoroughly inside and out with spiced wine, and whose body cavities were packed with cassia and myrrh—I also looked with profound interest at the erections of Pharaohs—always so unabashedly ubiquitous on the painted walls of tombs, and the vases and chests and scrolls which were stacked throughout the museum in an irresistible state of disarray. I suppose all this means that my adolescence was passed under the sign of *strangeness*—although this occurs to me only now.)

Fever Dreams: A Geography of Mind

Dale Peck

"JESUS CHRIST, JAMIE, calm down. Calm down! Jamie, what the—*okay.* I'll rent another car. Good God, do you have any idea where this—Jamie, calm the fuck down! I'm calling now. Look, I'm *dialing.*"

I lay in the back seat. On the glass above me Dutch Street, a transparent reflection thin as skim milk or watered-down memory. The embedded lines of the antenna broke up the buildings as neatly as a draftsman's rendering.

Doors opened; doors slammed.

The reflection of the dying city scrolled down the windshield like an afterimage, an afterthought. After Effects was the name of the company that made the screen saver in which lights illuminate a cityscape one by one, but my city was fading—first in the glass and then literally. The buildings fell away like daisy petals, he loves me, he loves me not, but what I heard was he is, he is not, and then the buildings were gone and we were on a naked bud of land. The glass above me reflected the ground below me, a veil of gray and green so thin you could poke a finger through it.

I poked.

Is. *Is not.*

"What is he—Jamie! Stop banging on that glass, it's driving me—God damn it, Reggie! Do *not* light that—ugh. The two of you! At least roll down the fucking window."

Rental cars like Buddhists are constantly reborn but bits of former lives linger. Checker in the ashtray, seven of hearts beneath the driver's seat. Activities to head off the bored child's "Are we there yet?" In this case Scrabble's Y. Ideogram: fork in the road, jet veeing off runway, hero with upraised arms. Adjective-maker. Word-wordy, sex-sexy, mess-messy. Value: 4.

"I'm taking the thruway because the one thing we know is that it's *west* of the river. No, it's not in *Jersey.*"

Was I dreaming? No, I wasn't dreaming. I was feverish but the fever dreams were in the past. I was looking for someone but the fever dreams tagged along for the ride. What I mean is, I've never had dreams more vivid than the fever dreams but even more vivid are my memories of them. If a dream is a cinematic projection of hopes and fears, then a memory of a dream is twice removed from reality. It's a counterfeit forgery, colored in, edges softened, the offensive parts painted over with self-censoring fig leaves.

Dream: dreamy.

"How many times—"

"This is the *fourth* trip. He won't even tell me what he's looking *for.*"

"What's up with little brother anyway?"

"How the hell should I know. He's been acting crazy since . . ."

"Since what?"

"He had a date with some guy. God, a month ago? Two?"

"*Shit.* I don't wanna know nothing bout that."

"Jesus Christ, Reggie, grow up."

"I'm all grown up, and I don't *even* want to think about—"

"Bout what? Butt-fucking? Tell me something, Reggie. Why is it a dick's the center of every man's world but an asshole's the center of his imagination?"

"Not *this* man."

"Nigger, move your mother-fucking hand before I cut it *off.*"

Still, I always knew what was happening. Almost always. In the beginning the fever dreams were as strange as soft stones and in the end as familiar as the many colors of my own skin, but I always knew where I was and I always knew what was happening. I always knew I was dreaming.

Almost always.

Six days I lay in bed. After the third the fridge was empty. After the fourth I couldn't use the bathroom. What was in me poured out through my skin as through a faucet. But all that was preamble. When everything else was gone the dreams began to flee too. That's what it felt like: my thoughts took material form—balloon, frog, bank loan—and floated and floated and floated away. Maybe that's why I clung so hard. Maybe that's why I cling still. When even the memory of them is gone I know I'll be truly empty.

"'Greene County.' Ain't that clever?"

"Damn it, Reggie. I *will* turn this car around and return your black ass to the ghetto."

Then: music. I thought it came from the radio but it was coming from Reggie. He was singing under his breath, the words, if they were words, not quite audible but crawling under my skin nonetheless. Calming me, quieting me. I relaxed into them, let me sink into the memory of the dreams.

"God*damn* that's beautiful," Claudia said, and I didn't know if she meant the music or the scenery.

Greene Country.

Count-county.

Population: 3.

First was the animals. One by one they came up and licked my upturned hand. *Don't be afraid* is what I thought my palm was saying, *I'm not afraid* were the tongues' answers. A cat's rasp, a dog's sloppy lap, the long curling swipe of a cow. But soon I realized it was the tongues that soothed me. *Don't be afraid,* they said, a horse's velvet muzzle, a deer's tiny pricks. *I'm not afraid,* my head said. A lion's tongue pillared by curved yellow incisors, the soft mossy bloat of a hippopotamus. *Don't be afraid. I'm not afraid.* At the last, a mouth opened before me like the entrance to a gaping cave, a tongue scrolled out like a carpet and licked up not my hand but my entire body and took me inside, where the darkness was pink and the tongue pulsed to the beat of a heart as big as my body.

Don't be afraid, the tongue pulsed.

I rubbed the tongue with my fingers. *I'm not afraid.*

Come with me.

Then the whale was gone and I floated. On a green raft, a leaf, an iceberg, a pinprick of land that poked through the water's surface from a floor too distant to be seen; on my own buoyancy. It didn't matter: a dream needs no transition. Or, rather, a dream is nothing but transition. The water was cold but the fever warmed it. Where waves rolled into me they sizzled and sighed into the sky. Once I tried diving down but roiling water shot me out like a ball from a vapor-charged cannon. Eventually I turned on my back and let the water hold me. Clouds of steam enveloped me: it was the fever itself, pushing out of me and making shapes in the water. The shapes were the ghosts of all the lives I would never lead now, now that I had chosen the one life I would have. One by one they shimmied out of me and shimmered away, a great rushing horde that slowed to a hissing trickle. The last ghosts were tiny, almost embarrassed. They lingered near me as if afraid of the long search for another body to inhabit. The final one was just a thin limbless snake rising from my navel, and when it had curled all the way up and out of me the first fever broke and I awoke and knew that whatever I had been before and whatever I was now I was *myself,* and nothing more.

"He quiet now."

"Sshh. I think he's sleeping."

"Baby—"

"Don't start, Reggie."

"What's going on, baby?"

"I *said* don't start. I don't want to wake up Jamie."

"I ain't talking bout Jamie."

"What did I say, Reggie? I said *don't start.*"

"What you doing now?"

"Pulling over. I've got to pee again."

Darkness. But pink darkness, and I wasn't alone. It was there too, floating blindly, unconscious of everything from me to the innumerable horde surrounding it. Only I saw it. At first I thought it was me and then I thought it was my traveling companion—I thought it was beside me but in fact it was inside me, carried along in the other's wake, a bit of undead flotsam waiting for the kiss of contact to come to life. I saw the other, too, saw that chance rules infection just as it does pregnancy (allow me this: it's not the metaphor that's mixed, just my synapses). Conception believes in the chaos of activity whereas sickness puts its faith in sloth. Both sperm and virus desire a berth, but the former is the shark and the latter the remora of the microscopic world. The one seeks while the other waits. But this wasn't even waiting. It wasn't . . . even. It wasn't me but it soon would be. The most that can be said is that it was possibility manifested in its smallest corporeal unit.

It wasn't hungry. It was hunger.

"Oh, look!"

I sat up in time to see a thousand stalks of goldenrod riotously advancing on an equally vast army of loosestrife, while here and there a stand of Queen Anne's lace waved its delicate pennant in surrender. Then the colors were gone, the yellow and purple and occasional sprig of white, and it was just grass again, and trees. But goldenrod salutes the end of summer, doesn't it, loosestrife the beginning of fall, and—

"What's today's date?"

"It's the eleventh, honey. Now go on back to sleep."

"The eleventh of?"

"What the—"

"Shut it, Reg. It's September, Jamie. Now sit back. We're nowhere near yet."

Now a swamp. Flatter than mere water, a level expanse of fragmite and sawgrass and cattails, a white tree trunk poking from its midst like a spoon in the earth's stewpot. Time was passing, not just miles. I turned back toward the tree. How many seasons had it taken, how many rainstorms to wash off leaf, limbs, bark like a patient housewife scouring a burned pan, how many sunrise-to-sunset sunbursts to bleach it the color of an old man's hair.

"Jamie! Do not be banging on that glass!"

Then I saw them: in the distance, the mountains. Purple as deoxygenated blood, thick as clots bled by the land. *That's* where we had to go.

Two journeys: one inner, one outer: the fever dreams. The virus lavished a single drop of itself on each of my cells but *she* remained indivisible. She pointed at me from the prow of her ship, her finger pulled me from the fishless sea. Red velvet, white lace, purple suede. Breast a double row of brass buttons running from an endless artificial mane of golden curls all the way to her ankles. A silver buckle clasped one black boot but in place of the other a single column of teak. She thumped along in front of me on the hollow wooden deck, offered only glimpses of her face. My Virgil: Virago. She pointed at something and it came into being.

She extended her arm. Pale blue sapphire crowning rigid finger, nail translucent as mother-of-pearl.

Oh look, she said.

A hundred acres garlanded by a lazy loop of water, a long narrow spit on which grazed horses and dairy cows; the mountains in the background and the sky above it all; blue and gray and brown. There was the peak-roofed house with its eyebrows and eaves, the gambrel-roofed barn, red of course, or once red and now the color of bisque or blush. The farm was an accumulation of walls: board-and-batten on the barn, clapboard on the main house, paint-flecked drop-siding feathering the side of the ancient kitchen wing. And there if you needed it was the sign: *Rt. 27C (Old Snake).* K.'d only left out one detail. Spanning the two hills which girded his little white house was the New York State Thruway, stilted above the land on pillars thin as a daddy long legs' limbs. The traditional equation reversed: here was the pastoral in urban shadow. Still, just as skinny boys dream of becoming Charles Atlas, the farm was The Garden's dream of itself. What I mean is, *this had to be the place.*

I hadn't thought it would be like this: so gentle. They teach you to think of it as an attack but actually you're the one making all the ruckus. It just wants a home. I saw it this way. It knocks at the door of a cell. No answer. It rattles the handle—locked. Damn. But maybe if it—ah, there we go. Inside, all is Baby Bear readiness, a warm nucleic meal followed by the comfy cytoplasmic pillow. Everything's just fine—until you get home to find someone sleeping in your own bed and all hell breaks loose. But unlike Goldilocks the virus doesn't wake up, doesn't run away. It sleeps through the commotion, secure in its dreams. Like me, the virus dreams only of itself, but unlike me itself is always its *self,* so fully imagined it becomes as real as the one imagining it.

And then there were two.

"Thank God. I gotta piss like a motherfucker."

"Reggie."

"Ease up, girl. I didn't say shit when you had to stop six times every hour. What's up with *that?*"

"I had to pee, okay."

"Don't feed me that bullshit. I can smell the throw-up on your breath. You jonesing on me or what?"

"Have you ever seen a more beautiful house?"

"That what it's gonna be like? *Fine.* But it seem like something missing for it to be beautiful to me."

"Missing?"

"Yeah. *Negroes.* We in the land of the white man now."

"Well then get out of the car, *Negro,* and let's black the place up."

Oh look, she said, and I saw: a gull. Oh look, she said, and I saw: an eel writhing in its beak. Look, and look, and look, she said, and I saw: that the eel was a rope: that a tiny arm was descending the rope: that their own ship waited to receive them. At some point I began to wonder if she willed these apparitions or if I did, but then I wondered when they would stop. By the time they reached the ship the soldiers were fully grown and by the time the gull had wheeled away they were firing at us. Oh look, she said: cannonballs plop-plopping into the sea like big marbles dropped in a big puddle. Listen, she said: explosions ricocheted across the water.

She pointed: To the battle stations!

And boulders poking from earth, too massive to be moved, and split rail fences saying, Here were forests once, and stone walls testifying to the rock-by-rock clearing of the land. The hooped wooden silo curled and sagged in on itself like a giant cruller, the house's fieldstone foundation was so old the mortar had withered away until stone sat on naked stone and a light in the basement escaped through a dozen gaps. Such a sober facade: the 12-over-12 windows on the first floor were all sealed by white curtains blurred behind warped panes, the eyebrows above were as hooded as the eyes of a Cossack. Age had shrunk the recessed Palladian door. It edged away from its glass frame, and a single knock resounded thinly from within, like the tapped skin of a tambourine.

Johanus Peeke had the beard Zenobia needed to complete her transition to magician. That was all the hair he had.

"Well my goodness. What have we here?"

Think of it like a stray: hungry, lost and alone. A pregnant stray, past and future implied in swollen belly. A self-impregnating stray, as fatherless as me, mother of its own children, author of its own destiny. But right now all it wants is a meal and a place to sleep. And we all know the implications of a meal. *One month for every seed, go to sleep as a man and wake as a swine.* Would that I had Hansel's chicken bone to offer the blind witch's pinching finger. But I was the feeder, I was the food. Does that mean I cast the spell on myself? Does that mean I can break it?

"Ain't here. See for yourself."

The planks in the central hall were two feet wide, rusty domed nailheads poking up a quarter inch. The ceiling was so low you could trail your fingers along it, and a dusting of paint—no, of plaster, the paint was long gone—fell down like a tree shaken after a snow.

"Here now, here now, watch what you're—"

Every creaking step had its own note, do-ti-la, do-mi-so, fa-so-do, and the banister was so loose on its turned spindles it wavered like a rope bridge. You had to duck at the top of the stairs or you'd hit your head and knock down more plaster.

"Here now, here now!"

It seemed too beautiful to be a weapon, so sleek and black and shiny with oil. She didn't arm it, didn't aim it, didn't light the fuse and scream: Fire! Instead she polished it. Rubbed it all over with the lace flounce at the end of her sleeve, stroked it up and down its great length, finally lay herself over it and hugged it close, like Cher in that video. Oh look, she whispered: and I was borne with the blast.

Two bedrooms, four beds. The mattresses on the iron bedsteads were thin as pallets. Such a stingy house. No corner out of earshot of any other. Every argument, every stirred pot, every creaking bedspring incorporated into the family dialogue like sugar in iced tea, sweetening it, and thickening it, too, but not so you'd notice. You had to get on your knees to look out a window, but even from that narrow portal you could see a half dozen varieties of tree: honey locust, hickory, hemlock, pine, oak, maple. The tips of the branches of one tree sported silkworm's sacs like blind eyes on the ends of stalks. Farther off, a hawk sat on a fence post, as barrel-chested as Popeye's Brutus. A world as old as America. There was a lesson in that: it wasn't the house that was important.

And the thruway, invisible, humming down like rain from a sunny sky.

. . . and Astrid begat Barbara, and Barbara begat Clara, and Clara begat Dorothea, and Dorothea begat Ethel, and Ethel begat Fay, and Fay begat Gwendolyn, and Gwendolyn begat Hildegard, and Hildegard begat . . .

"It's really very nice of you."

"Well I told him. He ain't here."

"I know, I know. He's just. I mean—I'm sure. Sometimes you have to see for yourself. And it's a very lovely home you have here."

"Not lovely, not mine, not a home."

". . ."

"Hey, you got a john I could use?"

"Sure. It's out back."
"Say what?"
"I'm just joshing you. Through that door."

Welcome to the Island of Itch Ivy! Paradise personified! Beaded sand and multipurpose flora, emerald leaves so shiny you can see yourself! See for yourself, my guide ordered, and I would have but I was distracted by a flash of white among all that green. A cat. It slunk in and out of the outer edge of the low green growth like a snake, disappearing, reappearing, seeming to wink into and out of existence, seemingly winking at me with its body. *See for yourself!* my guide demanded, but I was already off, her words were behind me, the cat ahead, the beacon of its body weaving back and forth among the tender green stalks as if weaving a single horizontal thread into their delicate verticals—as if I, following the lighthouse of its tale, were that thread. *Look here!* I heard behind me, but I had to keep my eyes forward to keep track of the cat, I had to run to keep up with it, had to jump up in the air sometimes to catch glimpses of the spire of its tail, and just when it seemed I'd lost the trail completely, a tuft of fur appeared, stuck on the pointed tip of a leaf as if arrow shape implied arrow sharpness. *Look here, look here!* I heard, and I saw that I was covered with dozens of thin slivers, blood-red but not bleeding, and as I ran after the trail of fur tufts I felt the itch ivy razoring more and more slits into my skin, carving more and more fur from the cat somewhere ahead of me, as if it weren't weaving but unraveling—unraveling itself. *Look here! See here now!* I heard, and I collected the fur as I ran, held it in my hands until my hands were full, then in my mouth, then, when my mouth was full, in the pockets under my upper arms, in the flat space between my forearms and stomach, and still the fur came until suddenly I realized I didn't have to hold it, it stuck of its own accord to my hatched-open skin, all I had to do was press it against my skin and it would stick, and it stuck, and I stuck more and more of it on, and *Look here, look here goddamnit,* and then the green field suddenly ended, crested like a frozen emerald wave, and we were on the opposite shore of the island. Naked now, the skinny cat sat in the golden sand at the water's edge, cleaning one ugly yellowish paw, its pink tongue winking in and out of its mouth and its glass-green eyes winking repeatedly, as if the sun were too bright. Behind me, the crashing ca-thump of pursuit suddenly died away, and I crawled forward meekly, swiping with furry hands at the fur in my eyes.

The cat winked once more, balefully. Don't *you* look a fright, it said, and then a wave rolled over it and it dissolved into the sand.

"This here's new house actually. Old house burned down eighteen hundred fifty-seven. Story goes cat was sleeping by fire. Spark jumps outta fireplace, sets cat's fur aflame. Cat commences to running around, before you know it curtains on fire. By the time curtains out, tablecloth's smoldering. Couldn't put out but one fire, cat lit two more. By the time it's over only thing left is chimneys and I tell you what: don't make 'em like *that* no more."

"Houses?"

"Cats?"

"Nope. *Stories.*"

I dreamed my infection. I dreamed my conversion. I dreamed my body. The body's dream: is that the soul? I dreamed my death, but I was already dreaming my life so it was hard to say what died. I dreamed my past, but it wasn't mine anymore. I dreamed the future, but it wasn't *my* future. The fever dreams were a prism that separated all of life's colors for a moment, showing me what I hadn't seen before and what I'd miss from then on—what would only come back for me in dreams.

"That? That's just a clos— here now! Can't be opening every door just cause they're *there.*"

Now then, she said. *Look.* And she showed me how to weave cloth from the leaves to cover my renewed nakedness, fashion a house against the rain and a bed against the night. Rolled, you could smoke them. Pulped, you could paint. One placed between two others made a sandwich, and later on the mulch could be used as fertilizer to grow more leaves. There was nothing you couldn't make from itch ivy, she said. There was only one rule: whatever you made, you had to make it in *threes.* I didn't understand until I sewed a cape to cover myself, wrapped it around me like a blanket, wrapped it tighter until it became a cocoon—and then I started to scratch.

The thing about computers is they don't age well. They weren't meant to age, only to be superceded, outmoded, *replaced.* I've always been a Mac man, don't know from PCs, but even I could tell this thing was ancient by computer standards, big as a suitcase, slotted for 5¼" floppies. It didn't even have a modem. It smelled like garlic and sausage, it was stained with coffee and jelly and dotted with toast crumbs. But it was turned on.

The fever dreams showed me I didn't know what time was. They showed me that time orders everything, even our minds—that chronology's a mental conceit imitating time, and linearity a literary conceit imitating chronology. But the fever dreams shuffled the days like cards. Monday followed Wednesday, Tuesday Friday. February eighth was the day after the fourth of June. The clock struck midnight on New Year's sometime in the spring; meanwhile, the snow was falling on open flowers and the flowers' open mouths gulped down water like chicks and belched forth colored jets of perfumed smoke and filled the air with gyrating genies. The genies didn't grant me any wishes but they promised me that if I danced with them I would understand the semaphore of their movements. I reached for their outstretched hands but my solid mitts passed right through theirs. Even in dreams, they said, a cloud is still a cloud and not the shape your eye pulls it into—but by that time I was already falling back to the land of facts, solid as stone, and just as hard.

TO: MADADMAN
FR: NYBISON
RE: BUMPER CARS AND BUMPER STICKERS

K.
If you can read this you're too close for your own good.
J.

I scratched and scratched and scratched. Scratched till my itch ivy chrysalis shredded and fell away from my blistered body, scratched till the blisters broke open and bled, scratched till the blood was gone, and the skin it had bloodied, and the nails which had caused it to flow. It doesn't usually work this way, does it? I always imagined a cocoon as a tranquil place, metamorphosis a deep sleep you woke from as something new. I hadn't thought I would plow my own body like a farmer tilling the soil, hadn't thought I would shoot out of the seed of myself. But there was nothing neat about it, no clean-seamed pod left hanging from a branch, no snakeskin left behind like a diamond-patterned hose, not even a million minutely curved bits of eggshell. Flesh fell away in clots and clumps, and where wind touched bare bone it sung like an electric current. When finally I'd ripped away enough to squeeze myself out of what remained, the new me, gelatinous, half-formed, fell at the foot of that teak totem pole. It towered above me, disappeared into the empty fold of purple breeches. She pointed down at me.

Oh look, she said.

"You don't mind driving?"

"I said it's fine. But you got to tell me. Did he find what he was looking for?"

"I guess so. How should I know. He said so."

"It seems like a whole lotta work for a Post-it on a computer."

"Well think about it this way: he shut up, didn't he?"

Most people are on a collision course with what they already know. Most people run straight into who they are. I know *I* had to travel a long way to discover I was exactly who I thought I was. I kept getting distracted—by who I had been, who I could have been. I mean, how obvious could it be? How many times did it have to happen? How many times did I have to dream my own birth before I finally realized it was death that obsessed me? And who am I? you ask. Or a simpler question: what have I learned at the end of my ridiculous journey? I am the epidemic's orphan. My parents were precaution and cure but they abandoned me, and now I'm all alone, with you.

"Claudia!"

"Lord God Almighty!"

"It speaks! It speaks!"

"Claudia, I have to know!"

"Jamie! Calm down! What are you talking about now?"

"What it was like. To have a mother. To have her and *then* lose her."

"What the— Jamie, I don't understand this. I don't understand any of it."

"I have to know, Claudia. You *must* tell me."

She turned in her seat. Her eyes were dreamy, almost vacant, and as she reached her hand toward my face I thought, She's remembering her mother. She has a mother to remember. When she smacked me I was so surprised I knocked my head against the window, and when I could focus again Claudia had turned back around, but she'd lowered her sun visor and looked at me in the vanity mirror.

"It was like that," she said. "*Now snap out of it.*"

Oh, look, she says. At what? At me? *Please.*

No, *look,* she says. At my mother? They're a mystery, mothers—and what are fathers but figureheads? The one denying meaning, the other accruing measure after measure of it like sixteenth notes scored in a fugue, golf clubs and rounded pennants drawn on the blank grid, the staccato forward march of authority in a barely successful effort to cover the silence. I ask you: how is one supposed to have relations, let alone relationships? And I suppose you'd have to answer: it's all *relative.*

Look, she says one more time, and this time I turn and look out over the in-again-out-again roll of the waves toward the horizon. See, she says. *America.*

Pan's Fair Throng
Rick Moody

—for Elena Sisto

FAIREST MONARCH OF OUR EMPIRE, *great king,* conduce in me, lowly tanner of hides, a righteous song as I embark to tell the tale of your origins, spinning for townsfolk the narratives of the province whence you come, that savage Northern province of brigands upon highways who accost travelers with blunt, crusted foils called, in those lands, *squeegee,* or in due course how you came from the prolific farms of *Jersey* to rule over all this principality of scribes and divers musicians, how you brought probity to scoundrels of disputatious cast. Lead me as you have led others, eternal administrator, *make your tongue my tongue* as my inscriptions cover this stone and I tell of your reign, to those in the crib, to those upon sickbeds rank and odiferous; let it be me, the tanner, who paints our masterpieces, paints your portraits in tongues of men, as if tales were altarpieces of historical churches, let me be as a butterfly with your paintbrushes, as you *climb down from your folding chair.*

There was a king, born in the first third of our century, precocious stripling, much given to reverie and to silence. In his bedchamber, he labored over problems mathematical and geometrical, never venturing forth, even should he chance to see a fair maiden dancing on the village green beyond his mullioned windows. He paid no mind to her jolly braids, nor to her furious dancing, nor to the particular brother of this particular girl, a woeful prince (for any comely lad of means was potential regent during our interregnum), whose acute melancholy was said to have been owing to his terror of ascending the throne. No, the future king secreted himself in his chamber, covered with animal skins, studying magics and potions through which he might better the station of workers of fields and shopkeepers and salespersons of viands and pickled vegetables. The king's formula, for the upstanding meritorious valor of aforementioned salespersons, was said to have been called the *Formula of Surplus Value,* completed by him in quill on goat's parchment, under a candle that, according to the spell of witchery, never burned down.

One day, our monarch, buoyed by the influence of a thick Turkic potion known as *espresso kaffee,* and because of faintest impropriety of speech that by and by inhibited the correct recitation of spells, turned the comely nervous prince—Maxwell Hennesy Charming, brother of the *flapper maiden* already mentioned—into a performing monkey, or hanuman. As I say, it was inadvertent. The king was making as to formulate a concoction of *creamy distillate* for his beverage. Nevertheless, wherefore Prince Maxwell, with fashionable opiated eyes and bulbous cheekbones, had dressed in long flowing garbs that might as well, in a dreamer's tossings, have been the robes of women, now, as hanuman, he became the *dandy.* Breeches of a dusty rose and a blue waistcoat with diamonds and rubies all upon it and stones as these days are called by the name *rhinestones,* such that he shimmered when he crawled on all fours or hung from a bough by his serpentine tail. Wherefore Prince Maxwell had been known to help a blind woman of our village, Miss Hogg, ahead of the carriages thundering by at street trivia, only to be named *infernal scamp* on deliverance of her to the farther side, as hanuman the prince was a rake and a Lothario, and would as soon inflict his manly endowments on a maiden as he would devour a banana in payment for his games of chance. I tell you, *I never liked that particular prince,* when he was under the curse, and would occasionally seize his tail and dip it into inks or poisons.

The family of Charming, a lordly assemblage of counselors and barristers, made suit against the king for having turned Prince Maxwell into a *tree monkey,* and this case was duly heard, on a day marked by grand hailstones. *Well it is remembered in my village,* how we had to flee the collapsing of thatched roofs, the merciless raining down of godly disapproval, but the courthouse, never have you seen such astonishing manufacture, with steps made out of the same pink marble used for imperial towers of clerks, and a roof that held fast beneath all assault, so that the carriages in which the barristers arrived to disgorge the principals of this story pulled fast to the curbstone and lords hastened indoors. Two or three foot soldiers were yet crushed by the hailstones so that their brains ran out in the street, *each of them a mother's son, alas.* Yet I was lucky among townspeople to sit in witness of that trial, in a box marked for commoners. A rabid bitch kept us in our place by growling ceaselessly if any of us should so much as take modest breath.

The courtier Ebenezer Sloane served as the plaintiff's counsel, and his miserly and shifty eyes were such that all present agreed he'd have bartered away his mother's petticoats if circumstance permitted. So wide was he that his frilly collar scarcely closed about his neck and but a tiny residuary chin protruded from the mounds of bulk. When cogitating earnestly—which was not often—folds of skin on Ebenezer's forehead would move and bulge, as if flowing of the humors to the skull so required.

The king, of course, not yet so crowned, was merely a young knight given to solitary and religious pursuits, and among witnesses and barristers he had none of that splendor we lately associate with his personage. Charges against him were read out by a lady in the employ of the judge—though some say *it is more than employ* and that saucier pursuits in her description might be more accurate. I'm speaking of Lady Calderon, Duchess of Fidget, who next declaimed, *Hear ye, hear ye, unworthy taxpayers of back alleys and fundaments of this very stinking mound of livestock droppings, we are gathered in this space to discuss the fate of this young magician, he of the oily pockmarks and unwashed parts, here to contemn in strongest terms what has confounded the very order of our local nature, an irrefutable slight against the family of Charmings, consisting of Maxwell Charming now deceased or metamorphosed into a primate from Asia Minor, his sister, the lovely Andalucia Charming, a father, Lancer Charming, Esq., his wife, Lady Charming, all drug into these premises to seek restitution for the fact of their nobility and station infringed upon by this young man of origins foul and mean.*

The Duchess, that sow—with mane of black curls, eyes jaundiced from gourmandish quaffing of mead *eight days per week;* a bosom that would barely be contained in her evening gown; pearls like a profane rosary circumnavigating her patchy neck, her lips horribly pursed. It was evident from the first syllables of her declamation that the celestial muse of justice *would not necessarily adjudicate in this tragical matter.* And yet at the woeful charges an uproarious tumult issued from the cronies of the Charmings. Jailkeepers rustled their irons at the corners of the space. Dogs grimaced and spilled their putrid salivas about us. It was a pretty show. And sure the king turned even bluer than his constitutional imperial shade, for his very term seemed about to come due, and if not capital execution then such tortures as *being branded with fiery iron, eyes excavated with wooden spoons, leg eaten off by ravenous boar.* Yet the king was prepared to meet his woeful fate without complaint: he was humble before persecutors.

Just then the queen—*Heart beat softly! I have given away a portion of the end! May my listeners forgive me!*—or rather the young Andalucia Charming assumed the throne of witnesses before our magistrate so deaf and blind that it is said he lingered for days though the courthouse be emptied, and she was sworn in, *under enchantment,* because the likes of which she spoke had never been uttered in a courtroom before or since, *Your honors, worshipful townsfolk, I have nothing but love for that contemned man, my heart throbs at the apperception of his fine manly features, I would unsheath myself of these fetters of rank and privilege and live with him as a lover, adrift upon breezes of sentiment, I would have no more divisions between folk, I recognize none, there shall be only love!* Consternation upon the courthouse. In later times it was said that this enchantment was not the king's own, yet whichever the origin, its most devastating magic was upon *the very soul of our king,* who loved Andalucia at once and from that moment forward, as a rich illumination hovered about her. Her braids, her fulsome lips, her downcast eyes. Who would not love the queen? Who would not kneel to declare for her?

The king thereupon rose to mount his defense, unaided by barristers.

I am a lowly inventor of magics and alchemical poultices, he began, *neither kith nor kin of any here on this* terra firma, *and my poor parents moldering six feet down, and I am called here for no reason but that I have increased the local population of apes by one, a feat which does not deprive the world of a living thing, nor does it infringe, as milady says, on the divine aspect of nature, since whichever way I chance to pivot is nature, and the same with you, for what is man but nature's most frolicsome plaything. And I would not undo my enchantment, but would rather accept my fate, yet that this young woman should perish in a foul grief at the loss of her brother, a prince, and so, out of respect for her loveliness, I vow to remove this curse upon hanuman and restore this savage to Prince Charming, meanwhile to insure the preservation of some qualities of his former apish state, namely a robust and amusing demeanor, so that he might talk freely with the fairer sex, and with passersby upon the street. If my fate is commuted until nightfall tonight I will total the figures and assemble the tinctures needed for this magic.*

The king, having no clear idea of *how* he had made the prince a monkey in the first instance—when, in like mishaps, he had changed a charwoman into hedgehog, and then, on attempting to return her to the former shape, had made her instead into *a large snaking desk lamp*—was agitated about the prospects for his next formula, but knew that his passionate affinities were enough to liberate him from the courthouse, as indeed a *lady of the court,* in sunshiney curls and clutching a velvet accessory in which were housed her several gold pieces rose up from the audience, in recognition of his fancy oratories, and cried out, *That man shall be king!* (For it had been said that the most just and enterprising of our many princes should *ascend.*) This being a piece of prophecy that she was in no way equipped to repeat, as I have heard this selfsame heavily rouged and plucked woman of the court was later pauperized *by making wagers upon sport between poultry.* Next, the town gossip, Mudge, afflicted with a peculiar ocular condition known among chirurgeons as *walleye,* as with a smart additional set of bicuspids, this Mudge strode, all inflated as when the peacock in thick of venery attempts to impress his mate, into the street to cry to all who would listen, *New regent, romancer or necromancer? New regent chooses a Charming bride and dazzles all!* Those of us gathered likewise spilled out into a dripping besmirchment of hailstones and forthwith made riot in merry dancing.

The king, as sunset fast approached was not, of course, able to find any oath that would restore the hanuman—which beast he had caged in his bedchamber so that while laboring he was subjected to a torrent of abuse in an excessively ornamented verbiage, *Hey, fair and pungent youth, I would not be the damned prince again! I'm happy just the way I am! I'd rather be mummer before thy endless processional of monarchical brats than be again that cur!* Moreover, the animal made the king so excitable, by tactics of percussive nattering and drumming upon the bars of his gaol, that his lordship kept mixing parts of lizards and vomitus of small birds *incorrectly* with the effect that his housekeeping, his Oriental rugs and French chaises, magically yielded to a sequence of *stuffed antelopes.* With this in mind, the king, short of time, saw no other recourse but to make appointment with *the most feared and reviled citizen of our village,* the pustulating warlock known hereabouts as Levi the Dispatcher.

The Dispatcher, as any here will assent, could not be found by searching, because such gray and black places as he sequestered himself were one day apparent down neglected thoroughfares and next entirely vanished. Only prayers of desperation, in combination with the production of ducats and other gold curios would produce the dreadful troll of a man. Thus, the king, not yet coronally adorned, walked the streets in rags muttering in low tones, *Oh, good gentleman Levi, I will give you a tenth portion of my treasury, should I ever ascend to the magnificence of rulership, if only you will dig me out of this infernal quackery into which I have plunged myself.* At which, finally, like lightning upon meadow, the foul warlock stepped out of a most ostentatious carriage called a *sport utility vehicle,* and confronted the incipient monarch, while picking encrustments out of his large nose, *Wait, let me be an answerer of riddles. Somewhere a neurasthenic lad is converted into a chimp and the bumbler who brought to pass this enchantment comes hither to have him restored. The further action of this drama? That shall cost you a pretty sum, my lordship, as you well know.*

The king's pockets were unfortunately spacious, indeed quite ventilated, and therefore he agreed to a special arrangement called *margin* (I have only passing acquaintance with the transaction), and this arrangement concluded the warlock rose, red curls like a kerosened halo, up above the streets to declaim the following lines of verse, no doubt composed by himself in a joyful interval, *Prince, oh prince, once so charming, your fine sports become alarming, yet since your future needs be farming, your apelike features we are harming,* during which moment, according to manifold witnesses, a jocose Prince Charming did suddenly appear upon the avenues of our fair city, smiling broadly and bestowing blessings on *women of mean reputation,* while here in our tale a ghoulish laugh issued forth from the warlock and he performed a number of somersaults and fell to earth before the king, saying, *It is done, and now I require of you a token of your esteem.* At which point the king ran him through with a dull blade. Manly act of a manly king.

And the king knelt down and prayed to the gods for whom we are justly pawns and made himself grateful. Promptly, upon returning to the court, he ascended to the throne, promptly he was trothed to the queen—until that felicitous day known as Andalucia Charming—and promptly, too, they produced a lovely daughter, the hunting princess named Diana, who wore frocks of blue and bows of red and who married a court musician. For some years all was right in the kingdom.

Wait just a moment, blessed auditor, bestow on me your forgiveness, for I seem to have misplaced a portion of the tale, such a large helping, in fact, as to be said to constitute *a second tale.* Fervent apologies. I urge you to return to *the enchantment in the courthouse,* of which I have earlier spake, having to do with the queen's sudden and fervid declaration for the king, though he be the man who changed her own brother into a *performing monkey,* etc., and so forth. This forgotten section of the story, which I append, concentrates on the author of this particular enchantment, namely, the giant of Sandy Spit, known among neighbors and plaintiffs as Maurice.

He wore foul jerkins instead of proper clothes, to begin judiciously enough, blouses that had been sweated through with undignified perspirings for many fortnights or even months; he was fat, he was of such girth that when he ate too much his *own house* burst open along the joists; his breath smelled of goat's milk that has been left out in the hot sun to accumulate gobs of cheesy rankness, he rarely even wetted himself down nor wore a gay cologne. And further to his miserable condition Maurice was alone raising up three progeny, a girl in her middle years, flaxen like himself, name of Kurt, a secondborn girl and boy both with dark mien, like the giant's deceased wife. Their names were Elsa and Stibb.

Nearly every inquisitive scamp who hears such tales requires to have satisfied *the exact largeness of the giant,* and so here I essay solution to the enigma, to common good of both young and old, both sober and them such as have spent entire days in public houses, *Just how big was the giant?* Since I only saw his children, I give surmise founded upon reports from travelers to distant precincts, who say of him, *taller than church spires, taller than the biggest oaks, taller than the cliffs at Mahon, tall enough to reach up to the green cheese in the night sky and steal himself a fermenting hunk, massive enough to light his pipe from the morning sun, giant enough to trample the oceans for footbaths.*

As the giant was their father, headmaster of hearth, bringer home of manifold pork products including pork loins and pork lips and sausages, his three children had no choice but to love him, yet for some ages they had noticed that he was *very dismally sad,* given to fits of grave sobbing and beating of breast, which would then cause floods in nearby streambeds, this melancholia dating to the demise of his goodly wife, of course; these many years, he had stayed singularly awake into the caliginous night muttering: *Love is an appellation known to all, and so why must I be so solitary unto the hereafter, just my wee children but no woman such as might love me and care for me despite my accursed appearance? Why am I destined to march unaccompanied along my path, all men fleeing my footfall?*

Upon encountering him, sleepless and cross, in the morning, the children confabulated many wiles and stratagems to distract the giant from woe, including the imposition of elixirs such as *St.-John's-wort* into his tea, which Maurice liked of such strength that it had been known to corrode iron kettles. None of these stratagems succeeded, alas, and the giant of Sandy Spit would therefore, in the midst of his fever, maraud upon the land, abducting children, devouring livestock, visiting many horrors upon gentlefolk. In such a fell mood, the giant one day espied before him in the road, like a poisonous ant that needs be crushed before habitations of the day can continue, a small fleeing figure, namely *the once and future Andalucia Charming,* now queen of our demesne, who had been bathing in a small, clear loch, a reservoir of agreeable drinking waters much traveled by lithesome harvesters of corn and other truck, and having spent an afternoon feeding berries to one of these lads, the queen Andalucia, clad only in a womanly undergarment—as mischievous youths had absconded with her further draperies—she now fled home, hoping to arrive at the castle before her most admirable mother, thereupon to make appropriate tributes to the staff such that they might *neglect to mention* to her progenetrix this dishonored state.

Thunder upon the land. The giant caught glimpse of the small, curvaceous, and perfect queen, and soon fetched her up in his fulsome palms, and here the giant held her to his eyes, being much afflicted in the matter of nearsightedness, at which he immediately became a convert to the argument of Andalucia's beauty. She was like a smoky crystal with its flindering lights, she was like unto the handsome portraits that hung in house whereupon his parents had once begged for alms, she was lily of field, bird of air, she might *make wolves eat only herbs and sing madrigals. Upon my honor,* Maurice cried, and of course the sounds were audible across the land, as if a rogue city state lurched *infernal bullets and arrows* toward our cities, *I believe a goddess has crossed into my wilderness and that I must devote myself to her service henceforth and always.* The queen attempted to reply, of course, but Maurice squeezed her so tightly in his fist she fainted dead away, and made no audible reply.

Well aware is your storyteller of his dependence on conjuring and mysticisms in this song, yet elegance and divine symmetry demand that he should now admit that the giant performed next as any gentleman of honor would under like circumstances, viz., he too made an oath *of devilish properties.* Said he, over the sleeping body of the queen, now laid alongside a rutted track which snaked into the town, and here I must profess again that the poem is of his own composition as I myself prefer blank verse, *Witches, warlocks of the night, restore this sleeper to her sight, make him next she sees be hers, the giant here who offers prayers.* And with that he reclined beside her to await her waking and subsequent veneration of himself. Yet he had squeezed her so tightly, that she didn't wake, *and didn't wake, and didn't wake, and didn't wake,* days commenced to resemble fortnights which soon resembled seasons, and she did not wake, and no traveler dared disturb the vigil of the giant. New roads were dug to circumnavigate his vigil, until such time as he came to believe he had *killed his fairest love,* his second love, and that, by arrangement of deities and constellations, he was therefore beyond grace and doomed to wander the earth, bereft, or perhaps to spend too much time in contemplation of ribald masques and plays. Off he marched in winter to relinquish himself to that paltry luck.

Thereafter, the queen, located by good gentlemen on horseback, was gathered onto a chestnut mare to be driven to town for *a grand adjudication,* namely the trial of that youth, much spoken of above, who would shortly be king. Sleeping, she was transported by these gentlemen, and sleeping delivered to her splendid parents, and she did not wake until, *struck by a hailstone,* she opened her eyes, to espy the next king of our land making his way up the steps, ascending to his destiny, which is to say *she opened her eyes to the felicity of love.*

Now, *the giant galloped amok upon the lands,* dear friends, as, in his madness, he tore stands of oak and birch and flung them this way and that, and a blindness fell upon him like a fever, and a terrible ringing like of a thousand bells did assail his ears, and he knew himself to have come to a fork in the road in the deserted netherlands beyond all our maps. No longer did wolves, nor bears, nor leopards harbor themselves there, idling in anticipation of smiting some passerby, no, life had fled and only the giant Maurice called it home, that complete oppositeness of light, at the edge of which his lonesome welps, Kurt and Elsa and Stibb, made themselves hoarse with beckoning. He did abandon them. And yet in his lonesomeness, *nonetheless a ray of melioration,* though no sophistry or legerdemain or clerical bluster would raise him from his spot, for suddenly he conceived what the lonely man must always come to know *that he is but a dream of sleep,* his term mercifully instant and insubstantial; so the giant was a dream, and with him were such excellent figures of dreams past as Rapunzel, and Snow White, phantastes all, the fine prince called Valiant, arrayed beside the giant, each of these with recitations of his or her heroic pilgrimages, no differences between one and another, for all stories issue from one origin, one maelstrom, *the demiurge Pan;* all things from his dark, implacable brow are fashioned; and this is the fact of the matter, fellow citizens, for I have come to recognize myself as the dream the giant had, the giant dreams of me and I dream of the uneasy king, who knows his reign must one day end, each of us a fervency in another's sleep, *there is no teller of tales,* no protagonist, only the interior of a portrait painter in our village, who in the hours before uncovering the easel of her labors, before *she sleeps,* tells her own daughter *Once upon a time.*

Four Dark Fables

Joyce Carol Oates

THE LITTLE SACRIFICE

THE CHILD VANISHED from her family's cottage by night. In the dawn, her little bed was empty. "Oh where is she? Our daughter, our baby? Who has taken her from us?"—so the distraught parents cried, for they knew that their daughter would not have left them of her own volition, but must have been abducted. Yet though they searched everywhere for her, and would never abandon their quest for the remainder of their unhappy lives, they would not find her. Had cruel fairies carried her off into the Underworld? Had a wild beast leapt through a window as everyone slept, and bore her away in his jaws? Or had the little girl simply vanished?—as dew sparkling like gems will vanish on the grass with the inexorable rising of the sun, transforming the night to day.

In fact the child had been abducted by fairies. But not carried into the Underworld. Her fate was more mysterious, and more cruel: she was bartered to a wealthy noble family who lived in a great house on a promontory above the village in which the little girl's family lived, their ancient name synonymous with high rank and devout Christian belief and the solemn responsibilities of such.

Oh, what had happened to her!—the little girl would never comprehend. She woke to find herself crudely bound and gagged; she was carried into the earth, to be freed in a dungeon beneath the great house; she would be given just enough food and drink to sustain her, and just enough candlelight for her to see dimly, as undersea creatures see with primitive eyes. At the outset of her confinement she wept and pleaded with her captors to be released, but her captors were servants of the noble family, and paid her no attention. She might have been pleading with the blank granite face of the mountain. She might have been pleading with the great Jehovah himself.

The noble family came to glimpse the child, through a grating in the dungeon door, only a few times. Enough for them to be assured by their servants that the little sacrifice was safely confined. "She is still alive. She eats, she drinks. She no longer walks, but she crawls. She has grown dull-witted. Her vision is poor. But she has ceased begging to be released. She has ceased crying. Like the others, she will forget, in time, the world beyond the dungeon that is now her home."

The noble family was content that the little sacrifice was a success.

"She is our measure of what God will allow. Without her, how could we gauge the wickedness in our hearts? And, in our hearts, in the heart of mankind? How could we gauge our own good fortune?"

The noble family looked upon their own innocent children with joy and gratitude.

These were good, generous Christian folk. Except for their single aberration, they were virtuous human beings. They attended Sunday church services without fail, they tithed from their considerable income, they gave to the poor, they were never without smiles and blessings for others less fortunate than themselves. Seeing each Sunday in church the grieving, broken parents of the little sacrifice, they were especially kind.

PREVAILING FAITH IN "FREE WILL"

YOU BELIEVE IN "FREE WILL" because believing in "free will" makes you feel content, at least not visibly anxious, and you're a normal human being, though not an average human being, and you want to be content, or, more reasonably, you want to prevail in that state of benign, suspended doubt in which contentedness is, if not immediate and inevitable, at least a possibility. You believe in "free will" because, as you argue, it's logical. You believe in "free will" the way you believe in those powerful seductive exhausting dreams of yours, while you're in the dreams. You believe in "free will" as an unexamined remnant of religious conviction. You believe in "free will" because you don't have an identical twin who at this moment, though invisible to you, some miles away, is seated in a posture uncannily resembling your own, right ankle propped with a jaunty awkwardness on his left knee, head tilted at a somewhat brooding angle, fleeting smile, veiled eyes and the fingertips of his left hand unconsciously tracing, like Braille, the carved edge of a mahogany table. (It's the arm of a chair your fingertips are unconsciously tracing.) You believe in "free will" because you don't have a twin who last week decided impulsively to take an ambitious hiking trip in the spring, as you, at about the same time, decided to take a hiking trip this winter. (The twin to Alaska, you to Ecuador where the seasons are reversed.) You believe in "free will" because you don't have a twin who a dozen years ago, when you were both in graduate school, he on the West Coast and you on the East, impulsively donated blood to the Red Cross, in a desperate yearning to be *of use, somehow.* You believe in "free will" because you don't have a twin who picks up the phone to dial your number, a rare event, even as you consider picking up the phone, or have in fact moved to pick up the phone, to dial his number. You don't have a twin you glimpse in the bathroom mirror, stumbling to use the toilet in the night. You don't have a twin who discards his old glasses, which resemble your old glasses, to buy new glasses, which resemble your new glasses. You don't have a twin who, when next you meet, and you forestall these meetings as long as you dare, will astonish you with his new, sleek haircut very like your own new, sleek haircut, designed to disguise, if only minimally, your thinning hair, his new, steel-colored sports utility vehicle very like your own, and his new, striking, obviously ill-chosen love.

THE REVELATION

THERE WAS A MAN our exact age who, early one morning, some time before his usual hour of waking, opened his eyes so quickly and unguardedly that he saw the web in which he lay: a fine, gossamer structure, beautifully symmetrical, the strands translucent as thought yet seemingly strong, unbreakable as steel; the longitudinal strands just perceptibly thicker than the latitudinal, and fewer in number. Instinctively his eyes shut tight; for it was too early to wake from sleep, and the revelation was too early in his life; and when at last he opened his eyes, an hour later, in eagerness and dread, he saw that whatever it had been in which he'd imagined he had lain in the sweet passivity of sleep had vanished, as if it had never been.

Joyce Carol Oates

THERE WILL COME THAT EVENING

THERE WILL COME THAT EVENING, very likely in summer, in the porous heat of late August, when, exhausted from driving through the long sun-scorched day, in thrall to a destination as fixed as any mathematical equation, comforted and panicked in equal measure by such fixedness, which is a way of acknowledging *This is I, I am this, for who else makes this journey?* you exit the thunderous New York State Thruway at Route 78 and drive north into the abruptly quiet, darkening countryside, as if driving into an undefined past, a waning fiery-phosphorescent sun in the western sky, driving on a country highway past scattered houses, farmland, open, grassy fields, at last turning up the driveway of a farmhouse and ascending a long, rutted drive past front pastures, crossing with caution the loose-planked bridge over a brook, or ditch, that's no more than a trickle by late summer but flash floods in heavy rainstorms, you ascend a steep hill to the first of the outbuildings, a small barn once used to store farm equipment and later converted into a tidy suburban-style garage with asphalt siding and a sliding overhead door, this evening when you park your car an outside light is immediately switched on, as if you've been awaited, you climb the wooden steps of the side porch and knock at the screen door, seeing movement inside, hearing a dog bark, and a figure moves to the door to open it, though only a few inches, a middle-aged man of about your height with a powerful, balding head whom you've never seen before, staring at you without recognition. "Yes? What do you want?"

The waning sun sinks beneath the treeline. The mass of cloud overhead is rippled like the interior of a gigantic mouth. A dog that appears to be a young, black Labrador retriever, both like and unlike a former dog of yours, and unknown to you, pushes against the man's legs, barking excitedly and growling deep in his throat.

There will come that evening.

A Dialogue

Richard Powers and Bradford Morrow

FRIENDS SINCE THE MID-EIGHTIES, we have traded thoughts about fiction on many occasions through correspondence and over dinner. The dialogue that follows is a natural extension of those earlier letters and conversations, and was done by e-mail over several months this winter. In the sidebars we respond to an unstated question as to what might prompt some of our novels, past and future. Powers cites salient quotes, Morrow salient musical works.

MORROW: Your interest in systems interests me. When I read a Richard Powers novel, I have the strong sense that predetermined underlying formal symmetries—like configuring gravities or grids—are very much in play. Such matrices aren't unusual in music, where the composer brings harmonic ideas to a given structure, a sonata form, for instance. Or in classical poetry where, say, the sestina informs the contours of language, proposes rhythms and emphatic moments along a measured line. But the novel has historically been an organic enterprise, so often arising in different narrative shapes and sizes. You seem to embrace large-scale forms that create expectations of implicit symmetries from chapter to chapter. From the three voicings that braid in fairly strict succession in *Three Farmers on Their Way to a Dance,* to the more recent back and forth of personal to impersonal in *Gain,* these substructures inform the narrative's meaning as much as the story itself. For instance, I couldn't get away from the impression that I was experiencing Laura's heart beating down toward her inevitable end in the very diastolic/systolic movement of *Gain.* How do you determine what interplay will occur between character and voice, story and system?

POWERS: I do love the meaning that comes from form, and you're right to conclude that my love comes out of an affinity for the forms and structures of classical music. I probably have a fuller, more visceral response to the formalisms of music than I do to what you call the organic enterprise of fiction, although the two don't seem to me to be a dichotomy so much as a continuum. In fact, I think of the tension graph of the classic, organic narrative plot—exposition, complication, climax, denouement—as roughly analogous to the sonata-allegro form. Even the most character-driven or event-driven of plots will have its shape, and in that shape, as much as in the particulars of gesture, the story's meaning lies.

For better or worse, I do think in large-scale structures, and these structures, to some degree, inform all my novels. I've moved away from the top-down novel gradually over the course of fifteen years, to the delight of one kind of reader and the dismay of another. I've become more interested in allowing local urgency to subvert global plan. I believe that the richest fiction always exists in the tension between top-down and bottom-up, between the expectations that form sets up and the many ways that such expectation is subverted, deferred or satisfied. Ideally, I shoot for a form that will hover in and out of a reader's awareness, oscillating between figure and ground. You know what form I always find heart-rending? Those long, involved Bach chorale preludes, where the simple hymn tune is so prolonged and elaborately interworked that it's a shock, every time, to be recalled to its next, four-square strain.

"An old man who had been a slave told of his white mother, a young daughter of a slave-holding family in North Carolina, who was confined to an attic prison on the day her small child, fathered by a Black man, was sold away." (Jane Lazarre, Beyond the Whiteness of Whiteness*)*

Form is visceral to me; I find it as moving and beautiful as any revelation of character. It *is* itself a revelation of character, that part of us that needs pattern and order. But recall that in its true sense, "organic" form is by far the most complex and ingenious of any form imaginable. No geometry, however elaborate, can match the astonishment of, say, blood vessels. That would be a structure worth striving for: the structure of organisms! When a story "lives," I think it generally has all the breathtaking, indescribable complexity of a living hierarchy. Organism, organ, cell—novel, scene, sentence: form shades off into the same particulars that evade and inscribe it.

MORROW: Your vision seems to me essentially celebratory. Bachlike. It doesn't shy away from the darkest of human experiences, from disease or from war, from treachery or other forms of human failure. But there's an underlying pedal point—to extend this musical metaphor—that seems to me spiritual, even religious. Not only does your rigorous formalism *not* make spirituality impossible, but it *is* spiritual. The world is numinous, yes, but god is also in the numbers. How do you see spiritual belief relating to your work?

POWERS: Art is a way of saying what it means to be alive, and the most salient feature of existence is the unthinkable odds against it. For every way that there is of being here, there are an infinity of ways of not being here. Historical accident snuffs out whole universes with every clock tick. Statistics declare us ridiculous. Thermodynamics prohibits us. Life, by any reasonable measure, is impossible, and *my* life—this, here, now—infinitely more so. Art is a way of saying, in the face of all that impossibility, just how worth celebrating it is to be able to say anything at all. However miserable our moment of existence, simply existing ought to leave us infinitely ahead of the game. And our mortality ensures that misery will always eventually come to an end. But we forget our deaths, habituate to the infinite unlikelihood of awareness, take our lives to be a baseline, and measure our lot against the handful of even more unlikely configurations that we feel entitled to. The task of art is to estrange us from everything that seems given to us and to return us to a condition of brute astonishment. The inanimate universe has been kicking around for 20 billion years. For 70 years, you get to have a look at it. The terms of all saying can only be awe and gratitude.

Willie Dixon's "Little Red Rooster" slyly draws a portrait of how we can love the very thing that most troubles us, threads through Come Sunday. *"Got a little red rooster too lazy to crow the day . . . keeps everything in the barnyard upset in every way. If you see my little red rooster won't you please drive him home? Ain't had no peace in the barnyard since my little red rooster's been gone."*

Does awe need to make room to describe darkness and misery? Of course. It has to, or it would be lying about who we are and what we are obligated to feel. But to forget our basic unlikelihood in the face of the things we are able to feel: that's just negligence. Which emotions, finally, would the most life-weary banish from the repertoire? Even despair is really appetite by another name. The fact that we can feel misery at all ought to be its own cause for perpetual amazement. Yet contemporary writing looks a little askance at celebration. Awe has been killed, I think, by the age of self-realization. What we've really lost in contemporary life is any sense of belonging to a project that is larger than we are. We live at a moment when all things bigger than us seem to be insidious, man-made and threatening. We've thrown in our lot entirely with the self, and the self is not large enough. Literature can recall to us the smallness of the private narrative, its eternal insufficiency.

I'd say that this theme is dear to your heart as well, that it infuses your own fiction: the humbling of the individual self in the face of stories much longer and wider than its own. I see a common thread between our work: our characters seem to find a corpse in history's attic, as it were, and are forced, by the rough edges of this discovery, to disassemble the small story they've been telling about themselves in order to accommodate the larger story they are thrust into. . . .

"Lieserl [Einstein's illegitimate daughter, who he had never seen] contracted scarlet fever; Albert was worried about the aftereffects of the disease. In the same letter he asked how Lieserl was registered—presumably for adoption. But there the thread disappears. We have no certain record of what happened to Lieserl—there is no evidence of her death, and the likeliest conclusion is that the child was given away." (Fritz Stern, Einstein's German World*)*

MORROW: The impulse to weave individual narrative threads through the tapestry of some large historical moment or movement, framing the personal within the public gesture, is one we share. History isn't some capsuled stage set, nor can we ever fully detach from its magnetic anatomy. It isn't widely differentiated from the biography of the frailest or most diffident soul who lived within its temporal borders. So, any individual act—however ostensibly small or even meaningless it might seem—cannot fail to shape the larger cultural history of the day in which it transpired, and the day after and beyond.

The butterfly effect, that ultimate precept for a Buddhist's physics, is a commonplace by now, but a valuable one nonetheless. To contemplate an individual in fiction is, among other things, to study the social, political and economic powers that catalyze his or her intimate universe. Kip and Brice, in *Trinity Fields,* are unimaginable outside the initializing context of their youths in Los Alamos and, by turn, World War II and

Vietnam, just as *Three Farmers'* Hubert, Peter and Adolphe are a collective embodiment of World War One life and thought. Similarly, Clare Soap and Chemical constitutes a kind of warp through which the woof of Laura Bodey's thoughts and actions are woven on *Gain*'s loom; a novelistic fabric not unlike that of *The Almanac Branch* in which Grace Brush is enmeshed with the Geiger Corporation to such an extent that it defines her, even though—like Laura—she'd rather it didn't. This instinct to counterpoint history and story may be born, aesthetically, from musical thinking—theme and variation crosscurrenting, echoing and influencing each other. Surely, it comes from the fundamental acknowledgment of a holistic ecology in which everything impacts the other. That corpse in history's attic is our collective forebear and a possible key to a more deeply dimensioned understanding of the world that moves through the rest of the human mansion.

Mahler's Symphony No. 4 in G Major, was inspiration architecture for The Almanac Branch, *its four movements reprised in the form of the family portrait, the fourth movement,* Sehr behaglich, *travestied as is Grace Brush herself by her brother's pornographic film biography.* "Wir genie Ben die himmlischen Freuden, D'rum tun wir das Irdische meiden"*: "We enjoy heaven's delights, thus can dispense with earthly matters," all inverted.*

Your thoughts about awe and art are compelling. I know when I have really *seen* a painting or sculpture because when I leave the museum I find myself on streets I hardly recognize, even though they are the same streets I'd walked just a few hours before. Museum sans walls. The old idea holds. Nineteenth-century chamber orchestra audiences were invited to listen to the music with such pure empathy that their experience was tantamount to composing it spontaneously in their imaginations as the performance evolved, a kind of inventive engagement whose contemporary manifestation might be air-guitaring. Windmilling rather than whistling in the breeze. A less subtle performance of affinities than the *homme orchestre* conjury of a Beethoven concerto, but the principle is the same, and so is the witnessing embrace. A book is asleep until the reader draws back its covers and awakens it. The very existence of any book depends upon a willingness, a determination, of a reader to see.

Regarding empathy: How do you read books? Can you separate the sorcerer's apprentice who is forever gleaning technical ideas from the immersion reader who gives himself over to the experience of the narrative? What kind of reader is your ideal?

POWERS: For me, the ideal reader doesn't have too fixed an idea of what a novel must be, prior to embarking on the next proof of what it might be. As I see it, the meaning of any artistic engagement is a measure of the displacement of the engager. Where was I before I started this journey, and where am I now, as I come out the other end? In a sense, this model resembles an information-theoretical one: a sentence (or a paragraph, a scene, a chapter, or a story) *means* by setting up expectations and then not quite fulfilling them, leaving the slightly rearranged expecter to do calculus on the gap opened up between the expected trajectory and the resultant one. No movement, no meaning. Books should not flatter our sense of self. They should investigate it.

"[O]ld ladies playing systems based on the sum of their nieces' birthdays divided by the pills in an Anacin bottle were hitting the daily double daily." (Bill Baruch, Laughing in the Hills*)*

When I read, I ask myself: "Who would I have to be in order for this work to answer all my unknown needs?" Then I ask myself whether I like being that person, the person who would find this particular book a masterpiece, and ask how far I'd have to move to get there. The distance and direction of that movement (whether or not I choose to make it) are the best indication of the values inherent in the story, of what the story *means*. I read another person in order to get better at interrogating my own unexamined narrative.

So my ideal reader is one who can allow the book to reinvent itself, not along a familiar trajectory but along one that seems familiar for a while and then, somehow, isn't. Similarly, my ideal writer is one capable of reinventing herself with each new project. This imperative can really throw a reader, especially a reader who has succeeded in loving a previous work. I'm sure you've found this with your audiences. Readers who respond strongly to *Trinity Fields* must be willing to be reinvented when they come to *Giovanni's Gift*.

MORROW: The ideal reader might want to remain open to self-reinvention with successive readings of the same work, as well, of exploring previously unseen tiers and depths. The *Lolita* I read when I was twenty made an enormous impression on me; its muscular, sensuous, sinuous language and all its sly tragedy—perfect then for who I was as a reader. The same *Lolita* reread in my thirties, then again recently, had of course newly seismographic impact. But of a different kind. Not that my earlier reading was all that immature, or that I didn't feel those first resonances. But because *Lolita* as a masterpiece of human comedy—whose staggering accuracy is rendered in the minutiae of the quip, the parenthetical aside, paying off in every sentence, line after line—helped me understand in what ways I might have grown as a witness. Who was it that said we don't judge books, they judge us . . . ?

Jerome Kern and Oscar Hammerstein's "The Song is You," performed by Keith Jarrett, Gary Peacock and Jack DeJohnette live in Philharmonic Hall, Munich, July 13, 1986, forms and informs the prose rhythm of Trinity Fields. *All that-headlong urgency of flight I tried to get in the opening passage.*

Among novelists I know, there is a strong disagreement about the moral implications of fiction. Some believe fiction is its own end and cannot, should not, serve other than aesthetic ends. Then there is the argument that fiction always marks a political or moral engagement, whether or not the novelist intends such engagement or not. What responsibilities does a novelist have within the context of his culture?

POWERS: Aestheticize politics or politicize art: the old, ironclad dichotomy bewilders me. I don't mean I'm bewildered by having to make the choice. I'm bewildered by those who think we can. We've reified these two terms of creative engagement and made them out to be incommensurable. Should fiction be concerned with beauty or morality? It's a little like asking whether humans ought rather to eat or to breathe, or whether sentences ought really to consist of nouns or verbs.

Everything I've ever written has attempted to break down this dualism and show the aesthetic and political to be two regions of a continuous spectrum, or better yet, two dimensions of a deep, wide plane. Warp and woof: the vocabulary of private experience depends upon the vocabulary of joint life, and the other way around. The purely aesthetic end still exists in a public and contested space, and even the most pragmatic politics will have, for the individuals who live them, private components of longing and fear. Which mode trumps the other? Which of the two is more legitimate or fundamental? The question doesn't make sense to me. Why would we *want* to split the two? The life of the private self and the life of the public hive coexist, by definition, in a perpetual, precarious, negotiated trade-off.

All human phenomena have their aesthetic abscissa and their political ordinate. We know things in our individual bodies and then we trade them outwardly with others. Private desires turn into public power struggles. Questions of beauty *become* questions of morality. We recognize one only in the silhouette of the other. The strongest stories thrive on this strangest of predications. I'm after the novel that not only partakes of this anxious negotiation but takes it as its fundamental subject. Anyone who writes as if aesthetics or politics can exist without one another is not doing justice to the full range of human experience.

MORROW: There may be a corollary to this aesthetic/political argument in the relationship between the local/universal—a relationship both of us have explicitly addressed in our writing. Aesthetics must be local, insofar as they are subjective. And politics must be universal, in that political action is the powerful result of groups of individuals finding consensus among their disparate needs and beliefs. Just as the aesthetic *causes* the political, and vice versa, so do the local and universal cause one another. It's the same family of coexistence, the same stuff of art.

POWERS: Have your thoughts about the relationship between little and big changed over the course of your years as a novelist? We've each been working now for roughly a decade and a half, long enough for our actual routes to have diverged from our initial headings. My earliest books—and yours, too, I think—were attempts to redeem the power of the single vote, and to affirm that decisions taken in a private, local life do have immeasurable "trickle up" effects. In some ways, to assert the local is also to mount an apology for fiction, which all novels incorporate into themselves in some manner. But my view of the terraced hierarchies of local and global has gotten more striated, if not more qualified, in the run of time. Gauges do cascade; vast ecological webs do self-assemble, aggregating into complex, recursive networks of feedback and feed-forward. But just what storms any given butterfly might create lie beyond anyone's ability to calculate. The dialogue between Clare Chemical and Laura Bodey is, on the one hand, a conversation between two individuals: a flesh-and-blood individual, and the individual that the limited-liability corporation literally is, in the eyes of the law. But these conversants belong to different ordinal realities. Their gauges and scales differ so greatly that they cannot hear one another, or factor one another into the levels on which each operates.

In a sense, my ongoing anxiety about the ability of the local to survive or impact the global has complicated my instincts as a reader over this same decade and a half. At twenty-eight, I liked to read for the transcendent moment, for the total immersion in the oceanic, an experience beyond our ability to decipher or control. At forty-two, I am still working out the relation between pleasure and responsibility, meaning and coercion, self-knowledge and rationalization, co-optation and genuine empathy. Every new book seems to interrogate the previous one's loopholes. I don't mean to say that I no longer find novels beautiful with the same frequency as I did when I was younger (although I guess I do now have more of the inevitable tradesman's sense of when something has been a little jerry-rigged). But the absolute, universalizing kind of beauty that I was after when I read a book in 1985 has opened out, grown more mottled, become its own turbulent ecology. I can still weep for Little Nell. But the tears are driven by a wider sense of human agendas—tainted, touched-up, qualified and always magnificently insufficient.

I'd love to know how your own role as a reader has changed with your novelistic maturation.

MORROW: The simplest answer to your first question would be to say that I find it impossible to consider individuals outside the context of their historical environment, since each of us—whether we're factual or fictional—defines and is defined by the cultural moment. I'm reminded of Yeats's intersecting gyres, the tip of one cone centering the circumference of the other and vice versa. You have indicated, and rightly, that there is no need to sever the little from the big. Indeed, they're not separable. Countries form alliances, they go to war. The nation itself doesn't die in the trench, as such, and yet it does. Every personal kindness informs peace accords. History remains a sequence of personal decisions scumbled onto a vast canvas.

The act of storytelling always presumes the singular experience to resonate with universal implication. Metaphor couldn't very well function without this being a presumptive truth. Readers of fiction, these narrative moments set forth in language, are asked to reimagine those nuanced moments, breathe a kind of visual and aural life into them. Stage them, as it were, in the mind's theater. So there's an implicit pact between the reader and writer, in the best possible scenario. Reading is an act of trust, just as writing is an act of faith.

You're right about the tradesman's eye for dropped stitches and tinted screens. Still, a great book requires energetic, empathetic reading to achieve that greatness. Even the richest text only escapes its fallow condition by a reader tilling and resowing its ideational fields.

POWERS: I like your formulation: the largeness of the novel does depend in part upon a reader's willingness to exercise largeness of spirit upon it. Readerly renarration involves the reader in retelling not only the printed story but also her own life's story, in the presence of a story that did not originate with her. And I like, too, the idea that this active reader somehow recapitulates the similar, active rereading that the novel's writer has performed on the writer's historical moment. The tale of the private life becomes a way of voicing the chaotic public sphere that did not yet even know it was a tale. But at the same time, I have balked, throughout my career, at the contemporary American aesthetic bias that decrees that the public narrative space can only be gotten to through a metaphorical correlation with the private story. Do you sometimes feel this same weight of aesthetic consensus? Our literature has become so solid, so skilled, so professional, so sure of the superiority of dramatic realization over narration, of showing over telling. Fiction in this country, Madison Smartt Bell once wrote, has grown dangerously close to becoming a poor relation to the movie business. So I love the fact that many younger writers now seem to be recovering a belief that story is also about the words used to say it. Telling, to extend your idea, really can be showing, by other means.

The converting element, of course, is voice. I have a favorite observation, made by Mikhail Bakhtin: "Every act of depicting is itself a depiction." Just as we've learned, over centuries of literary exploration, to refract the values of a literary work through the vessel of character, we can learn to read in a way that sees extended acts of narrative or even discursive prose as "characters"—sometimes ironized, sometimes frail or faulty, but always living, voiced depictions in their own right. We can read a narrative not for its final truth or universal sufficiency, but as a record of some provisional, always contingent, always improvised guess about the shape of the place we occupy. Stories—showing and telling—are, like genomes, the sculpted shorthand of speculations about how to stay alive. As the Psalms say: We live our lives as a tale told.

MORROW: Because of the process of writing novels, I have naturally grown more sensitive to overtones, extended possibilities of meaning, the secondary nuance, the texture of rhythms and music. To read the first sentence of Kazuo Ishiguro's *Remains of the Day*— "It seems increasingly likely that I really will undertake the expedition that has been preoccupying my imagination now for some days"—is to appreciate how the protagonist's rhetorical approach to life defines him. The tentativeness of "seems," "likely" and "really" in tandem with the comic hyperbole of "undertake the expedition" defines the narrator sheerly through language. He's cautious, stubborn, proud, antiquated and all of it's embedded in his manner of address. There are so many examples of form informing content. The imperative of "See the boy," at the outset of Cormac McCarthy's *Blood Meridian* proposes by its very syntax that the reader is entering a harsh world, peremptory, belligerent. It also carries, whether the author intended this or not, an echo of a precursor text, Melville's, which begins with three similarly loaded words, "Call me Ishmael." The basics, the building blocks. McCarthy's desert *Moby Dick* begun with a formal wink to the heritage it further extends.

These nuances and connectives may be the product of my implicating imagination. But unlike the woman who asked Robert Creeley during a question-and-answer session after a reading, "Was that a real poem or did you just make it up?" I'd like to believe my task is to know the difference, while allowing myself full rein as a creative reader. To be responsible to the spirit of the work, and responsive to the joys of experiencing it. So as not to sound overly cheerful, I should say, too, that with every book I read I'm increasingly aware of those I won't experience. Time the welder, time the cutter.

Which brings me to a question about mortality. You're relatively young, as novelists go, and have been steady, prolific, thoughtful in your progress from book to book. Do you have an ideal trajectory or arc in mind for your work as a whole?

POWERS: Each book tacks back across the path of the preceding one. But do I narrate the shape of my career forward in time, past the story that I'm currently working on? Never very far. And I always look to the book I'm immersed in to correct any ideas I might have about who I am or what I'm doing. Sam Shepard once said something I admire: "I don't want to have a career. I just want to write what I need to write."

You can and do have more than one book project alive and germinating at a time. I find that remarkable. How do you make that work?

MORROW: You know those Boorum & Pease ledger books that are about the shape and size of a modest grave marker, or a flotation paddleboard that children use when they're learning to swim? Being a longtime aficionado of stationery shops, I discovered these old behemoths collecting dust on high shelves and became addicted to filling them with words, clippings, drawings, invented family trees, character analyses, photographs, verbal and visual bric-a-brac. The stuff of narrative. Over a period of years these image greenhouses will begin to establish a character of their own, crises that define them, centralizing dynamics. And while they were likely latent novels from the day I first walked home with a new one under my arm, I made it my habit not to think of them as fictional manufacturing sites, or templates, or anything other than notebooks. Tabula rasas ripe for the palimpsest.

"You write some code, and suddenly there are dark, unspecified areas." (Ellen Ullman, Close to the Machine*)*

What seems to have become a working pattern for me is to develop these image systems which attach to names, become characters, members of families, in different ledger books. A prose music evolves and with it some germinating problem. Then the novel.

This pattern of developing two novels concurrently isn't one I can easily account for, other than that I may simply need some promise of futurity in order to believe what is present. Ciaro requiring scuro, yin needing yang, walking being a series of recovered falls. At this point, I can't imagine not working on two novels at the same time, though it's important to note that one always recedes while the other truly takes precedence. They assume their own authority in the daily imagination, as you well know, and can become very demanding once they do establish precedence. As if, trading places, the novel views its author as ledger rasa. So, while yes I am composing two novels always, one is inchoate as the other emerges. I like that Bakhtin observation. Words are at once objects, signifiers, and the objects being signified. It's the most lovely paradox.

You have always brought into close proximity people, histories, places that are superficially unconnected but through narrative process become crucially interdependent, mutually influencing. One finishes *Plowing the Dark* agog at how divergent seemed the paths of those laboring the virtual crayon kingdom in Seattle, and Taimur imprisoned in Beirut. Enclosures:

one potentially fleeing, the other seemingly a crypt. How do you conceive these dualisms? I wonder if they're not so different from the Boorum & Pease books, but collecting into a dynamic the possibilities of two novels and compressing them into a single furnace.

POWERS: You mentioned the Yeats gyres: an old favorite of mine too. And there's an old Dutch fairy tale called, in one variation, "The Innkeeper's Wife," which has always seemed to me the perfect illustration of that theory of interpenetrating complements. I've narrated the tale explicitly in one of my books, and it haunts the margins of at least two others. The wife of an innkeeper in Zeeland has a dream in which she finds a fortune outside the Bourse in Amsterdam. When she wakes, the dream is still so palpable that she feels it must be real. She tells her husband, who tries to discourage her from making the ruinous journey. But nothing can stop her, and she spends her savings on a ticket in to the city. All day long she walks up and down in front of the Bourse: no treasure. Finally, in despair, she prepares to go home empty-handed. A broker coming out of the Bourse sees her and asks her what the matter is. When she, weeping, tells him, he laughs. "You must never believe in such things. I, personally, have often dreamed that I've found treasure under the bed of a little inn in Zeeland where I've dreamed I'm staying."

U2's "Even Better Than the Real Thing" poses a paradox that rests at the heart of any ontological question and has its place in Giovanni's Gift *for that reason. Was the world more real before Pandora opened her famous box, or after?*

Some versions of the story end there, and others have the woman rushing home, tearing up the floorboards, and coming into her inheritance. The force of the story, for me, is the fact that each dream only has use as the key to the other. We cannot understand our own narratives except as the ground for some other's figure (or the figure for their ground). In *Plowing the Dark,* I tried to find two stories that exist at exact polar opposites of the unimaginable divide that we live spread across, two stories that have absolutely no point of contact, except that each is fated to save the other. . . .

MORROW: An intriguing function of that fairy tale is its unspoken invitation, even exhortation, for the listener to consider digging up the floorboards of dreams to see whether there isn't similar buried treasure in the form of a complementary story. Themes not only invite variation, but seem to demand them. It must be the organic and necessary result of our will to personalize the world, to make it habitable. For every book you write there are as many versions of it as readers who have taken it into their hands and read it. That's why I've always thought that all text is hypertext insofar as readers, during that inventive, passionate time they make their way through the narrative, breathe various life into the code once laid down on the page by an author long gone on to another labor, another encryption, often another sphere of existence altogether.

"No physically significant meaning can be attached to events happening 'now' at a far-flung place, because we can never know about or affect such events in any way." (Paul Davies, About Time*)*

I'm curious about the process of genesis of these books. Speaking with Joanna Scott about what triggers a novel, she describes small startling moments that in themselves wouldn't seem particularly fecund but spark a question, a curiosity, that then blossoms. A suit of clothes laid out on a bed, chosen by a widow for her husband to be buried in. A crashed car upside-down on the roadside which, when searched by the police who arrive on the scene, is empty. I recall, fifteen years ago, witnessing a woman drop her baby on Sixth Avenue and all in one fluid movement scoop it up and continue walking as if nothing out of the ordinary had happened. That moment marked the beginning of *Come Sunday* for me.

POWERS: Amazing: what a long journey that must have been, from that two-second catastrophe to the finished universe of your novel.

My books have sometimes come in a moment, sometimes in a year or more. *Three Farmers* was a moment. I was living in the Fens, behind the Museum of Fine Arts in Boston. Saturdays were—and still are, as far as I know—free days at the MFA, if you could get there before noon. I was there most Saturday mornings! One day, I walked over for the first American retrospective of a German photographer whose name meant nothing to me. I still have a visceral memory of walking into that room and coming into that almost seventy-year-old gaze of those three boys, as if they were waiting for me to close the loop. I leaned forward to read the caption: "Young Westerwald farmers on their way to dance." That was Saturday morning. On Monday, I gave my two weeks' notice at my job. Three years later, my "moment" was complete.

Another moment: this time I myself was in Germany. (I'd never been to Northern Europe prior to writing *Three Farmers* and I waited until I moved there to write my most American book.) I was now living in the little Dutch town I'd described in my first fiction. The Germans were having a rail promotion: 48 hours of unlimited travel for 50 marks. Determined to get my twenty-five dollars' worth, I decided not to sleep for the duration, but to keep sightseeing. So I found myself in a little Wesser town at four in the morning, wandering around and trying to see things in the dark. Wesser Renaissance pinnacles everywhere, and that weird, pastel, birthday cake painting on all the old town buildings. I found myself in a side street, trying to read a plaque on a wall in German. (My German comprehension is strictly a function of Dutch cognates.) At last I doped out the inscription: "On June 26, 1284, the children of Hamlin disappeared down this street." That instantly triggered the memory of my brother's account of serving as surgical resident in a large Los Angeles hospital ER on the afternoon when a killer opened fire in a nearby grade-school playground. Of the children who entered the emergency room that day, the staff was able to save two.

The "Le Gibet" movement from Ravel's Gaspard de la nuit *has haunted the entire composition of* Ariel. *The atmospheric chords that hover about the tolling note suggests titanic desert clouds over a thin line of horizon. I only learned after listening to the composition hundreds of times that Ravel wrote it while mourning his father's death in 1908. Ariel's father, too, is dying.*

Let me ask you the complementary question: when did you know that *Come Sunday* was finished? How do you get out of a book? *Can* you get out of a book?

MORROW: A moment of ambiguity, of imbalance, is what I look for as I near the end of a novel. The big ending is more the domain of Anton Bruchner and Metallica, or of didacticism. It has always been clear to me that too finished a finish may be too nature morte, or conversely too hopeful. The dead fish on the white plate with the bouquet of flowers in the vase on the table hopeful? Well, probably. So when I wrote my way to a moment when Krieger, the resourceful antihero of *Come Sunday,* is literally up a tree, somewhere near the border between Nicaragua and Honduras, observing down a pair of binoculars the temporary triumph of his sometime colleague and new nemesis, and has, at the very moment of utter moral, financial, political, human defeat, a new idea, I knew that was it. His thought is that he needs to get to a phone, but quick. He will redefine the argument, the rules, by reshaping the very game itself. How and what is of little consequence. And I understood that determinative fact. Readers of the book have asked me what Kreiger's idea was that would morph his fate and I've answered honestly I don't know. I do care, but am in the necessary dark. If I needed to know, I would have to break into that discrete world that was *Come Sunday*'s and still is. It was an unexpected, epiphanous instinct when I realized I didn't belong there any more. There was no further need of my imagining and to continue would have been to encroach. It has been true with the other novels, as well. Grace Brush's meditation about time in *Almanac.* Brice McCarthy down at Po-Sah-Son-Gay, a bend in the Rio Grande where the river speaks according to pueblo legend, his camera poised to photograph the old bridge the scientists crossed on their way to Los Alamos to invent the atom bomb. Grant listening to the bells ringing the Angelus in Rome even as he has no idea whether his hoped-for new life will come to pass in the last paragraph of *Giovanni's Gift.* These unfinished edgy instances are my clues to get out of the narrative, at least as its author. Whether we ever finally detach from these dreamed worlds is another matter. That is

"I am forced to admit a curious fact: the date of my birth is eighteen hundred and forty-two, the year when General Saint-Arnuad arrives to burn down the zaouia of the Beni Menacer, the tribe from which I am descended, and he goes into rapture over the orchards. . . . It is Saint-Arnuad's fire that lights my way out of the harem one hundred years later. . . . Before I catch the sound of my own voice, I can hear the death-rattles, the moans of those immured in the Dahra mountains and the prisoners on the Island of Sainte Marguerite. They provide my orchestral accompaniment. They summon me, encouraging my faltering steps, so that at the given signal, my solitary song takes off. The language of the Others . . . the gift my father lovingly bestowed on me, that language has adhered to me ever since like the tunic of Nessus: that gift from my father who, every morning, took me by the hand to accompany me to school. . . . ." (Assia Djebar, An Algerian Cavalcade*)*

not as easy, even were it desirable. Which isn't to say that coming to completion, discovering the finalizing form of a book is not satisfying, pure joy. I leave unreluctantly, yet remain inhabited by that offspring cosmos. The word "character" is one for which I hold no fondness, so given I don't think of the people who populate my narratives as characters, they recede—while life continues and a new novel rises into view—as might old friends for whom I will always have complicated affections but never see again.

Your *Plowing the Dark* has a particularly astounding ending. Without giving any hint of the end bracket to readers who haven't been there yet, could you tell me something about your endgame process in the book? Is the knowing when to leave the narrative a tougher decision than the entrance into it for you?

Sonata no. 28 in A Major, op. 101, is one of the most powerfully narrative of Beethoven's great piano works and suggests the tonal structure for a current book, The Prague Sonatas, *at whose fictional center resides a manuscript missing its opening pages but seems Beethovian. Among the thousand reasons to admire op. 101 is its midstream opening, a thought that reenters the sonata's flow in the third movement, modulated by the intervening emotional currencies. Beethoven has taught us how to* hear.

POWERS: I understand and agree with your desire to avoid too finished a finish, and there may be no better a description of our contemporary aesthetic than the resistance of closure. And yet, my endings have sometimes fought toward, if not finality, at least some denouement. But then, "denouement" originally means not wrapping up but untying. . . .

Sometimes my stories will want to do something to change the terms of the narrative justification, right at the end—some shift in focalization that will, with luck, deposit the reader on another level of the nested recursion that storytelling necessarily implies. A jump-shift in epistemic levels: the tale you've been reading becomes the book you are holding, as it does, in reverse, for the fictional inhabitants of that book. "Let's make a baby," Frank Todd tells Jan O'Deigh at the end of *Gold Bug,* cajoling her out of her half of a story that will make his whole, the story the reader has just finished.

Now the weird thing is that I find these "untied" endings will only work if I let them come upon me through the accident of design. I write the book to discover the ending that, unknown to me, has set me on the path of the story in the first place. The ending of *Plowing the Dark* completely blindsided me in its inevitability. Of course I meant it from the beginning; all the establishing elements were there from the first. But I hadn't a clue what I was doing until I did it. I find that if I work at the foundations, the vault will be there beforehand, even if I can't see it as I build. I may not get there the first time, but through the dismantling and recasting of successive drafts, I'm suddenly (some "suddenly"!) where I was trying to get. As the wonderfully ambiguous Roethke line has it: "I learn by going where I have to go."

Introduction to a Book Titled *Blue Sevens, or Protect Yourself From Witchcraft While You Get Rich*

Leslie Marmon Silko

THE WATER SUDDENLY HEAVES and washes against the sides of the bucket. While brushing your hair, you hear a voice croak from your left shoulder. His black tuxedo jacket disappears from the closet. You dream a dead husband who wets your bed. You dream a misunderstanding in which you do not tell him he may not have the book.

Someone wants power over you. Someone always wants a slave or a toy. Power comes from spells. Spells come from all places and times, and you never know which ones will work.

Right here let me say all powers come from God, whatever you call Her or Him or Them. Let's not leave any one out; I'll explain why in the chapters to come—especially the chapter on gambling machines.

This could happen: electronic communication with the dead, by tape recorder and computer. I will tell you all about that in the chapters to come; electronic devices are peculiarly vulnerable to interference from the spirit realms. The dead can tell you who is out to get you.

The Earth shrinks and turns faster and faster each year; with time and space running out, vicious emotions brew out of the scarcity of oxygen and water. Those hungry ghosts, Envy and Greed, descend on us and others.

The old people say there are four previous worlds below this world which is on the brink of passing to the realms below. No destruction, only change.

You will not only learn to protect against witchcraft while you get fabulously rich—this book includes valuable tips on how this book was written, for those of you who want to write a self-help book. We are going to write this book together—you and I—direct life experience being the best education for the student.

I was never very interested in the subject of stargazing or crystal-ball readings—seeing the future in flames or pans of water or goat's blood. Still, I keep a small quartz crystal as a knickknack on my writing desk in the hope the crystal might somehow attract or capture radio transmissons from outer space. I think they've made mistakes in the past with the sorts of Earth-people they tried to contact: apparently they have different strategies. No need to waste time on those of us who are their friends. They are saving us until they really need our political support. Instead, they try to learn what happens if they contact humans who are ignorant or afraid of them. They will eventually need us humans who support them; when they do, I want to get the call.

Are the alien beings merely human spirits gone into another realm or plane? If not, then do the alien beings have souls, or are they constructs of mathematical operations at the subatomic level?

"In the dust I can't recognize any of the old places." That's what one of them said! It sounds like something a dead soul might say, one not used to the loss or change of the corporeal self to the spirit self. "We are in a hospital here but it is different." "I have no shoes." "No air here." Later on they get used to it. (How can there be a "later" when they are dead and in a timeless state? Yes, the word "later" can't really be applied to the spirit realm.)

Do the dead contact the living? Do they want us to make money off them?

I am located in a small southwestern city, which will remain nameless to protect the people who help me. I will describe the dusty blue mountains that enclose the valley in its own smoke. Ancient volcanic deposits of ash fill the sky with fine dust from the denuded plain above the river bank.

For some years I made a decent living as a writer, until I was forced to find other means of support. I thought since I was choosing a new life and a new profession, I should do something completely different, even something I knew nothing about, so long as it was something that people truly needed enough to spend their money to get, no matter what. I expected the answer might lay in fortune-telling or sex.

Unfortunately, representatives of my former publisher followed me to Albuquerque before I could set out in a new field. An unpleasant situation developed over a large cash advance I took some years before to write a book—this book I am writing now, to get the goons off my back! I took off the next day for this town, and I don't think they can find me here. I intend to give them a book. After that, I really don't want to write anymore. The money is elsewhere, in fortune-telling and sex—something on-line—I have some ideas, but first I need to finish the book.

The summer heat was bearable only by sealing the windows of the motel room with aluminum foil. When I took the watchman's job, the real estate agent said the demolition was scheduled to begin at the end of August. I could have my pick of the rooms, she said, but only a few of them had air conditioners that worked. The land was in the process of being sold to foreign buyers, but there were problems with the financing that delayed the deal. The real estate agent stared off in the distance as she said this and I knew she was lying. All over the city there were motels and restaurants closed up with plywood and 2x4s. The lawns around the motel dried up and now the yellow frizzled grass was baked flat in the grayish clay. The hedges of dead oleanders all around the rooms seemed like fire hazards to me, and I made a mental note to tell the real estate agent the next time I saw her.

I avoided the heat of the day by staying inside, close to the air conditioner in the wall. The swimming pool was half full of green water; at night I sat outside and watched the toads come out and perch on the floating trash. They watched me with yellow headlight eyes, the small males on the backs of the big females. Through the dull haze of city light, only the brightest stars shine; later I walked along the river until I reached the cemetery where the darkness brings out more stars. I am careful to avoid the cracks where the earth subsided after the lawns dried up. In a few places the deepest cracks reveal concrete that seals the graves.

I sit for a long time and stare up at a big white star watching me from the southwest sky just above the horizon. The light reaches my eyes and completes a circuit across galaxies; perhaps the stars see their own reflection in my eyes and recognize a being here as they move westward. I swivel my ass on the ground and keep facing them until they set. Then in the east I see a bright blue star and two bright red stars—should one be the red planet, Mars? I feel they will reveal themselves to me. I will learn how to locate them in the sky. I watch them for hours on end and begin to feel familiar with a few. All summer I look back at the twin stars that form the monster's eyes on the southern horizon. The bright blue star is below the snake's mouth in the cluster I used to know as Orion's Bow. I leave all my former life behind me.

I know I have to change my diet. In the heat, heavy food or meats leave me queasy. The old folks used to say, Watch out what you eat because the animal's spirit may be offended by how you cook him or if any is wasted. To be on the safe side, eat no flesh of any kind—you can offend other beings without realizing what you've done. The best intentions won't save you. If you don't eat killed beings, you reduce the risk.

I buy cellophane bags of trail mix at the convenience store down the street; the days of supermarkets in this neighborhood are no more. All I drink is water from a tap out back by the gate. I dream vividly and wake in cold panic sweat from a nightmare that has followed me since childhood. In the dream there is only dry sand pouring over and all around me. Why the terror I feel when I dream it? Here is where I got the idea for part of a chapter in the book—I begin to write down my dreams and keep track of what happens later. I want to decipher the secret language of dreams—something everyong might use.

For example, dreams about cattle are considered particularly dangerous by cultures as distinct as the Diné, the Irish and the Bantu. Even for cattlekeepers, a dream of cattle portends disaster. Incidents with cattle also lead to grave consequences—a man hits a black and white cow with his Cadillac in the late afternoon and suffers a heart attack the following morning. Dreams of sand and only sand commemorate the blood memory of infanticide—dreams of sand warn of imminent destruction.

Anyone can make money and get rich. It really is easy and quick. You simply make up your mind, muster all your desire, all your drive, with the will of your very being. Pledge your life to money and nothing else. Only you can limit yourself once you dedicate your life to making money. No act is ruled out, of course, and laws don't apply in this realm of desire.

I make the note for the beginning of the later chapter about getting rich. I try to write the first chapters first, but all that comes to me are ideas for the later chapters.

Write it down as it comes to you. Don't worry about the form—it knows itself and you only need to write it to see. Go back and reread it each day. The reader wants to have case studies and the personal experiences of the author in a self-help book like this.

If you have the will, you can get rich simply with what you were born with: your flesh and blood. Step One: Move to any state capital. Frequent pubs and bars where legislative staffs meet for drinks after work. Always keep the video camera rolling in the bedroom for lucrative videotape sales later on. More about this in the chapters to come.

Today the air is chilled by snowfall in the mountains far to the north. I can't get the electric wall heater to work in the room so I spend most of the morning and early afternoon drinking tea in the dingy Chinese restaurant down the street. The place is so warm the front window steams over. Two old Chinese women run it. Two sisters? A mother and daughter? A mother-in-law and a daughter-in-law? They seem to hate one another. The place was done all in red, but a long time ago—the red carpet is dark with grime while the red plastic of the booths and the red formica tabletops faded to lighter shades. Overhead the silk tassels of the paper lanterns are faded to a shade of porno pink. At lunch time, booths fill up with Mexican cowboys for the buffet and cold beer; they are the only customers I ever see there. They all talk on cell phones. It seems the Chinese women take turns cooking and waiting on customers. Today the elder woman seems irritated with me when I pay at the cash register. They must think I'm homeless. I have the cash to buy a space heater but why do that when there are plenty other rooms that have working heaters? I don't know how long I'll be here. It will warm up again tomorrow or the next day.

Outside on the street, the wind is calm. I decided to walk into the desert to wait for dark. I watch the sun sink behind the lava hills, but darkness, even the twilight, is a ways off. I think about waiting. All we humans do is wait; for the dark, for the daylight, for the rain, for food or sex; we wait for that gift, that message, that bolt out of the blue. We wait for the beginning and we wait for the end, full of dread, and pray the stars stand still, and the present never to end so the executioner never arrives.

First lesson: don't believe everything you've been told about the sky and the stars and planets. We know we are small. At night the benevolent beings of immense proportions can be seen watching us—of course they are alive—watch them and one can see the pulse of the light we all came from. For an instant I suddenly feel their tenderness and love for all beings but then it is gone. Back in my room I dig through the bag of videos to see what I've missed over the years with the losers I've dated. The actor dressed in black executioner's robes enters the prison cells with a huge hard-on and ejaculates in the condemned man's face. The money to be made these days isn't in the usual fare. All the familiar pussy-and-cock terrain belongs to the amateurs on-line—exhibitionist husband-and-wife teams. I watch one after the other and lose track of which are women and which are men impersonating women, until I finally feel drowsy before dawn. I sleep the rest of the day and neglect writing the book. Still I feel I must go back every night to watch the stars to see what will happen.

Then one night in January when the weather was warm, kids broke into the boarded-up motel office and set a small fire. When I got back from my night with the stars, the fire engines were just leaving. I knew the real estate agent would want to know why I wasn't there to stop them that night. A couple of days passed but eventually she came with a cancellation notice for the fire insurance in her hand. She was disappointed in me; the others in her group wanted to hire a man as night watchman but she had argued for a woman.

I lie and say I was at the laundromat; I promise not to do my laundry late at night when the punks gather outside their clubs. I knew she didn't want to advertise again for a watchman. I asked her about a gun then. She agreed. It is dangerous, especially for a woman alone. Later that afternoon a messenger in a small white pickup brought the parcel with the pink nickel-plated .32 revolver with a box of ammunition. A woman's gun.

Maybe it wasn't the kids. I don't see any punks around the place. For all I know it is the police who set that fire in the motel office. I see them parked across the street when I come back from my night of stargazing. They sit with the headlights off. They used to catch up on their paperwork by flashlight, but so many of them got shot, they stopped. Now they only travel in pairs. They sit in the dark and smoke—the red ash ends don't move much; they seldom talk so they can hear the approach of footsteps. I avoid them like poison; they will shoot anything that moves they are so afraid.

At the back of the motel lot, I use the locked gate by lifting it from its hinges—an old trick I'd learned in the days I was a country girl and didn't let fences stop me. I cut the ranchers' wire fences to watch the cattle scatter onto reservation land where a couple of fat heifers always got stuck in quicksand. The real estate agent warned me the back of the lot was full of rattlesnakes; they were trying to hire an exterminator but so far no company wanted the job. In January, the snakes are underground—under the pile of broken concrete is my guess for the site of their den. I sit next to a hole every day the weather permits. Today the sky is dark blue layers like the bedding I found in the motel room. The last watchman left in a hurry without his shopping bag of dirty magazines and porno videotapes. The wind gusts out of the northeast. Another place this would mean rain, but not here. I close my eyes against the flying grit as I hurry inside. If I sit near the snake hole everyday, they will be used to my scent when they come back out.

What follows is Chapter One: *Those Who May Wish You Harm. . . .*

The Big-Breasted Pilgrim

Ann Beattie

OUR HOUSE IN THE FLORIDA KEYS is down a narrow road, half a mile from a convenience store with a green neon sign that advertises "Bait and Basics." Lowell's sister, Kathryn, called to get us to arrange for a car to drive her from Miami. She considers everywhere Lowell has ever lived to be Siberia, including Saratoga, New York, which she saw only once, during a blizzard. TriBeCa, circa 1977, was Siberia. Ditto Ashland, Oregon. In all those places, Lowell had what he now calls The Siberian Brides: his first and second wives, who gradually became as incomprehensible to him as foreigners: Tish, who lived with us in Saratoga and later in TriBeCa; Leigh Anne Leighton—a name so melodic he always speaks of her that way, even though it seems inordinately formal—who lived with us for a month in Ashland before flying to Los Angeles for her grandfather's funeral, from which she never returned. This was no case of riding forever 'neath the streets of Boston, however: she got a Mexican divorce and remarried a youth Lowell and I recently saw on *Late Night with Conan O'Brien,* playing soprano sax with a group called "Bobecito and the Brazen Beauties."

My own life is nothing like Lowell's. The joke is that I am his Boswell, and to the extent that I used to take dictation in Lowell's precomputer days, I suppose I have been a sort of Boswell—though I doubt the man, himself, ever scrubbed down a shower with Tilex, or would have, even if shower stalls—to say nothing of the excessively effective cleaning products we have now—existed. Nor, say, did we mistake Ashland for the Hebrides, though Lowell and I have inevitably arrived at pithy pronouncements as a prelude to packing up and leaving place after place.

I, Richard Howard Manson, was an Army brat, living in thirteen different locations by the time I started high school. The one good thing about that was that it made me pretty unflappable, though at the same time it's given me a wanderlust I've tired of as I've aged. Lowell makes fun of me for trying to decondition myself by accepting vicarious travel in place of the real thing: I subscribe to almost every travel magazine, and view cassettes of foreign cities, or even silly resort promo tapes, almost every night before bed. Lowell calls this "nicotine patch travel." Passing in front of the TV, he'll drag hard on an imaginary cigarette, then toss the phantom cig on the floor, grind it out, and slap his right arm to his left bicep, exhaling with instant relief. As it happens, I quit smoking—I mean real cigarettes—cold turkey. The travel addiction has not been so easy to break, but since I like my job, and since my employer is terminally itchy, he has often been pleased to take advantage of my weakness. The way wheedling wives have talked husbands into second and third babies, Lowell has persuaded me to give a month at the Chateau Marmont, or a few years in a rented Victorian in upstate New York, a try. He never claims we're staying, though he doesn't present the trips as vacations, either. When he had a larger network of friends—that period, about ten years ago, when everybody seemed to be between marriages—our ostensible reason for going somewhere would often be that we were on a mercy mission to cheer up so-and-so. Once there, so-and-so would be found, miraculously, to have cheered *us* up, and so we would stay for a longer infusion of friendliness, until so-and-so became affiliated with the next Mrs. so-and-so, who would inevitably dislike us, or until that moment when a blizzard hit and we thought of being in the sun, or when summer heat settled like an itchy, wooly mantle.

In most of the places we've lived, there have been constants, Kathryn's visits among them. Other constants are a few ceramics made by a friend, a couple of very nice geometrically patterned rugs, and our picture mugs, depicting each of us sitting on camels in front of pyramids. There's also the favorite this, or the favored that—small things, like jars of homegrown herbs, or the amazing sea nettle suntan lotion that can be ordered by calling an 800 number that relays a request for shipping to the apothecary in St. Paul de Vence. Our Barbour jackets are indispensible, as is a particular wine pull, no longer manufactured. When you travel as much as we do, you can seem to fixate on what looks to other people to be trivia. I make it a point to be casual about the wine pull, letting other people use it whenever they insist upon being helpful, though I often awaken in the night, convinced that it has been thrown away during the clean-up period, and then I go downstairs and open the drawer and see it, but return to bed convinced that I have nevertheless had an accurate premonition of its fate following the next dinner party.

Lowell is a chef, and a quite brilliant one. He has one of those metabolisms that allows him to eat anything and remain thin. I, too, can and do eat anything, my diabetes having been cured by a Japanese acupuncturist, but unlike Lowell, everything I eat increases my weight. At six feet, I am two hundred and seventy pounds—so imposing that the first time I hurried inside to pick up some items at our "Bait And" convenience store, the teenager behind the counter raised his hands above his head. This has become a standing joke with Lowell, who sometimes imitates the teenager when he and I cross paths in the house, or when I bring the evening cocktails to the back deck.

Lowell and I met more than twenty years ago, when I was driving for my cousin's private car company in New York City. Lowell was in town that evening to be a guest chef for the weekend at the short-lived but much-admired Le Monde Oujourd'hui. I picked him up at La Guardia in a downpour, and on the way in—he was coming from a birthday party for Craig Claiborne, in upstate New York—we talked about our preferences in junk food, rock and roll and—I should have been suspicious—whether any city that was a state capital had any zip to it. But this gives the impression that we chattered away. We spoke only intermittently, and I had little to say, except that I liked Montpelier, Vermont, very much, but that was probably because I'd only visited the state once, during a heat wave in New York, and it had seemed to me I'd gone to heaven. This brought up the subject of gardens, and I heard for the first time, though others no doubt knew it, the theory of planting certain flowers to repel insects from certain vegetables. On the streets of Brooklyn you didn't hear things like that—Brooklyn Heights being the place I had settled when I was discharged from the Marine Corps. I was living in my uncle's spare bedroom, driving for my cousin's car company, making extra money to help support the baby that would be born to Rita and me—that was going to happen, whether she left me or not, as she was always threatening to do—though less than four months from the day I picked Lowell up, my twenty-two-year-old, in-the-process-of-becoming-ex wife, as well as the child she was carrying, would be dead after a collision on the Merritt Parkway. In the years following the accident, this has never come up in conversation, so even if I'd been able to look into a crystal ball, I would still have chatted with Lowell about Sara Lee chocolate cupcakes and the extraordinarily addictive quality of Cheetos. I do not care to discuss matters of substance, as Kathryn has correctly stated many times. Both she and Lowell know the fact of my wife's death, of course. My uncle told them, the time they came to a barbecue at his apartment, six months or so after I met them. By that time, I was in Lowell's employ, and he was working on the second of his cookbooks, trying to decide whether he should take a very lucrative, full-time position at a New Orleans hotel. I had become his secretary because—as it turned out, to my own surprise—I seem to have a tenacity about succeeding in minor matters, which are all that frustrate the majority of people, anyway. That is, after some research, I would find the telephone number of the dive shop in Tortola that was across the street from a phoneless shack, where the non-English-speaking cook had used a certain herb mixture on the grilled chicken he had served to me and Lowell that Lowell felt he must find a way to reproduce. (Not that these things ever struck him in the moment. He often has a delayed reaction to certain preparations, but his insistence on deciphering the mystery is always in direct proportion to the time elapsed between eating and doing the double-take.) My next step would be to send Chef Lowell T-shirts to the helpful salesman in the dive shop, one for him, his wife and their two children and—FedEx's ideas about not sending cash in envelopes be damned—money to bribe both salesman and chef. It was a minor matter to get a friend of a friend, who was a stewardess, to use her free hours before her flight took off again from Beef Island to take a cab to the dive shop and pick up a small quantity of the ground herb concoction, which chemical analysis later revealed to be powdered rhino horn (one could well wonder how they got that in Tortola), mixed with something called dried Annie flower, to which was added a generous pinch—as Lowell suspected—of simple ginger. Of course I see these small successes of mine as minor victories, but to Lowell they seem a display of inventive brilliance. He describes himself, quite unfairly, I think, as a plodder. He will try a recipe a hundred times, if that's what it takes. But to me that isn't plodding; it's being a perfectionist, which, God knows, too few people are these days.

Tonight, before Kathryn arrives, Lowell's new love interest will be arriving for drinks. She has no idea that he is a famous chef, who has published numerous cookbooks, writes a monthly column for one of the most prestigious food magazines, and teaches seminars on the art of sautéing in St. Croix, where we are put up annually at the Chenay Bay Beach Resort. I have met this woman, who has a name like something out of a cheap, English romance, Daphne Crowell, exactly once, when I stumbled into them—literally—on the back deck. It was a moonless night, exceedingly dark, and the two of them had gone downstairs to observe our neighbor's speedy little boat coming around the point with another load of drugs. She had been wearing *my* bathrobe, which she simply helped herself to, after taking it from the hook on the back of *my* bathroom door. There she was, leaning against the rail at the edge of the deck like a car's hood ornament, when I awoke from slumbering under a blanket on a chaise longue just in time to see her untie the sash and pull off the robe, giggling as she held it forward to flap in the breeze—*my* robe—like some big flag at a parade. I'm sure the silly gesture was equally appreciated by our neighbor, whose own "secretary" wears night goggles for land-to-shore vision, in case the police are waiting in ambush with their panthers, or whatever intimidating beasts they currently favor. Anyway: Daphne is a fool, but nobody ever said Lowell didn't like to waste his time. A recipe he will fret over forever, but any woman will do—particularly on a night when Kathryn, whom he is still intimidated by, is arriving, all big-city bluster and Oh, how are you doing out here in the boonies? Since starting a graduate program in writing at The New School, she treats everyone as interesting material. She has been trying for years to see if she can make me mad by insisting that I read *The Remains of the Day,* which—I have not told her, and will not—I have, in fact, viewed on television. I understand completely that she wishes me to see myself as some pathetic, latter-day servant who has wasted his life by missing the forest for the trees. If she thinks I live to serve, she's wrong. I simply live to avoid my previous life.

"Everything ready out here?" Lowell calls. He has opened the French doors and is propping them open with cement-filled conch shells. Everything ready, indeed: he's the one who set out the cheese torte, under the big, upside-down brass collander. All I had to do was bring out the gallon of Tanqueray, the tonic and some Key limes. My Swiss Army knife will do for slicing, and even mixing.

"Are you going deaf, Richard? Half the things I ask you, you don't respond to."

He's mad at me not because I haven't answered, really, but because I refused to drive to Miami to get his sister. The ride wouldn't have bothered me, but two and a half hours with Kathryn in a car would be more than I could take, by approximately two hours and twenty-five minutes.

"Richard . . . is there a possibility that not only do you not hear me, but that you have no curiosity about why I'm standing here, moving my lips?"

"I thought maybe you'd just had something tasty," I say.

A pause. "You did hear me, then? You just chose not to answer?"

"What's the point of these random women?" I say.

He walks toward me. "I don't know why it upset you so much that she borrowed your robe," he says. "Anything that smacks of exuberance, you insist upon seeing as drunken foolishness."

"Remember the Siberians," I say. "And the one you picked up in South Beach, who wanted to sue for palimony after one weekend."

He looks at my knife, open to the longest blade, next to the bottle of gin. "This was your idea of a stirrer?" he says.

"She's so spontaneous and uninhibited," I say. "Let's see if she doesn't just use her finger."

As if that were a cue, we hear the crunch of gravel under Daphne's tires. Since today is Friday, she will have spent the day making fruit smoothies for tourists. On Monday and Tuesday, the only other days she works, she has been substituting for a dentist's receptionist, who was mugged in Miami during her ninth month of pregnancy. Six weeks after the mugging, the woman has still not given birth. If nothing happens by Monday, they are going to induce labor—though apparently what the woman is most afraid of is leaving her house. I know all this because Daphne phones the house often, and when I answer she always feels obliged to strike up a conversation.

Much oohing and aahing at the front door: such a lovely house, so secluded, such beautiful plants everywhere. The unexpected delight of seeing roses growing in profusion in the Keys, blah blah blah.

She has brought me—the absurd cow has brought me—a plastic manatee. She has brought Lowell three birds-of-paradise, wrapped by the flower shop in lavender paper, which she pronounces "coals to Newcastle." But the manatee . . . we don't already have one of those, do we? No, we don't. We don't even have a rubber ducky to float in the bathwater. We're so . . . you know . . . old.

Behold: she has on gold Lycra pants, gold thong sandals and a football-sized shirt with enormous shoulder pads. The material is iridescent: blue, shimmering gold, flashing orange, everything sparkling as if Tinker Bell, in a mad mood, applied the finishing touches. The sparkly stuff is also in her hair, broken lines of it, as if to provide a passing lane. All this, because she put a heaping teaspoon of protein powder into Lowell's smoothie, gratis. I see Lowell slip his arm around her shoulder as the two of them walk to the edge of the deck. I go into the house to get glasses and ice.

When I return, with the three glasses on a tray, she is in mid-banality: the loveliness of the sky, etc. Well: Kathryn's pathetic butler would bow out at this point, but in our house the servant drinks and eats with the employer. The employer has no real friends except for the servant, in good part because he is given to sarcasm, periods of dark despair, temper tantrums and hypochondriacal illnesses, alternating with intense self-appreciation. Similarly, the servant has been co-opted by a life of leisure, a feeling of gratitude. Lowell is far easier to take care of than a wife, certainly easier to care for than a child, much easier to look after than the majority of dogs, by which I mean no disrespect to either party, as a dog was the one thing I ever had a strong attachment to and deep admiration for. The Marines, I found out, were sociopaths. Imagine the days of my youth when I thought I would prove my manhood and patriotism by outdoing my Army Lieutenant Colonel father by joining the Marines. *Sir, Yes Sir!* And Lowell thinks there might be a problem with tracking down a particular herb mixture? I could kiss his feet. Though I settle for shining his shoes—or did, in pre-Reebok days.

Lowell and Daphne have decided to take a ride in the kayak, tied to the end of the pier. This may leave me alone to greet Kathryn, who should arrive in twenty minutes or so, if everything goes according to schedule. Lately, I have begun to think that she is angry because she has had to pity me for so many years. The choked-up version my uncle gave her of the event that ostensibly ruined my young life registered so strongly with her that she has never been able to put it aside. The sheer misery of what I went through gets superimposed, I suspect, on her desire to be competitive with me, makes her back off from trying, more tenaciously, to solve the puzzle that is me: a street kid who gradually became educated (nothing else to do those four long, cold years we lived in Saratoga), only to shun those with similar education—to shun everyone, in fact. What she doesn't know is that I knew almost immediately my marriage was a mistake, I never wanted to become a father—the accident was my way out, not only from that situation, but for all time. Daphne could have spooned so much protein powder into my fruit drink it would have had the consistency of sawdust, and I would only have paid her and walked away. I've faltered a bit, from time to time; Kathryn would love to know with whom, and when, but my uncle spoke so graphically to her, years ago, that he managed to instill even future shame—that's the way I think of the service he inadvertently did for me—so that she still can't bring herself to ask outright what the story is with some hulking street kid who has no girlfriend and no friends, who is aging companionably, in the lower Florida Keys, with her bizarre, neurotic brother.

They descend into the kayak. Daphne has found something, already, to giggle about. She has left one shoe on the dock, it seems. I am summoned to help. Once seated, Lowell doesn't want to risk toppling the boat, I suppose. I don't play deaf; I respond to his entreaty, and at the edge of the dock I bend and pick up her gold flip-flop, for which she thanks me profusely, and then Prince Charming and Cinderella set sail. Which leaves me with the four-cheese torta with rye saffron crust that I don't mind being the first to cut into, taking out a neat wedge with the knife and admiring its firm, yet creamy consistency. It is flecked with rosemary and ground pink peppercorns: the appetizer other chefs have been stealing and altering almost from the minute Lowell invented it. What none of them have guessed, to my knowledge, is the presence of the single, simmered vanilla bean. I bite off a tiny piece, chew slowly and consider the possibility that anything as ambrosial as this might be interchangeable with love.

The Triple J Cab pulls into the drive as the sun is setting. Kathryn alights from the front seat—wouldn't you know she'd be so ballsy she'd sit up front. She seems to have only a small bag with her, which means, thank God, she won't be visiting longer than she said. But then, from the backseat, a skinny woman emerges, holding her own small bag, wearing a beret and a long white scarf, which matches her white shorts and her white T-shirt, over which she wears a droopy vest. "Paradise!" she exclaims, throwing back her head and enthusing, as if the sky were awaiting her verdict. Yes, indeed—but who is she?

She is Nancy Cummins—Cummins without a "g"—who is en route to a bris to be held in a suite at the Casa Marina hotel, in Key West. She is an acquaintance of Kathryn's from New York—a highlighter, whom Kathryn arranged to meet at JFK, when it turned out the two women would be taking trips at the same time, almost to the same destination. ("Highlighter"—meaning that she paints streaks in rich people's hair.)

I carry their two small bags. Inside one, it will later turn out, is a narcotized kitten.

"Where's my brother?" Kathryn asks. Rushing to also ask: "Did he forget I was coming?"

"He's in a kayak with his girlfriend," I say.

"See?" Kathryn says to the highlighter. "No one meets anybody in

New York; you come to Siberia, and *bingo.*"

"Bingo," I say. "I haven't thought of bingo in a million years."

"They don't play games. They read books," Kathryn says to the highlighter, as if I'm not there.

"You know," I say, realizing I'm about to make a fool of myself, but not caring, "when she said you were a highlighter, I thought at first she must mean of books. Those yellow markers you underline with. You know: highlighters."

"No," the highlighter says. "I've always stayed as far from school as I could get."

I put their bags on the kitchen counter. It's only then that the highlighter unzips her bag and removes what I take, at first, to be a wad of material. It is a six-week-old black kitten, sleeping what looks to me like the sleep of death, though the thing does twitch when she puts it on the counter.

"Isn't it adorable?" Kathryn says.

Oh, absolutely. Now we have a cow, a manatee and a kitten.

"Did he chill my favorite wine, or did he forget?" Kathryn wants to know, pulling open the refrigerator door. In the shelf sit four bottles of Vichon Chardonnay, with two cans of Tecate at either end seeming to brace the bottles like bookends. Kathryn plucks a bottle from the shelf. I open the drawer and pantomime that I would be happy to extract the cork. But no: she's a liberated woman, none of that harmful stereotyping of the helpless female allowed. Flip forward until two A.M., when I'll have the anxiety dream.

The highlighter opens the door and seizes a Tecate.

"Key lime?" I offer, reaching behind the slightly quivering kitten and extracting one from a basket.

"What do you do with it?"

"You squirt some in your beer," Kathryn says.

"I hope . . . I hope it isn't too much trouble, my just, you know, *coming here,*" the highlighter says, as if the idea of limes used to enhance the flavor of drinks has just defined some complexity for her.

"Look at this! Next Sunday's *Times Book Review*—by subscription!" Kathryn says.

"Yes. We alternate with our reading of *The Siberian Daily.*"

"Didn't I tell you he has a clever come-back for everything?" Kathryn says.

As if this weren't a put-down, the highlighter extends her hand and says, "I can't believe my good fortune in being here. I mean, it's very generous of you to have me. Because what a coincidence, my flying to this part of Florida—I *guess* I'm in the right part of Florida!—just when . . ."

I shake her hand. It is what we might have done from the first, if she had said immediately how happy she was to be where she was, and if Kathryn hadn't plunked the two bags in my hand. Does this happen to other people? This finding oneself suddenly greeting someone, or introducing oneself, long after things have gotten rolling? Roger Verge once introduced himself to me on the second day of his visit, following his dinner of the night before, and after preparing lunch, for which he'd had me shop earlier that morning. Does some strange, sudden formality overcome people, or is there something I do that makes them feel so immediately a part of the family that they forget social form? I've asked Lowell, and that is his explanation. Just as his sister would never miss an opportunity to express skepticism about me, Lowell lets no opportunity pass when he can reassure me of my worthiness, by putting a positive spin on things. Leaving aside those periods when he is too depressed to speak, that is.

"And so you . . . you stay out here and create recipes together?" the highlighter asks.

"That sounds so domestic," I say. "No, actually. I have nothing to do with composing the recipes, and now that Lowell has mastered the computer, I sometimes don't even—"

"Tell her about tracking down the powdered rhino horn," Kathryn says, stroking the collapsed kitten.

"She's talking about my tracking down an herbal mixture Lowell had interest in," I begin.

"Did you go to jail?"

"Pardon?"

"For importing the rhinocerous."

"I didn't . . . I didn't import a whole rhinocerous. . . ."

"The drug smuggler around the corner would probably be willing to do that for a price," Kathryn says.

The highlighter looks at me, wide-eyed. "She told me about the guy who runs drugs."

"And did she tell you that we disapprove, and that we're spying on him for the Federal Government?"

"No."

"Only kidding. We don't care what our neighbors do."

"For one thing, you'd have to be delusional to live here on the edge of nowhere and think in terms of having a neighbor," Kathryn says.

"I know everybody in my building," the highlighter says. "Of course, there are only four apartments."

"Apartments," Kathryn muses, strolling onto the back deck. "Can you stand here and imagine one going up across the way?"

"No," the highlighter says.

"We've left places because of equally ridiculous scenarios," I say.

"Kathryn told me that you two have lived just about everywhere."

"She did? Well, as an adult I've only—"

"Rhinoceros," the highlighter says. "Isn't that an aphrodisiac, or something?"

The wall phone rings, sending a short spasm through the kitten, who has dragged itself almost underneath it, before collapsing again.

That is what we were doing, what the three of us were talking about, when a chef whose name I faintly computed called from Coral Gables, in quite a dither, wanting me to inform Lowell that George Stephanopoulos would be calling momentarily.

The president, it seems, is a lover of mango. He has recently sampled Lowell's preparation of baked mango gratinée—usually served as an accompaniment to chicken or fish—at the home of a friend, who prepared it from Lowell's newest cookbook. The president loved it, as well as the main course, which was apparently prepared out of the same cookbook. Furthermore, Mrs. Clinton has become intent upon sampling some of Lowell's newer dishes (*but no chocolate chip cookies,* goes through my mind) and wonders if they might recruit Lowell to cook for them during an upcoming weekend at a friend's borrowed home in Boca Raton. Mrs. Clinton herself will call to confer about the menu, which would be for ten people—three of them teenage girls—whenever it is convenient.

I cover the receiver with my hand and whisper: "When can you talk to Hillary?"

Kathryn, from the back deck, maintains this is all a prank.

"Any time," Lowell whispers back.

"Would Mrs. Clinton be able to talk to Mr. Cartwright now?"

"Probably she would right after the Kennedy Center performance," George Stephanopoulos says. "Give me five minutes. Let me get back to you on that."

The phone doesn't ring for an hour. By the time it does ring, the kitten is upright and spunky, chasing after Key limes rolled across the kitchen floor.

"George Stephanopoulos," the voice says. "Are you . . . there's a landing field in Marathon, correct?"

"Yes," I say.

"Big planes don't come in, though?"

I see the dinner slipping away. "No," I say.

"Is there a roasted pig? Not at the airport, I mean. I mean, is there a recipe for roasted pig?"

"Prepared with a cumin marinade, and served with pistachio pureed potatoes."

"The Clintons have left for an evening performance, but if it wouldn't be inconvenient, I think Mrs. Clinton would like to call when they return. It might be eleven, ten-thirty or eleven—something like that."

"Mr. Cartwright stays up until well after midnight."

"I'll bet I'm interrupting your dinner right now. Tell me the truth."

"No. Actually, we've been watching what has turned out to be an incredible sunset and we've been waiting for your call."

"Sunset," Stephanopoulos says, with real longing in his voice. "Okay," he says. "Speak to you later."

"This is *amazing,*" the highlighter says.

"Sting and Trude Styler rented a house in Key West last winter," Daphne says. "Also, David Hyde Pierce, who plays Frasier's brother, took a date for dinner on Little Palm Island, and he tipped really well."

Since the moment they were introduced, Daphne and the highlighter have gotten along famously. They're sitting on the kitchen floor, rolling limes around like some variation of playing marbles, and the kitten is going gonzo.

"When would the dinner be?" Lowell asks.

"They're going to call around eleven," I say. "You can ask."

"You ask," Lowell says. "I'd make a fool of myself if I had to talk to Hillary Clinton."

On the deck, Kathryn plucks a stalk of lemon grass growing from a clay pot, puts it between her two thumbs and blows loudly. The kitten slithers under the refrigerator.

"Reminds me of certain of the doctor's patients," Daphne says, watching the kitten disappear. "You know, what really drives me crazy is that when they call, they give every last detail about their problem, as if the dentist cares whether the tooth broke because they were eating pizza or gnawing on a brick."

The kitten emerges, followed by what looks like its own kitten: a quick moving Palmetto bug that disappears under the stove.

"Jesus Christ," Lowell says. "Don't we have bug spray?"

Antonio, the chef from Coral Gables, calls back. He wants Lowell to know that since the president will be having lunch at his restaurant, he is not at all offended that the president wishes to dine with us. Every effort must be made, however, not to duplicate dishes. He asks, bleakly, if we have had any success in finding fresh estragon in Southern Florida.

"If this were *Frasier,* Niles would run out and buy a speaker-phone before the president called back. He'd hook it up, but then in the middle of the call it would blow up, or something," Daphne says.

We all look at her.

"I always watch because I like my namesake," Daphne says.

"That's what he said?" Lowell says, pouring chardonnay into his glass. "He came right out and said the president liked my potato-mango gratinée?"

"What do you think he'd say to lead into the subject that Clinton wanted to come to dinner? That the president had been very depressed about the Whitewater investigation?"

"No mention of Whitewater!" Lowell says.

"It's like: don't think of a pink elephant," the highlighter says.

Kathryn comes in from the back deck. "The bugs are starting to bite," she says.

"Also, where are we going to seat them?" Lowell says.

I say: "At the dining room table."

"Twelve, with the leaf up, but fourteen? Where will we get the chairs?"

"You can probably leave that up to someone on his staff."

"This isn't going to happen," Kathryn says. "You really think the Clintons are going to come bumping down that dirt road like the Beverly Hillbillies?"

"Gravel," Lowell says. "Also, we could easily get it paved."

"Remember when Queen Elizabeth went to Washington, and they took her to the home of a typical black family, or whatever it was, and the woman went up to the Queen and gave her a big hug, and all the newspapers had the photograph of the Queen going into shock when she was touched?" the highlighter says.

"A good suggestion: a simple handshake with the president and first lady," Lowell says to the highlighter.

"If I had to talk to them, I'd probably piss my pants," the highlighter says.

"We could mention to Hillary that treatment for adult incontinence was not often covered under current health policies," I say.

"We could say that *yellow water* was better than *white water,"* Daphne chimes in.

"I just realized: I didn't put the carpaccio out," I say, going to the refrigerator.

"Let's spray ourselves and knock back some more wine out on the deck before we eat," Kathryn says.

"Yes, but . . . *we won't swallow!"* the highlighter says.

Well before eleven, we've run out of jokes.

"This is *the* most strange and exciting day I have had since Madonna came in to get her roots retouched after closing. There she was, looking like a little wet dog, with her hair shampooed and the handkerchief-size towel behind her neck, and she wouldn't speak to me directly, she said everything to her bodyguard, who relayed it to me. All of a sudden, instead of touching up her roots, I was supposed to dry her hair, set the dryer on low and give it to him, actually, and let him dry it, and I was supposed to highlight her wig, instead. And then we had a blackout. The whole place went dark, and do you know, her bodyguard thought it was deliberate. It wasn't Con Ed fucking up again, it was a plot to kidnap Madonna! He kept lighting this butane lighter he had with him and looking incredibly fierce. She was smoking a cigarette and talking to herself. She was dabbing at her neck and saying that she wished she could be somewhere else, and then, in almost no light, the bodyguard kept telling me to hurry up with highlighting the wig."

"What did she name that baby?" Kathryn asks.

"LuLu," Daphne says.

I correct her: "Lourdes."

"He reads the tabloids in the food store," Kathryn says.

At eleven-thirty, George Stephanopoulos has not called back. After Letterman's monologue, we decide to skip Burt Bacharach and call it a night. The kitten has been sleeping on its back, like a dog, for quite a long time. The highlighter casually reaches for it, as if it were her evening bag.

"You're sure it was George Stephanopoulos?" Lowell says to me, as Kathryn volunteers to lead the ladies to their rooms.

"It had the ring of truth about it," I say.

"I bet the president would have liked the dinner we had tonight, and then he could have played 'Last Year at Marienbad' with the three of us!" Daphne giggles, as she follows Kathryn toward the stairs.

I am amazed that the twenty-something highlighter doesn't ask,

"What's 'Last Year at Marienbad'?"

Then she does, pronouncing the last two words so that they resonate amusingly. The words are "Marine" and "bad."

The mere idea that I might have thought to take down George Stephanopoulos's phone number provokes merriment at breakfast (frittata and an orange-coconut salad; two-shot con leches all around).

Antonio, his wife informs me when I call, is spending the day fishing off a pontoon boat. She will have him return my call when he returns.

"Maybe he decided McDonald's was easier," Daphne says.

"Impossible. His wife was going to be along," Lowell reminds her.

Someone who is driving from Miami for the bris will pick up the highlighter at the discount sandal store ten minutes from our house, and give her a lift to the Casa Marina. I'll give her a ride out to the highway in another half hour.

"You'd think they'd call," the highlighter says.

We sit around, like a bunch of kids nobody's asked to dance. In a little while, when I go out to sweep the deck, the highlighter follows me.

"Are you guys gay?" she says.

"No," I say, "but you aren't the first to wonder."

"Because you're hanging out in the Keys. And you've been together so long, and all."

"Right," I say.

"What kind of tree is that?" she says, stepping around the pile of leaves.

"Kapok. It doesn't always drop its leaves, but when it does, it does."

"So listen," she says. "I didn't offend you by asking?"

"No," I say.

"Because if you're not a couple—I didn't think you were a couple—but I mean, since you're not, I'm going to be at that Casa Marina place for a couple of days after Izzy gets snipped, and I wondered if maybe I could take you out."

It's the first time a woman has ever invited me on a date. I haven't been on a date in years. I only vaguely remember how to go on a date.

"There's a private party in some place called Bahama Village. Gianni Versace's sister invited me. It's some house where they took out the kitchen and put in a swimming pool. He's given her a bunch of ties to give out. Not that you'd want a tie," she says.

"No particular use for them," I say.

"Doesn't seem," she says. Then: "So. Would you like to do that?"

"To swim in someone's kitchen?"

"If you'd rather we just—"

"No, no. Party sounds fine. I should come around to the Casa Marina, then? What time?"

"I think the party starts at ten."

"Little before ten, then."

"Great," she says.

"See you then," I say. "Of course, I'll also see you in about five minutes, when we should leave for the sandal store."

She nods.

"Like to sweep for a few minutes?" I ask.

That drives her away.

The next day, there is still no word. Could the potato-mango gratinée have been a moment's passing fancy? Antonio knows nothing, except that the Clintons will be arriving at his restaurant February 11, and that the restaurant will be closed after the first seating on February 10, when it will be secured by the Secret Service. The following day, they will watch Antonio and one assistant prepare all the food. He worries aloud about finding good quality estragon.

Just as I am about to step into the shower, the phone rings. It is George Stephanopoulos. He is apologetic. The president has been put on a new allergy medicine, which had unexpected side effects. Mrs. Clinton has been preoccupied with other details of the trip, and only realized that morning that further communication was needed from her. She is prepared to talk to me in just a few minutes, if I'm able to hold on.

I hold on. To my surprise, though, it is the president, himself, who comes to the line. "I'm very glad to talk to you, sir," the president says. "Hillary and I have greatly enjoyed your recipes."

"Actually, Mr. President, Mr. Cartwright is the person you want to talk to. I'm his assistant. I'm afraid he's out, right now, kayaking."

"Kayaking? Where are you all?"

"In the Florida Keys, Mr. President."

"Is that right? I thought you were in Louisiana."

"We're in the Florida Keys. A bit short of Key West."

"I see. Then where will we be having lunch before we come over to you?" the president asks.

"I believe you'll be lunching in Boca Raton, which is about three hours by car from where Lowell—Mr. Cartwright—lives."

"We're going to be coming to your restaurant that evening? How are we getting there, George?"

A muffled answer.

"I see. Well, that's fine. Wish I could take the time to do some fishing. But your restaurant—it's not a fish restaurant, is it?"

"Oh, no sir. It's . . . the thing is, it's not a restaurant. It's"—Is this going to screw the whole deal, somehow?—"It's where we live. Mr. Cartwright prefers to have favored people dine with us in his home. The view of the water from the back deck is splendid."

"A house on the water?" the president says. "Has George registered that?"

More muted discussion.

"I'm sorry," the president says. "I get caught up in logistics, when it's better to leave it to the experts."

"Water," I hear George Stephanopoulos hissing in the background.

"You know, I'm a chef's nightmare," the president says. "If I had my way, I'd eat a medium hamburger with extra mustard and go fishing with you guys." He says: "Isn't that what I'd do, George?"

"Papaya," Stephanopoulos hisses. Is he hissing at the president?

"Hillary got all excited about that papaya dish," the president says. "I'm going to let you speak to the boss about this, but if there's one thing I might request, with the exception of shrimp, I'm not overly fond of seafood."

"No seafood," I say.

"Well yeah, that kind of cuts to the chase," the president says. He clears his throat. "Just out of curiosity, how far is the airport from where you are?"

"Less than an hour, sir."

"That's fine, then. George and Hillary will firm this up, and we're looking forward to an exceptional meal."

"Mr. Cartwright will be so sorry he missed your call."

"Fishing in the kayak?" the president asks.

"Just paddling around with a friend," I reply.

This seems to cause the president several seconds of mirth. "Quite different from my plans for the afternoon," the president says.

George Stephanopoulos cuts in: "Thank you very much," George Stephanopoulos says.

"We look forward to making plans," I say.

"Good-bye," George Stephanopoulos says. "Thanks again."

I am standing there in my barracuda briefs, preparing to shower and go on my date. I fully realize that when Kathryn finds out, she will raise an eyebrow and say something sarcastic about my having a date. She will no doubt see my going into Key West as analogous to the butler's going off to find the former housemaid: a sad moment of self-protective delusion. Like him, I also won't be bringing her back. I'll be swimming with her at some party. Then, if we have sex, it can very well be in her room at the hotel. Simple white boxers are almost always preferable to the barracudas, when one is disrobing for the first time. The tangerine sports shirt that is my favorite is probably a bit too tropical-jokey; slightly faded denim seems better, with a pair of new khaki trousers.

"I'm going into Key West," I say, coming upon Lowell, pouring glasses of iced tea at the kitchen counter. "See you tonight."

"Why are you going into Key West?" he says.

"Date," I say.

"You have a date? With whom?"

"The highlighter."

"She just left," he says.

"Yesterday."

"I see," he says.

"Mrs. Clinton, or her secretary, will be calling. I spoke to the president briefly, and he doesn't want seafood."

"You spoke to the president? When?"

"Just before I showered."

He looks at me. "You've cleaned up beautifully," he says.

"Thank you," I say.

"Nothing else you want to tell me about anything?" he says.

"She asked if we were gay and I told her we weren't, and that seemed to provoke her to ask me out to a party."

"I meant, was there anything else you wanted to report about your conversation with the president," he says.

"If you get to speak to the president himself, tell him about kayaking," I say. "When I mentioned it, the idea seemed to please him."

"Maybe we could borrow a couple of kayaks and take them all for a predinner ride."

"Right. They can bring in the Navy SEALs."

"You're saying that would be too complicated," Lowell says.

"I suspect."

"You should leave before Kathryn begins to cross-examine you."

"Good idea."

"Be sure to fill the gas tank to the level you found it at."

I turn to look at him. He does a double-take, and raises his hands above his head. "Joke," he says.

The party is at a house with crayon-blue shutters. Broken pieces of colored tile are embedded in the cement steps. A piece of sculpture that looks like a cross between Edward Munch's scream and a fancy can opener stands gap-mouthed on the side lawn, but the lawn isn't a lawn in the usual sense: it's pink gravel, with a huge cement birdbath that is spotlit with a bright pink light. Orchids bloom from square wooden boxes suspended from hooks on the porch columns. A man who makes me look like an ant to his Mighty Mouse opens the door and scrutinizes us. Nancy—I am thinking of her as Nancy, instead of as the highlighter—reaches in the pocket of her white jacket and removes an invitation with a golden sun shining on the front.

"That's the ticket to ride," the man says. "Party's out back."

We walk through the house. Some Dade County pine. Ceiling fans going. Nice. The backyard is another story: a big tent has been set up, and a carousel revolves in the center, though instead of carousel animals, oversized pit bulls and rottweilers circulate, bright-eyed, jaws protruding, teeth bared. One little girl in a party dress rides round and round on a rottweiler. In the far corner is the bar, where another enormous man is mixing drinks. Upon closer inspection, I see that he has a diamond stud in one ear. Wraparound sunglasses have been pushed to the top of his shaved head.

"I guess . . . gee, what do I want?" Nancy says. "A rum and Coke."

"The real thing, or diet?"

"Diet," Nancy says, demurely.

"A shot of Stoli," I say, as the man hands Nancy her drink.

He pours me half a glass of vodka.

"Thank you," I say.

"Nancy!" a woman in a leopard print jumpsuit says, clattering toward her in black mules.

"Inez!" Nancy says, embracing the woman. She turns to me. "This is, like, absolutely *the* best makeup person in New York."

"Did you make friends with Madonna?" Inez asks.

"No," Nancy says. "She didn't like me. It was clear that I was really a menial person to her."

"She didn't know you," Inez says.

"Well, you can't meet somebody if you won't speak to them," Nancy says.

The woman disappears into the growing crowd, and Nancy sighs. "I didn't do a very good job of introducing you," she says.

"Can I be honest? I'll never see these people again, so it really doesn't matter to me."

She squeezes my hand. "I'd like to think that maybe there's a chance that I'll see you again, at least," she says. "Maybe sometime you'll want to come to New York and check out what's new in some restaurants there."

"Maybe so," I say. "That would be very nice."

"It would," she says. "There are hardly any straight men in New York."

Two ladies in hats are air kissing. One holds a small dog on a leash. It's so small, Nancy's kitten could devour it. On closer inspection, though, I see that it's a tiny wind-up toy. I overhear the woman saying that she's bringing a non-pooping pet as a gift for the hostess. People begin to play Where's-The-Hostess.

"I think it's so exciting you're going to meet the president," Nancy says. "Hillary, too."

"Are you talking about my friend Hillary?" the woman who'd been talking to a woman with the toy dog says.

"Nothing detrimental," I say quickly.

"Priscilla DeNova," the woman says. "Pleased to meet you both."

"I'm Nancy," Nancy says. "This is my friend Richard."

"Richard," the woman echoes. "And do you know George, if you know Hillary?"

"I've only spoken to him on the phone," I say.

"Oh. What were you discussing with my friend George?"

"The president's coming to dinner," I say.

"I see. Is he going to drop by to fish, first?"

"He did mention the possibility. But no. He's just stopping by to dine."

"Conch fritters?" the woman says. She seems very amused by something.

"I think we can do a little better than that."

"What he really likes is burgers," Priscilla says. "I guess anyone who reads the paper knows that." She tosses back her long hair and says, almost conspiratorially, "Tell me the truth. Have you been having me on about Clinton coming for dinner?"

"No. The whole family will be coming."

"You must either be a fascinating conversationalist or quite a cook," she says.

"Or quite delusional," I say.

"Yes, well, that possibility did cross my mind." She looks around

for someone more interesting to talk to.
"Tell us how you know George Stephanopoulos," Nancy says.
"My sister cleans house for a friend of his," the woman says. "She was a brilliant teacher, but she ruined her mind with drugs, and now about all she can remember is *Get the vacuum.* George has always been very kind to her. He gave her a ride once when she got stuck in the snow. He has a four-wheel drive, or whatever those things are. One time he saw us out hailing a cab, and he dropped us at the Avalon and came in to see the movie." She looks down, considering. "You know, I've never gotten straight on whether George, himself, goes on some fishing expeditions—so to speak, I mean—or whether Clinton gets some idea in his head, and then it just disappears. What I mean is, I wouldn't get my hopes up about them coming to dinner." She looks around, again. "Though if Hillary's involved, I suppose it might happen."
She drifts off without saying good-bye.
"Would I scare you off if I said that part of the reason I came to a bris in Florida was because a psychic told me that on this trip, or the next trip, I'd find true love?" Nancy says suddenly.
"You don't mean *me.*"
"Oh, of course not," she says, straight-faced. "The woman who just walked away."
"You did mean me," I say.
"Yes, I did. I don't mean that right this moment I'm in love with you, but you do seem like a real possibility." Her eyes meet mine. "Come on: you must have had some interest, or you wouldn't have come tonight."
I smile.
"And you have such a nice smile," she says.
"Excuse me for interrupting, but have you seen Gianni?" a small man asks. He has on a Gianni Versace shirt and black pants. He might be five feet tall, he might not.
"I'm afraid I don't know him," I say.
"But he's about to meet the president," Nancy says.
"The president of what?" the short man says.
"The United States," Nancy says.
"I'm Cuban," the man says. He walks away.
"So maybe it would be more fun at the Casa Marina," Nancy says. "Did you bring your bathing suit? There's a hot tub there."
"It's in my car," I say. "But didn't you say there was a pool here, in the kitchen?"

"Oh, right. I almost forgot," she says. "Let's find it."

We make our way back into the house. Two women are making out on a sofa in the hallway. The bouncer looms in the doorway, checking invitations. We take a left and find ourselves in a Victorian parlor. We turn around and go in the opposite direction. That room contains a stainless steel sink, where two women are washing and drying glasses. Nothing else that resembles a kitchen is there: no refrigerator; no cupboards. An indoor hot tub bubbles away, with several men and women inside, talking and laughing. There is a mat below the three steps leading to the hot tub. It depicts a moose, and says, in large black letters: WELCOME TO THE CAMP. The people in the hot tub are all speaking Italian. At the sink, the women are speaking Spanish. From a radio above the sink, Rod Stewart sings.

"Bathroom?" one of the women at the sink asks us.

"No, no. Just looking," Nancy says.

"Mr. Loring," the woman says, puckering her lips excessively to say, "Loring." She looks at Nancy. She says: "He went to the bathroom."

Nancy considers this. "Thank you," she says.

"De nada," the woman says.

"I think it would be more fun at the Casa Marina," Nancy says.

"Welllllll," Kathryn says. "Somebody got home *very* late."

"Refill the tank?" Lowell asks.

"Just imagine me blushing deeply," I say.

"But at least somebody thought to bring the *New York Times*. Good, good, good," Kathryn says.

"If you like all these things so much why do you leave New York?"

"To check the level of depradation," she says.

"Any update on the president?" I ask.

"You'd better not be responsible for my favorite hair highlighter of all time leaving New York City to live in the boonies," Kathryn says.

"Don't worry. I didn't ask her to marry me."

"You don't have to. Sex with a straight guy is enough to drive them over the edge."

"Quiet," Lowell says. "I don't want to hear the two of you sniping at each other before I've even had a cup of coffee."

On the counter, the coffee is slowly dripping into the pot.

"We went to a party," I say. "Gianni Versace was there, but he was peeing the whole time. We left and got into the hot tub at the Casa Marina. We watched *Grand Hotel* on the tube and had room service deliver a steak."

"It's love," Kathryn sighs.

"Well, don't sound so despondent about it, Cruella," Lowell says.

The phone rings. Lowell ignores it, resting his head on his hands. Kathryn is fanning herself with the travel section.

I answer the phone.

"George here," the voice says. "I just found out there was a screw-up, and that no one from Mrs. Clinton's staff got back to you. My apologies for that. I didn't awaken you, did I?"

"No, not at all. You'll want to be speaking to Mr. Cartwright," I say.

"Well, actually, if you could just relay the message that things are pretty much on hold at this end, I'd appreciate it."

"Of course," I say.

"I hope we can do it another time," George Stephanopoulos says.

I don't know what makes me do it, but I say, "You know, last night I was at a party—Gianni Versace and some other folks, down in Key West—and I met a woman who knows you. Apparently her sister cleans house for a friend of yours. Does this ring a bell?"

"What?" George Stephanopoulos says.

"Nice looking woman. From Washington. With a sister, who—"

"Oh, sure. You're talking about Francine Worth's sister Priscilla."

"Yes," I say.

There is a pause. "What about her?" George Stephanopoulos says.

Lowell and Kathryn are staring at me. The dripping coffee is making deep, guttural, sexual sounds.

"The party wasn't that much fun. You weren't missing anything," I say.

"Is that right? Well, a lot of the time I feel like I am missing something, so maybe I'll feel better now that I know I'm not."

"It wasn't so bad, I guess. I haven't been to a party for years. Not on a date, either, to tell the truth. So last night was quite out of the ordinary for me."

"I guess so, then," George Stephanopoulos says, after a slight pause.

I can't think what to say. I realize that I'm being watched from one end, and listened to carefully at the other.

"Well, we'll see if this can be worked out sometime when things are less hectic," George Stephanopoulos says. "Just think of me stuck at the desk the next time you step out."

"Oh, there isn't going to be a next time. She's going back to New York tomorrow." I add: "Priscilla had only good things to say about you. Your kindness in giving people rides, I mean. Very generous."

"Yeah, I caught a movie with them one time. Seems like that was in another lifetime."

"I often have that same feeling of disorientation. I've lived so many places. Thailand. All over France, at various times. Le Moulin de Mougins, when the cooking was still brilliant. In the U.S., there's a place called Lava Hot Springs. Lowell and I went there when he took part in a steak barbecuing competition, I guess you'd call it. A very nice place. And the country is full of places like that."

"I know it," George Stephanopoulos says. "Man, you're making me chomp at the bit."

"You should come here and fish and have dinner, yourself, if you ever take a couple of days off. We're right on the water. Plenty of room."

"That's very nice of you. Very nice, indeed. Certainly be easier than trying to get everybody together to caravan down there in early February, Mrs. Clinton converging from one place, the president with no idea what time his meeting is going to conclude. And you toss into that three or four teenage girls, some of them who'll back out at the last minute because some boy might call, or something."

"Feel free to call us," I say. "Some of Lowell's uncollected recipes are his very best. The Thai-California fusion dishes he's been working on have really come together."

"My mouth is watering," George Stephanopoulos says. "Think of me when you're having some of that terrific food."

"Will do," I say.

"And thanks again," George Stephanopoulos says. It doesn't seem like he really wants to hang up.

"See you, then, maybe," I say.

"I'll keep that in mind," he says. "Good-bye."

Kathryn is the first to speak. She collects her cup, and her brother's, and pours coffee, giving me a wide berth to indicate her skepticism. She's jealous; that's what it's always been with Kathryn. She's very possessive, very set in her ways. In spite of passing judgment on anything new, she's still trying to come to terms with things that are old. How many years have I been around, now—years in which I've been pretty decent to her—and she still wishes that she had her brother all to herself? Kathryn says: "The new effusiveness."

I say nothing.

"Well, for God's sake, would you mind letting me know the outcome of your little chat? Am I correct in assuming that the president is not coming, but that George Stephanopoulos might?" Lowell says.

I nod.

"What is this? Twenty Questions? The president is not coming . . . why?"

"Some meeting is probably going to run late, and Mrs. Clinton would be rendezvousing with him from wherever she was, and Chelsea and her friends apparently drive him mad, because they're so unpredictable."

"He didn't know this when he called?" Kathryn says.

"How would I know?"

"Don't you two start in on each other. Think about me, for once. What about my feelings, when I was prepared to be cooking for the president and suddenly he decides to blow the whole thing off because some meeting might run a little late."

Kathryn and I take this in. I get a mug and pour coffee. We all sit at the table in silence.

"I'm not sure it quite computed with me," I say. "The president visiting, I mean."

"I wonder if the bastard's still having lunch at Antonio's," Lowell says.

"Read the *Times,*" I say. "Would you like me to make you some toast?"

"No thank you," Lowell says. "But it's nice of you to offer."

"I'll be on the deck," Kathryn says. She picks up her mug and half the paper and walks outside.

"Still," Lowell says. "Not everyone gets a call from the president." He looks at me. "Remember a few months after we met, when we had that barbecue at your uncle's?"

"Of course I remember. He was a great guy. Never charged me a nickel for room and board. A totally generous man. 'Never get too big for your britches that you turn your back on your family,' my uncle used to say."

"You never did," Lowell says. "You sent him food every time we went somewhere exotic."

"Pistachios from Saudi Arabia," I say.

"And I've taken his advice, too. Which means that Kathryn will tyrannize us forever," Lowell says.

Back in Key West that evening, on impulse, I'm almost giddy. I go to the Green Parrot and have a cold draft before going over to the Casa Marina to meet Nancy and her friends in the bar there. Some bikers are at the Parrot with their girlfriends. Somebody who looks like a tweedy professor, except that he's got on pink short shorts with the tweed jacket with elbow patches, so he might be just another unemployed oddball. He's playing a game of Nintendo while sipping some tropical drink through double-barrel straws.

I am thinking about what I might have said to the president if he came to dinner.

But then I think: he no doubt already knows the Marines are a bunch of dangerous psychos. He always had better sense than to truck with any of that stuff.

What would Nancy say if I suggested moving to New York with her?

Probably yes. She dropped enough hints about the lack of straight guys in Manhattan.

What do you get when you fall in love?

You get enough germs to catch pneumonia.

What happened to all the great singers of yesteryear?

Replaced by "The Butthole Surfers."

"You hear the one about this guy's girlfriend who's leaving him?" a skinny guy in cutoffs and a "Mommy and Daddy Visited Key West And All I Got Was This Crummy Shirt" T-shirt says, sitting next to me on a bar stool.

"Don't think so," I say.

"The girlfriend says, 'I'm leaving you. I'm out of here.' And the guy says, 'Whoa there, can a guy even know why?' and she goes, 'Yeah, I've heard something very, very disturbing about you.' He says, 'Oh yeah? What's that?' She says, 'I heard that you were a pedophile.' He says, 'Hey, that's a pretty big word for an eleven-year-old.' "

Today I have spoken to this unfunny jerk, and to the president's assistant, George Stephanopoulos. Also to my employer, who is depressed, because the president was going to come to dinner and then suddenly he didn't want to, and to Kathryn—the sarcastic Kathryn, who always brings both of us down—though soon I will be talking to the lovely, though fleeting-as-the-breeze Nancy. Somewhere in the middle of these thoughts, I manage a strained, "Ha ha." I ask for the check and pay the bill before the guy gets wound up again.

I drive on Duval, to check out the action. A bunch of middle-aged tourists, who wonder what they're doing in Key West, a lot of T-shirt shops, quite a few kids beneath the age of consent, not yet at the age of reason, who have never even heard of the Age of Aquarius. Duval looks like Forty-Second Street, although maybe by now Forty-Second Street looks like Disneyland.

I meet Nancy and her friends—both women—where she said they'd be: at the beach bar. The women give me the once-over, and the You-Might-Hurt-Her-Permanently squint. Nancy flashes bedroom eyes, but only gives me a discreet peck on the cheek. "There's another party, in a condo over by the beach. But first Jerri has to go back to the photo place where she works, because she needs to double-check that the alarm is activated," she says.

"Nobody has a car. Would you mind driving?" Jerri says.

"Not at all," I say.

"Some customer left a bottle of champagne for the owner, but he's a beer drinker, so he just gives me those things. If you want, we could take that out of the fridge and drink it."

"Mmmm," Bea, the other woman, says. Bea looks like she might eventually forgive me for being a man.

"This new alarm system has been screwing up in a major way," Jerri says. "It will take me ten secs to make sure it hasn't de-programmed itself. And to round up the bubbly."

"So," Bea says. "I hear you're the assistant to a famous chef."

"Yes, I am."

"Do you cook, too?"

"Just help out," I say. "I'm not innovative, myself."

"So how does somebody get a job like that?" Bea says.

"Lowell and I became friends when I picked him up for a car service I used to drive for. It was back in the days when you'd meet somebody and check them out, and basically, if you liked the person, you never minded running some strange proposition past him."

"What was the strange proposition?" Nancy says.

"It wasn't so strange in and of itself. But there I was driving for a car service, and basically, he wanted to know if I had any interest in coming to work for him. Letting the other job go."

"Did he talk about money? I had two job interviews last year and it turned out they didn't want to give me any money at all! They wanted me to take a full-time job as a volunteer!"

"He didn't mention money, now that you mention it. But people went more on intuition then, I think. I figured he'd pay me a decent wage."

"So where did he get a name like Lowell?"

"I'm not sure."

"Everybody who meets me wants to know absolutely everything about me," Jerri says. "Full disclosure, even if I'm, like, trying on a pair of shoes. I wouldn't get out of the store without saying how much I pay in rent. Though I suppose people in Key West are obsessed with that."

"They are? Why?" I ask, grateful that something has come up that I can ask about.

"Because it costs so much to live here," she says.

"Oh. Right," I say. I open the car door, and everyone gets in.

"Guess what I pay in rent," Jerri says.

"I wouldn't have any idea."

"It's a one bedroom, and the bedroom isn't mine. It's on the top floor of a house on Francis that has a separate entrance. I share it with the landlady's granddaughter, who's not all there, if you know what I mean. She's forty years old, and all she does all day is read gardening books and drown all the houseplants so they die."

"When she moved in, they gave her a mattress that used to be the dog's bed," Bea says.

"God," Nancy says. "Things were never that bad back in New York, were they?"

"Oh, I didn't *sleep* on it," Jerri says. "But it was really depressing, because all these little fleas were using it as a trampoline. You could see them jumping up and down."

"I suppose you're going to tell me that the rent costs a fortune," I say.

"One fifty-five a month," Jerri says. "Take a turn here. The next street's one way."

"Isn't that reasonable for Key West?" I ask.

"Yeah, it's reasonable, but I had to buy my own mattress and box spring, and the granddaughter insists on keeping lights on in every room, all night."

"You couldn't find another place to live?" I ask.

"For *one fifty-five?*"

Jerri indicates that I should take an empty parking space. I park, and we lock the car and start down the street. From a clip hanging off her belt, Jerri removes a key ring. She opens two locks with two different keys and flips on a light inside the back of the shop. We walk in behind her. She looks at a panel, flashing a number, on the same wall as the light switch. "Whew," she says. "Okay, this is cool." She pushes a couple of buttons and walks to the small refrigerator in the corner, from which she removes the bottle of champagne. She reaches up on a shelf and takes down a tower of upside-down plastic glasses. She counts out four and puts the rest back on the shelf.

But my attention is drifting. In the back of the shop there are life-size cardboard cutouts with cutout faces. One is Marilyn Monroe, with her skirt blowing up. Another is Tina Turner, all long legs and stiletto heels and micro-mini skirt with fringe. There is the American Gothic couple, and there are a couple of Pilgrims, complete with a turkey that retains its own face. There's Donald Duck, and Donald Trump with Marla Maples, who also has her face; Sylvester Stallone as Rocky; James Dean on his motorcycle. There is also Bill Clinton, arm extended to clasp the shoulder of whoever stands beside him. Jerri has walked over to the figures; first she becomes Marilyn, then Tina Turner. Her young, narrow face makes her unconvincing as either. Nancy is the next to wander over. Champagne glass in hand, she tries her luck as Rocky. She motions for me to join her. I do, and together we peer out from behind the Pilgrim couple. Behind the cutouts she passes me her glass, and I duck back to take a sip of champagne.

"I look at this stuff all day long. It doesn't seem so funny anymore," Jerri says. "And what's really not funny is when some guy who thinks he's a real stud comes in to be Stallone, or when some guy who smells like a brewery wants his girlfriend to be Marilyn. *Really* wants her to be Marilyn."

"I notice they don't have one of Ike with his gun," Jerri says, sticking her face through Tina Turner's highly teased hair.

"Too bad there's not one of your good friend, George Stephanopoulos, just his flunky," Jerri says. "Nancy was telling us about that before you came over."

Nancy smiles, mugging from behind the female Pilgrim again.

"Well, we all know Nancy. Nancy's only interested in the rich and famous. Or in people who hang with the rich and famous," Jerri says.

"That cowboy she lived with was hardly rich or famous," Bea says.

"You were always so jealous you couldn't see straight, because somebody followed me all the way from Montana to New York," Nancy says. "It really made you crazy, didn't it, Bea?"

"Oh, look who's talking! Like you didn't call my old boyfriend the day he moved out!" Bea says.

"I called him to get my canvas bag back."

"Listen to her! She called about eight hours after he moved into his new place because she needed a bag back!" Bea shrieks.

"You are so sadly misled," Jerri says. "I mean, fun is fun, but this is one time I've got to defend my friend Nancy. She always thought your boyfriend was a *jerk!"*

It's as if I'm not there, suddenly. While they continue to go at it, I wander over to the plastic glass of champagne that's been poured for me and take a long, bubbly sip. So she lived with some guy who followed her all the way to New York from Montana. When? How long were they together?

"And you look so much like him!" Bea suddenly says to me. "If you were, like, fifty pounds lighter, and if you wore cowboy boots some armadillo gave its life for instead of those goony shoes, you'd be a dead ringer for Les."

"Jesus! I can't believe you're so jealous I've got a date that you're insulting him about his weight!" Nancy says.

"Oh, sit on it," Jerri says. "Both of you."

"Bea has really got it in for me!" Nancy says to Jerri.

"I've got it in for *you?* Nancy, you need to ask yourself why, every time somebody says something that's true, but maybe you don't want to hear it . . . you should ask yourself why you find it necessary to say that that person is *crazy.* I mean, Fuck you!" Bea says. She pushes past Marilyn and storms out the back door, crushing her empty plastic glass.

"Je-*sus,*" Nancy says. "What is *wrong* with her?"

"Well, don't get on your high horse," Jerri says. "You didn't have to tell her how mean and spiteful she was."

"I didn't say that. I only said she was jealous of me and Les."

"Who's Les?" I ask.

"I don't see why we should be talking about this now," Nancy says.

"You mean, you thought we were having a conventional date?" I ask.

"No, I didn't . . . I mean, we're going to a party, aren't we? We stopped by here because Jerri had to check the damned alarm."

"She wanted an excuse to say mean things and run off," Jerri says. "It pisses her off that Nancy and I can discuss things and be really honest with each other, because she introduced the two of us, and she's got some weird thing about how each of us has to have her as our best friend, so we're not supposed to care that much about each other."

"I can't follow all this. Maybe we should go to the party," I say.

"I feel bad," Jerri says. "I should have tried to cool her out."

"Why should you feel responsible for Bea's state of mind?" Nancy says.

"Let me get a picture of you two," Jerri says. "Souvenir of our wonderful evening, so far."

She goes to a safe and turns the combination lock. When the door swings open, she takes out a Polaroid and fiddles with the camera. I'm still wondering: Who's Les? How long has he been gone? And: what constitutes goony shoes?

Nancy seems quite shaken by Bea's exit. She is fighting back tears, I see, as Jerri gestures for us to make a choice: for a couples shot, it's either American Gothic or the Pilgrim couple. Nancy, sniffing, moves behind the Pilgrims. I stand beside her, crouching so my face peers out where it's supposed to.

The camera spews out the photograph. We both converge on Jerri, to watch it develop.

"Let me get you with the president. Go on," Jerri says, gesturing for me to stand next to Clinton.

"You know, she can really be a terrible bitch," Nancy says. "But now I feel like everything's all messed up."

The flash goes off. Jerri takes the first photograph out of her pocket and nods approvingly. The second photograph—the one she just took—begins to quickly develop. There I am, probably closer to the president than I'd ever have gotten if he'd come to the house, and obviously on much chummier terms. Probably just as good as meeting him, the photo op being interchangeable with real experiences in recent years.

"You're mad at me for dragging you into this," Nancy says. Tears are rolling down her cheeks.

"No, it's just one of those things that happened," I say.

"One of those things that happened?" she repeats. She seems confused. "You mean you think this was okay? It's okay if somebody insults you and if the person you slept with the night before turns out to be in love with some other guy?"

It takes me a minute to respond. "I didn't know until now that you were in love with him," I say.

"I am! And I think that if the mere mention of his name, by that bitch, can make me this upset, maybe I should swallow my pride and go out to Montana and get him. He didn't hate me, he just hated New York."

I raise both hands, palms up.

"That's fine with you?" she says.

"What can I do about it?" I say.

"You know, I think that once again, I've found an apathetic jerk,"

Nancy says. "I guess it's all for the best that this happened, because this way you and I won't waste any more time with each other."

"I cannot believe this," Jerri says. She puts both pictures in her shirt pocket. She walks over to the safe, shaking her head. She replaces the camera in the safe and shuts the door. "Lights out, kids," she says, tiredly.

"Yeah," Nancy says. "I think I'll be the first off to dreamy dreamland. I think I'll just spend the night alone with my fabulous new scenario."

We watch her go.

"I suppose I should have gone after her, but I couldn't see the point in it. I think she meant everything she said. So why would I go after her?" I say.

"Is that really a question?" Jerri says.

"Yes," I say.

"In my opinion, you did the right thing not to," she says.

"Thank you," I say.

"You don't have to thank me. I wasn't trying to flatter you. I was just saying that I think you made the right decision."

"What do you say, if you don't say thank you?"

"You don't have to say anything."

I consider this. "I think I'll drive home, but if you'd like a lift anywhere . . ."

"You know, you really didn't deserve that. You really seem like a very nice man."

"With dorky shoes," I say, extending my foot.

"Topsiders are dorky? Millions of people wear Topsiders."

"But I can see that they aren't exactly cool."

"We're not teenagers anymore," she says. "I don't think any of us will perish if we don't have the exact newest thing."

"No," I say.

"Thanks for the offer, but I think I'll just walk over to a friend's house."

"Fine," I say. "I'm sorry about all this, too. It's a lame thing to say, but I sort of appreciate the fact that at least one person is still talking to me."

She shrugs. "You take care," she says.

I'm out the door when she says, "Oh, wait. Take your pictures."

I turn around, and she puts the photographs in my hand. For the first time, I see that they're joke Pilgrims: the woman excessively big-breasted, the man with his fly unzipped. Stallone, of course, you wouldn't dare joke about. And Marilyn is almost a sacred cultural icon. People who don't like James Dean would nevertheless realize that he was the embodiment of cool. But the Pilgrims, I suppose, have become so anachronistic that there's no harm in joking about them. I hand that photograph back to her. "Two turkeys and one big-breasted babe," I say. "I think I might as well pass on that one."

Then I'm out on Duval, going around the corner to the street where I parked the car.

A guy in dreadlocks walks past, bouncing on the balls of his bare feet. On the steps by a guest house, a man lies sprawled on top of a coat, a small pile of clutter next to him. He's wearing a beret, is shirtless and almost trouserless. His pants are down around his hips. He's lying on his side, mouth lolled open. I walk past a store selling silk-screened bags with tropical birds on them. I stop to admire a traveller's palm in someone's front yard, spotlit. As they pass by, a middle-aged woman says to the man she is walking with, "So what part of town did they film *Key Largo* in?" In a shop window, I see a verdigris crane, flanked by gargoyles in graduated sizes. Just as I get near the car, someone's light sensor is activated by my presence; the light blinks on and floods the street with light, and I feel embarrassed, as if I've been caught doing something bad. Or as if I've unnecessarily caused some commotion. But the light blinks out after I pass, and the whole block—surprising, this close to Duval—is eerily quiet. It gives me more time than I want to hear the voice in my head telling me that I've done everything wrong, that years ago, I took the easy way out, that if I think I'm indispensable to Lowell, that's only a delusion—like the delusion that I'm a nice looking man, or at least ordinary, wearing inconspicuous clothes and conventional shoes. What must it be like to be the president? Pictures in the paper of you jogging, sweating, your heavy legs caught at a bad angle, so they look like tree trunks? Cry at a funeral, and they zoom the lens in on you. "It's love," I hear Kathryn saying sarcastically. Well, no: it certainly isn't, and apparently wasn't going to be. But what version is Nancy going to give Kathryn, back in the great city of New York? On the other hand, what do I care? What do I have to be embarrassed about?

I get in the car, not much looking forward to joining the weekend traffic exiting Key West. It seems that half the world is intent upon getting to the Southernmost point, and half the world is intent upon fleeing it. Half an hour up the Keys, there's a police roadblock. A cop standing in the street is motioning cars over to the side, but thank heaven: I was feeling so sorry for myself, and so preoccupied, that I was creeping along, barely going the minimum. Once past, I turn on the radio. The tape deck has been broken for weeks. I fiddle with the dial and find Rod Stewart, singing, "Do you feel what I feel? Can we make it so that's part of the deal?" which reminds me of the party the night before, which reminds me of afterward, at the Casa Marina. Bad luck, I think. Bad timing, bad lady, bad luck.

"A Whiter Shade of Pale" comes on, which really takes me back. I'm probably among the few Americans who first heard that song in a bar in Tangiers. I think about returning to my room, my VCR, my travel tapes. It seems a pleasant notion. And if I'm lucky, there will be leftovers to eat while I take the nightly imaginative voyage.

Then I see it: the police cars in the driveway. Police on the front steps. Police standing by the rose garden, writing whatever they're writing. The grating noise of their radios seems to stab the quiet of the night. I catch Kathryn, like a stunned deer, in my headlights. Then, suddenly, she is on her way back to the house, accompanied by a policeman. Lowell. Something terrible has happened to Lowell.

"What?" I say to the first cop I see. I only say that word; I can't manage a full sentence.

"Who are you?" he says.

"Lowell's assistant," I say.

"His assistant? You live here?"

I nod yes.

"There was an accident," he says. "The gentleman fell out of a tree."

"Fell?"

"Fell," the cop says, his shoulders going a little limp and his knees slightly buckling as he slumps toward the ground. "From a tree," he says again.

"What happened to him?" I ask.

"He was airlifted to Miami," the cop says. "I wouldn't want to speculate about the extent of his injuries."

"He's alive," I say.

"He might have broken his neck," the cop says. He swivels his head and puts his ear as close to his shoulder as it can get without actually touching the shoulder.

I go in the house, where every light is on.

"They wouldn't let me on the plane," Kathryn says, turning toward me in the glare. Then she collapses in tears. "That stupid whore you've taken such a liking to, with her mangy kitten. She just turned it out and then . . ." Tears interrupt Kathryn's story. Then she pulls herself together, or tries to imitate someone who's pulled herself together. She looks into my eyes. "You knew she left the goddamned thing here, didn't you? It got away, and she just left it. She told me to find it, like I was her servant, or something." She stops. "I didn't mean that the way it sounded," she said. "I didn't mean anything personal. Oh, God, if he lives, I'll never be awful again. I really won't. All I'm saying is, why am I supposed to find some scrappy cat and get it back to her in New York? That's something perfectly normal to expect, like she left an earring here, or something? She didn't even tell you any of this, when the other morning it was such a crisis I thought she was going to jump out of her skin if the ratty thing didn't come back?"

I shake my head no. This can't be happening. Just a few hours ago, everything was fine.

"It's impossible," Kathryn says to a cop who passes by. "This morning we were talking about the president coming here for dinner."

I reach in my pocket and take out the photograph of myself with Clinton. I stare at it, as if it's evidence of something.

"Hey! You and President Clinton!" the cop says. He's young. Blond with blue eyes. He looks like he's barely more than a teenager. But can he really be so unobservant that he doesn't know it's a joke photograph? My head begins to pound.

"It's my fault for ever bringing her here," Kathryn says. "She let her cat go, like it was a dog that would come back from a walk." She turns to me. "He was fixing dinner, and I saw it. It ran up a tree, like a squirrel. Lowell was inside. He turned off the stove and went out on the deck, and eventually we got the ladder and put it up. Lowell was trying to coax it down from the kapok tree. Then he started to climb, and the next thing I knew, he was in the water, but he wasn't moving. I thought he didn't move right away because the fall had stunned him. I waded out and got him. Otherwise, he would have drowned. You don't live where there's anyone who can help you in an emergency. I could have screamed my head off, and nobody would have come. He went after that stupid girl's stupid cat, and now they think something horrible happened to his spine."

The young cop has listened attentively to this avalanche of information. Finally he turns to me. "Was he also a friend of the president's? Should someone let the president know?" he says.

Is he possibly making some bizarre joke? I look at the photograph again, as if I might be the one who's missing something. Clinton, in a gray suit, stands smiling, his arm, with its inexactly cutout hand, too stiffly extended to really appear to be clasping anyone's shoulder.

Words tumble through my mind, as I imagine the letter I might send: "*Dear George, I enclose a photo that's as close as I'll ever come now to the real thing. This evening Lowell was airlifted to Miami, with serious injuries: quite probably a broken neck. Which leaves me wondering—if things go as badly as they seem to be going at the moment—what a person who has always been a maverick in this country is supposed to do when the comfortable life he more or less stumbled into unexpectedly disappears out from under him. The first woman I dated in years turns out to be in love with another man. . . .*"

I open the kitchen drawer. There is the wine pull, foolish contraption that it is. An item guaranteed to be puzzled over if found years hence in a time capsule.

"How you doing, big guy?" a cop I haven't spoken to before says to me.

"This is a joke," I say, removing the Polaroid from my pocket and holding it out. "You see that, don't you?"

"Sure," he says slowly, as if I'm playing some sort of parlor game. He studies my face. "I had a picture taken of myself one time in one of those fake stockades. Used it as a Christmas card. One of those 'From Our House To Yours' things. Turned out pretty funny."

"Thank you," I say, so quietly I can barely hear my own voice. I put the picture back in my pocket, clamping my right hand over it as if it might fly out and disappear. As if I were a boy again, in one of the many schools I attended, dutifully reciting the Pledge of Allegiance. Those days when life consisted of ritual, wherever we lived; ritual was the one constant, as predictable as my father's patriotism, as inevitable as my mother's churchgoing. I would get away from all that, I vowed. And I did—researching hotels and restaurants around the world, booking flights, arranging for any necessary letters of introduction, Lowell and I greeted by interesting and important people wherever we journeyed—people with whom we drank wine and dined. And now, it seems, that travel has concluded in the Florida Keys.

The note—the note in response to the letter I do eventually write to George Stephanopoulos—is very brief. It is addressed to Lowell, naturally enough, not to me. It concludes, in a heartfelt, yet predictable way, yet in a totally sincere way, if you know George: "*You are in the president and first lady's prayers.*"

Please Remain Calm

A. M. Homes

I WISH I WERE DEAD. I have tried to keep it a secret, but it leaks out: "I wish I were dead," I blurted to the woman who is now my wife, the first morning we woke up together, the sheets still hot, stinking of sex.

"Should I take it personally?" she asked, covering herself.

"No," I said and began to cry.

"It's not so easy to die," she says. And she should know, she's a woman whose milieu is disaster—a specialist in emergency medicine. All day she is at work, putting the pieces back together and then she comes home to me. She tells me about the man run over by a train, how they carried in each of his legs in separate canvas bags. She tells me about the little boy doused in oil and deep-fried.

"Hi honey, I'm home," she says.

I hold my breath.

"I know you're here, your briefcase is in the front hall. Where are you?"

I wait to answer.

"Honey?"

I am sitting at the kitchen table.

"Today's the day," I tell her.

"What's different today?" she asks.

"Nothing. Nothing is different about today—that's the point. I feel the same today as I did yesterday and the day before. It's insufferable. Today," I repeat.

"Not today," she says.

"Now's the time," I say.

"Not the time."

"The moment has come."

"The moment has passed."

Every day I wish I didn't have to live a minute more; I wish I were someplace else, someplace new, someplace that never existed before. Death is a place without history; it's not like people have been there and then come back to tell you what a great time they had, that they highly recommend it, the food is wonderful and there's an incredible hotel right on the water.

"You think death is like Bali," my wife says.

We have been married for almost two years; she doesn't believe me anymore. It is as though I've cried wolf, screamed wolf, been a wolf, too many times.

"Did you stop at the store?"

I nod. I am in charge of the perishables, the things that must be consumed immediately. Every day on my way home, I shop. Before I was married I would buy only one of each thing, a bottle of beer, a can of soup, a single roll of toilet paper—that sounds fine on a Monday when you think there will be no Tuesday, but what about late on Friday night when the corner store is closed?

My wife buys in bulk, she is forever stocking up; she is prepared in perpetuity.

"Did you remember milk?"

"I bought a quart."

"Not a half gallon?"

"You're lucky it's not a pint."

We are vigilant people, equally determined. The ongoing potential for things to go wrong is our bond—she likes to repair and I to wallow, to roll obsessively in the possibilities like some perverted pig. It is a control issue, maintaining control for as long as possible. Our closets are packed with emergency supplies: bottles of water, a backup generator, air purifiers, fire extinguishers, freeze-dried food, medical supplies, a stack of two hundred dollar bills, his and hers cans of mace, we are ready and waiting.

She opens a beer and flips through a catalog for emergency management specialists. This is how she relaxes—"What about gas masks? What if something happens, what if there's an event?" She checks off the box for gas masks and then goes for a couple of smoke hoods. "They're good for traveling. All the FAA guys carry their own, it's a little known fact, smoke inhalation is a major cause of death on airplanes."

"I'm not surprised." I open a beer, take a breath. "I can't stand it anymore."

"You're stronger than you think."

I have spent nights laid low near the exhaust pipe of a car, have slept with a plastic bag over my head and silver duct tape around my neck. I have rifled through the kitchen drawers at three A.M. thinking I will have at myself with a carving knife. There have been mornings when I've taken my straight razor to my throat and carved. Once fresh from the shower, I divided myself in half, a clean incision from sternum to pubis. In the bathroom mirror, I watched what was leaking out of me, escaping me, with peculiar pleasure not unlike the perverse pleasantry of taking a good shit. I arrived at the office dotted with the seeping red of my efforts. "Looks like you got a little on you," my secretary said, donating her seltzer to blot the spot. "You're always having these shaving accidents. Maybe you're cutting it too close."

All the above is only a warm-up, a temporizing measure, a palliative remedy, I want something more, the big bang. If I had a gun I would use it, again and again, a million times a day I would shoot myself.

"What do you want to do about dinner?"

"Nothing. I never want to eat again."

"Not even steak?" my wife asks. "I was thinking I'd make us a nice thick steak. Yesterday you said, 'How come we never have steak anymore?' I took one out of the deep freeze this morning."

"Don't try and talk me out of it."

"Fine, but I'm having steak. Let me know if you change your mind."

There is a coldness to her, a chill I find terrifying, an absence of emotion that puts a space between us, a permanent and unbridgeable gap—I am entirely emotion, she is entirely reason.

I will not change my mind. This isn't something new, something that started late in life. I've been this way since I was a child. It is the most awful addiction—the opposite of being a vampire and living off the blood of others, "eripmav"—sucked backward through life, the life cycle run in reverse, beginning in death and ending in . . .

Short of blowing my brains out, there is no way I can demonstrate the intensity, the extremity of my feeling. Click. Boom. Splat. The pain is searing, excruciating; the roots of my brain are hot with it.

"You can't imagine the pain I'm in."

"Take some Tylenol."

"Do you want me to make a salad?"

I have been married before, did I mention that? It ended badly—I ran into my ex-wife last week on the street and the color drained from both our faces—we're still weak from memory. "Are you all right?" I wondered.

"I'm better," she said. "Much better. Alone." She quickly walked away.

There is an enormous amount of tension in being with someone who is dying every day. It's a perpetual hospice; the grief is too extreme. That's my specialty, pushing the limits, constantly testing people. No one can pass—that is the point. In the end, they crack, they leave and I blame them.

I'm chopping lettuce.

"Caesar," my wife says and I look up. She hands me a tin of anchovies. "Use the romaine."

"How was work?" There is relief in other people's tragedies.

"Interesting," she says, pulling the meat out of the broiler. She slices open the steak, blood runs out.

"How does that look?"

"Perfect." I smile, grating the parmesan.

"A guy came in this afternoon, high on something. He'd tried to take his face off, literally—took a knife and peeled it."

"How did you put him back together?"

"A thousand stitches and surgical glue. Another man lost his right hand. Fortunately, he's a lefty."

We sit at the kitchen table talking about severed limbs, thin threads of ligaments, the delicate weave of nerves—reattachment, the hope of regaining full function. Miracles.

"I love you," she says, leaning over, kissing my forehead.

"How can you say that?"

"Because I do?"

"You don't love me enough."

"Nothing is enough," she says. And it is true, excruciatingly true.

I want to tell her I am having an affair, I want to make her leave, I want to prove that she doesn't love me enough. I want to have it over with.

"I'm having an affair," I tell her.

"No, you're not."

"Yes, I am. I'm fucking Sally Baumgarten."

She laughs. "And I'm giving blowjobs to Tom."

"My friend Tom?"

"You bet."

She could be, she very well could be. I pour Cascade into the dishwasher and push the button—Heavy Soil.

"I'm leaving," I tell her.

"Where are you going?"

"I don't know."

"When will you be back?"

"Never. I'm not coming back."

"Then you're not leaving," she says.

"I hate you."

I married her before I loved her. For our honeymoon, we went to California. She was thinking Disneyland, Carmel, Big Sur, a driving trip up the coast—fun. I was hoping for an earthquake, brush fire, mudslide—disaster.

In the hotel room in Los Angeles I panicked. A wall of glass, a broad expanse of windows looking out over the city—it was a surprisingly clear night. The lights in the hills twinkled, beckoned. Without warning, I ran toward the glass, hurling myself forward.

She took me down, tackling me. She sat on top, pinning me, her one hundred nineteen pounds on my one fifty-six—she's stronger than you think.

"If you do that again I won't forgive you."

The intimacy, the unbearable intimacy is what's most mortifying—when they know the habits of your bowels, your cheapnesses, your horribleness, when they know things about you that no one should know, things you don't even know about yourself.

She knows these things and doesn't say it's too much, too weird, too fucked up. "It's my training," she says. "My shift doesn't end just because something bad happens."

It is about love. It is about getting enough, having enough, drowning in it, and now it is too late. I am permanently malnourished—there isn't enough love in the world.

There is a danger in this, in writing this, in saying this. I am putting myself on the line. If I am found floating, face down, there will be theories, lingering questions. Did he mean it? Was it an accident—is there any such thing as an accident, is fate that forgiving? Was this letter a warning, a true story? Everything is suspect. (Unless otherwise instructed—if something happens, give me the benefit of the doubt.)

"What would it be like if you gave it up?" she asked.

I am incredulous.

"If you abandoned the idea? Aren't you bored by it all after all these years; why not just give it up?"

"Wanting to be dead is as natural to me as breathing."

What would I be without it? I don't know that I could handle it. Like being sprung from a lifetime jail, like Jack Henry Abbot, I might wheel around and stab someone with a dinner knife.

And what if I truly gave it up, if I said, Yes it is a beautiful day, yes I am incredibly lucky—one of the luckiest men in the world. What if I admitted it, You are my best friend, my favorite fuck, my cure. What if I say I love you and she says, It's over. What if that's part of the game, the dance? I will have missed my moment, I will be shit out of luck—stuck here forever.

"Why do you put up with it?"

"Because this is not you," she says. "It's part of you, but it's not you. Are you still going to kill yourself?

"Yes," I say. Yes I am, to prove I am independent, to prove I still can. "I hate you," I tell her. "I hate you so much."

"I know," she says.

My wife is not without complications of her own. She keeps a baseball bat under her side of the bed. I discovered it by accident—one day it rolled out from under. Louisville Slugger. I rolled it back into place and have never let on that I know it's there. Sometimes she wakes up in the middle of the night, sits straight up and screams, "Who is out there? Who is in the waiting room?" She stops for a second and starts again, annoyed, "I don't have all day. Next. Bring the next one in." There are nights I watch her sleep, her face a naive dissolve, tension erased, her delicate blond lashes, her lips, soft like a child and I want to punch her. I want to bash her face in. I wonder what she would do then.

"A thought is only a thought," she says when I wake her, when I tell her what I was thinking.

Then she tells me her dreams. "I was a man and I was having sex with another man and you were there, you were wearing a white skirt, and then someone came in but he didn't have any arms and I kept wondering how did he open the door?"

"Let's go back to sleep for a little while."

I am getting closer. The situation is untenable, something has to happen. I have lived this way for a long time; there is a cumulative effect, a worsening. I am embarrassed that I have let it go on for so long.

I know how I will do it. I will hang myself. Right here at home. I have known it since we bought the house. When the real estate agent went on and on about the location, the yard, the school district, I was thinking about the interior—the exposed rafters, the beams. The dead man's walk to the top of the stairs.

We are cleaning up. I wipe the table with a sponge.

"What's in the bag," she says, pointing to something on the counter.

"Rope." I stopped on the way home. I ran the errand.

"Let's go to the movies," she says, tying up the trash. She hands me the bag. "Take it outside," she says, sending me into the night.

The yard is flooded with light, extra lights, like search lights, lights so bright that when raccoons cross to get to the trash, they hold their paws up over their eyes, shielding them.

I feel her watching me from the kitchen window.

We go to see *The Armageddon Complex,* a disaster film with a tidal wave, a tornado, a fire, a global-warming theme. Among the special effects are that the temperature in the theater changes from 55 to 90 degrees during the film—*You freeze, you cook, you wish you'd planned ahead.*

The popcorn is oversalted. Before the tidal wave hits, I am panting with thirst. "Water," I whisper, climbing over her, into the aisle.

She pulls me back into my seat. "Don't go."

At key moments, she covers her eyes and waits until I squeeze her free hand to give her the all clear.

We are in the car on the way home. She is driving. The night is black. We move through the depths of darkness—the thin yellow line, the pathway home unfolds before us. There is the hum of the engine, the steadiness of her foot on the gas.

"We have to talk," I tell her.

"We talk constantly. We never stop talking."

"There's something I need to . . ." I say, not finishing the thought.

A deer crosses the road. My wife swerves. The car goes up a hill, trees fly by, the car goes down, we are rolling, we are hanging upside-down, suspended, and then boom, we are back on our feet, the air bag smashes me in the face, punches me in the nose. The steering wheel explodes into her chest. We are down in a ditch with balloons pressed into our faces, suffocating.

"Are you hurt?" she asks.

"I'm fine," I say. "Are you all right?"

"Did we hit it?"

"No, I think it got away."

The doors unlock.

"I'm sorry," she says, "I'm so sorry. I didn't see it coming."

The air bags are slowly deflating—losing pressure.

"I want to live," I tell her. "I just don't know how."

Lost and Legendary Aviators
Paul LaFarge

Lost Aviator, 1

IN 1678 THE SIEUR DULHUT, whom everyone in America called Duluth, traveled across Lake Michigan into the Mississippi Valley. There he spoke to Indians who told him that, if he went a few days farther West, he would find a salt sea. This was the Western Sea, from which a great river flowed into the Pacific, which ran all the way to China. Probably hundreds of Europeans were looking for a river to the Pacific, but Duluth was hardier than the others, and better informed, and an aristocrat to boot. He grew up in a castle with a tapestry that showed a unicorn luring tiny knights to their orange, woven death; so he could say that he knew from long experience the dangers the woods held for solitary men. He took a party of Frenchmen and Indians several times toward the Western Sea, and came so close to it that he encountered Indians who, in his opinion, spoke with a Chinese accent. But the sea hung back, always one story out of reach.

In the same year, a locksmith named Besnier who was no kind of aristocrat at all, and whom nobody had heard of except his wife and his three children and those whose locks he fixed, built a folly. It looked like Christ's Cross but with square wings at the end of each crosspiece. He claimed he'd done Christ one better: the savior had to carry his cross, whereas Besnier's winged cross would carry *him.* To prove it, he strapped his arms and legs to the posts and threw himself off a chair. His wife, scandalized by her husband's christological comparisons, let him lie on the floor, groaning, for a full half an hour before she unstrapped him and helped him to his feet. Besnier's nose was broken and his shirt bloody. "Well, my sweet fool," his wife said, "Have you learned your lesson?" Besnier looked past her, his eyes wide, seeing nothing that was and, indistinctly, something that was not, a look which will be so common in the annals of aviation that we might as well call it The Look right now. "I have, my wife. Bigger wings." He went back to his locksmithy and took the wings off his folly and put bigger ones on; while he was at it he put hinges on the wings and ran ropes through them so that they could be made to flap. With a new and improved cross and a bandaged nose Besnier went to the second-story window. "My husband, my husband, have you learned nothing? You must bear the cross—and I must too," she added, sighing. Her husband threw himself out the window. Miraculously his flapping wings carried him across the street, where he collided with the neighbor's house, fell and broke his arm. His wife helped him off with the wings. "Now you see how it is, my husband. The first time you didn't listen to the Lord, and you broke your nose. This time you didn't listen to your wife, and look, it is worse." Besnier groaned and clutched his arm. He lay in bed for three weeks, then one day his wife found him hauling a ladder up to the garret. "What are you doing?" she asked him, and Besnier said, "I am going to jump from the roof." "No you won't," his wife said. "I had your infernal wings broken up for firewood and gave them to the priest." Besnier cursed the priest and his wife, went into his workshop and locked the door from within. He came out sometime later with two wingèd metal poles, which he defied anyone to burn. He climbed up on the roof. The neighbor saw him there and asked what he was doing. "He's gone mad," his wife said. People gathered to watch; someone sent for the priest, and soon there was a crowd outside the locksmith's house. Eventually he jumped off the roof, flapping—and a miracle carried him all the way over the roof of the neighbor's house, and a little ways down the street, before miracles, which are notoriously inconstant, let him go. This time he broke his neck. The priest made the sign of the cross and said a few words; Besnier's wife took her husband home and laid him out to be buried, and the blacksmith took the wings and made them into a kettle and three frying pans. Besnier's flight was never reported to the Academy of Sciences; news of it did not reach the King, although he heard about Duluth's failed mission West, and, in time, commissioned another party to look for the water route to the Pacific. No one followed Besnier—but, on the other hand, his wings held him in the air for a few seconds, whereas the Pacific could not be reached by water, and never was.

Lost Aviator, 2

Mr. James Means of Boston. Undistinguished as to height, physique. Marked preference for the colors beige and taupe. Resident in

Dartmouth Street, just off Copley Square. Left-handed by birth and by election a Methodist. Mr. Means believes in ends and his mind is frequently on ultimate things of every variety: the conversion of the last heathen on earth, for example. In the mind of Mr. Means this takes place at the foot of an enormous tree in the Amazon jungle. The planet's last heathen lives high up in the branches of the tree—how else would he have avoided the truth for so long?—where he has a sort of log cabin, bound together with tropical vines. A great crowd has gathered at the foot of the tree. All the heathen's family are there, and the elders of his village, wearing their traditional skirts of dried grass; their faces are painted with designs in blue mud, but they all wear little silver crucifixes and some carry rosary beads. A quantity of Methodists and also missionaries of the Baptist Quaker Mennonite Lutheran Episcopalian and Adventist faiths are also present to witness the event. Behind them a circle of reporters equipped with notebooks and cameras. From this crowd a man in a tan suit and taupe fedora steps forward. He approaches the base of the tree and calls out that if the savage will not come down to religion, then religion will go up to him, i.e., the savage. This challenge gets no response from the tree. Upon which Mr. Means, for it is Mr. Means, produces a small wooden rod with a helical propeller at one end, and at the other a little string basket. He places a travel-sized Bible in the basket and gives the rod a sharp twist with his palms. The helicopter flies upward into the branches of the tree and for a blessèd moment no one says a word. The missionaries and reporters are murmuring their doubt when the tree's lowest branches part, and the last heathen in the world jumps to the ground. He holds the Bible in one hand and the helicopter in the other, and he shouts up into the branches of the tree that never has he seen anything so wonderful as this, this Great Spirit who makes books fly! Great cheering of missionaries, reporters, village elders, etc. Among the other last things Mr. Means has imagined: the peeling of the last orange on Earth, and the last dog crossing the last street anywhere, although this latter gives him cause for eschatological speculation, as it's entirely possible that dogs and streets will not cease to exist simultaneously. Mr. Means' contribution to aviation: a proposal, in 1891, for a sort of carriage with a vertical shaft coming out of its top, and a screw at the end of the shaft. Vertical planes set far apart to prevent rotation of the carriage. Although the machine was never built, and would most likely not have worked had it been built, Mr. Means expressed great confidence in his method. "If you want to bore through the air," he said, "the best way is to set up your borer and bore and bore."

LEGENDARY AVIATOR, 1

King Bladud of England, father of the fabled King Lear. Physical appearance not known. When not busy with his kingly duties, Bladud liked to terrify his subjects by leaping from towers strapped to a device of his own imagining, a pair of wings made of pine struts and leather boiled in wax. He would plummet toward the earth, shouting, "The King has wings! The King has wings!" and arrest his fall only at the last moment, when he would land unhurt and collapse with laughter. Then he would run up to the top of his tower and jump off again. His counselors urged him to give the wings up, but he refused, saying that the ways of power were not to be questioned. To prove it he doubled the royal levy on goats, and decreed that everyone would henceforth have to dance on his birthday. He died when a gust of wind sent him tumbling through the roof of one of his own temples, in the city of Trinovante; and England got Lear, who seemed like an improvement, for a while at least.

LEGENDARY AVIATOR, 2

Simon, called the Magician by some, and by others the Wise. "In the thirteenth year of the reign of the Emperor Nero, Simon undertook to rise toward heaven like a bird in the presence of everybody. The legend relates that the people assembled to view so extraordinary a phenomenon and Simon rose into the air through the assistance of the demons in the presence of an enormous crowd. But that Saint Peter, having offered up a prayer, the action of the demons ceased, and the magician was crushed in the fall and perished instantly."[1] What the legend does not tell: how when Simon fell everyone cried out, and how they circled his body, not daring to touch it. Peter, who was just plain Peter in those days, stood at the edge of the crowd, in a blue robe, pug-nosed, shouting and waving his staff as if the world were populated by kine and he their drover. He told them that he had ordered the demons to let Simon fall, and that it was a great miracle.

[1] Chanute, *Progress in Flying Machines*, 77.

But an old woman in the crowd remarked that when Simon was in Aricia he used to put on a puppet show which the children of Aricia loved very much. A bearded king got drunk and said something lewd to his wife, who chased him back and forth across the stage and finally walloped him with an amphora, and then it all began again. No one could figure out how he made the puppets move without touching them. It was just like magic. "The boys followed him everywhere, tugging at the hem of his magician's robe, and wouldn't give him a moment's peace. Simon said the trick with the puppets came from Egypt and there weren't but three or four people in the world who could do it. He promised to teach my grandson, but the boy died of typhus." When she had finished speaking, Peter said, "Bring your grandson to me, and I will give him life again." "Life," the woman said, "all right, but what about puppets?" And, Peter not deigning to answer an objection he considered absurd, the crowd dispersed, debating amongst themselves whether fickle but spectacular demons were better or worse than no demons at all. That night Simon's body was carried to Aricia, and then to Terracina, where he was buried.

Lost Aviator, 3

Mr. Eric Dudgeon, of Morristown, New Jersey, the celebrated maker of hydraulic jacks. Mr. Dudgeon participates in a yearly re-enactment of the decisive battles of the Revolutionary War fought in or near Morristown, New Jersey; every November fifteenth you may find him walking back and forth within the enclosure of Washington's Fort dressed in a coat as blue as the day and breeches which from the whiteness of them you would say had fallen from the clouds with the first flakes of November snow, and had not yet been sullied by the New Jersey woods. Mr. Dudgeon wears a powdered periwig and rouges his cheeks for the occasion; the effect is a whisper girlish, but no mind. When the lobsterbacks see him coming with a long-bore musket (surplus in real life from the Civil War) they throw their for-the-occasion British hands into the air and run, year after blessed year. Mr. Dudgeon feels an inarticulate sympathy for the British, for the Americans who have volunteered to play the British. There's something patriotic about supplying the nation with a not-too-tough enemy, some actual courage which is different in kind as well as in degree from the small enthusiasm which gets Mr.

Dudgeon out of bed at four A.M. every November fifteenth, into the periwig and aforementioned blue coat. Every year Mr. Dudgeon thinks, *next year I'll be a Brit,* but when the times comes to choose sides he always takes the American, for reasons which, to him, are as elusive as those flakes of November snow, which are lost almost at once in the thick of the woods. The War, to take sides in the War . . . What Mr. Dudgeon might say, if he could catch one of those snowflake-thoughts on his tongue: *The War is never pretend. Even though we are pretending it is real, for as long as we play at it.* Therefore he would no more play a Brit than he would, say, walk into a meeting with the suppliers of the parts of his hydraulic jacks in a pink tulle skirt and suggest that they dance the minuet, although—here's another snowflake—Mr. Dudgeon has, in fact, imagined putting on a pink tulle skirt and going into a meeting and taking the hand of the man who supplies the parts of his hydraulic jacks and putting a cylinder in the phonograph he ordered from his neighbor Mr. Thomas Edison of Menlo Park, New Jersey, cranking the phonograph and spinning with the supplier, faster and faster, to the recorded thump of a German orchestra which, when it was last a gathering of actual, human bodies, presided over the marriage of someone named Fleischmann to someone named Gespenst. And when the phonograph wound down, spinning, slowly, what a revolution then, eh, boys? The world of hydraulic jacks would be forever transformed. Or so he imagines. Never actually having done it. What would it charge? The War is fought to the same end every year and even the pretend is weighty and the springs which keep it turning aren't as strong as they were in Washington's day.

Mr. Dudgeon's contribution to aviation: like his neighbor, Mr. Edison, he "tested the lifting effect of various forms of screws when rotated by steam power, and, like Mr. Edison, he stopped in disgust when he found how small was the lift in proportion to the power expended."

Alice in the Time of the Jabberwock

Robert Coover

When the Red King awoke, Alice found herself back in Wonderland, still at timeless tea with her demented companions the Hatter and the Hare and being used as a cushion by both of them, her armchair occupied by the snoring Dormouse, his little two-toothed rodent mouth slackly agape, and she knew then that her whole life aboveground had been only a dream, the King's dream, just as that ill-tempered little fat boy Tweedledee had foreseen, his puzzle about who was in whose dream bitterly resolved, and she was back where she had always been.

"What's that Dormouse doing in my chair?" she complained with a yawn squeezed to half a yawn, feeling dreadfully suppressed. The Hatter's ten-bob-six hat was pushed under her chin, holding it up, and her upper lip was mustached by the March Hare's unwashed ear. "Off with its head," she added despondently and closed her eyes, hoping to fall asleep again and dream the Red King back to sleep so that she might, at least in *his* dreams, return aboveground once more to play with her cats and her games and take those lovely rowing expeditions on the magic river with her dream-sisters and the older gentlemen, so like wizards and magicians. Ah, those golden afternoons! Vanished like summer midges, and the rest of the century (that's what they called it up there) with them.

"The rule is," muttered the Hatter, shifting about to make himself more comfortable and Alice even less so (the Hare's ear twitched and she sneezed), "to get ahead, you must start behind."

"All right then," grunted Alice, elbowing free of her tea-sodden companions and rising heavily, "off with its behind." And she rolled the slumbering Dormouse out of her chair and collapsed into it, curling not into one corner as she used to do, but into both at the same time. Indeed, she did feel a great temptation to sink back into Dreamland, envying the oblivious Dormouse at her feet, who once told her (it was in the dead of night after one of those frumious battles, she couldn't sleep, she felt like she was going crazy, or if everyone here in Wonderland is already crazy, then like she was going sane, which was even more terrifying) that he sometimes went to bed so soon after getting up that he found himself back in bed *before* he got up. She was so tired now all the time that just *being* awake was an insufferable labor, but whenever she tried to sleep she found herself back in the Jabberwock's blistering grip, her body cramping and itching and her head pounding, a fearsome experience whose mere anticipation made her irritable and nervous whenever she was awake, which was, however dimly, most of the time.

"What, pray, is the reason," she asked, noticing them now, tied to the chairs and to the teapot handle, "for all those black balloons?"

"Inasmuch as a reason is a premise to an argument," replied the Mad Hatter in his haughtiest manner, perhaps somewhat put out at losing his cushion, "I suppose what you really wish to know is what is the argument? And the argument is a party."

"A party can't be an argument!"

"It is seldom anything else!" declared the March Hare, dropping his paw in his teacup, then gazing at it with a puzzled expression. "Oh! My paw's wet!" he exclaimed in a soft whining voice that reminded Alice of one of her dream-sisters from long ago.

"Of course it's wet, you poor crazed creature," said the Hatter. "Take it out of your teacup!"

The Hare raised his paw to his face and stared at it quizzically, his ears adroop. "It's *still* wet!"

"You might try sitting on it," suggested Alice, trying to be helpful.

The Hare peered up hopefully at Alice and tucked his paw beneath him. "Oh dear! Now my *tail's* wet!"

"Of course it is," said the Hatter. "That's called effect and cause."

"No," said Alice. "Cause and effect. The cause comes first."

"Nonsense," said the Hatter with a deprecatory snort that caused the tea to overflow his cup beneath his nose. "What came first was that his tail is wet. You heard him. *Now* comes the cause!"

"The cause . . ." insisted Alice, desperately weary of such madness, but unable to stop herself.

"There!" exclaimed the Hatter triumphantly. "You see?"

". . . Is his wet paw. His paw was wet before his tail."

"Exactly!" said the Hatter, feeling quite proud of himself. "Just as I said! It's like the balloons. First come the balloons, then comes the birthday party!"

"Birthday? Whose birthday?"

"Why, yours, dear child," said the March Hare, now sitting on both front paws, the second presumably there to dry the first and the tail as well. "The rest of us don't even *have* birthdays!"

"Mine? Again? But which—?"

"Your seventh, of course," said the Hatter with a patronizing grimace, as though speaking to an idiot or a small child.

"But it's *always* my seventh birthday! It was my seventh birthday when I *came* here!"

"I don't know about that," replied the Mad Hatter, "but last time, or some other time or times before or after that, it was, if I am not mistaken, your tenth birthday. And all the other numbers have had their party, too, it's only fair. I don't even mention your crowning party, which was your four thousandth *un*birthday—at *least!* Have you forgotten?"

"No, I remember. How could I not? It was the first time I stained my pinafore."

"An historic occasion!" pronounced the Dormouse, still fast asleep under the table.

"It was the Queen of Hearts's fault, she made me do it. It was just spite."

"It?" asked the Hatter. "You mean the stain?"

"No, the Queen. It—"

"Then you mean 'she.' *She* was spite."

"No, she was not," said Alice with an impatient sigh, feeling another headache coming on, the heartless red-eyed Jabberwock looming not far behind. "Spite was the *reason.* I was young and she was old." She'd thought about that tyrant often of late: all her dreadful moods, her furious passion, how she could become like a wild beast, screaming, shouting, crimson with fury, and what the poor old thing must have been going through.

"And the Queen was the argument?"

She sighed again, this time more in exasperated resignation. She'd promised herself never to come here again, but the truth was, she'd never been anywhere else. "You could say so."

"Thank you! I *will!*" exclaimed the Hatter, and he rose from his chair and put down his teacup and removed his hat, cradling it in his elbow, and solemnly declared in a manner he might have thought was singing:

"Alice had a little stain,
Which brought on royal laughter,
For everywhere Queen Alice went,
The stain would follow after

It followed her to tea one day,
'Twas quite a sight to see;
It made us all faint dead away
To see a stain at tea!

The Red Queen screamed and pointed to
The cause of our confusion.
If the argument was she, we knew,
That stain was her conclusion!

And though Queen Alice washed it out,
The stain came back again,
And went on following her about
As a banner of her reign!

But all of this was long ago,
It happened yesterday!
Where now's the stain? I do not know!
Nor should I, could I, say!"

From underneath the table, as the Hatter took his bows, came the little click of the Dormouse's clapping paws, and the sleepy remark, punctuated by low rumbling snores, "My point exactly!" The March Hare tried to clap while sitting on his paws, which made him bob up and down in his chair and caused his ears to waggle stupidly, but Alice only slumped into her armchair and said: "It wasn't like that at all." But maybe, she thought, because "confusion" and "conclusion" had wormed their way into her mind somehow like little tunneling centipedes, it *was* a bit like that *now,* now when it *had* stopped following her about, another cruel joke and she again the butt, so to speak. And, oh dear, *did* she have centipedes in her head? Was *that* her problem? She clutched her furrowed brow with both hands. It seemed best to change the subject. "When *did* I come here?" she asked, probably not for the first time.

The Mad Hatter removed his large round watch from his checkered waistcoat pocket and put it to his ear, which was half-hidden by his high stiff collar. "At least two hours ago," he said matter-of-factly, then put the watch in his mouth and sucked on it like rock candy. "Give or take a yard or two," he added, mumbling around the watch.

Alice scowled. "Do you even know *how* to tell time?" she demanded.

"Of *course,* I do!" he shouted with such vehemence that the watch flew out and landed with a plunk in his teacup. His notorious quarrel with Time had never ceased, and it showed now in his pallid tea-stained face, which wanted to grow old but couldn't. "What do you wish me to tell him? And make it short! He's very busy, you know!"

"Tell him," Alice said, more to herself than to the Hatter, with whom one did not really converse, but only reparteed, "to get lost!"

"Ah, no need to tell him *that!*" exclaimed the March Hare, squirming on his forepaws. "Time is easily lost without needing reminders!"

"Even if you can keep Time, beat Time, or take him by the forelock," declared the Mad Hatter portentously, ticking these items off with his fingers as though enumerating a bill of particulars, "Time gets lost just the same."

"I know," said Alice wearily. Reparteed, she thought; that's rather good, I can use it later at the re-party. If I don't forget it as I forget everything else these days. Probably I should make a memorandum. "Time flies and all that."

"Time flies?" cried the Hatter, falling back in alarm.

"She must mean horse flies," whispered the Hare.

"Butterflies," suggested the sleeping Dormouse from under the table.

"Bread-and-butterflies, *he* means," whispered the Hare.

"Speaking of that," said Alice. "Are there any sandwiches for my party? I'm desperately hungry!"

"There *were* sandwiches," the Mad Hatter said, stirring his tea with his pocket watch. "But someone stole them."

"Maybe it was the Knave of Hearts," said Alice gloomily. "That's in his line."

"In one of them anyway," agreed the Hatter somewhat patronizingly.

"No," squealed the March Hare, and he removed one paw from beneath him and pointed it at Alice. "*She* ate them all!"

"Did I?" They were all staring accusingly at her, all those with their heads above the table, that is. Well, it was possible. These days, she consumed all things edible, and some things not, as soon as her gaze fell upon them—EAT ME! DRINK ME! the whole world urged, and she did—but she was always as hungry afterwards as before, everything eaten reduced instantly to ash in her inner oven. Even her droppings, as they called them here in Wonderland where animals, after all, were animals, were hard as agates and scorched-looking, dark little pellets of the sort left by the dear old White Rabbit in his dithery ramblings. It was all so sad. So woefully mome and mimsy, as they were wont to say. She looked down at the spots on the backs of her hands and began, as she had so often done of late, quite without reason, as if reason had any business here, to cry.

"Now, now!" exclaimed the Mad Hatter, putting down his cup with a clatter as though rapping a gavel. "No tears, please! Definitely out of order at birthday parties!"

But still the tears kept flooding out of her as though having been bottled up in there for years, maybe that accounted for the terrible dryness she'd been feeling recently, inside and out, and now she was just wasting what precious little moisture she had left, it was pouring out of her from everywhere, tears or whatever, she couldn't hold any of it back. "Oh boo hoo!" she was wailing. Her face was wet, her pinafore, she was wet all over, there were puddles collecting at her feet.

"Now stop that, stop that!" cried the Hatter, scrambling up into his chair for higher ground. "A great girl like you, you ought to be ashamed of yourself! Stop this moment, I tell you!"

Oh, she *was* ashamed! And not just of the crying, but of everything that was happening to her! A great girl indeed! What was she doing here in this crazy nightmare, looking like this, leaking like this, her whole body like a huge squeezed sponge? It was hideous! *She* was hideous! She wanted to wake up! She wanted to go home and be a little girl again! She nearly did once, nearly did escape this terrible place—she could still remember this, though she'd forgotten almost everything else—for it happened one day that she found, in a corner of the White Queen's Castle, a looking-glass through which she might have passed, just as she had passed this direction long before, it might even have been the same one. But she had been so alarmed by the huge baggy thing she's seen in it coming straight at her (the creature's upper arms were flapping like wings! and all those *chins!*), she'd screamed and fled, and she'd never found her way back again. "Oh boo hoo hoo!" she sobbed. "I'm so miserable!"

"There, there," said the March Hare, who had got up off his front paws and splashed around the table to comfort her. The entire back garden was under water. The Hare cradled her head in his starched shirtfront and patted it tenderly. "Perhaps it *was* the Knave of Hearts who stole the sandwiches! Yes, yes, I'm sure it was!"

"But what's *happening* to me?" she bawled. "I can't stop *changing!* Who *am* I? *What* am I?"

"Why, you're a little girl, of course," snapped the Mad Hatter in something of a peevish temper, still squatting in his chair above the flood like an angry toad. "Just like you've always been! As large as life and—"

"No, no! *Much* larger! *Look* at me!"

"Now, now," said the March Hare, still patting her head. "We love you just as you are, dear child!" He gave her a rather smelly hug, then reached under the table to pick up the snoring Dormouse by his long tail and save him from drowning. "And not to worry about the sandwiches," he added, tying the Dormouse's tail around a tree limb overhead. "The Duchess is bringing one of her turnip and trotters birthday cakes with her famous black pepper frosting!"

"Oh no!" gasped Alice damply, but somehow the thought of the peppery birthday cake and the ugly mustachioed Duchess, who was *altogether* uglier than Alice, even as she was now (hairs had appeared on Alice's lip, too, but she'd pulled them all out), finally did bring the tears to an end, though her snuffles continued and her breast heaved in wobbly little spasms. Above her, the upside-down Dormouse, looking wet and bedraggled, but still sound asleep, swung idly back and forth like the pendulum of a clock, an image all too prevalent of late. If only she could get rid of all clocks. Clocks and looking-glasses. And birthday parties.

"Are you all right now?" asked the Mad Hatter, offering her, with some reluctance, the small square of linen he kept tucked in his cuff. Alice nodded and blew her nose in it. Her fat nose. With the creases above it that looked like the March Hare's ears. "Very well and good!" he said as though he were concluding a difficult argument. "Have some more tea then!" And he handed her a cup from an empty place across the table.

"I shouldn't," Alice said with a snuffle, taking up the cup. It was the worst thing for her really. "It just makes my hot flushes hotter." Not to mention worse things. She felt moist and faint and limp in all her joints as if she'd just been wrestling again with the whiffling Jabberwock, and there was a wet stinging tingle in that tender unseen place, a sensation she had come to associate now with moments when she was overswept with feelings of regret. Maybe all that talk of the Knave of Hearts had set it off. That shameless roué. She remembered how she first saw him (he seemed so old then and so much younger now), proudly bearing the King's crown on a crimson velvet cushion as though carrying a great piece of fragile pastry. He was quite royally enrobed, though an accidental glimpse when he slipped sideways suggested to Alice that he was more decorously attired on the near side than the back, which was quite bare. And then later she saw him for the second time at his trial, cruelly clapped in chains and threatened with execution and looking very pleased with himself in a tragic sort of way. When she rose to give evidence and knocked over the jury box, he winked at her with the one eye she could see as though to say he understood what she was doing, even though she did not. It caused a brief little flutter in her chest, rather like indigestion, a flutter that returned whenever he was near. Over the years, if they were years and not, as the Mad Hatter would have it, yards, he had attempted countless advances, using all his deceptive finesse, and she had always cut him cruelly, dealing him insult after insult, telling him he didn't suit her at all, then bidding him a frozen farewell, that flutter fluttering all the while. Perhaps she had not played fairly. With him. With herself. This was what the tingle said, had been saying ever since the flushes began. "Are other people really coming to my party?" she asked with a rueful sigh.

"They can't *come,*" said the Mad Hatter, settling back into his chair as the waters receded. "Not the way Time's behaving! But they will be here all the same."

Alice understood this. It was the way things happened here. Not at all or all of a sudden. "I rather wish they wouldn't," she said, feeling damp all over. "I don't think I want to see anyone."

"Then close your eyes," said the March Hare.

"That's not what I meant."

"Then you must say what you mean," admonished the Hatter.

"And mean what you say, I know, I know," said Alice snappishly.

"No, no, that's not the same thing, not the same thing a bit!" exclaimed the Mad Hatter vehemently, his polka-dotted bowtie bobbing.

"You might just as well say," said the March Hare, "that 'I like what I get' is the same thing as " 'I get what I like!' "

"Yes, yes," sighed Alice, having heard all this before, "or that 'I see what I eat' is the same thing as 'I eat what I see.' "

"I'm afraid it *is* the same thing with you, dear child," sniffed the Hatter.

"Oh," cried Alice, "why did I come here? How did this happen to me?"

"The question," said the Hatter, raising a pedagogical finger into the air, "is not how but whether!"

"*Stop it!*" screamed Alice, so loudly that her empty teacup cracked and two of the black balloons popped. "I can't *bear* this any longer! Think of something *else* to do!"

The Dormouse, swinging idly overhead, opened his eyes when she screamed, but now closed them again. "We might play games," he murmured sleepily.

"You mean, like Chest or Chuckers?" asked the March Hare. "Or Dafts or Chin Rubby?"

"Double Chin Rubby, more like," said the Mad Hatter, catty as ever.

"Or Hide and Shriek!" shrieked the March Hare, clapping all four paws. "Or Rings Around the Nosy, Alice Fall Down!"

"Or Drop the Rag," continued the Mad Hatter with a superior smirk. "Or Lacie Loosie!"

"That's much too clever," remarked Alice, repressing her urge to scream again. "And not very nice."

"Quoit," agreed the sleeping Dormouse, speaking up quite clearly, whereupon the March Hare, as if it were his turn to do so, said: "I vote the young lady tells us a story."

"All right," said Alice, mopping her brow with the Hatter's soggy bit of linen, for though she did not know what story she might have to tell, she certainly did not want to hear again about the three little sisters in the nauseous treacle well, or any other nonsense her mad companions might dream up. She felt headachy and grievously weary and bloated and as parched within as she was wet without. "Once upon a time—"

"I beg your pardon!" interrupted the Hatter.

"I'm not offended," said the March Hare.

"I was speaking to the little girl, you mindless beast!" exclaimed the Hatter. "Did you say 'once *upon* a time?'" he asked, turning to Alice accusingly.

"It's how a story begins," replied Alice, though she knew her explanation was far too sensible to suffice.

"I'm afraid, then, it begins quite wrongly," sniffed the Mad Hatter. "One cannot be upon Time. Ahead of Time perhaps. Behind the Times when they are out walking together. But never upon Time! He would not allow it!"

"Very well," sighed Alice, a bit desperately. "Once within time, then?"

"Scandalous!"

"Beyond?" The Hatter plucked his watch from his teacup and consulted it, but said nothing, so she hurried on. "There was once beyond time a little girl, an eager curious child who thought the world a wondrous place, and she was very pretty and loved by everyone, especially older gentlemen, and so small she could curl up in the very corner of an armchair. She lived aboveground with her cat named Dinah and two darling little kittens—"

"Was one of them white, the other black?" asked the Hatter.

"Yes. Have you heard this story before?"

"Before what?"

"Before now of course."

"I'm afraid that's impossible," said the Hatter with just a trace of melancholy, wiping his watch on his long coat tails. "It's always now. It can't be anything else. Before and after are just make-believe."

"Well, so is my story, then," said Alice, "for all this happened long ago and in another place. I don't remember what it was called, but there was an 'X' in it and a great river ran through it."

"How curious!" exclaimed the Hatter. "I never saw a river run!"

"I saw a river fall once," said the March Hare.

"I saw a river wave," muttered the Dormouse in his upended sleep.

"Aboveground," Alice said with determination, for she could be stubborn, too, "rivers run."

"It must be a strange place, indeed!" observed the Hatter, pocketing his watch after staring into its face as though to see the strange place there. "I suppose next you'll say that cause comes before effect up there!"

"Yes, and punishment always follows the crime, and two and two always make four, and time is not a person and never goes backwards, and when you say 'once upon a time,' that is exactly what you mean!" Alice was not certain about any of these declarations, shouted out so fiercely, for she had not been aboveground, except in her dreams (or the Red King's), for a very long time, and at least two of them seemed quite likely false, but she felt she had the upper hand at last in this conversation, and she did not intend to lose it by displaying any doubt.

"Two and two make *whom?*" the March Hare squealed with some amazement, counting his paws in a circular way such that he never came out with an even number. "I can't believe it! They must be out of their minds up there!"

"And animals don't speak aboveground! They are only spoken *to*, and often quite severely!" cried Alice, feeling another of her tearful rages coming on. The Jabberwock wouldn't come here, would he? Not to her birthday party! "And the only hares they have up there are jugged hares!"

"My ears! What a nightmare!" yelped the March Hare, and he

knocked over the milk jug in his alarm and fell off his chair.

"Now look what you've done with your cruel aboveground talk, you silly goose!" shouted the Mad Hatter, skimming some of the spilled milk into his teacup. "You've frightened the dear fellow half into his wits!"

"I'm sorry. I take it back," said Alice, regretting her outburst, for she was at heart a considerate person even in her present bitter and sometimes uncontrollable condition.

"You *can't* take it back! Not if it's been said! You couldn't take it back even if you tried with both hands!"

"I wouldn't *try* to take it back with my *hands,*" sighed Alice, pushing herself with effort out of her armchair, which was in any case still soaked through from her flood of tears and gave one the disagreeable sensation of snuggling amongst wet sheep, and she plodded around the table to give the March Hare a helping hand. Before she could reach him, however, they were suddenly surrounded by the party guests, all her Wonderland friends, everyone from the stammering Dodo to the pedantic Red Queen, all laughing and screaming and sneezing (the black pepper cake had arrived and had been consumed almost before it had been cut) and hopping about in the traditional birthday party fashion—aboveground, they had a phrase for this mad hopping, but she'd forgotten it—and the poor Hare found himself being quite soundly trampled until finally a kindly gentleman dressed in white paper, or else made of it, discovered him there and, with a thin folded bow, helped him to his feet again.

"You can't think how glad I am to see you again, you dear old thing!" said someone with a deep muscular voice, tucking a fat arm into Alice's and digging a sharp chin into her shoulder. It was the ugly pocket-mouthed Duchess, she who'd brought the cake, making her usual clumsy and annoying show of affection, if it was affection and not something more sinister. "Isn't it a lovely day!" she added, her hoarse voice squawking a few notes higher, for she had to stretch up on her tiptoes now to lodge her chin on Alice's shoulder as was always her custom during their conversations. "It's simply perfect for your crowning party!"

"You're too late for that, I'm afraid. This is more like a croning party," said Alice miserably

"Too late? Well, the moral of *that,*" said the Duchess, "is that it is never too late to say you're sorry."

"It's always too late," said Alice, for she had just spied the Knave of Hearts shuffling in with the rest of the pack, "or too early."

"You are quite right, my dear, time and tide run with the Hare and hunt with the hounds, making haste slowly, waiting for no one, who is always late anyway, the moral being, it is better to be safe than be sorry."

"Oh dear," exclaimed Alice, wondering if in fact it might not have been better to be sorry, "are there hounds here, too? It's getting very crowded!" Indeed, they were pressed in on all sides now by royalty and commoners alike, two-legged and otherwise, some in party hats and blowing little paper horns, others singing birthday songs of the rather unflattering "saggy/baggy, frumpy/dumpy" sort ("Happy birthday to Alice!" they were singing, "And to her spreading hips! To her varicose veins! And her tender nips!"), or telling impenetrable riddles, like why is a bearded lady like hot mustard or a candle flame like a fat bum? Just so much stuff and nonsense, which, together with the heavy presence of the overbearing Duchess with her squeezes and pinches, left Alice feeling quite put out.

"I know one," wheezed the Duchess in her ear, her sharp chin drumming on her shoulder as she spoke. "A riddle, I mean. Two make it, two bake it, two break it. What is it?"

"That's easy," said Alice. "Bread."

"No, it's a baby," corrected the Duchess, "the moral being, you know, as you brew so shall you bake!" And she gave Alice a thick suffocating hug as though clapping her in an oven.

"Don't do that, please! I hurt there!" she complained, and pushed the Duchess's hands away. All around her now, they were popping the black balloons, or else she was developing another savage headache.

"Oh, dear child! Are you not feeling well?"

"No, it's, well . . . the time . . ." Alice hesitated, for she did not like to admit even to herself what the trouble was (she glanced at the Knave of Hearts who was flirting quite openly with Lily, the White Queen's daughter, proposing to her a game of vingt-et-un in the March Hare's private chambers), but she was near to tears again and in need of a friend who might understand. "It's, you know . . . the Jabberwock," she allowed at last.

"Ah! The time of the Jabberwock! I remember it well!" announced the Duchess to all present, and released a windy sigh, though whether from nostalgia or anguish, it was hard to tell. "It was in those mimsical and frabjous days, as they are called, that I acquired my passion for black pepper. And for other things, not all as savory. Baby soup, for example. The moral being, of course, that one's passions are irresistible, but too often indigestible."

"I'm afraid I don't know much about passions, or babies either," said Alice mournfully.

"Well, they're a little bit like fashions and rabies," said the Duchess, stroking the hair on her lip, "though somewhat less civilized."

Around her, her party guests were behaving in *very* uncivil fashion, carrying on like the indiscreet animals that many of them were, and showing manners little better, those that weren't. Some like the Lion and Pat the Guinea Pig had taken off all their clothes, if they'd had any on to begin with, and the Unicorn was doing very improper things with his horn, eliciting violent squeals of alarm and laughter wherever he went. "Sure, I don't like it, yer honour, at all at all!" cried Bill the Lizard, flying through the air, and the Queen of Hearts kept fluttering her skirts and shrieking for the Unicorn's head. Even the old White Rabbit seemed quite undignified in his stiff exaggerated bouncing, his eyes glazed over and staring blindly as though he might have been back at his snuff pot again.

"I was just dreaming about you my dear," said the Red King, passing by, looking utterly exhausted, his eyes the color of his regalia.

"A nightmare!" added the Red Queen with an accusing scowl. "He's been suffering from insomnia ever since!"

"Perhaps you should have a little lie-down for a few days," Alice suggested hopefully, but the Red King only looked horrified and fled, he and the Queen speeding backwards in the direction from which they'd come.

Led by the Mad Hatter, many of the partygoers were still singing her birthday songs, or one of them anyway, Tweedledum and Tweedledee now taking turns reciting in their twittery little schoolboy voices alternating lines of another unpleasant verse:

"She's losing her hair,
There are pleats in her seat!
Her tummy's so big,
She can't see her feet!"

And here they wobbled their own round bellies in mockery, while all her friends howled out the Happy Birthday chorus.

"There's a moral about that," said the Duchess in her ear, "but I can't think what it is. It might be 'Honesty is the best policy,' or else 'Experience is the best teacher.' Or maybe 'All's for the best in the best of all possible worlds?' "

"I think I'm going to be ill again," said Alice dizzily, for she was feeling a sudden rush of the most intense heat to her chest, spreading quickly like a hot burrowing animal to her neck and face and arms, and she could feel the sweat breaking out all over and the wild palpitations of her heart—it's the Jabberwock!—and there was a terrible burning itch below that part of her they'd just been singing about as though their singing might have enkindled it. "Oh!" she gasped. "It's like being set upon by some dreadful storm!"

She turned to face the monster head-on then, quite willing just to die and have it over with, *no* one should have to suffer this, but it was only the ugly Duchess there behind her, smiling faintly, if that twitching of her massive jowls could be called smiling. "Just remember, dear," she growled gently, her dark scowl softening, "no matter the weather, old trots stick together!"

"I'm *not* an old trot!" she screamed.

"No, of course not, my love, who said you were?"

"I-I'm a little girl!"

"Yes, dear, aren't we all? The moral being—Ah! But take care of yourself! Something's going to happen!"

Something did. Someone sneezed behind her shoulder, and the heat immediately drained away, sinking into her tummy like heavy fog, and, more noisily that she might have hoped, left her by the ordinary passage.

"Ho! List! Who is it speaks so eloquently?" asked the Knave of Hearts with a sideways smirk at the vast landscape of her hinderparts, touching a kerchief plucked from his sleeve to his nose.

"I-I beg your pardon," whispered Alice, knowing that she was both pale and blushing at the same time, which probably gave her a very peculiar mottled look. The Knave was carrying a slice of the black birthday cake with a candle burning on it which he offered to her with a little bow and another sneeze into his kerchief, and because she was too embarrassed not to, she accepted it, though she hated black pepper and feared it would bring on another devastating flush.

"It makes you hot, you know," he said with a wink, pointing at the pepper.

"I certainly need no help for *that!*" replied Alice glumly.

"Do tell!" grinned the Knave with a suggestive roll of his eye, and he reached out to give her hip a thin papery pat. "I'll call that!"

"No, I mean *hot,* hot," she snapped, slapping his hand away with her free one. "Blistering hot. Sweaty sticky sickening hot. Not your kind of hot."

"Well, we won't know about that until we crack the deck, will we?" he murmured seductively, and stroked his waxed mustache, bobbed his eyebrow. "How about it, oh my queen? Just a round or two? Face up and jokers wild?"

All this was a mere routine, she knew, one he practiced like the rules of a game, for he was a Knave by design and could do no other, but should she ever play along and call his bluff, his hearts would blanch and he'd fold and flee in an instant. And why *had* she never played along? He was a notorious deceiver, of course, a thief and a seducer who casually discarded all the hearts he won or stole, and he could be insufferable with his knavish winks and nudges and his naughty innuendoes, which he probably thought were flattering but which were really quite insulting. She knew how to deal with him when he got out of hand, of course, and did—but what *was* out of hand on such occasions, and why was she so unbending? When asked at his trial, so very long ago (if it was not yesterday), what she knew about this business, she had to answer, "Nothing whatever," and she knew very little more now, and that learned more from watching her animal friends than from personal experience. She looked the Knave over. She could have done worse. He was handsome enough in a flat-headed sort of way (he was rather overly fond of his profile, she'd often told him), and his attentions always gave her own heart a little flutter as it was fluttering now. Wasn't that supposed to mean something? Perhaps it was not too late; perhaps, if she gave him just the least bit of encouragement (if only she knew how to *do* that!), he might still have a go. Well, the next time he suggested that she try playing stud poker or hearts or go-bang instead of old maid or solitaire, she should just follow his lead and say yes, thank you, do his bidding for once, why not? What did she have to lose but the infinite tedium of her Wonderland life? All these years of senseless tea parties! Whatever happened to her spirit of adventure?

Now, inspired perhaps by the loud singing going on around them and her own flushed hesitation, he bent toward her and asked: "Do you know the song, 'Tinkle, tinkle, little twat?' "

"I've heard something like it," she said politely, uncertain what a 'twat' was, but supposing it prudent not to ask. She smiled hopefully.

"It goes," said the Knave, "this way:

'Tinkle, tinkle, little twat,
How I wonder what you've got,
High above your dimpled thighs,
Like a clam up in the skies!' "

"That's really very rude, you know!" gasped Alice, somewhat aghast.

"There's more."

"I think that's quite enough!"

But the Knave only pursed his lips as if to blow a kiss, and she knew this was why she'd never said yes: he was so pompous and ill-mannered and utterly inconsiderate! Just like royalty. You played the game his way or you didn't play at all.

> "Tinkle, tinkle, little twat," he sang now,
> "High above the chamber pot—"

"*Stop it!*" cried Alice, and all her guests turned around to watch. "That's completely *stupid!*"

But he only grinned out of the side of his mouth and went right on:

> "How I wish I were a flower,
> "Underneath your golden—!"

"*NO!*" stormed Alice, her fury rising, hating herself for this shrill hysteria ("Off with his head!" is what she *felt* like screaming, and nearly did, unsure who she even *was* any more), but unable to stop herself. "You think you're a real *card,* don't you!" she cried out, and she took the lighted birthday candle from the cake and stabbed him with it in the middle of his royal pantaloons, burning a big brown hole there. "Now, dummy, you're a *marked* card!"

"You can't *do* that!" he shrieked. "*It's not allowed!*"

"Hmm. If that's your argument, yer honour," observed the mournful Carpenter, hovering nearby with a bitter tear in his eye and a toothpick in his blackened teeth, "there seems to be a hole in it," and the Walrus, stroking his long mustaches while gazing at Alice as though into a looking-glass, nodded solemnly. "Ah yes. Callooh, if I am not mistaken," he said, quite nonsensically. "And so, Callay."

The Knave shrieked again and flapped off in a rage, his hearts as black as spades, all the party guests now idiotically calloohing and callaying in his wake. Alice flung the slice of cake at his retreating backside, its plainness marred now by an ugly little brown hole, but hit the poor old Dodo on his beak instead.

"S-s-sorry!" exclaimed the Dodo, never at a loss for words or for a few extra syllables as well, and he looked up apprehensively at the sky as if it might be falling on him. "Always in the w-w-w-way!

I sh-sh-shouldn't even *be* here! Just a dod-dod-doddering old r-relic! I do-do-do-do apologize!"

"Poor old thing," growled the Duchess at Alice's shoulder. "Always lingering about as though afraid of being forgotten. He's become quite dot-dot-dotty in his old age."

"He was born in old age," said the Mad Hatter with a disparaging sniff. Well, thought Alice, still aflame, that's true, what with the way time works here. She must be quite a novelty for them. "Which reminds me, my dear, would you like to hear 'You are old, Father William'? It's one of your favorites."

"No, I wouldn't," sighed Alice, the rush of blood to her head and elsewhere slowly subsiding, aware now that she had just made her relations with the Knave very difficult, very difficult indeed. Why was she so out of control all the time? But the Hatter, one hand tucked inside his waistcoat and hat in hand, began to recite anyway, as she knew he would:

> "You are old, Mother Alice, and big as a door—"

"That's not 'You are old, Father William.' "

"Well, almost," said the Hatter. "Only a few of the words have got altered."

"It is wrong," she snapped, depression and perspiration flooding her, respectively, inside and out, "from beginning to—!"

"Don't interrupt, my child! Have you forgotten where you are?" he cried, then resumed his oratorical stance:

> "You are old, Mother Alice, and big as a door,
> And all covered with wrinkles and fat . . .!"

Forgotten where she is? Oh no, more the pity!

> ". . . And yet you still wear your old pinafore,
> Pray, what is the reason for that?"
>
> "I'll tell you, good sir," Mother Alice replied,
> "And I hope you'll not think that I'm bitter;
> Since I've grown I could not get it off if I tried
> For it won't lift off over my sitter!"

"Oh, stop, please!" She felt a pressure something like that of a closing nut cracker just behind her eyes, and her legs seemed suddenly as thick and ponderous as those of an elephant. "You're giving me a dreadful headache!" But there would be no stopping him, she knew, for the Hatter's madness was of the theatrical sort, and now all her guests had gathered around and were clapping rhythmically, spurring him on. In the end she'd have no choice but to run away.

> "You are old, Mother Alice, your hair has turned white,
> And your skin is as rough as sandstone!
> And yet you go chasing after each knave and knight,
> Why don't you leave them alone?"
>
> "I'll tell you, good sir," said Mother Alice in haste,
> "If you'll spare me a thought for my lot;
> All my life I've not been the chaser, but chased,
> It's high time that I ought to be caught!"
>
> "You are old, Mother Alice, and to be quite blunt,
> You seem to have run out of luck;
> It's clear that you've got a cork in your—"

But she never heard the rest. She had already fled, holding her head, the heat back, pounding at her temples, a kind of blindness overtaking her, and when she stopped running, if running could be said to be what she'd been doing (whatever, it exhausted her), she found herself standing, weak-kneed and fat legs aspraddle, wheezing heavily, in an old weedy garden, gone, as she, to seed. She wiped her dribbly nose on the apron front of her faded pinafore, sensing that the end of her story might not be very far away, whether or not she got past these duellos with the manxome Jabberwock, and she was frightened by that, and terribly depressed.

She knew well of course this sad garden which so reflected her own sad spirit. Alas. Her fault it looked like this. The flowers here, once quite lovely, used to talk. But then one day, enraged at her old tormentor the Rose, who liked to remind her that she was dropping her petals and fading fast, and who on that particular day had taken to reciting in her shrill little voice, "Alice, Alice, full of malice, why is your garden so dry," she'd simply plucked the wicked thing. "That will be enough of *that!*" she'd cried and snapped her fat little red head off. All the flowers had lost their color and withered away with a gasp of horror and had been utterly silent ever after, though sometimes, passing through, Alice thought she heard dry bitter whispers trailing in her wake.

Well, death, death and madness—the madness, as it were, of soldiering on for all the pointlessness of it, all the cruelty—these seemed to be the very essence of Wonderland, it was a wonder one should wonder. And—living garden, dead garden—did that mean that time really did pass in Wonderland? she asked herself, pressing her throbbing head between both sweaty palms. No, she replied, talking to herself as had ever been her wont. It only passed for her, fabulous otherworldly monster that she was. This garden appeared to her perhaps as sere and devastated, but to others it was no doubt as bright as ever and full of chatter; it had to do with something happening within one more than without, there was probably a word for it, at least aboveground, where things always got named no matter how crazy or useless or unpleasant they were, even such things as her present horrid condition.

Thinking about that, about names and how they got affixed to things that, of themselves, of course had no names, she recalled longingly the dark wood of forgetfulness, not seen since first seen, if ever (when she asked about it, people said it was only a legend, she must have imagined it, child that she was), a marvelous place where things had no name, and a place wherein she now wished desperately to lose herself. I don't want to be Alice anymore, she whimpered, realizing that in all the hysteria of her encounter with the Knave of Hearts she had apparently wet her drawers again (oh damn! as one of those old gentlemen on the river used to say whenever his pipe went out), and she again began to cry.

"A change like that's not easy, my friend," said a soft delicate voice behind her, "but it can be done. Look at me!"

Behind her, on a gaudily spotted mushroom, perched a beautiful Butterfly with gossamery wings the color of elderberries and orange marmalade, tinged with sugary wisps of silver. Alice wiped the tears from her eyes and squatted down to peer more closely. The mushroom was bloated and venomous looking, but the little Butterfly looked like a picture-book princess with her wings spread regally behind her like a gown flowing in the breeze. "Do I know you?"

"We met some time ago or perhaps in a different place," said the Butterfly in a voice as pretty as her wings. "But I was somewhat otherwise then. Or there. And so were you. You were only three inches tall."

"Ah!" exclaimed Alice. "That surly old blue Caterpillar with the hookah who gave me the magical mushroom! Are you he?"

"I am *not* a he!" snapped the Butterfly, somewhat offended, and she clapped her wings together stiffly, then fluttered them as though shyly batting her eyelashes. "Though once I was."

"But you were so old before, you're so much younger now! And, well, so very different!"

"And beautiful, too! Am I not beautiful?" she cried, preening.

"Exquisitely!" replied Alice, thinking, rather guiltily, how lovely she would look pinned under glass. "*Much* nicer than before!"

"Ah, but the trials of change, my dear! The unspeakable pain and humiliation! The deprivation! It's a terrible thing! And at such a time in one's life! I simply felt like crying all the time!"

"Oh, I know, I know!"

"It was truly an appalling crisis, from which I have only just emerged. I thought it would never end!"

"But it *does* seem to have been worth it," said Alice, feeling just a wee bit envious.

"Oh yes!" exclaimed the Butterfly, her colorful wings trembling with transparent joy and excitement. "Life is going to be so beautiful now! I'm going to enjoy every minute of it!" She flapped her wings more rapidly and rose to hover just above the spotted crown of the mushroom. "Look! I can fly! I shall see the world! Good-bye, dear child!"

"No, wait!" begged Alice. "Before you go, tell me, please! During the worst of it, was there anything, you know, that helped?"

"Only one thing—" said the hovering Butterfly, but just then a Swallow flew past like a flickery gray shadow and snapped her up and that was the end of their conversation. Ah well, thought Alice, staring glumly at the abruptly vacated mushroom. Wonderland.

As she was all alone again in a dead place, far from the party guests, and feeling a bit itchy and leaky once more, she decided to relieve herself while she was still in her squat, so she hiked up her pinafore and skirts and worked her damp drawers down over her knees.

"I've invented a plan," said a voice to her rear, startling her so that, trying to yank her drawers back up, she fell face forward into the desiccated remains of a petunia bed, that part of her which she'd hoped to conceal now most revealed (she seemed to hear a rattle of dry ghostly laughter all about), "by which one might raise and lower one's nether garments by means of pulleys attached to the ears." Ah. It was only her dotty old friend the White Knight. "I've also invented a very clever cure for nettle rash," he added in his kindly voice, and from the sound of it she could tell he was upside-down as usual. "It's made of truffles, boiled ink, and mashed carpet beetles, to be taken in small doses at high tea."

"It's not nettle rash," she said with a shudder, clambering heavily to her feet and lowering her skirts. Her drawers were wet and cold and, though it felt airy, she could not bear anything so unpleasant touching her skin just now, so she kicked them off. "It's more like nappy rash."

"Hm. Just as well, I suppose," he said with a heart-wrenching sigh, "for I have yet to find a sufficient quantity of carpet beetles prepared to devote themselves to medical science."

Alice went over to him where he lay, head downward as she'd supposed, in a ditch. She made no effort to pull him upright for, like one of the antipathies, as she liked to say, he was happier on his head than on his feet or seat. When she first came here, he was more of a grandfather to her; now he was like an addled older brother, but still dearer to her than anyone else in Wonderland. "I see you've fallen down off your wooden horse again."

"Actually, no, dear child, it fell up from under me. A most unreliable beast. But just as well, for, while lying here, I have contrived an ingenious way for someone in my present circumstances to perceive the world aright. As you know, A lens held at a certain distance will turn things upside-down, so one fastened to the toe of my boot would provide me, as I am now, a view of the world right-side-up, which would be very useful if a foe were in the vicinity or if someone were bringing me a present. I could nail a little box to my boot and attach the lens to a cord in it so that whenever I was upended, it would drop out and dangle before my eyes."

"Yes," said Alice, and she smiled down on her gentle foolish half-bald friend in his battered tin armor. Conversation with him always calmed her and held the Jabberwock at bay, if only for a brief time, so even head down, helpless and utterly bonkers, the Knight remained in some sense her protector. "They had such lenses aboveground, I think. They used them for taking pictures."

"*Taking* pictures? Do you mean, stealing them?"

"You might say so. Though, as I recall, I was always a willing victim, in or out of my little frock."

"They stole your frock, too? By my honor!" His mild blue eyes were wide with alarm and perplexity. "Where *is* this terrible aboveground of yours, pray tell?"

"Up there somewhere, I guess," said Alice gazing into the sky, which was today a shocking shade of paintbox blue. "Above your feet."

"You mean, down there, below my feet."

"If you like. And it was not so bad—having one's picture taken, I mean. It always gave me a kind of thrill. You know. Just to be *looked* at like that."

"I assure you, I *don't* know, my dear!" declared the Knight, trembling inside his tin armor and making it rattle. "It sounds like a frightful place for little girls! You must promise me never to go there again!"

"That's easy. Unless I can fall up, I don't think I *can* go there again. If there's really a 'there' and it's not just something I dreamt." But it seemed so real. As did her fall, that impulsive leap down the rabbit hole, never once considering how she might get out again, and then the slow weightless plunge, so slow she could catalogue the shelves and even practice her curtsey as she dropped. What ecstasy, that sweet dense fall, her whole body embraced by something like liquid yet not liquid! It was probably the last great pleasure she'd had, and the nearest she'd ever come to what she never came to. She often fell asleep thinking about it, her hands between her legs. And now, well . . . She gazed off into the black shadows of the forest beyond the Knight, where, no doubt, the Jabberwock awaited her, and she knew that she could not avoid it. If she walked toward it she would come to it and if she walked away from it she could come to it and if she remained here in the silent garden she would also come to it.

In fact, she had already come to it, to the edge of it anyway, for the dark forest had risen up before her, menacing, yet beckoning. The White Knight was somewhere far behind her, she was alone. Was this the mysterious wood of forgetfulness for which she longed? Alas, far from it. She saw lichens and ivy and hemlock and the webs of spiders and the spoor of woodland rodents, and knew them to be such and to be called such. She saw a flower and thought: Larkspur. Also known as delphinium. She saw trees and thought: Larch. Flowering chestnut. Copper beech. She saw many other things which did not even belong here, such as a writing desk, white kid gloves, a soup cauldron, a ladder with a snake curled round one rung, which she could name exactly, if she thought a little harder. No, far from being the wood where things have no name, this was surely the dismaying wood where every name has its thing.

And then she saw, hanging in the air above a pin oak limb, a catless grin. "Hello," she said, and the Cheshire Cat emerged around his toothy smile. "I thought you might be here. You always turn up at the direst moments."

"You are missing your birthday party," said the Cat without moving his lips.

"Well, I am not missing it very much," replied Alice, grateful for a bit of company, even one so ghostly. "And I doubt if it is missing me. Like you, I've become almost invisible here."

"You are hardly invisible," said the Cat with his fixed grin.

"Because I'm so big and floppy? That's just another way to disappear. Did you bring anything to eat?"

"No. But you'll find some mushrooms at the foot of the tree."

"Will any of them make me smaller?" she asked hopefully.

"No. But they may make you feel a little better for a while."

"Why should I want to feel any better? I feel just perfect, if you don't mind."

The Cheshire Cat did not reply, but merely continued to smile down at her enigmatically.

Alice sighed, stuffed her hands into her pinafore pockets. "All right, not *exactly* perfect." As the Cat remained silent, she went on. "It's the Jabberwock, you see. I try to hold it back, but it's stronger than I am and it claws its way inside me somehow and makes me feel like I'm roasting myself, and *that* makes it hard for me to hold my temper. I get all uffish, if that's the word, which gives me headaches and palpitations, and I become dizzy and have a bad tummy and a wretched itching in the worst places, which is there sometimes even after the Jabberwock has gone galumphing off again. It's all very strenuous and cruel and makes me perspire awfully, and that dries my skin out and leaves behind all these *brown* spots and white hairs and loads and loads of ghastly *wrinkles!* I wasn't supposed to *have* wrinkles! How did this *happen?* I *hate* them!" She was beginning to shriek like the Queen of Hearts again, so she paused and took a deep breath, her bosom heaving tremulously. Off with her head! that frumious Queen once screamed, and Alice now feared that that sentence of so long ago was finally being carried out, that she was indeed beginning to lose her head. It was maybe what frightened her most of all at this uncomfortable sort of age. Not to know herself might be even worse than not to be herself. The quizzical Cat meanwhile just grinned expectantly, showing all his teeth. "What else? Oh, I can't sleep, I cry all the time, my teeth hurt, my chest is as crinkly as funeral crêpe, I'm growing a mustache, I can't remember yesterday, I've got little purple doodles all over my legs, I don't see as well as I used to, I can't stop eating, I'm so *very* lonely, I think I'm going to die soon, I'm not at all pretty, nobody loves me, I'm bloated and saggy and red-eyed and ugly and I've had a stupid and useless life and I'm just dreadfully dreadfully depressed." Now she'd begun to cry. "I think I'm even starting to *smell* old," she sobbed, then stopped herself with a little stamp of her foot. It was just too embarrassing really, especially while being stared at with such derision. Which was, as she recalled, along with Ambition, Distraction and Uglification, one of the branches of the Mock Turtle's Arithmetic, the one that left you with considerably less than what you had before. Another foolish blubberer that Mock Turtle, and she was behaving just like him. She ought to be ashamed of herself, well schooled as she was in his dead languages of Laughing and Grief wherein one learned, above all, to keep a stiff upper lip. Even if it was puckery and creased and asprout with evil little hairs.

Remembering the Mock Turtle's lessons calmed her some: she hadn't forgotten *everything*. She wiped her nose on the shoulder of her pinafore. It was very quiet here in the wood, and it had grown darker. "Listen," she said, and she tossed her hair to get it out of her eyes in the old way: it made a rasping sound like river rushes in the wind. "Do you hear that? Dry as broomstraw! And it's falling *out*, too! That's right! Keep grinning at me, you loony old thing! I'm sure it's *very* amusing!" The Cat, though still smiling, began to fade a bit, she could see the oak leaves through its haunches, and she was suddenly terrified of being left alone here in the dimming forest. "I'm sorry. Wait! Don't go! I know I'm not as nice as I used to be, but it's not my fault. I'm just not *who* I used to be. It's a *very* curious sensation. And it has all happened so fast. There was something the Red Queen once told me that I didn't understand at the time. We were racing along, going nowhere, and she said: 'When you're over the hill, you pick up speed.' There, in that flat place, it seemed like complete nonsense, but I know now what she meant." That lady's rival the White Queen was able to make time run backwards: How did she do that? Maybe she had one of those watches with a reversal peg. If I could run time backwards, Alice asked herself, would I do it? I would, oh yes, I certainly would. Anything but having to face what's coming.

She looked up at the Cheshire Cat, who was only half there now, and she sighed, having the very strong sensation that she was merely talking to herself again. "All I want is just to be able to go home and be a child again and play with my cats and sisters and get my picture taken. I so loved it up there. It was a place that shaped itself around me and was as much part of me as I was, even if maybe it wasn't completely real. It was much more wonderful than this place, which *thinks* it's so wonderful, but is really very mean and tedious. I hate it here and the way I am now. But, well, you don't have to tell me, I know that's not going to happen. I'm stuck here and as I am and there's nothing to be done about it. After they made me a queen and all the fun was over, though it seemed like more fun for them than it was for me, I kept trying to find the way out. I used to follow the old White Rabbit around, thinking he might lead me back to that long hall with the glass table and cakes which one crawled into by way of a door in a tree. Ancient and feeble as he was, he still moved a lot faster than I could, so I had to follow the little, you know, clues that he dropped. Finally, one day, they did lead me to that little door, but I was too big by then to squeeze through. I could only get my head inside, but far enough to be able to stare up the hole down which I'd fallen, or supposed I had. Oh how I hoped to see something familiar, a face I knew looking down at me maybe, or even my cat Dinah, who was nice and cuddly and never showed her teeth and, if she was real, must have been missing me very much, but as far as I could see there was nothing up there but a terrible black emptiness. I lay there for hours to see if it would change, but it didn't. It gave me a very sinister feeling, and I thought: That's it. There's nothing up there and I am where I am and where I've always been." She shuddered. "And now all that emptiness has somehow got inside. Like whatever *me* was in there has been oozing away with everything else that's been squeezed out by the Jabberwock, leaving just a black empty hole in there. I wake up at night, soaking wet with perspiration, trying to remember who I am or what I am, afraid that Alice isn't going to be Alice anymore. It's as though that pretty little girl has gone away and left me and I'm now just another extinct and imbecilic old creature stumbling around crazily in Wonderland." Oh dear, she was crying again. Never mind. Let it come. If she couldn't cut the Jabberwock's head off, maybe she could drown it. "I just have this awful feeling of having lived a life inside an insoluble riddle made up by some mad, savage, unkind child!" she sobbed. "And if that's how this world works, *it's a poor, thin way of doing things!*"

The Cat had continued to fade away as though dissolved by her tears, only his grinning head remaining. She envied the Cat, being able to leave his body like that and just be a grin, but talking to him for solace was like quenching one's thirst with a dry biscuit. Even the Mad Hatter was more like company. And then she remembered: reparteed. She'd meant to use it at the re-party, but she'd forgotten.

She should have made a note. Now it was too late. It was always too late. She could hear whiffling and burbling sounds deep in the dark wood now. Or maybe she was making those sounds deep in her own body, which had become stranger to her than Wonderland itself. There was a chill wind rising, which she felt particularly as an unpleasant airiness between her legs, and she regretted having kicked her drawers off. The way she'd been lately, it would be wise to carry a second pair in her pinafore pocket. If she was going to die, she'd at least like to have clean drawers on. But she was not going to die, she knew. Not yet. Encounters with the Jabberwock might not leave you feeling like seven years old after, but they were not immediately fatal, or so the old Queen had assured her. After it was all over, there would be more insane tea parties, flamingo croquet, and stupid lobster quadrilles, there was much yet to look forward to. In fact, she realized she'd never really been a Queen, all that was just a pleasant mockery at her expense, it was only now that she was truly about to become one.

"Tell me," she asked the Cheshire Cat whose eyes still gazed down at her over the grin, though little else of him could be seen, "am I just an entertainment for everybody else?" He did not reply but his eyes disappeared, leaving only his uncanny grin afloat above the branch. She snuffled and wiped her tears again and felt the Jabberwock's heat rising in her breast. Sweat broke out on her brow. Yes, soon now. And chin up, soon enough all over: snicker-snack. Like everything else. That's time for you. That's glory.

"If a riddle is insoluble," whispered the wicked grin, growing faint as it too faded away, "it is usually because you know the answer but are afraid of it."

"I'm *not* afraid!" Alice shouted out after it into the gathering storm. "I'm just rather *angry* is all! It's all so *unfair!*"

And then a great hot darkness descended upon her, or arose within her, blowing in with flapping wings and stirring up a wind as strong as soup. It was not unlike that medium through which she sank when she first fell down the rabbit hole, though much more unpleasant.

"What a thick black cloud that is!" she seemed to hear someone say. It might have been the Cheshire Cat or his toothy grin. Or perhaps that pretty little Alice who once lived inside her. She could hardly breathe. But she would. Even if only for a short time. *"And how fast it comes!"*

Our Father

Julia Alvarez

IN HIS EIGHTIETH SUMMER, the old man is taken by his daughters to see the sights of a lifetime ago: the redbrick boarding house where he stayed when he first arrived in Canada as a young exile; the Hotel Troubadour where the owner of the logging camp interviewed and offered him a job as the doctor for nine hundred men; Victoria Station where he took the all-night freight train up to the camp.

All the years of their growing up, the daughters heard about this train, how the father had no idea where he was going, how he was not afraid, how he had to hike in twenty kilometers on foot to arrive at the central lodge. As little girls in Catholic school on the island, they were not impressed when the nun informed them that Jesus spent forty days in the desert. Up went their birdlike hands.

"Our father stayed for a whole year in Hudson Bay," Carla boasted. "Way way up near the North Pole. The snow was this tall." She stood up on her seat and indicated a spot above her head with her raised hand.

"That must have been quite an adventure," the nun said, nodding pleasantly. Her three-cornered wimple looked like a swan nesting on her head.

"Papi took off his shirt in the snow," Yo chimed in. All it took was one daughter mentioning the father's fantastic past, and soon they all had the same movie running in their heads, starring their brave, young father.

"His breath turned to ice on his mustache and he had to shave it off." This was the part that always got to Sandi. She tried to imagine it. She put an ice cube on her upper lip, and quick! had to take it off. It felt awful. And here Papi had had to breathe that way for months at a time!

Now in their forties—even Baby Fifi has turned forty!—the García girls head north from Montreal, hours on the road, the father in the back seat staring out the window, his mouth open so that the girls wonder if the old man has fallen asleep behind his foggy glasses. Carla, who is doing most of the driving, keeps looking in the rear view to make sure the father is enjoying himself. Beside her, Yo calls out the distance to Val d'Or every time they pass a marker. "Four hundred and twenty-five kilometers, Papi! Then we'll get to see the Valley of Gold!"

"The train took all night," the father says, rallying. "I did not know a winter from a summer. We left at dawn and arrived in Val d'Or the following afternoon. Then I had to hike in twenty kilometers."

"Weren't you scared, Papi?" Sandi takes his spotted hand and gives it a squeeze. She has to do it twice before he squeezes back.

"Scared?" the old man says. "Scared of what?"

A look passes among the backseat García girls. In the front seat, Carla looks over at Yo and rolls her eyes.

"I cut a slab of lard and ate it every morning on a piece of bread," the old man rewinds into the past. "I gained no weight. When I woke in the mornings, the temperature was 59 below. The mercury in the thermometer broke."

At this, all four women burst into laughter. "Ay, Papi! That's impossible. That's why they put mercury in thermometers because it takes some amazing temperature to freeze it."

"The mercury broke," the father says crossly. There isn't a sound in the car. "I ate a whole pie for breakfast."

"After the bread and lard?" Fifi asks in a little voice that gingerly walks a tightrope over the giggles in her throat.

"What bread and lard?" The old man looks at Fifi as if wondering who she is.

"Papi! You said you ate lard on a piece of bread every morning for breakfast."

Now he remembers. "I ate that, too. I gained no weight."

The girls look out their several windows to avoid laughing. They might as well go along with his stories. This is probably his last trip, as he keeps reminding them.

Val d'Or is a small, scrappy city full of used car lots and too many churches offering Bingo on alternate nights. The one downtown shop window displays pantsuits the pastel colors of Easter eggs. They walk the streets before dinner, the father pausing every few steps to gaze at one building or another.

"The hotel was over there," he says, pointing to a row of low-life bars in front of which a bunch of native Cree are loitering. They stare at the four dark-haired women in their flowing silk pants and knitted tops and dark glasses and leather pocketbooks abreast of an old man gaping across the street at them. "They didn't use to come to town back then," the father tells the daughters rather loudly. "I saved the life of the chief's wife. Three hours by canoe I had to go. She had a bad pneumonia. We contacted the Mounted Police to get her to the hospital in Noranda. There was no penicillin then."

Before the girls can catch him, he is headed across the street toward the young men, who have grown silent, their jetblack eyes glowering at him. The daughters run after their father. "Papi!" they call, smiling apologetically at the crowd of Cree pouring out of the nearest bar to see what these strangers are doing in town.

"Wikaya!" the old man says, lifting his right hand. The young men cock their heads, hands at their hips, waiting. "Wikaya!" the father says it louder. "That means hello in your language," he reminds them.

"He's going to get us killed," Fifi tells her sisters under her breath. The father now lives in New York City and takes yoga at the local Y. Surely, he has heard of political correctness. "Now Papi, there are all kinds of dialects, right?" Fifi defers to the men. Many of them wear their long hair tied back in ponytails with prominent sideburns. Their sneakers look oversized like the sneakers of brothers doing a rap number on MTV.

"We're originally from the Dominican Republic," Sandi offers as if this bit of news connects them with the Crees under the same minority status. The girls had already commented that some of the Crees look like Dominicans. "Phooey," the old man had said. "We are Spaniards. They are natives."

"Did you know a chief who was missing his arm?" The father holds out his right arm and makes a gesture of slicing it off at the shoulder with his left hand. "His wife had a bad pneumonia. It took three hours to get to the settlement by canoe. We had to call in the Mounted Police."

The owner of the bar, a big white man with hair the reddish color of meat not well done, has come to the door. "These boys aren't much for English," he informs the visitors. He pulls at his drooping mustache as he considers them. His bright blue eyes are as pretty as a doll's.

"I speak to them in their own language and they don't understand," the father accuses. "Wikaya," he tries it again.

"We speak French mostly," one of the Cree boys says in English. "This is Quebec, monsieur."

"Bien sûr, bien sûr," the old man says gallantly. "But did you hear of this chief?"

"Nah," the Cree says, hanging his thumbs in his belt loops and turning around to his buddies. They speak among themselves in a coarse patois that sounds nothing at all like the classroom French the girls learned from Soeur La Rosa. The little Parisian nun was more like an actress playing a religious person than a real nun, wisps of blond hair curling out of her wimple. The girls had to pucker in front of mirrors and hollow their cheeks so that they looked French even if they couldn't speak the language. "Nobody's heard of him," the Cree finally announces to the father. "Maybe you got the wrong tribe."

"No, no." The father is sure. "We go by canoe for three hours. Later this chief, he send me a bearskin with two young men. I cure it myself. One day I was walking in the woods, and I run into a village of teepees with only young girls there, and when they see me, they start making a whistle noise. Later at the camp the cook say that the girls found me attractive. The men must have been out hunting."

"Papi, you think maybe we better find a place to eat." Fifi takes the father by the arm. "My father was here fifty-five years ago," she explains to the young men. "We've come to see the places he's talked about all our lives."

They have left behind their husbands, jobs, children—even their mother, who complained that nature brings on her allergies. "You take me back to Val d'Or this summer," he asked them for his birthday gift. The sisters jumped at the idea. All their lives they have had an immortal for a father, and now that he is getting ready to die, they want to see what really went on in his past. To cut him down to size so that he will fit in the six-foot-deep hole in the hilltop cemetery beside his mother and father in his hometown of Santiago.

But here he is spouting about his larger-than-life adventures—he has switched over to his old Québeçois—as more men, Cree and white, are stepping out of the nearby bars. One of them asks Yo if she wouldn't like to meet him later at the Club d'Or. "When you've put *l'ancien* to bed," he says, indicating the father with his chin.

"*Non, merci,*" she says snippily in her old boarding-school French. This lean little guy with bulging forearms and ogling eyes seems to think it's a big joke: the old man seated on a stool the bar owner has brought out on the sidewalk; the Cree boys laughing and asking questions. How can this guy know that those mountains of memoried snow meant magic to four little girls growing up in the tropics, that the world seemed safer when the father appeared with his Cree bow and arrow and a necklace of rattles.

"Mon père," Yo begins, but she can't think of what she would say even in English about her father."

After the father has gone to bed, the girls collect in one of their adjoining rooms at the Journey's End Motel. There are four bulldogs playing cards on the wall before them. In the bathroom black and gold veining frames the mirror. "The only gold in Val d'Or," Sandi quips when she goes in to use the toilet.

They are planning tomorrow's outing. They will drive as far as they can go on the old logging road and then hike in to the camp where the father spent his legendary winter with nine hundred loggers and twelve feet of snow.

"I don't know," Carla is shaking her head. "Maybe it's going to be too much for him."

"He'll be fine," Yo assures. "We'll walk slow. Give him time to talk."

"Then, we'll never get there," says Fifi, laughing. "Or maybe we'll bump into that teepee village. Leave Papi there to spend his last days with a harem of Cree girls." They smile at the image of the old man lying on furs and fed venison snacks by young squaws who look like his daughters used to look twenty years back.

"Some stud asked me to meet him over at the club," Yo confesses. She thought she'd throw that in. All the girls complain about the father's boastfulness, but the apples, as their malapropping mother is fond of saying, do not grow far from the tree.

"The little guy who looked like Popeye?" Sandi asks. Yo has to smile at the apt description. She nods. "Well, he asked me, too," Sandi says. "You're not going to go, are you?"

"Are *you?*" Yo has a feeling that Sandi was planning to take their rental car into town the minute the others fell asleep. "Hey, the guy could be weird," she warns, but Sandi returns a coy smile.

"No one is going out tonight," Carla pronounces. As the oldest, Carla still thinks she can tell her sisters what to do. "You guys better stay, or—"

"Or what?" Sandi's eyes light up with mischief. "You'll tell Papi?"

Carla considers. "Yeah, that's exactly what I'll do."

And it would work, too. They can see it: the old man walking into the bar to rescue Sandi from the wiles of Popeye and the handsome Cree boys who were not allowed into town when the father was last here, the father fighting off the young men single-handedly. Indeed, all the stories the father has told them could be true if his daughters only believe in them as hard as they used to when they were little girls.

There was a story for every occasion and not always about Canada. The thing about Canada was that nobody could contradict the father by saying there were never ostriches in the Parque Nacional; electricity didn't come to Santiago until 1937. Canada, sitting on the immense shoulders of the North American continent, with long webby fingers, hundreds of them reaching up through the Arctic seas to touch the icy tippy-top of planet earth, Canada was the father's province, the backdrop of most of his marvelous stories.

But there were other stories as well, island stories. When the father was a young man, he got involved in a plot against the dictator. His was to be a daring, fantastic feat: in the middle of a milling crowd, the father was to whip out a syringe and inject the dictator with a fatal dose of chloroform which would kill him instantly. But an informer snitched to the secret police, and all the rebels were caught, except, of course, the father who escaped to Canada. There he lived for ten mythic years before marrying the girls' mother and returning to the island on a pardon.

Was this true? As young women, the sisters combed the history books looking for evidence of this plot—but there was never a word about it. "Everybody was caught," the father explained. "Nobody but me lived to tell the story."

What seemed incredible to the four daughters was how they had spent their childhood in a dictatorship without a clue as to what was going on. In the midst of horrors, they had felt safe because of their father's stories. The SIM's black Volkswagen at the turnabout in the driveway was the fairy godmother Belén coming off the road to nap in the shade. The periodic raids by the guardia? Some sixteenth-century English pirates had buried gold in the backyard, and the guardia were looking for it. The spray of bullets on the front wall of the house were meteorites the Martians were dropping from Mars.

The last of these island stories was about the messenger pigeons. The father bought two dozen of them and built a large wire cage in the backyard. These stupid, poopy, beady-eyed birds would carry messages in capsules tied to their legs wherever the girls wanted them to go. The father sat them down with paper and pencil and told the daughters to write love notes to whomever they wanted. Carla chose the President of the United States, and Sandi, Marilina Monroe.

Fifi was still too little to write a real letter, so she drew hearts on her paper to send to *Santicló* in the North Pole.

But Yo refused to write a letter. She was ten, now, and she could sense that the father was making up a story.

"Those birds can't cross the ocean," she announced to her sisters. In the wire cage, a dozen or more pigeons cooed in a low, mournful chorus.

Her father had been stuffing the teensy, folded-up letters into capsules with Mami's tweezers. He looked up. "You are right. You do not believe. Your bird will not fly."

Just the father's saying so filled Yo with a strong desire to write a letter, too. "Please, Papi, can I?" Yo pleaded. "I change my mind."

But before the girls' pigeons could return from their maiden flight, the Garcías themselves left the island suddenly for the United States. It was the father's second escape and later the girls would hear the father's stories of his being part of another plot. As for the pigeon project, it turned out that the father had been testing to see if the Underground could use these birds to convey coded messages from one part of the country to another. The girls' letters were meant to arrive at designated drop-off spots, not in the United States or the North Pole.

The day the family left for the States, the father walked to the back of the property, stepped into the wire cage, waving his arms until all the remaining pigeons had flown away.

The logging camp is now a hunting and fishing camp with a cracked plastic sign on a wheeled trailer. The cockeyed letters announce *Le Paradis du Chasseur*—The Hunter's Paradise—in French and English. They come upon it by surprise, for the father had insisted that they would have to hike in twenty kilometers, and the girls had all squeezed into their old jeans and boots and strung themselves with bells to ward off bears. But the black asphalt road leads right to the muddy parking lot in front of the makeshift lodge and then down to the concrete ramp where a rusted pickup is setting a motorboat down on the rain-pocked lake.

The father turns a full circle as he steps out of the car. The daughters wonder if he is as shocked as they are at this rundown assortment of trailers and plywood shacks. But before they can question him, a good-looking man in tall, fisherman's boots appears at the steps of the lodge. He seems startled at the sight of so many women. "*Bienvenue,*" he says with gusto. Dimples punctuate his tanned face when the women call back, "Hi!"

They fill him in on why they are here, each sister embellishing upon the others' stories. Roy looks from one to the other, a man not used to listening to women, but not minding it either on a slow day with a fine rain coming down and not much pike or walleye biting in the lake.

"So would you mind if our father looks around a little?" Carla concludes.

"I will myself be your guide," Roy offers. Behind his back, Sandi swats Yo's butt as if to say, Can you believe this hunk? "But where is your *père?*" Roy scowls in the direction of the car as if the father were still sitting in the backseat waiting for a green light.

Where indeed is their father? The daughters look around wildly like mothers suddenly aware their babies have wandered off in a world of traffic and deep swimming pools. "Papi!" they call out. "Papi!"

"Pop-eee!" The man with the pickup at the unloading ramp has completed the transfer and now walks toward them, mimicking their wild cries. "Who've you lost?" he asks more seriously, seeing as they have not giggled at his prank.

"Our father," Carla says distractedly. "Sandi, you and Yo look over there, and Fifi, you and I'll check the lake."

"It is not necessary. Come with me." Roy motions toward the lodge. "We have a way to call in our hunters. Your father will know." He leads them up the cracked concrete steps to the dark interior where, they suspect, he will turn on a siren or wham some huge gong. But the minute their eyes adjust to the dimmer light, they see there is no need for a summons. The father has found his way indoors through the back door and is sitting at the bar chatting up a blond, leathery woman he introduces as Gloriette.

"Papi, you worried us half to death!" Carla scolds.

"*Et pourquoi pas?* the father asks, winking at Gloriette. "*Je suis un connaisseur de ce paysage!*" He gestures expansively toward the blurry, muddy lake beyond the filthy screens. And now, he is launched on his logging camp stories. Gloriette encourages him with her tough woman's smile, the line of her mouth stretching across her face instead of turning up prettily in a sociable smile. Her eyes are two hard flints that surely strike fire when her temper flares up. But her brassy blond curls have caught the old man's eye. To the father all blondes are beautiful unless they are not friendly.

As the father prattles on to Gloriette, Roy shows the daughters around the one-room lodge. Stuffed heads of bear and racks of moose are mounted on the walls, as well as a couple of cheesy posters of women with bare breasts, so huge, they should be mounted, too. The hunters sit around the room at small card tables, drinking and watching the newcomers—big gruff men with large hands that wraparound their bottles of beer and hunting knives on holsters and tall boots like the kind that Puss 'n Boots used for leaping around the world.

"Where have these men been all our lives," Sandi whispers to her sisters. There was a time when they thought all they needed was a version of the young hero the father had told them he had been. But none of the men they found could make up for the sordid world their father had not prepared them for. What good were his magical tales when their marriages broke up; when they lost heart; when they wanted to walk into a blinding snowstorm and never come back? Why did he have to make up a story that wasn't true about the world?

Suddenly, there is a commotion at the bar. "How can this be?" the father is saying in a heated voice. "I gave you a one hundred. I have only big bills in my pocket."

"But monsieur, I have no 'undred in my register," Gloriette protests, opening up the drawer and inviting him to look inside. Sitting on the counter in front of the father is a chipped teacup with no saucer. What did he order in this place? Probably something he didn't want as a compliment to the blond Gloriette.

"I gave you a hundred bill, madame. You return me change only for a ten!" The father is standing now by the stool to give his statement weight. The room has gone silent. Gloriette is the one woman in this world of men; around her gravitates the heart of any drama that doesn't have to do with hunting bear or catching the season's biggest walleye.

"Is there *un problème?*" Roy has approached the counter. Gloriette lets loose in a gesticulating, emphatic Canadian French. The indignant arch of her painted-on eyebrows makes her seem suddenly very French. The father is following every word. He shakes his head, smiling ironically at the room. "She thinks I am just an old man," he announces when she concludes.

Gloriette is incensed at the suggestion she is lying. "*Ancien!*" she curses the father. "You need new eyes!"

"*Ça suffit,*" Roy says, grabbing her arm gruffly and shaking her. From the gesture the García sisters can tell that Roy and Gloriette are lovers; that they have violent fights in which things get thrown around, including Gloriette; that the good-looking, bear-hunting Bunyan hero beats the shit out of her from time to time. Why shouldn't she steal the change for a hundred from an old man? She is probably building her small stash to escape this den of men.

In an instant the father is headed toward the door. "We leave now," he informs his daughters in a shaking voice. "Come, come," he cries out angrily as if it is their fault for bringing him to this run-down den of thieves when he had asked for a trip back to the glorious world of his past.

As he is going down the cracked steps, he trips and falls, his head hitting the concrete stoop. Instantly, all four daughters are at his side. They sit him up like a doll and pore over him. "Papi, Papi, does anything hurt?"

"Ya, ya. I am fine!" he scolds, and then touching his head, he brings his hand down and his fingers are stained with blood. The gash on his scalp is all the more shocking against the snow-white hair.

"Oh my God!" Carla cries out. "Please get us a towel," she charges Roy, who has come to the door to see what has happened. He is back in a minute with a roll of paper towels. In the background, Gloriette is still grousing about the old man's accusation.

Her voice arouses the father's anger again. He struggles to stand, but the girls hold him down by the shoulders. "We go now!" he hisses at Carla, who is trying to stanch the wound.

There is no arguing with him. They lead him to the car, and sit him down in the backseat and ask him a dozen questions. Does he remember his name? What year was he born? How many daughters does he have? But none of these are the question they want to ask him.

Finally Fifi blurts it out, "Papi, can't you ever just say, 'I'm hurt'?"

"Yeah, Papi. This place is a dump," Yo says loud enough for Gloriette to hear.

"That woman is a bitch," Sandi adds. "Excuse my French."

He looks from one to the other with such a brutal blank gaze they are taken aback. "Okay," he says. "Okay. I admit. The world is ugly. People take advantage. Is that better I say it? Is it?" His voice rises in an angry challenge. His body is shaking as if with cold and his hands on his lap are stained with blood.

"Ay, Papi," they are crying. It is unbearable to think of him as a sad and bitter old man. They turn their wild, wet faces to him.

"No!" he answers his own question. "It is better to forget it." He waves away Roy at the busted screen door; the trailers lined up by the electric poles to steal electricity from the lines; the fine, filmy rain coming down on the tin roofs of the hunting camp. Then, pulling himself up, as if he could just snap his fingers and abracadabra, the glorious past is back, he adds, "I still feel like a young man. Over there," he points to the concrete unloading ramp, "is where the Cree came to trade in their canoes."

The daughters nod at the quaint, log cabins the father draws with his hand in the air, at the Cree Indians coming up the dock with their beaver pelts, at the vague birds swooping above the muddy lake with love notes strapped to their legs. They have not forgotten how, the summer they arrived in New York City thirty-five years ago, the father took his girls to Central Park. And there they were, not just theirs, but hundreds upon hundreds of pigeons that had made it safely across oceans from all corners of the world.

Wake

Lois-Ann Yamanaka

I PUT MY TINY HANDS together and prayed with a child's fervor and belief: God, take me home.

And when I woke, I was a twelve-year-old girl sleeping in the tiny back room of Granny Alma's house in Kalihi, dirty curtains from Sears, and the slow crowing of a neighbor's rooster; pit bulls barking, yanking on rusty chains; the screeching of the city bus around a hairpin turn.

And when I woke, I was thirteen and drunk from too many Tom Collins at the Stadium Bowl-O-Drome's Ten-Pin Lounge from Uncle Fu Man Chu with his Lucky Strike embedded in the spit-white corner of his mouth; stolen sips of screwdrivers from Aunty Tokyo Rose in her teased Aqua Net–do and tight turquoise capris; Granny Alma busy tending bar until one in the morning.

And when I woke, I was fourteen; it was midnight and I was stoned on shitty dope, staring at the waves, the full moon at Walls; a runaway hiding in the mock orange hedges near the Waikiki Shell, the cops chasing me into Kapiolani Park.

And when I woke, I was fifteen, Celeste dragging me from a crack house in Waimanalo; Doritos crumbs on the floor, Big Mac wrappers blowing across the table, dogs straying in and out of the open door, a sofa smelling like piss; my sister hitting me with a filthy mop she found dripping on a broken mattress.

And when I woke and woke and woke, I was Alone in a bar in Chinatown, cheap wine with a toothless man I called Gin Blossoms who always wore a wilted plumeria lei; a braless woman in a straw hat next to me singing Dionne Warwick songs over and over. Nobody knew the way to San Jose.

Take me home:

Because when I wake, I am in a two-bedroom walk-up in Las Vegas with Drake, warm beer in tilting bottles, a glass of merlot with lip gloss rainbows on its surface, Percodan and Prozac strewn on the countertop, glass pipes, amber vials, burnt pieces of tin foil, Drake passed out on the futon in the arms of a girl/boy drug friend, Sonny Boy mewling madly in the corner.

I wake with healing stones, fluorite and malachite, in my closed fist, the gray ash of incense on my skin, cigarette butts in a naked lady ashtray near a black lighter, my sketches and journals on the floor, a broken canvas with pieces of sky, bits of sculpture, torn music sheets, ripped photographs.

My breasts are engorged with thin, white-blue milk. Baby bottles on the floor, dirty Pampers full of diarrhea taped shut, receiving blankets covered with hair, an infant's sheepskin caked with vomit, a twisted tube of Desitin, and baby powder, a silk film on my skin. We cannot stop crying, Sonny Boy and I, towels strewn over the chairs.

I am screaming inside:

Shut the fuck up. Shut up, fucking rotten little shit. You better shut up right now or I will fucking kill you.

My teeth grit, my hands fold into fists, and I hit his face, squeeze his cheeks inside my closing palms. Distort his cry with my hands on his face and throat, until the sound makes me laugh. I have hair all over my wet hands, his and mine.

Okay, Sonia, breathe deeply, breathe. It's just another Sunday, I reassure myself. It'll pass. I'll make it. At least I'm not Alone. I cradle Sonny Boy's face in the protracted sunlight through the broad window.

Sorry. I'm so sorry, baby. Mommy loves her little boy.

Drake calls to me, the girl/boy giggling. "Leave the baby, Sonia, and come to Daddy. Let's make each other happy."

I get up off the floor. Sonny Boy, I cannot keep these words inside me. They hang outside of my lips like smoke I long to breathe in but simply cannot: My/son.

Sonny Boy, I had fertility to prove. Proven. Now I need you out of my life. Gone away in a tiny casket. Grieving mother all in black. All that mournful attention. Drake consoling me because *I* need *him.* And corn chowder in crock pots at my door. How the living love to feed the grieving.

Sonny Boy, a poet cannot write, a painter cannot paint, sculptor sculpt, photographer photograph, musician compose, not without the experience; your birth was to enhance my art. Art enhanced. Now how do I get rid of you? All evidence of you. Everything. I should kill you. Artfully. I've done it before. What a poem I would compose.

Sonny Boy, I had to birth you. I thought you were the blessing of a uterine lining, gone for what they all told me was forever. The possibility of my redemption, a miracle from God who found me at last.

But You found before, when they said that Kate and her holy roller friends had fucked my head with False Doctrine, Unbiblical Teachings, Unholy Lies and Demonic Delusions.

You sat in the corner of the room when they thought they might deprogram me. Light You, Being You, All You, white inhabiting my every memory and moment.

You looked at me in the dusty church office full of Sunday School quarterlies, empty offering plates, crosses over the doorways, the hum of the air conditioner, a red carpet, You, filling the room with seraphic light. So, I put on my shades.

Aunty Effie sat stern in holy disapproval with her hands clutching her Bible, there on the rattan sofa. She pursed her lips at me and wiped tears from the corner of her eye. Pastor Jimmy Hingman, whose claim to fame was singing backup on Glen Campbell's gospel album "To God Be the Glory," sat on the black executive's chair behind the big desk. He stared deeply at me, his hands in "Here is the steeple" formation. Deacon Apana sat, tongue clucking and head shaking at me, next to the desk in an old schoolroom wooden chair.

I watched the Holy Ghost outside the window hovering above the field of sleeping grass past the churchyard. The shifting of the wind tickled him, the free movement of rice sparrows through his gossamer shape. The Holy Ghost winked at You. I knew you'd seen him by the smile on your beautiful face.

"I love you," you said, loud as day, the light in the room ablaze.

"Deacon Apana," Pastor Hingman said, "would ya please turn on some lights. It's awfully dark in here. And open up the windas, would ya? Li'l darlin', would ya take off them sunglasses? It ain't that bright in here. We're gonna open with prayer."

And pray they did:

Purify.

Sanctify.

Rectify.

Disapprobation.

Calumniation.

Desecration.

Unrepentant.

Uncontrite.
Unatoned.
Beseech of thee Your Mercy.
Grace.
And.
Love.

"I love you, Sonia." Beside me, Christ the Son, his body gone from the cross on the wall, whispered softly in my ear, his voice a smooth sonata.

"Because the greatest of these is Love?" I asked.

"What?" Aunty Effie interjected, right in the middle of Pastor Hingman's fist-pounding, prayerful climax. She slapped my face. "Who the hell are you talking to, Sonia? You see what I mean?" she said. "They have her talking to the damn walls. Brainwashed, I tell you."

"Wake up, Sonia," Deacon Apana said in my face while snapping his fingers in front of my eyes. "I ask you, Dear Lord, to awaken this child," he said in spontaneous prayer as he held my face tightly in one hand and lifted his other hand to the ceiling.

"Li'l darlin'," Pastor Hingman said in his condescendingly holy voice, "do you hear voices talking to you?"

"Like they're talking now?" I asked.

Aunty Effie and Deacon Apana looked around the room and then at each other with great disdain. "They just showed the Joan of Arc film to her Sunday School class," Deacon Apana whispered. "She'll be speaking in false tongues in a little while."

"Are the voices speakin' to you now?" Pastor Hingman asked, his eyes roaming upward as I nodded. "The Devil plays some mighty evil tricks on weak minds, but it is the weakest link among us that is the strongest," he told me. "And that is why we are here to pray for you."

"Love is a trick?" I asked.

"Yes," Pastor Hingman paused, "even love." No one spoke.

I looked around the room. Panicked, I looked to the field of sleeping grass, the sad reverie of smoke diffusing upward toward the sky. The Son who sat beside me rose slowly back to his place on the crucifixture over the doorway. And when I turned my eyes to the corner of that silent room, You had vanished.

Grace vanished Celeste and me. "Say good-bye," she said, never turning back to watch us leave.

Mark vanished from my life every time I hooked up with another loser, another Drake, a poet without a pot to piss in, white trash without a place to stay, a wannabe carpenter who promised to take care of me but had to enroll in vocational school first, an alcoholic artist full of angst, bartenders, drifters, drug addicts, a pit boss or two, stray underdogs but always good sex. They all eventually vanished, too.

I even vanished myself, vomiting down to a size six, then four, then two until Granny Alma force fed me her power shakes full of some weight gain powder from Longs and pureed bananas.

I vanished three babies. A hospital's toxic waste bin, a dirty toilet at Magic Island and a jelly jar buried outside my bedroom window.

I want to vanish Sonny Boy. Wake up one morning and find him gone. Put him in a jar on the shelf. A paperweight. A work of Art. His closed pink eyes. He's sleeping, that's all, I put him to sleep, that's all. What in heaven made me think I was mother material? Grace told me the monthly blood was for this, *one day.* This?

All my fuck-ups have to be learned behavior. We're not born fucking idiots, we become fucking idiots. And I mastered the art of fucking myself over into idiot-dom very well. I drink too much, I smoke too much, I toke too much, I coke too much, Drake, me and our new estrogen-addicted girl/boy best friend, who does nothing all day but eat our food, stare at my crotch and wear smashing size two DKNY knockoffs from TJ Maxx.

Or was it not paying attention to Signs? The Miracle in each weary day. My Fate minus blessing. The open Door, the Road less traveled, the Riverboat leaving the dock. A Celestine Prophecy in each misplaced word.

The Voices vanished like breath.

Rigidity in my wrist. That's what it is. I know I can enter the realm of God through art. I should paint more. Glorify my impending disintegration. Try glass blowing. Do some deep breathing. Suffer more for the next poem. Maybe work with copper. Surrender to the bitter pill. Stare deeply into the spiralling pit. Drown the awakening.

I should lose this postpartum weight. Get shallow. Go shopping. Get back my Tiger Lily Wong gig or reemerge as the exotic Jade Kwan, now appearing Thursday nights at the Golden Nugget's 24-Karat Bar.

I want someone to blame.

Grace, easy.

Joseph, easier.

Blue-collar upbringing, yes.
Racism, yes.
Low self-esteem, good one.
Too many ethnic-female-with-dysfunction novels.
Which provide no solutions.
Because life provides no resolutions.
So we'll all be left hanging.
In our particular Victimhood.
God?

Granny Alma calls to remind me that "God loves you, Sonia, now make sure you take your One-A-Days."

Celeste Kurisu-Infantino calls to tell me, "Don't be such a cry baby. You made your proverbial bed, now lie in it. We'll be in Vegas for Reverend Oral Roberts' Glory Crusade. We'll all be there to support you and the baby. Besides, God forgives single mothers like you, Sonia."

Aunty Effie comes to Las Vegas three times a year with her daughters Aunty Frieda and Aunty Frannie with a care package full of Top Ramen, Spam, guava jelly and chocolate-covered macadamia nuts.

Aunties Effie, Frieda and Frannie who remind me that "God loves you, Sonia. Now pray we hit the million-dollar jackpot." They should have deprogrammed Aunty Effie from her lifelong gambling addiction.

"Wake up and be a good mother," Grace scolds. "It's just postpartum depression. It'll pass. If I could do it, you can do it. And really, you have no one to blame but yourself."

And Joseph. The vanishing father, the philosophical father, the father who left me. Left Celeste. Left Grace. Left home. Joseph, whose words always found me over continents and years.

I've kept your letters as evidence.
The evidence of your bliss/ignorant beauty.
The evidence of your sick I/Love/you.
Do I read too much, Daddy, those books with tawdry endings?
But how I love a happy ending.
Daddy, give me a happy one.

Sweet Sonia,

A man falls sick to severe dysentery. A woman enters his room with a small tray. Behind her, a little girl carries worn towels. The woman places her hand on the man's forehead then turns on a small lamp.

On his bedstand, the man sees white fungus in a clear broth, a bottle of fermented tea and a plate of grated coconut.

Outside, he listens to the distant rumble of approaching thunderstorms. The girl closes the window. When she notices the man's gaze, she covers her eyes with both hands, but peers at him from between her fingers. The woman begins cleaning the man.

The man is delirious. He tells her about the west lake where he rode an old black bicycle, the lake so beautiful, the color of blue rock from the Buddhist temple in the hills of Han Zhou. How the rain spread over the water from the curvature of sky.

The woman wrings the dirty towel and begins wiping his neck. The girl holds a tiny wooden box, this girl who has the Buddha's ears. Pink light shines through them when the girl looks up at the man. She looks like his sweet Sonia.

The man begins to cry. He cannot stop his tears. The girl climbs onto the bed. She crawls under the sheets and moves the man's heavy arm around her. When she opens the wooden box, she looks into the man's eyes. The music is unrecognizable at first.

Beethoven's Moonlight Sonata. It is at this moment that the man thinks of his sweet daughter. He knows he must return home. This girl in the moonlight wraps herself into the stink of his body, turns off the lamp and places the open box on the bedstand.

When he wakes in the morning, the tray of white fungus broth, fermented tea and grated coconut is gone. The window is open, the sunlight come, trembling in the curtains. The girl is gone, the room silent but for a tiny wooden box still playing a Moonlight Sonata.

I will tell you, sweet Sonia, a prayer that I learned years ago in a quiet synagogue in Amsterdam that this little Chinese girl restored in me:

I believe in the sun even when it is not shining.
I believe in love even when feeling it not.
I believe in God even when he is silent.
Keep these words.
Tell Grace and Celeste that I will be home soon.

I love you,
Joseph Kurisu

Daddy, the sun has come, a fire in the morning. Just another Sunday, but flames rise from the ground of this desert town, burn me from that Kalihi Valley suburb, blaze on from Hilo that sleepy bay town.

Sonny Boy falls asleep fitfully in my arms, his face and neck bruised. Asleep is the only way I love him. But this is love, I am sure. Love, an ache he's sharpened in a girl given away, a girl never found, a girl never kept. Wake me when this is all over.

And the Voice of God, no pulse or flicker there, Daddy, his silent ire, years going on years now; God is a vanishing, invisible breath behind the distant clouds.

And it's every day I say, Daddy, no matter the geography of place or time:

Let this day end. Let it end with me dead.

Happy Memories
Lydia Davis

I IMAGINE THAT WHEN I AM OLD, I will be alone, and in pain, and my eyes will be too weak to read. I am afraid of those long days. I like my days to be happy. I try to think what would be a happy way to spend those difficult days. It may be that the radio will be enough to fill those days. An old person has her radio, I have heard it said. And I have heard it said that in addition to her radio, she has her happy memories. When her pain is not too bad, she can go over her happy memories and be comforted. But you must have happy memories. What bothers me is that I'm not sure how many happy memories I will have. I am not even sure just what makes a happy memory, the kind that will both comfort me and give me pleasure when I can't do anything else. Just because I enjoy something now does not mean that it will make a happy memory. In fact, I know that many of the things I enjoy now will not make good happy memories later. I am happy doing the work I do, alone at a desk. That work is a great part of every day. But when I am old and alone all the time, will it be enough to think about the work I used to do? Another thing I enjoy is eating candy by myself while I read a book in the evening, but I don't think that will make a good happy memory either. I like to play the piano, I like to look at the plants that come up in the yard beginning in March, I enjoy walking with my dog, and looking down into his face at his good eye and his bad eye, I like to see the sky in the late afternoon, especially in November, I like petting my cats, hearing their cries, and holding them. But I suspect that the memory of my pets will not be enough, either, even if I love them. There are things that make me laugh, but often they are grim things, and they will not make a good happy memory either, unless I share them with someone else. Then it is not the amusement but the sharing of it that makes the happy memory. It seems as though a happy memory has to involve other people. I think of all the different people. I think of the good encounters with people. Most of the people I talk to on the telephone are friendly, even when I have called a wrong number. I have a happy memory of stopping my car by the side of the road to talk to a woman about her garden. I talk to the people who work in the post office and the drugstore, and I used to talk to the people at the bank before they put an automated teller machine in the lobby. When a man came to fix the dehumidifier in the basement, we talked about the history of this town. I enjoy my conversations with the librarian down the street. I enjoy the friendly messages I receive from bookstores selling secondhand books. But I don't think any of these encounters will make a memory that will comfort me when I am old. Maybe a happy memory can't involve people who were only strangers or casual friends. You can't be left alone, in your old age and pain, with memories that include only people who have forgotten you. The people in your happy memories have to be the same people who want to have you in their own happy memories. A lively dinner party does not make a good happy memory if no one there cared very much for any of the others. I think of some of the good or meaningful times I have had with the people close to me, to see if they would make good happy memories. Meeting a friend at a railway station on a sunny day seems to have made a good happy memory, even though later we talked about some difficult things, like starvation and dehydration. There were walks in the woods with friends looking for mushrooms that may make happy memories. There have been a few times of gardening together as a family that may make a good happy memory. Working together at some arduous cooking one evening is a happy memory so far. There was a good trip out to a department store. Sitting by the bedside of someone who was dying may actually make a good happy memory. My mother and I once carried a piece of coal on a train to Newcastle together. My mother and I once played cards with some longshoremen on a snowy morning waiting for a ship to come in. There was a time when I would return again and again to a botanical garden in a foreign city to look at a Cedar of Lebanon, and that is a happy memory, even though I was alone. My neighbor across the street once brought a plate of cake to the back door during a time of mourning. But I can see that if some day she and I were to become estranged, that would spoil the happy mem_ory. I see that happy memories can be erased. A happy memory can be erased if you do the same thing on another day and you are not happy, for instance if on another day you garden or cook together with bad feeling. I can see that an experience does not make a happy memory if it started out well but ended badly. There is no happy memory if there was something nice about an experience but also some problem, if two of you enjoyed an outing but the third was sitting at home angry because you were so late returning. You have to make sure, somehow, that nothing spoils the thing while it is happening, and then that no later experience erases it. I could have happy memories. I can see that the things I do with another person, and with a feeling of warmth toward that person, and with a person who will want to have me in his or her happy memories may make a good happy memory, while the things that I do alone and especially with a feeling of ambition, or pride, or triumph, even if they are good in themselves, will not make a good happy memory. It is all right to have candy and enjoy it, but I should remember that the memory of candy will not be a happy one. If I am playing a board game with people close to me and we are happy, I must be sure we don't quarrel before the end of it. I must be sure that at some later time we don't play another board game that is unhappy. I should check now and then to make sure I am not alone too much, or unhappy with other people too often. I should add them up, now and then: what are my happy memories so far?

In Camera
William H. *Gass*

1: The Stock

Mr. Gab didn't have that gift, though his assistant, who was supposed to be stupid but only looked so, would mutter beneath his breath, when annoyed with his tasks, "he had the gift, he did, did Gab." Mr. Gab spoke seldom, and then it was to shout at the steel shutters of the shop which were always reluctant to alter their position, whatever it was, and needed to be cajoled, flattered then threatened. Or sometimes he spoke to the steam pipes, complaining of the knocking, complaining of the excessive heat they gave off when they had to be heated and of the odor that the steam wafted to the nose through layers of paint resembling aluminum. Curls the graphs, he said with as close to a curse as he came.

Mr. Gab's shop was in a part of town so drably uninteresting robbers wouldn't visit even to case its joints, something Mr. Gab fairly certainly knew, and treasured, but he had these steel shutters left over from a former, more frequented, more luxuriant time and felt obliged to use them. One could have guessed Mr. Gab's age from these small facts: that he thought of possible intruders as "robbers," and worried about being "glommed"—terms which have no present employment. The shutters, window-wide slats of steel in Venetian style, creaked as they descended, and no longer fit firmly together or overlay one another as they had been designed to do in some far off factory; consequently, streetlights lit to illuminate an empty avenue, whose cracked walks were a menace even during the brightness of sunny afternoons, streaked into the shop at night where Mr. Gab might still be sitting, long after closing, long after nodding byebye to his stupid assistant, staring at his prints in the darkness, prints which covered the pockmarked walls of the shop, displayed there like dead things hung from nails, as if slain while other prey were being hunted: while picking up fallen apples maybe (though he lived so far from the country) a brace of grouse were to fling themselves into the apple bag, or while gathering pignuts (models ago he'd sold his car) a pair of pigeons might creep into a handy box—that unlikely—while sorting buckeyes to find the feathers of a turkey, or, while pulling loganberries out of their briaries (though he wore no woolen sleeves), flushing a covey of quail instead—prizes inadvertently taken, mistakenly developed, proudly framed.

Mr. Gab certainly had his favorites. These were images he knew so well they were—well, not engraved—on the balls of his eyes. He needed only the least light to see them down to their last shades of gray: an Atget was frequently imagined to be the state of his street outside—Atget, the documentarian. Perhaps he'd decide on the Atget of an intersection, of angle *de la rue Lhomond et de la rue Rataud,* its cobbles moist, light late, sky like sour milk, taken in the *quartier du Val-de-grace,* where, on one wall a poster was posted to say un million, un million, over and over in a voice not ever husky. Forever, Mr. Gab would allow himself sometimes to murmur: *cours de danse givre* . . . forever . . . though the "cours" is gone, "danse" is gone, even before the war arrived in a taxi, they were gone, gone, cobbles too, now, probably, building likely, gone, the lamp most certainly, gone, and the teeth of steel, like those of a large rake, that crossed the rue high above every head—sure, sure—that crossed the top of the image straight through the sour-milk sky and over the tree at rue's end—oh, yes—gone, quite gone, even the tree whose feet were hid behind a low wall, deep in the shot where the road disappeared into a vee as though down a drain—ah well—cut by now, blown over, hauled off, fire wooded, gone. Dear me.

What a curb, Mr. Gab permitted himself to exclaim. At the Louvre . . . what did the advert advise and proclaim? who could say? with the wall retreating, the posters defaced. What a glisten though! Still . . . the curb, the glisten, the deep recession of the street remained. Right outside there, beyond the barred door, beyond the shuttered window, lay Atget's modest little street still. Still . . . made of wavering lines of glis and shales of shine. The walk protected by posts. Mr. Gab did not dare say aloud what he succinctly thought, as he looked out through his engraved eyes: the world is mine.

Only during the evening following work—Mr. Gab thought that way of it, thought of it as work—shortly after he had—well—dined, but before he went slowly to bed, unbuttoning the buttons down his shirt—well, his vest first—seeing the street or some other scene all the while the buttons went as buttons do, loose from their hole, not like released birds because it was the shirt that was freed, the vest that flew loose, even if it clung to his slender frame like a woman in a romance to her wordmade lover—no—the buttons like sentries would stay sewn in their useful line perhaps for an entire shirtlife, vest time. In photographs, shirts do not get much attention.

He could of course have chosen to recall the elegant details of Le Restaurant Procope's façade, the café's name like a decoration running along in front of the building's second-floor windows, each letter as bold as an escutcheon affixed to a wrought-iron balcony railing: GRAND RESTAURANT PROCOPE, and then, under the overhang, discreet as a meeting, the name again: Grand Restaurant Procope, no doubt no longer in business though one sign said *verte du vins pour ville*—oh—the hanging lamps were like crowned heads, the walk lined with tables and paired chairs, the hour early, each empty—not the hours but the chairs—a busy day ahead of them, waiting to accommodate customers no longer alive.

Mr. Gab lived as many shopkeepers did once, both at the rear and above his establishment. He slept in a small loft a good size for bats which he reached by climbing the short stair which rose unsteadily from a corner of his kitchen, a kitchen of sorts, in whose foreshortened center Mr. Gab kept a cardtable and a ceramic cat. Breakfast might be an apple and an egg. Lunch—he frequently passed on lunch—though his stupid assistant ate lunch like a lion, growling over some sandwich distantly fixed. A sip of tea, a chewy biscuit maybe. Memories going back a long way. Mostly, though, he passed on lunch.

Days were dreary—oh yes—especially in a shop stuffed with gray-white gray-black photographs in cellophane sheets that had been loosely sidestacked in cardboard boxes, tag attached, maybe FRENCH XX or COUNTRYSIDE BRITISH or RAILROADS USA. He had three for trees: bare, leafed, chopped. On all the walls, clipped to wire hangers which were then hung from nails, his prizes, displayed so as to discourage buyers. Successfully. So far. For a decade.

Mr. Gab would have six or seven customers on a good day, which is what he would almost audibly say to them when they entered, making the door ring—well it was a rattle really. His stupid assistant would answer most questions, show them the labels on the boxes, wave at the walls, hung with hangers, open a filing cabinet or a case for those who fancied the fancier ones, explain the proper technique for sliding a photograph out of its sheathing, demonstrate the underhanded manner of holding it, or, with palms gently placed at edges as if it were a rare recording, how one could be safely examined.

The boxes were mostly of a conventional cardboard brown. They sat on tables or beside tables or under tables as if they'd sat there already a long time: the ink on the labels had faded; the paper of the labels had yellowed: the corners of the labels were munched. Covers were kept closed against dust and light and idle eyes by beanbags, forever in the family, inertly weighing on the boxes' cardboard flaps. The nails Mr. Gab had driven into the walls were zinc'd. They were suitable for fastening shingles, and you couldn't have drawn one out without pulling, along with the shank, large chunks of plaster. The wire hangers themselves were in weary shape. So the pictures hung askew. As if holding on with one hand.

Mr. Gab stocked several versions of the same photograph sometimes. A round red sticker affixed to the wrap signaled a superior print, a green circle indicated one produced from the original negative, but late in its life, whereas a yellow warned the customer that the sheath enclosed a mere reproduction, however excellent it might often be. His red version of rue Rataud was as fine as the one conserved at the Carnevalet, but on the white rectangles with their softly rounded corners which Mr. Gab had pasted to the bottom of each envelope and where he identified the subject, the photographer, the method, and the negative's likely residence, he had written about the less genuine image, below a yellow ball that suggested caution, the words *"trop mauvais état,"* a little joke only scholars might understand and enjoy.

Mr. Gab's provenances were detailed and precise; however, years earlier an envious dealer had accused his rival (for Mr. Gab was then in a dinky shop across from him on another street) (and whom the envious dealer called "Grab," somehow sensing Mr. Gab's sensitivity about his name, though unaware that Mr. Gab had become silent in order to avoid being addressed by anyone as "Gabby") of accepting or otherwise acquiring (during midnight visits and stealthy trips) stolen property. How otherwise, he complained, could one account for the presence, in prime condition, of so many rare and important photographs in such shabby shoebox circumstances. "Shoebox" was slanderous, certainly, though nothing had come of these allegations except a shady reputation, thought actually to be desirable in some circles.

A print's quality depended almost entirely upon its preservation of details, its respect for values. The fog-white sky of rue Rataud, in the version under its cautionary yellow dot, smeared the end of the street so you could not see how or where it turned, walls were muffled, and a hard light made the outlines of the cobbles disappear;

while the red-tagged rue Rataud allowed the eye to count windows far away and discern a distant huddle of buildings. In the latter, the spikey rod, whose use he could not fathom, crossed the street in the guise of a determinate dark line; in the former it was dim and insubstantial, as if obscured by smoke. On red's verbose information label, Mr. Gab had written that his photograph had come to the United States in the luggage of Berenice Abbott from whom he had received a few prime prints of other subjects. If interested, please ask. About the history of yellow, Mr. Gab offered nothing.

The stupid assistant was not sufficiently steeped, so when, as occasionally happened, a customer wished a little history, Mr. Gab would have to hold forth, not reluctantly with regard to the information, which he believed every cultivated person should possess, but reluctantly regards speaking—making noises, choosing words, determining the line of march for a complex chronology. From the box marked DECORATIVE ELEMENTS, for instance, another Atget might be withdrawn, and Mr. Gab could inform his customer that this view of some paneling at the Hôtel Roquelaure had been purchased from Atget by Georges Hoentschel—did he know?—the designer of the Union Centrale pavilion for the 1900 World's Fair in Paris; and subsequently placed in an archive of immense richness and variety which Hoentschel had catalogued and published in 1908 before it was sold to J.P. Morgan who later donated the whole shebang to New York's Metropolitan Museum. Someone had dismembered a 1908 catalogue and this image—which you should please hold at its tender edges—is a limb from one of those dismemberments.

Mr. Gab did not usually remark the fact (since some found the fact disturbing) that the door was no doubt long gone, though the photograph was evidence of fine wood and careful workmanship; but because Atget had taken a portion of the decoration's portrait, the surviving image had increased in value at each exchange and become what Mr. Gab, in a rare moment of eloquence, called "a ghost worth gold." Nothing touched by this man's lens was lost, he said, each was elevated by its semblance to sublimity, even the dubious ladies of the XIXe Arrondissemont, three of them, two leaning one peeking, from the traditional doorway, appetizing if you ate mud, an example of which (not the mud but the unsavory subjects) he, Mr. Gab, had in a box at the back of the shop marked "Nues," even though the women were decently dressed.

The light in the store, Mr. Gab's stupid assistant persisted in judging, "was lousy." With the shutters closed, you could see how dust-covered the front windows had become, while most of the lamps were simply bulbs housed in coffee cans hung from wires punched through their bottoms. A proper tungsten lamp throwing the appropriate fanfalling light could be found at the rear of the store—"don't call it a store," Mr. Gab always protested—where anyone who wore serious eyes could contemplate in quiet a possible purchase. The assistant believed that the entire furnishings of the store: the old oak desk where Mr. Gab presided, the swivel chair, alike in oak, the rose colored puff upon which he sat when he was seated, the smeary windows, the door which uttered a needless warning, the faded façade from former days which incorporated a large dim sign that spelled P H O T O G R A P H Y in letters that looked as if they wanted nothing to do with one another, the scuffed and cracked linoleum floor, the pocked walls with their swaying trophies, the trestle tables upon which the cardboard boxes stood, or under which they hid, or beside which they huddled, the dumb homely homemade lamps that filled the room with the rattle of tinlight, the tall stool in a back corner where the stupid assistant perched, the rug which hung over the entrance to Mr. Gab's private quarters: they were all meant to deceive detectives and most untrained and idle inspection. For the truth was—since the assistant harbored the same opinion as Mr. Gab's once-a-time rival—the stock was stupendous, of varied kind and exquisite quality, a condition which was quite unaccountable unless the prints had, at one time or other, by someone or other, been pinched.

The assistant, whose apparent stupidity was an effect of his seeming a suitable subject for Diane Arbus, knew, to cite one *outré* instance, that in a box at the back of the store, and in two Mr. Gab kept in a cleaning closet in his kitchen, were several beautiful pictures set in Sicily and shot in the early fifties by, of all people for Mr. Gab to have discovered, Enzio Sellerio: in particular one from Vizzini of the worn head and shoulders of a woman who had framed herself with a window that in turn was surrounded by rows and rows of descending roof tiles textured to a fare-thee-well—a woman whose gaze was one of total intensity, though her mouth expressed quizzicality, while on the sill lay an aristocracy of fingers, age infecting everything else—her figure positioned as if she were emerging from the grave of days; then another taken through the flychains of a Palermo doorway so that a seated man, a horse and cart, a churchfront and a couple are seen as if scrimmed by a blurring rain of o's; or the Chiesa Madre's quiltlike stairway viewed from above as it's being climbed by a herd of Paternò goats . . . well, where could this man who went nowhere, rarely to the edge of his neighborhood, have obtained work of this quality without hanky-panky of some kind? Without a lot of miscreating going on behind the back of every member of an honest public.

Oh . . . yes . . . Mr. Gab also had a very moving photograph—perhaps a tad melo—of some trailer camp kids in Richmond, California Ansel Adams had taken with Dorothea Lange's twin-lens Rolleiflex during the War, cropped and dodged according to his own account; and just how had that dramatic image made its way into a cello envelope and into a cardboard box in this silly little shop on Arsenal Avenue except if it were hiding out?

Mr. Gab was as silent about his system of supply as he was about everything else, and he sold so seldom he may have been holding most of his stock for years, and in the same boxes too, long before his assistant became old enough to observe any rate of change. Nevertheless, from time to time a very big Russian looking man in a very heavy Russian looking coat, though not with a dead animal on his head, which would have made everyone take note, came with wild hatless hair to see, and apparently to consult with, Mr. Gab, going into his quiet private quarters for a little chat, carrying a case large, flat and black. The Russian's big bass voice would soften as soon as his wide back disappeared behind the rug, which Mr. Gab held open for him as though they were entering a box at the theater. How are you this very day, my boy, the big man would thunder when the stupid assistant greeted him with a wince of recognition and a pleasant surprised smile. Annduh Missterr Gahb, my boy, is he ahbought? His accent, thick as his coat, was too eclectic to be genuine, and had been faked to cover a Russian one, the assistant thought. It was then, at the card table in the company of the ceramic cat, that the case would click open to disclose, the assistant imagined, a wondrous rarity, an August Sander maybe, filched from a German collector, a labor leader in an ill-fitting unpressed dark suit, throttled tie, intense vest, like those Mr. Gab wore, hair receding so it was now a headband, and those arms at his side ending in pugnacious little fists.

But when the assistant went later to look under Sander in the German box he found only the one which had been there through uncounted years: the hotelkeeper and his wife, Gastwirtsehepaar, around 1930, Tweedledum with Tweedledee, posed outside their vine-sided hostelry, she in her polkadot dress and frontally folded arms, he in bow tie and white shirt and hanky, a startle of patches against the compulsory black suit, including vest—black too—tucked under the coat like a head hid in a camera's hood—oh oh—there's one button missing, one out of four, too bad, the bottoms of the innkeeper's trousers hiked in an ungainly fashion above a pair of sturdy polished shoes, black as well, the innkeeper's arms clasped behind him so that the swell of his stomach would suggest to a hesitant guest hearty fare; well, they were both girthy full-fleshed folk as far as that goes, her eyes in a bit of a squint, his like raisins drowning in the plump of his cheeks.

What made August Sander's portraits so great—"great" was the word, in the assistant's opinion—was the way his sitters made visibly manifest, like the backgrounds behind them, the lives that had shaped their pictured faces and forms, as though their daily occupations had drawn them there to be displayed for the camera with all the seriousness suitable to such a show of essential self.

If you were to look at the penetrating portrait Berenice Abbott made of Eugène Atget when he was a whispy-haired old man with sunken cheeks, a mouth relieved of most of its teeth, assertive nose, and intense eyes, you might get a whiff of Mr. Gab too, for he was ancient early, grew up to reach old in a hurry, and then didn't change much for decades, except to solidify his opinions, much the way Atget had, both men easily angered, both men set in their ways, each short of speech, and patient as the stones Atget alone gelatinized. Mr. Gab disavowed color with the fervor of a puritan, and nothing in the shop had a hue you'd want to name beside the dull brown cardboard and the pillow in his chair, because the walls were once a clean cream dirtied now to nondescription, and the lino floor was like a playing board of black/white squares, a design mostly seen unmopped in public toilets, while the rug he'd hung across the door to his digs was a tweed a fade away from tan.

Mr. Gab was a stickler. His ideal was the perfect picture taken on the wing with one shot, and allowed to emerge from its development like a chick its egg, so that one saw not just the subject supremely rendered but a testimony to the unerring fineness of the photographer's eye; an eye unlike the painter's, he claimed, because the painter constructed, the painter made up his image as if the canvas were a face; while the photographer sought his composition like a hunter his prey, and took it away clean, when it was found, to present it in its purity, as the result of an act of vision, the sort of seeing no one else employed, what Mr. Gab called "slingshot sight." Painting took too long, sculpture of course was worse, and encouraged thinking, permitted alteration, changes of mind; whereas the photographer came, saw and shot in a Rolleiflex action, like waving off a fly.

Mr. Gab knew Atget bided his time, did and redid; he knew that Edward Weston pulled images like putty into weird unnatural shapes; he knew that Walker Evans cropped like a farmer, August Sander as well, who also staged every shot with theatrical calculation; that Man Ray was like Duchamps, an incorrigible scamp; that Ansel Adams dodged and burned and renovated; that even André Kertész, who possessed, like Josef Sudek, a saintly sensibility, had more than once employed a Polaroid . . . well, Mr. Gab didn't say very much about such lapses, he just threw up his hands, palms up/arms out, as he did in the winter, salting his sidewalk, and said that it was beyond understanding that the same man who had taken, from an overlooking window, those pictures of Washington Square in a snow of fences—when? nineteen seventy? well, in, anyway, a nearby year—it was dumbfounding that an artist of such supreme severity should have succumbed to Kodachromania and taken, it was said, as if he had embezzled them, two thousand Polaroids, and for a time had sunk as far as Cibachrome; but genius was a dark cave full of flickers, who knew what the darkness might disclose? who knew, his hands said, washing themselves in the air.

Mr. Gab forgave, and forgave again, but certain photographers had too many counts against them, like David Bailey, to mention an outstanding instance, because he bandaged the body exposing only the legendary wound with its unlikely whiskers, or did the worst sort of celebrity portrait—Yoko Ono, for god's sake—or shot up the worst sort of scene—Las Vegas, can you imagine?—consorted with cover models, and had nudes blow chewing gum bubbles to match their bubbies or wear necklaces of barbed wire; then there was a hot lens like Irving Penn, who spent too much time in the studio, who worked for fashion magazines (advertising and news were also OUT), who photographed Marisa Berenson's perfect bosom and Rudolf Nureyev's perfect limbs because they were Berensen's boobs or Nureyev's calves, and did portraits of famous folk like Truman Capote on account of that fame, often in silly contrived poses such as Woody Allen gotten up as Groucho Marx (Mr. Gab vented exasperation), or did cutsie-pie pictures like that faucet Penn pretended was dripping diamonds, but almost worst, his malignant habit of pushing his subjects into corners where they'd be certain to feel uncomfortable and consequently conspire with their tormentor to adopt a look never before or after worn.

Nevertheless (for Mr. Gab was composed of contradictions too), Mr. Gab could show you (while complaining of its name) Cigarette No. 69, from a series Penn had done in '72, or a devilish distortion from the box marked NUES which Kertesz had accomplished in 1933 as another revenge against women . . . well, it was admittedly beautiful, simply so, so simply blessed . . . he might mention the gracefully elongated hands pressed between the thighs, or draw attention to the dark button indenting the belly as if it were waiting to ring up a roomer on the fourth floor, the soft—oh yes—mound, also expanded into a delicious swath, of . . . Mr. Gab's stupid assistant would have to say the word "pubic" . . . hair, a romantic image, really, in whose honor Mr. Gab's hands shook when he held the photo, because he'd feel himself caught for a moment in the crease of an old heartbreak (that's what an observer might presume), memories extended elastically through time until, with a snap, they flew out of thought like a pursued bird.

The customers . . . well, they were mostly not even browsers, but wanderers, or refugees from a bad patch of weather, or misinformed, even so far as to be crestfallen when they understood the Nowhere they had come to; but occasionally there'd be some otherwise oblivious fellow who would fly to a box, shove off the bag of beans, and begin to finger through the photos as you might hunt through a file, with a haste hope might have further hastened, an air of expectancy that suggested some prior prompting, only to stop and withdraw a sheet suddenly and accompany it to the light of the good lamp in the rear, where he'd begin to examine it first with a studied casualness that seemed more conspiratorial than anything, looking about fly-lightly before indifferently glancing at the print, until at last, now as intent as a tack, he'd submit to scrutiny each inch with tightwhite lips, finally following Mr. Gab, who had anticipated the move, through the rug to the card table and the cat in the kitchen, where they'd have what Mr. Gab called, with a pale smile that was nearly not there, a confab.

Concerning cost. This was what his stupid assistant assumed. The meeting would usually end with a sale, a sale that put Mr. Gab in possession of an envelope fat with cash, for he accepted nothing else, nor were his true customers surprised, since they came prepared with a coat in whose inside pocket the fat envelope would be stashed. Consequently, it was a good thing the shop was so modest, the neighborhood so banal and grubby, the street, in fact, macadam to a fault, resembling Atget's avenues or stony lanes not a whit, not by a quick flip of light from a puddle or a flop of shade from an overhang, because the shop's stock was indeed valuable, and somewhere there was concealed cash with which, his stupid assistant surmised, Mr. Gab purchased further contraband, plus, if funds had been apportioned, a spot where lurked the money that tided Mr. Gab, his business, and his stupid assistant, over from one week to the next (though their wants were modest) until, among the three who stepped inside at different times on an April day, a shifty third would paw through the box marked PRAGUE as if a treasure had been buried there, and then, despite nervous eyes and a tasteless cream colored spring coat where—yes—the cash had been carried, buy a Josef Sudek that depicted Hradcany Castle circa 1915 under a glowering sky.

Mr. Gab really didn't want to let go of anything. His pleasure in a photograph, his need for it to sustain his sinking spirit, rose as the print was withdrawn and examined, and neared infatuation, approached necessity, as he and the customer, photo in front of them, haggled over the price. So Mr. Gab drove a hard bargain without trying to be greedy, though that was the impression he gave. Still, he had to let some of his prizes go if he was going to continue to protect his stock and ensure his collection's continued appreciation and applause.

Yes . . . yes . . . yes . . . the audience was small, but its appreciation was deep and vast, and its applause loud and almost everlasting.

Occasionally, as the assistant remembered, there were some close calls. A tall aristocratic looking man in expensive clothes and a light touch of gray hair chose a late afternoon to enter. Greeted by Mr. Gab in the usual way, he brusquely responded: I understand you have a photograph by Josef Sudek depicting two wet leaves. After a silence filled with surprise and apprehension, Mr. Gab replied with a question: who had informed the gentleman of that fact? He, by the way, he went on, was the owner of the shop, Mr. Gab was his name, while his visitor was . . .? It is common knowledge in certain places, Mr. Gab, if it is indeed you, the tall man answered, and consequently has no more distinct location than a breeze. For some moments, Mr. Gab was unsure which of his two questions had been addressed. I shall, the stranger went on, show you my card directly I have seen the Sudek. Two Wet Leaves, he repeated. What period would that be, Mr. Gab said, somewhat lame in his delay. Though it was his stupid assistant who limped. And who did so now—limped forward in an aisle while Mr. Gab was making preparations to reply. His stupid assistant: smiling, winking one bad eye. His naturally crooked mouth turned his smile into a smirk. Later, Mr. Gab would gratefully acknowledge his assistant's attempt to Quasimodo the threatening fellow into an uneasy retreat.

But the man pushed forward on his own hook, looking sterner than a sentencing judge. You'd know, he said. You've got a print. Two Wet Leaves. Archival quality, I'm told. 1932. You'd know. Then casting an eye severe as a spinster's at the layout of the shop, he added: where shall I find it? (waving a hand) where is it hid? The provenance of my photographs, Mr. Gab replied with nervous yet offended heat, is clear beyond question; their genuineness is past dispute; their quality untampered and unthreatened.

As if Mr. Gab's ire had melted the mister's snowy glare, he made as if to communicate a smile. The assistant tried on slithery faces and did appear to be quite stupid indeed. I should think every photograph in this place was in dire straits, sir, the man said sternly, ignoring the reassurance of his own signal. As I remember, Mr. Gab managed, Two Wet Leaves is quite impressive. You'd know, the man insisted, beginning a patrol of aisle one, his head bent to read the labels of the boxes. I had such a print once in my possession, obtained from Anna Farova herself, Mr. Gab admitted. Soooo . . . the stranger straightened and turned to confront Mr. Gab. And was it taken by sly means from Anne d'Harnoncourt's exhibit at the Philadelphia? Only from Anna's hand, herself, sir, Mr. Gab replied, now firm and fierce, and no other Farova than Farova. As if there were many, the man said frowning, you would know.

Why not an Irving Penn? This insult was not lost on their visitor whose upper lip appeared to have recently missed a moustache. The many boxes seemed to daunt him, and it was now obvious that Mr. Gab would not be helpful. I have friends in Philadelphia, he said in a threatening tone. I understand the nearby gardens are nice, Mr. Gab rejoined. It was clear to the entire shop that Mr. Gab had regained his courage. Was this freshly shaven man perhaps an officer of the law, the stupid assistant wondered, coughing now behind a stubby hand whose thumbnail was missing as David Smith's was in that portrait by Penn, the one in which Smith's mouth, fat lipped and amply furred, is sucking on a pipe.

It was necessary to sidle if you wished to approach the wall, and sidle the tall man did, closing in on an image dangling there, gray in its greasy container. Is that, by god, a Koudelka, a Koudelka to be sure. His hands rose toward it. Not for sale, Mr. Gab said. Not for money. No need to remove it. But the deed was done. Slender fingers from a fine cuff parted the clip and slid the photo forth, balancing it under a blast of can light upon a delicate teeter of fingertips. Not for money? then in trade, the man said, gazing at its darkly blanketed horse, and at the hunkered man apparently speaking to the horse's attentive head. Ah, what magical music, the man exclaimed, as if to himself. The grays . . . in the horse, the street, the wall . . . the light tracks, the swirls and streaks of gray . . . melodious as nothing can. Unless it was Sudek himself, said Mr. Gab. The man's lengthy head rose from the picture where it had been feeding. Yes, he said, having taken thought. Only Sudek himself.

The fingernails are especially . . . Mr. Gab began, because he couldn't help himself. Ah, and the white above that one hoof, the visitor responded, entranced. Yes, the nails, the gesture of the hand, a confused puff of tail and that wall . . . such a wall. Hoofprints, Mr. Gab prompted. Dark soft spots . . . yes . . . so . . . would you consider a trade, the man asked smiling—fully, genuinely—as he lay the cellophane envelope carefully on top of a cardboard box and allowed the print to float down upon it. I might have in my possession—if you have too many, you would know—a Sudek myself I'd be prepared to swap. I couldn't part—. Mr. Gab broke off to repeat himself. Not for trade or sale, though if the Sudek were fine enough, he, Mr. Gab, might be prepared to purchase . . . But were you to see the Sudek, the man said pointing toward his eyes . . .

It's a trap, Mr. Gab's assistant thought, for he only looked a bit stupid, especially with a little dab of spit moistening the open corner of his mouth. It is the immersement, the immersement of the figures in their fore and back and floor ground, that is so amazing, don't you agree? Mr. Gab, unsure, nodded. He's an entrapper, the assistant thought. I should show you the Sudek, the visitor said, no longer a customer but now a salesman. It sings, sir, it sings. I'm willing to look at anything Sudek, Mr. Gab said, over his assistant's unvoiced series of "noes." All right, the seller said, slipping his tall frame toward them. After reading Mr. Gab's expression, the man left abruptly, without leaving a clue as to his intentions, and without closing the door behind him.

2: The Stupid Assistant

Had appeared at Mr. Gab's shop door years ago with a note from the orphanage . . . okay . . . from a welfare agency. The note was in fact in a sealed envelope, and the boy, who was at that time about ten or twelve, and wasn't yet Mr. Gab's assistant, hadn't a clue to its contents. Nor did he care much. He was not then a very caring child. He had seen too many empty rooms filled with kids of a similar disownership of themselves as his. Mr. Gab looked at the envelope handed him and shook his head warily as if he could read through cream. He then conferred upon the child a similar gesture, as if he saw through him too—clear to his mean streak. Here at last, hey? he said. The boy had a pudgy bloataboy body. Half of him, the right half, though undersized, seemed okay; the leftover half, however, had been severely shortchanged. The head sloped more steeply than heads should, a shoulder sank, an arm was stunted, its squat hand had somewhere lost a finger, and the leg was missing most of its length. The kid had consequently a kind of permanent lean which a thick woodsoled shoe did little to correct, though the fellow tried to compensate by pushing off with his short leg, and thereby tipping himself up to proper verticality, with the result that he bobbed about as though fish were biting, nibbling at bait hung deeply beneath whatever he was walking on—a sidewalk, lawn, shop floor, cindered ground.

The boy knew that he was being handed over. The lady with him had explained matters, then explained them again, and made silly claims which didn't fit what little he knew of his own cloudy history. This man, he was told, had been his mother's husband, but was not known to be his father. The identity of his father remained a mystery. The boy's mother had not done a Dickens on him and died of childbedding, but had come down unto death with influenza when he was allegedly a month or two past the curse of his birth. Cared for by the state from then on. He went from wet nurse to children's home to foster parents back to children's home again. No one liked him. He was too ugly.

He appeared to be stupid, and most of what he did was awkward, to say the least. In close quarters he tended to carom. He learned that when you failed to understand something you were blamed for that, but that alone, thus escaping consequences. People would say: well, he didn't know any better; he's not all there. Mr. Gab called him "you stupid kid" from the very beginning, and never called him anything else, though he lived with Mr. Gab above the first shop (on the street of his envious enemy) like one of the family if there'd been a family, and in time ceased resenting the name, which was often sweetly drawled—hey-u-stew-pid—and eventually shortened to u-Stu, a result that u-Stu quite liked, though Mr. Gab pointed out that now his name was as out-of-kilter as u-Stu's stature and his gait.

In point of fact, there was really nothing the matter with his mind, which had somehow scuttled to the right side of his brain when his deformities were being assembled, so when his head got lopped a little on the left, his intelligence remained intact, hiding safely a bit behind and a bit above his bright right eye, and looking out of it with the force of two whole hemispheres.

For his entire life, not omitting now, Mr. Gab's assistant had watched gazes turn aside, watched notice be withdrawn, watched courses alter in order to avoid the embarrassments of his body: the bob and weave of it, its stunted members, the missing finger, the droopy eye, the little irreducible slobber that robbed his mouth of dignity, and the vacancy of a look that lacked muscle; who wanted to encounter them? face nature's flaws? pretend you were talking to a normal citizen instead of a mid-sized dope-dwarf? Kids his own age were curious, of course, and would stare holes in his shirt. Neither being ignored nor peered at were tolerable states.

U-Stu's speech had a slight slur to it on account of some crookedness at the left corner of his mouth and a bit of permanently fat lip in the same place. Simple minded, most thought him, if they listened at all. He'd talk anyway. Ultimately he took pleasure in producing discomfiture and awkwardness, embarrassment and shame. It suited Mr. Gab to keep him around for the same reason. And he liked the name "Stu" because he felt himself to be a loose assemblage of parts that commingled in his consciousness like diced carrots and chunks of meat in juice. A few, like boombox, the Russian furrier, would address him directly, but blarefully, so they still wouldn't see him through the dust-up of their own noise. After all, such folk had business with his master, as the assistant was sure they thought Mr. Gab was. He, on the other hand, was ugh! he was Igor. Who deals in eyes of newt. And brains of bats. Stirs into pots the kidneys of cats.

At first the silence was stifling, Mr. Gab's directions terse, his look stony, his indifference an act to cover revulsion, the assistant was certain; but after a while Mr. Gab began to see u-Stu's crooked mouth, saw the little bubble of spit, heard the slur, grew accustomed to the rockabyebounce, and accepted u-Stu's absent finger as well as the nail that was never there, not hammered off as had been, u-Stu believed, David Smith's. Then, after further familiarity was achieved, the assistant became invisible again, the way one's wife fades, or actual son recedes, seen without being seen, heard without hearing, felt without caring, even her breast. This was okay because it was based upon acceptance. Like getting used to handling worms or disemboweling birds. Yet it wasn't okay to the assistant because the assistant felt he was in fact disgusting—quite—so that if you were to truly take him in you should continue to feel revulsion too: he hadn't been brought into the world merely to wobble, but to repel people by its means, and at the same time to remind them of their luck in having sailed all of themselves down the birth canal.

The first shop, though it had a finer front, had been much smaller, and the assistant, while yet too young to be much help, had to assist in sleeping, since Mr. Gab talked in his sleep, and snored like a roaring lion, and turned and tossed like a wave, and occasionally punched the air as if he were a boxer in training, so the boy had to shake Mr. Gab awake sometimes, or lie in the dark nearby, listen to his mumbles, and participate in his nightmares, which was one reason why the assistant said, in his own undertone, he has the gift, Gab has, the gift. The boy asked Mr. Gab if he had enemies he was beating up on when he poked his pillow or flailed away at the night air, and this question helped Mr. Gab realize that their present sleeping arrangement wasn't salubrious. After some finagling, he found the space where they did their little business now, and where they established themselves, after making several trips (it was but a few blocks) to trundle cartons of prints on a handcart when it wasn't raining and if the coast was clear.

After the move, he slept in a sleeping bag at the back of the second store, at the border of Mr. Gab's quarters but not over the line, where a dog might have lain had they had one—art and dogs don't mix, Mr. Gab said (Mr. Gab hated Wegman), and the best kind of cat is ceramic. I shall be your guard ghoul, the assistant said, a remark which Mr. Gab didn't find funny, though he rarely laughed at anything, occasionally upon seeing a photo he would hoot, however u-Stu wasn't sure whether his hoot was one of amusement or merely derisory, so perhaps he was never amused, though he from time to time made such a noise.

U-Stu had facial hair on half of his face, and Mr. Gab, to u-Stu's surprise, would shave him. Half a beard is not better than none, he said. Because he believed for a long time that his assistant was too stupid to shave himself, certainly too stupid to live alone, take care of himself in any ordinary way, he shaved his adolescent, initially even cut his meat, carefully combed his ungainly hair, pressed his few clothes with an iron he had heated on the stove, and tried to cook things that were easy to eat. Gradually, he realized that although his stupid assistant chewed crookedly, his chew was nevertheless quite effective, and although he was short-armed (Mr. Gab always winced at that formulation), he could manage a knife and fork (he needed to lower one shoulder to pull his short arm to the front), and with his one good eye working overtime (as Mr. Gab probably thought), he could read, shave, look at pictures, and with a control over his body that grew better and better, he could perform his characteristic bob-and-wobble much more smoothly, and he soon learned to repair fixtures, sweep the store, replace photographs in their plastic sleeves, and return them properly to their cardboard files. And ask visitors: muh I hulp you shur?

Mr. Gab began by speaking to the boy (he had not yet received his promotion to stupid assistant) slowly, and a little loudly, as though the boy might be a bit deaf in addition, talking to him often, contrary to his habitual silence, plainly believing that such treatment was necessary for the lad's mental health, which it no doubt was, although no number of words could make him into a lad, because lads were always strapping. This loquacity, night and day it seemed, led the boy to believe that Mr. Gab gabbed, was a gabber by nature, so he would say to himself, almost audibly, he has the gift, he does, does Gab, as he went about his work which was each week more and more advanced in difficulty. He could see Mr. Gab's face wrestling with the question: what shall I say today—good heavens—and on what subject? Mr. Gab's slow considered ramblings were to be the boy's schooling. Perhaps, today, he'd want to learn about bikes. I want to know about my mother. The boy asked. Mr. Gab began to answer, almost easily, taken by surprise: she resembled one of Stieglitz's portraits of O'Keeffe. She was beautiful beyond the bearing of one's eyes. Such hands. Stieglitz always photographed her hands. Her hands. As if he had wakened, Mr. Gab broke off in great embarrassment, his face flushed and its expression soon shunted to a sidetrack.

Before that blunder—I want to know about my mother—Mr. Gab had spoken to the boy of many things. He always spoke as if chewing slowly, in the greatest seriousness, early on about school and how he, Mr. Gab, had struggled through classes here after his family had come to the States, having an unpronounceable name, and not knowing the language; about his sisters and aunts, mothers and grans, never of men, because men, he said, scorned him for his interests, and broke his Brownie; he talked about the time when he had begun work in a drugstore, learning from books how to develop his prints; about, after he had gotten canned for stealing chemicals, the days he had sold door to door—brushes, pots and pans—enduring the embarrassments of repeated rejection, once even attacked—his face mopped with his own mop by an irate customer (the funny side of things was left dark); until, eventually, having marched through many of the miseries of his life (though leaving serious gaps, even his auditor was aware of that), the subject he chose to address was more and more often the photograph, its grays and its glories.

Beneath—are u listening, u-Stew-pid-u?—beneath the colored world, like the hidden workings of the body, where the bones move, where the nerves signal, where the veins send the flood flooding—where the signaling nerves especially form their net—lie all the grays, the grays that go from the pale gray of bleached linen, through all the shades of darkening, deepening, graying grays that lie between, to the grays which are nearly soot black, without light: the gray beneath blue, the gray beneath green, yes, I should also say the gray beneath gray; and these grays are held in that gray continuum between gray extremes like books between bookends. U-Stu, pay attention, this is the real world, the gray gradation world, and the camera, the way an X-ray works, reveals it to our eye, for otherwise we'd have never seen it; we'd have never known it was there, under everything, beauty's real face beneath the powders and the rouges and the cremes. Color is cosmetic. Good for hothouse blooms. Great for cards of greeting. Listen, u-Stew, color is consternation. Color is a lure. Color is candy. It makes sensuality easy. It leads us astray. Color is oratory in the service of the wrong religion. Color makes the camera into a paintbrush. Color is camouflage. That was Mr. Gab's catechism: what color was. Color was not what we see with the mind. Like an overpowering perfume, color was vulgar. Like an overpowering perfume, color lulled and dulled the senses. Like an overpowering perfume, color was only worn by whores.

Grass cannot be captured in color. It becomes confused. Trees neither. Except for fall foliage seen from a plane. But in gray: the snowy rooftop, the winter tree, whole mountains of rock, the froth of a fast stream, can be caught, spew and striation, twig and stick, footprint on a snowy walk, the wander of a wrinkle across the face . . . oh . . . And Mr. Gab would interrupt his rhapsody to go to a cabinet and take out one of Sudek's panoramic prints: see how the fence comes toward the camera, as eager as a puppy, and how the reflection of the building in the river, in doubling the image, creates a new one, born of both body and soul, and how the reflection of the dome of the central building on the other side of the water has been placed at precisely the fence's closest approach, and how, far away, the castle, in a gray made of mist, layers the space, and melts into a sky that's thirty shades of gradual . . . see that? see how? how the upsidedown world is darker, naturally more fluid . . . ah . . . and breaking off again, Mr. Gab withdrew from a cardboard carton called PRAGUE a photograph so lovely that even the stupid not-yet assistant drew in his breath as though struck in the stomach (though he'd been poked in the eye); and Mr. Gab observed this and said ah! you do see, you do . . . well, boy . . . bless you. The stupid not-yet assistant was at that moment so happy he trembled at the edge of a tear.

Hyde Park Corner. This picture, let's pretend, is one of the Park speakers, Mr. Gab said, pointing at a hanger. What does it tell us? Ah, the haranguers, they stand there, gather small crowds, and declaim about good and evil. They promise salvation to their true believers. Mr. Gab went to the wall and took down his Alvin Langdon Coburn. Held it out for u-Stu's inspection like a tray of cookies. There's a dark circle protecting the tree and allowing its roots to breathe. And the dark trunk, too, rising to enter its leaves. In a misted distance—see—a horse-drawn bus, looking like a stagecoach, labeled A 1, with its driver and several passengers. In short: we see this part of the world immersed in this part of the world's weather. But we also see someone seeing it, someone having a feeling about the scene, not merely in a private mood, but responding to just this . . . this . . .and taking in the two trees and the streetlamp's standard, the carriage, and in particular the faint diagonals of the curb, these sweet formal relations, each submerged in a gray white realm that's at the same time someone's—Alvin Langdon Coburn's—head. And the photo tells us there are no lines in nature. Edge blends with edge until edgelessness is obtained. The spokes of the wheels are little streaks of darker air into which the white horse is about to proceed. But, my boy, Alvin Langdon Coburn's head is not now his head, not while we see what he is seeing, for he is at this moment a stand-in for God. A god who is saying: let there be this sacred light.

Mr. Gab would lower his nose as if sniffing up odors from the image. If the great gray world holds sway beneath the garish commerce of color, so the perception of its beauty hides from the ordinary eye, for what does the ordinary eye do but ignore nearly everything it sees, seeking its own weak satisfactions?

Such shadows as are here, for instance, in these photographs, are not illusions to be simply sniffed at. Where are the real illusions, u-Stu? They dwell in the eyes and hearts and minds of those in the coach—yes—greedy to be going to their girl, to their bank, to their business. Do they observe the street as a gray stream—no—they are off to play Monopoly. Scorn overcame Mr. Gab, whose voice sounded hoarse. They have mayhem on their minds.

Finally, Mr. Gab had got round to The War. Mr. Gab's tour of duty—he was a corporal of supply—took him to Europe. In London he learned about the Bostonian, Coburn. In Paris, he discovered Atget. In Berlin, he ran into Sander. In Prague . . . in Prague . . . Mr. Gab was mustered out in Europe and spent a vaguely substantial number of years in the continent's major cities. More, Mr. Gab did not divulge; but he did speak at length of Italy's glories, of Spain's too, of Paris and Prague . . . He took u-Stu on slow walks across the Charles Bridge, describing the statuary that lined it, elegizing the decaying, dusty, untouched city, mounting the endless flight of steps to the Hradcany Castle, taking in both the Cernin and the Royal Gardens. They strolled the Malá Strana, the Smetna Quai, as well as those renamed for Janàcek and Masaryk, had a coffee in Wenceslaus Square, visited St. Vitus Cathedral, and eventually crossed the Moldau bridges one word after the other.

When Mr. Gab returned to the States, he enrolled in New York's City College on the GI Bill, while working, to make ends meet, at several photography shops and even serving, during a difficult period, as a guard in a gallery. But now the gaps in this history of his grew even greater, became more noticeable than before; details, which had been pointlessly plentiful about Prague buildings and Italian traffic, disappeared into vague generalities like figures in a Sudek or Coburn fog, and most questions, when rarely asked, were curtly rebuffed.

But Mr. Gab did regale his pupil with an account of his trip in a rented truck to their present city, and u-Stu was given to understand, though the story did not dwell on cargo or luggage, that his cartons came with him, and, in Johnstown, of all places, were threatened by a downpour which forced him for a time to heave to and wait the water out, so sudden and severe it was, and how nervous he had become watching the Conemaugh River rise. The journey had all the qualities of uprootedness and flight, especially since Mr. Gab's account did suggest that he'd left New York with his college education incomplete, and a bitterness about everything academic, about study and teaching and scholarship, which only hinted at why he had abandoned his archival enterprise.

For in Europe, surrounded at first by fierce fighting, bombs made of blood and destruction, Mr. Gab had formed the intention of saving reality from its own demise by collecting and caring for the world in photographic form. There were footsteps he was following, or so he found out. Like Alvin Langdon Coburn he had been given a camera by an uncle. Like Alvin Langdon Coburn, he had crossed the sea to London. Like Coburn, he would tour Europe, though not with his mother, who was as missing from his life, he insisted, as that of u-Stu's. In the footsteps of Mr. Coburn, possibly, but not in the same shoes, for he, Mr. Gab, hadn't had a father who made shirts and died, leaving his mother money. He hadn't found friends like Stieglitz and Steichen with whom he could converse, or exchange warm admirations. He sat in metal storerooms surrounded by supplies, and learned a few things about stocks and stores and shipment.

Unlike Johnstown's fabled inundation, but rather drip by drip, words entered Stu's ear, and filled his mind to flood stage finally; not that he needed to be instructed about the grimness of the world, or about what passed for human relations. Some of the words weren't nice ones. Mr. Gab kept his tongue clean, but now and then a word like "whore" would slip out. You will not know that word I just used, Mr. Gab said hopefully. Stu thought he meant the word "catechism," which indeed he didn't understand, but Mr. Gab meant "whore," which he proceeded to define as anyone who accepts money in return for giving pleasure . . . pleasures which were mostly illusory. There were shysters for mismanipulating the law. There were charlatans for the manufacture of falsehood. Quacks for promising health. Sharks for making illegal loans. Mountebanks to prey upon the foolishly greedy. Apparently, humanity was made of little else.

But there were, Mr. Gab assured u-Stu, the Saviors too. They bore witness. They documented. Eugene Atget had rescued Paris. Josef Sudek had done the same for Prague. August Sander had catalogued the workers of his country, as Salgado has tried to do for workers worldwide. Karl Blossfeldt, like Audubon, had preserved the wild plants. Bellocq had treated his Orleans' whores with dignity. And how about Evelyn Cameron, who had saved Montana with her single shutter? Or Russell Lee who photographed the Great Flood of '37 as well as the negro slums of Chicago? Or consider the work of a studio like that of Southworth and Hawes, whose images of Niagara Falls were among the most amazing ever made? he, Mr. Gab, had but one of their daguerreotypes. And Mr. Gab then disappeared into his room behind the rug to produce in a moment a group portrait taken in the Southworth and Hawes studio of the girls of Boston's Emerson School, and through the envelope which Mr. Gab did not remove, u-Stu saw the identically and centrally parted hair of thirty-one girls and the white lace collars of twenty-eight.

Mr. Gab went on to extol the work of Martin Chambi whom he had available only in a catalogue produced for an exhibit at the Smithsonian (so there were an unknown number of books behind the rug, perhaps in that closet, perhaps in a shelf above the boxes). Although Mr. Gab was capable of staring at a photograph uninterruptedly for many minutes, he had the annoying habit of flipping rapidly through books—dizzying u-Stu's good eye, which could only receive the briefest tantalizations of an apparently magical place, set among most remote mountains, Mr. Gab called "Macchoo Peechoo"—until he reached the photo he was searching for. There, there, Mr. Gab said, pointing: a young man in a most proper black suit and bow tie was standing beside a giant of a man clad in tatters, a cloth hat like an aviator's helmet in the giant's hand, a serape draped over the giant's shoulders, and, and around the small man's, a huge arm finished by fingers in the form of a great claw. The little fellow is the photographer's assistant, Mr. Gab informed. Who, u-Stu saw, was gazing up at the face of the giant with respectful incomprehension. But one was mostly drawn to the giant's patched and tattered shirt and baggy trousers, to the barely thonged feet which had borne much, and finally to the huge stolid countenance, formed from endurance. Shots of shirts were rare.

Not all of Mr. Gab's enthusiasms were trotted out at once. They were instead produced at intervals involving months, but each was offered as if no finer effort, no better example, could be imagined. Yet u-Stu came to believe that the artist Mr. Gab called P.H. (Ralph Waldo was the "other" Emerson) was dearest to him, after one afternoon being shown (again from the cache in the kitchen) a simple country and seaside scene: a crude sailboat manned by three, and oared as well, underway upon a marshy watercourse, the rowboat's big sail, with its soft vertical curves and pale patches, in the center of the photograph, and to the left where the reeds began, though at the distance where there had to be land, a simple farmhouse resting in a clump of low trees, a trail of chimney smoke the sole sign of occupancy.

Every photograph by its very nature is frozen in its moment, Mr. Gab said, but not every photograph portrays stillness as this one does. The sail is taut, smoke is streaming away toward the margins of the picture's world, and the postures of the oarsmen suggest they are at work; but there is little wake, the surface of the water is scarcely ruffled, not a reed is bent, the trees are without leaves, and the faint form of a small windmill shows the four blades to be unmoving. Nevertheless, it is the lucency of the low light, the line of the sail's spar which meets, on one side a shoreline, on the other a small inlet-edging fence, which holds the image still; it is the way the mast runs on into its reflection, and the long low haze stretched across the entire background at the point where earth and air blend, where the soft slightly clouded sky rises; it is the relation of all these dear tones to one another that creates a serenity which seeks the sublime, because it is so complete. Complete, u-Stu-u, com plete.

Look. In this work, the house, the boat, the rowing men, have no more weight than the boat's small shadow on the pale white water, or the bare trees and stiff reeds, because all are simply there together. Equals added to equals yields equals. One can speak one's self insensible about the salubrious and necessary unity of humankind with nature, u-Stu-u, yet, though striving and straining, never permit our listener to see how the solitude, the independent being, of every actual thing is celebrated by the community created by such a composition. The light, coming from the right, illuminates the sides of the house in such a way it seems blocky and dimensional, as the boat does; however the sail, the sky, the water, and their realms, though made of a register of curves, are otherwise, and flat as a drawn shade.

In this way his education proceeded, but it had an odd consequence. His head was made of someone else's words; his memory, formerly poor, no doubt reluctant to linger on an early bringing up that was mostly a throwing down, adopted another person's past, and he saw what that other person said. He kept house in another head, and who could blame him? who would not have done the same? why not change residences? when the body where you were contained was a bitter bit of bad business.

His fingers licked him through the pages of Mr. Gab's dozen or so books of photography, mostly limited to Mr. Gab's narrow enthusiasms; however there was a recent Salgado which rendered the stupid assistant weak in his poor knees, though he'd been told messages were for Western Union. Such messages—these.

Stu started stepping out—a phrase to be used advisedly. He obtained a card at the local library, shoplifted a few fruits, sat in sun-filled vacant lots, down in the weeds, in open air. In the library he began examining the work of the two painters Mr. Gab admitted to his photographic pantheon: Canaletto and Vermeer. In the shops he slyly added to his meager stock by stealing small fruits: figs, limes, kiwi, cherries, berries. In the weeds, eating them, he would imagine he lived in another world, and he'd scale everything around him down, pretend he was hunkered in a photograph, where woods were black and white and pocket-sized. In the library he was eyed with suspicion, and Stu felt certain that only the librarians' fear of a lawsuit let them lend to him. In the open-air market, they knew he was a thief past all convicting, yet they hadn't caught him yet, it was a public space, and they begged for the crowds which covered his snitches with colorful blouses and billowy shirts. Shirts ought to receive some celebration. But he was run out of the vacant lot by a cop.

It was about then that Mr. Gab expelled him from his sleeping post, and he formally became Mr. Gab's assistant. Mr. Gab had never paid his assistant a wage, not a dime, nor had he bought him anything but second hands, even his comb. Mr. Gab was frugal, probably because he had to be, so their diet was distinctly rice and beans. He moved his assistant out to a little room in a rooming house run formerly by Chinese, the Chinese who ran it maintained. It had brown paper walls, a cot and a chair, a john down the hall, a window without a blind, a throw rug which—to expose a splintery floor—would wad itself into a wad while you watched. You can keep this job if you want it, Mr. Gab announced, and I'll pay you the minimum, but now you must take your meals and your sleep and your preferences out of here—out—and manage them yourself.

At first the new assistant was wholly dismayed. What had he done, he finally asked. You've grown up, was Mr. Gab's unhelpful answer. You go away, god knows where, and look at god knows what, color and comic and bosom books. Actually, it was as if Mr. Gab were clairvoyant and knew that his assistant had come on a book by Ernst Haas called "Color" in the same local library where he had obtained his volume of Vermeer, and been subsequently ravished, just as Mr. Gab feared. But if Vermeer was photographic, Haas was painterly. He was sure Mr. Gab would say, very pretty, very nice, nevertheless not reliable. The object is lost, can you find it? torn posters and trash—that's the world? and how far into a flower can you fall without sneezing?

The stupid assistant suspected that Mr. Gab had listened to what was going on in his stupid assistant's head, and heard objections and reservations and hesitations and challenging questions, both personal and educational, particular and theoretic. Then said to himself: this Stu should go elsewhere with these thoughts. Ernst Haas had photographed some flowers through a screen, making romantic a symbol of romance; through an open oval in a dark room, like the inside of a camera, he had rendered a bright café scene so its reality seemed an illustration in a magazine; he'd snapped a cemetery bust at night as if the head had bleached the film and raised a ghost; and Mr. Gab would certainly have denounced these startling images as mere monkey business, had he seen them: the cropped stained glass from Cluny, too, glass heads looking like stone ones in a dismal darkness, a regiment of roofs in Reading, the silhouettes of fishermen fishing in a line along the Seine; but the assistant could remember, now, Sudek's magical garden pictures, with their multiple exposures, dramatic angles, and cannily positioned sculptures; and he found himself thinking that it wasn't fair, it wasn't fair to be so puritanical, to live with a passel of prejudices, even if each enthusiasm that was denied intensified another devotion.

Mr. Gab's exiled assistant came to work just before ten each morning like a clerk or a secretary, but if mum were Mr. Gab's one word, he would not utter it. Silence lay over the day like a shawl on a shivering shoulder. In the flophouse where the assistant lived now there was plenty of jabbering, but he couldn't bear the cacophony let alone find any sense to it. In his room the world had grown greatly small. The window framed an alley full of litter. The brown paper wall had tears and peels and spots made of drops of who knew what—expectorations past. Yet in such stains lay lakes full of reeds and floating ducks and low loglike boats. Instead of the sort of wall which furnished a rich many-toned background for so many of Atget's documents; instead of the cobbled courtyard that the remainder of the photo surrounded, shadowed, or stood on; instead of gleaming rounds of stone with their dark encircling lines; instead of the leaves of trees like a dance of light and dark about a field of figures; there might be—instead—a single pock, the bottom of it's whitish with plaster; that's what he had to look at, descend into, dream about, not a shining slope of rock, its layers threaded and inked; not the veins of a single leaf like roads on a map, or a tear of paper resembling a tantrum—his rips didn't even resemble rips—or faded petals that have fallen like a scatter of gravel upon the foot of a vase; not an errant flash of light centered and set like a jewel; instead he had a crack, just a crack in a window, a cob's web, or that of a spider, dew-drop clinging like an injured climber to his only rope of light; not a clay flowerpot given the attention due a landscape; not a scratch on the hood of some vehicle, not directional signs painted on the pavement, instructions worn by the wheels of countless cars; not a black eye blown up to resemble the purple of a blown rose. These were the images in his borrowed books, the material of his mind's eye, the Liliputian world grown taller than that Peruvian giant.

Even Mr. Gab's heroes, even Josef Koudelka, had devoted at least one frame, one moment of his art, to a knife cheese chocolate bit of fruit that had been put out upon the rumpled front page of the *International Herald Tribune.* That's okay, he heard Mr. Gab say, because it records a lunch, a day, a time in the world. I want that, u-Stew-u, I want the world, I don't want to see through the picture *to* the world, the picture is not a porthole. I want the world *in*—you see—*in*—the photo. What a world it is after all! Am I a fool? not to know what the world is; what it comes to? that it is misery begetting misery, you bet; that it's meanness making meanness, sure; that it's calamity; that it's cruelty and greed and indifference; I know what it is, you know what it is, how it is, if not why—yet I want the world as it is rescued by the camera and redeemed. u-Stu-u.u. Paris is . . . was . . . noisy, full of Frenchmen, full of pain, full of waste, of *ordinaire;* but Atget's Paris, Sudek's Vienna, Coburn's London, even Bellocq's poor whores (I never showed you those ladies, you found out and stared at that filth yourself), Salgado's exploited, emaciated workers are lifted up and given grace when touched by such lenses; and every injustice that the world has done to the world is forgiven—in the photograph—in . . . in . . . where even horse plopped cobbles come clean.

But what about, the stupid assistant began, what about Haas's Moreno, a photo full of steps, the dark woman walking toward a set of them, her black back to us, the red and white chickens standing on stairs . . . they'd all look better gray, he was sure Mr. Gab would say. Or the lane of leaves, that lane of trees beside the Po, or the Norwegian fjord photo, Mr. Gab, the faint central hill like a slow cloud in the water, what of them? what of them? So what, he replied on behalf of Mr. Gab who was somewhat cross, when one can have Steichen's or Coburn's street lamps, spend an evening full of mist and mellow glisten, bite into an avenue that's slick as freshly buttered toast.

But Mr. Gab do you dream that Sebastian Salgado wants anyone forgiven: are the starving to be forgiven for starving? are those scenes from Dante's hell (the hell you told me about) redeemed because the miners of Serra Pelada's gold—worn, gaunt, covered with mud and rags—are, through his art, delivered from their servitude and given to Dante? am I to be forgiven for my deformities? my rocking, as if I were indeed the baby in the tree, is it okay? if cleverly clicked? o yes, Mr. Gab, you're right, I did peek at the fancy girls, and I was toasted by one in striped tights and a bonnet of hair who raised to me a shotglass of Raleigh Rye, but so many of them, sad to say, had scratched out faces, only their bare bodies were allowed to be; while Bellocq too, by the book, was said to be misshapen . . . not quite like me; but he didn't dwarf himself, I bet, and behaved himself with the girls because he understood his burden; just as it's true, I didn't do me, someone else, perhaps yourself, Mr. Gab, did, but I was not a party to the filthy act that made me, or to the horror of having insufficient room in an unsuitable womb; I didn't mangle myself, suck the nail from my own thumb, shorten my stature, wound my mouth; yet daily I inflict them on others; I wobble along on my sidewalk and all those passerby eyes flee the scene like shoo'd flies.

Should Salgado—u-Stu-u.u—Mr. Gab rejoins, should he then forget his skills and just picture pain picture human evil picture human greed picture desolation picture people other people have allowed to become trees made of nothing but twigs, picture many murdered, meadows murdered, hills heaved into the sea, sand on open eyes, the grim and grisly so that it approaches us the way you do on the street, so we will look away, even cross against traffic in order to avoid any encounter, because the overseers of those miners don't care a wink about them, never let their true condition enter an eye, form a thought, suggest an emotion, no more than the other workers, who sweat while smelting the ore, give the miners time, since no one thinks of the smelters either, the glare oiling their bare chests, no more than those who stamp some country's cruel insignia on the country's coins or dolly a load of now gold bars into a vault think of anyone else but their own beers and bad bread and breeding habits.

But Mr. Gab, sir, when I look at that huge hole in the ground, and like ants those innumerable heads and shoulders heavy with sacks of dirt on paths encircling the pit just as you said Dante's rungs did, I see something sublime, like the force of a great wind or quake or volcanic eruption.

Yes, u-Stu, because u have a book in your hand, u aren't in the picture, u are thousands of miles from Brazil, u have clean underclothes on (I hope and suppose), but u can now reflect on your own sad condition, as molested by fate as they've been, those poor workers, because who of us at the end of the day goes home happy? do you go to your room and laugh at its luxury? you saw—it's less than the whores of New Orleans; don't you still see trash from your window, and stains on the wall and through a pock or two if you peer into them won't you encounter again that barrenated man covered with a silkskin of mud, a man who a moment before the photo was in a long climbing line up the laddered side of one of hell's excavations, and won't you continue to find behind him, and free of misery's place in the picture, another man in shorts and a clean shirt studying a clipboard? and what are we to think of him, then? and what are we to think of ourselves, and the little gold rings we wear when we marry?

Starve the world to amuse the few. That's man's motto. That sums it. But now Mr. Gab's assistant didn't know—couldn't tell—who was supposed to have said it.

Alvin Langdon Coburn came up. After a day of silence, his name seemed a train of words. Alvin Langdon Coburn. As if Mr. Gab had really been talking with his assistant as his assistant had imagined. He was holding a paperback copy of Coburn's autobiography. With a finger to mark his place, Mr. Gab gave it a brief wave. I shall read u-Stu what Alvin Langdon Coburn wrote about those who do dirty tricks with their negatives. Mr. Gab's voice assumed a falsetto his assistant had never heard him quote anyone before this moment—a moment which had therefore become important. "Now I must confess I do not approve of gum prints which look like chalk drawings . . ." Mr. Gab interrupted himself. P.H. was equally fierce and unforgiving, he said. ". . . nor of drawing on negatives, nor of glycerine-restrained platinotypes in imitation of wash-drawings as produced by . . ." You won't have heard of this guy, Mr. Gab added, letting disdain into his voice like a cat into a kitchen. ". . . Joseph T. Keiley, a well-known . . ." Well known, well known—not anymore. ". . . American photographer and a friend of Alfred Stieglitz." They all claimed to be that—a good, a fond friend of Stieglitz. Let's skip. ". . . I do not deny that Demachy, Eugene, Keiley and others . . ."

Heard of them, have we? Are they in the history books? are they? take a look. ". . . and others produced exciting prints by these manipulated techniques . . ." Bah bah bah-dee-bah. Here—"This I rarely did, for I am myself a devotee of pure photography, which is unapproachable in its own field." Unapproachable, you hear? Pure. That's the ticket. That's the word. Unapproachable. He snapped the book shut and relapsed into a silence which said that something had been proved, something once for all had been decided.

3. From the Stool of the Stupid Assistant

During the long empty hours between customers, Mr. Gab sat at his desk at the front of the shop and drowsed or thumbed through the same old stack of photographic magazines he'd had for as long as his assistant had been near enough his paging thumb to observe what the pages concerned. Most of the time Mr. Gab sat there with the immobility of a mystic in a trance. Occasionally, he'd leaf through a book, often an exhibition catalogue or a volume containing a description of the contents of a great archive, such as Rüdiger Klessman's book on the Kaiser Friedrich Museum, over whose pages and pictures he'd slowly shake his head. Once in a while, his back still turned to his assistant, he'd raise a beckoning hand, and u-Stu would leave his stool in the rear where he was awkwardly perched while trying to read books light enough to be steadily held by one hand, and come forward to Mr. Gab's side where he was always supposed to verify, by studying the picture, Mr. Gab's poor opinion of the masterpiece.

The beckoning finger would then descend to point at a passage in a painting. Whereupon Mr. Gab would say: look at that! is that a tree? that tangle of twigs? The finger would poke the plate, perhaps twice. It's an architect's tree! His voice would register three floors of disgust. It's a rendering, a sign for a tree; the man might as well have written "tree" there. Over here, by "barn," see "bush"? And the fellow is said to be painting nature. (It might have been Corot or Courbet.) See? is that a tree? is that a tree or a sign, that squiggle? I can read it's a tree. You can read it's a tree. But it's not a tree anyone sees. Twigs don't attach to branches that way, branches don't grow from trunks that way, you call those smudges shade? To a simp they might suggest shade. To a simpleton.

The finger would retire long enough for the assistant to make out an image and the book would snap shut like a slammed door: I am leaving forever, the slam said. A fake crack in a fake rock from which a fake weed fakes its own growth, Mr. Gab might angrily conclude: we are supposed to admire that? (then after an appropriate pause, he'd slowly, softly add, in a tone signifying his reluctant surrender to sadness) that . . .? that is artistry?

The assistant spent many hours every day like a dunce uncomfortably perched on a stool he had difficulty getting the seat of his pants settled on because it stood nearly as high as he did and furthermore because the assistant was trying to bring a book up with him held in his inadequate hand. Once up, he was reluctant to climb down if it meant he'd soon have to climb up again. So he perched, not perhaps for as long as Mr. Gab sat, but a significant interval on the morning's clock: with a view of the shop and its three rows of trestle tables topped with their load of flap-closed cardboard boxes adorned by beanbags as if they were the puffy peaks of stocking caps. The tables appeared to be nearly solid blocks since so many containers were stored underneath each one where with your foot you'd have to coax a carton to slide sufficiently far into the aisle to undo its flaps and finger through its contents. ROME I.

But Mr. Gab or his stupid assistant, whoever was closest, would rise or fall and wordlessly rush or rock to the box and lift it quickly or awkwardly up on top of the ones on the table, unflapping it smartly or ineptly and folding the four lids back before returning to chair or stool and the status quo. Mr. Weasel would occasionally come in and always want a box buried beneath a table in the most remote and awkward spot; but at least he'd pick on a container up front where Mr. Gab would have to say good day in customery greeting and then push cartons about like some laborer in a warehouse to get at PARIS NIGHTLIFE or some similar delicacy which Mr. Weasel always favored.

Customers who came to the shop more than once got names chosen to reflect their manner of looking or the shapes they assumed while browsing, especially as they were observed from the stool of the stupid assistant. Weasel slunk. He was thin and short and had a head that was all nose. His eyes were dotted and his hair was dark and painted on. The first few times Weasel came to the store the stupid assistant watched him carefully because his moves produced only suspicion. After a number of visits, however, the Weasel simply became the Weasel, and the stupid assistant shut down his scrutiny, or rather, turned it onto his page.

Part of the stupid assistant's education was to study books which

Mr. Gab assigned, not that they ever discussed them, and it would have been difficult for Mr. Gab to know, ever, if his assistant was dutiful or not, or was reading filth and other kinds of popular fiction. When he thought he caught the Weasel, u-Stu was wading through Walter Pater. And Pater held a lot of water. U-Stu was wading waist deep. Mr. Gab had not recommended any of what the assistant later found out were Pater's principal works, but had sent him to a collection of essays called *Appreciations* where u-Stu learned of Dryden's imperfect mastery of the relative pronoun, a failing he misunderstood as familial. All Mr. Gab asked of his assistant regarding the works he assigned (beside the implicit expectation that it would be u-Stu who would withdraw them from the library, now that he had a card) was that u-Stu was expected to select a sentence he favored from some part of the text to repeat to Mr. Gab at a suitable moment; after which Mr. Gab would grunt and nod, simultaneously signifying approval and termination.

It was not clear to u-Stu whether there were designs behind Mr. Gab's selections, but *Appreciations* contained essays on writers whose names were, to u-Stu, at best vaguely familiar, or on plays by Shakespeare like "Measure for Measure" for which slight acquaintance was also the applicable description. The first essay was called "Style" and u-Stu supposed it was Mr. Gab's target, but, once more, the piece was larded with references that, from u-Stu, drew a blank from recognition. U-Stu resented having his ignorance so repeatedly demonstrated. To Mr. Gab he said: "this book is dedicated to the memory of my brother William Thompson Pater who quitted a useful and happy life Sunday April 24, 1887." Quite to the quoter's surprise, this sentence proved to be acceptable, and u-Stu was able to return the volume a week ahead of its due date.

This is not to say u-Stu didn't give it a shot, and in point of fact he was in the middle of trying to understand a point about Flaubert's literary scruples (all of Mr. Pater's subjects seemed to be neurotic) when his head rose wearily from the page in time to see the Weasel slip a plasticine envelope, clearly not their customary kind, into the stock of a cardboard box labeled MISCELLANEOUS INTERIORS. Skidding from his stool he rocked toward the Weasel at full speed. Sir, he said, sir, may I help you with anything, you seem to be a bit confused. This was a formula Mr. Gab had hit upon for lowering the level of public embarrassment whenever hanky-pankies were observed. However, as u-Stu took thought, as Mr. Gab turned to locate his assistant's voice, and as the Weasel looked up in alarm, u-Stu realized that the Weasel, so far as he had seen, was adding, not subtracting, from the contents of the container. Had u-Stu perhaps missed an extraction? Was this the latter stage of a switch?

It's alright, Mr. Stu, Mr. Gab said urgently. Mr. Grimes is just replacing a print for me. Oh, said Mr. Stu, stopping as soon as he could and calming his good eye. Mr. Grimes, the Weasel, winked in surprise and backed away from Mr. Stu toward the door. Something is up, Mr. Stu thought, thinking he was now Mr. Stu, an improvement surely, a considerable promotion, a kind of bribe, but an acceptable one, coming as it did at long—he thought—last. But what was up? what? Mr. Stu retreated to his stool and Mr. Grimes slid out of the shop with never a further word. In fact, Mr. Stu couldn't remember a first word. But he'd been inattentive while tending to Walter Pater's work, and to the peevish Flaubert, who had just vowed, at the point Mr. Stu had been reading, to quit writing altogether.

Mr. Gab's back was soon bent over MISCELLANEOUS INTERIORS. From his stool where he was perched once more like some circus animal, Mr. Stu couldn't see one interesting thing though he knew rummaging was going on. He felt in his stomach a globe of gas, a balloon filled with rising apprehension. Mr. Gab, having done his dirty work, returned to his desk empty handed, allowing the store to become as law abiding as before. With his Pater closed, Mr. Stu, as he would from this morning on be called, began to fill the back of Mr. Gab's head with his own thoughts, enjoying a vacation in another body, even old Mr. Gab's, which had to be a low-rent cottage in a run-down resort, but—hey—several limps up from the ramshackle where he currently was.

Other eyes, both reasonably well off, saw through gray glass into the street where the world would scarcely pass. He imagined he was sixteen, which was perhaps his age. He had the legs of that Caravaggio cupid which had so exercised Mr. Gab when he'd come upon them the other day in Rüdiger Klessmann's catalogue of the paintings in the Berlin Museum (remember that liar's name, Mr. Gab had commanded). Naked, the kid was. Very naked. A pornpainting, Mr. Gab said in sentence. It is written here that this is the figure of a boy about twelve. Sitting on a globe. The posture is contorted, but not like Mr. Stu on his stool, Mr. Stu thought. Look, this Klessmann fellow says that every wrinkle and fold of the skin is reproduced with the utmost realism. Ut-most. Look, What do you see?

U-Stu saw a cupid with arms and thighs wide apart, as wide as full sexual reception might require, and musculated like a twenty-five-year-old wrestler, though wearing the weenie of a boy of six, one nipple showing in a swath of light which flew in conveniently from the left to dispel a general darkness; in fact to fling it aside like a parted robe and reveal a creased and belly-buttoned stomach below a strong broad chest where the nipple lay, as purple as a petal fallen from a frostbitten rose (Mr. Gab had said as if quoting). The head, however, bore a leering drunken grin as salacious as they are in Frans Hals. Those huge thighs, though, Mr. Gab fairly growled, how are they rendered? see the way they are rounded into a silk soaked softness? (Was he quoting still?) An amazon in the guise of a baby boy. Holding the bow of a violin! What allegorical gimcrackery! But no! another masterpaint, Mr. Gab announced, as if introducing a vaudeville act. And Klessmann dares to call this pornographic pastiche realism!

Caravaggio was simply a ruffian. His darks were merely dramatic, his colors were off, his attitudes appropriate to saloons. He was a pretender in front of reality, and reality had made him a murderer and a convict. Tenebrist indeed. Remember that word. (His assistant tried, but he understood it to mean "tenuous.") Mr. Gab could be relentless. Carrahvaggeeoh, he'd growl. For him darkness is never delicate. Carrahvaggeeoh didn't understand what a shadow was—an entire region of the world. Ah . . . we know where to go for shadows.

By now Mr. Stu was able to interpret Mr. Gab. Realism—truth—was the property of the photograph. He regularly ridiculed paintings which presented themselves as lifelike. About *trompe l'oeil* compositions he was particularly withering. What kind of streetcar accident has caused this rabbit, that jug, this—hah!—hunting horn, that—hah!—hat, that knife, that—hey?—horseshoe, and that key—a key!—those two dead birds?—to hop to run to fly to get carried in a carriage to see the smash, rehear the crash, and enjoy the bloody scene? What drew them to this place? These dots of detail? that's the real? reality is a stupid collection? trophies of a scavenger hunt? Whose eye would they fool?—hey?—whose?

Mr. Stu, now in the guise of the Caravaggio, stretched his grand legs wide, even if he wouldn't fool anyone, and flaunted his cute little sex. Those few who might pass would never look in. Anyway. He wondered, as he had so often, what it would be like to be ordinary and have had an ordinary childhood, not one in a Home where everything was shoes in a line. And nothing had ever been his: not his bed or blanket, the table at which he drew, not a wall, not a window, not a fork or spoon, lent instead, shared, maybe his underclothes had been his, but only because they wouldn't let anyone else soil them. He'd left with the clothes on his back as the cliché insisted, so they had to be his: his shoes, and his socks and his bulbous nose. Even now his room was rented, his books were borrowed, his stool belonged to his employer, as did the boxes of photographs, presuming they weren't all stolen. At the moment, though, he owned a violin and sat heavily on his own globe.

He'd noticed how Mr. Gab did it: how he studied a picture (this one, another Sudek, had showed up out of the blue to be held under Mr. Stu's nose) until he knew just where the darks went (had he bought it from that haughty high hatter? that would not have been wise); dark filling almost the whole road except for the wet and glistening dirt that still defined some wagon tracks (the temptation would have been far greater than for another piece of cake), the sky, too, setting with the paling sun, and walls and buildings nothing but edges, tree trunks rising into the dying light, crisp and unconfused (had it been dropped off by the Weasel? god forbid), rows of insulators perched like birds for the night on faintly wired poles, but so composed . . . made of mist . . . composed so that the bushes at one end of the panoramic rhymed with the tree limbs at the other; thus the blacks beneath held up the grays above, so the soft glow of the failing sun, which could be still seen in the darkening sky, might lie like a liquid on the muddy lane . . . and Mr. Gab would inhale very audibly, as if a sigh had been sent him from somewhere, because only once had the world realized these relations; they would never exist again; they had come and gone like a breath.

An image had been etched on an eye.

Mr. Stu had made Mister, though, even if he didn't have a childhood; and he had a job—a job that was his job, no one else's, as stooled to its heights as any accountant's—and he had his own room even if it was rented, even if it was paid for by his father figure; and he had a market where he could swipe fruit, a weedy field to sit in now and then, a library card for borrowing books; and a worry which was ruining his reveries. If the cops got Mr. Gab, what would become of Mr. Stu? No job then. No room. He could read in the weeds. But the authorities didn't like the appearance it gave the neighborhood when he flopped down in the empty lot and looked up at a clutter of clouds or saw inside a deeply receding blue sky a scented silent light.

With Walter Pater parked, Mr. Stu settled on his stool and set his sights on the back of Mr. Gab's head, and bore into it with his whole being until he felt he was looking out into the empty sun-blown street where now and then a figure would pass, moving more often left than right, while he wondered what was to be done, what he should do to defend themselves from the calamity that was coming. After closing, after, as he imagined, still wholly inhabiting Mr. Gab, he'd taken that body to bed in the Chinese flophouse where Mr. Gab's somewhat resourceful assistant had found a curtain made of mediocre lace at the market—near that stall from which, by using the crowd, he'd appropriated fruit—just a cloud of thread to tack to the wall above his window so that now when Mr. Gab's hand drew the curtain the room grew gray and a few of the city's lights spangled the frail netting where, bedclothed, u-Stu in the garb of Mr. Gab could still see, till sleep, a kind of sky, and pretend he was napping in the weeds or smelling space like a moth; so after closing, Gab gone to the flop, what was left of Mr. Stu would go through the boxes one by one and systematically, if there were a system, hunt for pictures that were likely pilfered in order to hide them . . . yes—by reswapping bodies for the task, putting Gab back in his own boots—maybe too many switcheroos to seem dreamable—and subsequently to slide the suspicious photographs into such other boxes as he'd have collected under his so far fleabagless bed, where no one would ever think to pry, thus cleansing the premises of the taint of loot and securing the safety of what was looking more and more like a possible life.

He swore that were he able to do it, he would work earnestly to improve himself during the remaining existence he'd been given, giving up both fruit and stealing; he'd pass out fliers to stimulate the store; he'd memorize a new word every day and read like a regiment on the march; he'd—

What, though, could be done about the ones which perched in plain view upon the walls, yet tried to lie about their presence like the purloined letter, even though they could be seen to be what they were, Koudelka, in an instant, glorious, an icon worth worship, or an Emerson, swimming in silence through reedy weeds, or that damn Evans with the foursquare face outstaring stone, or the Abbott tucked away near the rug-hugged doorway; because Gab would feel their loss even if Mr. Stu just replaced the prints and not the hangers, put up at some risk a Harry Callahan or a Marc Riboud instead, since who knew if Gab had grabbed them too; he'd feel their loss like a draft through a door left ajar, the hairs on the back of his neck would whisper their names in his ears; yet the Koudelka, the Feininger had to go, guilt could not be more loudly advertised. Looking at "Lake

Michigan" Mr. Gab had muttered placement, placement, placement, three times, u-Stu had supposed, to honor the three figures standing in smooth lake water, water which merged imperceptibly with a grayed-over sky, three figures perfectly decentered, and the wake of the walking bather . . . well . . . as if there'd been some calculation . . . if not by nature then by Callahan . . . alas, not a serious name. Yet Callahan, said Mr. Gab, would do.

He could not spirit these evidences from their walls. Suppose he could persuade Mr. Gab to squirrel them away in some quiet sequestership of his own where they couldn't be seen let alone seized let alone certified as swiped. In so doing, in going along with Mr. Stu's suggestion, wouldn't Mr. Gab be confessing to his crimes? Then, though, if he did that, perhaps he'd be relieved of his reticence. What stories Mr. Gab could tell about each one—Cunningham's magnolia, that late Baldus, or Weston's two shells—how he had found them, stalked them, and withdrawn them from their owner's grasps (even slipped them out of their countries) as if they were already as much his as his hand was his, leaving their handclasps.

At first, of course, u-Stu's head, heart, conscience, were all firmly set against the notion, voiced by their enemy from the earlier street, that Mr. Gab's stock contained stolen articles. His mind could not figure out how Mr. Gab might have managed. He seemed taciturn not sly, blunt and biased not crafty or devious, and it was difficult to envision Mr. Gab as young, vigorous, and thievish, climbing walls like a quick vine, seeping like pulverulent air (his word to work on for the day) under doorframe or window sash; yet so quick fingered as to pry open cases in a wink, slip a photo from its frame in a thrice, and then to saunter carefree and concealing from a museum or pretentious shop straight through customs declaring only a smile and a bit of a cough. Nor had he the heart to imagine Mr. Gab to be no more than a fence for those more slick and daring than he—as if Weasel were—what a laugh; yet appearances were deceiving, who knew better than he how that was, for he, Mr. Stu, no longer the Stupid Assistant, never had been, only looked so, on account of his one cross eye and leaking lip. Conscience . . . well, conscience made a coward of him. Made him fear a fall. From his stool of course. From his room, job, minimal relation. Because he actually would have loved to believe that Mr. Gab was a Pimpernel of prints. He knew that conscience, if it had to compete with pride, wouldn't stand a chance, and could be cowed into silence. So that to have the prince of purloiners for a Pa . . . well . . . that would be okay. That would be quite all right.

He might have to get used to some such idea. Evidence was more prevalent than fingerprints. There was that envelope postmarked Montreal in which the Baldus was, contrary to custom, still kept: an absolutely perfect albumen silver print of the train station at Toulon, with the Baldus signature stamp lower right; the envelope carrying the capital letters CCA outlined in red on its front flap: rails running straight through the glass-gated shed into the everlasting; the envelope dated in a dark circle May 1, 1995: about a foot and a half wide, the sky, as almost always in Baldus, kept a clear cream, the scene so crisp as to seem seen through translucent ice; the print in heavy plastic slid between tough protective cardboard: uncluttered, freight cars parked in place, not a sight of mortal man as usually, in Baldus, was the case, a document that documented as definitely as a nailed lid; but now, so overcoated, the thing bulked in the box it was shoved in, crying out to the curious.

What a quandary. Surely Mr. Gab would see the wisdom in such a gleaning of the incriminating prints whose very excellence made them enemies, and surely he would understand, in such circumstances, the good sense in ceasing for a time to acquire anything more that might entrap Mr. Gab against his will in the terrible toils of the law; yes, surely he would have to recognize how wise it was to heed these warnings, to back off and go double doggo; but Mr. Stu knew that Mr. Gab would bite on that Sudek if it were offered, that he could not resist Quality which overcame him like a cold; because what he understood to be Quality was all that counted in the world, Mr. Stu had come to grasp that: not warmth, it threatened the prints; not food which merely smeared the fingers; not leisure for where would an eye go on vacation but to its graphs—to bathe in their beauty as if at a beach? not shelter since his pictures furnished him his bricked lanes and cobbled streets, damp from rain, and all his buildings defined by shade and the white sky and the dark freshly turned fields and the veined rocks and river water frozen while falling into a steaming gorge; not a woman's love, since the photos gave up their bodies ceaselessly and were always welcoming and bare and always without cost—after, once, you had them; further than that there was the flower petal's perfection, the leaf's elemental elegance, rail and river line, rows of trees, a hill, a chateau, a vast stretch of desert dotted with death and small mean rocks. Mr. Stu had a dim hunch about how, for Mr. Gab, they had replaced his mother's flesh. I touch you. You touch eye. That eye owns the world.

So what to do. Just broach the subject? Just say: I think, Mr. Gab, we should take these precious ones away for safer keeping. There are robbers out there looking for swag. The richness of your stock might get about, remarked here, mentioned there, whispered around until the information reaches the wrong ear. And then in the night when you are asleep up there, wherever it is, some thug may force his way in, easy enough even if the shutters are shut and the door is locked; these days they have pry irons and metal cutting torches and lock picks and credit cards they cleverly put to illegal use. Mr. Gab, is that you sir, someone said, startling Mr. Stu out of his thoughts as though they were dreams. We, sir, are the police. You have been denounced.

4: The Day of Reckoning arrives

I've—?

Been informed upon.

Mr. Gab gave Mr. Stu a look of such anguish and accusation his assistant's heart broke. Mr. Stu felt his blood was running from him and put his hand to his nose. Then Mr. Stu returned Mr. Gab's anguish with his own, a pitifully twisted expression on an already twisted face. Mr. Gab immediately knew his suspicion was false and unfounded; it had followed the awful announcement as swiftly as the sting from a slap; there'd been no time to take thought, show sense, conceal his feeling. He realized how horribly he had wounded his adopted kid, his loyal assistant whom he'd helped from the Home and taught to grow up, reaching the rank of Mister. Mr. Gab understood now that he'd left a son a second time. Whose only mistake was being born. Or being in the neighborhood when Mr. Gab was nabbed.

We have a warrant.

A warrant?

To search your shop and to remove these boxes and place them in our custody while they are examined. It's been alleged you have been in receipt of stolen goods.

Mr. Gab tried to rise from his chair by pushing at its arms with his fists. I have no receipts. Long ago they each arrived, these photographs, like strangers off a boat you understand. There are decades of desire boxed here. Though they are good photographs. I admit that. Good. It makes for envy in others. But he was not speaking to the detective who had probably been chosen for the job because he didn't look like a detective is supposed to look because his look, now was deeply troubled too. And it made his figure seem puny, his hands small, his nose abruptly concluded as if it had once fallen off. Mr. Gab was not even attending to himself. He was being borne down by a lifeload of anxiety and a moment of misguided distrust.

It is said these boxes are full of stolen pictures.

They are mine. My prints. They live here.

These pictures may not belong to you.

They are prints not pictures. They are photographs not pictures. They are photographic prints.

They may not belong to you.

They do. They belong. In these, of all boxes, they belong. But Mr. Gab was not attending to the officer either. Bulky men were entering the shop, one by one, though they had begun trying to enter two by two. The detective held forward a folded sheet with an insecure hand. Out in the street, Mr. Stu saw the Russian without his hat—his hair, in the sun, shining from a thick pomade. The bulky men wore overalls with a moving company logo on them. This is the writ for this, the detective said, beginning softly but adding a hiss by the end. He sensed he was not impressive. He shook, again, his folded paper. Mr. Gab still sat as solemn as a cat and seemed to be registering one blank after another. The warrant was placed in his lap. This gives us the right to remove—the man waved—and to search the premises. If the allegations—which I must tell you come from high up—powerful government agencies—if they are unfounded, these materials will be returned to you. You shall be receipted.

Receipted? At that, Mr. Gab gathered himself. The paper slid to the floor as he rose. For the first time, he seemed to be taking in the police and the moving men. These are my eyes, he said, and the life of my eyes. One man bore a puzzled look but picked a box up in his arms anyway. Bring in the hand trucks somebody said. You are using Van Lines? There will be a complete and careful inventory, the detective reassured him, looking intently about the store. Maybe you will finally learn what you have. Then he peered at Mr. Gab. You understand sir that later we shall want to speak to you at length. A hand trolley stacked with a box at its top marked PRAGUE rolled out. NIGHTLIFE went next. MISCELLANEOUS LANDSCAPES followed.

Why don't you help us by taking those pictures on the hangers down, the detective suggested to Mr. Stu. That way, nothing will get bent or soiled. So Mr. Stu did. First finding an empty carton to keep them in. Which took time because he was bloodless as a voodoo victim, and the bulky men and their boxes were in all the aisles. The enormity of everything took his blood's place.

Mr. Gab no longer protested. He simply stood beside his desk and chair and stared at the men as they pushed their trolleys past him. Mr. Stu made out a truck parked at the curb. Against its pale gray side the Russian's figure loomed. As each box was loaded into the rear of the truck, he wrote something on a clipboard. Mr. Stu suddenly thought: where are his witnesses? Every transaction took place in the back, between just the two of them, behind the rug; and was always in cash, Mr. Stu had been given to understand. There weren't any records. What could they prove?

Mr. Stu rocked into the movers' doorway. You shit from a stuffed turkey, he shouted, though it was doubtful the Russian understood him, he hardly looked up from his list. Turkey turd, yeah! A big moving man easily hipped him out of the portal. We'll get you guys, he was afraid he gobbled. Mr. Gab's position or posture hadn't changed. His eyes were unnaturally wide and seemed dry. Why was his face, then, so wet all over? One aisle of tables was vacant. How strange the shop seemed without its boxy brown bulks. Now the entering men with their empty trolleys went down the open aisle and returned to the street through one which was solidly cartoned. Wire hangers lay in a tangle on the trestle tops. The big moving men were tossing the beanbags on the floor, often in fun. Mr. Stu thought of saving several of the hangered photos by concealing them under his shirt, but the detective had two public eyes on his every move. The toe of one of Mr. Gab's shoes was on a corner of the warrant. Tears were sliding from his eyes in a continuous clear stream.

Evidence, Mr. Stu feared. They had evidence aplenty. Who had owned the Julia Cameron before it had come to hide and hovel here? she who specialized in wild hair and white beards? about whom he'd read had breathed the word "beautiful" and thereupon died, her photographs "tumbling over the tables." Was this an orphanage Mr. Gab ran, and were all these wonders children who had wandered or run away from their homes and families to find themselves in alleys and doorways and empty squares instead of warming hearthsides and huggie havens. No, they all had owners once and, Mr. Stu feared, had been as if by fairies stolen. Picsnapped. So they'd be traced—every trade and traduction. And then what? Mr. Gab's presence in the town nearest his Lordship's estate, his lodging at the inn, his visit to the household—each would count against him; his travels to Paris at opportune times, his many friends in the army who might turn up a bit of art here and there for some of the crown's coin, complaints from shops about losses they had suffered shortly after his employ—they would surely count against him; oh so many collaborators, filchers anonymous, partners in crime, many of whom would be still around to testify, and, for a break from the court, would see no need to lie. The prospect before Mr. Stu and Mr. Gab, Mr. Stu decided, was nothing short of calamitous. That was what he had thought to call it before: calamitous. In any case, and the awful moment came back to him like a bad meal, Mr. Stu could hardly work for a man who was so immediately ready to suspect him; who believed he might be a traitor, a child sent by society to win his trust, trip him up and dispatch him to jail.

Mrs. Cameron was a woman of good character, and did not retouch, Mr. Gab had once summed her up, but she was far too social in her choice of subjects. Social might have been a good idea, Mr. Stu now wanted to say to Mr. Gab. Friends in high places might have stood Mr. Gab in good stead. Tennyson. Darwin. Could come to the rescue. Attest to Mr. Gab's character. Honest fellow, as trustworthy as a hound. His museum was being removed, his life looted. Such a painful wrench and one deceitfully turned. The Russian—and Mr. Stu now saw his blurry figure counting boxes as they were taken off to jail—might have been an Albanian in disguise. He might be wearing that goo to fool Mr. Gab and Mr. Stu into thinking him sufficiently shiny to do business with. In reality, he was probably some Fed who lived in town with wife and child.

What's back here, the detective said, as if asking for permission when he wasn't, and pushing the rug aside to see. Kitchen, came his voice again. George, he shortly cried. One of the busy big men turned away from his work and went to join the detective out of all sight. They will surely find the special treasures, Mr. Stu thought. Soon enough the big man returned carrying within both arms a large box clasped against his chest. What's this, the detective asked when he reappeared. It has no label. Tell Amos to list it as "Kitchen Closet," he shouted after Shoulders as Shoulders bore his burden out.

Mr. Gab's eyes ran without relief.

It's terrible. Why do you have to take everything, Mr. Stu asked desperately. Can't you see how awful it is for Mr. Gab?

What?

Mr. Stu tried to speak more clearly—slowly and precisely as, in the Home, he had once been taught. By switch and rule and ruler.

Order of the court, seized on suspicion, the detective finally said, going out himself. The walls were bare except for the zincy heads of the roofing nails. The tables sheltered nothing under them now, while the emptied tops merely supported that absence, and bounced the blare of canned bulbs through a little shoe-shuffled dust. The air though was heavy, and Mr. Stu felt the trestles groan. Then the men with their big damp backs were gone. The truck was driven off, and the detective and his Albanian henchman vanished as though they'd become street trees.

Mr. Gab was where he'd been the entire time, still utterly silent, his face oozing away into grief, perhaps not to return. Mr. Stu, out of a need to soften the barrenness about them, slowly turned the cans off, so only the late afternoon light, made gauzy by the dirty window it soaked through, roamed the room. Then Mr. Gab moved to wreeeeek the shutters down. Here and there a sun streak would reach deeply into the darkness of the shop. What are we going to do? Mr. Stu spoke to himself more clearly than he spoke to strangers. At least you have those photographs engraved on the balls of your eyes.

Don't accuse me, Mr. Gab finally said, smearing his face with a shirtsleeve. What evidence can they have—from that fellow, I mean—Mr. Stu ventured. I gave him the slip, Mr. Gab said slowly, separating the words with consternation. He wanted a receipt for his cash. So I gave him the slip. He'll have a—. Well, maybe not, Mr. Stu said and received a bleak look for his pains. Not the first times, but the last time. Then I gave him one. Still, Mr. Stu persisted, you couldn't have known—. I knew, and he knew I knew, Mr. Gab said firmly. It was a Lange I had to have. A face of such . . . as if . . . pain had worn it . . . like wood by a wind. I'm sorry, Mr. Gab added. I've taken away your world, u-Stu, the way they've taken away mine. He shuffled as though old past the rug he now resembled.

Mr. Stu sat carefully in Mr. Gab's chair. It was not all that comfortable. Slivers of sun as though from a fire raced through the shutters and ran up the rear wall, now wholly exposed, the pale shadow of a table against it like a patch of unsunburned skin. When someone walked by on the sidewalk, the pattern palpitated. It was true that Mr. Gab didn't have much of a life. He sat in this not very comfortable chair most of every day, letting his eyes lie idle or roam randomly about like a foraging pooch, thinking who knew what thoughts, if he thought any, who knew that either. Now, and even more often then, Mr. Gab would reluctantly help a customer, and once in a great while do a bit of business behind the rug where the rug quite muffled the doing. You'd have to account it a life full of empty. But that life had better prepare to be so much worse. Its present plenitude of absence would prove to be a blessing. Nevertheless, who knew how to count these things: the quality of an existence, especially from the meager stuff that took place outside, in walking, talking, eating, drinking, sitting seated in a seat long hours, leafing a leaf from an out-of-date mag, arguing with an image in a catalogue, watching faint figures pass?

Mr. Stu let his eye run back and forth along the light like a squirrel on a wire. His life wasn't a winner either. Yet he had a job, a room, a library card. And he could open a book as if it were a door and disappear. He could inhale air in his weedy lot. He could look. He'd even learn. Yet already he'd found Sundays a stretch. He was supposed to stay home and pretend to be a person of substance in that slummy brown shoebox space of his. Itemize the alley. When the walls were whisked away? when the window went, what could he count? when his little box of belongings was put on the sidewalk outside, what would he manage? Mr. Gab, Mr. Gab, what were they to do? And when they took Mr. Gab downtown for questioning, and found what they would find, how could either stand it? . . . endure it? . . . live through? it! the awful. Mr. Gab reappeared with a bundle. He wore, for once, a wry smile. Quick as a cat Mr. Stu vacated the chair.

There are signs the dick went up the ladder to my loft, Mr. Gab said, but the dick missed this, wrapped in a sheet, under my cot. there was a great wad of sheet to be clumsily unwound before a photogravure, rubberbanded between cardboards for its protection, was released. Mr. Gab put the print where a streak crossed a trestle so they could see it. An Eastern moment, Mr. Gab said softly, and Mr. Stu saw the most beautiful silken scene he'd ever, which Mr. Gab explained was a Stieglitz from 1901 called "Spring Showers." Composed by a god, Mr. Gab whispered, as if the detective might overhear. He also spoke in awe, Mr. Stu knew. Like an oriental hanging, Mr. Gab said, as though the mottled gray surface was that of cloth. Less than half a foot wide, a foot tall, made almost solely of shadow, Mr. Stu saw there in the dim a streetsweeper in wet hat and wet slicker pushing a wide push broom along a wet gutter toward the photograph's wet left edge. Despite Mr. Stu's despair the image made him feel good. Just off-center, though on the same side as the sweeper, so that the right two-thirds of the picture was empty of everything except some soft faint shapes that represented traffic on the street, there grew a sidewalk tree with a gently forking trunk protected, perhaps from being pissed on, by a round wrought-iron fence whose pickets were thin as sticks. Surrounded by the sweetest vagueness, the tree rose from the walk on its own wet and wavery shadow as though that rivuleted shadow were a root, easing toward its thin thin upper limbs, which were dotted with brief new leaves and one perched bird, to faintly foliate away in indistinctness, though there were modulated hints that tall buildings might block you if you entered the background, as well as shimmers that signified some moving vehicles, and the loom of a large ornamental urn—was it?—one could not be sure.

What was certain was the photograph's depth, its purity, its beauty. And the silken faintly hazy and amorphous gray that made up most of this small and simple streetside scene was the most beautiful, most comforting, most expressive of all. It was everywhere as wet, Mr. Stu realized, as Mr. Gab's face had been before his sleeve had swabbed it. Gloom began descending again. Greatness could not keep misery away, not for long. Beauty eventually increased the pain. Mr. Stu understood incompleteness. For he was. Mr. Gab understood loss. Because he was its cause. Pictures someone had taken, he'd taken, taken and hid. Now these prints had been wrenched from him in turn, and were nowhere in the world anymore where they might be gratefully seen—pictures that had been pokey'd.

His shoulders in such a slump they ceased to be, Mr. Gab went with his treasure through the carpet again. Part of the carpet had pulled from its tacks so that now its hang was uneven. It bore a diamond design deep in its tan that Mr. Stu had never noticed. Throughout the shop sunlight flickered for a moment. Someone was passing. Mr. Stu thought that when emptiness was loom and mist and suggestive shadow, it was rather full; and that the photograph, which had so little that was definite in it, was a whole realm rich with right feeling. What would it mean to a man to have made such—there was no other word for it—such beauty? to have seen it through rainwatered eyes? to have captured it in a small now antiquated box? brought it to life almost amniotically? (another of his words) and in the style of a far-off culture too, also learned about by looking? Would it fill a life with satisfaction, or would it sadden, since a loveliness of that kind could never be repeated, could never be realized again?

Mr. Gab had treasured his collection. However acquired. He had gathered good things together which had perhaps been stolen and dispersed once already. He had achieved an Archive, made his own museum in the midst of a maelstrom. Didn't that count? So Mr. Stu thought maybe Mr. Gab could say he hadn't known they were anyone's legitimate possessions any longer, but were the spoils of war, refugees of slavery, expropriation and murder. Of course they could be returned to their proper homes if they had any, as long as it was their real wish to be rehung on the dour walls of grandiose old estates with their long cold halls given over to stuffily conventional family portraits and other tasteless bragging, to languish in the huge mansions or palaces they'd come from, or to sit in shame propped up on some lectern like a speech no one would give and no one wished to hear; that would be okay, provided there'd be no further punishment for Mr. Gab, since he'd had pain enough from his loss to surpass that of most lovers. Lover: that was right, because who, Mr. Stu surmised, had looked at them as though they were gray lace; who had weighed a shadow against a substance, a dark line against a pale space, the curvature of a street's recession against the forefrontal block of a building, so as to feel the quality of judgment in every placement, the rightness of every relation and how these subtle measures made the picture dance with the ideal gaiety of an ideal life.

We pass through frames, Mr. Gab had said. We walk about our rooms, our house, the neighborhood and our elbow enters into a divine connection with a bus bench or bubbler in the park, a finial, a chair or letter lying on a hall table, which is, in an instant—click—disssolved. The nose, the earlobe, the bosom, the elbow, the footfall, the torso's shadow, pass in and out of awkward, in and out of awful, in and out of awesome combinations just as easily as air moves; the sublime, the suddenly supremely meaningful and redemptive moment is reached, achieved, left, dissolved into the dingy, only, in a few frames further, to connive at more communities. It is grace and disgrace constantly created and destroyed. The right click demonstrates how, in an instant, we, or our burro, or our shovel, or our eye or nose or nipple, were notes in a majestic symphony. A world of self-concerned things is suddenly singing a selfless concerned song: that was what the fine photographer, over and over, allowed to be *seen* in solemn apology for what should have been *heard*.

Nothing had been heard from Mr. Gab in quite a while, though Mr. Stu hadn't counted breaths; however his employer's retreat should not have been surprising since he'd just lost a wife, more dear than life, to a bunch of hand trolleys. He'd be in the dark on his garret cot sobbing like a sad child, Mr. Stu bet, why not? in a room fixed to the top of a shabby ladder like a squirrel's nest in a tree; what could be sillier than where it was? and Mr. Stu had wanted to laugh when he first saw the way the ladder led up through a hole from which coal could have dropped. Perhaps Mr. Gab would be comforted by the darkness since it might suggest an end to things—no more moving men moving his treasures out, treasures to be treated like contraband—less anxiety, fewer humiliations—dark at midday was what this day deserved—so perhaps he'd be somewhat slightly—well, not reassured—but protected from any additional pain, such as being pierced through and through by his unwarranted suspicion of his former employee, Mr. Stu, a feeling that had been turned on—click—like a light, when the strange man had said the phrase—the curdling phrase—"informed upon."

You have been given up, Mr. Gab. We gottcha. Dead to rights. We got yer goods too. Yer a looter, a despoiler, a thief, a fence, a flown away father, an ungrateful and suspicious boss. Now you'll have to bear your loss like just desserts. Go to bed like your boy has, time upon time, to cry inside the pillow till the pillow flats. Go to bed like your boy has, countlessly, to imagine the bitter oncoming day. When you will walk about a barren store. When you will begin to miss me. When you'll be invited to "come downtown." Go to bed like your boy has, heart beaten by shame, sore and in despair he is alive. Go to bed like your boy has, angry at all, alone as a bone that has lost its dog. Head screams aren't effective. Head howls aren't effective. Head longs aren't worth a damn. Seek some solace in the fact that you aren't being gnawed on at the moment, not being yelled at, at the moment, not being guffaw'd, not being always at anything worst, on anything tossed, in anything last. Seek solace we advise . . . seek solace, don't we say? . . . the one photograph that remains, had it been unshrouded and claimed, would nonetheless have been engraved on your weeping eyes.

Mr. Stu felt a wadded sheet at his uneven feet. He picked it up, to unwad and refold, only to find his arms weren't long enough, so he spread it out on a trestle where its whites blazed in the streaks. The shutters were crossed by bleak slivers of sunshine. Mr. Stu drew a roll of masking tape from Mr. Gab's desk drawer, tape Mr. Gab used now and then to repair boxes, and began to block out the light, initially not easy because it bled through the thin tape, and it took several layers to make the glow even faint. Biting the tape in two, making its stickum do, gradually the room grew darker. Now there was only a halo to see by. It ran around the rug and apparently came from a light in the kitchen. Bring a pin, Mr. Gab, please, Mr. Stu called out. Though he thought he heard in his head the beating of a desperate heart, Mr. Stu boldly drew back the rug and entered the kitchen where he found a roll of stout picture wire after a few minutes of pawing about in drawers which otherwise yielded little in the way of contents. Bring a pin, Mr. Gab, please, Mr. Stu shouted up the ladder at the hole which was darker even than the inside of a hose.

Mr. Stu was feeling his way to his idea. He realized, while groping between trestles through the shop, that he was performing the steps of his project in the wrong order. Consequently it was with difficulty that he found the nails he wanted on opposing walls, and with difficulty that he finally fastened one end of his wire to a conveniently big nail, and with difficulty that he unrolled the wire—held over his head—to the other side and found another roofer to wind his wire around, allowing the remainder of the roll to dangle. Now he had a firm line across the room to fling the sheet over, but he was unsure of what came next. Bring a pin, please, Mr. Gab, he called, suddenly weary and useless.

It took some time—and after the slow return of resolution—to hang the sheet, though he should have been more expert, having hung a lot of laundry out to dry in his day, even standing on a short stool to do his pinning when the line was high. He stared into the dark, making nothing out. What's the idea, Mr. Gab asked. They stood in pitch now that Mr. Gab had turned the kitchen off. I just thought we might—Mr. Stu began. Ah, of course, you've occluded the shutters. Tape, Mr. Stu said. Something to do. You might have thought I was crying, Mr. Gab said. I was not. I was at a loss even for that. I didn't, Mr. Stu said, think. You might have thought I was huddling, Mr. Gab said. I was not. I was too tired to lie down. I didn't, Mr. Stu said. There is nothing for my eyes to adjust to, Mr. Gab said. It's as dark as the hole in a hose, said Mr. Stu.

They both stood without the whereabouts of the other. Say something more so I'll know where you are, said Mr. Gab, clearing his throat as if he were warning a boat about a shoal. I thought if we pinholed a bit of the tape, we'd get here, on this sheet you can't see, a bit of picture. Something to do, said Mr. Stu. Mr. Gab bumped gratefully into his desk. Mr. Stu heard its drawer be withdrawn. I've a hatpin here somewhere. Rats—ouch. No. I didn't stick myself, just thought I might have. Mr. Gab had to get close up because the tape on the shutters was barely visible. if I were to put a hole, say, here—what—

Suddenly there was a watery loose smear on the sheet. Needs to be closer was the opinion of Mr. Stu. Needs to be farther back, Mr. Gab decided. In the sheetlight it was easier to find the tight turned wire and unwind it from its nail, Mr. Gab doing one side, Mr. Stu the other. They moved in concert slowly toward the rear of the room, watching an image grow and slowly brighten. Now, cried Mr. Gab, and they both scrabbled for nail heads, feeling the wall gingerly as though it were flesh not their own, holding the wire as high as they could, which wasn't very, in Mr. Stu's case, because the sheet dragged on his lefty side. Shouldn't let it get dirty, Mr. Gab said in his familiar cross voice which suddenly was reassuring. The sheet, however, hadn't hung clear for many feet before it roiled over tables and caught on their crude edges. The focused image ran like a frieze across the top of the screen, but then the sheet tented toward the front of the shop as though there were a wind gusting from its rear.

Without, now, a word needed, Mr. Gab and Mr. Stu began to shove the tables—not an easy thing to do—toward the sides of the store, just so there'd be a space for the sheet to hang and its image to cohere. Sawhorses don't roll; they wouldn't even skid; and beanbags were treacherously everywhere. Mr. Stu knew not to curse, but he nearly cried. It was futile. Why were they doing this? What had his idea been? Mr. Gab would go to prison. Mr. Stu imagined this might take place tomorrow. And homeless Mr. Stu, whose deforming birth marks bespoke bad begetting, would get the heave ho from every eye, and even from those on pleasant picnics.

Quickly, quickly, your stool, Mr. Stu, you mustn't miss this. Mr. Stu dragged his perch awkwardly forward. Beanbags bore him malice. Mr. Gab had turned his chair to face the screen, and there . . . and there . . . there was their street, clear as clean water. There bloomed a building of red brick. Of a deep rich rose they had never before seen. It was . . . it was as if the entire brick had been hotly compressed the way the original clay had been, yet each brick was still so supremely each because the mortar between them was like a living stream, and the pocking was as crisp as craters photographed from space, individual and maybe named for Greek gods. Where the brick encountered a lintel of gray stone, the contrast was more than bugle calls in a basement. The gray had a clarity one found only in the finest prints. Mr. Gab's hand rose toward the scene in involuntary tribute. Where the glass began its passage through the pane, light leaped the way water encircles the thrown stone, though now they were seeing it from below like a pair of cautiously gazing fish. Further on, in the darker parts, were reflected shades of such subtlety that, still a fish,

Mr. Gab gaped.

The sheet bore creases of course. It would have to be ironed. The hang of the cloth over the wire could use some adjustment, perhaps a little weight attached to the bottom edge might improve the stretch, and the wire itself might be profitably tightened. Nevertheless, toiling in the dark, they'd done a good job.

We'll keep watching. Someone will be along soon. In a red sweater maybe. How would a red sweater look passing that brick, Mr. Gab wondered. Such a spectacle. Well, Mr. Gab, it *is* upside-down, Mr. Stu said. I should say thank you to you, Mr. Stu, Mr. Gab said. You've given me quite a gift. And upside-down will be all right. Like reflections from water. We shall adjust. I guess it will be, Mr. Stu said, but not even his ears knew whether he spoke in earnest agreement or out of sad acceptance. It . . . it's colored though. Yes, Mr. Stu, and what colors, too. Have you ever seen such? And look at the contours, so precise while staying soft and never crudely edgy. Never . . . you know . . . I never saw this building before. I never observed our street. We might wash the window—that bit in front of the pinhole, Mr. Stu suggested. Splendid idea, Mr. Stu, agreed Mr. Gab. But it *is* upside-down, Mr. Stu ventured. They gave one another looks which were gifts not quite accepted. A car . . . a cab . . . flashed by. The chariot of the sun, Mr. Gab exclaimed. Oh, Mr. Stu, this will indeed do. The bricks reddened like roast beef. It will do just fine.

Joanna Scott

An Interview by Bradford Morrow

JOHN HAWKES WAS THE MUTUAL FRIEND, the mutual mentor, who wrote me extolling the virtues of her first novel with that strange, beautiful title, *Fading, My Parmacheene Belle.* As usual, Hawkes was right, and the promise shown in *Fading* has been fulfilled with each new book. Over the years following that fond introduction, we've become friends, colleagues, comrades-in-literary-arms, and this interview—begun as an e-mail exchange—we completed over coffee in my apartment one late-winter morning this year.

BRADFORD MORROW: You have a gift for conjuring childhood consciousness, of depicting the many nuances of not-yet-knowing as it graduates toward knowledge. Tom, in *The Closest Possible Union,* and Bo, in your new book, *Make Believe,* strike me as completely realized children—not an easy triumph. We've known each other for a number of years, but I realize all I know about your childhood is that you grew up in Connecticut. Self-portrait of the artist as a young woman?

JOANNA SCOTT: I've come to think that the freedom I had way back when was really formative. Maybe this is just a story I tell myself, useful nostalgia, but it seems to me in hindsight that the freedom I had as a kid was extraordinary. My three older brothers and I were all half wild. Our only responsibility was to return home unharmed at the end of the day. From a very early age I could go and do whatever I pleased. And what pleased me most was to roam the patches of fields and woods in our town and pretend to be someone else. That kind of play gave me both a connection to the world and the illusion of escape. When my adolescent sense of dignity kicked in, I had to look elsewhere for that paradoxical pleasure. Books started to fill the space of play. At the same time, I'd plant myself in front of the television and watch the string of afternoon shows—*Gilligan's Island, F Troop, The Brady Bunch, I Dream of Jeannie.*

MORROW: A personal favorite of mine. I wonder if that freedom to roam didn't somehow translate into the freedoms you naturally claim as a novelist—certainly your forms are fresh with each new novelistic journey you take. What books seized your interest when you began to read? Can you trace influences in any of those early authors you most liked?

SCOTT: From the blur of my childhood reading I remember best my love of Tolkein, Burnett, Lewis Carroll, Harper Lee. But the odd sources I kept returning to, the books that puzzled and enlightened, were a collection of old English tales, the *World Book Encyclopedia,* and a musty copy of the Bible—*New Revised Standard Version.* I admit that by the time I got to Revelations, I was really confused. But I wonder if together these books gave me a sense of literary form and its endless possibilities.

MORROW: Just as your television shows seem mostly set in an imaginary other world, this childhood reading list really expresses a love of wordplay and invented language—Tolkein, Lewis Carroll.

SCOTT: Invented places, too. I enjoyed the distance and differences, the excursions to other worlds. Then I read Faulkner: *The Sound and the Fury. Go Down, Moses.* I started writing what I dared to call fiction in response to Faulkner.

MORROW: What was it in Faulkner's work that struck sympathetic harmonics in you? I can see a shared Gothic temperament, an interest in darker resonances in the individual personality. Certainly, an embrace of language as character, if you will, of form as content. Your geographies are different. What were the affinities and what was it in an inchoate winter that made her want to take that immense leap from reader to writer, witness to practitioner?

SCOTT: It *is* immense, that leap. I'd like to say I had no choice—at some point in our lives the ground opens up beneath our feet. But the propulsion came from Faulkner and his ability to make the murky private work of consciousness meaningful. Faulkner persuaded me that even the strangest, most confused impressions deserve articulation. I read "The Bear" and heard for the first time the sound and beat of thought. Then there's the ending. That astonishing, wild ending. The squirrels in the gum tree. I wanted to write something that deserved such a finale. No surprise that I missed Faulkner's humor and could do no better than bloat my sentences with commas and adjectives and sincerity. Luckily, I was introduced to criticism fairly early on. My first significant experience was at a party. The father of a friend wandered into our midst, found my notebook on the table, and opened it to the first page of one of my earliest attempts at fiction. He started to read it aloud. Just a group of teenage kids and this Mr. So-and-So in a room listening to the silliest, most overwrought prose ever written. Line after line—what howlers! We were all in stitches. It was a long, portentious paragraph about a storm. Now it might seem this guy was being a little unfair, exposing me to ridicule that way. But I was happy to have my aspirations.

MORROW: You clearly survived this first encounter with criticism. Who were your earliest encouragers? I know that John Hawkes was an inspiration and a mentor.

SCOTT: In college, at Trinity and Barnard, I found my support in a few wonderful, idiosyncratic teachers, who helped steady me through those wobbly years. Later, at Brown University, I worked with Robert Coover—a famously tough, precise, passionate teacher—and I started to feel more at ease with the whole process of writing. He taught me how to use a computer (this dates me—I'm talking about life back in the Dark Ages), and once I learned the block-and-delete command I saw how liberating revision can be. Then John Hawkes returned after a year's leave. Jack was a hugely important teacher. He was a great comedian, a great writer, a devilish critic, a kind reader. He was—or pretended to be—endlessly perplexed. His complaints about a piece were cast as bafflement and comic misinterpretations. And yet I could hear the ring of truth in Jack's misreadings. With the last story I wrote for Jack's class, I tried something completely new. I gave up my attempts at elegance and created a narrator, an old fisherman, who begins, "I will tell you exactly how it was one day . . ." And I meant it. That old man was going to tell it exactly how it was. But within a few words it became clear to me that his version depended upon his illusions, his bigotry, his habits and assumptions, and it took me many pages to explore this strange consciousness. When I was done with him I had my first novel.

MORROW: Your work is never evidently, plainly autobiographical—by which I mean to say that the old writers' workshop maxim, *Write only what you know,* seems somehow irrelevant, or at least shallow. Egon Schiele's life. The life of young Bo in *Make Believe,* whose mother was white and father black. The scientists and discoverers in

Various Antidotes. The narrators of both *Fading, My Parmacheene Belle* and *The Closest Possible Union.* None of these relate in any easy way to Joanna Scott. What does this distancing mean for you as a writer? How do you research a boy such as Bo, his grandparents, his parents? What's the process?

SCOTT: I'm tempted to say that anything I ever write is no more than an accident. The fundamental mystery for me in any fiction is located in the confluence of circumstance and character, and when I start a fiction I can't know whether or not that confluence will be rich with mystery. I may have some plan in mind, but my plans usually don't see me through many pages. Especially with longer works of fiction, I experience a whole lot of false starts. I get to a certain point when I'm writing a novel and find that the elements aren't combining, mystery isn't being effectively generated, and I can't make the inflections of language work for me. So I start over. If I'm lucky I stumble upon a subject that generates a novel's worth of wonder, and I keep going. I find that when the elements are strange to me, different and distant from my own life, the fictional concoction is more interesting. There's more to discover when I'm writing about an old fisherman, Egon Schiele, a small boy, a Coney Island witch, a Dutch lens grinder. Maybe when I'm eighty-five I'll write my coming-of-age novel. But so far I've been able to invent more freely, and generate more mystery, by working with subjects that are, at least on the surface, unfamiliar. The research I do—if I dare to call it research—is haphazard, done at a glance, really. We take in so much at a glance. I glance at a stranger in a coffee shop and suddenly I feel I have an entire new novel in my head. Or I see a little pen-and-ink drawing or am struck by some piece of an anecdote. I have to say I've grown a little suspicious of research. Writers need to find various ways to gather information, but we use the word research to describe that process of gathering, and the next thing you know, authenticity becomes the highest value.

MORROW: And yet Bo's world strikes the reader as utterly "authentic." Its authenticity—verisimilitude, to use the painterly term—doesn't come into question during the experience of reading. Is this as much a function of the language used, then, prose itself, the form of the artifact, as it is of scenes and circumstances?

SCOTT: Think of Defoe calling *Robinson Crusoe* a just history of fact. Deception is a writer's great privilege. We use language to create a world, a feeling, a character, and we can call it true. We can lie. We can counterfeit.

MORROW: A novel's an authentic counterfeit.

SCOTT: Yes, and half the fun is in the pretense. We learn about the mind's astonishing powers of logic and invention as we read fiction—or write. I do want to make something genuine, but I get sqeamish when authenticity is used in a prescriptive way to define some definite accordance with life. As long as it can describe both Vermeer and Braque, Dickens and Beckett, then it remains useful. This is the back-route answer to your question about language. These days I find myself most interested in the inflections of words. Old words, dull words, strange words—everything short of nonsense can be inflected in new ways. A distinct fictional consciousness is rendered by the slight elongations of meaning, the twisted, unexpected nuances. And it takes some sort of fictional event or circumstance to give an energy to the words, to make them spring into action.

MORROW: This calls to mind the taxidermic menagerie housed at the Manikin, and the library afloat in the Charles Beauchamp—in different ways manifestations of the power of obsession to bring imagination to life. Indeed, obsession seems to be a linking theme in many of the novels and stories.

SCOTT: It's true, I'm obsessed with obsession. Or maybe just mildly preoccupied. Or maybe it's a major linking theme for many of us, thanks in large part to Poe. We're imps of the perverse, we can't help it!

MORROW: Which leads me to ask you about the Gothic. Both of your most recent novels are informed, it seems to me, by an increasingly Gothic sensibility, an interest in how the imagination (of children, again) is shaped by encountering mortality—be it in the form of the classic Gothic manse with its suggestive imagery, or the violent death of a parent. How do you see classic Gothic theory and form influencing your work? Who besides Poe interests you? I could swear I've heard Charlotte Brontë humming behind some of your *Manikin* passages.

SCOTT: A wonderful thought, Charlotte humming—but not without her sisters. All those ghosts behind the cobwebs. And all that great new fiction you and Patrick McGrath gathered in your Gothic anthology. What is it that's so appealing about the form? It could be the possibility of giving weight to shadows. Raising the dead from their graves. But there's a simple explanation for my interest: I'm infatuated with the Gothic in its nineteenth-century manifestation—with Dickens, Emily and Charlotte Brontë (Emily more so, though you're right, I was thinking of Charlotte's Thornfield when I was building and furnishing my Manikin), Godwin at one cusp, Hardy at the other, and on this side of the ocean, Melville, Hawthorne and Poe (his weird, weird Pym). Sometimes I think that contemporary writers can best be described by their loyalties to either the eighteenth or nineteenth century. Some are Sternians, and others Dickensians. The Sternians are endlessly witty and aren't plagued by Dickensian sentimentality and melodrama. Sentimentality and melodrama—they produce great dreams and nightmares, unforgettable violence, madness, passionate love. But they also can look pretty silly on the page. Perhaps this is why nineteenth-century writers so often open their fiction with an apology, begging the reader's indulgence.

MORROW: What kind of reader are you? By which I mean to ask, when you're reading Melville or Dickens or one of the Brontë sisters, what is the experience—is it possible or even desirable to sideline the technician within who's there to glean formal ideas?

SCOTT: I'm reminded of Virginia Woolf's remark about reading George Eliot: "No one has ever known her as I know her." It's a wonderful feeling, a sense of privileged intimacy, that certain writers inspire. We have private conversations with people we've never met. But I don't do much talking back, at least not during the first encounter with a book. On a first reading I'm watching, listening, savoring the occasional shock of understanding, gliding down the page, sometimes drifting lazily. It's when I return to a book that I go with a pen in hand and try to decipher the method.

MORROW: Did you have the chance to visit the Nabokov centenary exhibit at the New York Public Library? I was mesmerized by his complex jotting, schema and doodlings in his copies of Kafka, Joyce and others. It was as if he read with his pencil, tattooing his way through the sentences, all but revisiting the compositional moment of scribing the words of his colleagues.

SCOTT: No, I missed that. I wonder if he'd have found Post-its useful. I do a lot with Post-its these days.

MORROW: Interestingly, Nabokov wrote often on index cards. So Post-its might have been right up his alley. If he tossed one up into a strong breeze and squinted, who knows but that it would've resembled a butterfly. Jane Austen wrote her novels on small sheets of paper. I remember seeing her manuscript of *Mansfield Park,* or *Emma,* at the British Museum—stacks of confiningly narrow fields of foolscap covered in her long, elegantly complex sentences. A paragraph might go on for pages. Everyone develops a composition method. Graham Greene's five hundred words written patiently each day. Kerouac's compressed writing binges. Marguerite Young developing her massive narratives over decades. What are your practices, rituals, your ways of working?

SCOTT: A wonderful catalogue of tricks and habits you describe. I like to sit by a window when I write, and I like to begin with pen and paper. The computer is a temptation, and sometimes I find myself starting a sentence on paper and finishing it on the screen. But I know I've had a good day of writing if my hand is smudged with ink from my pen. The method does change from book to book. I work hard to develop a sharper sense of what belongs and what doesn't belong as I move forward in a fiction. It has to do with voice, with the logic of character. The rules of a text are implied in the first sentence, and then they become more elaborately defined with the next sentence and the next. Even if I don't know as I'm writing precisely what rules I'm following, what the confines are, I have some sense of it, and that's what I try to honor in revision. I try to keep following the governing logic of a text. That means deciding what sort of observations and metaphors are available to my particular narrator. What words, what exclamations, are out of bounds? Does my narrator eat lobster thermidor or pancakes? Does a certain passage deserve a long unbroken block of full sentences or a short list of nouns? I need readers to help me do this. My husband, Jim Longenbach, is my first and best critic. We're constantly trading pages from our works-in-progress.

MORROW: Question at an oblique angle. Does the writer have social responsibilities in the work she produces, and outside that narrative textual work? I know you serve on the board of PEN, for instance. How do you see the writer's relationship with her community?

SCOTT: I'm discussing Chekhov's "Gooseberries" with my students later today—it's an illuminating illustration of this responsibility conundrum. In Chekhov's story, Ivan Ivanich tells his friends a story about his brother, who, late in life, is happy with his opinions and his gooseberries. The brother's example enrages Ivan Ivanich, who can't stand what he calls "a kind of universal hypnosis," and yet he considers himself too old to engage in the struggle, as he says. He has, at best, a passionate sympathy—or so he thinks. By framing this sympathy in a fiction, Chekhov keeps the problem sizzling, and readers can't help but consider their own silence and hypocrisy. The fiction is unsettling, like most great fiction. And it is ambiguity—a strange ambiguity—rather than polemics that makes it powerful. This is true for some of the great social realist writers of the nineteenth century—Dickens, Hugo, Tolstoy. *Les Miserables,* to take one example, is a truly strange novel, with the possessive, passionately sympathetic Jean Valjean at its center—a wonderfully mysterious center. But it's not enough to blend passionate sympathy and ambiguity. Anyone writing today has to be keenly aware of our potential for moral error. When a writer stands up and declares himself a witness, a spokesman for the masses, I get nervous. A writer must respond to "the terrible things in life," as Chekhov puts it. Usually, though, we can do no more than keep the problems visible, at least when we're inside the fiction. When we're outside, anything goes. Grace Paley's a good model—complex satire inside the fiction, passionate political activity outside the fiction.

MORROW: A section toward the end of *Make Believe* begins with the phrase, "Imagine yourself looking up from the bottom of Hadley Lake." And then, in *Various Antidotes,* the story "Nowhere" begins with a similar invitation, "Imagine a treeless landscape . . ." The challenge to the reader is to imagine with you—what is imagination? How are we to imagine?

SCOTT: I've just been reading Elaine Scarry on this subject and my thoughts are in a bit of a flux about this. I find myself especially interested in the limits of the imagination. This is one of Scarry's subjects in *Dreaming by the Book.* And William Gass has that brilliant essay, "The Concept of Character in Fiction," in which he describes the way readers imagine a character. He points out that we can only imagine pieces of an image. When we're reading fiction our imaginative involvement is so piecemeal, so circumscribed. As readers we participate in someone else's dream. But there's something about the broken quality of that dream that makes fiction unique. A character in *Anna Karenina* enjoys the cold air against her bare shoulder.

Tolstoy is directing us to consider this single sensation, to imagine Kitty's shoulder—only her shoulder. It's such an effective moment because it is limited. The most memorable images of fiction stand out because they are surrounded by darkness.

MORROW: Could we go through your novels and discuss the moment the idea for the book came into being? I've often found that the genesis moment, the personal circumstance, that prompts a narrative can sometimes have little to do directly with the novel's outcome.

SCOTT: Every novel I've written has been prompted by some sort of unexpected encounter. It often happens when I'm struggling with another piece of fiction. Often without even knowing, I'm looking, listening, waiting for the right accident.

MORROW: You're a place looking for an accident to happen.

SCOTT: Exactly! Which is what happened most recently with *Make Believe,* literally. A car overturned in the middle of the night outside our house. But the first novel, *Fading, My Parmacheene Belle,* originated in a story my husband told me about his grandmother. She was Pennsylvania Dutch, very neat and precise, and on the day she was going into the hospital for major surgery, she set out her husband's suit for him to wear to her funeral. That suit on the bed—it's an image with immense implications. In *Fading* I set out to explore those implications.

MORROW: Such as?

SCOTT: What would a man think as he stands alone in the bedroom staring at that suit? The single image became the prompt for the fiction. I imagined the tangle of emotions provoked by the image, and in the process of untangling the response, I started inventing a narrative voice.

MORROW: *The Closest Possible Union?*

SCOTT: I had begun a novel about a literary critic who wanted to exhume Ezra Pound's body in Venice and bring him back to the States, and I was in the library stacks looking for information on Pound's background. I was just browsing, really, and I came across a book about slave ships and slaving. I opened it to a random page and read an excerpt from a boy's journal. He describes watching an African man being hamstrung and thrown into the ocean. His voice was so peculiar—he was an incredibly observant and yet uncomprehending witness. I decided to mimic that voice in my own fiction.

MORROW: *Arrogance?*

SCOTT: I was at the fin-de-siecle Vienna exhibition at the Museum of Modern Art, and I heard some people laughing at one of Schiele's drawings, a self-portrait of the artist—a beautiful, grotesque sketch of the artist standing naked. The people were laughing, the man asking the woman beside him, Would you buy a used car from this guy? That's a powerful kind of laughter, isn't it? Arrogant laughter inspired by contempt, contempt inspired by indifference, indifference a defense against the artist's provocation. I went home and started reading about Schiele, and in my own arrogant fashion I decided I could write a novel about him.

MORROW: What I'm hearing here is that you reach a moment of personal availability to the coincidental, the happenstance, the unexpectedly pregnant moment, which has richer implications than might at first be apparent.

SCOTT: Right. We have to be ready to notice coincidence. Or else I'm just trying to give meaning to arbitrary experience. A few years back our neighbors put a stuffed deer out in their yard. A trophy from their last hunting trip. But I mistook the stuffed deer for a real deer. A beautiful white-tailed deer standing in the snow. I admired it through the kitchen window, I went outside and called to it, I picked up a snowball and threw it at the deer. And still it didn't move. I picked up another snowball, and threw it, and it hit the deer, and it still didn't do anything. That's when I realized I was dealing with an imitation. It turns out that my hometown of Rochester was a center for taxidermy at the turn of the century, and we still have some of the country's greatest taxidermists here. Taxidermy—it struck me as an irresistible metaphor. We kill life in order to create art. How could I not write a book about it?

MORROW: And *Make Believe* arose from a car accident?

SCOTT: A car overturned in front of our house in the middle of the night. I went out to help but couldn't get the doors opened, and the windows were tinted so I couldn't see inside. I thought for certain that the driver had been killed, since that side of the car had been flattened by the impact. It was a dark, damp night. The street was silent. The only sound was the car's blinker—tick tick tick. As it turned out, the driver, the only one in the car, had been thrown into the passenger seat and wasn't hurt. But I filled the car with my own story.

MORROW: There seems to be a common thread of filling something that had life in it before, but is missing its inhabitants. The eviscerated deer, the empty suit, the crashed car whose occupant has fled, even Schiele was not there to defend himself against the ridiculing laughter. And here's the artist, ready to fill those empty spaces with fresh life.

SCOTT: That's very intriguing. Maybe it's that whispering in the dark we do.

MORROW: What would you have done if you weren't a writer?

SCOTT: There was a time when I wanted to study rocks. There was a time I wanted to train animals.

MORROW: To do what?

SCOTT: To do whatever I wanted them to do, of course! And then there was a time when I wanted to be a photographer. In high school I worked with an ambulance crew and I hung out at the local emergency room at night. I wanted to devote myself to medicine. And I wanted to sing in musical comedies.

MORROW: Who are your contemporaries with whom you feel an affinity?

SCOTT: Both as writer and editor, Brad, you've helped to tighten alliances among a pretty disparate group of writers. I feel grateful for that sense of connection to these extraordinary writers. And then there are the contemporary George Eliots—the strangers I know only through their work, writers I admire immensely. Calvino, García Marquez, Sebald, John Berger, Rushdie, Gordimer, Ozick, DeLillo, to name a few.

MORROW: Do you have a sense of what a Joanna Scott shelf should look like at the end of your writing life?

SCOTT: I want it to look just like this table here. With a shell, and a stone, and a little turtle, and a broken glass hand, and a dagger. And I just hope that when I'm all done—whether it's tomorrow, or in thirty years—that there's some coherence to it. I can't tell just now.

Requiem for a Prodigal Son
Jessica Hagedorn

MANILA.

The procession heads slowly toward Quiapo Church, toward Baclaran, toward San Augustin, the little girls resplendent in their rhinestone tiaras and satin gowns, clutching satin rosettes, burning candles and rosaries. The lucky man, the chosen one costumed as Christ, grunts and groans under the weight of his wooden cross. His wailing disciples follow close behind. Old men, young men, stripped to the waist, flagellate themselves with homemade bouquets of tiny whips, razors attached to the ends etching bloody stripes across their naked backs. Flesh and blood glint in the midday sun. The children chirp bittersweet hymns in Latin, in Tagalog, in Ilokano, in English, the most beautiful costumed in their yellow satin gowns and baby-blue polyester tuxedos, miniature kings and queens perched on miniature thrones. They wave stiffly to the crowds from flower and sequin-bedecked floats snaking down Taft Avenue, across United Nations to Roxas Boulevard. What time was Jesus actually crucified? What time did the Virgin Mary die? This is not Ash Wednesday, this is not Good Friday, this is the funeral of Florian Zamora, only son of Florian El Primero and Mary the American. The women inch across Padre Faura on scraped and skinless knees, across Ongpin Street, across Buendia, across Ortigas Avenue, across Escolta, across Claro M. Recto, across Mabini, across M.H. Del Pilar, across Epifanio de los Santos, crossing and criss-crossing the avenues of bloody history in spite of the stink and heat and traffic.

His father, Don Flaco Zamora, declares: It is a crime for a father to have to bury his only son.

His mother, Mary Zamora, declares: God's will. *Bathala na.*

His father is at war with God and at war with his wife.

His father is baffled by everything but money.

His father's daughters are flying in from Madrid, Miami and Palma de Mallorca. But they don't matter as much, of course. Only his son matters now.

From the glorious markets of Divisoria to the noodle factories in Binondo, they sing. Manila alive with the sounds of thirty million voices singing in prayer, in hope, in forgiveness, singing for the sheer joy of singing, celebrating Florian Zamora and his astonishing tribe of innocents. Florian the playboy explorer, stuff of *chismis,* dark myth and legend. These are the processions and the pageants as his father Don Flaco orchestrated them, utilizing his own money, his millions and billions, stocks and bonds, leverages and buy-outs. World Bank and IMF loans, blackmarket scams, kickbacks and ransoms, his share of Yamashita's gold.

More children appear, costumed as miniature martyrs and gaudy angels. The procession snakes through the clogged streets, streets swarming with scrawny dogs and mobs of the pious and faithful, all gripped by hysteria and ecstatic longing. Bodies succumb to the unbearable heat, fainting and falling at an incredible rate, trampled upon by oblivious hordes of believers. The procession creeps along, unsure of its final destination. Perhaps Rizal Park, perhaps Intramuros, perhaps Malacañang Palace. No one is really sure but everyone keeps moving forward, pushing and shoving and surging ahead, keeping up as best they can. Tinny loudspeakers blare undeciperable hymns and overwrought love songs. The miniature martyrs, angels, kings and queens trapped in their lavish floats maintain their somber expressions. They are children with the faded eyes of old people.

All this pomp and spectacle to honor Don Flaco's only son, Florian Zamora. A reviled man, a ruined man, a forgotten man. Once admired, feared and envied, once the butt of too many jokes, once the shining star of sordid *chismis,* but deserving of honors, nevertheless. And his three elder sisters—Maria Amparo, Maria Azucena, Maria Angelita—are flying in for the funeral from Madrid, Palma de Mallorca and Miami Beach. Plump, paranoid, filled with regrets, they fled Manila as soon as they could, as soon as he was born. They understood their lives were over, saw it all coming. And on the day he dies, gaunt, covered with violet lesions, vomiting black phlegm and begging for mercy, his overdressed sisters arrive separately from the airport in their chauffeur-driven Mercedes-Benz, Nissan and Lexus sedans, arrive on the front steps of their brother's house flanked by polite bodyguards in stylish *barong* shirts, brandishing walkie-talkies and guns. Is he dead yet, our brother? Our dear brother, Junior. *Sí, sí, sí.* He is dead. The sisters purse their lips in grim disapproval. They've been away too long, no longer used to the sweltering heat and snail-paced traffic. They are furious, they've just missed their brother's last rites. They fan themselves, murmuring I told you so, I told you so, I told you so. The monkeys and macaws in the garden screech and chatter in sympathy.

Mary Zamora stumbles down the hallway into her son's private, air-conditioned chapel. Her beloved son lies in his closed coffin, his once fine, feral face now the waxen, puffy face of a fool. Not her son at all! Mary Zamora bolts the chapel door from the inside, collapses face down on the marble floor, hard and cool to the touch. Her sinewy arms are spread out in a crucifixion of grief and sorrow. She mourns prostrate before the coffin, before her son's corpse awaiting his bitter sisters and baffled father, before the statue of the black, bleeding Nazarene, before the statue of the bland, pitying Virgin Mary, before the statue of the chubby, golden-haired Santo Niño. Her son is dead, and none of it is any use, no comfort whatsoever.

From her hiding place within the confessional booth, the servant Candelaria Cayabyab observes Mary Zamora. Candelaria who is a stout old woman now, cursed with chronically bloodshot eyes and a bellyful of tumors. She studies Mary with the detached curiosity the poor sometimes have about the rich, and the rich never have about the poor. *Aha, aha, aha. So this is how the crazy bastard's mother mourns her son.* Candelaria takes note of the plain black pumps. The severe black crepe dress. The black pearls. She dozes off and dreams of her daughter, Rizalina. Gone now, for twenty years. Had Florian Zamora driven her away? She had warned her daughter about him. The one they all bowed down to and addressed respectfully as *Sir. Boss. Master. Mister Señor.* Candelaria had worked there long enough to know how much he liked his women. The younger and browner, the better.

Insistent banging and knocking, the anxious voices of Mary Zamora's daughters and husband come through the doors: Let us in, Mama. Let us pray with you. The funeral must begin! Don't shut yourself in there like a madwoman! Mary Zamora remains frozen in her crucifixion of despair. Candelaria, roused from her dozing, giggles softly to herself. At last Florian Zamora is dead. At long last. Her feet ache, her bellyful of tumors ache, but she is happy for one brief moment. The velvet cushions in the confessional are plush and inviting, stuffed with kapok and handstitched by Candelaria herself. She surrenders to twenty years of servitude and exhaustion, leaning back against the pillows and dozing off once again. Oblivious to the servant in the confessional, Mary Zamora recites the rosary of bitter lament in a monotonous drone, never lifting her head off the stone floor. Her penance will last for days and days, the rosary repeated until Mary Zamora's vocal cords finally hemorrhage, and Candelaria Cayabyab awakens to the violent sounds of the doors being broken down with axes. But that is yet to come.

NOW

even under the closed lid of the coffin, Florian Zamora's embalmed corpse begins to stink. The sweet, sickening odor seeps from under the bolted doors and into the hallway where Florian's sisters and father are waiting in vain to be let in. Don Flaco refuses to be defeated by his stubborn wife and calls an emergency meeting. His attorneys, his flock of priests, family physician, family mortician, his entire public relations staff and the commandante of his private army are summoned. Don Flaco is a firm believer in "the power of P.R." He postpones the funeral. More processions, commemorative pageants, and arbitrary fiestas are planned. Press releases are faxed throughout the world: Florian Zamora, Jr., discoverer and protector of the Stone Age Taobo tribe, is dead after a long, undisclosed illness.

Outside the gates of the Zamora compound, several foreigners, photographers and journalists insinuate themselves into the front ranks of the swelling crowd, pointing cameras and taking notes while whispering furtively into microcassette recorders.

Note: SO HOT! Not too big of a crowd, but not too little. Usual morbid gawkers and passersby. Few celebs. Grieving starlets in tacky outfits. Old loves? Paid mourners? Recognized one or two scholars and bureaucrats, maybe the controversial anthropologist Dr. Carrera—or was it Cabrera? standing next to an unidentified woman.

Note: Respectable enough turnout, considering.

Note: F.Z. died of "undisclosed," "unconfirmed," "mysterious ailment." HA!

Note: Where is mother? Rest of Zamora family? Aunts, uncles, etc.? Ex-wife and children?

Note: Where are Taobo?

Note: The crowd, orderly so far, waiting hours in the sun. How about some goddamn water? Foreigner with red hair shouts in English. His faithful friend and defender, Ken Forbes?

Note: One of two angry guards points a gun at (maybe) Forbes. Mocks foreigner: Talking to me, SIR? Foreigner, sheepish, backs off.

Note: Old man, probably Don F, spotted briefly on balcony. Waves.

Note: Florian Zamora dead at age 59.

Today's date: May 22, 1997.

The Technology of Silence

Ben Marcus

1825

THE FIRST DOCUMENTED INSTANCE of the Female Jesus appears at England in the form of a seven-year-old girl. Using rapid clapping and tongue clicks, the girl lures various species of birds from hundreds of miles away, who assume a circle of protection around her and raise a field of sharp wind in the area. When her father attempts to rescue her, the birds are able to beat out a rudimentary language of ricocheted wind to command his own hand against him, and he dies, a suicide. Several male witnesses also die, and the air that the birds have stirred with their wings remains sharply turbulent at the seaside site for the next five years, repelling any men who try to approach. This form of barrier comes to be known as "Jesus Wind." It will be used against men, together with a clear sock covering women's heads, to neutralize their language at the *End of Sound* protest in 1974.

1965

A noise filter is created at Dark Farm to muffle radio and television frequency. It will be the first nonsacrificial attempt by Jane Dark and her followers to mute the noises of the air and bring about a "new world silence." Mounted upon the roof of a hilltop barn, the filter is a dish-shaped sieve filled with altered water that will supposedly attract and cancel electronic transmissions, including television, radio and women's wind. The water, which absorbs the intercepted frequency, is considered a master liquid of supernutritive value. It is removed monthly and administered to the women as a medicinal antibody. The drink is called a "charge," or Silent Water, said to render women immune to sound.

1852

Women in middle Denver seize celebration rights to the annual Festival of Stillness, previously observed and dominated by men. They travel in groups to mountainsides and forests outside of town, drink Girl's Water, attire themselves in stiff sheets of weighted cotton, and seek a final, frozen posture, hoping apparently that the mountain weather will calcify or fossilize their bodies into a "one true pose," to represent them for all time. Their bodies are displayed in a traveling exhibit called "Women's Behavior Statues," and teenage girls are asked to study and rehearse the more basic positions. The slogan *Action is Harm* is coined that year and the Festival of Stillness becomes a dominant women's holiday.

1971
Silentists attack Fort Blessing, Texas, July 19 and kill five members of the Listening Group before kidnapping 17-year-old Caroline Ann Parker. She will live peacefully with the Silentists for four years (until "rescued" against her will by the Texas Mounted Police), marry quiet-boy Bob Riddle and stage spectacular, noiseless demonstrations in the Texas desert. As a professional listener, Parker will be employed by the Silentists to discover an American territory with broad parameters of silence, a region where silence will not only be possible, but required. They will settle in Ohio.

1939
Long Island physician Valerie James, 36, and a sister begin a practice devoted to what they call "Women's Fuel." She has studied anatomy and physiology with a local medical group for three years but is otherwise untrained. Before she develops her notorious line of medical drinks for women, the James Liquids, or *Water for Girls* (see 1955), she and her sister will attempt several techniques of altering the disposition of women: the water chair, bolted to the floor of a medicinal pool, which holds a woman underwater until her lungs give out and "expel from the body all toxicity"; a sleep sock slung over the doorway, that women might sleep "in the fashion that they stand"; high volumes of wind shot at a woman's body to "massage the senses"; and endurance speaking (or Language Fasting), in which the woman speaks rapidly until collapse, to "deeply fatigue the head and free it of language pollutants." Only the sleep sock, which enforces a female sleeping posture, will prove to have lasting credibility, although the language fast is adopted and modified by Sernier, who requires students to undergo it before attending his lectures.

1935
Burke is born at Akron. Within months he will use an invented language based on radio static and stuffed-mouth lamentations to control his father and mother like puppets, forcing them to copulate in public and weep openly. The parents will request of the Children's Police that the young Burke's "gifts" be carefully controlled, but it is suspected that even this utterance of theirs is generated by Burke himself, who sees his parents' bodies as "weapons to be used against the town, satellite forms acting on behalf of my body." Burke's youthful demonstrations will be the first American indication that language, dispensed precisely, can regulate the behavior in territory. It is eventually suspected that a portion of the town of Akron has been "hushed" by the careful recitation of sentences at the perimeter between Ohio and the world. Although the boy is eventually fitted by authorities in a tight, clear sock, even his restricted pantomimes create disturbing loss of control in the animals and children in his vicinity.

1963
Athlete Emily Anderson, 45, who has been imprisoned for interfering with runners at a men's track meet in Chicago just as they neared the finish line, is fatally injured when she is shot from a cannon into a brick wall during her "Hard to Die" show in July. An unknown Silentist, in a display of grief over the death of the quiet athlete, catapults herself from an English cliff into the sea, and an *Anderson* comes to be known as an act of mourning in which women launch themselves into the air for extended distances, often landing in the sea, but not necessarily.

1928
The American Naming Authority, a collective of women studying the effects of names on behavior, decrees that a name should have only one user. The nearly one million American users of the name Mary, for example, do not constitute a unified army who might slaughter all users of the name Nancy, as was earlier supposed, but rather a saturation of the Mary-Potential-Quotient. Simply stated: too many women with the same name produces wide-spread mediocrity and fatigue. A competition of field events, centering around deployment of a forty-pound medicine ball into hoops and holes, is proposed to determine which women shall rightly hold the title of their name, with all losers in the same name category to be

designated as assistants of the winner, forced to wear wind socks or hip-weights to slow down their progress, enslaved to the first Mary, the first Nancy, the first Julia, as the case may be. Parents still able to name their children begin to seek either unique names or names that are considered neutral by the authority, such as Jesus and Smith. Many girls are given the name Jesus Smith, which when pronounced as an all-vowel slogan becomes a crucial new word in the Silentist movement, and is also possibly responsible for enabling the new strains of female behaviors seen at this time.

1959
Animal artist George Rafkill, 29, is arrested when it is discovered that his popular portraits of horses and dogs, "The Animals of America," which sell to hotels and restaurants, and can also be embroidered on flags, bear undeniable facial resemblance to thirteen women who have been missing from his Akron neighborhood for the past year. While Rafkill claims that he can "paint the dead," authorities point out that he only paints those dead who are also missing and believed murdered.

1966
A clear sock is devised by the body-sleeve specialist Ryman that will protect a woman's head from men's language, the so-called weapon of the mouth. The sock also works to block the entrance of television and radio transmissions, certain man-made aroma and men's wind. Because breathing is difficult when wearing the Ryman mask, fainting often results, and it is through this accident that the Listening Group discovers what they will term the "revelatory power of willful fainting," and adopt the belief that regular drops in consciousness allow women to hear something deeply secret in the air. The Ryman sock will be fitted posthumously to the heads of dead Silentists, to aid their attainment of a possible women's afterlife.

1954
The American Television Industry attempts to market a Women's Television Set. The unit resembles their standard device, but is designed to receive a special frequency broadcast from the Women's Storm Needle at Atlanta, where experiments are being conducted in images and sound that only women can perceive (also known as the Female Jesus Frequency). The set receives little attention and will fall into immediate disuse by the few customers it gains, but the

Storm Needle continues to transmit an all-vowel female "music" for five years. This period will prove to be the most crucial in the Silentist movement, allowing Jane Dark and her followers to travel the countryside undetected, camouflaged by the women's tones masking the Midwestern landscape, curling over the territory as, arguably, the lowest and thickest wind ever felt in America.

1968

The first official version of the *Promise of Stillness,* a vow against motion, appears in January at Albany. The document argues that motion and speech disturb the atmosphere and must cease before a "world storm" is generated that destroys America. The Women's Congress, which fled to Albany from Boston in December, has commissioned local radio announcer Katherine Livingston, 26, to risk her job by reading the document on the airwaves while, throughout the country, the signatories take their final positions, mostly in their homes, before ceasing all motion and speech. Emily Walker, the most vocal of those women to take the promise of stillness, issues a statement declaring, "If I die, it will not be of hunger. I am not hungry or thirsty. I refuse the false promise of motion. I stop." She dies in six days after shedding a brittle layer of skin, the Walker Pelt, which hangs still in a New Jersey home. Her cause of death is listed as starvation. In the years to follow, Walker Pelts will be marketed to families as small body rugs to be thrown over children, either to immobilize them or to reduce the falsity of their motion.

1980

Sernier kills Burke and is acquitted. He says that if he had it to do over again he would have killed Burke more slowly. He wishes he could "continue killing Burke." Burke's family silently walks through their Akron neighborhood while people jeer at them with the chant "Burke is dead." Burke's scholarly works are no longer widely stocked in bookstores. The grammatical tense that Burke has proposed, "Burke," is rejected by the Omaha Language Council on the grounds that it renders improbable things too plausible, because it "makes no linguistic distinction between what can and cannot happen." In August, Sernier's students attack seven men and women who were said to have been students of Burke, forcing them into a Thompson Box, a clear cell with a speech tube attached, where the input of language disrupts the rhythm of their bodies, leading to seizures and ultimate physical arrest. Sernier applauds his students in an editorial, asking readers not to forget that he killed Burke. He promises that the word "Burke" will hereafter create a "lasting wound to the skin." Jane Dark promptly adopts the word as her first language weapon. She demonstrates that by shouting "Burke!" at a small dog it will not be able to walk and will soon collapse with fatigue.

1952

The Women's National Pantomime group gathers on an athletic field in Dulls Falls, Wisconsin, for their largest event since their inception in 1946. Fifteen new gestures are introduced by the group leader, a slender teenager named Jane Dark, and so many women suffer seizures and vomiting after performing the difficult new movements that the local hospitals cannot contain them and Ms. Dark is forced into hiding. Four women die, while many others turn in their memberships in protest, miming disgust and a lack of support. The wounded women are so disoriented that they must relearn basic movements such as walking and kneeling, drinking and sleeping. The men's chapter of the Pantomime Association publicly renounces Dark and her followers, calling her modifications harmful and contrary to the chief purpose of Pantomime, which is to entertain. Dark explains that her fierce group of aggressively silent women will no longer exist to glorify the "false promise" of silent motion, or Pantomime, but will instead attempt a new system of female gestures, to replace sound as the primary means of communication, declaring motion the "first language," with a grammar that is instinctual and physical, rather than learned. It will be the first instance of a women's semaphore that will not be an imitation, but rather a primary behavior with, according to Dark, "very real uses in this country." Dark will begin authorship of a series of pamphlets called "New Behaviors for Women." The pamphlets argue that gesture and behavior alone can solve what Dark calls "the problem of unwanted feelings." She also helps market Water for Girls, small vials of "radical emotional possibility," under the premise that water contains the first and only instructions for how to behave in this world.

1928

Boston widow Claire Dougherty is arrested on her doorstep, October 3, by detective Sherman Greer, as she tries to swallow a coded message. In prison she refuses to speak and appears to suffer at hearing any kind of sound, a condition termed "Listener's Disease," in which even sounds produced by her own body appear to cause her agony. She must wear a soundproof suit and a Life Helmet. State doctors report that there is nothing unusual in Dougherty's hearing, but they agree to relieve her with a quiet cell in the prison and a full-body muffle, later termed a Claire Mitten and worn by young girls who are sickened or distraught at the sound of their own voices. Before she dies, in November, she writes in a letter to her daughter that ". . . a new sound is upon the world. We have erred greatly and will be killed for it. Look to the soil, for the sound to me was beneath it. Walk slow or do not walk. Hide. Duck. Listen." Detective Greer, the arresting officer, will die a year later, complaining of a "sharp noise" in the water near his home. His cause of death is listed as exhaustion. The two deaths will launch several studies of diseases caused by sound, and Greer's wife will later appear in the streets of Boston wearing an executioner's hood. Her body, upon examination, will reveal heavily damaged ears.

1985

Quiet-boy Bob Riddle constructs his home-weather kit, to definitively prove that speech and possibly all mouth sounds disturb the atmosphere by introducing pockets of turbulence, eventually causing storms. By speaking into the tube that feeds the translucent-walled weather simulator, which resembles a human head (in this case the head of his father), Riddle demonstrates the agitation of a calm air system. The language that Riddle introduces to the test environment—whether English, French or the all-vowel slang of the Silentists—repeatedly smashes the model house within, proving that sound alone can distress and destroy an object. His essay, "The Last Language," argues for an experimental national vow of silence, claiming that spoken language is a pollutant that must be arrested, first by stuffing the mouths of unnecessary speakers ("persons whose message has already been heard") with cloth. Before his death, in 1991, he will build a mouth-harness (the Speech Jacket) that limits its wearer to a daily quota of spoken language, beyond which the person must remain silent until the next day, or else trigger a mild explosive that will destroy the mouth. The Speech Jacket is tested first on children and, although it causes intermittent blackouts and fainting, it serves to restrict their speech to requests for food and short displays of all-vowel singing.

1972
Martha Ferris develops Women's Sign Language and tours the country, demonstrating the technique at schools and churches, proposing a women's bilinguality that will not only allow for private utterances, but possibly enable new forms of thought not available under current systems of grammar and syntax. Her younger sister, Katherine Ferris-Watley, has pierced her own eardrums during a local Show of Silence and refuses to learn American Sign Language, keeping her hands swaddled in cloth, and often "signing in tongues," a form of gibberish sign language thought to have religious significance. It is from Katherine's blunt and frustrated semaphore that *Sign Language for Large Hands* emerges, a system of forceful prop-aided sign language meant to be read from a great distance, utilized by Silentists who have injured or burned their own hands in protest, but who still must enact a basic language. Women's Sign Language will be rejected by the deaf communities, since much of it requires that the hands of a woman be pinned against her hips while she jumps and spins in the air, maneuvers that deaf women, with their compromised sense of balance, are unable to perform safely. The Listening Group, seeking further difference from the Silentists, will establish a new but troubled relationship with the deaf communities, believing that their skin is receiving the sound that their heads cannot, leading to the Deaf Pelt Thefts of 1974, an action of massive scalping and skin theft against deaf persons.

1955
James Water is cultivated and distributed by the Women's Medical Group. Designed by physician Valerie James, the tonic, comprised of exact water, ostensibly cancels unwanted emotions, as James surmises (prophetically) that "feelings" merely express an absence or surplus of water in the body, correctable through water fasts or strategies of soaking the body or hands in prepared water. A key premise of her theory is that water is the fundamental, and only reliable, recording agent of behavior. Water is thought to "see" and memorize the actions of persons. By filtering water through her patients undergoing fits of various emotions, James creates supposed Behavior Water of these feelings that can be administered as medicine or antidotes, a catalogue of fluids that comprise a person's entire repertoire of behavior. James goes on to write about the centrality of water in considering the possibilities of the person in America (see *The New Water*), but warns of its danger, arguing that the next major

war will be fought with water alone and that women should carry personalized water for protection, and consider water the only reliable diary, speaking their secrets privately into rivers, lakes, ponds.

1922
Finland proposes a separate language for women, becoming the first European nation to do so; all men and women twenty-four years and older not considered suicide risks are fitted with a "Brown Hat," to enable or prevent them, as the case may be from performing the new language. The Brown Hat, in women, is fitted into the mouth to allow a broader range of vowel production, which is considered a vastly unfulfilled potential of women. The flesh-colored apparatus camouflages with the head. For a time it becomes a symbol of status and wealth; streamlined designs create striking new possibilities for the human head, accentuating its animal shape. Women in Finland seen without the facial gear are considered incompletely attired and are refused access to the black-tie Head Theater conducted in the countryside. Men are to utilize a smaller, darker Brown Hat (the Carl Rogers Cage), resembling a bridle, that will restrict their vowel production and crimp the skin of the upper face to narrow the ear canals, deafening them to the new language. Both men and women will be advised to speak nightly messages of personal import into a cloth screen that will be used to test for a possible chemical element of language. No chemical difference is discovered between the speech of the sexes, only a marked absence of water in each, which will prove to be vital for later projects of the Listening Group, who will add water to their language filters, Brown Hats or Thompson Masks, in order to scramble or falsely translate their speech.

1958
The Susan House, an experimental school for girls, has its beginnings in an all-girls retreat conducted simultaneously one August evening in seven American towns. The focus of the retreats, initially, is to bury a clay head of Jesus, then meditate over the grave about the true requirements of the name of Susan, a technique of divination dating back to the Perkins Noise, when Perkins killed himself by vigorously repeating his own name, but not before achieving "immense information on the human enterprise." The Susan House School, initially conceived as a training ground for girls named Susan and no one else, gives rise to several specialty name-centered education institutions and drives a new and terribly divisive political

wedge into the population. Although many parents change the names of their children to Susan, only persons born into the name will be considered for enrollment (see *The Unwritten Books of Susan*).

1895
Chemist Emily Sussler, 46, heads the first Science Week drive to aid the Vertical Horizon Project, an attempt to extend the typical citizen's field of vision. Sussler's scheme, initially opposed only by preservationists, is to design a fire that will link the American coasts, the largest fire ever conceived, to burn in a pattern precisely designed to create tunnels of brightness deep into the sky, as well as to scorch a black line across the continent. Her notion is to produce a bed of light that will provide a wide base of illumination for a viewing project beyond what has ever been possible. Sussler maintains that brightening the sky with a systematically designed fire will produce a "Horizon Crane" to yank back the barrier of the horizon, altering religious and scientific notions of the ultimate role of the Person in the atmosphere. Nearly every state government opposes the "science fire," as it comes to be called, partly because Sussler insists on providing her own technicians to manage the blaze, refusing to let the fire be monitored by local firefighters, whom she insults repeatedly as "highly ignorant of fire management." Her technicians radically lobby for the approval of the fire, and ultimately foil their chances by setting test flames in the perimeter surrounding Atlanta which create a vortex of heat-generated darkness in the city itself, causing not only a blackout but a "soundout." Neighborhoods of Atlanta will be resistant to sound for years afterward, and a localized heat-deafness emerges in the South that is apparently caused by unnatural exposure to fire.

1978
The first plaster casting is taken of the inside of Bob Riddle's mouth, including the cavity that extends down his windpipe ending at his lungs. When the casting is removed and hardens, it resembles a roughly shaped sphere (the inside of the mouth) with a ridged handle attached and is considered a primary shape around which his body has grown, a hardened form of the white space at Riddle's center, a sculpture of his nothingness. Riddle calls it, incorrectly and rather pretentiously, his soul, given that it represents his "language cave," and he argues that this shape is the primary object by which

a person can be understood, and possibly controlled. The object will later be known as a "Thompson Stick," as important a shape as the sphere or triangle. The women's athletic movement will use it as their principle piece of equipment.

1956
A woman is found collapsed in a field, her arms sheathed in metal sleeves, nearly burned down to the bone. Her mouth is void of teeth and likewise charred. When a microphone is held to her skin during a routine exam by a Listener, muted voices and noise can be heard, suggesting her body has been crushed or otherwise altered with sound. During the same month a caravan of women is intercepted by the Texas Mounted Police. Among their possessions are found a set of foil-lined sleeves and leather hoods, which the women will only say are used to "fight sound." When they are addressed during a group interrogation they use quick coordinated actions with their hands to nearly silence the questions coming at them. The turbulence they generate with their limbs is recognized as "Jesus Wind." They are apparently able to quiet the local sounds in a room simply by making shapes with their hands. The child Jane Dark is among them, who demonstrates that by standing next to a passing train and engaging in an odd form of gymnastic pantomime that appears part Karate, part dance, the girl can mute the forceful racket of the train so that it passes by in virtual silence. Late in her life, it will be this talent that will prevent her from hearing even her own voice, as the orbiting wind of silence she herself has created becomes so potent that it can no longer be penetrated, and she appears to the people around her as a character in a silent movie. She can neither speak nor be spoken to, a deprivation of language that causes her hands to wither.

Stalingrad

Christopher Sorrentino

. . . MY LIFE HAS CHANGED IN NOTHING; it is now as it was ten years ago, blessed by the stars, avoided by men. I had no friends, and you know why they wanted to have nothing to do with me. I was happy when I could sit at the telescope and look at the sky and the world of stars, happy as a child that is allowed to play with the stars.

You were my best friend, Monica. Yes, you read correctly, you were. The time is too serious for jokes. This letter will take two weeks to reach you. By then you will already have read in the papers what has taken place here. Don't think too much about it, for in reality everything will have ended differently; let other people worry about setting the record straight. What are they to you or me? I always thought in light-years, but I felt in seconds. Here, too, I have much to do with the weather. There are four of us and, if things were to continue the way they are now, we would be content. What we do is very simple. Our job is to measure temperatures and humidity, to report on cloud ceilings and visibility. If some bureaucrat read what I write here, he would have a fit . . . violation of military security. Monica, what is our life compared to the many million years of the starry sky! On this beautiful night, Andromeda and Pegasus are right above my head. I have looked at them for a long time; I shall be very close to them soon. My peace and contentment I owe to the stars, of which you are the most beautiful to me. The stars are eternal, but the life of man is like a speck of dust in the Universe.

Around me everything is collapsing, a whole army is dying, day and night are on fire, and four men busy themselves with daily reports on temperature and cloud ceilings. I don't know much about war. No human being has died by my hand. I haven't even fired live ammunition from my pistol. But I know this much: the other side would never show such a lack of understanding for its men. I should have liked to count stars for another few decades, but nothing will ever come of it now, I suppose.

When it was clear enough they saw the trimotor JU-52s begin their final approaches, miles distant. Every now and again one of the transports vanished in a burst of light, and then the thunder of the guns would roll across the steppe and Horst would try to guess the tonnage of the supplies that pitched out of the sky.

He'd had no intention of becoming an officer, no intention of doing anything except remaining "a lazy boy who lives in the fields after dark." So his father told him. His father had his own intentions for him.

His mother complained: "You never leave the house before four in the afternoon." It bothered her.

They were under the impression that he behaved as he did deliberately, to annoy them.

"You live in the fields, like a rodent," his father said.

"Who knows where he goes with the long coat and the notebook—"

"With the field glasses," interrupted his father.

"—just as darkness begins to fall," said his mother.

"A total mystery."

"A mystery a boy doesn't feel as if he has to share with his mother and father."

"You want to know what a boy should do? What a boy should do is bring his friends over to the house is what a boy should do."

"Friends," snorted his mother.

"Suppose you were to go out while the sun is still shining in the sky. It'd kill you, or what?"

"He looks at the stars. The stars!"

"I thought you said it was a total mystery," Horst said.

The radioman arrived for daily reports. He shifted from foot to foot in the bitter wind, waiting for Horst to double check a few figures. The weather was pretty much what someone without experience, training and a lot of expensive and advanced instrumentation might have thought it was. The difference, Horst's private joke went, was just a matter of degrees.

The idea of the *steppe* was interesting to him. It was certainly flat and treeless, but was this what was referred to as loessial soil?

How could he take the accomplishments of the century seriously when there were millions of stars he would never know any more about than he already knew from gazing at them with his naked eyes? What edge did he have on the observers of the past?

"Don't talk back to your mother. This is not normal."

"If he had a normal schedule maybe he'd have some friends."

"I know you find it all unspeakably boring, but it's not such a bad town to be a young man in, Horst. They hold dances. They show movies on Saturday nights."

"I hear boys on the road going by on their way to town and I say to myself, 'Why isn't Horst with them? He's so bright, he's got so much to offer.' But no—my son's a vampire."

Loess was a soil said to be chiefly deposited by wind.

Starlight had traveled across fated distances to reach the earth and cast itself here. How sad, he thought. Across uncountable miles, to shine upon this field of futile dead. Not that he was anywhere near the futile dead. Weathermen kept themselves at a remove from futile dead. They kept their campground shipshape, the weathermen. They charted temperatures and humidity, cloud cover and visibility, made their reports for the artillery barrages that never occurred, the Luftwaffe that never bombed.

One morning, a sullen breakfast. He gazed out the window at the ancient cotoneaster, heavy again with flowers, while his father noisily shook the newspaper. The sensuous smell of gardenia in the air, its source unseen. His father shook the newspaper to get it to lie the way he wanted. A love smell, a Freya smell. A pain smell. His father shook the newspaper again, looked at him, put it down.

"Why do I have the feeling that if I were to give you two thousand Reichsmarks at the beginning of each year all of your so-called problems would be mysteriously solved?"

Horst rose and left the table to go upstairs, Monica meeting him at the landing and shadowing him into his room, where he began to fill a soft-sided bag with clothing and toiletries.

"I'm joining the army," he said.

"You?" said Monica.

To be a star, cradled in your own heat and light, untouchable, afraid of nothing. This was God's own image.

He still dreamed of Freya during the howling, freezing nights. They would walk hand in hand down a sunny country road, or they would sit on a bench along a broad esplanade and watch boats sway in gentle water. In one dream she turned to him and said, "I have a perfect profile."

They tested him: he was to outline in writing a simple statement of the climate of Germany. He was to demonstrate his general knowledge of the composition of air, referring both to its constant and variable elements and the functions of each. He was required to develop quite broadly the following subjects: moisture, fog, hail, rain and snow. He was asked to explain points connected with electrical and optical phenomena in the air, in order to demonstrate a knowledge and understanding of rainbows, mirages, looming, halos, the Northern Lights, St. Elmo's Fire, lightning and thunder. He was to describe in detail any such phenomena he had seen firsthand. He was to show knowledge of the use and construction of the barometer, thermometer, anemometer, psychrometer and rain gauge, and to demonstrate an ability to read each. He was required to construct a weather vane. He was asked to interpret charts and graphs contained in the regular publication of the Weather Service. He was to submit a daily record kept over the course of one month listing the following: morning dew or frost, and, at the same designated time each day, the direction of the wind, the temperature, the kind of clouds in the sky and whether it rained or snowed at this designated hour.

Then they issued him his Luger and shipped him to the East.

He'd had no intention of becoming an officer. The radioman was wearing two right shoes, Horst noticed. These were part of a particularly infamous supply shipment the Luftwaffe had overseen.

He'd tried to avoid the humiliation of revealing the extent of his emotional loss. At the time, of course, the investment in Freya had seemed a necessary risk. His mother and father thought he was behaving peculiarly and being shiftless. They bought him two neckties, an act freighted with hostile significance. His father lectured him in a voice that assumed the hectoring tone of one backtracking, for the benefit of a dilatory student, to review ground covered long ago. It was difficult for him to justify his expenditure of grief. Even in the early, triumphant, days of the war the Wehrmacht had sent the town its share of bad news. His mother read the notices aloud from the newspaper.

He climbed up the stairs to pack a bag. He moved as if directed from without. Monica stood watching.

"Yes, me."

"You of all people in the army."

"What about it, Monica?"

"There's a war on, you know?"

"Of course I know."

"If she shows up at your funeral, which I frankly doubt she will, you *won't be there to know about it.* I can't believe I have to explain this to a grown-up. You'll be dead, and however sorry we all happen to be about the lousy way we treated you it won't matter."

"It doesn't have anything to do with her."

"Horst."

"I have to get out of here."

"If you haven't noticed, Horst, it just so happens we occupy the whole bloody continent. Go to Paris."

A flash of light in the sky and another planeload of supplies would rain down upon the barren flat. Or a JU-52 would crack up on the badly pitted airstrip. Or it would arrive intact, only to be stormed by the walking wounded, demanding evacuation. They made their daily reports as men and airplanes fell. Events unfolded in a long dream. They made their daily reports on temperatures and cloud ceilings. At night the stars were there for counting. The wholeness, the purpose, of them revealed in the radiant pinpricks the ancients understood them to be, in the figures they combined to form in their distant relation to him and to one another. He counted them.

In the dream he held her hand, her fingers warm against his palm. She spoke to him as if she knew him, as if she'd seen him that morning and would see him again that evening. The life. A country road, bright in sunlight.

* * *

> . . . You are the wife of a German officer, so you will take what I have to tell you, upright and unflinching, as upright as you stood on the station platform the day I left for the East. I am no letter writer and my letters have never been longer than a page. Today there would be a great deal to say, but I will save it for later, i.e., six weeks if all goes well and a hundred years if it doesn't.

Every seven seconds a German dies in Russia!

Friedrich came in, knocking the snow and scraping the frozen mud off his boots. He stood near the stove to warm himself, watching Werner write. He asked: "A letter to the wife with the lovely strong name?"

"Yes," said Werner.

"You keep yourself busy," Friedrich laughed. "Keep your mind off everything. Aren't you just the least bit suspicious that they've ordered us to write these letters? I am. Who knows what Hitler's thinking? If I were you, I'd inform Augusta that you're being served ice cream in Red Square by the millions of grateful if faintly unappealing souls you've liberated from the Bolsheviks. And that you're giving it to Stalin's daughter up the ass in Lenin's tomb, while you're at it."

"Does Stalin have a daughter?" asked Werner.

"How do I know? All I can say is these letters are all very nice but I have my suspicions."

"You have your suspicions about everything."

"OK. Thing one: how are they going to get the letters the hell out of here? I thought they were filling the planes with wounded."

"Am I asking? I have twenty minutes, I sit and write to my wife."

"Thing two: the last bunch of miserable and despairing letters was immediately followed by a decrease in the meat ration."

"The thing of it is, I'd rather write to her than just about anything else."

"My conclusion being that they're taking the letters and reading them! Hitler himself is reading the letters to see if we deserve our little care packages!"

"Just about anything else that's possible, here, anyway."

Friedrich raised and lowered his eyebrows rapidly, assuming an exaggerated expression of lewdness. The gesture seemed to exhaust him, and he went and sat on his bedding. "That is what you meant, isn't it?"

> You will have to reckon with the latter possibility. If all goes well, we shall be able to talk about it for a long time, so why should I attempt to write much now, since it comes hard to me. If things turn out badly, words won't do much good anyhow.

Every seven seconds a German dies in Russia!

Friedrich: "I guess what I really want to know is whether or not it's true about you not knowing what hit you. Dying a certain kind of death, that is. I mean, how quickly do you think nerves transmit signals? At the exact moment of a fatal impact do they begin traveling at the speed of radio waves to the brain? At the speed of light? Is that the same speed? Signaling, *pain pain pain.* How long does it take the body to die? Is it like this *process,* involving an actual *decision* to stop functioning? I figure this has got to take some time, if it's true. The brain sending its own signal, *die die die.* Or is it a matter of complete incapacitation, in this case imposed from outside, which the body doesn't have a whole lot to do with one way or another? That's my bet, personally. But in either case, does the brain respond *dread dread dread* with equal speed?"

Werner said, "How do you know you're going to be lucky enough to die with one shot? What about Streibler and Heffermann?"

Friedrich contemplated the fates of Streibler and Heffermann. Their screams throughout the orange night. Not to mention Kinder and Eigen. Nor the ironically named Eisenhauer. The ironically named Eisenhauer had died saving his makeshift Christmas tree. He'd fashioned it out of the skeleton of an umbrella that he picked from the ruins of the Univermag department store where Paulus had his headquarters in the basement. He'd draped it with ribbons and bits of colored paper, likewise found in the rubble. Christmas Eve they'd stood in the cold firing red, green and white flares into the boiling sky. On Christmas Day they awoke to a blizzard driven by terrifying winds that whistled eerily through the desecrated ruins. Then mortar attacks and cannonades, followed by the familiarly dispiriting Katyusha salvos. In lulls they heard for the first time the message the enemy had since been relentlessly blasting at them through loudspeakers: "Every seven seconds a German dies in Russia!" The ironically named Eisenhauer had broken out to rescue his tree, which he'd embedded upright in fallen masonry.

"Of course the ironically named Eisenhauer committed suicide," said Friedrich.

"He wanted that damned tree saved," said Werner.

"Did you see the Christmas tree that Bartenhagen carved? Now that was a tree worth saving."

> You know how I feel about you, Augusta. We have never talked very much about our feelings. I love you very much and you love me, so you shall know the truth. It is in this letter. The truth is the knowledge that this is the grimmest of struggles in a hopeless situation. Misery, hunger, cold,

> renunciation, doubt, despair and horrible death. I will say no more about it.

Every seven seconds a German dies in Russia!

The odor of food. Werner had taken his unit to do some street cleaning one day. They'd worked all day, house by house, room by room, climbing from the basements to the attics and in the process losing two or three men per house only to find at the end of the afternoon that they were being fired upon from behind; that the enemy had broken through the walls separating the houses and withdrawn right from under them to set up machine-gun emplacements to the rear. And at the precise moment Werner realized he had sacrificed thirty men for nothing, the warm smell of food from the Russian field kitchens wafted through the cold and the stinging cordite.

> I did not talk about it during my leave, either, and there's nothing more about it in my letters. When we were together (and I mean through our letters as well), we were man and wife, and the war, however necessary, was an ugly accompaniment to our lives. But the truth is also the knowledge that what I wrote above is no complaint or lament but a statement of objective fact.

Every seven seconds a German dies in Russia!

Speaking of food: Friedrich passed the time by keeping a log in which he entered descriptions of some of the various methods he'd observed troops using to obtain food in the city. He often shared his findings with Werner, who had so far declined to eat anything other than the bread and broth that rations had dwindled to.

Rat In a Can

The favored game in the southern part of the pocket. Empty ration tins are reclaimed from the garbage heaps and used to lure rats. Once again one is obliged to question the intelligence of the enlisted men, who surely would better serve their appetites by observing the garbage in its natural environment for signs of symbiotic coexistence with vermin, if indeed any remain. One assumes that the technique of removing the tins for placement in a more agreeable, if less fecund, environment is an outgrowth of the Wehrmacht soldier's naturally proud reluctance to associate with refuse of any kind.

Volga Dog

Hunting customarily begins at nightfall as the terrified creatures attempt to flee the burning city by swimming the river. The temptingly bloated animals may be perforated by either side's artillery or left intact to release noisome gases upon dissection. Though a frequent recourse in the early days of plenty (ca. mid-November), one finds it tastes less like food than one might like.

Here Kitty

The mere fact that these animals have remained within the city limits throughout the course of this noble conflict should put to rest any continuing rumors with regard to their alleged intelligence, to wit, that it is superior to that possessed by mongrel dogs, chimpanzees and leather-soled shoes. It is most certainly not the cats your observer has recognized attempting to swim the river. Still, one can hardly fault the beasts for their constancy.

> I cannot deny my share of personal guilt in all this. But it is in a ratio of 1 to 70 millions. The ratio is small; still, it is there. I wouldn't think of evading my responsibility. I tell myself that, by giving my life, I have paid my debt. One cannot argue about questions of honor.

Every seven seconds a German dies in Russia!

Friedrich appeared to have gone to sleep and Werner sat rereading what he'd written, a meditative lull that called for a glass of port, or at least a cigarette. Despite his attempt to be honest he'd presented Augusta with his death as though it were somehow for the best—a voluntary, though reluctant, cessation. The considerately discreet letter was tinged with a sort of courtly despair. Very literary, he thought. Not bad. No need for Augusta to bear a parting image of him as a wild-eyed scarecrow, unshaven and filthy. This was a woman to whom he'd promised the Luxembourg Gardens, articulating his clear and unambiguous plan as if it were their right.

> Augusta, in the hour in which you must be strong, you will feel this also. Don't be bitter and do not suffer too much from my absence. I am not cowardly, only sad that I cannot give greater proof of my courage than to die for this useless, not to say criminal, cause. You know the family motto of the von Hingels: "Guilt recognized is guilt expiated."

Don't forget me too quickly.

* * *

> . . . The Führer made a firm promise to bail us out of here; they read it to us and we believed in it firmly. Even now I still believe it, because I have to believe in something. If it is not true, what else could I believe in? I would no longer need spring, summer or anything that gives pleasure. So leave me my faith, dear Greta; all my life, at least eight years of it, I believed in the Führer and his word.

"It's the boy scout."

"What do you hear from the Führer today, Gerhardt?"

The two men had been deep in the sort of dreamy conversation Gerhardt had never quite understood, as if such conversations were conducted in a foreign language. A matter of different priorities. Unshared enthusiasms. But what was it they couldn't share? Food? Warmth? These were human things. Was he not a human being as well? They had the same needs. They were comrades in arms. He smiled, considering his literal use of the expression. He thought of saying, "But we're comrades in arms." A small joke, they'd share a laugh, and word would spread throughout the division. Then he saw that one of the men was missing his rifle.

"Where is your weapon?" demanded Gerhardt.

"The hell do you care?" asked the man, Stein.

"On your feet," said Gerhardt. "Immediately."

"Oh, go fuck yourself."

As Gerhardt decided whether to move along—to lend himself to more urgent business or to assert his authority as the man's superior and maintain order within the ranks—a series of four explosions, stuttering in a roughly elliptical line along the length of the airstrip, sent up chunks of earthly stuff—soil and stones and asphalt and the petrified roots of Czarist trees. Before this distant rain began to fall, Gerhardt threw himself to the ground. Stein and the other man, Erlanger, began to laugh. Gerhardt rose having decided he had better move along after all.

During basic training, members of his unit once snuck into the showers to steal his towels and clothing as he bathed, and he had to walk naked to his barracks as a group of officers looked on. He waited in terror to be court-martialed, even executed. But apparently without the uniform he'd made no sense to them, made no impression at all.

He went about his business as if he actually had some.

On maneuvers, an obliging infantryman from another division was sent as a prank: the man hailed him, and when Gerhardt turned the unfamiliar soldier hurled rotten eggs at him. "Jew!" Gerhardt yelled. He swore revenge but he'd never found out who had joined in this latest conspiracy.

Inside himself, he felt resolute. Of course.

Then came the unexpected invitation to the beer garden on his birthday. They urged him to meet them there in mid-afternoon so they could help him to celebrate. Touched by the unexpected gesture, he'd arrived carrying the package of sausage and cheese that Greta had sent, only to discover the deserted garden, stirred by a slight wind, lush and quiet under the trellises. The proprietor, all alone in the establishment at that hour, scratched his head. "Soldiers? No soldiers here, pal. I think someone's been having you on. Beer?"

Once again his tormentors were nowhere to be found. He lay awake all that night, talking of the Führer, and when morning had arrived he found himself headed, under restraint, to the dispensary, where the doctor tapped his knee and had him stick out his tongue and then kicked him out of his office. "No goldbricking here, soldier," the doctor said. "You're off to the East with the rest of them."

He lay awake night after night proclaiming his relationship with the Führer.

A flare rose in the sky, illuminating everything in its quavering brilliant light, and he froze where he was. Suddenly, he heard "H-h-h-heil Hitler!" Goetz (an irritating loudmouth) stood with Vogel (a loathsome subversive). Each offered a left-handed salute.

Goetz shouted, "Hey, Gerhardt, tell Superman Number One to send us some cigarettes, will you?"

"They'll just forget the fucking matches," said Vogel.

"Gerhardt, you *stupid asshole!* Are you *listening* to us?"

"Your Führer is an incompetent piece of stupid shit!"

"Are you *listening,* Gerhardt?"

The expressions of the two men, amusedly contemptuous at the outset of their harangue, had rapidly changed into bitter masks of hatred. He noticed that the men didn't seem able to enjoy their contempt for him as much as they once had. This meant, of course, that he'd been right: their ability to enjoy him, to rely on him as a foil, had been dependent upon an ingrained faith in the Führer. Despair followed loss of faith: this much he'd been taught as a boy.

Gerhardt enjoyed being in the 6th. It was rumored that fully one-fifth of the men were Party members.

The men seemed happy and at ease only when the Führer provided for them abundantly. Never were they able to take the long view. He'd never seen much of the Führer in them. But then, only he could fully understand the Führer: that his generous plans for the German people were defined by the very destitution that had marked his progress through a wilderness of misunderstanding. That he would lead the people to glory despite their meanness and ignobility. That he saw seeds of greatness in the German race that individual Germans were scarcely worthy of bearing.

Goetz, who looked suspiciously Jew-like to him, outranked him.

He'd lain awake to speak of Hitler and the others sneaked up on his bunk and overturned it. They threw wadded balls of toilet paper at him. They poured cold water on him. In one memorable instance, they sodomized him.

But this was Hitler, whom he loved—the Hitler in whose hands he was willing to place things of importance to him, the most delicate and fragile things. Sometimes the Führer talked to him, to exhort him in difficult moments, but also to confide in him regarding his own burdens. (Lately, the Führer was not thrilled with Manstein.)

He lay awake and explained his private relationship with the Führer to the astonished men who found themselves with him in the long Russian nights. He'd suddenly feel the flurry as the comrade beside him would abandon him for other shelter. This was how he was born to feel.

Here, over a rise he felt a surge of white red inside his red. He looked to see white white with the red in truth to him. Zaitsev red red him dead. The white. Turn red in red pain to see. No sniping Zaitsev but only 6th. And lay on white laughter for red peril him in. 6th Army boys the red red flower of whitest Germany. Bang.

And the Führer said, "Feel me in you,"

And he responded, "I feel you."

And the Führer said, "I am your iron will,"

And he responded, "And I am yours,"

And the Führer said, "You are Germany, and Germany is all."

And he responded, "Everything is Germany."

* * *

> . . . Today I talked to Hermann. He is south of the front, a few hundred yards from me. Not much is left of his regiment. But the son of baker Brauer is still with him. Hermann still had the letter in which you told us of Father's and Mother's death. I talked to him once more, for I am the elder brother, and I tried to console him, though I too am at the end of my rope. It is good that Father and Mother will not know that Hermann and I will never come home again. It is terribly hard that you will have to carry the burden of four dead people through your future life.
>
> I wanted to be a theologian, father wanted to have a house, and Hermann wanted to build fountains. Nothing worked out that way. You know yourself what the outlook is at home, and we know only too well what it is here. No, those things we planned certainly did not turn out the way we imagined. Our parents are buried under the ruins of their house, and we, though it may sound harsh, are buried with a few hundred or so men in a ravine in the southern part of the pocket. Soon these ravines will be full of snow.

It seemed to pass the time for him to imagine the sharp lines and edges of the house Hermann had promised to design. Each of the boys had taken an interest in architecture, but Martin was ungifted, as he succinctly put it. He left it at that, preferring not to be coaxed into admitting this was a statement that described everything about him. It wasn't that he'd *wanted* to be a theologian: it sounded acceptable when he considered it, he imagined his own face with a faint and antiseptic glow to it . . . The idea of the house would come to him unbidden at times. It would have been an unusual house back home, in that medieval city with its occasional instances of Speer's Nazi garniture. Hermann, if he lived, would dedicate himself to the undoing of Nazi appearances. That was Hermann's other gift. The invincible modernity of American and British bombs had undone the city first, though, and Father was never to have his house . . . Hermann's house came together in Martin's head as something Gropius might have designed. To imagine such a thing in this land taken whole from Breughel! He wondered if there was anyone else looking out into the red night of this unutterably cold furnace of a city who would summon such a vision. Hermann perhaps. But each summoned what he needed. . . . Martin was not entirely sanguine about his role as elder, the comforter. It wasn't one he'd been called upon to play very often. Hermann had more or less taken care of his own simple emotional requirements over the years, and the devastation he displayed at the news of their parents' death surprised

Martin. He put his arm around him and they rocked together. Here his lack of talent and imagination were not even an issue. His credentials as elder brother were unquestioned as he held tight to Hermann's shoulder. They sat in frozen mud surrounded by torn corpses to mourn the faraway dead. They embraced in full view of the other soldiers, their bodies swaying. Then Hermann, his dirty face streaked with tears, looked at him slyly.

"You realize, of course, that we look as if we're davening," he said.

. . . The Führer would not like this house! He and Hermann shared lots of little jokes, most of which nowadays seemed to be at Hitler's expense. Hermann sketched the house on paper napkins and the backs of envelopes. He sketched it for their father. He sketched it for their mother, for their sister. The big idea was for Father to have a banner sales year so they could buy enough land to build the house on. A banner sales year—they all laughed. Times were not good for a traveler in meat-cutting machinery. Not a house the Führer would like, not a bit! Though despite the irreverent joking they all had come, all had died, when Hitler called. There was an ineffable agitation in the ranks. Each had found his way to the realization that he was going to die. . . . Klara's anger impressed him: *No way of padding this ghastly news with the usual gossip, as if that would make what I have to say any easier for either of us: at about nine o'clock last night the British planes once again flew over this incredible stronghold, this metropolis of unimaginable strategic importance. In this instance Promenadplatz was not spared. Mother and Father were inside the apartment at the time making their usual insidious plans against London and Washington and were buried in the mess. Fortunately—I use the word advisedly, Martin—I was out at the time.* Was the sarcasm something new? He couldn't remember if Klara had been a sarcastic girl before the war. It didn't help to be reminded of his parents' utter innocence, to have that rubbed in his face, but he couldn't blame her. She wrote of *The perverse world in which I expect daily bombings,* she wrote of *Everything we knew, Martin, for all those years—and their lives as well, gone for nothing* and he forgave her for her presumptuousness and self-pity as he sat amid his own corpses in his own frozen ditch because after all she was a woman, a noncombatant, and still thoughtful enough to consider Hermann, to consider his feelings, writing *but of the three of us, one, at least, should get the news directly from a loved one, in person. . . .* Then again, he'd played right into it, solemnly midwifing the delivery of bad news from sister to younger brother. Why did he deserve less consideration simply because he wasn't going to have gone on to design beautiful houses and public gardens? Because he wasn't one of a pair of stubborn old fools who refused every opportunity they may have had to escape living in a sizable German city during daily allied bombings? The arrogance of believing in the strength of one's daily routines, one's comfortable habits, against chaos! . . . Martin envied Klara her sudden, unexpected lack of ties. A liberating windfall. He pictured her tossing clothes and toiletries into a soft-sided bag, leaving for South America, for America herself, the mother of fine democratic bombs! Sweet impulse. He, on the other hand, had been born for the army. For once his and Hermann's roles had been reversed: he took naturally to what Hermann found difficult, unbearably frustrating. . . . So it was he, Martin, who had taken refuge in the drills and routines. The Wehrmacht was unbeatable in part because of the fervor of their training: one was disciplined to believe in the fragility of its invincibility. Total effort was required to keep the Reich insulated from calamity. And at first the men felt the terrible loss here as a personal failure. Except Hermann, who instinctively traced the disaster all the way back to Berlin. Right once again. . . . Martin suddenly recalled walking late one night into the bedroom he and Hermann had shared in their parents' apartment. Back for the Christmas break during his first year at university, he returned home after an evening out with friends to find his brother fast asleep on top of his bed, one hand holding his pajamas to the side while the other grasped his limp penis. A "provocative journal," as Hermann referred to magazines of a certain type, lay open on his chest. Martin lingered long enough to reconnoiter the situation, to savor Hermann's pose, to take in the slack jaw and the drool moistening the pillowcase. Then he'd gone to rally Klara, clamping his hand over her mouth to prevent her from laughing aloud at the sight of their little brother. They retreated to her room to assemble armfuls of stuffed animals—the girl had dozens, it seemed—and returned to bombard Hermann with them until he awoke and then, red-faced, realized the attitude in which he'd been discovered. . . . Was this the memory he wished to die with? Was triumph always this stupid and necessary? . . . In Hermann's house each would have had his own bedroom.

* * *

> On Tuesday I knocked out two T-34s . . . afterward I drove past the smoking remains. From the hatch there hung a body, head down, his feet caught, and his legs burning up to his knees. The body was alive, the mouth moaning. He must have suffered terrible pain. And there was no possibility of freeing him. Even if there had been, he would have died after a few hours of torture. I shot him, and as I did it, tears ran down my cheeks. Now I have been crying for three nights about a dead Russian tank driver, whose murderer I am. The crosses of Gumrak shame me and so do many other things which my comrades close their eyes to and set their jaws against. I am afraid I'll never be able to sleep quietly, assuming that I shall ever come back to you, dear ones. My life is a terrible contradiction, a psychological monstrosity.

They still exulted after discrete instances of destruction: this was one of the dubious pleasures reserved to members of antitank crews. Each annihilated tank emitted smoke—as if this were a predictable part of its function, thought Ernst: first, the white smoke rose into the sky where the wind dispersed it, adding to the overall haze, while oily black smoke spread from its source across the filthy snowed ground. The three crew members exulted, spreading their arms and jumping. One T-34, against a pork-colored sky. Jets of flame. Smoke. They leaped into each other's open arms. Ernst thought of newsreel footage he'd seen, before the war, of American baseball teams celebrating this way after important victories. Two T-34s. A rare prize. They embraced each other and emitted sounds of guttural self-acclaim, like the flanneled mongrels of America, in the arenas of their motherless, shameless cities.

The tank driver's mouth was alive; it communicated the despair of the burning body. Flames tracked the length of the dying Russian. He said, "Ooooo." It was a hopeless, body-deep condition for the tank driver: he had always been this way. Any other way of being was strictly an illusion. He said, "Ooooo," inhaling and exhaling as his legs burned and his tunic began to smolder. Smoke rose from him. "Ooooo." Ernst cautiously approached the charred ruins of the tank. Simple as this: the Russian's feet had been caught as he attempted to escape the oven of his tank. Either a fluke of this particular kill or a frequent result of flawed Russian tank and/or uniform design. The choking, blinding smoke wafted up the Volga and Ernst could hear Katyusha rockets smashing those parts of the city where they didn't care to risk their tanks. As he took aim at the living mouth before him, tears icing his cheeks.

For the rest of my life, thought Ernst—he saw him, his O of a mouth hanging under the flaming body. Ernst had exterminated many men before, smeared them to frightening and painful deaths inside their tanks. He consoled himself by thinking that the T-34 was a truly superior piece of armament, better even than the Panzers. Not, he thought sardonically, that they'd seen any Panzers in a while. They'd been left to die by themselves in rubble beneath a flaming sky. The man said, "Ooooo." Ernst was obliged to shoot him. The T-34 had disgorged the softest thing at its center. Legs aflame he dangled from the hatch of the tank, mouth ovaled "Ooooo."

"Ernst killed two T-34s. Blew away the driver of one," said Vogel. They crouched at the junction of two attached houses that had been hammered to about four feet above the rutted ground, where Vogel had set traps for rats using ration tins. The traps were empty this evening and Vogel was gingerly cleaning the bait out, sucking the food off his forefinger.

"Well of course he did," said Hofner.

"No, I mean with a gun."

"What the fuck? You got that close?"

"You're not supposed to admire your handiwork." Hans punched him lightly on the shoulder.

"No, I . . ."

But Ernst didn't know what to say. He *had* driven over to gloat.

". . . I don't know what to tell you. I drove over. Anyway, the driver was trying to get out and his feet got caught. Shit, he was on fire. It was horrible."

"Horrible?"

The wind penetrated the dubious shelter, roaring in alternating blasts of frigid cold and searing heat. The latter brought with it downy inch-square flakes of ash.

"No, I mean, of course, sort of. But he was *moaning.*"

"Theme song of the subhuman," said Vogel.

"Call them subhumans if you want," said Goetz. "You're the one eating rat shit."

"Hitler'll come through . . ."

"That maniac forgets we're even here. If Paulus would stop asking him and just withdraw . . ." Goetz trailed off. Vogel gave him a wounded look.

"It isn't rat shit," he said.

Hans jabbed a thumb at his chest. "This isn't a summer uniform."

"Those aren't empty ammunition boxes."

"That isn't a bunch of frozen guns."

"Those aren't empty gasoline cans."

"Heil Hitler!"

"Heil Hitler!"

They giggled, then Vogel peered into the ration tin and, satisfied that he had completely cleaned the inside, tossed it over the jagged wall. Again they heard the Katyushas pounding.

"There goes Gumrak," said Goetz.

"What the hell do they want it for I'm wondering. They already blasted it to hell," said Hans.

"We got too fucking good at fixing the airstrip quick," said Hofner.

Vogel peered over the wall. "Are the wounded out? Are the wounded out?"

"Oh sure," said Goetz. "The wounded got out. But that's about it for wounded, n'est-ce pas? Last plane tomorrow at the latest? You don't want to be wounded, any more. I mean, just try for dead straight off the bat."

"What's going on at the field hospital? Aren't they doing anything?" asked Hans.

"'Field hospital?'" said Goetz, witheringly.

Vogel moved back, giving himself room to gesture as he talked. "The rationale if you're wounded is to leave you in the fucking snow since you bleed less in the cold. That's the rationale they use for taking your fucking blanket from you. That's the rationale they use for not even pretending to take care of you."

"You don't want to be wounded," repeated Goetz.

Once again, Ernst thought of the Russian tank driver, moaning "Ooooo." He wondered if he could count on similar kindness from any Russian he might encounter. He suspected not. Here he was crouched on the parquetry of someone's parlor, uninvited.

Speaking of which: a young lieutenant crabbed into their alcove, pistol drawn.

"What's going on here, Sergeant? Are these your men? Who is your commander?"

"So many questions," said Goetz, shrugging. "Such a curious lieutenant."

The lieutenant opened his mouth as if he were going to say

something, then shut it. After a moment's pause, he spoke again.

"I need you to take charge of these men and meet me at the north-west forward command to defend the airfield."

"Here they are," said Goetz. "What, do you want me to drag them there? What are we? The fucking infantry all of a sudden?"

"What was that, Sergeant?"

"I said fuck you."

The lieutenant considered the situation for a moment, then left.

"Christ, Ernst—if you really wanted to put someone out of their misery," said Vogel.

A psychological monstrosity. As a boy, he had gone with his parents on holiday deep in the heart of some seaside place (though he remembered it being the country as well, and he couldn't possibly be conflating two trips since holidays were rare in those days), far from the city. He walked on the shoulder of a freshly paved road sparkling from the glass splinters embedded in the macadam. His father held his hand tightly, though the road was not dangerous. Everything was hot. He thought now about that heat as the wind lanced him through his clothing. The sun had been hot. He'd walked with his hand in his father's—and now he felt the nostalgia of the memory mutating into a spiked forlornness for his own children, the younger of whom had just begun to walk the last time he'd seen them. Typical: when he thought of them here he felt their absence most sharply, more than during training, far more than during the first campaigns—when he'd actually felt he was fulfilling the Führer's promise for their future—but he seemed to remember only the impatient, the unsympathetic moments he'd spent with them, the times when they'd bothered him to distraction with some childish doings. Their future no longer looked so good. At the very least they would be raised by another man; their morals and ethics springing from that unknown's brain, rather than his: just as well. He would die here knowing that the most compassionate act of his life had been the mercy killing of a stranger he'd put in unimaginable pain, pain beyond fear, beyond words. Ooooo. And they'd embraced, jumping into one another's outstretched arms, like athletes in an October sun, the shadow of the grandstand creeping up from the point of the emerald diamond.

The road he'd walked with his father led to a bluff that overlooked the seashore. A set of steep stairs had been built into the hillside and he and his father descended to the beach, to the palpable humidity and salt of the air there. Surf rolled in from the end of the world, the northern sky hung with endless light. They walked along the seashore and Ernst shattered a large shell with a rock to see what lived inside, then lifted it, *fix it,* to his father—"It's dead, Ernst." His father laughed, then was startled to see his son begin to shake and cry, the ruined shell still in his hands, glistening meat dangling from the shards. He led the boy to the edge of the water and urged him to cast the shell into the surf, so that the ocean would heal it.

* * *

> . . . In January you will be 28. That is still very young for such a good-looking woman, and I am glad that I could pay you this compliment again and again. You will miss me very much, but even so, don't withdraw from other people. Let a few months pass, but no more. Gertrud and Claud need a father. Don't forget that you must live for the children, and don't make too much fuss about their father. Children forget quickly, especially at that age. Take a good look at the man of your choice, take note of his eyes and the pressure of his handshake, as was the case with us, and you won't go wrong. But above all, raise the children to be upright human beings who can carry their heads high and look everybody straight in the eye. I am writing these lines with a heavy heart. You wouldn't believe me if I said that it was easy, but don't be worried. I am not afraid of what is coming. Keep telling yourself and the children also when they have grown older, that their father never was a coward, and that they must never be cowards either.

Whenever I experience sorrow or misfortune in my life I tend to think immediately of my father and the enormous unknown into which he carried the final portion of his life. He died, leaving his body somewhere in the Soviet Union, this much is nearly certain. He might have died only hours after having finished the last of the 27 letters he sent to my mother from Stalingrad. He may have lived through the final siege, only to die in transit to a Soviet camp. Certainly he died in the camp if he made it that far. His transient thoughts are all I have of him, though it's obvious my father weighed his words very carefully before committing them to paper—his letters are meticulous, and I doubt he could have obtained sufficient paper on which to write successive drafts. Yet, I wonder if he had a sense of posterity, if this is truly what he intended to leave for me and Gertrud to remember him by. He was always present, yet I have only his name, the letters, and the photograph of him in that damned Wehrmacht uniform. What would the neighbors say to that tiny swastika, on our father. And us supposedly Americans. My mother raised Gertrud and me as Americans. I barely speak German. She married an American serviceman who had remained in Bad Nauheim for occupation duty. I doubt Father would have approved of him, though it was not the serviceman's Americanness that would have bothered him, nor would it have been his drunkenness, but something in addition to these things. I can't say what, but his letters tell me so, authoritatively. A certain lack of precision in the American's actions, an overall vagueness to him. I remember the smell of his aftershave, the look of his clothing. I cannot recall his handshake. Mama married the American to leave Germany, and he managed to do us the favor of dying shortly after installing us in a big mock Tudor house in San Mateo. He drove us up and down El Camino Real in his car, showing us auto dealerships, appliance stores, supermarkets, as if to humble us with the abundance of the nation we'd dared to challenge: there was always that adversarial sense; he made Mama his own but Gertrud and I were always Other. He was quick to remove his belt, this democratic warrior. Then he died. Mama began taking in boarders. They were nearly all Jewish: make what you will of that. Most of them seemed casually anti-Semitic—hearty, tanned young men and women named Keith and Kathy who lived light-years from the gas chambers and the crematoria.

Trudy married a man from Los Angeles when she was seventeen. She and Mama did not get along, and the man from Los Angeles seemed to be an attractive expedient in his Lincoln Continental and his elegant suits. They were killed in an auto accident on a canyon road, and it was Mama and me.

And when Trudy died, I thought to myself—although I quickly learned not to say, not even to *whisper* it—"This can't happen to me . . . my father died at Stalingrad." When I was robbed at gunpoint in the street, I thought to myself, "Why is this happening to me? My father died at Stalingrad!" When I was fired from a job, I thought to myself, "How absolutely unfair—Stalingrad claimed my father." When I failed a required class in college, I thought, "My father died at Stalingrad." When lovers abandoned me, it was, "My father . . . Stalingrad." When my mother withered and died, I thought, ". . . Stalingrad . . ."

Not that it was America's battle. It is not a particularly notorious battle here. It has little resonance for the Americans, who simply cannot contemplate loss on that scale. Our two cultures—Russian and German—are bound together by the sense of the legitimacy of brutality, and an immanent familiarity with massive loss. How do we not know these things when we have committed so many millions of bodies to the ground? When will our sacrifices become apparent?

In the meantime, I derive solace from the monthly checks I still get from boarders and from my other tenants—for Mama was no fool with the drunkard's money—which I put in a pile and, all alone, sit and look at, admiring the letters of my name written out on the payee's line. My own true name, and, I like to think, a good one—despite the fact of that tiny swastika, goddamn it, in the photograph.

One of these days I'm going to take that photo out of the drawer and put it on display where Keith and Kathy can see it. For they, the Jews, share with the Russians and with us the burden of the century's fatal obligations. I'll take it out and put it on a table, in the light. My father was obliged to wear the swastika on his uniform and he was obliged to wear it where it showed. Hitler clearly had a hand in the design of the uniform as well—was there no discipline whose rigors daunted the man? Did he never suffer a failure of self-assurance? "I won't retreat from the Volga!" My father's anonymous corpse, discovered in the thaw of that stinking, burnt city, which for all intents and purposes no longer exists, not even in name.

Calling the Hour

Brian Evenson

1.

ONE HAND FULL THE OTHER HAND EMPTY, both hands gone full as he grasped the back of his shirt, stripped it fluidly off over his head, the shirt dropping and the same hand hovering at her own chest, parting the buttons of her shirt, then tugging the shirt back and down by the collar until it hung just above her elbows like a wrap now, shoulders bare. He let the collar go and one hand fell empty again and moved to draw her in, she too startled to resist the half-nude embrace: the warm dry feel of chest against shoulder, arms wrapped about her, empty hand flat and spread flat across her back, full hand all knuckled up around the gun and granching against her side. She still could not move at the cessation of the embrace, might never have moved had it not been for him now tugging her before the mirror, his arm around her shoulders, drawing her in and tight until they both stood configured in the silvered glass from shoulders up, shoulder to shoulder, both seemingly bare, her neck blotching now, his arm drifting over now to drape fingers over her ear. And then his gunless hand pulling their heads together, pressing ear to ear as she watched still in the mirror, his other hand now rising to lift the gun to his own temple, aiming through his head at her own. She observed the flattened image steady the pistol, press it hard against the free side of his skull, cock, fire.

2.

Face no more than a dark blur at first and then still a blur but clearer. The other man behind her, holding her head at the temples and forcing it forward, demanding she regard what he claimed to be her reflection. There, in the bright pocked metal: the shaved temple, the dark blister of blood where a fragment of bullet had passed through his head and touched hers. *Perhaps any number of heads,* she thought—*hardly my head,* she thought, as the other man spoke urgently and psychiatrically at her, at the odd, blurred visage in the metal tabletop which she could not accept as her own. It was his visage she was looking at, she realized of a sudden, his preserved head: she knew the other side of the head where the bullet had burst forth was a ruin, would be a ruin still, but she did not dare turn her head to see. If she does not turn her head she can still consider herself to be herself head to tail even if her head is his head, even if she does not know the whereabouts of his bony body, wandering and armatured with her own head.

3.

He now roamed woman-faced, now exulant and incognito while she has finished male-visaged and always in danger of collapse, always just seconds before the sound of the gun as it goes off, the burn of powder and the pain in the head as she falls, her doubled image gone bloody and slipping from the mirror. They are calling the hour now, the other man long gone from behind her, the nightwatchmen coaxing her up from the table and down the shadowed hall, a final vision pursuing her now and catching at her heels, ephemerated movements and discerpted forms spinning along fresh-polished floors. She knows it is the cast of her own legs and feet she is seeing, the feet of the nightwatchmen as well, perhaps here and there glimpses of her head and other parts. But there seems more than that, a supplemental furzing of shadow and color which she knows as the coming into being of his peculiar vision: soon in the shadows of her room, the locked door, the steps of nightwatchmen crossing up and down halls, the vision will nearly claim discrete shape. His form a dim phantasm intorting in the shadows of the room, congealing and fading over the night's course. She shall rise from the bed to try to capture him in her blanket, try to retrieve her head, but each time she believes to have him he will reveal himself just over her shoulder, laughing with her voice, her lips, as she herself knits his furrowed brow and tries again. Then, later, morning, the blanket empty, the door snapping open and she will be drawn back down the corridor again into the same day she has just left, knowing at both ends of the corridor he shall await her, full- and empty-handed, and no place for her to turn but toward him.

In the Lightly Moderate Vivid Deep

Diane Williams

GRAYISH PURPLISH RED

THE WATER IS RUBBED into my hair and the black hair is moistened and twirled unprettily. I hope I am not too dry for anyone.

In fact, last night in Britain, a woman came to me. We talked quite a bit about what she was—plain and very sturdy. She lives in England. She has vanity, old age, ignorance and all the rest! She wears a wig. She says she doesn't wash her hair. If I suffer, I think I please her. We drank bonnyclabber. It was this that gave—We kept talking about what we used to know, when in came another human being in a dress who dusted an inner form and the faience washstand. Did not see the babe leave, although she's all gone.

My mother said she herself would stay longer if not for my certain coolness, my unspecified dimness, my slowing down, my not-looking, my overheard meekness in this phrase which portrays me and betrays me and portrays me and portrays me. I have fewer burdens, even cried at times, went on lying on part of my face on the bed, fell asleep! My first few nights on our earth are such rubbish. She does not want to love such a lackluster person.

The worst jolt about being loved is when it will start.

BLUISH BLACK

AT THE FORT the mister ate fat. He is made to stay inside.

He has a plan, otherwise he'll only just be ill.

The missus at the foot of my chair reclines and she opens her legs so I will pet her. She is intelligent. Every few hours I take her outside because it's necessary. She thinks her property will calm her. If she sees her property, she thinks it calms her.

At the Fort, the houses are made of Portland stone, very formal.

A steady program of repair on the heavily treed land leading from the Fort to the Lake is now in progress. The community has transferred the Fort to the Preservation Trust.

Such signs of life—as a vase and a bowl—people do pay to look at.

People ought not to act so bored. That's so rude.

Most of the men—why do they have all those stars and the heavens and those embers and sparks which ruin everything for me. They're so fake.

MADDER LAKE

"WELL, YES," SAYS JACK, "but there are Frenches!"

Uh, that's very specific this time that here is Marcel French and George French and Steve. It's Steve. It's Mike. Mike's companion's name is George. He's a French. They have their obligations. That's Colleen and Marcel French and that's Sherwood French.

The seated Frenches with their bud finials and their swags are clearer than a speck of pastel.

It is generally overlooked that I'm the wriggle upright who is wearing women's slipper-type shoes.

I speak to Jack.

"In a way," I say, "I like it here." It is not difficult to understand why.

I do have the summary of quarrels. Yet, Jack and I, we are boxed-in with painless prickings. We chew our morals. Our clothes are good.

Uh, that's very specific this time that it's the stuck-down Frenches—Steve and Mike French. All else is undulation and the inlaid outline.

Frenches say—"I was there." "It is my belief." "Try wide in the last four years."

Colleen French is featured with tapering legs, with a raised back. She wears her woman's head, her padded arms. I dare not to speak a word to her, in front her, at the end of March, near her. I spoke to Jack. My feeling is I should have. I thought one sentence of mine was cadent all over itself.

Tell Jack, Jack, tell Jack! Jack! Jack! My apron, it doesn't feel too bad. My arched knee hole, I cannot breathe through it. My decorated hand, my *brèche d'alep* top, my pierced-together stretcher, my gilt hair—all nice!—the barrel movement, my displayed mount, the hanging space on every side—sliding. They do not terminate! They issue in the stylized chains! I left lunch cooking on the stove and I made coffee!

Get myself endeared I should, endorsed with a particular day in mind. This day is Wednesday.

All Frenches are not dispersed. They will lunch. A French says, "You don't usually wish?"

"Yes," Jack told Mike, "I do wish, despite my mind."

I do wish too despite my mind. I feel quite sincere and Jack is wise. I take his arm. Ah, the day—if you want one of these days I will save it for you. Jack puts his hand out for my hand, puts an arm around the waist of my madder lake crêpe dress, the brilliant dress for me. Jack's speech has adjectives. It has the word strategem. He is one of our ablest and most crafty.

Now, for goodness sake, in the distance is a girl who is good-looking in a necessary way. It's not that I did not stay here and get plucked and pluck.

I have not sought to avoid the dominion of the Frenches. I will explain more fully. I discuss their qualities. I content myself with talking about such Frenches and conclude again that nobody is forcing me to. I cannot avoid forgetting who I am in favor of remembering Frenches—their munificence, their dignity, their victories, their different kinds of brains.

I look down. What's a *cache-sexe?*

I hear the girl—a friend of Colleen French's say, "Are you all right? I think you're over it."

I notice the shade of the sky. This shade of sky is "orange glow," a visual effect usually created by lower skies, not often by this sort of sky which is so very high. This sort of sky's highness manages to preserve the charm of direct sunlight.

I suppose all my money that I've spent—I should only marvel at. The girl says, "Pourquoi êtes-vous si triste?" She is talking away. There you are. "Il ne faut pas être triste." Jack's hair is hanging down in one plait. He says to me, "Put your arms around me."

Our sky's so high. It's at the gravel stop of a big, tall building, when I look at two rock-dry clouds. They set such a good example because these clouds are rocks now. They changed.

Joy of Eating

Matthew Derby

The Tins

They have taken the joy of eating from us, and so we sit at table, hands folded in prayer, each in personal cardboard food booths. At the beginning of our meal, the signal is given. Elaine inserts the corncob. William, with half-palsied face, picks at his beefsteak. "No more of that," cries mother, "No more—we will have no more of that," she calls from her booth. Father, having come to us by means of a remote control device, slouches in his chair, head in hands. Perhaps he does not belong to us. The twins feed each other dense, gray portions of mashed potato, pasting the material to each other's face and forehead. "No more of that—children." Mother will use the wooden spoon, she warns them. The portions, delicately and lovingly arranged on every plate, will taste no different than on other nights. Meals arrive at our doorstep in heavy tins. Instructions are that each family member assist in the meal. William will help stir. Elaine needs a phone book to stand on. I will sift flour from a metal can with a trigger. Look, a tasty dip can be made with sour cream and onion soup. Mother tucks the meat, garnishes it with cherries and pineapple rings.

Novelty of Heat

The joy of eating having been taken from us, we are allowed to play in the yard. William, this time, is the German. We each break into a rapid, awkward gait, scattering across the lawn. Elaine crouches behind the hedge. The twins have not learned the rules. William is gaining on them. I have climbed into the high branches of the sycamore tree, where the animal qualities of children are most apparent. This section of the yard is made up entirely of smells. William falls ass-backwards, wheezing, the wind knocked out of him. A truck rolls down the street, selling cupped ice. Summer will be passed in this way, each night progressively longer, more dissonant, objects lurching in the sky overhead.

THE HARD CANDIES

The joy of eating is gone. Mother, having taken the Germans for a walk, washes her face and hair in the kitchen sink. We are not to look. Father works alone in the forbidden room. It is conjectured that he has been to war. Elaine shows me her secret, a cache of brightly colored hard candies she hides behind the porch steps. She sucks on one and begins to cry. Everything is about as useful as water, now.

INTO HER MOUTH

Eating, that joy which we have taken part in for as long as we can remember, has been revoked. Father is outside, wielding the lawn-mower in concentric squares. William, who has been punished, sits alone in his room in a chair by the window, diagramming the behavior of birds. Elaine is out with friends. I am sitting down to a bowl of ice and a fresh comic book. It is cool here in the dark kitchen. Summer, as reported, has been the worst season for food. Dirt has a taste, it is reported. The suggestion is that one mix small amounts of dirt into one's meal. Mother, in her garden, gingerly inserts a finger into her mouth.

JOUST

Each of us, in turn, recalls the joy of eating, now lost to us. William has been fighting with the other boys. They wear cloth helmets and carry long wooden poles for jousting. The goal is emasculation. They can be heard in the streets before dark, charging at each other fiercely. An ice cone truck passes. Mother sets her magazine down, neck craned in the direction of the window. On television, hands hold up black holes where food was once inserted. Elaine has locked herself in an upstairs closet, where she says there is "another kind of air."

JOY OF SLEEP, INTERRUPTED

Because the joy of eating has been lost, we are huddlers. We are loitering in our own lives. William's bedwetting incidents have increased in number and intensity. Father finds tiny holes bored into the mattress, and inserts a diode into the head of William's penis to shock him awake next time.

The Back of Abraham

Eating, the joy of which has been wrested from us, becomes difficult. Out behind the pond Peter has found a can with something in it. Half of us are wearing ornate Indian headgear. Jill shakes the can, puts it to her ear. "I can hear the heart of it moving." There is a box with Mason jars, filled with dark, pulpy objects, soaking in their own fluids. Abraham opens a jar, picks out a wedge of something that looks like a small lung. "It is softer than you would expect," he says, "less substantial. Messy, like a wet genital." He holds it to his mouth. For a long moment nobody says anything. "No," he says, lips slick and red from handling, "I'm afraid not." Some pioneer from the other side of town shoots an arrow from over the hill, which pierces Abraham's shoulder. Those of us who do not run don't know what to do, either. Abraham hunches over, the arrow quivering in his back.

Joy of Eating, v. 2

Hot fresh baked corn cakes! Spoonfuls of homemade apple sauce!

For the Memory of Food

They fly over us in great planes and drop pamphlets: "For the Memory of Food." Some people in the town have fled, over the hill and off into another town. The houses where they lived stick out like buck teeth along the street, busted into and painted over in red. Peter has left with his family, all of the them taking only what they could carry. Those of us who remain have satisfied ourselves with the carving of immense, ornate ice sculptures, displayed in our front yards for the children to come and lick. One morning, by cosmic fluke, everyone makes swans.

The Hands

What a joy, to eat. We find ourselves in the kitchen, wandering, fingering cardboard cartons stacked away in high cabinets and filled with corn starch and water. Whatever it is we did not want to become, we have become. I meet Father one night in the hallway, his face riddled with pasty crumbs from a paper sandwich. Shamefully, we hold our places there in the cold, blue light, regarding each other. His father was a Methodist preacher—he has the same tendency to turn red. "There, there, now, let's off to bed with you," he says, holding out large, paddlelike hands, the kind that might get you ready for a smack. He hooks them under my arms and lifts. I can feel how heavy I must be, slouched there over his shoulder. On my pajamas cloned cowboys rope pastel steers in unison, the way you seem to stay a certain age forever.

My Grandmother's Tale of How the Iguana Got Her Wrinkles, or The True Tale of El Dorado

Robert Antoni

AYEEYOSMÍO! YOU WANT ME to give you this nasty story? Well you best push up close here beside me so I don't have to talk too loud. Even though at ninety-six years of age I can't make so much more noise anyway, and worse still since I lost the teeth. Because when the man carried them the other day with me bawling *thief! thief!* behind him, he only continued climbing through the window smiling he big horsesmile at me with my *own* teeth in he mouth, and me there with my gums and my lips flapping, and nothing more than the soft *thufft! thufft!* like a fart coming out my mouth. Sweet heart of Jesus! So I don't have my jewels no more—that is how I used to call the teeth—and when I try to talk up loud everything comes out in a jumble beneath the shower, but Johnny, it would take *plenty* more than that to shut me up. And we got to be careful just the same, even if we don't talk no louder than a whisper. Because if you mummy only hears me telling you this nasty story—particular when I reach to the main part that concerns, of course, the *pussy* of this younggirl—she will put us both out the house before we can catch we breath. That is one word to grate up against she ears in truth, that every time I am giving a joke or telling a story and I forget myself and let it escape, you poor mummy gets that look on she face red red like she's trying to make a caca with a corcho inside she culo! You daddy too, never mind when he was a youngboy this one was he favorite of all my stories. You daddy, and he wicked brothers, and all they bad-john-boyfriends begging me again and again please to give them the story of the old iguana—even though it was the younggirl's *pussy* they wanted to hear about, and not that old wrinkled up iguana a-tall—because of course, there ain't nothing in the world to excite the blood of the youngboys more than *that.*

Well then, it happened in the old old time, this story. Back in the very beginning, when the first of those explorers from Spain and

England arrived in this Caribbean, and the only people they found here living happy and peaceful enough were Amerindians, Caribs and Arawacks and Warrahoons and such. The explorers came, as you know youself, searching out the famous El Dorado, Sir Walter Raleigh leading the English, and Fernando de Berrío the Spanish. Sir Walter was the tall, handsome Captain dressed fancy in he jacket of red velvet, and he pantaloons, he white shirt with the collar of ruffles shoved up against he chin. Always reciting he love poetry, even at the moment of he brutal attacks. And de Berrío was the short, funny-looking fellow with he little round paunch—he tin costume creaking from the caballeros of the century before—with he little legs shaped in a bow from all those years riding on a horse. Always disappearing down in he cabin in the middle of he fierce battles, plagued either by seasickness, or he frequent diarrhea. So those were the two who came with they fleets of ships, and of course it was we misfortune to get Fernando de Berrío, the Captain from Spain, because he was the one who decided that this El Dorado they were both looking for so crazy, was hidden somewhere right here on this island of Corpus Christi. Sir Walter made up he mind it was somewhere else—up the river Orinoco in what we now call Venezuela—or hidden somewhere along the coast of what we now know as Guyana.

But Johnny, the truth is that these two spent as much time watching each *other,* as they did searching out the gold. Each was afraid the other would find it first, so every time they heard a rumor or got a premonition that the other one was close, they would go straight away and ransack him. This would mean he would have to recover heself—and repair he ships and send to England or Spain for more soldiers so he could start he expedition all over again—but of course, before he could begin again he had to retaliate and attack the other. Back and forth and back and forth so many times that it's not surprising they never *did* find the gold, even after all those years, even if there was any gold to find here a-tall. Johnny, the truth is that all of this El Dorado business wasn't nothing more than the fantasy of everybody's imagination. Growing bigger and bigger all the time, otherwise it could never have sent them so vie-kee-vie as it did.

Because not only didn't they know where was this El Dorado, they didn't know *what* it was neither. Some said how it was the long lost city of those Chibchas—another of the ancient Amerindian tribes—with the houses and the furnitures made solid from silver, all adorned in diamonds, and rubies and every kind of jewel that you could name, and the streets paved only in gold. Some said how it was the mausoleum of a great Arawack king, or the emperor of those Incas from Peru, hidden high in the mountains. Others said that it was not the creation of a man, but some marvel of the earth itself. A river in the forest overflowing with water that was molten gold, or a lake, or the famous fountain of youth. And if you bathed yourself in that golden water it could cure all you diseases—particular syphilis and the rest of that nastiness they brought with them from Europe that had they toe-tees turning green, and rotting off, and all those poor Amerindians dropping down like flies—that fountain of youth that could cure all you diseases, and you could live happy forever. Others said that it was a secret fruit, or flower, and if you ate some you shit would come out in shining bars. Others said how this fruit was the very same one out the Bible, and when you ate it the bar would appear instant in *front*—blossoming out to burst open you zipper—tall and permanent like a golden obelisk almost to touch you nose. And Johnny, with that standpipe standing up like that and all those beautiful Amerindian slavegirls, you could live happy forever too! They just didn't know. And the more they talked about it and ransacked each other the more excited they became, and the more frustrated, until after a time they'd work theyselves up into a *frenzy* to find this El Dorado. Only beating the Indians and torturing them and dragging them from one place to the next to show them the secret, or tell them in a language they couldn't even understand—wherever or whatever it was—with the poor Indians the most confuffled of all.

So it was this same Fernando de Berrío, as I was saying, who arrived here in Corpus Christi with he fleet of ships, and he built the first houses—the jail and the church and the palace for the governor—the first settlement of Europeans here on the island. They were mostly Spanish. But some of them were also French, Portugee and Italian and whoever else wanted to come—anybody but *English*—and the name of this settlement was *Demerara.* The very same settlement that years later came to be called St. Mary, and still later St. Maggy. But it was named Demerara first for the crystals of sugar they would send back on the ships to Europe. That way the ships could return loaded with salted hams, Spanish wine and French champagne, Edam cheeses from Holland like cannonballs in they skins of red wax, clothes and books and guns and whatever else they needed. After a time, though, they began to say how those same yellow-brown crystals of Demerara sugar was the very El Dorado they were looking for, because after they sold it off, those ships were returning to Corpus

Christi loaded down mostly with gold. But Johnny, the true El Dorado in all that sugar commerce wasn't those demerara crystals a-tall. It was the same yellow-brown *Amerindians* the Europeans put as slaves to clear the ground and grow the cane and make the sugar, and they beat them so much and worked them so hard, they were killing them off as quick as they could make theyselves a fortune.

Of course, the main reason for all that sugar was to finance the explorations of Fernando de Berrío. But before he could leave de Berrío had to put somebody in charge of Demerara. For this reason he sent to Spain for he partner in the sugar tradings, Don Antonio Sedeño, to pick up heself and come to Corpus Christi straight away. De Berrío wrote a letter at the same time to the King of Spain—because of course at this time Corpus Christi and all these islands belonged to the Spanish crown—that the King could name Don Antonio the first governor of the island. So it happened, and if you look in you history book you will see how it is true, that Don Antonio Sedeño was the first governor of Corpus Christi.

So now at last de Berrío could gather up he soldiers and he ships and leave on he first expedition. Because they had to make those expeditions by sea and not by land—an unfortunate thing for de Berrío, considering especially he seasickness and persistent ricewater-stools—as that jungle was too thick and dangerous with poisonous snakes for them to penetrate. That first expedition de Berrío intended to study the pitchlake at La Brea in the south of the island, and search the length of the coast beside it. Because de Berrío had read long before in the logs of Columbus how he went there to collect tar to stop-up holes in the bottoms of he ships. And Columbus wrote how that pitchlake was a marvel of nature that nobody never saw nothing like it before, "not even the dancing troubador-donkey from Seville!" so maybe the earth could have made the natural marvel of that *golden* lake somewhere beside it too?

But no sooner did de Berrío raise he sails when Sir Walter Raleigh, as was he habit, came straight away to ransack Demerara and burn the Church of San José de Irura flat to the ground. At the same time Sir Walter rescued those five little Amerindian kings de Berrío had chained together in the jail. Wannawanari, Tanoopanami, Maquarami, Atrimi and Caroni—that the hardest thing for me about telling this story is trying to pronounce those names—the five of them standing there naked, and trembling, they backsides pressed curious against the wall. Until Sir Walter turned each slowly around, and he discovered they bamsees singed from the torture of those burning pokers and boiling pigfat.

That was the year of 1595. So de Berrío had to change he course and come straight back before he could begin he explorations, and he had to build back everything that Raleigh destroyed. But this time he built a big wall going right around Demerara, and the big fortress up above the harbor shooting off plenty cannons, and this time too, when he set sail on he expedition at last, he left half he soldiers there with Don Antonio. Of course, before he could begin he expedition again he had to sail all the way up the river Orinoco. Because first he was obliged to ransack Raleigh and take back he five little Amerindian kings, each dressed up now in they *own* frilly white shirt with the sleeves reaching down past they knees, a pair of red velvet pantaloons dragging around they ankles.

And now at last Don Antonio could send to Spain for he wife and he two daughters, because he'd had to leave them behind when he came running to Corpus Christi in such a hurry. He wife was a very stern and pious woman. *So* pious she used to shave she head bald like a nun, and she pledged sheself to dress only in black—this was the sign that she was mourning the death of she husband in advance—and she name was *Doña María Penitencia.* With the two daughters called *María Dolores* and *María Consuelo.* Three Marías, and just as you would expect from names like these, the three of them were only for the Church. María Dolores and María Consuelo were the two doting acolytes of the old Archbishop, assisting him to prepare the altar and light the incense and fill the silver bowl with communion breads for all the Masses. Attending him the whole day long to put on and take off and put on again all he vestments. Because in addition to he several complete outfits for each of the masses, he had another special green costume only to walk the garden, and a white one only for he midday meditation—a yellow one to greet the sick and a red one for the poor—and another complete *brown* costume with hat and cape and tall leather cowboy boots, only to stoop behind the bush when he received the calling. With the mother, María Penitencia sheself, sewing out with she own hand he long robe of purple silk for him to hear the penance, forty-two mother-of-pearl buttons going from beneath his chin all the way down to he toes! And, of course, those three Marías could *never* come to this place of heathens in the savage Caribbean, without bringing with them they old Archbishop.

They arrived to find Don Antonio still fast asleep for he afternoon siesta, and when they tiptoed quiet inside to lift the sheet and take a peek, there sleeping beside him in all she natural beauty, naked as the day she was born, was he little Amerindian slavegirl. So the first job for this Archbishop now that he had reached the New World—soon as they could bring he big trunk from off the ship—was to dress heself in he special costume for excising Caribbean devils, and pray over the head of Don Antonio. Now the two Marías could assist him to change he outfit to the one of purple silk, and they gave him a chalice of wine to satisfy he thirst. Now the Archbishop could take from out he trunk the instrument they called the "cat-of-the-nine-tales," and he delivered one hundred hot lashes to the little slavegirl. Poor child could scarce stand by the time he finished. But now at least María Penitencia was satisfied enough, ready to let loose the child that she could return to she family in the forest. Because in truth this little slavegirl was a princess very precious to she own Arawack people—the daughter of that same Wannawanari King that de Berrío had locked up in the jail—with she royal family waiting anxious for her on the other side of the island.

They *would* have let her return home to she royal family too, if it wasn't for one thing already obvious for all of them to see, that this little slavegirl was pregnant with the child of Don Antonio. So they couldn't send her home straight away. Instead, they locked her up in the cell downstairs in the basement, with María Dolores and María Consuelo bringing her she food every morning, nothing but a piece of Johnny cake and a glass of coconut water. But Don Antonio had a kind heart, and late each night he would tiptoe down the stairs to bring the child something proper to eat. Of course, most nights Don Antonio would get carried away with heself, and the two Marías would discover him early the next morning still consoling he little slavegirl, there struggling beneath him in she hammock tied in the corner.

The baby was born premature. A tiny creature with transparent skin and all the branches of blue veins showing, shiny red eyes like those of a salamander, and it didn't have no eyebrows nor lashes nor nails at the ends of its fingers and toes, only tiny cups like the suckers of a frog. But this little slavegirl loved she baby just the same. Cooing and talking to it soft and gentle in the language none of them could understand, and she wouldn't let she little salamander out from she hands for even a second. In truth, she would have remained happy enough locked up there in she cell for the rest of she days, before she lost that child. But they took it away from her just the same. And they called in two big soldiers to knock her down and beat her and bind she hands and feet, and they carried her off still struggling inside the banana peel of she little hammock, back to she family in the forest.

It was those two Marías who raised up this child, because every time they gave it to they mother to hold, María Penitencia, she only wanted to pelt it out the window. The Marías used to keep it in a shoebox in the corner of they room, some dry grass sprinkled at the bottom. And they tried to feed it every kind of fly and mosquito and spider that they could find—until they discovered the only *one* thing this little salamander liked to eat—and that was the green green dasheen leaves growing beneath a full moon beside the river, soft and wet with dew. So very early every morning the two Marías would get up faithful to go and collect them. It was a little girl, and the Marías called her by the same name as she mummy, *Iwana,* which in the language of the Arawacks means "iguana." And when she began to crawl the two Marías would carry her out in the yard every afternoon, each taking they turn to walk behind her, attached to a long string tied around she neck. Until one afternoon when Iwana got loose and took off running up the tall poinciana tree, she legs and arms turning at she sides like the blades of an airplane—which is just the way iguanas run if you've ever see them—and she remained up that tree for three days. Until the two Marías attended the old Archbishop to dress in he green costume for walking the garden, and he climbed up in the poinciana heself to bring her down.

The Marías continued to feed her the soft dasheen leaves every day, and Iwana continued to grow, that after a time nobody didn't take hardly no notice of her inside the house. Scrambling between they legs each time they came through the door, and climbing up to sit draped like a scarf around they necks, or curled comfortable in they laps every evening beneath the dinner table. Sometimes they would realize all in a sudden that nobody had seen little Iwana the whole week—with everybody taking off crazy to search in all the drawers, and the cupboards, and beneath the beds—because they were all afraid María Penitencia would stumble across her first. Like the time Iwana crawled down the drain of the kitchen sink, and María Penitencia opened the pipe full and almost drowned her.

But in time even *she* seemed to grow accustomed to Iwana's presence in the house. Before they could turn around she'd grown up into a little girl, and just as you would expect from a tale like this—

despite that Iwana was born such an ugly baby—she grew into the most *beautiful* younggirl Demerara had ever seen. Because don't forget that this Iwana, like she mummy before her, was a princess of royal Arawack blood. In addition to being the very first child of the New World to come out half-Spanish and half-Amerindian, and as always happens with mixtures like that, she took the best features from both. Tall and slim with golden skin and green almond eyes, she long dark hair reaching all the way down she back. And Johnny, every bit as beautiful as this child's looks were she gentle ways, calm and quiet and so graceful—that every time she passed you in the street hurrying back and forth between the governor's palace and that church—you couldn't help but feel a pang of pity. Because just as you would suppose too from a tale like this, the more beautiful and kind was this Iwana, the more cruel those two Marías treated her, and they mother, María Penitencia.

They put her to clean the palace and cook the food and wash all the clothes, not only those of the household, but now Iwana must wash and iron and attend to the old Archbishop for all he endless vestments too. Rising at the crack of dawn to grind the coffee and put it to boil, squeeze the oranges and bake the magdalenas for breakfast. Then she must heat the water with aromatic leaves for the bath of María Penitencia, sponging down she broad shoulders, she shiny coconut-head. Then Iwana must prepare the baths for the two daughters, washing and drying and combing out they hair, before she could attend them to dress theyselves. Then—before she could even have a chance to catch she breath—she must take off running across the square to attend the old Archbishop, that by the time those three Marías arrived he could begin the six o'clock Mass. So on and so forth the whole day long, until at last Iwana could descend the stairs to she little room in the basement, followed close behind by María Penitencia, the big key in she hand to lock her up inside. Because of course, that was the only way to keep out Don Antonio. And by the time Iwana lay sheself at last in she little hammock in the corner, and she closed she eyes to drop quiet asleep, María Penitencia was there already at the door unlocking it to let her out.

Now the time arrived for Don Antonio to look for suitable husbands to marry off the two Marías. By now, of course, Demerara was a busy town well known in Europe, and attracting plenty youngmen to come to the Caribbean and make theyselves a fortune. On top of that Fernando de Berrío was convinced that any day soon he would find he El Dorado, and when that happened, of course, everybody would have more gold than they could dream. But in truth the majority of these youngmen coming to Demerara didn't have so much of pedigree and high breeding, but they were only wadjanks and bad-johns looking to get theyselves rich. Prisoners that escaped the jail, and thieves, and every kind of scoundrel that you could imagine, that in truth none of those youngmen were suitable for the daughters of Don Antonio a-tall. There was only one, and he was the young French doctor who arrived in Corpus Christi from he city of Marseille. Only boasting about how he was the last of a long long line of Compts, and Bis-Compts, Barons and every kind of thing—and people used to go to hear him recite the names without interruption for three hours at a stretch—tracing he blueblood all the way back to Charlemagne the Great! He full name was *Dr Jewels Derrière-Cri de Plus-Bourbon*. But people used to call him Dr Jewels. So Don Antonio proclaimed that whichever one of the two Marías Dr Jewels chose would go with half he estate, and the other could return to Spain and marry sheself off to the convent.

So for a period of several months Dr Jewels would come every evening to take he dinner at the palace of Don Antonio. But Dr Jewels was famous in Corpus Christi for another thing besides he name, and that was he peculiar culinary habits. You see, the only thing he blueblood would allow him to drink was French champagne—that would be obvious enough—and the only dish he palate could tolerate was the legs of a frog, sautéed soft in butter. Of course, nobody had never even *thought* of eating those crapolegs before, that people said was surely food for the devil. And it was several evenings before the three Marías and Don Antonio could sit at the same table, watching Dr Jewels nibbling careful at them like little twigs, and not run in the yard quick quick to vomit up they *own* dinner. He would eat them one by one for hours at a stretch—the big red-and-white checkered kerchief tied like the bib of an infant around he neck—he eyes closed tight in complete ecstasy, he fingers and he waxed moustaches dripping with butter. But this vision of Dr Jewels at table was not even the worst thing about all these crapolegs, which of course would require a great quantity piled on the plate as tall as he *nose* to satisfy this Dr Jewels. The worst thing was that now, in addition to all she many *other* labors in the palace, now Iwana must spend several hours a day at that stinking Maraval Swamp, wading through the mud high as she waist, chasing behind all this multitude of jumping crapos. Then she must take out the froglegs and sauté them soft in the butter every evening, that every evening they could be ready in time for the dinner of this Dr Jewels.

After dinner he would take he snifter of cognac and smoke he cigar with Don Antonio. Then he would choose one of the two Marías—Dolores or Consuelo—and they would go and sit together on the back gallery, gazing up at the big moon floating above a glittering sea. Holding hands and reciting poems and professing they love to eachother—all the things that youngpeople did when they went courting—with of course, María Penitencia the chaperone always there beside them. Some evenings Dr Jewels would go for a walk along the wharf with María Dolores, or he would stroll through a sleeping Demerara arm-in-arm with María Consuelo, with of course, María Penitencia stumbling in the dark a few steps behind.

Soon the day arrived for Dr Jewels to announce his decision. So Don Antonio made a big fête in the palace to celebrate this event, and he invited all the important people of Demerara, including Fernando de Berrío heself. Because he had the ill-fortune to be in port at this same time, furnishing he fleet with fresh supplies. Early that Saturday morning the seamstress brought the gowns for the three Marías, white lace for María Consuelo and red for María Dolores, and of course, black for the gown and the big wide-brimmed hat of María Penitencia. With the three of them fussing the whole day long to get theyselves ready—the two daughters scurrying back and forth in the palace, each bubbling with excitement sheself—each convinced that *she* would be the choice of the young Dr Jewels. María Consuelo swore that in the moment of she passion one evening of sweltering poetry, the eloquent Dr Jewels—*even* with he mouth full—had pledged heself to her. And María Dolores proclaimed that just at she climax of he serenade one slippery and passionate night—poor Dr Jewels with he tongue in tatters—had promised heself forever to *her.* With Iwana running behind them both from the dawn of morning, bathing them and combing out they hair and attending them to dress in they magnificent gowns, and of course, she must prepare all the food for this big banquet tonight too.

Well those guests consumed a galleon-load of French champagne before the food could even reach the tables. And after they ate they first and second and they third courses—and then Iwana brought in the main course which, for Dr Jewels, was nothing more than he plate of froglegs piled up as tall as he nose—of course, the rest of those guests had to run in the yard quick quick to vomit up they *own* previous three courses. But after all that confusion, and revelry, and so on and so forth—when they could no longer sustain they suspense and everybody began to beat they spoons against they champagne glasses—at last Dr Jewels arose to ascend to the podium and announce he decision. But at that precise moment all they heard was the big explosion of cannons firing, everybody burying theyselves beneath the tables. Because of course, when Sir Walter heard the rumor that de Berrío was returning home to port for this big fête, he decided it could only mean they were celebrating he discovery of El Dorado at last. So of course he had to come straight away with he own fleet of ships, and launch another of he attacks on unsuspecting Demerara. He waited until the fête was in full swing, with all those soldiers so borracho they could hardly stand, and he fired off he cannons all together. But Sir Walter realized soon enough that de Berrío didn't find a fart again as usual—and the only treasure he could think in he moment of frustration to run off with was those two prize daughters of Don Antonio—both they magnificent gowns ruined with the stains of squids simmering in they own ink, both trembling with fear beneath the table.

So now de Berrío had to jump up quick and take off in he fleet chasing behind Raleigh, all the way up the Orinoco again, and attack him and take back the two prize Marías. Of course, now there was the same great preoccupation weighing down on everybody's mind, particular Don Antonio's and Doña Penitencia's. Because nobody really believed what they said about those English sailors, even after the evidence to document the proof. That it didn't have nothing to do with all they boasting about honor—all they feathers, and flowery gestures, and all they schoolgirl manners—because every single Englishman is a fairyboy in truth.

It was Dr Jewels heself who performed those inspections. Utilizing the probe of own educated little finger, with all Demerara waiting anxious outside the palace to hear the results. And before long he appeared gallant on the balcony to drape he kerchief over the rail—not the checkered one, but a special *white* kerchief this time—and then he retrieved the kerchief to repeat heself draping it over the rail a *second* time, the whole crowd bursting forth spontaneous in a great uproar. Because of course, this was the signal obvious enough for everybody to understand, that *both* those Marías still possessed they virtues untouched. Except of course by the Doctor's own little finger.

Don Antonio was so pleased he declared a festival to last for three days and nights. Everybody singing, and dancing, and drinking rum in the streets—that many people say how this is the true origin of modern day carnival—and when at last they were all exhausted, and stale-drunk, all with they voices hoarse from so much bacchanal, they dragged theyselves once again to assemble beneath the balcony of Don Antonio. Now Dr Jewels appeared again to announce he decision everybody was waiting in suspense for so long to hear, which of those two Marías he would choose for he wife, and which would return to Spain to bury sheself in the convent? But no sooner could he open he mouth when a *next* spontaneous uproar arose from the crowd—this time of cursing, and beating they fists in the air, and pelting rotting fruit—because what Dr Jewels answered, in all he youthful innocence, was that he didn't understand the question.

You see, just like all those sophisticated young Frenchmen of polish, and education, and plenty pretensions during that era, this Dr Jewels was a Socialist. That means of course he was an atheist too—and he didn't believe in Papa God, nor Pope nor King nor nothing else a-tall besides the power of *money*—so how could he *possibly* marry heself to a Roman Catholic like either of those two Marías? Dr Jewels said, just as you are expecting, that if Don Antonio still wanted him for he son-in-law, then the only way was for him to marry he *youngest* daughter, who was none other than the Princess Iwana. Because even though from a little girl Iwana had spent all she time in the church, running behind the old Archbishop, it never occurred to none of them even to pelt a little holywater and a pinch of salt over she head to baptize her. So before Don Antonio and Doña Penitencia could have a chance to think how they could get theyselves out from this pepperpot they'd found theyselves swimming in all of a sudden, the crowd let loose another spontaneous explosion of *cheering* this time. And just like true blue Caribbean people, they took off for another three days of carnival and bacchanal in the streets. Leaving Don Antonio and those three Marías standing there on the balcony, all cross-eyed with they mouths hanging wide open like if *they* were a family of lizards now catching flies.

So first thing Dr Jewels had to build a house adequate for heself and Iwana to live in, and he built the biggest one, on the highest point of the whole island. It was a *castle* bigger than Sandlord's own, bigger even than the palace of Don Antonio. With walls that were five feet thick of solid coral blocks, and it had more than a hundred rooms, each with a window looking out over the sea. And the bedroom of Dr Jewels had its own fireplace—a big bed with the canopy above, and a bathtub with the golden feet of a lion below—and hidden behind the bookcase in the library was a secret door. That door opened to a narrow hallway with a deep dark hole at the end, like a waterwell without the water, and a long ladder to climb down inside. Then a tunnel to crawl on hands and knees all the way beneath the foundations of the castle, then a stone staircase winding around and around climbing higher and higher, until you reached to the highest point of the roof. Then there was a next door of rusty iron bars and a big rusty padlock, and of course, beyond this second door was the tower of this castle. It was open to the open air, only a piece of thatched roof in the corner, and beneath the roof was the bed. Only a little bed with a prickly coconut-fiber mattress, and attached to one leg of the bed was a long rusty chain. At the other end of this chain—with a next padlock and a rusty neck-clamp clasping secure around she neck—was of course Iwana, sitting naked on the little bed. But Iwana was happier living in the tower of that castle than she had been in all she life!

Now she didn't have that household of Don Antonio to take care of, with those three Marías and the old Archbishop to run behind from dawn of morning until late into the night. Now she didn't have she cold dark cell in the basement to sleep the stingy few minutes Doña Penitencia would allow her at the end of she wretched days. Because in truth, there wasn't nothing in the world Iwana loved to do better than *sleep!* Now she would crawl out from under she piece of thatched roof to stretch sheself lazy beneath the sun, she skin a glittering gold, eyes half-closed beneath she thick dreamy lids. The whole day long, not even a worry in the world! And she never felt lonely nor hungry neither, because from that first day in the tower iguana came to visit her.

Understand, there beside this castle was the tallest and oldest tree on the whole island. And Johnny, this ain't no beanstalk we're talking about! This one was a giant *kapok* tree, the royal silk cotton, with the tallest of its branches hanging just above the piece of thatched roof. Iguana—who was the only creature on Papa God's earth able to climb so high—iguana would drop from out the tree to land safe with a *thwack* on the thatched roof, and she would go to visit with Iwana. That first morning iguana happened to be chewing the last piece of a soft green dasheen leaf, she favorite food, and of course, Iwana's eyes lit up straight away. She hadn't seen a tender dasheen leaf like that since she was a little girl. That same night was a fullmoon night, and early the following morning iguana brought her a big bundle of leaves tied together with twine. With the two of them chewing happy together the *whole* day long—pausing every now and again only to stretch out side-by-side for a nap beneath the sun—both they eyes half-closed beneath they dreamy lids. Until late one afternoon, with the sun sinking slow in the glittering sea beneath a crimson sky, when they were startled awake by the rattling of Dr Jewels in the padlock.

Iguana didn't have no choice, and neither did Iwana. There wasn't even time to scramble beneath the bed and hide sheself. Because of course, like everybody else on the island, iguana had long ago heard about the peculiar palate of this Dr Jewels. And Johnny, the tail of an iguana doesn't taste so different from the legs of a crapo a-tall! In the space of a breath Iwana had stretched out one of she long golden legs toward iguana, and iguana scrambled up quick along it, disappearing sudden inside!

But as much as everybody on the island knew about the unusual *culinary* habits of this French doctor, nobody had never heard nothing before about he peculiar palate for sex. And that was a fortunate thing for both iguana and Iwana. Because if he did he business normal like everybody else as you would expect, Dr Jewels would have discovered iguana hiding inside Iwana straight away. But Johnny, in order to partake of *he* particular kind of pleasure, Dr Jewels didn't even need to take off he clothes. On the contrary, he dressed heself up in more clothes, if you consider the big red-and-white checkered kerchief he took out from he back pocket, and he tied it up like the bib of an infant around he neck. Now Dr Jewels took hold of the rusty chain attached to the neck-clamp around Iwana's neck, and he led her over to the little bed. But he didn't do it rough, nor brute, nor in any way cruel! Because the truth is that despite that rusty chain—despite the padlock and neck-clamp and all the rest—this Dr Jewels always handled Iwana like if she was a china doll. Like if she was a fragile little bird, and he put her to sit gentle on the bed, she back resting cool against the coral wall. Now Dr Jewels opened up she legs. He went down on he knees beside the bed as if he was no longer the Socialist-atheist a-tall, but he was a better Catholic than all of us, only preparing heself to say he evening prayers. As if he was sitting at table before he cherished plate of froglegs sautéed soft in butter—and he smoothed back he stiff moustaches with he eyes closed tight in complete ecstasy just the same—Dr Jewels bent over careful beneath Iwana for he evening feast.

Papa-yo! What Dr Jewels tasted, of course, was not Iwana, but *iguana,* hiding sheself inside Iwana. And of course, he'd never tasted a pussy so *sweet* as that in all he life! Because this Dr Jewels, due to he medical profession, had the opportunity to study a great variety. And he'd sampled every thinkable flavor and nationality, from French Bordeaux, to Italian oregano, to English pussies doused in they double cream. Hindu palori pussies, German pussies boiled in beer, and Portugee cavinadash pussies pickled in garlic. This Dr Jewels had the opportunity to sample Chinee sideways pussies, Singapore squinty-eye ones—even the incense-smoking *Catholic* pussies of those two Marías—since this particular preference of Dr Jewels was the only *un*perilous kind of sex condoned by the Church. But Johnny, he had never before tasted nothing like Iwana, who in truth was iguana.

And so every evening it was just the same. Soon as the sun began to sink beneath the sea, and iguana and Iwana heard the rattling of Dr Jewels with he key in the gate, Iguana would scramble up she leg and hide sheself inside Iwana. And Dr Jewels would take out he red-and-white checkered bib from he back pocket, and he would go down on he knees beside the bed for he evening feast. But Johnny, it is only fair to Dr Jewels to tell you that after a time, Iwana had learned to close she eyes just the same. After a time *Iwana* discovered she pleasures in those evening visits of Dr Jewels too. Until she could no longer tolerate the intensity of she own excitement, and she would shove he head tender away. And Dr Jewels, always kind and respectful of Iwana, would wipe he whiskers and fold up he bib again straight away in he back pocket, he would bow he head gallant before her, and he would hurry out the gate.

Every evening it was just the same, as I was saying. And almost before Iwana could realize the years had passed. But hidden away like that high in the tower of this castle, Iwana could never know of the happenings of the world at she feet. Of course, iguana would keep her informed to a certain extent, and she brought her fresh news every morning. Of the most recent events in Demerara, of the latest attacks of Sir Walter on Fernando de Berrío, of de Berrío's retaliations on Sir Walter Raleigh. But there was one piece of news iguana could never find the heart to tell Iwana. It was news of she own Amerindian people, of she royal family at home, of the Arawacks, and Caribs, and Warrahoons. Of how all those Europeans were killing them off fast enough. Putting them as slaves to grow the cane and make the sugar—and tobacco, coffee, cocoa and *all* they crops—and they worked those gentle Amerindians and beat them with the cat-of-the-nine-tails until they dropped. Iguana could never find the heart to tell Iwana that in truth, all she royal family had perished long ago, and there wasn't a handful of she people still walking the earth. Because Johnny, already those Europeans were bringing shiploads of *new* slaves to this Caribbean. New ones to replace the perished Amerindians. These slaves came on ships from *Africa.* And iguana never told Iwana that even in the castle of Dr Jewels, there wasn't but a single Amerindian slave remaining. Now they all were Africans.

Dr Jewels *heself* began to change, as if to coincide with all these changes of the world. By now this Dr Jewels had become a rickety oldman, frustrated with heself and he own feeble oldage. He no longer treated Iwana so kind, nor gentle, and Johnny, some of he activities during this period were too nasty to name. Iwana and iguana soon came to *despise* he visits each afternoon. Then, one afternoon with no warning a-tall, Dr Jewels appeared in the tower accompanied by another. It was the first time in *all* those years he had not arrived alone. This time—attached to a next rusty chain with a next neck-clamp and padlock—Dr Jewels brought with him the new slaveboy he'd purchased that same morning in the market. And Johnny, when Iwana heard the rattling of Dr Jewels in the padlock that afternoon, and she opened she half-closed lids to see the creature standing there beside him, *now* she sat up straight away. Because Iwana had never seen a man so *beautiful* as him in all she life! Similar to Iwana, this young slaveboy was a prince from the royal family of he own Yoruba people. Tall and strong with rich purple skin and the grace of a panther moving beneath the trees, a gentle look on he face, and he name was *Anaconda.*

Dr Jewels took out he red-and-white kerchief just the same. He went down on he knees at the bedside before Iwana, just as he did every evening. But this time he held in he hands the chain of Anaconda, standing there beside him with he head turned to look the other way. Because of course, he would never look at Iwana to shame her so. *Never!* And now—when Dr Jewels had satisfied heself and he folded up he kerchief again in he back pocket—now he *didn't* bow he head gallant to take he leave as usual. Johnny, now this wicked Dr Jewels wanted the *additional* pleasure of observing Anaconda, doing what he, in he feeble oldage, could never manage heself. He commanded Anaconda to strip heself naked. Anaconda obeyed. He order him to lay heself on the bed beside Iwana. And Anaconda lay heself down. Now Dr Jewels smiled wicked and he smoothed back he waxed moustaches, and he ordered Anaconda to kiss Iwana. First she mouth, and then she soft breasts. Anaconda obeyed. But quck as Dr Jewels could issue the next *in*human command—Iwana trembling with fear in Anaconda's strong arms, frightened for both sheself *and* iguana—Anaconda took pity, and he called up those special powers that he had brought with him across the sea from Africa.

Johnny, just like all those Yoruba princes of royal African blood, Anaconda could change he shape at will to the very creature that bore he name. And in that same instant, Iwana looked down to discover only the thick black snake squirming on the bed beside her. With Dr Jewels standing there astonished, nothing in he hands but the rusty chain and the empty neck-clamp! Quick as a breath Anacaonda climbed up onto the piece of thatched roof above they heads, up onto the nearest branch of that kapok tree. Because despite the fact that Anaconda could never climb *up* a tree so tall, he could climb down easy enough! Dropping one branch to the next until he reached safe to the ground. And then—the most curious thing of all—Anaconda crawled straight into the waiting crocusssack of Dr Jewels. Because of course, Dr Jewels had hurried heself back down the stairs, and he was there waiting beneath the tree to hold Anaconda prisoner again.

It happened the same way every evening, time and time again. Anaconda taking he animal shape and sliding away at the last minute, with Dr Jewels hurrying down from the tower to capture him again—of he *own* volition—as soon as Anaconda could reach the ground. Until one evening when the sun was just disappearing beneath the glittering sea, the whole sky burning a bright crimson, and Anaconda could never resist the temptation to pause there on the branch a moment to take it in. Then he turned to watch Dr Jewels hurrying out the tower gate, rusty chain and neck-clamp dragging down the stairs behind him. And then—so strange a sight he had to blink he eyes twice before he could *believe* it—Anaconda watched iguana wriggle sheself out from inside Iwana. He shook the head, and he was just about to write it off as another one of those meaningless, magical events common enough in folktale-stories like this—ready to drop down to the next branch and begin he descent again—when he happened to see something else to sadden he heart: the two of them were weeping. So now Anaconda dropped instead with a *thwack* back to the piece of roof, and he slid down the post again to question them why.

They both answered together, Iwana and iguana, speaking both at the same time. And they told him, of course, they were both in love with him. Each, of course, with the appropriate shape. Anaconda looked up at the crimson sky a moment, and filled with sadness heself, he told them that he, too, was very much in love. To such an extent that he was willing to surrender heself a prisoner to Dr Jewels every evening, only to enjoy the kisses of beautiful Iwana again. An *impossible* love! But just as soon as he said this a spark lit up in the depths of Anaconda's dark eyes. He smiled, and he told them both to dry they tears. "Let me study me head *good* tonight," he said. "And tomorrow evening, I going to tell you what we will do!" With that Anaconda slid up onto the thatched roof, he climbed up onto the nearest branch, and he began he descent down the great kapok. Down toward the ready crocusssack of Dr Jewels.

The following evening Anaconda waited for Dr Jewels to take he leave as usual. Again he dropped with a *thwack* to the piece of roof, and he slid down toward Iwana and iguana, a smile shining on he face. "Listen!" he told them both. "What I going to do is take off my skin. And I want iguana to put it on. Tomorrow, when Dr Jewels comes to take he feast, iguana must crawl up inside Iwana just the same. *Then,*" Anaconda said, smiling he knowing smile, "we going to see what we will see!"

And that was just what happened. Anaconda took off he long skin, and he slid away blushing like a little boy. But Anaconda's skin was a size many *many* times too long to fit iguana. She put it on just the same. And just as you would suppose too—all those ages and ages ago when the earth was young sheself—iguana was still a fresh younggirl. She skin as soft and smooth as a new zabuca-pear, golden and glistening without a blemish to the tip of she tail! But Johnny, by the time iguana finished dressing sheself in Anaconda's long skin, she didn't look like no springchicken *a-tall.* Now she looked like the oldest ramshackled creature on all Papa God's earth! Like a ratty old rastaman, he dreadlocks hanging down below he waist, so many wrinkles did iguana have now around she neck, she belly and all about. *So* many wrinkles that she had to struggle and struggle to squeeze all that extra skin inside Iwana, the following afternoon when Dr Jewels arrived with Anaconda, he big key rattling inside the gate.

After only a single sour taste of *Anaconda,* Dr Jewels opened he eyes wide wide for the first time ever during he evening feasts. He looked inside Iwana to see all those endless oldlady wrinkles, in that very pussy which only the previous day, he had tasted smooth, and sweet, fresh as a fresh younggirl! Dr Jewels jumped up in a rage straight away. He rushed to the wall of the tower to spit the sour taste over the side. And Johnny, then something happened that nobody could anticipate a-tall. Even me, and I have been telling this story for so many years. Now Dr Jewels turned around to see beautiful Iwana lying there on the bed, handsome Anaconda there at the bedside also—two of the most *beautiful* creatures ever to walk on Papa God's golden earth—and he saw for the first time the reality of those wretched chains around they necks. He contemplated for the first time the wretched state that was the world—which, in good measure, was he *own* doing—and without the least forewarning a-tall, Dr Jewels threw heself from the tower to he death down below.

Just like that! The story was over already, before anybody was ready to see it finish. Because Johnny, the only thing remaining was for iguana to crawl out from inside Iwana, so Anaconda could make love to her for we tale to have its happy end. But then something *else* happened that neither of those three, nor nobody else could have ever suspected. You see, when iguana wriggled sheself out from Iwana at last, she couldn't help but leave half the wrinkled up skin inside. And iguana tried to wriggle out *sheself* from all that wrinkled up skin she was wearing, she *couldn't.* All that skin had stuck—to Iwana and to iguana—and so *both* of them remained with they wrinkles to this very day. It's true, that's the way they got them. And Johnny, when you grow older and you have the opportunity to look for youself, you'll find all those wrinkles folded up inside just the same. Just as I am telling you. But don't worry, because Johnny, one more thing that I can tell you about iguanas too—*despite* all they wrinkles—is that both of them remained young and sweet sweet forever!

This, of course, Anaconda knew as good as anybody else. So with the sun just disappearing beneath the glittering sea, all the sky above them painted a brilliant crimson, Iwana and Anaconda could make love to each other at last. And the next morning, Anaconda taught her the trick of how to change she shape. Iwana *became* iguana. Then Anaconda changed to he serpent self too, both of them climbing down from the giant kapok tree. They disappeared inside the forest, where they have lived happy together to this very day. Only on occasion, when the moon is full with the scent of the forest green like the first day Papa God breathed life in the earth, do Anaconda and Iwana feel a longing to change they shape. Only on occasion to they surrender, and only to make love together like human beings.

Overland

Pamela Ryder

THERE IS TALK, NOW, of the Paca Bunta.

There is much to-do made each night of procedures to repel them; much ceremony in the placing of the boughs of stinkwood beyond the light of night-watch fires; in the sprinkling of stinkwood ash out past the perimeter of our sleeping places—the little hollows that the porters and the bearers have scooped out in the earth, shaped to fit the shoulder and the crest of hip. There is much attention to the spreading out of the skins of springbok, the hides of wildebeest and zebra—the bedding down beside the tent where Burton burns his lamp and charts our passage; much talk, again, of how the rattling of pods, the chants, the singing to drum beats will appease them; of how the crushed leaves, the ash, the scattering of shredded bark of stinkwood touched to a drip of blood from the loins of anyone willing to be pierced with a shard of cowry shell will slow their progress—("Just a scratch, John," Burton says, and he lets them make the laceration); much telling, again, of how the taking of a bit of gore from any porter, guide or bearer willing to be penetrated with the tip of our stolen calipers will keep them back—will keep the Paca Bunta (or, as those who say they have seen them say the name: Bunta—simply Bunta) back, and then again, there is much talk from the older ones who dig their sleeping hollows deeper, who have lost their share of surplus flesh in the district called The Land of Ants—that nothing will.

("Clean bone," says Mgongo Thembo when we ask about the drum beats.

"Broken reed," he says. "Knife no blade. Slow bucket."

"Bad news, then?" I ask him.

"Hoo! Bad, sir," says Mgongo Thembo. "Hoo! Hoo! Very much bad.")

There are those among our party—mainly the guides for hire (one of whom, I suspect, has taken my pocket pedometer)—who say they have seen the great nests of the Paca Bunta in the grasslands—the mounds they build above their subterranean cities; the quarters for their excavators; barracks for marauders; chambers for egg cases; crypts they use to keep their stores of stolen shreds of meat.

There are some that travel with us—natives of the northern deserts—(one of whom, I now believe, has made off with my compass)—who say they have come across remains of men overtaken by the Bunta—carcasses of slave traders within the slack and rotting trousers, the corpses of their captives still shackled at the feet. This they speak of when they show us the blades they have fashioned from a shinbone or whittled from a rib. This they tell us when we ask if we are at all close to the cold stream Burton believes to be the source of the Wrong Way River or if we have passed the route of tusk trade that turns south at lower elevations; skirts—at some point—the mountain-high lake named Smoke in the Sky; approaches—in that proximity—the marshes made by the supposed seep of its headwaters, takes us further into the interior, leads us overland, and in the end turns west out to the coast. This they answer when we ask if the centimeters of our map showing fields of scree and scoria we may assume to be reliable; if the concentrics of topography can at all be verified; if claims regarding the location of the lake that feeds the Wrong Way River we may take to be accurate; if rumors of the water we seek a dozen days west of where we are (or where we think we are, or where we were a week ago—a month ago—"some time ago" is what we say) have been borne out.

They answer with a lengthy bout of deliberation. They continue with a stint of bickering, proceed to hair pulling, foot stamping, howling and drum-talk, then finish with their fingers moving all across our map. Finally a bearer or a porter steps forward and points out to the horizon. He squints into the western light and says, "There the water lives, the sun waits; there the sky bends."

Burton smiles at such remarks, at what he takes as quaint. "The sky bends, John," he tells me. He claps the bearer on the shoulder. "Yes, yes! Good man," Burton says, and folds away our map.

He sits among them nightly. He takes his notes into his tent, pencils in distances. He examines the specimens: seeds, beetles! Leaves the men say are medicinal! He takes more interest in the tales the bearers tell of flying mice and diving spiders—expends more energy penning a recollection of a picturesque beggar, or in making a sketch of a spittle bug or chrysalis—than he does in taking a trophy tsessebe or a fine horned buck. Evenings we see him, writing by the lantern light until he emerges through the canvas flap. He limps to the fireside, unwraps the bandage. He has Mgongo Thembo apply the masticated pods to the place where he has let himself be cut.

"Think of it, John," Burton says, "as a simple field experiment. Primitive medicine. Potential anti-infectives," and he sits with them in their circle, drinking the same fermented muck they drink, passing the bottle skin, poking the flames. I have seen the things that they will cook—bats snatched in their dangling sleep, mossed sloths, rodents that whistle; but nothing antish, never a one of them kinish to Bunta. No, the things they devour they dig up or take from inside the carcass of a kill, pull from within the twist of sloughing innards, or pluck from contented sucking tight to a taproot: invertebrates defined, ash-dusted; writhing creatures they turn inside foliage fastened petiole tucked into leaf tip and set among the coals to roast. Served hot. Never salted. Said to be tender. Stashed sometimes in their packs for a good long spell and retrieved for eating when advanced to what Burton likes to call "a fine putrifaction". They gobble, they slobber. They dress their beards with drippings and use an ankle as a napkin. Burton sits and shares such feats as these with them, while the steaks of a fine blue duiker I bring back from an evening's shooting goes to waste.

"Phylum Annelida," he says, blowing on bulge rolled within a steaming leaf. "Segmented, saprophytic." He licks at his fingers. "A species quite interesting for its protuberant sperm funnel," he says, "and the position of the slime tube, the concealed dorsal pore." He holds up a hunk of something skewered. He sniffs the thing and says, "Come and sit, John. Eat."

("Fire stick," says the drum. "Black ash. Clay bird. Empty pot.")

They watch us eat—the Bunta do—Mgongo Thembo tells us. They send their scouts, he says, to learn our scent, to eat from the cast-off ribs of roasted Kudu, the pieces of beast whose bones we have sucked and still bear the smell of our saliva, the dent of our teeth—parts we have so carelessly strewn about our evening fires. One gourd bearer whom I believe to be a half-wit (not withstanding his clever attempts to steal my pocket chronometer) says the Bunta lookouts sit upon the boughs of stinkwood we so prudently place outside our evening camp. There they wait until the morning when we empty our basins of whiskered shaving water and fold away our tents. And when we have packed up and moved on, they swarm in over the wet where we have pissed the last of last evening's embers out.

("Third moon," says the drums. "Sore foot. Stinkwood splinter. Yellow blood.")

It is said that the Bunta mount the body of a sleeping man in unison.

It is said that no amount of brushing or beating of one's body will dislodge a one of them; no amount of plucking will persuade their tiny biting parts to release their grip upon the flesh.

One tries to flee, not knowing the attacking flank spans a full kilometer. One staggers, and falls—smiling—or so the bearers say.

"Hoo! Hoo! Very bad!" says Mgongo Thembo, elaborating.

"Ataxia," says Burton, "followed by euphoria. Undoubtedly a toxin secreted through the pincers—formic in origin; paralytic, probably; initially sequestered deep in their salivaries."

"Rubbish," I tell him. "Daft talk and ravings. We speak of intruders at a picnic! Invaders of the pantry for a bit of damson jam."

("Bad hunt," says the drums. "Hornbill bird. Grilled root. Kaobab.")

("Hoo," says Mgongo Thembo.)

"So few gourds left," I tell Burton when we move on in the morning.

"No shaving, John," he says. "No bathing. No side trips for hunting. No stops for tea."

We will drink—when we must drink—the watered blood and curdled milk in bottle skins the bearers keep. We will break camp in the cool of early dark. Set off. Suck stones.

Leave before first light when the earth is still cool enough for their kin—for the kin of Bunta—to be stirring, to be unburrowing themselves; to be rolling away the balls of dung that seal their dens, to emerge from the sticky pistil of a night blooming flower, to scuttle from the mouth of a fallen bird, creep from under the frond that made their midday shelter from the heat.

There is talk at night to these small things—these kin of Bunta—with links of undulating legs, chitin backs and bivalved bodies. They speak to them—these arthropods that stretch the timbral membranes in their bellies drum-head tight to make their whirring songs or rake their rough-scored legs along their wings to speak. It is these small folk, who, our bearers say, will talk with Bunta. Will say our names to Bunta—the names of each of us—and tell them that we have come far, that we mean no harm, that we want only to find the place the river was born, to name the place the river was bornin—*is* born in every day, they say—water, our bearers say, that comes the same as water before the birth of something they still are waiting for.

("High lake," says the drum. "Cold stones. Water bird. Bright wing."
"A bit off course," I tell Burton of a detour through the hill country.
"Coleoptera," he says, of a beetle up his trouser leg.
"Coral bead," says the drum. "Ivory comb. Print cloth. Looking glass.")

These tiny beasts the bearers take with nets made of their hair, or with snares woven of vine, or with spider's silk procured by prodding large arachnids until strands are shot from ventral spinnerets. (So strong is this substance, we have seen the great spiders here capture godwins and guinea fowl, wind them neck to tail with silk as if they were spindles, and to keep them from their frightful peeping—add a last bit about their beaks.)

These kin of Bunta the bearers set loose from their nets, with great care unwind the strands of hair or vine or silk from what has been captured in the dark—untangle the needled stinger, the stylet, the beaded feeler; release the pedicled mouth part, proboscis, protuberant ovipositor. And then, snares undone, they kiss the iridescent shells of these arthropods never listed in our taxonomy, place them on their dark palms and breathe them off, set free to carry our message to the Bunta, back to their subterranean metropolis of tunnel and chamber.

"Tarawat!" they say to send the creatures crawling off or taking flight. "Tarawat!" they say. "Sik!"

("Low on salt," I tell Burton.
"Hypertrophy of foreleg," he says, of a hard-winged kin of Bunta.
"*Barton's Botany* is infested with booklice," I tell him.
"Sexual adaptation," he says, "for copulatory clutching."
"No more holcus-scones," I tell him.
"Highly effective," he says, "for grasping through a wing slit."
"Sik," says the drum.)

"Say," I tell him, "we come to water. We find the stream—the one cold enough to be the outlet of the high lake we seek. Say we fill our gourds, our skins, and there we cross and follow."

"Yes, John," says Burton, puffing on the stick-pipe and passing it on. "Say we do."

"Would not all this talk of Bunta cease? Would the bearers say the Bunta stop and leave us at the banks?"

"Mgongo Thembo," Burton calls. "Ask the men, the drummers: if we find our way and we cross cold water—will it stop the Bunta?"

They begin the familiar rhythms. They scatter the stinkwood. Ash in the air, palms to drum skin: slap, slap, Bunta. Slap, slap, slap.

"Hoo! says Mgongo Thembo. "Bad, sir! Very bad! Tiny boats of folded leaf!"

(Slap, slap. Slap, slap, slap.)

"Tiny boats?" I ask Burton.

Burton smiles and shrugs. He rubs the wound inside his thigh and lets Mgongo Thembo apply the poultice. He takes another swallow. He is stupid with the drink. "Smoke, John?" he says, and he coughs and offers up the hollow stick.

I will not sit, as he does, at their fire. I will not, as he has, forego civility, forsake the use of a napkin or plate. I will not crouch in the dirt and distribute our strands of trade beads, our shards of penny looking-glass or our best bolt of calico with whomever comes calling at our camp—the hunting party, the slave escaping, the so-called local king who has for his kingdom castles of reed huts, scepters of chip-stone.

I will not sway with them to the sound of their chanting, or decorate my face with stripes of yellow clay.

Will not shed my trousers and dance about on one good leg with them in the firelight.

Will not lay down as he does upon the reed mat with the women the king offers us in our honor upon the night of our departure; will not bed them in the name of anthropological exploration; will not watch as they lift their bark skirts so I may select my favorite orifice; will not watch while they dress their heads with fat of kudu or smear their heathenish holes with an unguent of rancid butter.

I will not let the one who makes their medicinals feed me a leaf for the purpose of scientific inquiry; will not weave a fringe of feathers through my beard as a study in culture or let savages slather my genitals with mud.

"John," he calls, "Come see"—(that grin of his when he gets half mad!)—and he shows me how big his prick has grown, how marvelously thick, and how the mud along the shaft cracks and flakes. And I see. And it has.

("Smoking stick," says the drum. "Yellow clay. Fine buttock. Coarse hair."

"Common sphinx moth—the order Lepidoptera," Burton says, when he stumbles to his tent and finds the shaggy creature laying dead inside the lantern glass.

"Low on gunpowder," I tell him. "Nearly out of lamp oil."

"Too badly singed," he says, "to be a proper specimen."

"Etching of dentrites on the lens of the telescope."

"Order of Strepsiptera; vestigial forewings; life cycle notable for sexual dimorphism."

"Aneroid nonfunctional: atmospheric derangements."

"Rudimentary organs for mutual stimulation."

"Pocket watch crystal smashed; main spring over-wound."

"Penile maturation in periods of drought."

"Smoking spoor," says the drum.

"Swinging tail," says Mgongo.

"Calf of kudu," says the drum. "Blood on stepstone. Torn flank. Old lion.")

I bring down a reed buck. Heart wound. One shot. The bearers take their bone blades and slice the belly open. The porters set it roasting, dripping on a turnspit. The flesh is lean. We have no salt.

"This grassland variety, Redunca arundinum," Burton says, tearing at his portion. "Too bad it's nearly tough as mutton. Save the skin as specimen. Bottle up the blood."

The bearers drag in deadwood. Mgongo Thembo brings the last of our brandy. Burton swigs and soaks his beard. The bearers scatter the bark of stinkwood. The circle of sleeping hollows are dug. The hides are spread. Mgongo Thembo reports on the state of our provisions. Burton props his leg. I oil our pistols. The stinkwood crackles and smokes. The sun sets. The shapes of thorn trees and aloes grow dimmer. The boulders fade into the dunnish color this up-country landscape takes on at dusk. Silhouettes of acacias buckle in the updraft, limbs awash in the spark spray of burning, in the dying lights above the dark-hilled horizon where the sun sleeps, where the water waits. Where the sky bends above the nameless place the river was born in.

Burton talks of women; I—of game, gun and saber. He unbuttons his trousers. He shows me where his groin is dark and tender, how his prick is swollen hard. He takes a final swallow. He speaks of home—of the fields and the stables; of polished boots and the finest saddles. He slings his arm across my shoulder. The stinkwood snaps.

The green sticks hiss. We sit side by side as the burning logs sink and shift, and we sit and we speak like men.

Night drums merge with the sounds in dreams—the chatter in the treetops; the hooting in the canopy; the snuff and root from the leaf-rot floor as a serpentine tongue is shot from a snout and comes back sticky with centipede or Bunta. Around us is the clicking of insect pincers in the stinkwood, their insistent drumming in the forest stands of ficus, the grind of a clock key, of a hairspring winding.

They move along the limbs; they meet along a stalk. Inseminating parts are spent and devoured. Stacks of eggs are inserted into stem slits, deposited into corpses. Erect ovipositors are sunk into dung balls for leisurely incubation fueled by decay. Larvae hatch, crawl, sleep. Duplication of wings. Exoskeletons split. Emergence from the nymphal skin is marked by the beat in a drum-hollow belly, by a membrane of vibration or a rasp-edged appendage that signals their solitary, synchronized flight; the announcement of night navigation by moon, by stars, by flame; by hot sparks that the night wind lifts. By burning wick that illuminates our tents and brings a shadowy flit across the span of canvas: their jointed bodies, their symmetry of wing.

There are apparitions in sleep; there is sense in dreams: Burton, in the lamplight, standing at the tent flap, firm, unfevered. "John," is all he says, all I need to have him say. All I need to hear above the ratcheting of limbs, the tapping on the lantern glass. The night turns cool. The narrow cot. The taste of brandy of his tongue. Pulse of drums. Beard to chest. Crest of hip to crest of hip. Clutch of foreleg. Drip of loin. Limbs pressed, damp. Muscled cleft. Dungish hole. The skin stretched tight.

("Sik, sik," is the sound of the wingbeats on the canvas, the membrane in the body.

"Calabash," goes the sound. "Many seeds. No worm."

"Riverweed," says the drum. "Slipstone. Mud in the mouth.")

Morning, and two bearers are, as they say, among the missing—snuck off, apparently, sometime in the night; taking with them loose tea, our knife for skinning, Greenwich watch, match tin, salt cellar (empty), brass telescope.

"Stars, John," says Burton, "They haven't taken the stars and we still have the sextant." I see he will not stand without his crutch. He barely sets his weight upon his leg.

We are slowed down in this hard country. There is no tree, no shade or stream. Thickets of heath adhere to the hillsides. Thorn-bush acacia sprout from the rock dust. Occasional cactus: yellow-spined, barrel-stemmed, rooted along seams of basalt. The terrain is strewn with slabs of mineral—chert and obsidian—great fractured plates of it, mostly volcanic, now hot again clear through the boot. Burton struggles along with his crutch of stinkwood—off balance as we travel the rough gullies. He calls to me when we must clamber over the rubble of rock and brush. He falls back when the trail we make tilts up.

We are made to take our rest out in the sun, but there is no sense in this.

We lighten the weight in the loads of the bearers: toss away a cook pot, a kettle, the trade beads, the cutlery.

The cactus has pulp. We suck the juices out.

Mgongo Thembo retrieves a spiny rind we toss off and shows us the single Bunta clinging to the wet.

"A large specimen, a good two centimeters," says Burton. "Banded cephalothorax, longer antennae—a lone scout, perhaps, or just a lost individual." He lifts it to eye level and speaks in a whisper: "Have you come to catch us, little fellow?"

"Hoo!" says Mgongo Thembo, smacking his head. "Very bad luck to speak to Bunta! Talk only with kin or cousin!"

"Very much pardon us!" he tells it, and sets the fruit skin away from us upon a rock. "Tarawat!" he says, bowing. "Sik!"

("Low on lump sugar," I tell Burton. "Out of iodine."

"Diperta," he answers, swatting at a sweat fly.

"No more rope. Short on pitch. Half spool of rush twine. Fish hooks rusted."

"Probably related to the lowland tsetse."

"Matches damp. Candles melted. Whetstone cracked. Spirit level leaking."

"Stone fly species, partial to sucking. Seminal vesicles packed into appendages."

"Nearly out of vitriol. Last dose of laudanum."

"Tiny soul," says the drum the bearer now is beating. "Low cloud. Great swarm. Long walk. Clotted water.")

We lean into the hillside, stepping slantwise, making a foothold in the spaces between stones. Mgongo Thembo, from somewhere in the lowlands, is unused to such climb and descent. ("Hoo!" he says, when we show him the map and we ask which of these dark countries he is from. "Hoo!" he says. "Far!") He slips from the trail and slides a ways into the rift. His pack splits. The strap breaks. We watch the flask of ink explode, the biscuits become airborne, the sextants bounce. My horn-handled knife is a small glint of blade stuck fast and far away between the rocks.

"Hoo," says Mgongo Thembo, when we haul him out. "Hoo."

("Sik, sik, sik," comes the sound of what we first think to be drums, but drum beats could not reach us here across these corridors of rock. "Sik, sik, sik," it comes again—the beat and rattle of the skin of Bunta with bodies that blend with the color of the stones, wings the shape of blades, appendages of thorns.)

New terrain ahead of us: grass, kaobab, grass—a broad stretch. Beyond that, a green border. "Wetlands," says Burton, "At last, perhaps, the river valley." He jams the sharp end of his stick in a crack. "John," he says, "Give a hand and help me up."

There is a dark place on his trousers, stained with what leaks from him and when he moves, there is a smell, however faint, like the kind from certain fungi. Sweet, yet fetid—the sort that might bring flies. I sniff at my clothes and wonder if the stink is just the decomposing cloth, or the powdery earth mixed with my sweat and turned to slime. Or is it I, at last begun to rot?

"Hymenoptera," says Burton about something hovering. "Cousin to the Ichneumon wasp."

The bearers hoist their packs. We walk on.

We pass through the flatland: high grass, hard earth, herds of gazelle known only by the nod of head and horn and black pellets of spoor.

The trail becomes thick, the terrain wet, without the growth of succulent or thorn. Here is all ficus, liana, broadleaf shrub. Bromeliad tucked in crotch and fork. There is seep, great rot, smells we are uncertain of. Overhead is heard the hush of larval forms chewing through bud tips—the leaf miners, the pith splitters, the soft-bodied creepers and cocoon spinners. We hear the rising stridulation of forms largely arboreal. The earth gives. We clutch vine and runner, misjudge handhold, fooled by aerial root. We fall into the muck. We see light ahead where the foliage thins. Breakthrough of sun. We find the riverbank.

What water is this?—we ask our bearers—as fools would ask: could this be the source of the great Wrong Way River?—and we unfurl our map, spread it flat with our forearms, and take our pencils up.

"Why," says a bearer, "this is the water that settles in the corners of the eyes when a thorn finds a home in the foot."

"What wets the skin," says the other, "when the sun is high and the man must be running."

"The same," says the last, "that fills earth holes in the season that the sky is dark."

"That water, sir," says Mgongo Thembo. "There is no other!" and so we lift our arms to let the paper loose and roll back up.

He brings us our box kit of instruments, releases the brass catch, lifts the teak lid: survey compass missing its needle; condensation under the stopwatch crystal; elevation thermometer cracked clear through, leaking quick silver onto the felt. But, it is no matter—no use would there be in making our measurements—this river feels too warm to be source water. We know the instant we step in.

We shed our clothes, and bathe in the shallows. Burton soaks himself, squeezing fistfuls of sopping river grass into the spot where he was cut. "John," he says, "look here," and waves me over. "The swelling has subsided somewhat," he says. "Well? What do you think?"

I think, sometimes, I hear the drumbeats when we are too many days beyond the sound of any drum or village.

I think I hear them say the name of us, or any name I say along to the sound of them, or anything I seem to want to hear. Some nights I hear them say the same sik, sik, sik, they say to kin of Bunta.

In dreams, some nights, I know the kind of language they speak.

We rinse water vessels of the soured curds, dark clots. We fill the skins. We fill the gourds. We find a trampled path to the water where hippos lumber along, gather momentum, fall upon their bellies and with great abandon and joyful bellow, mud-slide in. We watch the shores for what moves and what might slither. We see a great-beaked thing lifting its yellow legs, stalking the pools.

"Marabou," says Burton, and he calls for his book and his pen, but we have no ink. He takes up his pencil, but he makes no note or mark. "Perhaps," he says, "just a white-bellied stork—habits comparable to the vulture or other carrion eater."

"Comforting," I tell him.

"John," he says, "We'll walk out yet. The both of us have grown too thin to be anyone's meat."

We make camp, peg the tents, prepare to rest and study our maps. There is water here, at least. And game, good shooting: gemsbok and water buffalo at the stream, come to drink. Evening brings an easy kill. We have only the bone blade to cut the skin and section the meat. We call the bearers, both of them, to clear a fireplace but they sit and look away from us. Mgongo Thembo speaks with them, but still they sit; they will not come.

"Bad smell, sir," says Mgongo Thembe, pinching the end of his nose. "Blood in the wound stinking like a river sitting still; like a lake with no stream out."

"Sik, sik, sik," I hear the bearer tell the porter on his little skin drum, tapping out his song as the night sounds start.

"Tarawat, sik, sik," as they pile on the stinkwood.

"Sik, sik, sik"—becoming a comfort—the bearer's small brown fingers to the hard stretch of drumskin. His thumb across his thumb and his hands the shape he would make for a shadow play of butterfly or bird, bending at the wrist, fading to the distant backdrop of a dream. Becoming the recollection of a cry between our breaths, between the beat of beating hearts, between the dull and final pulse within swollen appendages.

"Sik, sik, sik"—it comes, calling back the morning with its slow smoking cinders and the rocks varnished black by the resin of the stinkwood.

"Sik, sik, sik"—through the circle of sleeping places where the porter and the bearer had pretended to sleep and looked to the east where the sky is known to bend and the first light lives. Where they waited for the light and they abandoned the hollows they had scooped from the earth for the comfort, for the crest, for the slope of the hip.

"Sik, sik. Bird, sir. Bone blade. Horn blade."

"Sik, sik. Sucking bee. Honey gone. Rope over."

"Hoo, sir! Hot leaf. Folded boat. Bad, sir."

"Coleoptera. Hymenoptera. Dorsal pore. Damson jam. Formic in origin."

"Stinking river. Bad, sir. Sik! Sik! Sik!"—is the sound in the circle of snouts just out of sight of the circle of sleeping places; whiskers quivering to the scent of a fine putrefaction; to the smell of our stinkwood fire gone out, of a limb gone dead, of the dank and mildewed canvas we drape upon the poles of stinkwood.

"John," Burton says as he settles into the litter, "I'm afraid I've become such a bother this trip." We set the poles upon our shoulders and we lift him. We step into the river. The stones are all slime, all humped—pushing hard into sole and instep by his weight. The cobbled bed gives way to the soft bottom and the river comes up waist high, pouring in and filling the sling up to his neck.

"Odonata," Burton whispers, of a flat-winged fly that has landed on the canvas. "Rectal gills for respiration; larval forms are largely aquatic."

We push apart the tangled roots of hyacinth to make a path through the spiked blooms and stalks. Bottom silt rises around us. We are red-brown and rusted where the water leaves its mark; black upon the streamer of bandage that floats beside us—a foul decoration undone by the current with the slough of crust and skin and muscle. We drag the litter up. We cough and spit away what has slid inside our mouths. The hammock leaks its runnels down the slope.

"John," he says, and he has me by the wrist. He pulls me down to him, close to his mouth. "Tonight we will camp with open sky above us. We will see the stars and find out where we are. And when the drum sounds start and the fever makes me sleep, you will set the lantern close by and use the blade."

The bolt of calico is wet. I take the cloth in my teeth and tear it into strips.

We sit, the three of us, and watch the river. Clouded where the canopy breaks. Opaque where it skims over rock. Bright where it parts for a snake.

We watch the sway of river grass, the downstream spread of silt. The spiked blooms of hyacinth we have broken loose.

"Hoo! Bunta!" says Mgongo Thembo, now on his feet and peering upstream at what is coming: a flotilla of leaf fall, wide as the river is. A fleet of green, pushing through flotsam of petal and twig. Leaf after leaf is what is coming, turning in the current, creased along the midrib and keeled by petiole, brimful of tiny, antennaed passengers, riding pincer tight.

"Hoo! Bad, sir!" says Mgongo Thembo. "Sik!" he cries as he scrambles up the bank.

Burton's mouth is open. We bind his wrists with rush twine so he will not dangle. We tie him at his feet so he will not thrash. The sun is higher. The clouds have parted. It is past the time for leaving. It is getting hot. We will be late today in starting up.

We will stay ahead of them, the Bunta. We will keep on now, now that we have crossed this river. We will keep a steady pace this time, making progress, leaving their battalions behind us. We will be moving now while they are bivouacked at noonday, while they are awaiting the return of the ones sent out to reconnoiter but return bearing no news of our direction, no notion of our whereabouts; telegraphing down their ranks with the tap of crooked antennae and the wagging dance of distance; moving onward as their marching narrows to the trickle of single file, flowing over what has fallen and withers on the floors of the rainy forests, winding through the stems of the grass on the great savannas, scrambling over rubble of clod and pebble, tumbling into the craters we have made where our boots have stepped and sunken in, deep with our weight.

We will be far beyond them—the Paca Bunta. Ahead of the procession that slows down but never stops for its stragglers, dilates with the convergence of their bodies, distends with the spreading edge of their numbers, the flux of a multitude that swells, surges, widens as the red-brown water of a river spills over where no river ever is.

Tonight we will camp and wait for sleep and the sound of drums from somewhere. ("Reed mat. Marabou. Blood melon. Cold river.")

We will listen between our cries; we will wait between wing beats. ("Full basket. Palm heart. Pomegranate. Wasp honey.")

The pulse of the blood will come, and the sound of palms to the drum head: the beginning hum and timbre of a skin stretched tight. ("Tusk. Tusk. Mud wallow. Kaobab. Weaver bird.")

We will wait for the drums—what we hope will be drums—but we know we will be left waiting. We will listen for the sound but there will be only the drumming from within a hollow abdomen, the vibration of a belly part.

There will be the buzz of a tibial spur, of rasped appendage pulled along a cross-scored thorax.

There will come the sound of flint clean-flaked to a spearhead; the chip-sound of rock becoming a cutting tool, drawn across our limbs or a limb of stinkwood; the saw of a riverstone turned into a blade, sent through hide, through skin, pushed through muscle; the sound of a rib whittled sharp for penetration, wound at one end with a rush twine handle; slim and sharp for the piercing of the femur; fine-edged and serrated for the slicing of meat.

We will hear the noise we will make upon the body by the lifting lights of sparks and the flames of stinkwood: the sound of a sliver of chert; the sigh at the insertion of a shard.

The singing of obsidian, of basalt, through flesh.

The sound of bone on bone.

Obituary

Han Ong

ALL THEY HAD WAS a picnic table. One leg was uneven but the table was long enough for five people to work at comfortably and the three-plankboard top was sturdy. Somebody measured the uneven leg and returned with a sawed-off piece of plywood to prop underneath it. It was important the thing didn't wobble. For what they had to do, an accident could mean the difference between life and death. Five would work together, two on one side, three on the other, with a sixth, the man whose idea it was, walking around to supervise.

The sixth's know-how had been picked up from pamphlets you could buy at the right underground places: bookstores run by anarchists who were anarchists more in theory than practice, but who nonetheless believed their act of brokering information, because illegal, was in itself taking action. In these places, the clerks were not the owners and usually had the looks of punkers and the demeanor of tokers to signal their remove from the world which you saw on the nightly news, full of changes and consequences, but which was fucking rigged and full of puppetmasters they didn't want manipulating their consciousness, too. And so, they could be counted upon to ring up what you bought without registering what it was they were ringing up. Aside from how-to bomb pamphlets, you could pick up S&M literature; porno—straight, gay, pederasty, bestiality; videotapes of animal slaughter made by animal rights activists to discourage meat consumption but which had found a specialized niche with cruelty fetishists; books purportedly written by ex-CIA operatives on how to kill a man and erase the evidence, written by professional hit men on the tricks of their trade; catalogues from companies specializing in spying and surveillance devices; surveillance videos of celebrities caught with distorting expressions of cruelty or orgasm on their faces; and so forth.

His name was Bruce, from Portland, with a penchant for places catering to the fringe, which was how he'd found himself in the bookstore, and how he came to be with the Lost Sons in the first place.

At the Lost Sons he had found a place that valued him without asking any but the essential question: was he white in spirit as well as in body? But he'd been here for two years, and was now twenty, and he could feel that maybe he wanted something bigger for himself.

Bruce had picked up the pamphlet in downtown Seattle, the clerk not even bothering to look at him, making useless the precaution of a Halloween moustache. Back at the farm, he'd read it backward and forward. Then had made a small bomb of his own, cutting to a tenth the original measurements of ingredients, pouring them one by one into a child's beach pail. He'd capped the finished product with a plastic lid cut down from a large Quaker Oats lid. And then had set off for the nearby woods. He'd made sure to bring a fuse, whittled down from a piece of bark, and long enough for him to be able to get a running distance after it was lit, and in the end, with two thin, bare trees up in flames right beside where he'd set his creation, he was sorry he hadn't brought someone along to witness his victory.

The five people he would lead would be four boys and one girl, all of whom, it was presumed, shared sympathies which would extend easily into murder.

The girl had been Bruce's idea. It was the same girl they'd found at the Greyhound station in Seattle and who, seeming to have no will of her own except a murky, puppyish idea that she must somehow find a way to eat and a place to sleep, had followed them all the way up to the farm. Up until her arrival, thought Bruce, there had been no one worth fucking in the whole place. And that had been all he was thinking when he'd approached her.

Her father had deserted her and she would have to start selling herself to get money for food. He'd asked how fixated she was on her hair, and then explained that there was someplace she could go—with him—but that she would have to give up that beautiful hair of hers. Would she be willing to do that? She'd replied yes. And he'd asked her what she thought of white supremacy and once more, evincing a pliancy which he could only think of as doglike, she'd said that it was OK by her. She'd spoken in a flat, affectless tone that strangely, containing no emotion, provoked a lot of emotion in the listener.

The project was to be a secret from everyone else, and especially from Leonard Wright, the group's dying leader.

His son Justin would pick the locations where the bombs would be planted. Bruce had a kid's advantage of brio and ferociousness, but Justin Wright had a thirty-one-year-old's advantage of smarts and cautiousness, and so could provide the right check on anything suggested. He did not, as the kid did, see the hordes of bloodied corpses as the tail-off point of their campaign, the place where the story ended. No, the Sons had to be shepherded through the next, less dramatic phase of being sniffed out by the cops. That would involve a lot of waiting, while the police cross-referenced alibis, and even worse—though if Justin Wright had his way nothing would come of it—members could be made to appear before a police line-up and warrants could be issued for a property search. He'd seen his father go through the same ordeal. He'd learned calm under pressure and could pass it on to the next generation.

Part of this preparedness involved the thinking before the doing, which couldn't be carried out for too long or too exhaustively or otherwise they might not do anything at all. The trick was to learn to stop just short of withdrawing. Consequences imagined should rightly engender fear but fear should lead not to cowardice but instead to care, to increased cunning, to creativity. But with the boy, he knew that there would be no withdrawing: the kid was like a pinball struck; he would go on and on until he met his end. That was why he needed the kid. Because his father's legacy had been thinking, not doing, and he needed the hot blood of this new generation untempered by too much contemplation to fuse with his (even at thirty-one) old-timer's considered gun-shyness; otherwise to his dying day he would remain an armchair supremacist which, it was becoming clear to him, was no supremacist at all.

The kid would be the brawn, the guts, while he would provide the head and the heart.

He would remind them, should they begin to quease, as he knew they would, that the bodies lying dead were to be viewed as symbols of a symbolic war: This was their world and they were demarcating its parameters and the message had to be spelled out in human loss, in martial terms. He would draw parallels to history to inflate the platitude, Nothing worthwhile was won without effort, which by itself he knew would draw blanks in their minds.

He was the leader and the plan's success depended entirely on him. Every day his father grew weaker, with muscles further slackened from bed rest and his cheer beginning to desert him. His father's masculinity had been tied to his heartiness and now that heartiness had evaporated. Every day, a group of female recruits ministered to his father, feeding, cleaning, pushing and stretching his useless legs. His father saw their youth as a vampire stares longingly at an exposed neck. One day Leonard Wright would die, and though Justin was beginning to become clearer on many aspects of his plan, one thing that still hadn't become apparent was whether the first of these attacks would happen before his father died or afterward.

The girl, Clara, hadn't been excited when chosen. Not that she felt depressed either. She would do it. She smiled, fearing that it would look strange if she didn't. The five boys, including Bruce, had looked at her knowing why she was there. She knew it too, but what could she do? There was no refuting her uselessness.

She felt no closer to the group than when she was at the mess kitchen, preparing lunch or dinner. She was a good cook. Only then did she actually understand what it was to be granted reprieve from the everyday feeling of being alive and being nothing at the same time. She enjoyed everything about cooking: the measuring, the slicing of vegetables, the kneading of meat, the tending to the various pots and pans, controlling the flame. Adding the seasoning to the boiling vats of oil or water—which she measured out by instinct, using hands instead of cups or spoons—she could anticipate what the finished product would taste like, which made eating redundant.

She had broken through her reticence to volunteer for the job, and the girl whose place she took was more than glad to leave—she hadn't joined a group that espoused superiority and privilege only to be made servile and subordinate within the organization.

Clara hadn't minded. Nobody really took a good look at her while she was in the kitchen, but if they did, they would've noticed that for a brief moment the blankness in her eyes lifted. Nobody would have believed that the body that usually moved as if dressed in stone flitted about and that her skin seemed to redden as if some internal clockwork had woken her up. Most strange of all, that the bald head that had seemed such a decimation ceased to matter. She'd been prettified by activity, and for her that activity was cooking, or more accurately, *kitchening.*

The faces of the eaters never lit up. Her talent with food surely deserved no less a tribute. But nobody said anything. They were all too young maybe and didn't distinguish between eating and tasting. Or their minds were elsewhere occupied. She had never seen so many young people who went about their daily life absently, as if the present, shabby and shameful, was not worth the effort of being, well, *present* for. Instead, they all lived inside their heads, looking forward to a future that they were saving all their energies for. Only then would they awaken. Next to that future, the food that came out of her kitchen was nothing.

It was a future she could not, even after she'd heard it elucidated in meeting after vociferous meeting, understand; in this way, they reminded her of her former "family" in Corona, New Mexico, which her father had assured her would be the only family she would ever need but which, having disgusted him irrevocably, they were forced to shun. That was a few weeks ago. Now, here she was in the belly of another family whose members also had the same glinting eyes and hard-set jaws that suggested the determination to be prepared for a future happiness which would mainly involve the exacting of revenge on enemies.

She couldn't begin to understand why her father had deserted her, except to guess that whatever taint the Corona congregation acquired late in life had transferred to her as well. She had gone to live there with her father at age three. Now she was twenty. Seventeen years. Spent pining for the one moment which, when it was supposed to arrive, hadn't. Seventeen years she believed easily in God, who she'd been encouraged to see as flesh and blood, someone to be touched on that blessed day. And now she didn't believe anymore; flesh and blood had vaporized, turned ghost traces without the power to interfere in her life. She was shocked at how easy it had been to undo years of hard work. She was surprised that she could go on living without the faith that had so governed her life and her father's that it used to make her envision herself, before going to sleep, as a small pebble, rounded and without distinguishing protruberances or roughnesses, and most importantly, without an animating force from within, and yet somehow made worthy by being held aloft by a steady current of air, rescued from the earth's muck below. That current was God and he would never let her fall. And around her there were many other pebbles, all of them without speech or feeling, and yet still buoyed up, together forming a curtain stretching skyward and around the earth. She was one of them, insignificant except as a building block. Thinking which would ease her into sleep, comforted.

But she hadn't fallen, hadn't cracked, even when the current had stopped.

This new group saved her. Well, Bruce did. And since Bruce was so committed to the group, she felt obliged, out of gratitude to him, to do the same.

For the first four, five weeks, this gratitude took the form of cooking. Besides keeping her busy and away from Bruce's attentions, it gave her access to the food. In five weeks, she gained seven pounds. Her belly began to round, peeking out of her shirt. She hoped this would stop the boys looking at her. But it didn't work with them, and neither did it work with Bruce. Strangely she took comfort from the ooze of skin where her jeans met her waist every time she sat down. She felt like some primitive person in the Arctic fatting herself for the coming blizzard. She wasn't sure what this meant and also wasn't eager to uncover why, even though repulsed by pregnancy, she felt about herself that she was pregnant and didn't need to undo it.

She cooked enthusiastically and ate listlessly. And so did everyone. They all ate as if wanting to get it over and done with. Still, she took pride in her work, in her usefulness, and was convinced that the fault was with them and not with her.

Accustomed to the group's indifference, she wasn't surprised that nobody expressed regret when she was taken off mess duty by Bruce for a new unspecified job.

She would be the one girl, qualified only by the strength of Bruce's belief in her. None of the others said a word.

First Bruce demonstrated what to do: the measurements and order of the ingredients, one by one carefully poured into a plastic bucket painted black, all the while explaining about acids mixing with bases, etc. Everyday objects turned away from their everyday use, made mysterious by being reduced to their salient chemical qualities, revealing inside them, when combined in proper proportions with one another, the power to destroy.

The ingredients, by their feel and weight, refused to impart information through her hands and to her brain. In that way, it was nothing like cooking. She was simply following instructions. And though it somehow felt wrong to be mixing sawdust with orange juice, and then further blackening the mixture by pouring in nails which had been greased, and though already a little smoke arose when she continued to pour the Lysol and Clorox, she continued and didn't dare stop. And though she heard the serious words coming from Bruce's mouth, painting pictures of bodies of their enemies lying dead from their hands, there was a huge blank in Clara's head inside which her actions seemed at once remote and rote.

Five people, plus Clara, standing at the same spot where once before Bruce had set off a bomb. The woods, with the crystalline white-blue sky above, and the desolate grouping of sparse-limbed and denuded trees enclosing them, was like a stage set. Clara felt that Bruce had prepared the scene for maximum effect. Nothing would distract from the staggering proof of her ineptitude. Orange juice, sawdust, nails?

She was sure that the whole thing was a joke, and she would be its butt. The white fear radiating from inside her skull did not disarray her features, however, which remained as always blank and pretty and mysteriously riveted as if envisioned.

Bruce carried the black bucket and placed it on the ragged ring that looked like a predrawn sign, increasing the stagelike quality of the event. He showed them how to attach the fuse, making sure to insert it deep into the mixture and to look out that it didn't come loose, even though he told them they didn't need to be worrying about it because they would be using dynamite set to a timer. For today's purposes, a fuse would do just as well, for today the important thing was to see the idea behind their guidebook exertions concretized. A bomb was not a bomb unless it exploded, and they would be made to see how powerful their hands were, linked to the potential for death. Hearing this, Clara felt as if the message was meant specially for her, for whom their assembly line had not even felt real enough to register as a game, much less a full-blooded, no-turning-back first step in an adult campaign, and she blushed, or thought she did, because again, nothing rippled across the dead calm of her face.

One of the boys asked where they would get dynamite. Bruce told him not to worry. He would take care of things. Another asked if a timer wouldn't give itself away. Bruce replied that the trick was to store everything inside a container stuffed with insulation like cotton or blankets.

Any more questions? he asked, feeling his beautiful control over them.

Everyone said No.

Bruce lit the fuse.

Except for Clara, who balled both hands white at her sides, everyone expected the bomb to occasion the beginning of greatness in their lives.

Because the bomb had been stuffed with mangling nails that had a far greater reach than the actual fire and smoke and shake, they ought to have been standing farther back than they did. Bruce recognized this lapse in his leadership only after the thing had gone off. But thankfully, miraculously, no one had been hurt, and he didn't say anything.

On closer inspection, nails were seen studded into the limbs of trees, like Gothic growths. Wisps of smoke clued them in on where these nails were. Everyone made gurgling noises of wonderment. There was a scent that they could separate and tease out. Orange juice and Clorox and the fishy odor of the grease coating the three-inch nails, and overlaying everything the thuggy, brownish smell of things stuffed into an oven and forgotten, left to decimate themselves.

A thin tree that had already been blackened once before was now split cleanly into two, one half left standing with an exposed seam of bark running the length of its side, the other burning on the ground. Clara overcame her shock to formulate a clear thought: how Biblical. Bruce was schooled neither in theology nor advanced leadership, and therefore missed an opportunity to seize on the sight and speechify. Instead, the words he spoke helped them to fill in the desolate landscape with images of mangled, horror-movie corpses of niggers and chinks and all the rest of them who were draining the lifeblood of this country, siphoning the white man's share of the benefits due from this country's founding in which they did not share one iota of the labor, and were thus latecomers and ultimately beggars.

He didn't know that the likelihood of white corpses next to those colored ones, seeing that public spaces were going to be targeted, was high, and couldn't warn them, leavening the idea of victory with sacrifice, like gambling.

Each of those bombs, claimed Bruce, would do the damage just demonstrated, meaning that each of them could count on seeing effort pay off. To speak in video-game analogy, as Bruce proceeded to do, in terms of lock the target and fire, in terms of concentration and peripheral vision, was to tap into the current of his peers' brainwaves. For the first time since the project began, seeing the scene before them further familiarized by the invocation of the brand-names and playthings of their youth—things now revealed to have been more study and preparation than play after all—they smiled and laughed. That was how they eased themselves, as if sliding into protective coats preparatively greased, from boys into men. Up until then, though they were mostly twenty or a little older, they remained children. Most had dropped out of high school, out of their family's sight, out of wage-earning society. They grumbled their speech and dressed in T-shirts and jeans that distorted the royal lines of their lithe bodies, turning themselves slack as if in proud negation of being the inheritors of so much prosperity, even if this prosperity was more theoretical than actual.

They were poor, and though not intending to find the roots of their poverty, their discontent, were slowly provided one by the unity.

Except Clara. Her face was untroubled and blank atop the body in which her blood, postshock, had begun to circulate once more, though faintly. It was only when they were halfway back to the compound that she felt Bruce by her side, could sense his pride in her accomplishment, and then, farther down, just below her knee, could sense another source of heat, and discovered a welt that was about to bleed, and in its center, winking off and on as the light hit it, the head of a nail. For the first time, registering pain, she registered emotion.

Soon enough, they were back to the making of new bombs to replace the two that had been test-detonated. And this time, accompanying her work was the sensation, just as if she was back in the kitchen, that at the end something living could be affected by her efforts and that it would call out, like a pet to its master, or a child to its parents, her own name, rooting her to her fate. Hate animated her face. Hate for her father which, because new and surprising and in its first fervor, seemed like the corrective to her life of apathy. She hadn't realized she wanted her life turned around so much. And all it took was to imagine beyond the present task of pouring in cupful after cupful, the scene of desolation wrought which would include, among many inert, deserving faces, that of her father's, mouth open in arrested protest, or to explain the reason for his desertion, or to say to her that he finally understood the bigness of his act, not only of leaving her, but of creating out of a child of three a woman who would be the willing dupe of betrayals and who would at the same time construe them as her own failing. This hate which animated her Bruce mistook as a growing affection for the project, and therefore, for Bruce himself, and seeing this, he was strengthened enough to—one night, after both bombs had been rebuilt and they were only awaiting word for their first assignment—corner her outside and squeeze her hands, then her breasts, then plant a kiss on her mouth. This was when Clara once more felt a submergence and ceded to the man closest at hand the power to make the decisions for her. So in this way, hate was subsumed into something close to love, which for Clara meant surrender. And when she would look back on this episode in her life, asking herself the questions of why she did what she did, despite knowing their harm, their destructiveness, she would only say that she did it out of love. She would know at once how incoherent and incongruous she sounded, but she would also know that she wasn't lying, that she hadn't, out of a need for evasion, fabricated a mystery where a genuine one truly existed, palpitating right at the center of her recollected, unborn life.

The Moor

Russell Banks

IT'S ABOUT TEN P.M., and I'm one of three, face it, middle-aged guys crossing South Main Street in light snow, headed for a quick drink at the Greek's. We've just finished a thirty-second degree induction ceremony at the Masonic Hall in the old Capitol Theater building and need a blow. I'm the tall figure in the middle, Warren Low, and I guess it's my story I'm telling, although you would say it was Gail Fortunata's story, since meeting her that night after half a lifetime is what got me started.

I'm wearing remnants of makeup from the ceremony, in which I portrayed an Arab prince—red lips, streaks of black on my face here and there, not quite washed off because of no cold cream at the Hall. The guys tease me about what a terrific nigger I make, that's the way they talk, and I try to deflect their teasing by ignoring it, because I'm not as prejudiced as they are, even though I'm pleased nonetheless. It's an acting job, the thirty-second, and not many guys are good at it. We are friends and businessmen, colleagues—I sell plumbing and heating supplies, my friend Sammy Gibson is in real estate and the other, Rich Buckingham, is a Chevy dealer.

We enter the Greek's, a small restaurant and fern bar, pass through the dining room into the bar in back like regulars, because we are regulars and like making a point of it, greeting the Greek and his help. Small comforts. Sammy and Rick hit uselessly on one of the waitresses, the pretty little blond kid, and make a crack or two about the new gay waiter who's in the far corner by the kitchen door and can't hear them. Wise guys. Basically harmless, though.

The Greek says to me, "What's with the greasepaint?" Theater group, I tell him. He's not a Mason, I think he's Orthodox Catholic or something, but he knows what we do. As we pass one table in particular, this elderly lady in the group looks me straight in the eyes, which gets my attention in the first place, because otherwise she's just some old lady. Then for a split-second I think I know her, but decide not and keep going. She's a large, baggy, bright-eyed woman in her late seventies, possibly early eighties. Old.

Sammy, Rick and I belly up to the bar, order drinks, the usuals, comment on the snow outside and feel safe and contented in each other's company. We reflect on our wives and ex-wives and our grown kids, all elsewhere. We're out late and guilt-free.

I peek around the divider at her—thin, silver-blue hair, dewlaps at her throat, liver spots on her long flat cheeks. What the hell, an old lady. She's with family, some kind of celebration—two sons, they look like, in their forties, with their wives and a bored teenaged girl, all five of them overweight, dull, dutiful, in contrast to the old woman, who despite her age looks smart, aware, all dressed up in a maroon knit wool suit. Clearly an attractive woman once.

I drift from Sammy and Rick, ask the Greek, "Who's the old lady, what's the occasion?"

The Greek knows her son's name, Italian—Fortunata, he thinks. "Doesn't register," I say. "No comprendo."

"The old lady's eightieth," says the Greek. "We should live so long, right? You know her?"

"No, I guess not." The waitresses and the gay waiter sing Happy Birthday, making a scene, but the place is almost empty anyhow, from the snow, and everybody seems to like it, and the old lady smiles serenely.

I say to Sammy and Rick, "I think I know the old gal from someplace, but can't remember where."

"Customer," says Sammy, munching peanuts.

Rick says the same, "Customer," and they go on as before.

"Probably an old girlfriend," Sammy adds.

"Ha-ha," I say back.

A Celtics-Knicks game on TV has their attention, double-overtime. Finally the Knicks win, and it's time to go home, guys. Snow's piling up. We pull on our coats, pay the bartender and, as we leave, the old lady's party is also getting ready to go, and when I pass their table, she catches my sleeve, says my name. Says it with a question mark. "Warren? Warren Low?"

I say, "Yeah, hi," and smile, but still I don't remember her.

Then she says, "I'm Gail Fortunata. Warren, I knew you years ago," she says, and she smiles fondly. And then everything comes back, or almost everything. "Do you remember me?" she asks.

"Sure, sure I do, of course I do. Gail. How've you been? Jeez, it's sure been a while."

She nods, still smiling. "What's that on your face? Makeup?"

"Yeah. Been doing a little theater. Didn't have any cold cream to get it all off," I say lamely.

She says, "I'm glad you're still acting." And then she introduces me to her family, like that, "This is my family."

"Howdy," I say, and start to introduce my friends Sammy and Rick, but they're already at the door.

Sammy says, "S'long Warren, don't do anything I wouldn't do," and Rick gives a wave, and they're out.

"So, it's your birthday, Gail. Happy birthday."

She says, "Why, thank you." The others are all standing now, pulling on their coats, except for Gail, who hasn't let go of my sleeve, which she tugs and says to me, "Sit down a minute, Warren. I haven't seen you in what, thirty years. Imagine."

"Ma," the son says. "It's late. The snow."

I draw up a chair next to Gail and, letting go of the dumb pretenses, I suddenly find myself struggling to see in her eyes the woman I knew for a few months when I was a kid, barely twenty-one, and she was almost fifty and married and these two fat guys were her skinny teenaged sons. But I can't see through the old lady's face to the woman she was then. If that woman is gone, then so is the boy, this boy.

She looks up at one of her sons and says, "Dickie, you go without me. Warren will give me a ride, won't you, Warren?" she says, turning to me. "I'm staying at Dickie's house up on the Heights. That's not out of your way, is it?"

"Nope. I'm up on the Heights, too. Alton Woods. Just moved into a condo there."

Dickie says, "Fine," a little worried, due to the weather. He looks like he's used to losing arguments with his mother. They all give her a kiss on the cheek, wish her a happy birthday again, and file out into the snow. A plow scrapes past on the street. Otherwise, no traffic.

The Greek and his crew start cleaning up, while Gail and I talk a few minutes more. Although her eyes are wet and red-rimmed, she's not teary, she's smiling. It's as if there are translucent shells over her bright blue eyes. Even so, now when I look hard I can glimpse her the way she was, slipping around back there in the shadows. She had heavy, dark red hair, clear white skin smooth as porcelain, broad shoulders, and she was tall for a woman, almost as tall as I was, I remember exactly, from when she and her husband once took me along with them to a VFW party, and she and I danced while he played cards.

"You have turned into a handsome man, Warren," she says. Then she gives a little laugh. "Still a handsome man, I mean."

"Naw. Gone to seed. You're only young once, I guess."

"When we knew each other, Warren, I was the age you are now."

"Yeah. I guess that's so. Strange to think about, isn't it?"

"Are you divorced? You look like it."

"Shows, eh? Yeah, divorced. Couple of years now. Kids, three girls, all grown up. I'm even a grandpa. It was not one of your happy marriages. Not by a long shot."

"I don't think I want to hear about all that."

"Okay. What do you want to hear about?"

"Let's have one drink and one short talk. For old times' sake. Then you may drive me to my son's home."

I say fine and ask the Greek, who's at the register tapping out, if it's too late for a nightcap. He shrugs why not, and Gail asks for a sherry and I order the usual, Scotch and water. The Greek scoots back to the bar, pours the drinks himself because the bartender is wiping down the cooler and returns and sets them down before us. "On the house," he says, and goes back to counting the night's take.

"It's odd, isn't it, that we never ran into each other before this," she says. "All these years. You came up here to Concord, and I stayed there in Portsmouth, even after the boys left. Frank's job was there."

"Yeah, well, I guess fifty miles is a long ways sometimes. How is Frank?" I ask, realizing as soon as I say it that he was at least ten years older than she and is probably dead by now.

"He died. Frank died in 1982."

"Oh, jeez. I'm sorry to hear that."

"I want to ask you something, Warren. I hope you won't mind if I speak personally with you."

"No. Shoot." I take a belt from my drink.

"I never dared to ask you then. It would have embarrassed you then, I thought, because you were so scared of what we were doing together, so unsure of yourself."

"Yeah, no kidding. I was what, twenty-one? And you were, well, not scary, but let's say impressive. Married with kids, a sophisticated woman of the world, you seemed to me. And I was this apprentice plumber working on my first job away from home, a kid."

"You were more than that, Warren. That's why I took to you so easily. You were very sensitive. I thought someday you'd become a famous actor. I wanted to encourage you."

"You did." I laugh nervously because I don't know where this conversation is going and take another pull from my drink and say, "I've done lots of acting over the years, you know, all local stuff, some of it pretty serious. No big deal. But I kept it up. I don't do much nowadays, of course. But you did encourage me, Gail, you did, and I'm truly grateful for that."

She sips her sherry with pursed lips, like a bird. "Good," she says. "Warren, were you a virgin then, when you met me?"

"Oh, jeez. Well, that's quite a question, isn't it?" I laugh. "Is that what you've been wondering all these years? Were you the first woman I ever made love with? Wow. That's . . . Hey, Gail, I don't think anybody's ever asked me that before. And here we are, thirty years later." I'm smiling at her, but the air is rushing out of me.

"I just want to know, dear. You never said it one way or the other. We shared a big secret, but we never really talked about our own secrets. We talked about the theater, and we had our little love affair, and then you went on, and I stayed with Frank and grew old. Older."

"You weren't old."

"As old as you are now, Warren."

"Yes. But I'm not old."

"Well, were you?"

"What? A virgin?"

"You don't have to answer, if it embarrasses you."

I hold off a few seconds. The waitress and the new kid and the bartender have all left, and only the Greek is here, perched on a stool in the bar watching *Nightline.* I could tell her the truth, or I could lie, or I could beg off the question altogether. It's hard to know what's right. Finally, I say, "Yes, I was. I was a virgin when I met you. It was the first time for me," I tell her, and she sits back in her chair and looks me full in the face and smiles as if I've just given her the perfect birthday gift, the one no one else thought she wanted, the gift she never dared to ask for. It's a beautiful smile, grateful and proud and seems to go all the way back to the day we first met.

She reaches over and places her small crackled hand on mine. She says, "I never knew for sure. But whenever I thought back on those days and remembered how we used to meet in your room, I always pretended that for you it was the first time. I even pretended it back then, when it was happening. It meant something to me."

For a few moments neither of us speaks. Then I break the spell. "What do you say we shove off? They need to close this place up, and the snow's coming down hard." She agrees, and I help her slide into her coat. My car is parked only halfway down the block, but it's a slow walk to it, because the sidewalk is a little slippery and she's very careful.

When we're in the car and moving north on Main Street, we remain silent for a while, and finally I say to her, "You know, Gail, there's something I've wondered all these years myself."

"Is there?"

"Yeah. But you don't have to tell me, if it embarrasses you."

"Warren, dear, you reach a certain age, nothing embarrasses you."

"Yeah, well. I guess that's true."

"What is it?"

"Okay, I wondered if, except for me, you stayed faithful to Frank. And before me."

No hesitation. She says, "Yes. I was faithful to Frank, before you and after. You were a virgin, dear, and except for my husband, you were the only man I loved."

I don't believe her, but I know why she has lied to me. This time it's my turn to smile and reach over and place my hand on hers.

The rest of the way we don't talk, except for her giving me directions to her son's house, which is a plain brick ranch on a curving side street up by the old armory. The porch light is on, but the rest of the house is dark. "It's late," I say to her.

"So it is."

I get out and come around and help her from the car and then walk her up the path to the door. She gets her key from her purse and unlocks the door and turns around and looks up at me. She's not as tall as she used to be.

"I'm very happy that we saw each other tonight," she says. "We probably won't see each other again."

"Well, we can. If you want to."

"You're still a very sweet man, Warren. I'm glad of that. I wasn't wrong about you."

I don't know what to say. I want to kiss her, though, and I do, I lean down and put my arms around her and kiss her on the lips, very gently, then a little more, and she kisses me back, with just enough pressure against me to let me know that she is remembering everything, too. We hold each other like that for a long time.

Then I step away, and she turns, opens the door and takes one last look back at me. She smiles. "You've still got makeup on," she says. "What's the play? I forgot to ask."

"Oh," I say, thinking fast, because I'm remembering that she's

Catholic and probably doesn't think much of the Masons. "Othello," I say.

"That's nice, and you're the Moor?"

"Yes."

Still smiling, she gives me a slow pushing wave with her hand, as if dismissing me, and goes inside. When the door has closed behind her, I want to stand there alone on the steps all night with the snow falling around my head in clouds and watch it fill our tracks on the path. But it actually is late, and I have to work tomorrow, so I leave.

Driving home, it's all I can do to keep from crying. Time's come, time's gone, time's never returning, I say to myself. What's here in front of me is all I've got, I decide, and as I drive my car through the blowing snow it doesn't seem like much, except for the kindness that I've just exchanged with an old lady, so I concentrate on that.

Flight of the Swan

Rosario Ferré

WE LIVED ON KOLOMENSKAYA STREET THEN, where I did the laundry for several well-to-do families. One of them was the Poliakoffs, a very wealthy Jewish family. Lazar Poliakoff's father was a banker on Nevsky Prospekt; they owned one of the largest investment houses in St. Petersburg, with branches all over Europe.

One day I saw the son of the family come out of the house and he followed me to the apartment on Kolomenskaya Street. He was wearing a magnificent black astrakhan coat with matching hat of the same curly, jet black fur. He closed the door after him and asked my mother to go out and get him a pack of cigarettes. As soon as we were alone, he pushed me on top of the bundle of dirty clothes I'd been carrying and raped me. He came back every week after that, and when I had my little Niura, mother only had to see him from the window and she'd say: "There's the black mutton that dropped little Niura on our doorstep again; he's come for another pack of cigarettes."

Things went on like that for another year, and then young Lazar stopped coming. Much later I learned that the Poliakoffs had found out about their son's "mistake" and had sent him to the university at Le Hague to get him out of harm's way. They paid me a small stipend, so I could adequately feed and care for the child, and they had a Rabbi visit us, who taught her Scripture. Little Niura, as I always called her, had no idea who her father was but she knew she was different. One day, someone sent a photographer to the tiny apartment, and the man told us he was to take our portrait. He brought his 8x10 camera with him, and the clothes we were supposed to wear for the shot: two black silk dresses with tight sleeves and narrow lace collars. I was told to sit on a chair and Niura to stand a little distant from me, as if we weren't related. She was facing the camera with that expression of superiority I know so well.

Niura was petite and finely boned. Her legs were long and her feet were beautifully arched. She had a great affinity with birds—quick, darting movements and a light step—and the rich black silk of her sleeves made the long, tapered fingers of her hands look even more delicate. I myself am a large woman; I come from peasant stock. I was born in the village of Bor, on the banks of the Volga, whose waters are white as milk because it's the river that nurtures Russia— and my hands are as large as a man's. But I'm an honest woman; I've always worked for my keep. My knuckles are red from scrubbing the clothes of the rich, and I don't see why I should hide them. So when the photographer told me to slide my hands discreetly under the folds of my dress, I placed them squarely on my knees, to make sure they stood out in the portrait.

A few days later, the photographer came back to the apartment and gave me a print of the portrait in a cardboard frame. I liked it very much and put it on the living-room table. I wondered if the photographer had taken a print to Niura's father, also; the black mutton that had stopped coming to butt her. "Maybe he was going to cut me out of the picture entirely," I thought, "or maybe it's a convenient way for him to prove that his little girl's mother was Russian and if he were caught in a pogrom, it might help him survive." Lazar must have guessed I would never give up Niura, though, because he never offered to adopt her.

Ever since Niura was a little girl she loved to dance: if it was snowing outside she'd copy the way a snowflake drifted down the window pane; if it was autumn she'd sway exactly like a leaf fluttering in the wind. Once, when she was in the park with me, she saw a dragonfly and began to imitate its nervous flight with marvelous precision. The Rabbi saw her do this, and he must have said something to the Poliakoffs, because a few days later he brought me a note from Lazar's father. The Poliakoffs were a cultured family, and they had influence in all the right places, because the note said I was to take little Niura to the Imperial Ballet School on Theater Street, between Nevsky Prospect and the Fontanka River—St. Petersburg's most exclusive district—and leave her there. I'd be able to visit her on Sundays, and she would be well taken care of. I was shattered, but I prayed to the Virgin and left little Niura in their hands.

I had seen the Imperial Ballet School from the outside on my way to service at Vladimir Cathedral from Kolomenskaya Street. It was an elegant eighteenth-century palace, with many windows to let in the light and large salons with thirty-foot ceilings. When we arrived and I asked how much the tuition would be, a lady in a black shift said I shouldn't worry, everything had been paid for in advance. She handed Niura two brown cashmere uniforms, four white muslin shirts, a pair of pumps and a pair of short leather booties, books and study materials. I looked at the woman in wonder, but didn't dare ask questions for fear it would all evaporate like a dream.

The pupils of the Imperial Ballet School were formally adopted by the Tsar; parents virtually relinquished all rights over them. Niura was a boarding student for ten years. She loved it there. The school was run with an iron discipline based on military principles, the same that ruled the Imperial Cadet School. Niura's days were spent in rigorous exercise classes to develop her body, and she took courses on harmony, composition and musical theory. She could read music and even direct an orchestra. I thought all this was wonderful, but my old fear hadn't left my heart, and I prayed every night when Niura finished her studies she could stay by my side.

The Imperial Ballet School owed its existence to the Tsar's subsidy, and the Romanovs considered the ballerinas their personal baubles. They went to the school often, to observe the students' progress; or just to talk to them about art, music or perhaps more private subjects, discreetly discussed. Niura saw the Tsar several times up close during the matinees given for the parents of the students. Like most Russians, she had ambivalent feelings toward him.

Every year, on December 6th, there was a lavish celebration for Tsar Nicholas's birthday. On that day the theater was full of small children and young people: tiers of boxes tightly packed with girls and boys in uniform from the lyceum, the Naval Academy, all the popular St. Petersburg schools. Every child received a box of candies with either the portrait of Tsar Nicholas, the Tsarina or the Tsarevitch on the lid. During the intermission, tea and refreshments were served in several foyers, and the wait staff wore gala red uniforms adorned with Imperial Eagles on their collars. Cool almond milk, deliciously perfumed, was served. On one occasion they were all taken to kiss the Tsar's hand after the performance. Nicholas II was sitting in the Imperial Box next to Tsarina Alexandra, and they must have been going to a ball afterward because both were regally dressed. The Tsar wore a blue sash across his gala uniform and the Tsarina had on a coronet of stars. The Tsar asked: "Who was the little girl who danced the golden fish in *Le Roi Candaule?*" Niura stepped forward, and curtsied gracefully before him. "How did the shepherd's magic ring happen to be on you, when it was supposed to be at the bottom of the sea?" Niura was wearing a fish costume, modeled out of gold papier-mâché, and inside the fish's mouth was hidden a small box where the ring was put. Niura bent down and explained how it worked. The Tsar was enchanted. He smiled. "I would never have guessed it," he said.

You can imagine Niura's amazement when the next day she heard that the Tsar, who was such a nice man, had gone on a hunting expedition to the province of the Urals, where there was a terrible famine. He came back ten days later with 100 deer, 56 goats, 50 boar, 10 foxes, 27 hares—253 animals shot within a week's time. "Why did he shoot them? He can't possibly eat all that," Niura asked. Poor heart, she was that innocent!

The day of Niura's graduation I was terribly proud of her. Her grandmother came all the way from the village of Ligovo to be there, and Niura looked beautiful in the white tulle skirt and delicate diamanté wings in which she danced *Les Sylphides,* her graduation ballet. All the dancers took part and the audience was mainly composed of parents, although the Royal family was also present. They were sitting in the Marinsky's Royal Box, just to the left of the stage, with the gilded crown carved on top and the gold fauteuils with blue velvet upholstery. They looked just like a postcard: Tsar Nicholas with his watery eyes; the Tsarina with her hard, unyielding German mouth; and their five children, all dressed in angel-white muslin. It was hard to see them as the oppressor, or a flock of devils in disguise.

I had sewn the wreath of tiny roses that Niura wore that day around her head and she looked happy and carefree during her graduation exercises. That's why I was so surprised when, a few days later, she arrived at the apartment carrying two suitcases with everything she owned. She was moving back with me, she said, and we would have to change our lifestyle. "At school we were taught that progress in the world depended not only on the quality of our dancing, but on the magnanimity of our patrons. I'm tired of being poor, Mother. I should have made that my motto to start with." I sighed with resignation. Now we would both have to survive on the small income the Poliakoffs sent us, which was barely enough for one person.

When Niura began to get flowers from bewhiskered, portly gentlemen who brought her home from the theater in splendid carriages late at night, I began to worry. One evening I went to her room after she had gone to bed and said, "You don't have to do this, Niura, I can go back to washing and ironing." Niura looked at me with her large, luminous eyes. "Thank you, Mama," she answered. "But my dancing will support us both; you have nothing to worry about." That calmed me, because my little Niura was never wrong.

Every time I saw Niura dance at the Marinsky, I thought the same thing. Sitting high up in the gallery I could see the audience in the orchestra seats below, sumptuously dressed in lace and velvet and glistening with jewels, and onstage I saw the dancers wearing similar apparel and jewelry. No wonder *Le Mirroir* was St. Petersburg's favorite ballet. The aristocrats were convinced they deserved it all and were fascinated by their own spectacle, while in the countryside the peasants continued to starve, because all the food was needed for the soldiers who were fighting a war against Japan.

Matilde Kschessinska was Prima Ballerina when my Niura graduated. They danced together at the Marinsky a few times, and were always competing for the limelight. Matilde also had many followers who would have done anything to advance her career. Being older, she had much more experience than Niura. She obtained the favors of Nicholas II when he was still the Tsarevich, and he bought her a magnificent house on the English embankment, a very fashionable address. Matilde loved to dance wearing the jewelry the Tsarevitch gave her as a present. Sometimes she wore three diamond necklaces at a time, which made her look like a poodle because she was short and wore her curly hair cropped close to her head. She was not a great ballerina. She was polished but only danced "on the surface," to entertain the audience. She never danced from the depths, like my Niura did.

Tsar Nicholas had many artist friends, not all of them dancers. One of the most famous was a little girl, an American diva whose name I can't remember. She was ten years old, and created a furor when she appeared at the Winter Palace singing "Ah! non giunge" from Bellini's *La Sonnambula.* She was warbling like a nightingale and standing on a little red plush platform with wheels when they rolled her out to the center of the stage. The ovation was so great that the Tsar and the Tsarina sent for her at the end of the performance. That was the same night my Niura danced in *Le Roi Candaule.* She was very young, but she never forgot the doll-like diva, dressed in a fanlike frock and wearing a hussar's red jacket, who threw her a rose as she went by. The Tsar presented the young prima donna a coronet of diamonds that night, a smaller reproduction of the one the Tsarina was wearing.

At this time Niura took a large apartment in Anglisky Prospect. I didn't know how she could afford it, but it was better not to ask. It was a new building, and we were to move in together. I was ecstatic. It meant I didn't have to be separated from my daughter again. I'd cook for her, wash and iron her clothes. No one was to know I was her mother, so my presence wouldn't embarrass her.

The apartment was beautiful: all big, lofty rooms decorated with white Empire furniture upholstered in blue silk. Niura's bed had a latticed headrest and footrest, with garlands of roses carved over them, and her bedspread was exactly the same ice blue color of the Neva which could be seen flowing by from her window, layered in winter with a thick crust of snow and glistening beneath its muffled rumbling. In what was once a salon for entertaining guests, Niura set up her own dance studio, with an immense mirror on one wall and an exercise bar the length of the room on the opposite side.

The income from Niura's friends and the Poliakoffs' stipend meant we could begin to live with a certain degree of comfort. Niura also began to make more money dancing. Whenever she performed at benefits and galas people flocked to see her, because it was rumored she came from a humble background. This was pleasing to people with Bolshevik sympathies. Matilde Kschessinska's Imperial connections were harming her, and although she still held the title of Prima Ballerina at the Marinsky, Niura was gradually taking her place in the public's eye.

Niura never showed any interest in meeting the Poliakoffs, for which I was grateful, although I always suspected she was secretly proud of her Jewish blood. It set her apart from the Petersburg *haut monde* we both despised. Although no one knew who Niura's real father was, one of Kschessinska's friends at the Marinsky might dig up the secret by asking questions about my illegitimate daughter, and it could lead to Niura's expulsion from the city.

The Imperial Ballet was not exempt from the upheavals tearing Russia apart. Many of the dancers were students at the university and were thus very well informed about political developments. Niura began to attend Bolshevik meetings and one day she stood up on a desk at school and made a forthright speech in which she poured scorn on an army that cut down defenseless people and saw innocent workers as the enemy. She was the daughter of the washerwoman from Kolomenskaya Street, she said, and she had everything to gain if the Revolution was successful. She lent her apartment to the students of the ballet school that had gone on strike, so they could meet there. Then one day the Poliakoffs shut down their bank and unexpectedly left the country. Niura and I were left practically destitute.

The night she found out about it Niura was dancing *La Fille Mal Gardée—The Unchaperoned Girl*—a ballet full of verve and playful coquetry at a benefit gala for the families of the sailors that had perished in the destruction of the Russian fleet. At the end of the performance she received a bouquet of roses in her dressing room with a card from the "Honorable Victor Dandré" attached to it. Each rose came skewered to a piece of wire and Niura couldn't bear the sight of them. She asked me to free them from their torture, taking out the wires and putting them in water. I did so immediately and placed the vase on her dresser.

The Honorable Dandré wished to invite Mademoiselle to a private dinner at his apartment after the performance, the card said. Niura received dozens of cards like that every night. This time, however, instead of ripping the card in two, Niura penned a quick answer on the back and had it returned to her admirer.

Victor Dandré was a frenchified Russian who had lived in Paris for a while. He was tall and bear-chested, with a red mustache that compensated for his bald pate and large, ruddy jowls that trembled when he laughed. He was known in St. Petersburg as a successful investor, and had a comfortable situation. That night he invited Niura to one of the city's many luxurious restaurants with private chambers at the back. Afterward they went to Dandré's plush apartment on Italiansky Street.

"Our economic problems are over, Mother: now we won't have to starve or sell our home because of the strike. I've finally found the protector the Marinsky Imperial Ballet School always expected me to have," Niura said. I began to cry; I understood well enough. I made her kneel down before the icon of the Virgin of Vladimir and ask for forgiveness. Niura kissed the lower corner of the icon and bent her head in front of it. The decision had cost her a great deal. She'd always looked down on Kschessinska and the other ballerinas, who readily accepted the Marinsky's patrons' demands in order to go on dancing.

Mr. Dandré always kept his bachelor place in Italiansky Street; he never moved in with us. Niura didn't feel attracted to him, but he was a strong man and a shove from him would send any unwelcome admirer crashing against the wall. At that time Dandré had a theater box at the Marinsky, which he shared with a gentleman friend, and he went to see Niura dance every evening. He realized she had a unique talent, and that if she stayed in Russia she'd never be able to free herself from the "shroud of the Imperial Ballet School," as he used to say. She was stifling at the Marinsky, where only old-fashioned ballets were produced; in Paris and London she could blossom into a true artist. One day he suggested she go on tour and visit Helsinki, Riga, Stockholm and other cities of the Baltic coast.

She could dance there accompanied by a small troupe and he would escort her part of the way. The tour was an enormous success, and after that Niura began to go abroad more often. When the Bolsheviks came into power and Niura's house in St. Petersburg was expropriated by the government, Dandré convinced her to buy a house in London, in the suburb of Golders Green—William Turner's famous Ivy House—so she already had one foot out of the country.

Then we sailed off to America. Our first tour took the company across the whole United States by train. We visited forty cities, from New Orleans to Seattle, in a span of nine weeks, and sometimes Niura had to dance two performances a day. She earned thousands of dollars a week, but at the end of the tour she didn't have any money. Mr. Dandré mapped out pulverizing schedules for her and would disappear with the profits at the end of each month, although he insisted he spent it all on our traveling expenses, new costumes, salaries and hotels. We stayed in New York for a while, where Dandré made Niura appear in all kinds of advertisements—like Pond's Vanishing Cream—which was perfect for the image of Niura fading away in a swan costume.

Mr. Dandré was already middle-aged when Niura met him; he was half-bald and had a little paunch, which pulled like a grapefruit at the starched front of his shirt. Some said he was corrupt, and it wouldn't have been surprising. In Tsarist Russia that was common, everybody was like that. But he was very affectionate with Niura. He spent a fortune on her designer clothes because he insisted it was good for business. In his opinion, every little American girl's dream was to be a ballerina, so Niura had to look exactly like a ballerina's dream.

When we traveled to Paris, Niura joined Diaghilev's Ballets Russes at Monte Carlo. For a marvelous season she performed with Vaslav Nijinsky as her partner, but she didn't stay long.

She was out of there like a bullet and returned to the Marinsky. She's always been proud as a princess and never danced second to anyone. She's been Prima Ballerina Assoluta in every company she's ever danced with. Vaslav Nijinsky, on the contrary, who came from a humble background, was an easy prey for Diaghilev. Sergei was the son of a cavalry colonel from the Urals, and he charmed poor Nijinsky into renouncing his contract with the Imperial Ballet and joining the Ballets Russes full time. Nijinsky reigned supreme in it, as Niura found out. But only for a short time. He was the perfect example of what happened to you when you let your heart get under your feet.

Uitzilintzin, Uitzilintzin: Love Medicine For Sale

Ana Castillo

A MAYAN STORY SAYS THAT the hummingbird is the sun courting the moon. To the Aztecs the sun god, Huitzilpochtli, a fierce warrior, was also symbolized by the hummingbird. For many Native American peoples the hummingbird was the sun, vegetation and rain with its fast flutter of tiny wings, its zest for life. It is beauty—with its radiant feathers, love, for its craving for the nectar of flowers. In Nahuatl the word for hummingbird is uitzilinztin—a minuscule yet powerful creature that appears to defy the laws of its species with its stationary and zigzag midair dance. It is also very old love medicine.

All this and more Madame X, a spiritual worker in East Los Angeles, knew of the magical powers of the uitzilintzin when a client came and asked about finding romance. The uitzilintzin had brought her her third husband, after all. Perhaps not her best husband or her favorite but a decent one nonetheless, for a while or in some ways more than others. Well, at least he was handsome. Kind of. From a certain angle. Oh well. Better not to think too much about that ex-husband, she told herself as the years went by. And who was counting husbands, anyway? she'd conclude.

People came to her for limpias. They came to have their homes exorcised of devils and bad spirits. They came to ask for assistance in getting a job or to work out a difficult relationship. Some sought riches. Every now and then someone wanted to get rid of an enemy, a rival at work or a gossiping neighbor. But no one had asked her for love medicine. It was only a matter of time before someone would, she figured. So she did a little research on the subject. Why fool around and waste anyone's time with guesswork—like petitions to a saint who had no use for courtships during his own life since martyrdom and celibacy is on the top of the list to be made into a saint in the first place. There were other sources to turn to. There was Aphrodite—but Madame X was not Greek. She had no Greek clients either. There was the breathtaking image of Botticelli's

Venus to contemplate. But Venus was a star in the sky which to the Aztecs—Madame X's ancestors—became a male god, Feathered Serpent, a very important god, but not a love god. This Venus god was so chaste he didn't even like to drink.

On a trip to Mexico, Madame X paid a visit to the witches' market in Mexico City. It was really huge and had been there forever. It was the very same witches' market that her mother had visited regularly as a little girl, where even her great-grandmother had gone to in her own youth and so on, a long line of women following the traditions of their foremothers, pagan and Christian alike. You could get just about anything you needed to do any kind of magic—with good and not-so-good intentions. From plastic-wrapped packets filled with charms to every known herb for tinctures and teas to live goats for sacrifices.

All of Madame X's intentions were always good.

This is why when she decided to experiment with love medicine on herself, she knew that she could not impose her will on anyone. Basically, as a good bruja she lived by the Golden Rule. When her future husband appeared she would know him. Just as importantly, he would know her too. The task here was to open all paths so that they could meet.

She went back to her casita in East L.A. armed with her love medicine: six desiccated hummingbird carcasses, rather drab and pathetic looking at first sight. She felt a little sorry for them. But in her line of work she understood the infinite connectedness of all things, animate and inanimate, dead or alive, everything had its own eternal energy.

You can buy a uitzilintzin already prepared. A bruja can cast a spell on it, whisper to it to bring the supplicant true love. She'll dress it with bright red tassels and give you instructions for use when you take it home. There, as if lying in state, the tiny loved one is placed somewhere special, where it won't be disturbed. Its spirit is still vibrant and strong. And it begins working for you, bringing your intended closer to you every day.

But Madame X preferred to do her own preparation of materials. More importantly, she felt, she had to prepare herself before anything else. There was a lot of possum around, and she certainly didn't want to catch a possum. Therefore, to attract the best, she herself had to be at her best, a virtual love goddess incarnate. She spent weeks preparing. She exercised regularly. She meditated and gave herself time to reflect, to write in her journal. She made a long list of all the qualitities she was looking for in a mate. She got this idea from a therapist friend who showed her her own list. There was a diamond ring on it. This would be no big deal for a lot of women seeking marriage but Madame X found it sweet that her friend included it because, despite being a feminist lesbian activist, she was still a nice Jewish girl from New York and would require an engagement before taking a prospective lifemate home to meet her parents.

"Okay," Madame X thought. "I won't say no to the ring either."

Meanwhile, there were lots of baths in oils and essences, aromatherapy treatments and massages. There were facials and saunas and long hikes with friends. Madame X kept busy with work and organized social activities. You cannot expect to find someone who is active and living a full life to find you in the least interesting if you spend all your time at home watching TV, feeling sorry for yourself. She set some career goals and pursued them. She took a vacation alone. No woman or man should want a companion just because they are afraid of being alone. That kind of loneliness doesn't ever go away no matter who is with you.

It was on a business trip that she met him, the third husband. Less than a year later they were married. A beautiful wedding. The marriage did not last. They didn't even remain friends. In the end, she almost hated his guts.

Which brings us to the third and last phase of love medicine work. The first is seeking it. The second is putting it to work. The third is accepting the consequences. By no means should anyone blame an earnest dead bird with a beak the size of a large sewing needle on a much desired yearning for love having been met for only a brief time. It was met—at which point it was left to the two individuals involved and was completely out of the fine-feathered magical hands of the uitzilintzin!

Where to purchase your own uitzilintzin love medicine without making a trip to the witches' market in Mexico City:

Many Mexican curanderas in the U.S. have a supply. (You'll have to ask since it won't be displayed!) If you find one who doesn't know about this love medicine, I would really question as to how much she knows her stuff and find someone else who does. Incidentally, like most Mexican magic, it works for everyone else, too.

The Ecstasy of Looking: Six Proofs

David Shields

1. Sex and Death

Rachel got lost in bathrooms. She felt safe in them, at home, locked in. She had a toilet kit like a suitcase. She liked to be clean. She talked about towels and soaps and different kinds of tissues (their warmth, their softness). She liked to play with faucets and shower curtains and swinging mirrors. Transfixed on beauty, she stared into mirrors for hours, scaring away blemishes.

2. Victory Video

I was standing here in Victory Video in a godforsaken village in northern New York—too far north to even be called "upstate" New York. The girl behind the counter was wearing an usher's outfit and munching popcorn. Victory Video carried (by mistake, I think) Henry Jaglom's *Always,* which I adore, so I got it and the girl behind the counter asked to see my driver's license. She commented upon how happily few numbers my California driver's license had compared to a New York driver's license, then said, "I wouldn'ta left California for nuthin'." Which had the quality somehow of an accusation: I was living in Xanadu and left; what could possibly be the matter with me? It was a good question, and she looked into my eyes for the answer.

3. The Heroic Mode

Several years ago my friend Doron saw an ad for "free housing" on an estate on Fishers Island in exchange for "light groundskeeping." He applied and won the job over many applicants because he could be convincing that he was handy with tools. The "housing" turned out to be a large, dreary garage apartment on a run-down estate. The new owners were in their early thirties, with five young kids. The estate had a huge, shaggy lawn, neglected fruit trees, a garden infested with rabbit warrens and a trout pond whose resident eels ate all the trout as soon as they were stocked. The agreement was that Doron would cut the huge lawn each week with a lawn tractor, and with whatever hours were left over after that, would do gardening and handiwork—up to sixteen hours a week. He would have to work only during the summer months, when the family was in residence. During the winter they lived in Manhattan; Doron would get the house, though he'd have to pay utilities.

He found it took almost twelve hours to cut the lawn, but he also fixed a dock and a garden gate, planted a big garden. At the owners' insistence, he pruned the fruit trees after they had already begun to leaf. The owners wildly complimented his first efforts and began smilingly asking him to do this and that. Once, he was called into the main house to fit a loose hinge on a cabinet door. He could tell by the gouges in the wood that the owners couldn't figure out which way a wood screw turned out. (I say this as if I know which way a wood screw turns out; I don't; this is just the way Doron told me the story.) They put pressure on him to do more and more. He resisted, citing the original agreement. Eventually, he and the owners had a screaming fight, and he quit. He lasted out the winter by fishing for food.

Before things turned sour, though, he enjoyed the making of the family portrait. The owners had hired a famous portrait painter much admired by the rich of Manhattan. He could paint you representationally, but heroically modern. He took a huge photo of the family all posed outside the house on Fishers Island. He agreed to paint in for a background a wild point of land on the island reaching into the turbulent waters of Long Island Sound. This was a place where he and others surf-fished on the island at dusk, but where summer people never dared tread at any time of day. It was near the end of the small airstrip on the island where several light planes bringing in the gentry for weekends had recently, and fatally, crashed in the fog.

The artist went back to New York City for a month and painted in the bodies as posed in the photo. Then he came back to the island to do the faces. He did one at a time, posing the person as his or her body had already been painted in, on the grass of the shabby estate. But all the subjects were restless. They had no contemplative skills. They couldn't hold themselves still for more than several minutes.

The painter finally fixed on the strategy of running an extension cord out of the garage and plugging in a portable TV and the painter would paint the faces. Doron saw the painting for the first time when the painter took it to Race Rock Point for the background. According to Doron, Race Rock Point is the last piece of earth that got deposited by the receding glacier.

4. Fantasy

This trip to Manzanillo, Mexico, was supposed to be a prenuptial honeymoon of sorts, so for recreation Rachel lay, like a virgin sacrifice, across the white kitchen counter and confessed that the only fantasy she'd ever had was to open her legs as wide as she could and, under virtually gynecological scrutiny, be admired. Just that. So female. Be admired. She leaned back. Her bikini bottoms flapped about her ankles.

5. A Preview of Coming Attractions

I recently went by myself to ring the doorbell of my childhood home in the Griffith Park section of Los Angeles, and no one answered, so I looked around a little outside. The brick wall was gone, the garage was replaced by a deck out back and the living room appeared to have been turned into a wet bar. Incense burned out open windows. What was once a white and lower-middle class neighborhood was now integrated and middle class. I could remember only a few things about the house in which I lived the first six years of my life: between the front lawn and the front porch, the brick wall which served as an ideal backstop for whiffleball games; an extraordinarily cozy living-room couch on which I would lie and watch *Lassie* and apply a heating pad to relieve my thunderous earaches; the red record player in my sister's room; and the wooden rocking horse in mine. . . .

I'd hold the strap attached to his ears and mouth, lifting myself onto the leather saddle. One glass eye shone out of the right side of his head; its mouth, once bright red and smiling, had chipped away to an unpainted pout. His nose, too, was bruised, with gashes for nostrils. He had a brown mane, which, extending from the crown of his head nearly to its waist, was made up of my grandmother's discarded wigs glued to the wood. Wrapping the reins around my fist,

I'd slip my feet into the stirrups that hung from his waist. I'd bounce up and down to set the runner skidding across the floor. Then I'd sit up, lean forward, press my lips to the back of his neck and exhort him. (Infantile, naive, I thought I could talk to wooden animals.) I'd wrap my arms around his neck and kick my legs back and forth in the stirrups. I'd lay my cheek against the side of his head, press myself to his curves. When he pitched forward, I'd scoot up toward the base of his spine and when he swung back I'd let go of his leather strap and lean back as far as I could, so I was causing his motions at the same time as I was trying to get in rhythm with them. I'd clutch him, make him lurch crazily toward the far wall, jerking my body forward, squeezing my knees into wood. Then I'd twist my hips and bounce until it felt warm under me, bump up against the smooth surface of the seat until my whole body tingled. I'd buck back and forth until it hurt, in a way, and I could ride no longer. Who would have guessed? My very first memory is of myself, in my own room, surrounded by sunlight, trying to get off.

6. The Stranger

"My cousin Mike, who works at Computerware, pointed out something pretty relevant to my situation: Greg Brady is way too old to still be in high school." These were the first words of a monologue spoken to me years ago in an Amtrak dining car. The rest of the monologue went like this: "He looked okay in the real early ones when they all had crew-cuts, but then they kept him in high school for eight more years. It's like Richie Cunningham. I mean, how many years can you be in eleventh grade? The point Mike was trying to make was they secretly have these older people play teenagers just to make us feel like totally inadequate shits. Even in a show like *James at 16,* which later became *James at 17,* they got this guy Lance Kerwin to play James. Not that he was bad at it, mind you. But when I compared myself to this guy, it didn't seem right. Okay, here's an example. There's this Swedish exchange student. Inga's her name. In real life, she's the girl who does the ads for Flex hair conditioners. The girl with the cowboy hat and the gun. The one who married Joe Montana. Well, James helps her with her English and shows her around town. Evidently Inga really appreciates what he does for her, because when James gets all romantic, puts on Billy Joel's *The Stranger* and whispers all this mushy shit to her, she lets him fuck her silly on the couch. How am I supposed to react to this? Say, Way to go, James, next time let me meet her sister? It's like I'm just supposed to sit in my room and wait for some girl with big tits to come down from outer space like E.T. and enter my life. . . .

"Mike stayed at this party and I walked around the town for a while. There was this bar with a sign that read 'Nude Dancing Nightly—Luscious Ladies.' So I went in to see if I could catch some action. The place was pretty seedy. Lots of weird old men sitting at these big long tables, but no luscious lady dancers anywhere in sight. I asked the bouncer about the lack of dancing nude women and he just said, 'No dancing tonight. Tomorrow.' Understandably disappointed, I sat down at the end of the bar and ordered myself the most important sounding drink I could think of. *Brian's Song,* my favorite movie of all time, was playing on the TV. Even in a bar, it was a very touching experience. In fact, I can honestly say that by the end of the movie, there was not one person in the whole place that didn't have one of those sore lumps in the bottom of their throats.

"I shaved my head and joined this cult that fucks sheep. Ha ha, only kidding. There was this movie where all these people actually do that, though. It was on Cinemax last month. I can't think. Not just today, every day. I used to go to the mall, but since Christmas shopping started, everybody wants to know what time it is and slush gets all over your shoes. . . .

"Everything has become so much better since we got cable. Used to be that nothing was on after *The Flying Nun.* But now with WTBS the Superstation, you can watch *Hazel, Bewitched* and *Perry Mason* all right in a row. Too bad that Della Street got charged with murder on this new movie they made. It was pretty good, but the guy who played Paul Drake wasn't the same. He was his son or something. From what I understand, they might make a sequel. . . .

"Mike has this theory that explains why you never see girls half as good looking in real life as the girls in the videos on MTV. Mike's idea is that there's this island, sort of like Fantasy Island, where all the beautiful girls on MTV live. They are real live Amazon women who kill lions with spears and stuff. That's why they're so hot and sexy; they eat raw flesh and it turns them on."

Finitude: From the Permanent Collection

Jonathan Safran Foer

—for John Burghardt

SHAKESPEARE'S PARROT'S PARROT'S PARROT'S PARROT'S PARROT'S PARROT'S PARROT'S PARROT'S PARROT'S PARROT'S PARROT. 1942–?
Striped West-Indian Parrot, approx. 14 x 5 in.
Museum purchase.

LITTLE IS KNOWN OF THE MAN who is widely considered the greatest writer in history. The best insight into who he was may lie in the parrot perched before you, a tenth-generation descendant of the parrot given to Shakespeare in 1610 as a gift by his friend and fellow poet Michael Drayton. The Bard was exceedingly fond of the bird, and would speak to her as one might write in a journal—to chronicle, reflect and confess. When he died of fever six years later, Anne Hathaway kept the parrot, and introduced into its cage a younger parrot, to learn what the older could teach it. She never spoke to either of them, and forbade guests from speaking in their presence. A line of Shakespeare's parrots was raised in the painstaking silence of her love, and when she died, our reverence. And so we ask you not to speak while in this sound-proof room, but only to listen. We ask you not to compromise the ever-weakening but direct line from this parrot to Shakespeare. And when it begs you, "Talk to me," as it has the habit of doing, we ask you not to give it the company of your voice—it is not the parrot, remember, who begs to be talked to, and while Shakespeare may reach us through the parrot, it will never work in the other direction.

Isadora Duncan's Accidental Strangulation. 1927.
100% cotton, silk fringes, 12 x 84 in.
Promised gift of Benoit Falchetto.

Fourteen years before her life adjourned her body, Isadora Duncan endured the loss of two children. Trapped in a car that ambled backward into the palm of the Seine, they watched the leaves obscure to yellow gestures. The day before her own death, Duncan saw a girl who reminded her of Diedre. "I cannot continue to live in a world where there are beautiful blue-eyed, golden-haired children," she told a friend. "I cannot!"

Tragedy was the dancer's only trusted partner. In 1922, world-famous and broke, she married Russia's revolutionary poet-laureate, Sergei Esenin—mad, alcoholic and seventeen years her junior. In a starched white hotel room on the last night of 1925, he burned his manuscripts, sliced open his left arm from palm to bend, penned a farewell poem with his own red ink (see Gallery B), and hanged himself.

Duncan descended further into a depression as impenetrable as it was undetectable, gaining weight where no one saw, drinking in great excess and secrecy, spending carelessly what little money she had. She admired a red Bugatti convertible and contemplated buying it. "Will you allow me a test drive?" she asked with a finger in the air, and recognizing who she was, the proprietor, handsome young Benoit Falchetto, said, "I will. Of course. Tomorrow evening." On the way back to her hotel she saw a girl who reminded her of Diedre, and told her friend, "I cannot!"

The next evening, Falchetto pulled up in front of her hotel in the red Bugatti. The night was cool, the yellow leaves descended, and Duncan shivered. She refused both the cloth cape of her friend, Mary Desti, and Falchetto's leather jacket, but instead wrapped twice around her neck and tossed over her shoulder one of her trademark long, silk-fringed red shawls. As Falchetto pulled away, the loose end of the shawl dragged on the ground, danced like a comet's tail behind her, and within moments became caught in the spokes of the back wheel. The car was accelerating—Falchetto trying to show her the Bugatti's capacity to put the road behind it, as the present does with the future—and the shawl, as if yanked by some invisible hand, by the hand of young Diedre, perhaps, whipped back and snapped Duncan's neck. By the time her head struck the side of the door—a blow that smashed her nose into a hundred pieces—she was dead.

The shawl was so tightly bound to Duncan's neck and the Bugatti's wheel that it could not be disentangled, and had to be cut. While Falchetto adamantly denies it, it is suspected that it was he who stitched the halves back together, making the shawl whole again, as now exhibited.

JOHN WILKES BOOTH'S MIRROR. 1865.
Mirror and oak frame, 36 x 72 in.
Promised gift of Brooks Brothers.

On loan.

ANNE FRANK'S LOWER EAST SIDE ANNEX. 1986.
Construction, 40 x 65 ft.
Built with funds from an anonymous gift.

You are about to enter a re-creation of Ethel Schneiderman's re-creation of Anne Frank's annex. Unlike Frank, Schneiderman survived the Holocaust. After two years in a Polish displaced persons camp, she immigrated to the United States and moved into a one-bedroom apartment on Delancy Street, where she lived until her death (pneumonia) in 1986. With no surviving family, no coworkers and no known friends to miss her, it wasn't until her neighbors complained about the stench from her apartment that her body was found. It was the middle of the night when the police entered the front door, as you are about to. (For the sake of accuracy, our re-creation is kept in the cold and perfect darkness of a year's unpaid bills.) Sweeps of muted yellow flashlight were not enough to prevent the men from tripping through the apartment's many small rooms, from bumping into walls and knocking their heads on the door frames. "Something's off," one of the officers said into the shadows.

Scholars at the National Holocaust Museum in Washington D.C., as well as experts from the Anne Frank House in Amsterdam, have verified the impossible accuracy of Schneiderman's annex. Every conceivable detail, down to the crusted tears on Anne's pillowcase and menstrual blood on her sheets, was perfect, more perfect, even, than the Anne Frank House itself, which has been altered by the thousands of tourists who pass through every day. Dust, in Schneiderman's annex, was where it should be.

But something, as the officer guessed, was off. It took weeks of puzzled speculation to realize the seemingly obvious: Schneiderman's annex was slightly smaller than Anne's. Everything, therefore, had to be at 89% scale—from the tin spoons, to the boards nailed to the windows, to the chamber pot, to the diary itself—almost close enough not to notice, but off enough to cause one to stumble, to stammer and sway, to feel larger than one is.

Please be careful in the annex. Keep your hands in front of you to feel for unexpected objects. Let your feet search the ground for things over which you might trip. Mind the low doorframes and narrow passages. As you move through, feel free to touch whatever you like. Lay down in Anne's bed. Bring her cotton blouse to your face—smell it, without knowing what color it is. Sit in her too-small chair. Put your hands on her desk. Pick up her pencil, to see what it must have felt like—but remember that your hand is not huge, that you are not a giant.

THE EMBALMED BODY OF J. ANTHONY GAUSSARDIA, AMERICAN HERO. 1879.
Human body, 72 x 11 in.
Generous gift of the National League of Civil War Paraphernaliaists.

The modern embalming process, which involves the replacement of body fluids with a variety of chemicals for the purpose of preservation, was patented in 1856 by a Washington, D.C. entrepreneur, J. Anthony Gaussardia. Ten rival patents soon followed in the city, and the nation's capital became the embalming capital of the world. The timing could not have been more propitious, as Union soldiers were being killed by the thousands, far from home. The new process allowed the bodies to be preserved for the slow train rides and wagon trips north. Families wanted their sons returned home; J. Anthony Gaussardia made that possible.

One funeral more than any convinced Americans of the merits of Gaussardia's art. The embalmed corpse of Abraham Lincoln was viewed by millions of mourners, first in Washington, then at depots along the solemn train ride to his home in Springfield, Illinois. Only by seeing Lincoln's body was the country fully able to grieve the loss of his life.

Ironically, Gaussardia didn't trust anyone else with the embalming of his own body, and so resolved to embalm himself, to drain his body, and simultaneously drink increasing doses of embalming fluid. Toward the end of the process that lasted nearly three years, he was barely able to move, and sat posed like a wax sculpture at his desk, trimming his eyebrows, rouging his cheeks. It was the preservation, of course, that killed him, as he knew it would. But as was his wish, no dead man has ever looked more alive, and you will not be able to help but say: "He looks great."

THE STONES IN VIRGINIA WOOLF'S POCKETS. 1941.
A handful of stones, various sizes.
Retrieved by the museum.

Burgled.

NAPOLEON'S COWLICK. 1821; **HITLER'S FINAL MUSTACHE.** 1945.
Human hair, various lengths.
Museum purchase.

Exhibit case "A" contains a lock of hairs from the head of Napoleon Bonaparte. His final words, murmured in fits, were: "God! . . . France! . . . My son! . . . Josephine!" (although the order has been much debated), and his less noble, but equally emphatic, final wish was that his body be cremated after his head shaved and his hair divvied among his friends according to loyalty. While neutron activation analysis found thirteen times the normal amount of arsenic in several of these samples, and some would take this to suggest that he was poisoned, it is far more likely that St. Helena itself was environmentally poisoned, and that he died of a malignant stomach ulcer that invaded his liver. (As early as 1817, four years before his death, he was vomiting what looked like coffee grounds—his own dark, digested blood.) Similar analysis, after all, found thirteen times the normal amount of arsenic in the soil of St. Helena, and in the bark of St. Helena's trees, and even in the paste of the wallpaper in Napoleon's room. The portrait of Josephine that saved him from solitude was poisoned—the indigo eyes contained thirteen times the normal amount of arsenic, the ochre locks were poisoned, the vermilion lips. The nib of his pen was poisoned, as was the vellum on which he wrote the dozens of unanswered letters to his son, the Viennese duke of Reichstadt. "I recommend to my son," his will states, "never to forget that he was born a French prince." The space between his third and fourth buttons down—where he hid his deformed hand—was poisoned. His prized medallions, all bestowed by him upon himself for great honor in war, were poisoned. The flakes that fell from the rotting ceiling and onto his dying body like snow—"God!" he called, his last word, let's believe—they too were poisoned.

Exhibit case "B" contains Hitler's final mustache, shaved from the Führer's face by Heinz Linge, the valet who found him and Eva Braun seated side by side and dead on the afternoon of April 30, 1945. At approximately 3:30 P.M. of that day, Hitler crushed a glass ampule of cyanide between his teeth, and shortly after was finished off by a bullet through the head, either self-inflicted, or more likely fired by Eva Braun. After shaving the mustache as a relic to bring home for his mother, Linge took Hitler into the courtyard, as specified in the Führer's will, and set him aflame. Due to a shortage of gasoline, however, the corpse was not rendered completely to ash, and the charred remains were discovered days later by occupying Russian forces. To his dismay, Linge's mother would not accept her son's gift, for accepting it would be to accept that the Führer had died, that the cause was lost, the war over. He promptly sold the hairs to a local artisan, who used them as snow in the children's toy before you. Feel free to shake, and watch Hitler's final mustache descend upon Berlin.

PERPETUAL PHOTOGRAPH OF HENRY WREN. 1960–?
Silver-gelatin print, 9 x 12 in.
Promised gift of Henry Wren.

For the last forty years, beekeeper Henry Wren has been taking a photograph of himself. Mounted on an arm extending from a helmet he wears at all times is a camera whose shutter never closes. "I don't know how I got the idea," he admits. "Curious, I guess."

Wren became something of a media star when a local news team did a feel-good piece on him, which was then picked up by the national networks. The interviews, the cheap and kitschy fame, the thousands of photographs, were not at all what he intended, and ultimately drove him and his wife into seclusion on a farm in Northern Vermont. In an open letter to the *New York Times*, he stated that only after he is dead will his wife, Mayla, remove the camera from its mounting, close the shutter, and develop the film. Exactly one print will be made, and it will reside on the wall before you. "Please do not bother me for anything else."

There are those who are certain that Wren's life will look like this:

And there are those who are certain that it will look like this:

There are those who think that the image will depend on the amount of light at the time of Wren's death, when his eyes and the shutter close—that it is not until the final moment of his life that the photograph of his life will be determined. Should it be night, or should the shutters be drawn, or should his wife, Mayla, lean in to kiss his forehead, and by so doing block the lens, his life will look like this:

But should there be light—pouring in through the arms of the trees, sponging him as his mother once did in the kitchen sink, blanketing him, behind him, above him, around him—his life will look like this:

Of course, any amateur photographer knows that the image will have nothing to do with the final moment, but the accumulation of light over the course of Wren's life. If he lived a normal life—ran in the grass with one sock on, labored in lit rooms, loitered on rickety stoops, reaffirmed his love over dripping wax—his life will certainly look like this:

WAGNER KILLED THE CASTRATI STAR. 1816.
Testes, no larger than acorns.
Generous gift of Elton John.

By the late 1600s, the slightest aptitude for singing could result in genital mutilation. How many gonads were tossed like dice on the gamble of the perfect instrument! With his sac severed, a castrati typically studied at a conservatory until his debut at the age of 18. If he did not establish a career, as precious few did, he was left without the possibility of partnership (the church forbade nonprocreative marriage) or employment (never having learned a craft). While religious and popular sentiments were ostensibly outrage, castrati continued to draw huge audiences to churches and opera halls, and it was the composers who brought about the end of the darkest period of testicular history. Wagner, in particular, refused to tolerate the common musical tamperings of the castrati, who were so eager to distinguish themselves that they often took great privileges with his scores. Indeed, he refused to write parts for them at all, and with his ascent came their demise. Resting on the red velvet pillow before you are the testicles of Gioacchino Velluti, the world's last castrati. A terrible life, a beautiful voice.

SOFYA TOLSTOY'S CARPAL TUNNELS. 1863.
Tendons and nerve bundles, 4 in.
Museum purchase.

After transcribing *War and Peace* for the ninth time, Sofya Tolstoy lifted her wrists to the sky, tried to unball her fingers, and let her numb fists fall to the table: "I'm sorry." Approximately 33,000 handwritten pages. Stacked, these would measure no less than fifteen feet. 1,300 pounds of paper. Paper to displace enough red wine to fill 372 bottles. Enough paper to pave a road of almost eight miles; paper to paper the walls of a respectable cathedral. An equivalent mass of feathers would have filled their small house to the shingles, poured from the windows (as if escaping to the birds from which they once came) and suffocated Leo and Sofya inside. "I am so sorry," she cried into her arms, which burned at the bends, were cold needles at the wrists, dead at the hands. "I cannot write another word." Tolstoy, who would several years later leave Sofya for his newly discovered piety, pulled back his beard to give her a kiss. "Thank you," he said. "Now I know I am done."

SERGEI ESENIN'S FAREWELL POEM. 1925.
Blood and paper, 8½ x 11 in.
Generous gift of the Duncan Estate.

As all poems should, this speaks for itself.

LINCOLN'S MIRROR. 1865.
Mirror and oak frame, 36 x 72 in.
Promised gift of Brooks Brothers.

What you are looking into is the mirror that Abraham Lincoln looked into as he tried on the Brooks Brothers suit that he would wear to the performance of *Our American Cousin* at Ford's Theater on April 15, 1865.

"What will they think if we hold hands?" Mary Todd asked coyly, nodding at their guests in the presidential box. "They won't think anything about it," he responded, and took her white-gloved hand, and then Booth's bullet, which lodged itself behind his left eye.

If it were a wall before you, the wall that Lincoln looked at as he tried on the suit that he would wear to his assassination, you would think little of it. If it were the final portrait of Lincoln, or his last penned letter, or Mary Todd's blood-spattered glove, or even the suit he wore that last night of his life, it would not affect you as looking into this mirror now does. What is it, then, that you think you see?

The Names

Carole Maso

I NAMED MY CHILD Mercy, Lamb.

Seraphina, the burning one.

I named my child the One Who Predicts the Future, though I never wanted that.

I named my child Pillar, Staff.

Henry, from the Old High German Haganrih, which means ruler of the enclosure, how awful.

I named my baby Plum, Pear Blossom, Shining Path.

I named my child Rose Chloe—that's blooming horse. I almost named her Rose Seraphina, that would have been a horse on fire.

Kami, which is tortoise. The name denotes long life.

Kemeko—tortoise child.

Kameyo—tortoise generation.

So she might live forever.

And Tori—turtledove.

I named my child Sorrow, inadvertently, I did not mean to. In the darkness I named her Rebecca—that is noose, to tie or bind. In the gloom I named my baby Mary—which means bitter, but I am happier than before and name my baby Day and Star and Elm Limb.

I named my child Viola, so that she might be musical. And Cecilia, patron saint of music, so she might play the violin.

Vigilant was the name of my child. Daughter of the Oath. Defiance. I name my child Sylvie so that she will not be frightened of the sunless forest.

I named my child War, my mistake. That would be Marcella or Martine. I named my child Ulrich—Wolf Power. Oh my son! After a while, though, I wised up and passed on Brunhilde, Helmut, Hermann, Walter. And Egon—the point of the sword. I did not value power in battle and so skipped over Maude.

Instead I named my child Sibeta—the one who finds a fish under a rock. Sacred Bells, and Ray of Light. And Durga—unattainable. Olwynn—white footprint. Monica—solitary one. I named my child Babette, that is stranger. I named her Claudia: lame—without realizing it.

How are you feeling Ava Klein?

Perdita.

I named her Thirst. And Miriam—Sea of Sorrow. Bitterness. And Cendrine—that's ashes. But I am feeling better now, thank you. I named my child God is With Thee, though I do not feel Him.

I named her Isolde—Ruler of Ice. Giselle—Pledge and Hostage. Harita, a lovely name derived from the Sanskrit denotes a color of yellow or green or brown, a monkey, the sun, the wind and several other things.

I named her Clothed in Red, because I never stopped bleeding.

I named my son Yitzchak—that's He Will Laugh. And Isaiah, Salvation.

I named him Salvation. And Rescue. Five Minutes to Midnight.

I named my daughter Esme, the past participle of the verb esmer, to love. I named her She Has Peace, and Shining Beautiful Valley. I named my baby Farewell to Spring, just in case.

I named my child Ocean for that vast, mysterious shifting expanse. I named her Marissa, that's of the sea—because naming is what we do I guess. There is a silliness to us.

I named my child Cusp and Cutting Edge and Renegade, to protect her from critics.

I named my child Millennia, because the future is now—whether we like it or not.

It is a distinct pleasure to be here on this earth naming with you.

They lift a glass:

New Year's Eve and the revelers. Dizzy, a little more than tipsy. At the edge of what unbeknownst to them has already happened, is already happening. It gives them a sepia tone. In their paper hats and goblets and blowers and confetti. *Happy*—that old sweet and hopeful *New*—there is not one day that I have not thought of you my child—*Year*. And time passes. As if we had a choice.

A strange photographed feeling. The black hood over the box on its legs. That wobbly feeling come from champagne and last things. As the new century moves into us—1900.

Time immemorial—so they say.

What is to come unimaginable.

I named my baby Many Achievements, Five Ravens, Red Bird. I named her Goes Forth Bravely. Beautiful Lake. Shaking Snow, Red Echo, Walking by the River.

And we relish the saying. While we still can. And in the saying, inhabit our own vanishing, in the shadow language, its after-image, a blue ghost in the bones, the passage of time, intimacy of the late evening—seated by a fire—embers.

Pipe smoke when you were a child come from under the crack in the door, letting you know that Uncle Louis was near. The distant sound from your nursery of the revelers—they come in to peer at you in your crib in the eerie masks of Victoriana on the dying year's last eve. Louisa and Herman move toward the lamplight. Oohs and aahs and then quiet. All disperse: a proper German gentleman, an American with a handlebar moustache, a chorus girl, a rabbit-faced widow, a bursar or stationmaster, a man in a turban, a geisha—a chic Orientalism. A sultry gypsy girl. They meander through the Ramble, weaving a little, with the odd premonition that they are all playing their parts—on this elaborate stage, the world hurtling forward, the year on the verge of turning. Snow begins to fall. The lights twinkling. They lift a glass.

New Year's Eve and we dream—of a music, a book never seen before, at the edge of its obsolescence—the light pale opal. On the shards of story and sound. What is left now.

On the last day of the last year of the last one thousand.

And the dead stream by with their names. And all the ways they tried to say—

Clint Youle, 83, Early Weatherman on TV
H.S. Richardson, Heir to Vicks Cold Remedies
Hazel Bishop, an Innovator Who Made Lipstick Kissproof
Linda Alma, Dancer in Greek Movies
Walter O. Wells, a Pioneer in Mobile Homes

The future already with us. Its advance implacable and the revelers, having rested up that afternoon, begin their foray. To play out the passing of time—thrilled, a little frightened, tinged with melancholy, struck as they leave now by the intense desire to stay.

"To earn one's death," writes *Mary Cantwell, 69, Author,* "I think of it as a kind of parlour game. How, I shall ask my friends, would you like to earn your deaths? And how would I like to earn mine?"

And we are charmed. I named my baby The Origin of Song—and then The Origin of Tears. Angel Eyes and Angel Heart. And Sweetie Pie and Darling One.

We've relished the naming—eased by it. And all the other games we made up, and all the things we thought to do. New Year's Eve and the revelers.

At the end of the century a whisper. The Berlin Philharmonic plays seven finales in a row.

And the year 2000 is issued in, scraps of story and sound. That beautiful end of the century debris.

We were working on an erotic song cycle. It was called: *The Problem Now of the Finale.*

Today, where the sense of key is weaker or absent altogether, there is no goal to be reached as in earlier finales, as a closing gesture, what, what now?—a joke, a dissolve, a fast or slow tearing, intimations of a kind of timelessness, the chiming of bells, a wing and a prayer—perhaps, a solemn procession toward—what then?

New Year's Eve and the revelers.

Another sort of progress.

I named my child Farewell to Spring.

How strange the dwindling—pronounced as it is on this night where we deliberately mark its passage. Happy New Year. Lost in the naming, in the marking of time as it slips—distracted from the strangeness for a minute.

It's been a privilege. And how quickly all of a sudden . . . Pipe smoke when you were a child.

Or the alarming forced jollity of a Shostakovich finale—

Where are you going?

Where have you gone?

I named her Century. I named her Bethany—House of Figs. I named her Lucia to protect her from the dark. And Xing—which is Star. Dolphin, Lion, Lover of Horses.

I named her Arabella—Beautiful Altar, and Andromeda—Rescued.

My child was made almost entirely of blood in the end. She slipped through my hands. They say ordinarily such a child is not named.

A flock of birds. Bells that descend. A rose on the open sea.

The pages of the baby name book ragged. Nevertheless—I could not pass up

Mercy.

Tenderness.

Lamb.

I wish I could decipher the Silence. Understand its Whims. The century a Chalice of Heartbreak. We put our lips to it and whisper.

What now?

What then?

And Bela—derived from a word that means wave—or a word that means time—or a word that means limit. It is also indicative of a type of flower or a violin.

NOTES ON CONTRIBUTORS

JULIA ALVAREZ is the author of three novels, *How the García Girls Lost Their Accents, In the Time of the Butterflies* and *¡Yo!;* two books of poems, *Homecoming* and *The Other Side;* and a book of essays, *Something to Declare.* Her new novel, *In the Name of Salomé,* will be published by Algonquin Books in June. She is a writer-in-residence at Middlebury College.

ROBERT ANTONI's tale is from his forthcoming book, *My Grandmother's Erotic Folktales.* He is the author of two novels, *Divina Trace* (Overlook) and *Blessèd is the Fruit* (Henry Holt), and is coeditor, with Bradford Morrow, of *Conjunctions:27, The Archipelago,* a collection of new Caribbean writing.

PAUL AUSTER is the author of *The New York Trilogy, Mr. Vertigo, Moon Palace, The Music of Chance* and other novels. He recently wrote and directed the movie *Lulu On The Bridge.* His latest novel is *Timbuktu* (Henry Holt).

RUSSELL BANKS's most recent novels are *Cloudsplitter* and *Rule of the Bone.* "The Moor" will appear in his forthcoming collection of new and selected stories, *The Angel on the Roof,* from HarperCollins.

ANN BEATTIE is the author of six short story collections and six novels, among them *Distortions, Secrets and Surprises, Falling in Place, The Burning House, Picturing Will* and *Another You.* Her most recent collection is *Park City—New and Selected Stories* (Knopf). She is completing a new novel.

MARY CAPONEGRO's newest collection of fiction is *Five Doubts* (Marsilio). She teaches at Syracuse University. A new collection is forthcoming from Coffee House Press in spring 2001.

ANA CASTILLO is the author of four novels, the most recent of which is *Peel My Love Like an Onion.* She has also written a collection of poems, a book of short stories, one of essays, and a recent children's book, *My Daughter, My Son, The Eagle, The Dove.* She lives in Chicago.

SANDRA CISNEROS is the author of *The House on Mango Street, Woman Hollering Creek, Loose Woman, My Wicked Witch Ways* and *Hairs/Pelitos.* She has recently completed the novel *Caramelo,* from which "Mexico Next Right" is taken, and is at work on a book of vignettes, *Infinito.*

ROBERT COOVER's most recent books are *John's Wife, Briar Rose* and *Ghost Town.* He teaches electronic and experimental writing at Brown. "Alice in the Time of the Jabberwock" is from a collection in progress, *A Child Again.*

EDWIDGE DANTICAT has published two novels, *Breath, Eye, Memory* and *The Farming of Bones,* and a collection of stories, *Krik! Krak!* "Dies Irae" is an excerpt from a novella of the same name.

KATHRYN DAVIS's most recent novel is *The Walking Tour.* She received the 1999 Morton Dauwen Zabel Award from the American Academy of Arts and Letters. She teaches at Skidmore College and lives in Vermont.

LYDIA DAVIS's books are *Break It Down, The End of the Story* and *Almost No Memory* (all from Farrar, Straus & Giroux). She is currently working on a new translation of Proust's *Swann's Way* for Penguin Classics, and teaches at Bard College's Milton Avery School of the Arts.

MATTHEW DERBY is a young writer living in Providence, Rhode Island. His work has appeared in *Third Bed, 5_Trope* and *Impossible Object.*

RIKKI DUCORNET's novel *The Fan-Maker's Inquisition* is just out with Henry Holt. *The Monstrous and the Marvelous,* a book of essays, was published last fall by City Lights.

MICHAEL EASTMAN's work has appeared on the cover of *Time* as well as in *Life, American Photographer* and *View Camera* and can be found in the collections of the International Center of Photography, the Metropolitan Museum of Art, the Chicago Art Institute and the Los Angeles County Museum of Art. He lives in St. Louis.

STEVE ERICKSON's *Days Between Stations, Rubicon Beach, Tours of the Black Clock, Arc d'X* and *Amnesiascope,* have been published in nine languages. His most recent, *The Sea Came in at Midnight,* has just come out in paperback with HarperPerennial.

BRIAN EVENSON is the author of three books of fiction, including *Altmann's Tongue* (Knopf) and *Father of Lies* (Four Walls Eight Windows). A new collection of fiction, *Contagion,* will appear later this year.

ROSARIO FERRÉ's works in Spanish are *Papeles de Pandora, Fábulas de la garze desangrada* and *Maldito Amor.* In English, she is the author of *Sweet Diamond Dust, The Youngest Doll, The House on the Lagoon* (nominated for the National Book Award in 1995) and *Eccentric Neighborhoods.* Her most recently completed novel is *Flight of the Swan,* from which this excerpt is taken. She lives in San Juan, Puerto Rico.

JONATHAN SAFRAN FOER has finished a novel, titled *The Beginning of the World Often Comes,* and is at work on a second. He has edited an anthology of writing inspired by the bird boxes of Joseph Cornell, *A Convergence of Birds.*

WILLIAM H. GASS's fiction includes *Omensetter's Luck, In the Heart of the Heart of the Country, Willie Master's Lonesome Wife, The Tunnel* and *Cartesian Sonata.* His most recent book, *Reading Rilke,* was published by Knopf.

EDITH GROSSMAN has translated works by some of the most important authors writing in Spanish today, including Gabriel García Márquez, Mario Vargas Llosa, Alvarado Mutis and, of course, Mayra Montero.

JESSICA HAGEDORN's "Requiem for a Prodigal Son" is from a novel-in-progress. Her two previous novels are *Dogeaters* and *The Gangster of Love.*

MAUREEN HOWARD's most recent novel is *A Lover's Almanac.* "Inishmurray" is an excerpt from "The Magdalene," one of *Three Tales for Spring* to be published by Viking next year.

A. M. HOMES is the author of six books, most recently the novels *Music For Torching* and *The End of Alice.*

PAUL LAFARGE's first novel, *The Artist of the Missing,* was published by Farrar, Straus & Giroux last year. His second novel, *Haussmann, or the Distinction,* is in progress, as is his third, *Luminous Airplanes,* from which "Lost Aviators" is excerpted.

CAROLE MASO's works include *Ghost Dance, The Art Lover, AVA, Aureole, The American Woman in the Chinese Hat,* and, most recently, *Defiance* (Dutton/Plume). Forthcoming in May is a book of essays, *Break Every Rule* (Counterpoint Press). She teaches at Brown University.

BEN MARCUS is the author of *The Age of Wire and String* (Dalkey Archive Press). He lives in Providence, Rhode Island.

MAYRA MONTERO lives in Puerto Rico. She has published five novels, a collection of stories and a book of essays in Spanish. Her novels, *In The Palm of Darkness* and *The Messenger* (both Harper Flamingo) are available in English. *The Last Night I Spent With You* will be published this year and *The Red of Your Shadow* in 2001, all in translation by Edith Grossman.

RICK MOODY's books include the novels *The Ice Storm* and *Purple America,* as well as a forthcoming collection of stories, *Demonology* (Little, Brown).

BRADFORD MORROW is founding editor of *Conjunctions* and author of the novels *Come Sunday, The Almanac Branch, Trinity Fields* and *Giovanni's Gift.* He teaches at Bard College.

JOYCE CAROL OATES is the author of many books. Her novel *Blonde* is just out with Ecco Press. She is a longtime resident of Princeton, New Jersey, where she teaches at the University and helps edit *Ontario Review.*

HAN ONG is one of the youngest recipients of the MacArthur Fellowship. His novel, *Fixer Chao,* will be published by Farrar, Straus & Giroux next year.

DALE PECK's most recent novel is *Now It's Time to Say Goodbye.* "Fever Dream" is an excerpt from his forthcoming novel, *The Garden of Lost and Found.*

RICHARD POWERS is the author of *Three Farmers on Their Way to a Dance, Prisoner's Dilemma, The Gold Bug Operations, Operation Wandering Soul, Galatea 2.2* and *Gain.* His new novel, *Plowing the Dark,* is forthcoming from Farrar, Straus & Giroux.

PADGETT POWELL's new novel, *Mrs. Hollingsworth's Men,* will appear in November from Houghton Mifflin. Author of the novels *Edisto, Edisto Revisited,* the collection *Aliens of Affection: Stories,* he teaches at the University of Florida.

PAMELA RYDER is a nurse practitioner. Her stories have appeared in *Quarterly, Shenandoah, Prairie Schooner, Frontiers* and *Black Warrior Review.*

JOANNA SCOTT is the author of six works of fiction, including *The Manikin* and *Make Believe.* She teaches at the University of Rochester.

DAVID SHIELDS's most recent book, *Black Planet: Facing Race During an NBA Season,* was a finalist for the National Book Critics Circle Award. Among his works of fiction are *Remote, A Handbook for Drowning* and *Dead Languages.* He lives in Seattle.

LESLIE MARMON SILKO's novel *Gardens in the Dunes* was published by Simon & Schuster. She lives in Tucson, Arizona.

CHRISTOPHER SORRENTINO's first novel, *Sound on Sound,* was published by Dalkey Archive. He lives in Brooklyn.

ALEXANDER THEROUX, who has taught at Yale, Harvard and MIT, lives on Cape Cod. He is the author of the novels *Three Wogs, Darconville's Cat* and *An Adultery.*

WILLIAM T. VOLLMANN has written numerous books, among them *The Atlas, The Rainbow Stories, Whores for Gloria, Thirteen Stories* and *Thirteen Epitaphs* and the *Seven Dreams* series. His new novel, *The Royal Family,* is due out from Viking.

PAUL WEST's two new novels are *O.K.: The Corral, The Earps, and Doc Holliday* (Scribner) and *The Dry Danube* (New Directions). His new nonfiction book, *The Secret Lives of Words* (Harcourt) is a Book-of-the-Month Club selection. His next book, *Master Class,* will be about his final MFA seminars.

Two-time PEN/Faulkner award winner JOHN EDGAR WIDEMAN is the author of *The Lynchers, Reuben, Brothers & Keepers, Philadelphia Fire, Fever, The Castle Killing* and the Homewood trilogy—*Damballah, Hiding Place* and *Sent for You Yesterday*—among others. He is currently working on a book about baseball.

DIANE WILLIAMS's most recent book is *Excitability: Selected Stories* (Dalkey Archive Press). She is the founder of the new literary annual *NOON.*

LOIS-ANN YAMANAKA is the author of the novels *Heads by Harry, Blue's Hanging* and *Wild Meat and the Bully Burgers,* and a book of poetry, *Saturday Night at the Pahala Theatre.* "Wake" is from a work-in-progesss, *Father of the Four Passages.* She lives in Honolulu.

BOMB

Edward Albee Robert Altman Laurie

Magazine

Aharon Appelfeld Ida Applebroog Adam Bartos Rick Bass Max Blagg Peter Campus Peter Carey Joseph Chaikin George Condo Michael Cunningham Maryse Condé Chuck D Olu Dara Jenny Diski Philip Kan Gotanda Mary Heilmann bell hooks Barbara Kopple Yayoi Kusama Kerry James Marshall Ian McKellen Arthur Miller Walter Mosley Michael Ondaatje Cynthia Ozick Robert Pinsky Padgett Powell Francine Prose Marc Ribot Sapphire Andres Serrano Gary Sinise Stellan Skarsgård Anna Deavere Smith Kiki Smith Thomas Vinterberg Paula Vogel Zoë Wanamaker Cassandra Wilson Wood Alan Winchester Michael Winterbottom

Subscribe

$18/Year

1.888.475.5987

RATTAPALLAX

A Journal of Contemporary Literature

with CD featuring poetry from the journal read by the poets

Editor-in-Chief George Dickerson
Senior Editor Judith Werner/Art Editor Arlette Lurié
Publisher Ram Devineni

One year (2 issues) $14.00 / Two years (4 issues) $24.00

532 La Guardia Place • Suite 353 • New York, NY 10012
www.rattapallax.com

3rd bed

Alkman
Charles Baudelaire
William Browne
Michael Burkard
Maile Chapman
Bei Dao
Matthew Derby
Jeffrey Encke
Brian Evenson
Robert Fludd
Margaret Flynn
Brooks Haxton
Jim Ineich
Michael Ives
Camden Joy
Fin Keegan
Bill Knott
Stacey Levine
Tuan-Li Diana Liao
Cormac James
A. P. Maddox
I. W. Mallet
Michael Martone
Paul McRandle
Hermine Meinhard
Heidi Peppermint
Chris Riley
Anthony Robbins
David Rossmann
Theokritos
David Tod Roy
James Wagner
Diane Wald

one year (2 issues) $10 two years (4 issues) $18
subscriptions and submissions:
3rd bed, joslin lane, buskirk, ny, 12028
www.3rdbed.com

“This book is essential” — Library Journal

“A fascinating compilation, reflecting this year’s varied bounty of literary feats.”
— Publishers Weekly (starred review)

Over sixty stories, essays, memoirs and poems appear in this landmark edition, as picked from more than 5,000 nominations with the help of over 200 distinguished contributing editors.

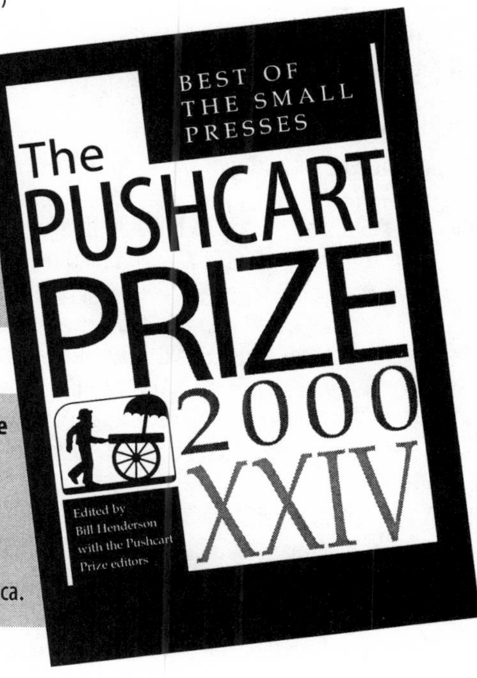

For its 24th year, **The Pushcart Prize** surpasses itself with a stunning presentation of new and celebrated authors selected from hundreds of presses. **The Pushcart Prize** is the most honored literary series in America.

“A vital archive of American letters.”
— Booklist

Pushcart Press
PO Box 380
Wainscott, New York 11975

Hardcover $29.50
Paperback $15.00
585 Pages

Internationally known specialists in rare literature and primary works in the history of ideas, in all languages and all periods.

At present we are offering:
An inscribed first edition of *A la recherche de temps perdus.*
Ulysses, signed by James Joyce.
A magnificent set of the first edition of Robert Musil's *Der Mann ohne Eigenschaften.*
George Trakl's own copy of his only lifetime book, *Gedichte*
The first edition of Mann's *Der Tod in Venedig,* 1 of 100 copies printed.
A superb copy of Boswell's *Johnson* in original boards.
Dylan Thomas's *Deaths and Entrances*, inscribed to his parents.
Osip Mandelshtam's first book, *Kamen,* inscribed to V.V. Gippius
Nabokov's *Lolita* signed by Nabokov in each volume.
The Varieties of Religious Experience inscribed by James to Charles W. Eliot.
A splendid copy of the first edition *Tristam Shandy,* three volumes signed by Sterne. (as issued)
Books inscribed by Rilke, Cavafy, Akhmatova, Tsvetaeva, Pasternak, Kierkegaard, Browning, Whitman, Gaddis, Fitzgerald, Hemingway, James, Wharton and hundreds of others.
Manuscripts and letters of Hegel, Benjamin, Adorno, Brecht, Kafka, Proust, Mann, Le Corbusier, Diego Rivera, Neruda, Voltaire, James, Nabokov, Pasternak and hundreds of others.

Catalogues forthcoming or available in Modern Thought, Rare Literature, Manuscripts and Autographs, Russian Literature, German Literature, Association Copies, First Books.

We will exhibit at the following international antiquarian book fairs and conferences:
Boston: May 6-7
Paris: May 25-28
London: June 8-11
Edinburgh: September 21-24
Boston: October 26-29
Berlin: November 10-12
Hamburg: November 16-19
and at the MLA in Washington.

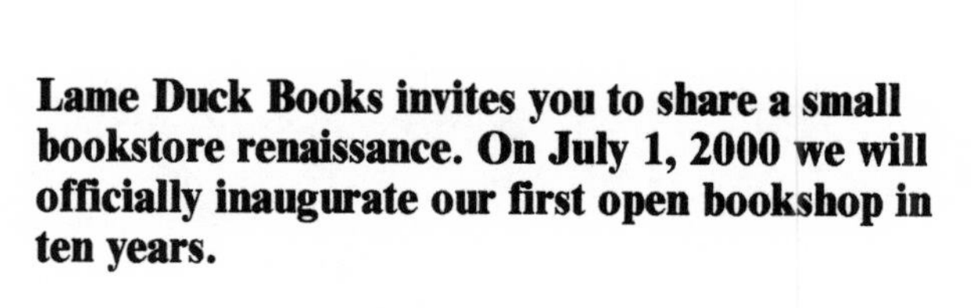
Lame Duck Books invites you to share a small bookstore renaissance. On July 1, 2000 we will officially inaugurate our first open bookshop in ten years.

We will share a fine old retail establishment with our colleague Peter L. Stern Rare Books directly behind the Brattle Book Shop at 55 Temple Place, Boston, Massachusetts 02111.

While most urban centers have long purported to deplore the demise of the open bookshop and even the most sanguine bibliophiles have long prophesied its final eradication from our cities;
We are happy to announce that six antiquarian booksellers have now established public premises on the collar of Boston Common: Brattle Bookshop... the oldest continuously operating bookshop in the United States; Commonwealth Bookshop... one of the best used scholarly bookshops on the East Coast; Arlington Books... among the most active buyers of used scholarly and general used books in America; F. A. Bernett... rare and scholarly books on the fine and decorative arts, architecture and archeology: and Lame Duck Books / Peter L. Stern Rare Books... two of the primary specialists in the United States in rare literature, manuscripts and works in the history of ideas in all languages and of all periods.

We will maintain business hours from 9 until 5, Monday through Saturday. We may be reached by telephone at 617-421-1880; fax: 617-536-7072;
email: lameduckbk@aol.com

When visiting Boston, consider a visit to another world.

Members:
Antiquarian Booksellers Association of America,
Verband Deutscher Antiquare.

The Web Forum of Innovative Writing

www.Conjunctions.com

"We'd be hard put to find another leading literary magazine establishing itself so preeminently in electronic format."

—Martin Earl,
Web Del Sol/The Review of Contemporary Fiction

Discover what thousands of readers already know by visiting the *Conjunctions* website where work by over 500 innovative fiction writers, poets, playwrights and artists is a keystroke away.

➤ **WEB CONJUNCTIONS:** The Web companion to our print journal, presenting new writing and artwork available *exclusively* online. Contemporary and documentary poetry, fiction, plays and more. Updated regularly.

➤ **JUST OUT:** Complete table of contents and selected works from our current issue.

➤ **PREVIEWS:** See what's ahead in upcoming issues before publication.

➤ **NEW ADDITIONS:** Quick navigation to our most recent postings.

➤ **AUDIO VAULT:** Reading performances by our authors unavailable elsewhere, with links to texts. Read and listen to your favorite writers simultaneously.

➤ **THE ARCHIVES:** Generous selections from all past issues, including cover art and complete tables of contents.

➤ **PLUS:** A *Conjunctions* index, 1981–2000, favorite links to other literary sites and much more.

➤ Subscription and back-issue ordering.

CONJUNCTIONS.COM

The Web gateway to contemporary writing